P9-CFB-640

Hawkspar

A NOVEL OF KORRE

Holly Lisle

A TOM DOHERTY ASSOCIATES BOOK
NEW YORK

TOR®

HAWKSPAR: A NOVEL OF KORRE

Copyright © 2008 by Holly Lisle

Maps by Ellisa Mitchell

A Tor Book
Published by Tom Doherty Associates, LLC
175 Fifth Avenue
New York, NY 10010

www.tor-forge.com

Tor® is a registered trademark of Tom Doherty Associates, LLC.

Library of Congress Cataloging-in-Publication Data

Lisle, Holly.
Hawspar: a novel of Korre / Holly Lisle—1st ed.
p.cm
"A Tom Doherty Associates book."
ISBN-13: 978-0-7653-0994-5
ISBN-10: 0-7653-0994-7
1. Women slaves—Fiction.   I. Title.
PS3562.I775H38 2008
813'.54--dc22   2008005223

First Edition: June 2008

Printed in the United States of America

0   9   8   7   6   5   4   3   2   1

Hawkspar

Tor Books by Holly Lisle

Talyn
Hawkspar

To Matthew, with all my love,
and,
in memory of Frank O'Brien Andrew, without whose assistance this book
would have existed, but would not have been as good

Acknowledgments

Some books are easy. This one was not. Writing it was an adventure, and as grand as adventures are once they're over, sitting in the (metaphorical) mud and icy rain in the middle of one, trying to figure out how to fix the broken wagon by inventing your own spare parts is no great fun. I owe thanks to the people who got me from the beginning of the adventure to the end.

Huge thanks to my agent, Robin Rue, whose help kept *Hawkspar* the book I wrote.

I also owe Matt, who kept me centered when all those deadlines landed at once, and kept me laughing, and who kept reminding me that he believed in me, and believed that I would, in fact, figure this out and make it all the way through.

And another thanks to the folks at Pocket Full of Words (http://hollylisle. com/writingdiary2), who cheered me on and frequently reminded me that they were waiting to read this. Remembering that there were people who wanted to know what happened helped enormously.

The World of

Korre

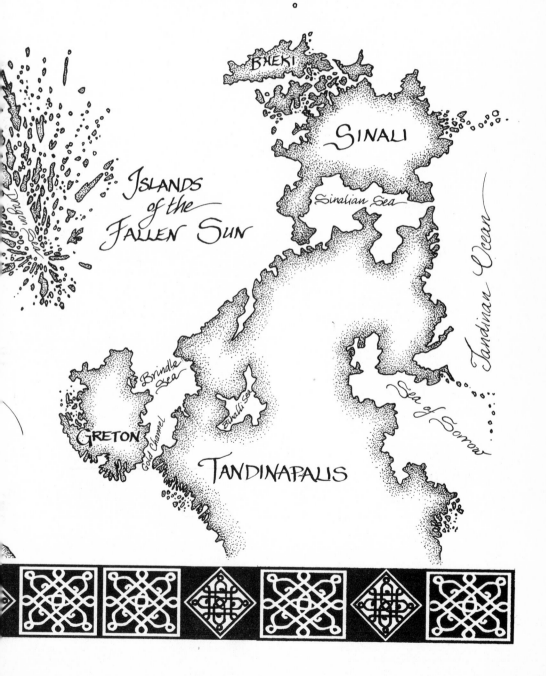

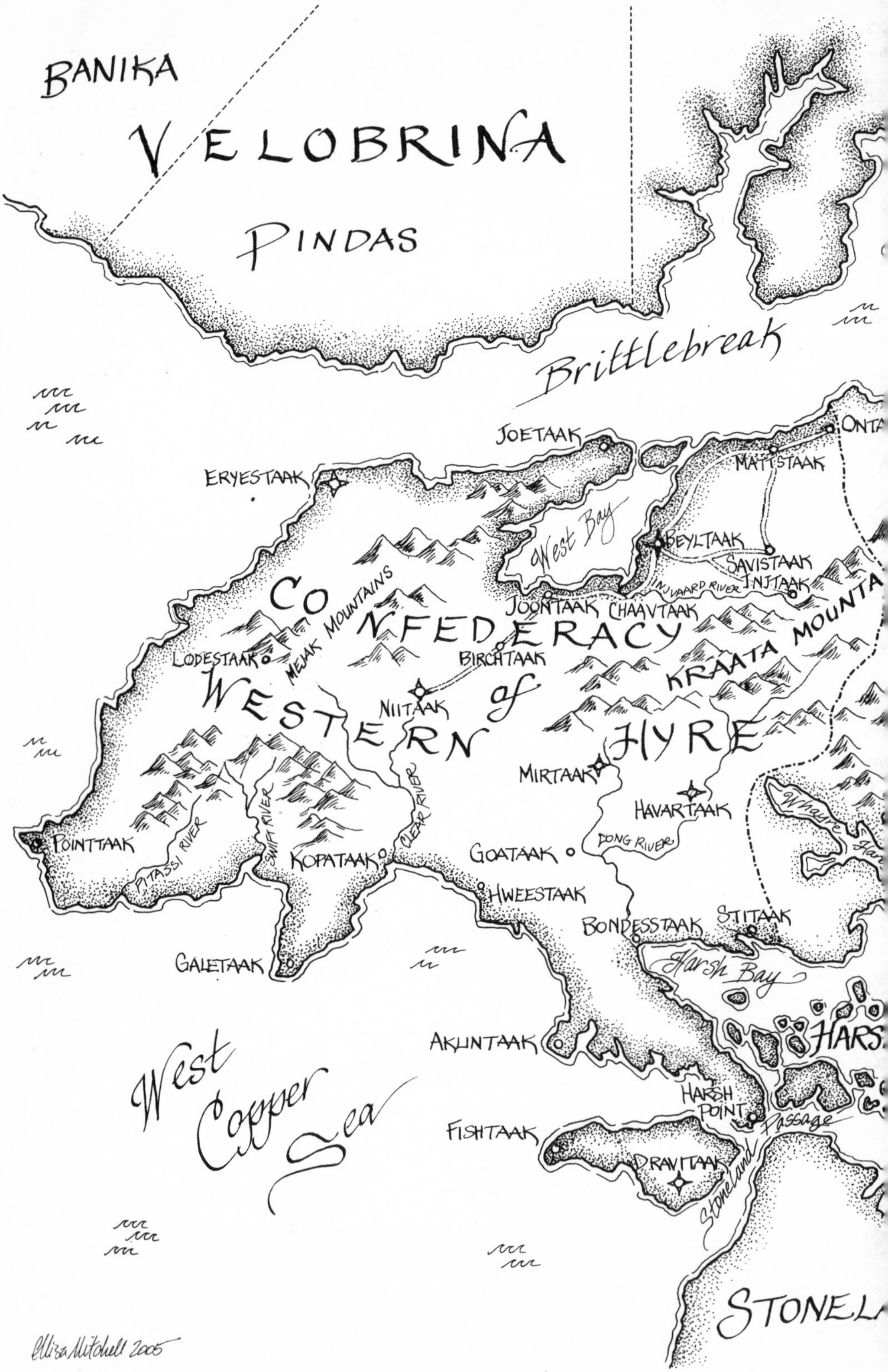

BANIKA

VELOBRINA

PINDAS

Brittlebreak

BANIKA — top left

JOETAAK ● ● ONTA

MATISTAAK

ERYESTAAK ✦

West Bay

DEYLTAAK

SAVISTAAK

INITAAK

INVAARD RIVER

JOONTAAK CHAAVTAAK

CO

NFEDERACY

MELAK MOUNTAINS

LODESTAAK ○

BIRCHTAAK

WESTERN

NIITAAK ✦

of

KRAATA MOUNTA

HYRE

MIRTAAK ✦

HAVARTAAK ✦

SWIFT RIVER

CLEAR RIVER

Whale Shor

POINTTAAK ●

PITASSI RIVER

GOATAAK ○

DONG RIVER

KOPATAAK ●

HWEESTAAK ●

BONDESSTAAK ● STITAAK ✦

GALETAAK

Harsh Bay

HARS

West

AKUNTAAK ●

HARSH

POINT

Copper

Passage

FISHTAAK ●

DRAVITAAK ✦

Stoneland

Sea

STONELA

Eliza Mitchell 2005

Hawkspar

Penitent

My jara came at me with a quick punch and sweep of her ban. We were practicing that morning with ban-vi-ri, which means "stick like self"—they're heavy wood staves cut to our height. The jara, taller than I, had better reach.

I was quicker for once, however, and feeling more aggressive. "Hai!" I shouted, and went over her sweep, already moving inside her defenses and punching with my ban before she could pull hers back to defend herself. "You overreached."

My ban smacked her ribs, and she yelped, and I spun the end overhand to catch her opposite shoulder a sharp downward blow. Done correctly, this will get through the padding of the rayan—the corded shoulder protectors that are a part of our penitent garb—and weaken the opponent's grip on her stick. Done perfectly, it will cause the arm to go numb and the stick to drop from the hand.

I, however, did it badly, because as I snapped my ban downward, out of the corner of my eye I caught sight of an Obsidian stepping into the doorway to the fighting floor, then moving toward us. Which meant that my attention wasn't fully on what I was doing. My blow bounced harmlessly, and left me with my stick up and entangled in the back of hers for an instant. The jara, for whom my secret name was Redbird, grinned, and used the opportunity to sweep me again and take my knees out from under me.

So it was that I found myself lying on my back with my head ringing from the rap on the floor when the Obsidian stopped beside us and stared down at me.

I had to guess she stared down at me—after all, she bore Obsidian Eyes, and it's impossible to tell what those featureless, glinting black stones are looking at. Everything, maybe—or nothing.

"Senior Penitent Ter Light Ranwi?" she said.

I scrambled to my feet, and bowed. "Yes, sera."

My heart was in my throat. The Obsidians are the warriors of the Ossalene Rite—silent and terrifying, dressed always in unrelieved black. They have fighting skills that defy the eyes and the mind, and what we see when they demonstrate skills for us or spar with us is only a portion of what they can do; they are rumored to walk on water and disappear and appear at will, to be able to kill with a fingertip touch or a whisper, to be able to see not just our sins of commission, but the sins in our thoughts.

As I had lately occupied myself by committing all manner of both sorts of sins, I could barely breathe as I stood before the Obsidian.

But she did not say, "I know what you've been doing." She did not say, "I know what you've been thinking." And she did not mention tossing me into a cage filled with starving rats.

All she said was, "Oracle Hawkspar commands you appear in her private chapel next bell."

And that was worse. All hopes I might have had of surviving the day fled.

The only thing that could have made me more panicked than having an Obsidian single me out for attention was discovering she did so in order to command me to face an oracle. In the oracle's private chapel at that, where none entered unbidden, and where only some who entered later exited.

Nor would I be standing before just any of the Nine Holies. Oracle Hawkspar was the Eyes of War, the Living Goddess of the Blade, whose words brought kings and commanders, dictators and despots—all bearing the wealth of nations—to the Oracle Tower to beg for her true telling of their futures.

Hawkspar was the commander of the Obsidians. She was, to us penitents, like Death incarnate.

She knew what I'd been doing, I thought. But she couldn't; if she'd known, I would already have been fed to the rats. Or perhaps she meant to make a spectacle of me. It would make sense.

I said only, "Yes, sera," for if a penitent speaks to an Obsidian, the only acceptable answers are "yes, sera" and "no, sera." My voice shook saying merely that; I was grateful no more words were required of me. In my ears, the two words I had said screamed my guilt.

Redbird's hand rested on my shoulder, silent comfort.

The Obsidian turned next to her. "Jara Light Ranwi?"

"Yes, sera."

"You will follow Ter Light Ranwi, and will see the Oracle Hawkspar when she is finished with the Ter."

Redbird's fingers tightened on my shoulder.

"Yes, sera."

The Obsidian flowed away without comment, and Redbird and I exchanged panicked looks. She, now ranked Senior Penitent Jara Light Ranwi, had been my closest friend since the day they chained her into the hold of the slave ship next to me. When we staggered off that ship, we stood side-by-side on the slave block in the market of the city below the Ossalene Citadel; we'd managed not to faint when a stone-eyed monk had touched us and told us in our own language that we were going with her; and we had managed to stay together through years of slavery within the Citadel, through the choosing that brought us as lowly penitents into the Ossalene Rite of the Cistavrian Order of Marosites, more commonly called the Order of Ossalenes.

We'd risen through the ranks. We'd put together a fine, fine conspiracy.

And now we had been found out. Hawkspar would not see mere penitents for anything less than the sort of overarching criminality that we'd committed.

"You haven't much time," Redbird whispered. She looked as pale and sick as I felt. "You can't go looking like that."

"Neither of us has much time."

I needed to present myself, clean-showered and in formal garb, in less than a bell. Redbird would have a little longer—as long as it would take the oracle to sentence me to death.

"I'm sorry," I told her.

"You'll never make it unless we run. I'll help you," she said.

We fled the fighting hall, and when we were clear of the Obsidian paths, raced to Ranwi Hall, up the spiral staircase from the common area into the cells, and into the cell we shared with two other Lights, Fawi Light Ranwi, and Ghoteh Light Ranwi.

Penitents are designated by bed color, cell name, and hall name. These change each time a penitent moves on, either to become an acolyte or to be sent from the Order; all the other penitents move up a bed, and their designations change. Bad months, when a sera or two dies, or something unspeakable happens with a group of acolytes, our designations changed half a dozen times. We learned not to get attached to names—but we'd already learned that when we were slaves. All slaves are called Slave. Nothing more—ever.

We were beaten for speaking our real names, for using nicknames for each other. But Redbird and I had developed a system. We found common items around the monastery: wild animals, birds, flowers wild and domesticated, bits and pieces of cookware. We marked each other and our other coconspirators with these hidden nicknames, and by so doing, managed to hold on to news of each other, to stay in touch, to pass messages, to keep friends—the very things I suspected the ever-changing rank names had been designed to prevent. Our hidden nicknames could be passed in casual conversation, along with a specific movement of the face. Whatever magic their terrifying Eyes gave them, the blind Ossalene sera, we had discovered, could not read facial expressions.

In our cell, which Redbird and I shared with two other penitents, we pulled our formal robes from the shelves. Then Redbird and I raced to the ground floor and to the penitents' bath, a large open room with one wall dedicated to showers. Water poured constantly from twenty dragon-shaped showerheads, then down a drain and into the garden irrigation system. We placed formal robes on the long, narrow changing table, stripped off our work clothes, and tossed them into the basket where the penitents assigned to laundry would gather them up. And we plunged into the icy downpour. I scrubbed quickly, soaping body, face and hair with the harsh lye-and-ash soap we penitents used, that the slaves made. When I was a slave, I had hated soap-making days.

Even terrified, though, I kept to my ritual. I sent the magic into the water. If all hope was gone for me, it still might remain for some of the girls in the monastery. I put everything I had into the little spell. And I prayed to a forbidden god that rescue would come in time to save even me. *For the love of Jostfar, by the hands of the Five Saints, save us before we perish.*

I did not let myself think about Oracle Hawkspar, or what she might want with me. I had served her for a season my second year as a penitent; I could be said to know her better than most, yet she remained a mystery to me, and she terrified me. With her stone Eyes that replaced her sacrificed human eyes, she saw what had been, what was, and what would be in the dealings of the great men of many nations, and if she was so moved, she would tell those who petitioned her what she saw.

Oftentimes she sent the mighty and the rich away with nothing. She was a harsh woman, cold and demanding, and if her visitors displeased her, she turned her back on them.

Most things displeased her. She did not like children at all, and the girls who were assigned to serve her, slaves and penitents alike, cowered at her slightest whisper of displeasure. In the season I spent serving her, I had wished one of the two of us dead every single day. The longer I served her, the more I didn't care which of the two that might be.

I stepped out of the shower shivering, and Redbird tossed me a coarse hemp towel pulled from the rack. A few flicks took care of my hair, what little of it there was. Slaves' heads are shaved, penitents must wear a fuzz no longer than the first joint of our first finger; acolytes' hair is cut as long as their longest finger. Seru wear a single twisted rope braid capped at the end with a hedu, or little metal ball. Oracles wear their hair in whatever fashion they like. The Oracle Hawkspar shaved her head like a slave. I could not guess what she meant to say by doing this.

Damp but with no time to get completely dry, I tossed my towel into the laundry bag. The seru were unforgiving of messes left lying; slaves and penitents kept ourselves and our quarters neat as a simple matter of survival.

Redbird helped me put on my formal garb of the Order of Ossalenes, which consists, even for one of my low station, of layers of cotton and silk, each wrapped precisely, every piece requiring a special tie or named and complicated knot or the precise and ordered crossing of bands. There are prayers to be said as each piece is donned—but neither Redbird nor I had time for that.

At the best of times, dressing is difficult to do well, and an appearance before the Oracle Hawkspar could never be considered the best of times. My hands shook so badly I ended up holding lengths of the thick brown silk away from my body while Redbird did the knot and tucked the ends, and both of us whispered Tonk curses. When all of my attire was perfect, I threaded the top edge of my beaded cepa, my rank apron, which is of the brilliant bloodred we call ter, beneath the outermost layer of my bo—my wrapped silk belt—and then folded it under the innermost layer so that both ends hung even with the skirt of my tabi.

"Is it straight?"

Redbird stood on tiptoe and peered out of one high ventilation slit. "It's going to have to do," she said. "The bell-slaves are heading into the tower now."

"Already?" My body went rigid with fear. I looked to Redbird, my mouth dry. "How about you? Will you be ready in time?"

She nodded.

I ran.

So the slaves and penitents and seru and oracles meditating in the central garden watched me hurtle over the cobbled paths, leaping flowerbeds that impeded my race to Oracle House, while I clattered like a mule in my wood-soled shoes.

Word of my behavior would no doubt reach Oracle Hawkspar well before I did.

And then the bell rang, and I was no longer merely indecorous, but also late.

I took the steps up to Oracle House two at a time, dodging Bloodstone seru who cluttered the broad stairs like great red birds—one *walks* in the Citadel, but most especially, one walks wherever oracles might be.

I had no doubt I would pay horribly for my sins, but there is no greater sin to an oracle than to present oneself late. I skidded into the vast entry hall, gasping for air.

One of the white-eyed Seru Moonstone crossed her arms over her chest and said, "You're late, and you've been running."

"Yes, sera."

"I could have you taken away this very minute and given ten lashes for being late, and a week of solitary prayer in a silent cell for the running."

"Yes, sera."

The Moonstone sighed heavily and turned away from me. "I have no doubt the blessed oracle will be able to do a better job of punishing you than I could ever hope to."

"Yes, sera."

"Go in, then. You've kept Oracle Hawkspar waiting, but she still wishes to see you. You know which quarters are hers?"

"Yes, sera." But my feet dragged.

"Go." She made shooing motions with her hands. "She said you were not to be announced."

I bowed the deep bow of a senior penitent, and the sister gave me the head nod that is all one of her station is required to give when dealing with one of mine.

Aaran

Aaran av Savissha, tracker for the Haakvaryn pack of Tonk wolf-ships, sat on the higharm, legs wrapped around the foremast, hands clutching ratlines. With his eyes closed, he tracked the fleeing slaver. "Two degrees northwest," he bellowed over the scream of the storm.

The runner slid down the ratlines, careened across the deck to Captain

Haakvar, and repeated Aaran's directions. Within moments, he was back on the ratlines, and Aaran felt the *Windsteed* aligning itself with the slaver. "Dead on," he yelled to the boy, a child who was one of the captain's multitude of nephews, and the boy gave him an excited smile. Then the child clambered back into the riggings and settled below Aaran on the lines, waiting the next message to the captain.

Aaran, his eyes once again open, squinted through the sheeting rain that battered him. He watched the *Windsteed* climb up one towering wall of water and slide down the next. They were close to their quarry. He hadn't caught sight of the slaver since it ran headlong into the storm, but he knew from the tracking spell he'd cast within the Hagedwar that the enemy and its cargo were less than half a league in front of them.

On deck and up in the lines, the sailors fought the storm—but it was less of a storm than the slaver fleeing them struggled through. The Tonk wolf-ships had an advantage. Aft in the steersman's castles, the windmen kept the worst of the storm at bay. The *Windsteed*'s windmen, bending the air with Hagedwar magic, surrounded the ship with a shield that filtered and channeled the storm—keeping the gale always behind and the sails always filled; smoothing the surface of the water, if not by much; making the waves the *Windsteed* fought less vicious than those ridden by the slaver.

Every advantage the windmen could confer brought the *Windsteed* closer to the holdful of captured, chained Tonk children bound for slaver markets in Sinali and Bheki.

Aaran and the trackers on the other three ships conferred within the Hagedwar—how best to bring the pack in for the attack, how to coordinate with the windmen for the safest arrival.

Then, bound by magic to his enemies, Aaran felt the slaver ship suddenly founder. At the same time, the tracker on the *Long Fang* gave the urgent message that they had men overboard from a rogue wave; that tracker stayed linked to the other three trackers, but his attention diverted to locating the men for the *Long Fang*.

Aaran shouted to his runner, "The Sinali mainmast has torn away, and we're closing fast! Tell the captain we'll be on top of them in minutes."

The boy launched himself down the lines again, and just a breath later, Aaran heard Haakvar shout the "Ready to board" order. The marines streamed up out of the lower decks and formed up, crouched at the center of the deck with boarding grapples and swords at the ready. Sailors reefed in the ringsails, snapsails, and squaresail, and the *Windsteed* slowed and crawled up the next wave on pillar and fansails. She crested to find herself almost on top of the slaver, a modified three-masted Sinali war frigate that was fighting to keep its prow to the onrushing water, with broken main and foremasts and sheets dragging through the sea like anchors, pulling the ship's port side toward the waves and dragging her starboard side downward.

Aaran could see sailors aboard the slaver fighting to cut the lines.

He closed his eyes—like most Tonk trained in the foreign magic of the Hagedwar, he could work within the patterns of sphere, cube, and tetrahedrons with open eyes, but coordinating with other trackers required deeper, more intense concentration. The *Sea Hawk,* running even with the *Windsteed,* had planned to board the slaver from forward starboard while the *Windsteed* boarded from forward port. *Sea Hawk* could not approach on the starboard side, though—the sails and masts that were sinking the slaver would foul her. The *Ethebet's Dagger* would board at aft portside, but like the *Sea Hawk,* the fourth member of the pack, the *Long Fang* would not be able to take her place on the aft starboard. But the *Long Fang* was still chasing down her missing sailors. With luck, she'd catch up quickly, but the tracker was sure the lost men could be saved.

The displaced *Sea Hawk* angled down the crest of the wave and fought her way to the port side of the *Windsteed* and the *Dagger.* When the *Sea Hawk* came even with the *Windsteed* and the *Dagger,* her marines crossed decks—a risky maneuver in bad seas.

The marines—tough, nimble men, went up the tall side of the frigate like spiders up their webs. From his viewpoint atop the crow's nest, Aaran could see them swinging over the top onto the deck. This was always the worst point—the place where the most men were lost—but because the slaver was foundering, few of its men could be spared for fighting. Most of the crew were cutting lines to free themselves from the broken mast and tangled sails.

The marines killed those few who opposed them, but most slid to the listing starboard side fast as they could and began working with the enemy to cut away the entangling lines, while a handful of the nearly sixty men who boarded went belowdecks to find the captives and free them.

The marines knew where the captives would be. Sinali slaver ships—even the modified ones—followed the same basic design. And that design kept chained slaves lying flat in a lightless, low-ceilinged hold one floor above the bilge.

Knowing where to find the stolen Tonk children wasn't the problem. Getting them to safety was.

Just as the marines belowdecks located the captive children, the marines and Sinali sailors above succeeded in freeing the slaver from the deadly tangle of masts and spars and sheets and lines, and the slaver righted itself—lower in the water than it had been and taking the waves badly. But upright for the moment at least.

Aaran, his job done, sent his runner down to the captain, who would most likely send the boy into Haakvar's quarters to wait out the storm. Aaran began to slide down the lines to offer his own services to the captain, whether to fight or to assist the windmen aft in keeping the storm at bay.

It was at that moment, hanging halfway down the ratlines in the midst of a gale, that pain screamed through the Hagedwar—sucking pain that almost pulled Aaran and the trackers of the *Ethebet's Dagger* and the *Sea Hawk* down with it.

He didn't have time to think—only time to react. He broke away from the connection he shared with the other three trackers to save his own life. And, unguarded, wide open, unprepared, he fell to a wave of magic unlike anything he'd ever felt. It blasted through the Hagedwar that enveloped him, slamming him in lungs and gut and heart all at once. A cry, unearthly and powerful, rose up out of the sea and wrapped itself around his brain, blinding him to all but the space between the worlds in which the Hagedwar lay. Aaran found himself in the danger zone between the relatively safe Feegash magic of the Hagedwar and the deadly magic of his own people. He hovered at the point where protected space bled into the View, where the siren songs of eternity flowed through him. The faint, fragile buffering of the Hagedwar shield didn't keep them out—they called to him, luring him toward solitary ecstasy and annihilation. Over their sweet music, which was nothing less than the breathing of the universe, a trail of desperate rhythms, of terror and pain and despair, pulled him north and east.

A captive Tonk girl begged for rescue, and—bound to her by blood and pain—countless others cried out in wordless horror.

The girl's plea was cast by intent, though, and it was clear in his mind as a dagger drawn across flesh: *For the love of Jostfar, by the hands of the Five Saints, save us before we perish.*

She was Tonk.

Enslaved.

Doomed.

Desperate for rescue.

Aaran shook himself free of the powerful spell she'd woven to find that he hung upside down in the ratlines, his legs tangled in rope, while two sailors and his cousin Tuuanir fought to free him.

"I'm all right," Aaran yelled over the screaming of the storm. "I'm all right. Av Yaddar, the tracker on the *Long Fang* is dead, though—he bound himself to one of the men overboard so he would not lose the lot of them, and he didn't pull back in time when sharks hit them and the man he'd marked died."

"Tracked him into death?" Tuua asked.

Aaran nodded.

They got Aaran down quickly, and he steadied himself as best he could in the churning seas and vicious winds. He dragged himself by steady-rope and rail to the captain. "I've located more slaves," he shouted, and Haakvar, at the tiller holding the ship tight to the struggling slaver, stared at him in dismay.

"More?"

"Yes, Captain. I cannot be sure of precisely how many, but nearly a hundred. Possibly more. One of them has a good grip on the View. She's used it to send out a rescue call that near knocked me senseless when we floated through its current."

"Her plea . . . has a current?" Haakvar frowned, clearly bewildered.

"She bound magic to the sea. I do not know how she did it, or how she holds it together, but it's a powerful current. We've passed it now, but I marked it before we moved beyond it. I could get us back to it again. We could find them."

Up on the deck of the slaver, Tonk marines fought with Sinalian sailors. In the *Windsteed*'s rigging, half the sailors hung from the ratlines, acting as a secondary force of archers, taking clear shots at the enemy when offered. In the slavehold below, other marines were gathering the freed children below the aft hatch that opened onto the archers' platform. No archers occupied the platform because while they fought with their masts and rigging, the Tonks deployed their smaller but better-trained forces.

When the fighting finished, the marines belowdecks would move the rescued children to the four waiting ships, and would strip the slaver of any worthwhile cargo it carried, as well.

Aaran said, "We could let the other three ships take captives and cargo from this slaver, and go after the slaves to the north on our own. They're desperate—something horrible is about to happen to them."

Aaran couldn't ignore the look of dismay Haakvar sent in his direction. "Aaran, lad, think about it. Can we, alone, run north, perhaps near the Fallen

Suns, certainly across Sinali shipping lanes, to rescue more than a hundred slaves from their unknown situation? We've taken storm damage, we've lost men, we'll have injuries. How am I to tell these men risking their lives right now to forgo their shares in the loot from this ship, or their share of the reward for the successful rescue of the captives, to run up north into Jostfar knows what?"

One massive wave crashed over the deck of the *Windsteed*, and everyone grabbed lines or masts or rails lest they be washed into the ocean.

The captain clung to the crew companionway rail, holding his footing. Rya Haakvar was a good man, but practical. He saw not grand goals, but the obstacles that stood before them; not a bird's wings, but its feet. He patted Aaran on the shoulder and said, "Am I to take tired and injured crew and exhausted windmen into the northern hells without a resupply, rest, or a chance to stand on dry land? What sort of captain would I be if I did that? Saints' sorrows, what sort of *man* would I be?"

Aaran sighed. He knew that Haakvar was right—that he stood on firm moral ground in refusing to chase Aaran's newest trail.

But Aaran could still feel the girl's desperation vibrating beneath his skin like the metal of a hard-rung bell. He couldn't stop feeling her. Just as her pain and terror had bound itself to the water, so it had bound itself to him.

He clung to the rigging and stared to the north. "I understand," Aaran said. "But I can feel edges and shards of their situation. I don't think they have much time."

At the back of his mind was the thought, never absent, that Aashka might be among them. That *she* might be almost out of time.

Haakvar said, "When we're on our way back to port with the children tucked away safe, come into my quarters and we'll chart your trail out and see where it leads. It might be that we can take the pack after these slaves you've found as soon as we've had a chance to resupply and refit. But perhaps not. No matter how desperate the situations of those who need us, we cannot save them all. We are too few, and those in need of rescue are too many."

Penitent

Through the heavy brass-bound doors at the back of the great room, Oracle Hawkspar had her living quarters, and to one side of that, her private chapel.

She sat on her bench, dressed in black garb identical to the fighting garb of the Obsidian seru, her head bowed. But when I stood in the doorway, her head came up and her face turned toward me.

I was surprised at how gaunt she had become, and how pale. Hawkspar had always been a lean woman; she had seemed to me one who in another time would have ridden astride a horse with a sword in her hand. No one could have mistaken her for Oracle Ruby, the Eyes of Family, whose vast, matronly girth no doubt made her seem motherly and welcoming to the women who sought her out for matters of the heart, childbirth, and the home—never mind how those of us who knew her found her.

Hawkspar had seemed hard and gaunt. Sharp-edged. But never worn, never frail. Nor had she seemed old; merely ageless.

"Sit, girl," she told me, and pointed to a place beside her on the worn rosewood bench.

I sat.

The oracle waved a hand in a casual fashion, and suddenly, silently, the walls, ceiling and floor around us glowed with a pale blue shimmer.

"Now we can talk," she said. "You don't want to be here." When I did not answer, she laughed. "That's all right, girl. When you hear why I've summoned you, you'll want to be here less."

There would be rats, I thought. Starving rats, a cage, and the Arena.

I said nothing.

She was watching me, but I—well-trained and terrified in the same moment—stared straight ahead.

"That's quite a remarkable conspiracy you have going on," she told me.

And there it was. The worst thing I could have feared, and she had wasted no time getting to it.

"You've been interesting to watch, with your bits of Ossalene magic twisted together with bits of Tonk magic—I'd have thought you too young to remember any Tonk magic when we got you—sending your rescue message into the sea. Through the showers, no less. Your plea for rescue has wended its way into the deep currents now."

I did not look at her. The air in her chapel was cool, but beads of sweat formed on my forehead and my upper lip and rolled down my spine. The palms of my hands felt slick; it was all I could do not to wipe them on my hakan-ara.

"And the number of young women you've managed to draw into this business with you . . . well, it leaves me breathless. For them to know they face a death sentence if they're caught, and then to follow you anyway? It speaks of your talent for leadership."

My talent for leading us all to our deaths.

"Your patience was most impressive, your plan to get your people into a position where their power could be turned to your advantage, well thought out."

She chuckled.

I could see nothing funny about the moment. I could think only of the other penitents who had trusted me—some of them now raised to acolytes, two in place among the Obsidians, and many of us moved at last into senior positions where we could hope for access that we had not previously had.

I had faith that the spell I spun into the water each morning as I showered—a spell that washed out into the gardens, and drained through the ground, and finally ran to the nearby sea—would summon help for us. Beyond faith, though, I had laid groundwork that would allow those of us bent on escape to steal onto an unguarded ship in the Citadel's secret harbor, should no help come. It would take longer that way. But I'd been sure we would succeed in reaching freedom.

I'd been sure.

"My laughter distresses you?"

A question. For which I would have to provide an answer. "Yes, Oracle."

"Let me tell you a little story, then, and at the end of it, perhaps you'll see why I laugh."

In spite of myself and years of training, I turned to look at her. Her face was turned toward mine. A tiny smile twitched at the corners of her thin lips. Her Eyes . . .

Hawkspar is a rare stone. It is golden-brown, layered with solid black and transparent amber bands, flecked with bits of gold. Its bands shift colors in the light, the gold gleams and glitters, the whole effect is rich and liquid and lovely. Polished hawkspar is beautiful—but two smooth, polished stones of hawkspar replacing a woman's natural eyes were not beautiful at all. The oracles and the sera, with their stone eyes, terrified those of us who knew Eyes lay in our own futures.

I stared at the cold stones, and felt the oracle looking at me. I knew that she could see me in some fashion: that was part of the magic of the Eyes. I had no idea what she could see.

But when I turned to her, she smiled at me as if she could see me as clearly as I saw her.

"I was twelve when the slavers came," she said. "They caught me away from my home, and thus had from me no more fight than I could provide alone. Compared to the fight they would have had from a taak full of furious Tonk, that was not much fight at all. I rode in the filthy slavehold in the bottom of one of their ships, and I lived, and the sera came down from the Citadel to the market, as they came for you. They took me, even though they worried over the meaning of the mark on the palm of my hand."

I had such a mark on my own palm—tattooed into the skin, faded and blurred with time. Three horizontal lines of differing lengths, the shortest on top, the longest on the bottom, and beneath the longest line, a curve like a cat's tail. I held out my left hand and looked down at it, and the oracle put her own left hand atop mine, palm up. The marks matched.

Her hand in mine felt like nothing but bird bones covered by cool, loose, papery skin.

"We are kin, you and I," she told me. And then, before I could consider how that fact might affect my future, she said, "To the best of my knowledge, I was the first Tonk ever to become a slave in the Citadel, and I proved a challenge for my masters. I had talents they wanted. I had Tonk magic, and a language they had never heard, and a dozen interesting, useful skills. But I was forever finding new ways to escape. I wanted no stone eyes; neither did I fancy a life lived within the Citadel's walls. I got out a number of times, the last time taking other young women with me."

"They didn't feed you to rats?"

She laughed. "I had something they wanted. I couldn't give it to them if I was dead. So they made me one of them instead. It was their first mistake, but not their last."

Inside of me, some little part of the terror that held me released its hold. She was something like me, was Hawkspar. She had once been kin, of a sort, and she had once planned her own escape. She had failed. I, too, had clearly failed. But I suddenly realized that I might yet live.

The oracle fell silent. She sat facing forward on the rosewood bench, stick thin, ghost pale. I watched her, and saw a quick flicker of amusement cross her face.

"Have you noticed how many of the Order have similar marks on their hands?"

"Yes, Oracle."

"That wasn't by accident. Only a few of the members of *my* conspiracy are still alive. But as other Tonks have become full seru in the Order, we've brought them into what we were doing. We never gave up on what we wanted—we simply discovered there was something bigger to fight for. Since then, we've been quietly buying up every Tonk girl from local slave markets. We buy a handful of the ones who appear in our local market, but have other buyers picking them up for us, too—we don't want it to be known that we're specifically looking for Tonk girls, because we could create the demand that would encourage slavers to hunt down more of them. The problem is bad enough already." She sighed. "We've been accelerating promotions of Tonk within the Order. Five Oracles are Tonk now, so we have a majority of one. That's enough for simple votes. All but a handful of old-guard Obsidians are Tonk, because we've worked very hard to get our people into that calling. Of the seru in the other specialties, we have either a majority, or at least parity."

I'd noticed a lot of young women bore tattoos on their left palm, as I did. I hadn't realized that *meant* anything, though. I didn't remember getting the mark. No one ever said anything about it. The girls and women whose hands bore the tattoos weren't treated differently than anyone else—not that I'd noticed, anyway.

But we had been, evidently. I sat staring at my hand, at the mysterious tattoo. Being Tonk meant something in here? What? Why?

I knew I'd *been* Tonk. I still spoke the language. It and more than twenty other Great Languages, plus as many local dialects as we could wrap our minds around, were drilled into every penitent as part of our daily training, which also included fighting, basic magic, history, and the duties and offices of the Cistavrian Order of Marosites, of which the Ossalenes were a small, solitary, and rich offshoot rite.

But it had never occurred to me that anyone but me still considered me Tonk. That my urgent prayers at sunrise and sunset, offered to a god other than Vran Vrota, the dual male and female god of the Marosites, might be offered by others as well.

It had never occurred to me to notice that most of the Obsidians wore tattoos on their left palm.

It had never occurred to me to notice a lot of things.

But perhaps the fact that no one thought to notice was part of the oracle's plan.

"You're wondering why we're doing this, no doubt," Hawkspar said.

"Yes, Oracle."

And she ran a finger over the mark on her own hand. "This mark is Eskuu," she said. "It tells you which clan of the Tonk you were born into. Did you know that?"

"No, Oracle."

"You and I are both Eskuu Tonk. We share a clan, a history, and blood. And we share a mission." She laughed softly. "You still say your prayers every day."

"All the penitents do," I said, my mouth dry with fear.

"They might," Hawkspar laughed, "but *you* still say the Tonk prayers, morning and evening. *Haabudaf aveerzak* each sunrise, *Gitaada* each sunset."

"You . . . knew?"

The oracle smiled a slow, secretive smile. "Oracles have sight unlike anything you can imagine. And with that sight, I have watched for my successor these long years—there was a girl thirty years ago who could have done what would need to be done, but our time to act had not yet come. The river had not yet flowed to the rapids. . . ."

She sighed. "You cannot understand what that means yet, but . . . you will. In any case, I have seen a great horror coming for a long time. But until now, anything we tried to do to stop it would have ended up discrediting the Order, and us, and wasting our one chance to end a hidden war and an unimaginable evil. Had it been the right time, I would have died and let that earlier girl inherit the Eyes. But I did not know if she could remain steadfast, and the time when the trouble would come was not yet clear to me."

I longed to ask the oracle what she wanted from me, but a penitent would never dare such forwardness. So I kept quiet.

"Times make the hero," the oracle said softly. She turned to me, lifted my chin with her cold, paper-skinned hand, and forced me to look at her Eyes. "The time has come for sacrifice," she told me. "For a young leader with a plan to become Hawkspar. The oracles will be told that you are the penitent the Hawkspar Eyes have chosen to be my successor."

That seemed to me a strange wording, and I am of a suspicious nature. "Am I?" I asked.

"No," the oracle said. She laughed out loud, merrily, and it occurred to me that before this meeting, I had never heard her laugh at all. She seemed in this blue-lit room very different from the oracle I had served for my season. I tried to imagine her as a young penitent planning her escape, but I kept seeing myself. "The Eyes would confer themselves on a senior acolyte, one who loves the Order above all and seeks advancement with her every step, and who would gladly serve the interests of the Citadel. Whereas you despise the Order and have already set into motion the mechanism of your escape."

"I do not want the Eyes, Blessed One," I said. "I have never wanted the Eyes."

She wrapped an arm around my shoulders and hugged me quickly.

"The Eyes of War would make you, arguably, the most powerful woman in the world, able to direct the courses of wars and declare the paths of peace. The Eyes of War can make their wearer a goddess, child, with powers you cannot conceive. Men will give you anything you ask if you will make them kings, and with the power of the Hawkspar Eyes, you can make a man a king, or make a king a pauper. Or a corpse."

"I never doubted that," I said, trying to sound humble and to avoid arguing. "But I . . . I love the sight of the sun, Oracle, and to see the stars. The colors and shapes of roses and daisies, the shimmer of glass, the beauty of clouds on a stormy day. The green of grass, the blue of sky. I fear blindness. And the pain." I looked into the Hawkspar Eyes, gleaming gold and brown in the old, thin face, and they held no emotion, no cue.

By all accounts, the oracles and the seru saw what mere humans could never see. The flow of time, the shape of magic, the links between what had been, what was, and what might be. Some said they could read our thoughts; others, that they could see what we would do, and sometimes punished us for sins in the future rather than sins in the past.

I did not know what they could do—nor did I care. What I knew was that no magical power equaled the beauty of the sun as it rose each morning and touched my face.

The seru—the Holy Wearers of the Sacred Eyes of Ossal—were blind to a one. When they became seru, they were taken to the Arena and in a ceremony attended only by other seru, their eyes were ripped out and the cold stone Eyes of a dead sera were removed and placed into their bleeding sockets, at which time they assumed their Eyes' names, and inherited their magic.

This was the future I was fighting so hard to escape. This was the future I'd been leading my courageous band of followers to escape. This was the reason I did illegal magic each day, the reason my allies and I had hidden stores of food, weapons, and supplies all around the Citadel.

Because neither I nor my fellow conspirators wanted to take Eyes.

I had no intention of hurrying myself into this hellish future. I was not even an acolyte; in theory, Oracle Eyes only went to acolytes who had attained the highest level. In theory, I could not be accepted for Oracle Eyes.

Not everyone shared my aversion to the Order and to becoming seru. Some of the penitents practiced walking about blindfolded so that they would be ready to assume their Eyes when the time came. Some talked endlessly about the ceremony and what it must be like. They eagerly sought out any work that they thought might win them favor and get them moved into Brevon Hall—the acolytes' house.

I had done none of that. I was senior penitent in spite of myself.

Hawkspar said, "The pain can be terrible, girl. The blindness is no joy. The nightmares are a terror. The moments of possession are horrible."

Pain I knew well enough. I'd been beaten more than once for my attitude or my actions. My back bore the tale of my infractions in raised and thickened scars.

Nightmares I already had. In my dreams, the slavers still came and ripped me from my mother's arms and murdered her before my eyes. In my dreams, I watched those who had threatened the Order tossed into the Arena in cages, and fed to starving rats.

Blindness I feared above all things, but I knew about it—knew it came with the Eyes.

But . . . *Possession? What possession?*

Hawkspar was still talking. "But you have *not* sought power, and when I offer it to you, you still don't want it—and this makes you special to me."

Not all that special, I thought. I didn't want the Eyes before you mentioned possession. Now? Now I will do anything—*anything*—to get myself out of whatever it is that you intend to do to me.

She said, "In you, I see someone like me. You will not sell your power to those who do not deserve your aid, you will not be swayed by the gold of kings or the lands and slaves of emperors or the seductions of Ossal. You will use this power for our people's fight."

Don't ask, don't ask, don't ask, don't ask, the little voice inside me screamed. But I broke every rule of the order, spoke as a penitent, out of turn, to an oracle, and asked, "What fight?"

And she did not strike me dead. Instead, she said, "The Tonk are in a war they do not know they're fighting. The men who took you slave and killed your family are part of a larger plot. You were not unique, your taking not an accident, but part of a plan by an enemy whose hand moves invisibly through a hundred other peoples. I am too old now to do what must be done. But I have worked my whole life to make the ground ready for your feet, to make the doors open for your hand."

"Not me," I said. "You haven't done this for me. You want someone else. I watched my family die, Oracle Hawkspar. I was so young—but my mother's face is with me always, the anguish in her eyes, her hands reaching out to pull me back from the barbarian who pulled me from her. My father is dead, my brothers and sister, dead or gone. I am alone."

"You are Tonk. Tonk are never alone. You touch your family, your people, morning and evening when you whisper your prayers. Can you not feel them beside you in those moments? Uplifting you? Strengthening you?"

I could. I whispered *"Haabudaf aveerzak"* to the rising sun, and all around me the voices of others seemed to whisper the same words. I could almost feel hands linking into mine, could almost imagine a place with great broad plains and free-running horses, and no stone walls to pin me to one place. "Yes," I told the oracle. "When I pray, I can feel them."

"Your family is all of the Tonk, and the Tonk are losing ground to an enemy who will see all who love freedom enslaved. Every virtue and ideal the Tonk value is in danger, child, and your sacrifice may save more than you can imagine. More than you can even comprehend until the moment when the Eyes accept you. You have a fire in you strong enough to control the Eyes instead of letting them control you. You have a talent for bringing together and making strong those who might otherwise live quietly and in fear. You have a hunger for freedom that you have pursued at risk of your own life."

Her voice broke. "You are Tonk, child. We are of one flesh and blood and spirit, you and I. If I could make these old bones young again, I would go out and fight. But all I can do is offer you the key to the gate I've been building my whole life, and beg you to take it and use it. The river has flowed past me; now it flows to you. Dare to step into it."

I imagined the ceremony of the Eyes, and horrors I did not want to contemplate. A lifetime of blindness. New nightmares. New pain. And the mystery of possession.

I wanted to tell her no. I wanted so very much to walk away. She had brought me in to ask me to take the Eyes, which meant I had some form of choice.

But she knew of my plans to escape, of the steps I had taken, and of the people I had involved. If I refused her, I could not hope that we would be permitted to proceed.

And if I refused but could not escape, some Moonstone sera or some Obsidian or some Amber would grow ill, and her Eyes would choose me to take her place, and I would suffer the same pain, the same dangers, the same loss—but for nothing.

I would save no one.

I would do nothing more than what the seru had been doing for the lifetime of the Ossalene Rite.

Perhaps outside the Citadel walls I did have a family who needed me. Perhaps I could find my way to freedom. Perhaps I could spend my life on something of value.

I was afraid of everything that would come.

But the future would come whether I chose the moment or not. It would take me and use me, or it would leave me behind.

So I chose.

"I will do as you ask, Oracle Hawkspar. I will become your disciple, and serve you until the Eyes come to me."

"I thought you had it in you to do that," she said. "Understand that you do not have much time. I have stretched my life long past its natural length. When the time comes—and it will come soon—I will simply let go of it, and within moments I will be gone. I will choose the day and hour of my death to give you and your plan the best chance to succeed—"

I interrupted her. For this, I knew I could have been beaten until I bled, but . . . "My plan? To escape?"

"I'm going to help you and everyone you've brought under your leadership escape. But you'll escape as the Oracle Hawkspar, and you'll take full seru with you—as many as you and I can bring into this. You'll have your freedom after a fashion. You're going to hunt down the invisible hand that is destroying the Tonk, and you're going to do your best to destroy it."

"Will I succeed?"

"Your chances are poor. But if you fail, the Tonk of the world will be gone within your lifetime." She shook her head slowly. "You cannot consider failure. You can only move forward and fight to succeed. I've started helping your plan already. I've strengthened the magic in your rescue plea, and have guided it to the currents the Eyes showed me. Someone has heard you. Someone will come."

Someone would come. Spoken from an oracle, my vague hope became a thing almost of solid fact. Someone would come, I would flee the Citadel, I would not die here.

And then the oracle stood and asked me a question I could not answer. She said, "What is your name, penitent?"

My name.

I had a name once.

It bound itself tight to pictures in my mind: of horses galloping in great thundering herds; of my mother singing to me in darkest night while outside our waxed felt walls a great storm raged; of my father walking beside me as I rode my first horse. I could see the faces of other children in these images—so many. My brothers and sisters, they might have been, but I had long ago forgotten.

My name died in fire and blood, when I watched my parents slaughtered and when I was bound with the other children around me and dragged to a ship and thrown into darkness.

In darkness I found weeping and prayer. I felt pain. Manacles around my ankles, a metal collar around my neck. Some around me coughed out their lives in the darkness and died—unheeded, untended, unmourned.

When darkness birthed me back into daylight, I stood naked on an auction block, blinded by daylight, and women from the Citadel of the Ossalenes came to the slave market and examined my teeth and my hands and feet. Something in me satisfied them, and money changed hands.

I became Slave.

And Slave I remained. Alongside Redbird, whose secret call for me was Mouse, I carried water, scrubbed floors, made soap, washed cloths for the oracles and the seru and the acolytes and the penitents. Along with other girls, some who arrived and stayed, some who were sold back to slavers because they were unsuitable for life in the Citadel, and some who would eventually be chosen as penitents, I toiled from first light until last, and ate my meager meals, and slept on a mat on a stone floor with two hundred others just like me. Evenings I studied with the rest of the slave girls at the feet of a succession of stone-eyed seru who taught the lot of us morning and evening prayers, manners and courtesies, languages, and the rudiments of unarmed combat.

We were all Slave, nothing but Slave, and beaten terribly if ever we confessed the names we had once borne.

The seru knew if ever we whispered those forbidden syllables. They always knew. So we earned scars on our backs, and we learned quickly that this was a sin we would not commit.

Words fall away if unused, and my name was nothing more than a word. I'd kept it hidden close to my heart, as I kept the images of the people who had loved me, but I never spoke my name, and no one else ever spoke it, and one day it was gone and I could not call it back.

"I have no name," I said. I stared down at my hands—at the blurring green-black lines that curled across my left palm. "I lost it," I said.

She sighed. "We got you young. So I suppose you have. Your name is somewhere inside of you. With time and effort, you'll find it."

"I hope so," I said.

"When you remember your name, take it back. It will give you strength against the Eyes. Remember that you are not the Eyes, and the Eyes are not you."

"I'll remember."

"Above all, find the enemies hidden behind puppets and masks who move to destroy our people. Destroy them before they can succeed."

"I will," I promised her.

She reached out a hand and touched me, and for a moment cold blue fire engulfed me. It stung me, and I could not catch my breath, and my head pounded and my eyes ached. And then she released me. "I have bound the Eyes to you. In what comes, they will act as if they have marked you as their own. This is a forbidden magic. Not even other oracles know of it. And you must never hint to anyone that I have done this, or you'll be killed instantly."

"I will keep my silence." I was good at keeping silence.

"Go, then. I will send word that the Eyes have chosen you, and that you are to be made an acolyte within the week."

3

Aaran

Aaran watched the burning wreck of the Sinali slaver sink into the sea. The storm had turned from a screaming nightmare into a relentless but harmless downpour, and all the wolf-ships had their water barrels on deck to take advantage of the bounty.

The rescued children—spread between the four wolf-ships—were freed of their shackles, fed, and given berths on the floor, where they slept in nests like exhausted puppies. Few if any of them had homes to return to; in most cases their taaks had been burned and any family members old enough to offer resistance had been murdered. But, in light of the slaver problems, the Tonk throughout Hyre had set up communicators who would find surviving family members or even distant kinsmen where they existed, and who would locate clansmen whose families would add these children to their own if they were left completely alone.

Several of Aaran's brothers and sisters had added orphans to their broods. In families with ten children or more, adding an extra mouth or three to feed created no problem.

Aaran passed quietly through their midst and joined his cousin, Tuua, in the ship's temple. Tuuanir av Savissha dryn Nakri was the ship's keeper. He was an Ethebettan scholar by preference, though he kept up with the other saints to make himself useful to any aboard ship who might seek his guidance. He and Aaran had grown up together in the nomadic Clan Viikuu Sogan, which drove caribou and Tonk horses between Miirtaak and Kopataak. They ran in the hills as boys, untouched by the horrors of the Feegash occupation and rebuilding that followed—events that were the greatest focus in the lives of taak-dwellers during the years of their childhood.

Best friends, they had chosen to accept the challenge of edaa together. For a season, they lived apart from the adults and children of their clan with the other young men undergoing the Tonk coming-of-age trial—they occupied an edaataak, an isolated hunting ground in which they lived in waxed-felt shaddas, provided their own food by hunting and fishing, sought the guidance of Jostfar and the saints in the paths their lives should follow, discussed matters great and small . . . and frequently behaved in a fashion that would never be condoned again, once they left the edaataak's confines.

Aaran still remembered his edaataak's experiments with the creation of alcoholic beverages (a moderate success), and the group's attempt to build a flying device (a terrifying failure).

But it was in the horrors that followed their edaa that Aaran and Tuua became men for real. Those had been the moments that set them on a shared path that led to the sea and to the wolf-ships.

Most of the things that bound the two of them as best friends had come before. All of the things that made them brothers came after.

Tuua, facing the door and writing in a thick bound journal, looked up when Aaran entered. "Ethebet save us, I thought we'd never see port again."

Aaran slid onto the fixed bench across the table from his cousin. "If Haakvar had not worked out his deal with the captain of the *Sea Hawk* over the distribution of the Sinali captives, I don't think we ever would have. I thought sure they were going to draw swords on each other."

"Who'd have thought Sinali slavers carried women of leisure aboard?"

"Who'd have thought they only carried three?" Aaran said.

Tuua laughed. "We'll not suffer too much for their lack of custom, I'm thinking. Midrid is not far, is it?"

Midrid, the nearest trading port that Aaran could find, lay seven days sailing due west, if the winds held or the windmen held up. "Not so far. And Haakvar got us good concessions for giving up the whore. Our pockets will thank us." He looked down at the table for a moment, then up at his cousin again. "I'm not going to be staying with the *Windsteed*."

Tuua looked stunned. "You're giving up on Aashka? You're going back to land?"

Aaran snorted. "Never." He sat on the hard bench, looking around the neatly stowed shelves of books, all held in by bands of gum-rope that kept them where they belonged, even in the worst seas. He'd read a handful of the volumes. Tuua had written a fair number of the books on the shelves, had memorized many of the remainder, and knew them all. "I found something while we were fighting the Sinalis. A connection to a hundred or more slaves in desperate danger. The Tonk girl who is sending out the distress signal doesn't have much time. She's about to face some horrible torture."

"So we make a quick reprovisioning stop, and then we go get them," Tuua said.

"That's what Haakvar said, until I tracked the girl's call back to its source for him and we went over the charts to figure out their position."

"And . . . ?"

"They're on an island in the northern Fallen Suns, close to the Dragon Sea."

Tuua gave a low whistle. "No."

"Yes. It's such an inhospitable area that all Haakvar has on his charts for that area is white space and the list of names of ships known to be lost while traversing the area."

"But you're sure Tonk slaves are there?"

"Yes."

"Then we go get them."

"Haakvar says we don't. That region is full of cannibals, necromancers, and petty island kings who demand tribute to pass through their waterways. He said he'd never get the full pack to sign on to a voyage into those waters, and without a full pack, he could be assured only that we'd never survive to save anyone. Then he said we couldn't afford to die for a useless gesture— the Sinalis have picked up their slaver activity on the north coast of Hyre, Wiiktaak was just burned to the ground yesterday, the children who weren't murdered are presumed stolen, and this pack owes its duty first to save those who can be saved."

Tuua sat up straight, studying his cousin with narrowed eyes. He pushed the book in which he wrote to one side without looking at it, then leaned forward. "Aaran Donin av Savissha dryn Tragyn, have you come to me seeking advice, or the guidance of Ethebet? For if you have, I offer my services."

Aaran shook his head. "Forget the formality. I already know what I'm going to do. I came in to find out if you'd do it with me."

"Tell me first that you're not going to mutiny and steal the ship."

Aaran laughed. "I'm not going to mutiny *or* steal the ship. I'm going to see if I can get a good rate on a captured ship, refit it as a wolf-ship, and then register as a privateer."

Tuua swore under his breath, invoking the Saints in unflattering ways. "I always suspected you were a madman," he said. "Aside from watching you trying to fly off the ledge in that horror of skin and branches you and those other fools built, though, this is the first time I've had proof."

"I know. I shouldn't consider it. But I'm going to. We joined the wolf-packs to save our people and stop the Sinalis, and these are our people. Tuua—I can hear this girl in my head. I can feel her under my skin. When I close my eyes, I can get glimpses of where she is, of the path to her. I can taste her fear and desperation—it's like metal and blood in my mouth."

He pressed his fists to his thighs, fighting the urge to pound the table in frustration. "*She* may be there. Aashka. She may be one of these captives. Something in me screams that this path, and this path alone, will take me to her."

Tuua studied his cousin for a moment, and Aaran couldn't read his expression. Then the keeper rose and went over to the shelves. He perused them for a moment and pulled a slender, black-bound volume from between the ropes. *"Atinak on Ethebet the Warrior,"* he said, and returned to his space on the bench. He thumbed through the pages, frowning a little as he did. And then, for just a moment, he read. "Yes. I thought so."

"Could I hope that you would share with me what you have discovered?"

Tuua read aloud: "Koorak the Spider-Legged, Jostfar's keeper and companion of Ethebet, stood at Ethebet's side on the day that she and the only three warriors who would wear her braid mounted horses to ride against an enemy of a thousand. This was in the days when Northmen plagued the Tonk and the Tand Plains were yet overrun with them.

"Koorak, knowing what she planned to do, had cast her lot with caribou bones, and had seen for her no future. So he told her, 'Stay and save your life, my beloved. If you go as only four, the moriiad will eat your flesh and drink your blood, and wear your bones in their hair and your teeth at their wrists. You cannot hope to succeed with only four.'

"Ethebet smiled down at him from astride her horse and said, 'Then come. Make us five and we shall rout them. Or if we do not, then we shall yet make such a show of it that none shall ever forget the tale.'"

Aaran said, "I thought the keepers had decided that Spider-Legs was a later fiction. Didn't you tell me that?"

Tuua gave him a disbelieving look. "That *misses the point,* you thick-headed ox. The *point* is, when a thing must be done, it must be done. But better to go with five than with four."

Aaran had spent long years listening to Tuua, and winding his way through Tuua's endless quoting and paraphrasing and referencing, all offered in place of answers that from a sensible man would consist of either "yes," or "no," or perhaps "I'll consider it."

"No, Tuua," Aaran said, "the *point* is that one of these days you'll actually answer a question and I'll fall over dead."

Tuua said, "I'm coming with you, you idiot. Of course I'm coming with you."

And that was why Aaran loved Tuua as his best friend. His trusted ally. His brother. "Good." He stood up. "You can contribute some of your share to the purchase of the ship, and to the refitting." He stepped over the bench and walked to the door. "And one of these days you're going to tell me how it is that *you* are the one who answers a question with fifty words when one will do, and leaves the asker no more certain of what you intend than before you opened your mouth—or your book—but *I'm* the thick-headed ox." He pulled the door open, but turned toward his cousin one last time. "In my case, of course, that would be *bull.* Not ox."

Aaran returned to his own berth in the crew cabin, stretched out in his hammock, and closed his eyes.

And slipped into the Hagedwar, building the forms and shapes of it. First he spun out the rich blue sphere that was the Banjgran—Infinite Eye of God. Within that, he cast the vibrant red cube called the Hunatrumit, the Flesh and Thought of Man, making sure all corners of the cube stayed within the borders limned by the sphere. Finally, he spun out of light and fire the pale yellow left-pointing tetrahedron that was the Sugritnaj—the Will of Soul, and intersecting through it the rich golden right-pointing tetrahedron of Grandolfit—the Will of God. The Hagedwar was foreign magic, from a people as far from the Tonk in philosophy as they were in geography. Fifteen years earlier, a Tonk Shielder named Talyn had discovered the secrets of the Hagedwar and turned them against the Feegash occupiers of Hyre, ridding the land of the foul bastards for good.

Talyn had then passed on what she'd discovered to as many Tonk as were willing to learn it, because unlike the Tonk magic, which could only be learned or used by those born with an innate talent for it, the Hagedwar could be taught to anyone who had patience and an ability to follow instructions. And unlike the Tonk magic, it could be used—more or less safely—by one person alone. The Hagedwar was not completely safe, but it was safer than stepping naked and alone into the View to listen to the songs the universe sang.

Aaran could use the Tonk magic. He'd been born with the talent and when he was old enough, it had manifested itself in him. But trackers worked alone, both on land and at sea, so he had learned to use the enemy magic, Silent Magic, as well.

Now, with the shield of the Hagedwar formed, with it cast around him to keep him from falling under the spell of the songs of creation that could lure him to leave his body behind while his soul wandered forever, he sought out the desperate cry that had so compelled him before. He tracked his markers back to the current.

And there she was.

He could not see her, though he could see through her eyes. He could not touch her, though he could feel through her hands. But he could hear her, because she could hear herself.

Her words when she spoke to others were foreign to him, but when she cried out to him, she spoke Tonk.

He strengthened the connection between them, searching for the thread that connected this stranger to Aashka. He could find nothing tangible, nothing that he could track directly. But for the first time since he lost her, he could feel a hint of the presence of his sister.

He had sworn an oath, and for the first time in long years, he caught a whiff of hope that he might live to fulfill that oath.

For that hope, he would cross seas filled with cannibals and enchanters and monsters—by swimming, if he could find no other way.

Penitent

Redbird sat down next to me at the long table where we took our meals. One of the seru led us in "Ritar, Ritar, Vran Vrota Megaro Nondi" (Vran Vrota, for All Your Blessings, Our Thanks Twice Over) and then the slaves carried out the bowls from which we would share our midday meal. Most were filled with hot tubers sliced thin, covered with bean gravy; some held fresh asparagus from the garden, lightly steamed and vibrantly green; and platters held sliced black bread and small crocks of nut butter to spread on it. And as always, we had clear water to drink.

We ate, for the most part, in silence, but some talking was forgiven if we kept our voices down.

"What did she say to you?" I asked Redbird.

"She requested that I take Obsidian Eyes. Immediately. That I become your protector. She said you were to be Hawkspar." Her voice dropped lower. "It does not have to be this way. We are so close. We can . . . finish what we've started. Tonight."

I'd thought of that very solution a hundred times throughout the morning, doing my regular studies and my regular chores as if nothing had happened, knowing that some time within the week, everything in my life would change.

We did not yet have a rescuer, but Hawkspar had said one had heard my plea and was coming; what if he came while I was receiving Eyes? What if he came and took all save me, and I was left behind?

What if I might hope to escape with my own eyes still intact?

What if all my coconspirators and I could reach freedom without being blinded and branded by the Order for the rest of our lives?

Even if he did not come in time to save us, we'd thought to save ourselves. We could slip aboard one of the ships down in the harbor of the town below the Citadel. We'd considered that option, even though we knew if we did so, we would have to pay with our bodies, traded by men and used as they chose. We had heard often enough about that trade—about the slave girls who had not been lucky enough to be bought by the Order, and who were probably dead of a hundred horrible diseases, and glad to be dead.

We could probably escape on one of those harbor ships—we had one coconspirator who had recently become an Obsidian, who had access to the gates that led out to the rest of the world. We could beg her to let us out, and hope that she remained loyal to us, and not to the Order.

"Did she tell you about . . . family?"

Redbird ate and nodded, saying nothing.

"She told me, too. I feel them out there. Every day, morning and night. You know when."

She nodded again. We did not talk about our secret prayers morning and evening. I knew she did them though, just as I did. No matter where we were, at sunrise we found time to face the sun and think—for we dared not say—*Haabudaf aveerzak,* and at sunset, *Gitaada.*

Hawkspar had known. The moment held magic in it. Somewhere out there, in my heart I felt others standing beside me. In that moment, I was never alone.

For that moment, for the possibility that it was more than simply my yearning heart pretending a feeling that did not exist in truth, I had to do what I had to do.

"I'm taking Eyes," I told Redbird. "You need not. You have a choice."

She looked from her plate over to me, her expression serious. "You are taking Eyes. Therefore, I am taking Eyes. The blessed oracle said you would need me. How much more truth is there in the world than that?"

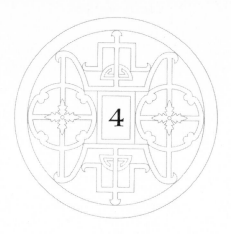

Aaran

The wolf-pack sailed into Port Midrid at dawn, with a clear sky behind it and busy docks before.

Aaran stood on the deck with the captain. "You'll leave us in a bad way if you go," Haakvar said. "We're not like to find another tracker of your caliber any time soon; you've been with us a long time, too."

Aaran nodded. "I can't save them all, Captain," he said, "but I believe I can save *these*."

"You're set on buying your own ship then, are you? And getting your papers, and taking on crew? I know you know the basics of it, lad, but have you thought out the particulars? You'll be crossing into the territories the Sinalis claim as their Empire. Whether they hold it in truth or only in the fiction of their legal papers and their twisted minds, if you're Tonk and they find you in the Fallen Suns, they'll kill you. No trades, no negotiations—and it won't matter if your commission from the Joint Council of Hyre is in order or not. Your papers are no good north of the equator and east of the Path of Stars. Those Sinalis'll call you a pirate and rip your innards out with a meat hook."

"I've thought of that."

"Have you considered the cannibals, then? Everyone knows the Fallen Suns are full of cannibals. And what of weird wizards? And sea monsters. Summoned storms, flying blood drinkers, headless women who will lure you to your death against reefs, walking dead? Those islands are the playground of the damned. Nothing good can come of going in there."

Aaran said, "All the more reason I have to go. Our people are trapped there. Slaves." He didn't tell Haakvar he thought Aashka might be there. He had worn that hope to threads with the captain years before; he could hope for nothing but a look of pity if he mentioned it again. Some things were better left unsaid—he didn't want word getting around that he was a madman when he was going to have to hire a crew to go with him. In the world of men and ships, mad captains were a health risk no sailor would choose to take.

"Then you're bound to do this?"

"I am."

Haakvar's eyes narrowed and he said, "You can stay on the *Windsteed* until cash-out, then. Make sure you have your next berth ready and your belongings cleared before cash-out, though, because once you have your money, I don't want you in my sight again. Unless you come to your senses before then."

Aaran was stunned. He and Haakvar has always worked well together, had eaten at table often, had shared ale and tales and a comfortable camaraderie. He'd expected the man to clap him on the back and wish him luck. He'd hoped Haakvar, who was rumored to be richer than taaklords and to own nearly half the ships that comprised the Tonk privateer fleet, would consider financing part of this venture. "I've done well by you for years," Aaran said. "And I'm heading off to save Tonk slaves no one else has gone after."

"You have done well by me. But now you're leaving me with neither a decent warning, nor a trained replacement, nor even a half-trained assistant. And no matter what you might believe, you're taking whichever fools you might find to follow you up north to die. You'll be wasting good men and at least one good ship, and I have no patience for that."

Aaran felt anger boiling in his belly, but he kept it locked down tight. Haakvar thought it well enough to run after the slaves that were easy to reach, but was willing to leave to die those unfortunates who had gone into darker lands. Aaran had always thought better of the captain than that. He said, "Then I'll be here until the share is divided."

"Keep yourself out of my sight until it is."

When he parted company from the captain, Aaran sought out Tuua, who was down in Ethebet's temple with the books.

"Trying to decide which part of the collection to negotiate as part of my severance," he said, grinning, as Aaran stepped through the doors.

"Consider none of it, and count yourself lucky with that," Aaran told him. By the time he'd finished describing his encounter with Haakvar, Tuua looked almost sick.

"I've *written* a dozen of these volumes," Tuua said. "I just days ago completed an analysis and gloss on Raakbaan av Finetaak's *Journeys of Ethebet: The Ten Essential Meditations.* I cannot leave any of my own writings behind; I haven't had a chance to take them to a temple to be copied and entered into the archives." He stared around the chapel walls, wild-eyed. "If they stay here, it will be as if they were never written."

"You don't have to come with me, Tuua. Perhaps this is a sign from Ethebet that at last the time has come for us to part company."

Tuua said, "I will seek Ethebet's guidance. Until I have done that, I don't know what else to say."

Aaran felt his heart sink. He had somehow imagined that Tuua would instantly declare that the books were mere books, and that his cousin mattered more. But books were Tuua's life and love.

Perhaps, after all, it *was* a sign that Ethebet had decided to set the two of them on different paths.

Aaran went to his own quarters and gathered up his kit. He had other belongings onboard, but if Haakvar suddenly decided not to let him board again, Aaran intended to have already removed those things he considered essential.

With his kit bag slung over his shoulder, he headed up to the deck. Thanks to Haakvar's temper, or his own stubbornness or stupidity, he was going to be stranded in Midrid. To his benefit, Midrid was a large, busy port. He had contacts around the town. But he decided he wanted to know where he would be staying before Haakvar had a chance to kick him off the *Windsteed.*

The docks were the usual jumble a man could find in any busy harbor, and while Aaran let his legs adjust to ground that didn't move beneath his feet, he walked the piers, simply taking it all in. After months of water and small islands, the busyness was alien to his eyes. Gamblers and whores and hucksters he found in plenty, and sailors fresh from the sea, and sailors weary from the land. Old men sat along the warehouses watching the ships that sat at anchor with wistful eyes. Old women and young scanned the horizon for a familiar mast, or a long-absent flag, a known blazon on sail.

This was Aaran's known terrain. This thin strip that lay between his home in the sea and the foreign world hidden away behind every port was always like coming home, and it was home in any harbor into which the sea washed him. He searched out familiar faces in the crowd—men with whom he'd shipped out, women who might welcome him for a meal or a toss between sheets. He saw some, and nodded, but did not stop to talk. He needed to find a place to stay—but not a place like the ones he had always stayed in before. He was to be a captain, taking on crew, and to hire decent officers he would have to stay in a place where captains—*good* captains—would stay.

He could find a room in one of the dockside taverns quick enough, and pay sailors' prices, and live with sailors' risks. Dockside, honesty was not a policy. Money flowed fast, ale faster, and the roughs that eyed his sea-staggered gait with narrowed eyes smiled a little as he passed. He could feel their interest in him and their assessment of his possible value versus his possible threat. He knew the game. He knew the rules.

Captains stayed inland, in fine rooms. Officers saw their wealth and knew they could trust their futures to these wealthy captains' ships.

Aaran wandered into the unknown world of Midrid proper. It was, beyond the rattrap structures built onto the piers and wharfs, a pretty place. It lay closer to the equator than any point in Hyre, and had trees and birds far different than those he knew from home. Midrid had no walls, either, which made it unlike the Tonk taaks. Its narrow, uneven, curving streets wandered in all directions, the products of ruminant surveyors, no doubt. The houses were all white wood planking, ship-built, tall roofed. Profusions of flowers hung from window boxes, and ribbons of laundry flapped on lines from house to house across the streets waved like banners to welcome home returning heroes.

From the high stories and side windows, he saw women leaning on sills and chatting house to house. In the streets below, children ran in mobs and scattered like chickens as he moved close.

In Trade tongue, he asked a woman where the nearest good inn might be found. Lips pursed, she looked him up and down—that narrow assessment outlanders got from homefolk—and at last decided he was a decent enough sort to warrant an answer. She pointed onward and up the hill, and told him to ask for Wayron Hogsmann, and the Buttered Bread.

Aaran thanked her. He did not toss her a coin as he would have had he gotten the same information from a child; customs differed from place to place, but he had yet to find a land where decent women took money from strange men as anything but an insult. Or an excuse for calling out the dogs.

The Buttered Bread spoke of wealth and comfort. It announced itself like a silk-dressed woman at a party—the inn was dressed in bright pink paint, with glittering lights showing from huge windows. It had a wide courtyard, a dozen liveried boys who were taking horses back to a stable or bringing them when called for, and greeters in the brightest orange shirts and breeches Aaran had ever seen stepping up to potential customers and asking them how they would wish to be served.

The customers themselves, women and men, expensively dressed in clothes of exotic cut and exquisite fabric, stepped in and out of the inn through a wall of glass-paned double doors that sat side-by-side, eight across.

Aaran had never seen the like. Marqal never sat beneath months of falling snow and ice, and its architecture suggested as much. But—Midrid had lived its whole history at peace, too. Not a single building had been built with war in mind. This place, if ever called to defend itself, would throw up pretty hands in despair and be overrun in an hour.

One of the greeters came up to him, judged his status quickly, and in Trade tongue asked if he would like a room for the night.

"Longer than that," Aaran said, "though I'm not sure how much longer. I'm going to have to buy and refit a ship and take on crew, and I've only just got into harbor."

The greeter permitted one eyebrow only the slightest arch of surprise. Aaran, dressed in the uniform of a Tonk ship's officer, knew he didn't look like a ship buyer, or a crew hirer. He looked like the sailor he'd always been.

But the greeter said, "We have captains' quarters open on the top floor if you'd like to inspect them, sir."

Aaran shook his head. "I'm not looking for anything so grand. This will be my first ship, and I need to save as much of my share as I can toward what I'll have to do. Let me have—" He hesitated. If Tuua were coming with him, the two of them could share a two-bunk room and save a great deal of money in the process.

But he couldn't be sure that Tuua would be joining him. "For tonight, let me have a one-bunk. I have someone who is considering investing with me in this venture—I'll not know for a day or two if he's coming in on it."

The greeter nodded. "We can easily move you to a two-bunk if you need. We have a comfortable number of open rooms at the moment."

Aaran studied the constant traffic around the front door and tried to imagine the place when it was full and busy. "Thank you."

"Private bath?"

Aaran thought of the luxury of a private bath, and the temptation pulled at him like a storm tide. "How much extra for the night."

"How will you be paying?"

"Horse cash."

"*Horse* cash. *Very* good, sir. Customers who pay in favored currencies get our discount. Your room will be three cash per night, half a cash extra with private bath."

"The parlor needs to be large enough to interview potential investors, crew, and suppliers. I'm also going to need names and directions for area shipwrights."

"The services we offer to captains who room with us include half price on all meals taken at table with one or more guests, so that you can entertain those with whom you wish to do business without impoverishing yourself; posting of the positions you have open on our board in the grand hall and on our boards down on the docks, for a mere pittance; and a greeter who will, for a modest sum, arrange interviews with you at times of your convenience."

"How much for the extras?"

"A one-time fee of ten horse cash for the job postings; a daily rate of one horse cash for the greeter; and as for meals, if you are careful to order the house ale or house wine, prices per guest at meals will be fixed at half a cash. Our house drinks are quite palatable even to the most selective."

That sounded reasonable. "Let me see the room, then."

"You get a two-bunk for us, did you?" a familiar voice shouted behind him.

Aaran spun, disbelieving. "Tuua?"

Tuua, a big pack slung over his back, came swaggering up the street. "I'm in," he said with a broad grin.

"Your first officer, Captain?"

"My temple keeper."

"Very good. A two-bunk, then, Captain, *with* private bath?"

Aaran glanced over at the man, knowing he must be radiating relief like a fire radiated heat. "Absolutely. All your captain services. A parlor room. I'll have my list to you in the morning."

"*Very* good, sir," the greeter said, and led the two of them through the grand glass doors.

"You're sure about this?" Aaran asked Tuua as they followed the greeter. "You'll make no friend of Haakvar for leaving his employ."

"I promised I'd help you find Aashka and bring her home. And if we have to move all the world ourselves, I'm with you until we do."

Penitent/Acolyte

The day I did not want came far too quickly. Obsidians came to the Ranwi building before first light. The penitent on hall duty in our dormitory watched me strip down to nothing but my tabi. I owned nothing, and would take nothing with me to the acolytes' house—not even the soltis on my feet.

"You're to be Hawkspar?" The girl who asked me had a fuzz of bright red hair, skin so pale it was almost transparent, and vivid green eyes.

She was Ter Hurry, a junior penitent, though of course that would change when I moved up. She was also one of mine—in on my escape plans, as desperate as I to flee the confines of the Citadel, and as fine a fighter as any of the Obsidians.

"I am," I told her. "Nothing has changed, though."

But I could not tell her more. Other girls, freed from work for the few minutes before they would go to bathe and then retire for the night, wandered in to stare at me. Word had evidently spread.

"Are you excited?" one asked. She was dark-eyed, dark-haired Fawi Catch, a senior penitent, but assuredly *not* one of mine. She loved the Order, and worse, had always been ambitious. She yearned for a place as an oracle, talked about the wonders of having Eyes, and talked far too often about how she would make changes if she attained an oracle's power. She thought our lives were too soft.

Few of the other penitents cared much for her, though she belonged to a little group of fanatical penitents who shared her vision of the future of the Citadel.

"No, I'm not excited," I said.

"You're to be a goddess," she said.

"So I'm told. My sense of it is that I'm to have my eyes ripped out and cold rocks—spelled with visions and pains and suffering I do not want—jammed into their places."

Fawi Catch said, "But you were chosen. This is what we live our lives for—to be *chosen*. To be made something more than we are. To be given names, and new sight, and to serve and to . . . to earn praise and honor for the Order."

"We *had* lives before the Ossalenes. We *had* names," I growled. "We had families and homes." I had more to say, but stopped myself. I had, after all, chosen this path. If I had not chosen it, I would have eventually been forced onto a path not of my choosing. Nonetheless, I had been called, and like the rest of the women who would one day take Eyes, I had in the end agreed to take them voluntarily. And I would do so for something bigger than the enrichment of the Order.

Instead, I left quietly, to a few whispered good wishes.

I walked the short distance from Ranwi Hall to Brevon Hall—the only acolyte hall. Redbird was already there, standing and waiting. First Acolyte Marit Brevon met me at the door, a bundle of acolyte garb in her arms.

I took my place beside Redbird.

"Welcome, acolytes," she said, looking at both of us, but handing me the bundle. "You're to be Acolyte Alsa Brevon until the new first acolyte," she nodded toward Redbird, "takes Eyes. I will step back to Betsin until you become Marit."

Which was not how matters should have been. Redbird and I were the newest acolytes, while Alsa was the second-ranked cell, and Marit was first.

I bowed to the first acolyte and said, "Permission to ask a question."

"You're an acolyte now. You don't have to ask," she said.

Of course. "How, then, am I made second acolyte? How is . . ." Names are always a problem. "How is the new Marit made Marit?" I asked her. "We should be Rono and Khern." These were the two lowest acolytes.

"You aren't an acolyte because you have what the Order sees as an aptitude or a vocation. You've already been chosen—and by the Hawkspar Eyes, no less. You're to be an oracle, she's to be Obsidian, and she will become Obsidian on the morrow. Hawkspar sends word that you will be Oracle within the month, though she will not tell us the day."

I had heard rumors that some of the oracles could make seru Eyes. I could not swear to it, but the rumor was fairly common among the slaves and penitents. However, for me to receive the Hawkspar Eyes, the current Hawkspar had to die. Oracle Eyes were unique.

So she knew she would die within the month?

I did not wish to step ahead of all the other acolytes, though, nor did I imagine that Redbird did. All penitents heard of the jealousy that sometimes led to . . . well, "accidents" in the acolyte hall, as women who had been chosen as acolytes for their vocation were passed over by Eyes who chose wearers who were younger or who appeared less qualified. I knew already that I had not been the true choice of the Hawkspar eyes, and I knew as well that some girl or woman within Brevon Hall *had* been. I was a pretender. The true heir to the Hawkspar Eyes—assuming she wanted them—would have cause for jealousy if she suspected the truth.

I must have looked worried, for Marit said, "It is the way of things. We all know it. We renounce possessions, we offer ourselves in service. We do not seek advancement; advancement chooses us. You know this, as does every woman here. You were chosen, they will accept." She shook her head slightly and added, "You must stay focused on your purpose." And she held up her left hand.

On her palm, she bore a mark similar to mine. She put the hand back down quickly, but tipped her head to one side and said, "Do we understand each other, then?"

I raised my own left hand and presented my palm to her. And raised my eyebrows. And shrugged.

Her head nodded almost imperceptibly. *Yes.*

"We understand each other," I said.

She was not one of my fellow conspirators, which suggested she was one of Hawkspar's conspiracy.

I wondered how many of us there were, what parts the others would play.

"Shower," she told me and smiled slightly. "As you usually do." And she left.

A chill ran down my spine. How many people knew about my magic?

Five years earlier, when I ascended from junior penitent to following penitent, I found myself in the class of Sera Rosestone Hano Sha, who gave us an overview of magic systems, including the Tonk Shield and View training.

The View is . . . well . . . everything. In Comparative Religion, we learned that to the Tonk it is nothing less than the body and soul of the universe. But that is because some Tonk are able to move within it, to work with it. To most other peoples, the View is the part of magic that will swallow and destroy the unwary. The Sera Rosestone explained to us how Tonk warriors banded together to enter the View with their minds, and how they used the energy they found there as weapons of offense and defense. She explained how other peoples who worked magic learned to create shields to protect themselves from the View, which was seductive and powerful, and which called in and swallowed the unwary.

She showed us briefly how to create a shield, and discussed how Tonk warriors discovered that they could reach into the View.

That day five years earlier, an idea I'd held in my mind about water and where it ran—how it always ran down, how it all ran to the sea—came together with bits of Tonk magic I had been taught as a child, bits of Ossalene magic I'd managed to pick up from watching older penitents and acolytes practicing, and from the discussions and demonstrations of Shield and View.

That day, for the first time, I bound magic to water and begged for rescue. I'd felt terribly clever.

Five years later, considering the breadth of the conspiracy I was discovering, I realized two things I had never considered before. That particular Sera Rosestone had a tattoo on the palm of her left hand. Not the same as mine. But similar.

And that she had given me exactly the information I needed to discover that I was one of those Tonk who could find the View—and exactly the demonstration I needed to protect myself while using it.

Five years earlier, I had felt terribly clever.

Five years later, standing in the icy shower building and binding my plea, I realized that it was entirely possible that the Sera Rosestone had taught my group as she had, hoping one or two of us would find our way into the View without getting ourselves killed doing it. That someone would do what I had done.

Had Hawkspar seen my actions? Could she see such a thing in the future?

Penitents were not permitted to use magic unsupervised, of course. And we were carefully and constantly watched, even when we were to all appearances completely alone. The Seru Onyx did not hear our thoughts, perhaps, but through the magic of their Eyes, they saw our every move, even through walls. They would descend like black-robed vultures upon even the least transgressor.

I'd used the shield Sera Rosestone had taught us, thinking it protected me from their watchful Eyes as well as from the View. Perhaps the protection I had derived from it had been other than magical in nature. Perhaps use of that spell had only put me under the protection of those who worked with Hawkspar to further her secret cause.

I felt uneasy as I created a glowing blue sphere in my mind's eye and wrapped it around myself, preparatory to moving into the View.

I was reaching for magic while facing for the first time the fact that within the month, I would become subject to the agonies through which the oracles and the seru suffer in order to share the magic of the Eyes. I had my own magic. Why couldn't I escape with my eyes intact and use that magic to seek out Oracle Hawkspar's invisible enemy hand?

I drew in breath, and imagined my toes sinking into the stone floor, digging roots down to the center of the world like the strong roots of a tree. I imagined pulling water up through my roots, drinking it in as trees drink, as flowers drink—drawing it up in a steady stream. I imagined myself filling with this water, filling until I was full to bursting, until I was like the statues in the gardens that spewed forth water from eyes and mouths and noses, from toes and fingertips and nipples and navels. And when I could feel my summoned magic stream through me as strongly as if it were the shower, I bound my will thrice around the water, and thrice times thrice bound spirit-water to real water, and when it was bound, in my mind I called out to whomever might hear me: *Come. Save us! Hurry, for we suffer and we die. For love of Jostfar, by the hands of the Five Saints, rescue us!*

And I sent my spirit-water and the real water pouring out the drain, through the pottery pipes of the Citadel, out of the Citadel and down the cliffs on which it sat, down into the bay, out into the sea. I sent it wherever it might go, praying with everything in me that someone with a strong arm and a fierce courage would hear my plea and follow my spell and my call back to me. To the Citadel. To rescue not just me, but every girl and woman within the thick Citadel walls who yearned for escape.

And while I was praying, all I could think was that I wanted my freedom. I wanted to flee.

At that moment, I wanted more than anything to renege on my word to Hawkspar, and take my allies and escape from the Citadel before any more of us were bound to the Ossalene Rite. I had no doubt panic suffused the plea I sent out.

When I stepped out of the shower, I got myself under control.

With my shower taken and my body clean and presentable, and with my magic done, I wiped down the shower, then put on the new and unfamiliar garb of the acolyte.

After underthings, I first donned the allar—which means *deceiver*. It was a shirt of the same cut as those worn by the Ossalenes, made of pale, heavy green linen and worn beneath the sleeveless tabi. It had long, full sleeves snugged tight at the wrists with long cuffs and a tall, padded collar called a tera that was designed to protect the throat, and I fumbled putting it on. The sleeves and their tight-buttoning cuffs initially resisted my attempts to fasten them, and when I'd hooked the tera closed, I felt as though I would choke. Rumor had it that fighting seru—the Obsidians and the Onyxes—as well as the oracles, wore a layer of hammered metal within the layers of padding in their tera. I tried to imagine inheriting a metal-lined collar, and my mind fled back to being chained in the darkness in the hold of that slave ship, lying between the dying and the dead. I wondered if Redbird would wear such a collar. I wondered how she would find the courage to put it on if she did.

I did not mind the pants. Except for the pale green color, acolyte pants were the same hakan-allar as those worn by seru and oracles. The hakan-allar were tremendously full and not bound at the ankles, the better to hide a fighter's movements.

Over shirt and pants, I put on a tabi and rayan like those I had worn as a penitent. But these, like all other acolyte garb save the cepa, were pale green. The color signified rebirth, according to the seru. While slaves wore the dark, dreary gray of dead ash and penitents wore the brown of freshly tilled earth, acolytes represented pale seedlings pushing their way out of the earth to become . . . well, whatever we were to become.

The seru wore colors that matched the Eyes they received. So both Obsidians and Onyxes wore black—though the Seru Onyx had white trim on their garb, and white bos to make them stand out. The Seru Rosestone wore rich fuchsia, the Seru Beryl had garb of deepest green, the Ambers put on rich yellow-gold, the Bloodstones deep red trimmed with black, the Moonstones white, and the Granites the many grays of doves with pale shading into dark, and edged with black.

I dressed with difficulty in the new and more complicated robes of the acolyte, then tossed my penitent tabi into the laundry bag, and stepped out into the common room and waited while Redbird tied up her second baruti.

"I suppose we have to go out there now," she said.

I didn't want to, either.

A group of acolytes, spending a few moments talking together before the bell sounded final prayers, stopped talking and turned to watch us walk in. Some of them nodded to us in silent greeting. Others frowned and turned away. Two of them were allies of mine, promoted before me but now ranked beneath me. To them I would tie a knot-message that we still worked toward our plan.

The previous Marit, now made Betsin, waited apart from them. She stepped toward us. "I must give you both your duties," she said. "Come with me."

She told us the lists of chores bound to the Marit and Alsa cells, all of which had to be completed before sunrise each day. Redbird and I repeated each chore thrice, assigning each chore to a separate finger and marking an image of it in our minds. From the time we are slaves, we change duties so often that the seru teach each of us this technique for remembering what is expected of us. Beatings are the other way they enforce memory, but the seru first give us the opportunity to learn without pain. Those of us with some sense of self-preservation take advantage of that opportunity.

As Betsin told me my last chore, she handed me a message tube that would hold a rolled knot-net. The tube bore the unbroken seal of Hawkspar. She said nothing as she handed it to me, nor did I say anything as I accepted it. If the oracle was choosing to send me a knot-message, it would be something that not even Betsin would dare to say out loud, if she even knew what it was.

The bell for prayer sounded, and Betsin said, "You'll find your prayer mat on the bottom shelf, next to your coal brazier. Be sure to remember to burn your prayer incense." And with a finger, she tapped the message tube.

So she did not think me a fool who on my first night as an acolyte would forget how to say my prayers.

I was, instead, to burn the knot-net when I had read it.

"It is tradition for the Marit to take prayers with the Alsa the night before the Marit takes Eyes," Betsin said.

We parted without another word, and Redbird and I entered my cell for the first time. I opened the door to my balcony, and a nearly full moon shone its light into my quarters. I went out to light my oil lamp from the central lamp on the floor. In the penitent cells, lamplighting had always been a Ghoteh duty, setting up the altar had always been the responsibility of the room Jara, preparing the incense had been the duty of the Fawi, and leading prayers had fallen to the Ter.

But after that night, where Redbird and I split duties silently, I realized that for as long as I was in the Citadel, all the duties of the cell would fall to me.

That night, though, I put out my prayer mat before the room's altar, while the sounds of the seru singing the "Office of Night" floated across the Citadel grounds. Redbird set the brazier on the center of the stone-topped altar, and opened it. A slave had cleaned it and filled it with fresh kindling and perfumed, fatty tree knots. I lit the kindling from my oil lamp, and dropped my wax incense into the little pile.

Then we both assumed the stance of prayer—kneeling, toes in our split-toed soltis splayed to let us rise quickly, knees forming the base of a wide triangle for balance, hands clutching the message tube—for in all things we remained a warrior order, and never chose positions of vulnerability. I broke the wax seal as the song "First Order of Night" ended, and the sera who sang first voice began the "Chant of Spirits."

I pulled out the carefully rolled knot-net, and unrolled it, and hooked the knot-stick that formed the top border on the hook that was at the edge of the altar for that purpose. Sometimes, after all, acolytes had to read the prayers they were to memorize before they learned them well enough to do them from memory.

And with my fingers sliding along the knots, with the moon shimmering fat and pale down on me, with the sweet first voice singing the solo "Chant of Spirits," I read:

> Oracles Sunspar and Windcrystal have expressed doubt that you are the true choice of the Hawkspar Eyes, and have asked that you be put through full trials. You will be brought to the tower tomorrow without other warning, so that the oracles may decide your fate. Prepare yourself.

Redbird had been reading the order after me. I turned to her, terrified, and saw my expression reflected on her face.

Oracle Sunspar was the Eyes of Secrets. Oracle Windcrystal was the Eyes of Justice. I recalled the history of the Ossalene Rite, and the lists of succession for the oracles. Very few nominations were ever sent to trials, and almost none were overturned, for oracles have long memories. The histories recounted a handful of violent successions, where a challenged heir, upon obtaining her Eyes, promptly removed those who had sent her to the trials. Methods of removal varied, but not in their cruelty or violence.

Our Order's oracles were mostly older women, closer to their own deaths, and guarded about their own survival, I supposed. Both Sunspar and Windcrystal were young, though, and from all rumors, zealous in their worship of Vran Vrota and consumed by their devotion to the rite established by our long-dead founder, Seruvra Ossal—which meant *Watcher of the Hand of*

Gods. Ossal was the blessed daughter of Vran Vrota who'd created the oracle Eyes, and many of the seru Eyes.

If those two oracles stood against me, then the Seru Onyx, the Eyes of Discipline, who policed the slaves, penitents, and acolytes, would stand against me, for Onyx served at the command of Oracle Windcrystal.

And the seru Bloodstone, the Eyes of Order, who knew everything everyone did, or found ways to find out, stood against me as well, for they served Oracle Sunspar, the Eyes of Secrets.

I was in deep trouble.

6

Aaran

"Where, then, is your ship docked?"

Aaran, sitting in the suite's captain chair, interviewing yet another potential officer he hoped to recruit, said, "I am still seeking a suitable vessel."

He didn't add that he hadn't yet been paid his shares for his previous voyage, and so had nothing but pocket change with which to purchase his vessel at the moment. For three full days, he'd been trying to put together a crew, and for three full days, Haakvar's malice had thwarted him. It seemed that every good Tonk sailor of officer potential had already heard about the madman who had abandoned a ship and crew that needed his skills to seek the opportunity to hare off into the Dragon Sea in search of death.

Aaran did his best to present the demeanor of a sane and capable master-tracker turning captain; he did his best to present his voyage as the heroic rescue of kidnapped, enslaved Tonk children, with a good secondary potential to bring back significant treasure in the process.

It didn't matter. First they came to the open call, or because Tuua, out actively looking for crew, had sent them, and they offered their skills and credentials. Second, they asked about his ship. Third, they put his name and mission together with Haakvar's "madman" label. And fourth, they walked out the door. Whether they did it laughing that they had allowed themselves to see the madman face-to-face, or whether they did it annoyed that they had wasted precious time that might have been spent elsewhere was the only variant he'd yet experienced in the play.

He sighed, and to save face, told the man before him, "Unfortunately, your qualifications don't meet my needs, so we don't need to take this discussion any further." He stood, and the prospective officer stood, too, awkwardly, and left with a bewildered expression on his face.

That was the first new type of exit Aaran had seen in three days, and he almost had to think it an improvement, because he got to be the rejector, rather than the one rejected.

He leaned back in the chair and rubbed his eyes. The Tonk captain's uniform he wore itched—it was new, and the fabric was stiff, and it fit him uncomfortably. He thought he looked very good in the rich emerald greens and blacks of the thing. But the uniform had not yet been tempered by the sea— and he began to fear it never would.

A boy poked his head through the door. Aaran, weary and dejected, recognized him as one of the two young wharf rats that Tuua had signed on as captain's runners. The boy was bright and cheerful, happy to have a place, and Aaran wished he could recall the boy's name.

He struggled with it for a moment, because a good captain knew every soul on his ship by name, and Aaran intended to be a good captain even in the small details.

Neeran. It was Neeran.

"What is it, Neeran?" he asked, and saw the boy's shoulders straighten with the acknowledgment that a ship's captain knew him by name.

"Keeper Tuua sent me with a message for you."

"Bring it in then, boy," Aaran said.

Neeran handed him a wax-sealed note, stamped with Tuua's seal.

The *Windsteed*'s cargo has been sold, the captives counted and sent off aboard ships back to Hyre, and our shares are to be divided in the morning. Get here earliest.

Aaran clapped the boy on the shoulder and said, "Good news at last." The tiny silver coin he pressed into the boy's hand earned him a delighted smile. "Go," he said. "Spend it or save it. On the morrow, we'll find ourselves a ship. Crew should come easier then."

He slept poorly, his dreams laden with vague portents of disasters. But the hotelier woke him early as he'd requested, so he shook off the nightmares, put on his master-tracker uniform, and jogged most of the way to the dock.

He got onto the *Windsteed* before the night watch shifted to day, and announced himself to the watch. They greeted him warmly enough.

"Captain said if you came aboard, you were to wait on the deck," one of the two men said.

Aaran had worked with both of them. They were decent men. One liked his ale too well, the other fancied women of inexpensive virtue when he was on land. But both were honest. "Captain still angry that I'm leaving?"

"He hasn't found a decent tracker yet, and has talked to one or two dozen of them. He vows you won't find ship or crew, and you'll come back with him when your foolish attempt to go against him fails."

"So . . . yes."

"If you want a clap on the back and a good-fellow-well-met from him, tell him you're planning on staying aboard after all."

"No."

"Then once you've got your share, you probably want to put a bit of distance between yourself and him. He hasn't said anything to any of us, of course, but he's been loud enough to his first."

Aaran waited, walking the deck with the watch, leaning on the rail watching the sun rise, hearing the familiar creaks and groans of the *Windsteed* as she sat at rest. She'd been home to him for years, and it was hard to think of having her sail away without him aboard; hard, too, to consider that he might never see any who sailed with her again.

But if he closed his eyes and used the Hagedwar to feel his way across the sea, he could find the girl who had called to him, and the others with her. He could feel that faint, gut-held promise of Aakasha after so long. He might cross the ocean and crawl his way through the Fallen Suns and for all of that, he could rescue the girl and discover that all he got from her regarding Aashka was a clue, a hint . . . or maybe even nothing. Even if that was the case, he was still going. He could not bring the captain with him; he'd tried. So now he had to take his chances on his own.

At last Haakvar came on deck. "I heard you were here. I'm doing shares in the common room. Come on."

Aaran followed him belowdecks, and into the central area where crew ate, played cards, whittled, talked about their lives, and told lies about women and fish. The armed day watch stood guard over two large strongboxes. Aaran hoped both of them were full.

The captain gave the common sailors their shares first, then graded sailors, and then specialists like Aaran and Tuua. He was paying in horse cash, which would make the money easy to spend anywhere. Tuua got a wad of horse cash thick as his wrist, and a bonus of half again as much. Both of the other specialists received the same.

Aaran did not. He got his share, but no bonus.

He looked Haakvar in the eye and said, "I tracked that last slaver across the sea through a storm the likes of which we've never sailed in before. The trackers on all three of the other wolf-ships lost their lines on it as soon as the weather got bad. I was the only one who managed to hang on to it throughout the whole chase. The only one, Haakvar. Without that ship, we would be out near a hundred children and every bit of treasure that you looted. So where's my bonus?"

"I'm saving it for when you sign your next set of papers with me, Aaran."

"You can't do that and you know it."

"I can."

"You want me to sign on with you again, you follow the track I found up to the northern Fallen Suns. The only reason I'm leaving now is that you won't do that."

"I *won't* do that. Didn't fancy the idea of dying in those hells when you shipped it past me, and I don't fancy it now."

"Then I won't sign on with you."

Haakvar stood and rested his palms flat on the table, his nose shoved in Aaran's face. "Then you have what you've earned. Get off my ship."

"The rule has always been share plus bonus for the specialists, and an extra half bonus for the tracker. Supposed to be a half bonus pitched in by any pack ships that benefited from the tracker, too—so considering my pitch-in would be three half bonuses from the others and a half bonus from you, I'm looking at missing my regular bonus, and two full extra bonuses."

Aaran grinned at him, and stood, and rested his own hands flat on the table. Eye-to-eye with Haakvar, who outweighed him two to one in hard muscle and heavy bone, he said, "You sure you don't want to pay a bonus to the tracker who won you and three other ships in your pack your richest prize of the voyage. You, who are supposedly in desperate need of a new tracker. Because, I swear, if word gets out that you shorted the man who got you where you needed to be through a ship-eater of a tempest, you're likely to never have another tracker worth the name step on board a ship with you again."

"You threatening me?"

"Simply trying to help you see your way to good business practices—ones that wouldn't leave you shorthanded and blind your next voyage out. I like the *Windsteed*. I'd hate to see her get left behind by ships with eyes."

They stood that way for a long time, with Haakvar glaring and Aaran not blinking, while all around Aaran a sense of creeping danger grew tighter and keener and closer. He wondered if Haakvar meant to have him killed when he stepped onto the docks, or maybe before; if he'd hired someone to rob him; if the captain planned to drop him in a weighted bag and throw him over the back of the ship right then.

But Haakvar said, "Three bonuses for him. Now," and one of the guards counted out the money. It was a huge pile.

"Understand this," Haakvar said. "You'll have no good name from me to any man who asks it. No aid from me or mine if we cross paths and you're in desperate need. Were you ablaze, I wouldn't piss on you to put you out. Do you understand?"

"Well enough," Aaran said, putting his money into his bag and shoving the bag down the front of his pants. "You've been quick enough to put a bad name on me already, and you've cost me good officers and good sailors. But I'll take my chances with the men who'll take their chances with me. For my part, I'm satisfied with that so far as you go no further with it. If you're threatening me harm—that I'll have to deal with. If you're satisfied with trying to give me a bad name, knowing that if I find what I think I'll find, you'll brand yourself a coward and a fool—and I'll help with the branding, I swear it—we can part in peace, and I'll wish you no ill will."

"Oh, if wishing's to be a part of it, I hope you're lining the bellies of a hundred cannibals by year's end. I wish you no end of hurt and suffering, and a bad death as a bow on the box. But I'll do nothing to bring your troubles about."

Aaran walked to the door. "Then, for all you wish me, I wish you twice as much." He left, and after him came the other specialists. None of them, including Tuua, said anything to him, nor he to them. Haakvar's ship wasn't the place, and right after that exchange wasn't the time.

All the men walked together, though. They would travel the docks togther to watch each other's backs until they'd put their money where it would be safe. And after that, Aaran and Tuua, with a payout that would let them invest in a sound shipwright, would take the next steps in their voyage.

"You didn't tell Haakvar you were leaving?"

"For all they know, I'm giving my time and future earnings to a nest of whores," Tuua said. He was unpacking books into one of the bolt-and-lock storage boxes the inn provided to patrons. Most of the books Aaran recognized as being Tuua's work. A few others were not.

"Does Haakvar know you took your books?"

"No. I didn't remove a single thing that I did not own—but I'll be dipped in oil and lit for a wick if I let him have things I *have* paid for. Or worse yet, things I've written. He didn't sign me to contribute to his temple, just to maintain it and serve its users."

Aaran studied his cousin with worry. Tuua was taking chances, and Aaran didn't want to spend any of his share of money or Tuua's paying off local justices and guards. He said, "Any chance he'll have you served for theft, whether you have a right to these or not?"

Tuua said, "Any keeper would walk into his temple and see that all the necessary books are in there. And a few oddities. It's a whole library even without these books, and Haakvar will have no cause for complaint. But Ethebet has a temple here, and keepers who fought the Feegash. And the Sinali. We're a brotherhood, you know—as tight as any of Ethebet's own. They'll not let a dozen new works fall into oblivion. Some of these replace works lost in the Feegash Purge." He smiled and added, "Captains may stand alone, but keepers don't. And Ethebet's keepers carry swords."

Aaran wanted a dockside war not at all. But Tuua had every right to fight for what belonged to him, and if it came down to swords, Aaran would be right there, standing shoulder to shoulder with him.

"The Ethebettans have taken a message to Haakvar by now, telling him that they'll be replacing me with another member for the next voyage. He has no real say in the matter. The temple rarely exercises its right to recall us, but it has that right."

"I fear we have such officers as we're going to get from these parts, anyway. Want to help me sign crew?"

Tuua flashed a grin at him. "Was it not Ethebet herself who said, 'Let the champion lead the warriors, and let the warriors follow'?"

Aaran looked at him with narrowed eyes. "You tell me."

Tuua headed for the shower. "Would I make up such a thing?"

"Yes."

Tuua laughed. "I've no wish to lie to crew. Enjoy the power of captaincy, my dear cousin. I'll help you look for a ship when you're ready, since apparently I'm to pay for half of that. In the meantime, however, I plan to go out in search of companionship of a feminine nature. It may be the last I'll ever have."

Acolyte

Two Obsidian seru woke me from sleep.

"I—it's still dark," I said, which was perhaps not the cleverest thing anyone has said to a sera. At least it wasn't something that would get me in trouble.

One sera was pulling items off my shelf—in the dark I could not see what exactly she was getting. Without the benefit—or hindrance—of sight, she had no trouble finding what she needed. The other said, "Get up. Dress in your best. We have little time before you are to go before the Oracles to be tested and confirmed."

"I thought acolytes were only to face trials after their oracles had a chance to train them."

"Generally that would be true. However, everyone has heard that Hawkspar is near death, and rumors have reached certain oracles' ears that you were not the sort of penitent who would ever have been chosen by Eyes of any rank, and certainly never by the Hawkspar Eyes. So you are to face trial, and if you fail, Oracle Hawkspar will also face trial."

I was frightened. Redbird, who had been away for much of the night, finally slept in the cell across from mine. I could hear her steady breathing. And in the two other cells, the Betsin and the Arna tried to sound like they were sleeping as well, but both clearly weren't.

"What am I to do?"

The Obsidian who held my garb said, "You are of very little importance in this matter, overall. From time to time the oracles challenge each other in order to change alliances and shift power among themselves. You are merely seen as a weakness in Oracle Hawkspar's previously unbreachable wall. The matter is, in fact, about her, not you."

"Yet I'm the one who will die in trials if I fail."

"Being disposable is never a pleasant experience," the other Obsidian said. I could hear no sympathy in her voice.

I dressed hurriedly. When I was finished, I asked, "Have I time for bread or a drink of water to settle my stomach? I'm afraid."

"You have no time for anything. They have demanded your presence in the Tower."

At mention of the Tower, fear coursed through me. I had never been in it. It was a place where only those who sought the assistance of the oracles, or those who had displeased them, ever trod.

We walked through the dark toward the Oracle Tower, cutting across paths, walking through gardens and over grass, taking the quickest route possible. The dew soaked through my soltis and chilled my feet, and made the hems of my hakan-allar heavy. I found myself missing my neat, easy-to-keep-dry penitent pants.

I did not know if the hour was late night or early morning. Weariness clouded my vision, and fear my thoughts. Outside the Citadel I heard the cries of small animals, and looked up to see the stars that glittered overhead. So far away, so very cold. If I survived, if I became Hawkspar, I would miss the stars, too.

We passed Oracle House and turned onto Tower Path.

Before me stood Oracle Tower. Unlike the gray stone from which the rest of the Citadel—from walls to halls to temples to outbuildings—had been built, the founder of the Ossalene Rite had created that tower entirely of a single block of deep green volcanic glass, carved at the base to mimic vines climbing its surface, and farther up, to show the faces of men and women peering from between the vines.

The faces often seemed alive, and always seemed to be watching, peering down on us from their high vantage. I'd noticed more than once that they never seemed to be in the same place, either. I hated walking past Oracle Tower, nor could I think of a single slave or penitent I had ever known who did not. The air surrounding it tasted like pain and fear.

It is a part of the magic of the Tower that only when someone who belongs within is present does it have doors. It is an otherwise solid mass of glass—no army could force its way inside uninvited, for there would be no inside to the tower. Nor could any who had no business there pass. The slaves and penitents have all heard this, as I had heard it. Yet I did not understand what that meant until the Obsidians pushed me forward.

"Touch the wall," one said.

I touched cool, smooth glass, and felt a vibration beneath my fingertips.

The glass curled away from me, shaping itself into an arching doorway. Light began to glow within the tower, and by it I could see stairs forming themselves in front of me, spiraling upward around the inside of smooth, glossy walls. I took a step back, frightened—the air that rolled out from the tower had a stink to it that drove like a spike straight into my brain. Something obscene waited inside, and I would have offered anything to be spared walking through that arch or up those stairs.

One of the Obsidians behind me said, "We may not pass."

The other said, "I was instructed by the Oracle Hawkspar to give you a single piece of advice. Hawkspar said: *To the damned, courage is better than truth.*"

I turned to stare at her. "What does that mean?"

"I could not say," she told me. "You'll have to discover its meaning on your own." And then she put her hand to the small of my back and shoved me forward. "Go. You are to wait until the Oracles join you. You would be well advised to pray."

I stumbled though the arch just as the seru rang the bells of Basmam, third quarter of dark, and I felt the doorway suck itself shut behind me. I refrained from turning only out of sheer willpower; I knew if I saw there was no longer a door behind me, I would panic. I would run. In the faintly green-glowing darkness of Oracle Tower, I sensed that panic would have consequences I could not imagine, and would not desire.

I had a long wait ahead of me before I could hope for the presence of the oracles. They rose at Noesmam, the last quarter of dark, and would be unlikely to enter the tower before the bells rang Dalmam, the first quarter of light.

From the chapel across the green, seru began chanting the "Prayers of the Dreaming Vran Vrota." These songs become so much a part of us that sometimes I dreamed them. They are beautiful, but like meditation and prayer and so many other things in our cloistered life, they take us away from who we are . . . and after time, I suspect they take who we are away from us.

Which is probably why they exist.

Within the glass walls, the chants were distorted, and the voices singing them sounded inhuman, as if they were sung by sharp-voiced angels. Or demons.

I did not look behind me, but slowly trod the steps.

I felt vibrations beneath my feet, heard liquid sounds all around me, and knew that beneath me, the stairs folded in upon themselves and the walls bled back into solidity, while before me, new stairs formed just out of my sight.

Around me, voices whispered.

To the damned, courage is better than truth.

I did not know, even yet, what the oracle had meant in sending me that message. But I knew to keep my hands close to my body, for the walls beside me rippled as I ascended, and faces flowed upward in the glass, watching me, and glass hands formed and reached out to touch me as I passed, then melted back into the surface again as I moved away. I knew not to look behind me, for as long as I did not look back, I could imagine a clear retreat still lay behind me. I knew to breathe slowly, as I had been trained to do since my days as a slave. I knew to cast a shield around myself as if I were going to do magic.

I knew to pray. But not to Vran Vrota, the hybrid god of people from a world far away from my own. I prayed to the Tonk god Jostfar, through Ethebet, the patron saint of warriors.

I reached the top of the stairs and found myself in a featureless open space that glowed with its own inner light. I settled myself on the floor, assuming the stance of prayer. I prayed for myself, and for Redbird who at first light would be taken to the Arena for Gata Ossala Shen, the Ceremony of Taking Eyes.

I prayed for rescue. I prayed that if I were to die, none of the rest of the penitents and acolytes, and even the sera, who had joined with me in our plan to win our freedom, would be punished for my sins. I prayed to live. I prayed to see my parents again.

At some point I must have fallen asleep, for I found myself on a broad, rolling plain, with the grass around me rippling in a gentle breeze. Wildflowers bloomed in astonishing profusion, in colors so beautiful I could not even name them. Horses galloped by me in a glorious, thundering stream. When the last of them vanished over a rise, I turned to see a woman watching me. She was dressed all in white, and her hair was the white of purest snow, done in a complicated braid unlike anything I had ever seen. Her eyes were blue, her lips full, and her face surprisingly young. The cut of her clothes reminded me of my mother. She smiled at me, and suddenly, I felt safe. I felt as if I had found my way home. She watched me, staying at a distance. I wanted to run to her, but at the same time, I knew I could not. When the time was right, she would come to me.

The time was not yet right.

I could almost believe I knew her.

A sickening smell woke me, a stench of decay and filth. As soon as I opened my eyes, I saw that the sun was rising. Its light filtered through the green wall, marking the east for me. I heard bells ringing, and below me, the moist sucking sounds of the tower opening a passage that would permit the oracles' entrance.

I needed the privy. I wanted to run.

I could do nothing but stand and face whatever came for me.

I heard feet stumping slowly up the stairs of the tower then, and short, harsh, panting breaths.

Hawkspar, as always wearing black, and nearly invisible within oracle's cloak and hood, came first.

She was followed by Oracle Tigereye, the ancient Eyes of Discovery, who was as gaunt as Hawkspar, but gorgeously dressed in robes of gold and green and brown, heavily embroidered, with jewels woven into place, and with a matching cloak and hood of exquisite make.

Following Tigereye came Ruby, wide as a plowhorse and probably as strong. The Eyes of Family had dressed in red and silver and shimmering white, with a red velvet cloak sparkling with diamonds and gleaming with cabochon rubies that matched her eyes. She'd had her girl dress her hair in a complex fashion of curls and braids and loops, and it spilled around her shoulders in a gleaming black waterfall.

Windcrystal, whom I could only think of as my enemy, though I hated to do so, followed. Her pale, transparent blue Eyes of Justice gleamed. She wore unadorned black.

Sunspar, her Eyes of Secrets glowing pale yellow, followed Windcrystal. She, too, wore black.

Oracle Sapphire, the Eyes of Magic, wore dramatic wide robes of embroidered purple. They were foreign things, not even cut in the fashion of the order's robes.

Behind her came Oracle Emerald, the Eyes of Growing Things. Wearing black.

Amethyst, the Eyes of Words. She wore white.

And finally Raxinan, whose Eyes of Compassion always made my skin crawl. They were clear as pure water, but full of thin lines of brightest red, as if someone had dropped tiny sticks in them. She wore simple robes of the Order, as plain as my own, without any symbol of her rank. But Raxinan was known for both her modesty and her piety, as well as for her deep and adoring devotion to the Order.

When all the oracles stood around the periphery of the room—with me in the center—a green glass table grew out of the floor, with the center cut out. The center sank, the table rose, and each oracle took a seat in a throne of green glass. And then they all stared down at me. At no point could I see them all, for they sat evenly around the circle. Was this what petitioning kings and emperors faced when they came to ask their favors? I wondered if they felt as small and frightened as I did.

Oracle Hawkspar cleared her throat, and I turned to face her. Her face twisted with anger. She said, "The oracles will ask you questions. Answer them in the manner that seems best to you."

And then she turned to the women with her. "I request your acceptance of my acolyte and Vran Vrota's chosen vessel."

Windcrystal said, "She is not devoted to the Ossalene Order. I am certain of this. I cast my lot against her."

Heads turned toward Windcrystal, and Tigereye said, "You cast your vote before it has even been called? You would not at least offer the girl the opportunity for testing?"

"I would not," Windcrystal said. "I know your choice, and I know her sort." The oracle's voice rose. "I will never believe Vran Vrota chose her! On three past occasions I have recommended to this body that she be cast out and sold for transgressions, and on each occasion I have been told that she committed no transgression. And yet I knew she did!" Now the oracle was actually shouting. "On two occasions, when you voted against me, I asked that she be disciplined with rats, and again many of you stood against me. I have taken my defeats quietly and abided by your vote, but she is not worthy to be an oracle. She is the worst kind of sinner, a selfish, headstrong girl who has no business in any position here, not even as the least of slaves."

I was stunned. I had always thought Windcrystal the kindest of the oracles. I had worked for her for a season following the season I spent with Hawkspar, and unlike Hawkspar, Windcrystal never had a harsh word to say to me. I worked hard for her; I was as obedient and quiet as I knew how to be; I tried with her more than in any other post I'd held to honor the Order and its ways. I'd done these things simply because she had been kind to me—or at least as kind as anyone within the Citadel ever had been.

Sunspar spoke next. "I believe that I will not vote for her. I believed Windcrystal's accounts of what she had observed before, and I still believe them to be true. But I would first have this acolyte tried, to see if Vran Vrota truly has marked her. I would, after all, not wish to be unjust."

"Of course," Hawkspar said. "And how would you see her tried?"

"I suggest the trial of the rats."

"Because justice will have its vengeance for being so many times overruled?" Hawkspar asked.

I could only think, *The trial of the rats? Yes, of course it will be that.*

"Because justice is tired of being flouted," Windcrystal offered.

The Oracle Ruby said, "She hides things. She lives a lie. She is not one of us, and will never be one of us. But by all means send her to be tried, if you dare. If Vran Vrota has any hand in her choosing, Hawkspar, I'll allow myself to be led by that."

"And your choice of trial?" Hawkspar asked.

"Oh, the rats. We have a good cage full of them that had been starving for one of the slaves, but the girl died before we could put her to them. They'll be ready by now."

Would no one speak for me?

Emerald then said, "I have no issue with the girl. Still, if we are not to take a vote now—and it seems to me that we could, and have this business settled quickly—then I, too, offer the trial by rats as the acceptable means of demonstrating that this candidate is genuine."

Hawkspar nodded. "I see. Have none of you any questions to ask her? Have you no wish to hear how she would present herself? You know I have not had time to train her, as each of you were trained, and as some of you are now training your acolytes. You know that I bring her before you as she is, without subtlety or deceit beyond whatever she might have naturally. When we entered this room, I told her to answer the questions you gave her as seemed best to her."

Oracle Windcrystal said, "You said that. But you did not tell her not to lie."

"Would you know if she lied, Windcrystal? Do you think the spirit of Vran Vrota within you could tell you that?"

"Of course I'd know if she lied."

"Then all I did was give her the opportunity to be dishonest if that was in her nature, so that you would see her as she truly is."

Hawkspar then sat with her head down, her hands folded before her. Waiting.

I waited, too, turning slowly within the center of the circle, hoping to catch some sign of compassion from those who held my future in their hands, but I was beginning to feel light-headed. They had wanted me sold. They had wanted me killed. How, then, had I lived long enough to find myself in a position where I seemed likely to be killed anyway?

I fidgeted, desperate for a trip to the privy, unable to speak unless addressed, and remembered my dream, and the woman in white who had seemed so kind.

Raxinan said, "With four prepared to send her to trial, perhaps you should withdraw her as your choice, Hawkspar. I would not like to see her fall to the rats."

"She is Vran Vrota's choice," Hawkspar said. "The Eyes themselves have called for her. Shall I deny the Holy Dyad what it wants so that I may pander to the egos of those here who for *selfish* motives do not like her?"

"Oh, no," Raxinan said, startled. "I would never suggest that. I simply do not wish to see the girl die."

"Nor do I," Hawkspar said. "But she will not. Vran Vrota and the Eyes are well pleased with her."

"Hah," Ruby said. "The Hawkspar Eyes? Those Eyes haven't had a choice in the Hawkspar vessel in generations. I cannot imagine the spineless gathering of oracles it must have taken to let you into this body."

"Can you not?" Tigereye, oldest of those present, said. "I was one of them, Ruby. I have found Hawkspar dedicated to our Order over these years, and of all of us, she alone maintains the selflessness of our Order as if she were still a penitent. The acolytes live gentler lives than she." The old woman stopped to cough, then said, "No one anywhere suggests that the good word of *Hawkspar* can be bought for a fine roll of silk or a supple slave girl."

I tried hard to make myself invisible. I had often heard exactly such things said about the Oracle Ruby. I did not suppose that they would be mentioned within a conclave of oracles, however, or even that this behavior might be questioned by anyone. We low to the ground dare not look up and question our masters.

I was discovering, though, that our masters were more than willing to question each other.

Raxinan said, "I have no questions I want to ask the girl. You have been an inspiration to me, Hawkspar, and I will trust in your Eyes' choice."

Amethyst had been quiet, too. "Hawkspar, you know you have my support."

Sapphire said, "And mine. I have never seen a problem with the girl. She is much as any other of them—if your Eyes have marked her, who am I to question?"

Tigereye said, "You have my support as well, Hawkspar."

My oracle said, "Then you are divided. Half for me, half against me. Vran Vrota will remember who stood where—be assured of that."

Emerald twisted her hands nervously. "It's not that I stand against you or the Hawkspar Eyes. I simply feel that, well, Sunspar and Windcrystal have access to information hidden even to the rest of us. If they stand against you . . . well . . . your . . . Vran . . . your Eyes' choice . . ." Her voice trailed off into silence.

Hawkspar rose slowly. "I could call a vote now, and with my vote, which I am entitled to cast, I could have the Hawkspar Eyes' choice for the next Hawkspar without forcing the girl to prove herself." She turned her face to Windcrystal and said, "Are those of you who stand against me prepared to face the consequences if my acolyte faces the rats successfully? There will, I assure you, be consequences."

Ruby said, "What consequences do you think you can carry off in your condition, you ragged crone?"

"I can call for the testing of *your* acolyte, for one thing, Ruby. I hear she warms your bed well, and she is a pretty thing—but I wonder how she would fare against any of our standard tests."

"Hawkspar can do that," Tigereye said. "And not only can she, but I would support her call if she did, Ruby. The rumors about your acolytes have been long standing. You have sold off three of your acolytes in past years for suddenly becoming displeasing to your Eyes or Vran Vrota—there are certain tests that you could be brought forward to face. Were I inclined to meddle, I would wonder how the Holy Dyad has such a difficult time discerning which woman among all of those in the Citadel will suit your Eyes, when for the rest of us, the Blessed All seems up to the task." Her voice grew both soft and terrible, and she said, "There are penalties for oracles who are guided not by the hands of Vran Vrota, but by their own appetites. And there are precedents throughout our long history which you would do well to remember."

To the damned, courage is better than truth, I thought.

If they chose to challenge Hawkspar's honesty—and I was sure they could do this, and would, if they began to suspect she had done what I *knew* she had done—then I would die, and she would die. Because she *was* lying. Further, the oracles could have some way of testing that lay beyond the straightforward trial by ordeal.

If Hawkspar and I both died and the Eyes went their own way, then whatever lay beyond the walls of the Citadel of the Ossalenes would be sacrificed as well. If, truly, we were to be the salvation of the Tonk people, then without us, such family as remained to me would die.

To the damned, courage is better than truth. Hawkspar had bound the Eyes to me. Or had claimed to. If she had not, then all was already lost

Windcrystal said, "How easy to threaten, to terrorize, to avoid facing a trial and at the same moment avoid proving your doubtful truth. But we would not face repercussions, because no goddess has ever looked twice at that blasphemer of yours."

Hawkspar said something else, her voice sharp—but I could not hear her words over the pounding of my own heart.

If all I had was lies waiting to be laid bare, or courage, I'd choose courage.

I said, "I'll face the rats."

All the oracles turned their faces to me. Sunlight poured through the green glass to the east. It turned them all ghastly, inhuman shades, and made their stone eyes glitter.

"What did you say?" Windcrystal asked me.

Louder, I said, "I volunteer to face the rats."

If silence were water, we would have all drowned.

Across from me, I saw Ruby shudder. Windcrystal's grip tightened on the edge of the table. Sunspar turned her face toward me and seemed to stare; I could not guess where she really looked or what she really saw. But— whatever it was, she did not like it. Emerald wrapped her arms around herself and shivered.

Before any of them could respond, Hawkspar stood and said, "Then it is decided. My acolyte will be stripped and bound and placed in the cage with starving rats for the time from one bell to the next. If she is devoured, we are agreed that she is untouched by Vran Vrota, and I will face the consequences for my choice of her. If she lives but is injured, she will be returned to slavery, to work here or be sold as the oracles shall choose, and I shall face such fate as you deem fitting. But if she faces the trial of rats unscathed, then the Dyad's touch on her is accepted—and I will claim right of redress for the questioning of the will of the Eyes and the Holy Dyad." She placed her hands flat on the table.

I did not get the feeling that she leaned on it because she was tired. Rather, I felt sure that she leaned on it because doing so made her menacing. She certainly frightened me.

"Are we agreed that I have presented the rules of trial of this acolyte by rats in true and full fashion?"

"I will forgo the trial," Sunspar said.

Hawkspar laughed. "I'm sure you would. But my acolyte, moved by the spirit of Ossal within her, has volunteered. It is now out of your hands. As is your own future. The accused who volunteers to face trial may not be denied." She repeated, "Are we agreed that I have presented the rules of this trial in true and full fashion?"

Four strong voices claimed agreement. Four less enthusiastic ones also as-
sented.

While the oracles voted me to the rat cage, I stood thinking about the
slaves and penitents I'd seen fed to rats—for the punishment would be
worthless if the rest of us did not witness it. The victim never survived. I had
never seen anything so horrible, or so drawn out and shameful and ghastly.

And by my own word, I had bound myself irrevocably to that fate. In the
Arena at that moment, Redbird was getting Obsidian Eyes so that she could
be my second, so that she could stand by me as my guard.

And I had thrown myself where the oracles had surely planned to throw
me anyway. But I had done it to myself—and possibly rendered the sacrifice
she was making worthless.

To the damned, courage is better than truth.

Courage. And a privy.

Aaran

Aaran and Tuua were on their fifth shipwright, and their fifth shipyard, and well past despair. A ship such as the one they needed—one that would carry a full crew and permit the rescue of more than one hundred slaves as well, would cost them most of everything they had merely as a down payment. They hadn't the credit with shipyards to get a good rate—on a ship that would meet their needs, the interest alone would sink them. Anything they might have gotten close to was too small.

Worse, though, Haakvar's poison had spread. Word of Aaran's mad destination, along with Haakvar's predictions for any who dared sail with him, had reached the ears of not just officers and sailors, but shipbuilders and moneylenders. And even worse, Haakvar had passed word through his entire fleet of ships that any shipwright or lender who aided Aaran would never have custom from him again.

In the first two yards, shipbuilders who gave him prices and showed him ships laughed in his face the instant he produced his papers and they learned his name. And then they sent runners to the other shipyards, so that when he and Tuua stepped onto the docks in the third and fourth yards, they were ushered off again before they could even state their business.

But Aaran refused to give up, and in the fifth yard they weren't chased away. They didn't identify themselves. They only said they needed a big, inexpensive ship, and right away.

"Ahh, you're the crazy ones, then," the shipwright said, and laughed. His name was Makkor Gurak-Golak-Dok-Hkukguh, or, as he translated for

Aaran with evident pride, Makkor Only-Hkukguh-Builds-a-Better-Boat. Hkukguh being his people's god of the sea.

Aaran gave Tuua a look, and the two of them started to turn away.

Makkor laughed. "Don't leave. Walk with me a bit, and let's talk about this. I don't like men who threaten me, so I'll listen to you two crazies just to give that arrogant Haakvar a bony fish to stick in his craw."

The shipwright was so bald that not only had he no hair on his head—he had neither eyebrows nor eyelashes. His ebony skin sheened blue in the midday sun. He had sons Aaran's age and older, but he didn't look old enough to have fathered the oldest of them. In Midrid, he was a minor legend. Evidently he was famous for one story that got longer and wilder every time Makkor told it. And as he'd been telling it for nearly forty years, it had evidently reached the point where it required a breakfast, a midday, and a full sit-down dinner with wine to get through.

Makkor walked them along his private dock. "I hear you pissed in Haakvar's beer, and now he has it in for you."

"That about sums it up," Aaran said glumly.

"I hear that you're on a fool's mission into the heart of calamity, with a date for your own demise."

"So we've been told," Tuua said.

"Going after a hundred stolen children, and them that stole them."

Aaran heard a change in Makkor's voice, and the hope in him that he'd thought dead twitched once. "Yes."

And Makkor looked at them sidelong, and walked to the far end of the dock without slowing at any of the piers in between. He stepped onto the last rickety finger pier, and said, "Follow."

Halfway to the end of Makkor's last pier, lined with ships that were, to a one, clearly salvage, the shipbuilder stopped. "Before I show you what I got, you tell me what you want. Just so I know which side of the stories is true."

Aaran took a deep breath. "We need room for a hundred passengers, though they can be close-berthed. We need room for a full complement of crew, a full complement of marines—I'd like to run with fifty crew and fifty marines if I can. Maybe more. We need arms storage, we need treasure storage, we need a good galley and berths for cooks for all shifts. We're going to be running hard through ugly waters and danger, so speed would be a good thing. We don't give a cold damn about looks."

"You really are going up the Path of Stars, through the Fallen Suns, and into the Dragon Sea."

"If we live long enough to get that far," Aaran told him.

"I have your ship. You won't like her, because you'll know her. But she'll do what you need her to do."

They walked all the way down to the end of the pier. The last ship.

"She's drowned salvage. An older Tonk wolf-ship—bigger and slower than the current builders are making them, but with a good knife hull and plenty of room for cargo. I've already done structural repairs on her, but haven't had time to shine her up or add any extras."

Aaran did know the ship, and Makkor was right—he didn't like her. She had been the *Kytaak Haar,* the *Loving Daughter,* and she had gone to the bottom of the sea in unknown circumstances, taking all hands with her, plus a rumored thirty rescued captives.

Tonk sailors did not salvage sunken ships. A ship that had betrayed the lives of those onboard once was not given a second chance.

But there were no more shipbuilders in Midrid, and not likely to be any other ships that would meet Aaran's needs in Makkor's shipyard, else he would have shown them.

Aaran and Tuua walked up the ramp, and stood on the deck, smelling old wood and new wood and drying varnish and the sea. And beneath them, mold and mildew and decaying food and some incredible stink that Aaran couldn't even put a name to.

When he stepped between the worlds, the Hagedwar would shield him from the spirits of the ship's dead. But the men aboard would feel their weight. They would know they sailed with the dead, and that the ship carried the curse of the despoiled grave.

"There won't be another one," Tuua said.

Aaran kept staring at the ship, feeling the presence of the disturbed dead pressing close to him. "I know."

The wolf had good lines. She'd been built a hundred and fifty years earlier of the best Tandinapalis timbers, peg-and-joinery fitted; hers was old-school craftsmanship that had taken a crew of artisans a good year to build.

Until a poor captain had taken her helm, she'd faithfully served a score of better captains and good crews.

Her stint beneath the waves showed, though. Aaran could see places where the decks had worn seaweed and barnacles, where paint had bubbled, where seaworms had worked the wood, where scum had established footholds. She smelled like death, and to more than just his nose.

Makkor said, "She's sound. Now. I got her hull back in shape, replaced bad timbers, got her seaworthy. She's not lovely, but with a good crew you could have her gleaming again before you left the harbor."

"Isn't the crew decides that. Any crew is good with the right captain."

They worked their way up to the captain's deck.

The shipwright ran a hand along the cabin door to the captain's quarters, a faraway look in his eyes. "So. You want to take my ship to the Fallen Suns?"

"You going to double its price when we tell you we do?" Aaran asked.

"No. For the right promise, I'll even give you a deal like you've never had."

He opened the door, and Aaran looked in. Death assaulted him and filled his nostrils. Aaran crossed the threshhold reluctantly and looked around. The quarters held the captain's berth, which was big, plus two small berths with cabinet-style privacy doors up in the loft for runners, a mapping table, and a spiral staircase down into the captain's attable. Mattresses had been replaced. Everything else had been wiped down, but not scrubbed. The stink would take muscle and sweat to clear.

"What promise?"

He and Tuua followed Makkor aft to the officers' quarters and the steersman's castle.

"Here's the thing. I sailed down here from Bheki with my brothers when I was not much more than a lad, with a shipload of friends looking for adventure. We came down through the Fallen Suns. Quite an adventure, that. I'll have to tell you the story. But coming through, I picked up a wife for myself."

Aaran felt his skin tingle at Makkor's mention of the Fallen Suns. Nobody had said his wild sailing stories were about the Fallen Suns.

"My wife died fifteen years back," Makkor continued. "And there's not another woman in these parts fit to kiss the ground where her feet walked. I'm a lonely man, and I want another wife. You bring me a girl from the Fallen Suns who speaks Terkak, a good, big dark-skinned girl with some fight to her who would like the looks of me and is willing to take a rich old man as a husband and keep him warm and happy nights, and I'll give you the ship for the cost of the repairs I've put into it. If you survive to get back here, of course."

Tuua and Aaran looked at each other. "The cost of repairs?"

"You don't want to try to cheat me, though, son. I've got friends in places you cannot imagine, and if you don't find me a good wife, you'll owe me the value of the ship—and that's a lot, even if she's a drowner. Not all captains or crews are as picky as the Tonk."

Aaran was looking around the officers' quarters. They were roomy enough, with decent storage, double-berth cabins, adequate light. They didn't have anything he could think of as luxuries. But the officers wouldn't be swinging in hammocks shoulder-to-shoulder in an open hold with forty other belching, farting men, either. He said, "It sounds possible, if you can tell us where we might hope to find the girl you're looking for. We're in a hurry, so the trip up we're doing at a dead run. The return trip, though, we should be able to make some time to stop off and look."

Makkor grinned broadly. "I have charts, I have our ship log, I have souvenirs . . . what the little piss-pants girls-in-beards around here don't realize is my two brothers and I and five of our best friends and a single master *did* that trip they won't even think about—every bit of it just as I tell it. We took my ship straight down the middle of the Fallen Suns, just because we could. I've been there, lads, and lived to tell the tale. Have no desire to go back. But by Hkukguh, they make good women in those parts."

They toured the rest of the ship. It was a good ship, with passenger quarters below and separate sleeping quarters for sailors and marines, with generous holds, a large, serviceable attable and cooking galley, and a reasonable, livable design. Makkor hadn't lied when he said getting the insides livable was going to occupy the crew during their free hours, though. The drowner stink clung to every board, and it would take stone polishing and good soap and oil rubs and hours upon hours of muscle and sweat to eliminate.

But the price was right.

So Aaran and Tuua sat for Makkor's story. It was a good story, hair-raising and chilling, and it had a ring of flat truth to Aaran. They took the charts Makkor offered them. They looked through the log.

And Aaran faced facts. Drowner or not, the whole of the ship had good lines. A thoughtful layout. Enough space for everything he had to have. It would do what Aaran needed it to do, or kill him in the process. It was the only ship he might hope to buy. He either took it, or turned his back on those slaves trapped in the Fallen Suns. And, his gut whispered, on Aashka.

So they paid Makkor earnest money on their promise—a hefty fee, a hundredth the value of the ship, much of which Makkor would give back at the end of the journey if they met their end of the bargain—and signed the contract that would give them the ship for his expenses, already enumerated and more than paid with earnest horse cash, if they survived the voyage and brought to Makkor a wife fitting the description he gave them.

They took the charts and the log to the local Ethebettan temple to pay scholars to copy the lot and have the whole back to them in a single day. They returned the originals to Makkor, and took possession of the ship.

They still had to pull together their crew.

As he carried his belongings onto the ship, as yet unnamed, Aaran could feel the girl calling to him. When he looked down at the water, he could feel her close to him. Desperate. Terrified. If he did not reach her in time, he might never find his sister. Even though he had no way to prove it, his damnable gut insisted that Tonk slave was the first true chance he'd ever had to find Aashka. He had no trouble believing she could be his only chance.

All he could think was, *Hurry.*

"It's bad luck to take a ship to sea unnamed," Tuua said when he came up the gangplank. "You have to call her something."

She couldn't carry her drowner name. "Every name I can think of speaks of danger and disaster," Aaran told him. The ship stank. She reeked. And though she might have been sound, all he could think of it was that he wished he could have afforded something new, something that did not carry with it the voices of the dead. He feared going to sea in a cursed ship.

"I know a name for her."

Aaran looked at him.

"You're all the talk in the harbor. So is your ship. And so is this journey. You're the Madman now, Aaran. In five languages, one need only say that word, and your voyage leaps into the conversation and silences all others."

Aaran watched the few sailors he'd hired coming aboard. Watched his two Tonk officers, of the minimum of twelve he'd need, walking down the shoddy finger pier, looking for him, looking for the ship in which they would be risking their lives and careers, and then recoiling.

"We can't call her Madman. *Sookyn* is no name for a ship."

"No," Tuua said. "That would miss the spirit of this venture. Call her *Taag av Sookyn.*"

"*Taag av Sookyn?*" Aaran thought about it for a moment, as he watched Neeran, the boy he'd taken on as a runner, come trotting along the pier. Neeran caught sight of him and waved and grinned. He, at least, was un-bothered by the look of the ship.

Aaran nodded. "*The Dare of the Madman,* eh? That works."

He put his hands on the rail. "We sign the rest of the crew here. We accept as officers the exiled once-Tonk we talked with yesterday. We take any-one else who will sign papers and sail with us—Tonk, Eastil, Kadino, Marqali. We make it clear that Tonk and non-Tonk alike earn full shares. We berth as officers any who are qualified and will swear oaths, whether they are Tonk or not." He heard Tuua gasp. "Oh, that's not all. We declare

Trade the official tongue of the voyage, not Tonk, though among such as speak Tonk, Tonk will be permitted. Our complement will be as mixed as the cities of the Eastil Republic, if need be. But we put out the final call to-day, we offer what we must to fill our berths, and we sail tomorrow."

"You *are* a madman," Tuua said.

"I might be," Aaran agreed. "But we're going to the Fallen Suns by the shortest route and the fastest pace. I'll stand by such men as will stand by me in my madness, and they'll need not be Tonk to earn my loyalty."

8

Acolyte

They kept me in a private cell away from everyone for three days. I was permitted prayer. I had regular food and water. But no one could speak to me, nor could I speak to them. I had no news of Redbird. I had no word from Hawkspar. I had only the silence of the cell, punctuated by the ringing of the bells, the songs of service, and from time to time, the sharp rap of a sera on the door, letting me know that it was my time to follow her to the shower.

On the fourth day, shortly after sunrise, I opened the door to find half a dozen of the Seru Onyx, instead of just one.

It was time, and I was not ready. I would never be ready.

Whatever reckless courage had driven me to volunteer myself as rat food was gone. The oracles who had spoken in my favor had seemed to take my volunteering as a sign of the Dyad speaking through me. Those who had spoken against me seemed, to my surprise, even more convinced.

Only I was near certain that I had been stricken by a passing madness. Fear had replaced courage, and brought with it a panicked strength. My eyes were clear, my legs were steady, and the thought foremost in my mind was that I could fight the Seru Onyx who surrounded me as we walked toward the Arena.

I could get in one good kick, perhaps, smash the nose of one sera. The others would try to subdue me, but I was skilled enough at the fighting arts that I thought I would be able to force them to kill me.

Death by Onyx would be a quicker, more merciful end than rats.

The Seru Onyx were usually silent in carrying out their duties. But the one walking at my right hand broke with expected taciturnity. Curiosity can become too much even for the Eyes of Discipline, I suppose. We were almost to the Arena when she asked me, "How come you to face the rats, Hawkspar's acolyte?"

"I volunteered," I admitted.

Around me, all the Seru Onyx stopped as one. Faces turned toward me, and black stone eyes without the faintest hint of life or light all seemed to focus on me.

"You *volunteered*," the same sera repeated in a flat, disbelieving voice. I realized she and I had been slaves together—I could see little of her face for the folds of her black hood, but her voice I knew well. "Why?"

They stood around me, all of them tall and strong and fierce, banmuhan-ri staffs—the longest and most dangerous—resting on the ground. I could feel their astonishment and their disbelief.

"I cannot say," I said. "The oracles were arguing among themselves, and I was listening to them. Four wanted to see me tried by rats before they would confirm me. Well, one said she would not confirm me, no matter what, while one said she did not care what happened to me, but she thought it proper to support Windcrystal and Sunspar in their votes. Four said they would confirm me without trial. My oracle said she could call for a vote right then; that she would cast the final vote herself and guarantee the majority." I sighed. "And when the matter was nearly decided in my favor, I volunteered to face the rats."

"Why?"

I shook my head. "They were challenging Hawkspar's honesty. Her devotion to the Order. They thought to try *her* for naming me her successor. It seemed like the right thing to do. At the time, at least. Now . . ." I felt my hands clenching in spite of my wishes. I took deep breaths.

The seru took small steps away from me. In case my madness was contagious, I supposed.

One said, "And the oracles still insisted that you face the test of rats?"

"They were prepared to reverse themselves once I volunteered," I said. "But they had already as much as called the Blessed Oracle Hawkspar a liar. She insisted that I be permitted to face the trial they had requested. She claimed the right to declare the consequences for those who challenged her if I succeeded."

The air around me changed. It was like stepping outside on a hot day, breathing in, and smelling a storm coming on the breeze. But there was nothing to smell, no breeze, nothing I could point to and say, *There. That was different.*

I had never felt such a thing before.

"Such as we can do to make the coming ordeal less onerous for you, we will do, Chosen of Hawkspar's Eyes and Vran Vrota," one of the Onyxes said.

"We are duty sworn to present you naked, weaponless, and bound before the audience in the Arena, and to see you in that fashion into the cage," a second said. "Please remember when you are Hawkspar that we acted not out of malice or agreement, but out of regretful obligation."

I considered that as we walked toward the Arena.

The Seru Onyx said nothing else. All of us togther proceeded to the staging area just beneath the main gate into the arena floor.

Someone had already carried out the rat cage. I could see it from where we stood, and all of a sudden I could not keep myself from shaking.

The rat cage is a box big enough to hold one large woman and perhaps fifty rats, if one cares little for breathing room. It is made of sturdy, close-woven wire to keep the rats in, bound over thick iron bars—to keep the victim in. The cage has one-way drop holes at each of the four top corners. The drop holes are short tubes with hinged doors in the middle; the hinges swing only one way. In. The rat-keepers on the outside can shove rats from their carrying cages into these tubes, and the beasts will slide down the metal and through the door without being able to gain purchase or crawl back out. They will drop on the girl or woman waiting for their arrival, teeth and claws ready when they land.

"Undress," one of the seru said, and pointed to the table where I should put my clothes.

I took off my robes slowly and carefully, folding each piece of clothing and placing it neatly in a squared stack. Even in that moment, I could not cast off Ossalene training and toss my clothing in a pile. I must act like I would be coming back to wear it.

When I stood naked before them, one of the Seru Onyx bound my wrists behind me, and then bound my elbows together tightly enough that my back arched and I had to breathe shallowly. While she tied my arms, one of the others tied my ankles and my knees.

And then we stood there.

Out in the Arena, I could see the raised gray stone tiers filling with slaves and penitents and seru. The oracles would come in last, marching across the sandy arena floor from the gate opposite the one where I stood. Oracle Hawkspar would announce the reason we were gathered; I was her acolyte, so she would have that right. None of the other oracles would speak. Doing so would be a breach of etiquette. No matter how my oracle chose to portray my situation, the rats—and through them Vran Vrota—would decide the case, proving all she said either true or false. I expected nothing more, therefore, than a bare recounting of facts from her—that question of my legitimacy had been raised, and that I had volunteered for this trial.

That truth, at least, ought to provide everyone present with a few moments of amusement.

"I don't want to do this," I whispered.

I had not intended anyone to hear me, but someone did.

"I don't blame you," the Sera Onyx closest to me said under her breath. "But you can't change your mind. Once the oracles have decided a thing, you cannot un-decide it for them."

The rat-keepers, four brawny Seru Onyx garbed from head to toe in hardened leather, with close-woven iron-wire cages over their faces to protect them should the rats escape, wheeled out the cart that held stacks of tiny individual cages, and parked it beside the cage where I would be placed.

Starving rats cannot be caged together, for the strongest will eat the weakest until only one rat is left. They'll not eat each other if any other food is provided, though. And ours were fed—when they were fed—bound live animals so they would know what to do when thrown into the cage.

I could hear them squeaking. Tiny hairs on my arms and the back of my neck rose, and my eyes filled with tears. I stood there, naked and tied and helpless, with the six Seru Onyx around me waiting for their cue to take me into the Arena and throw me into the cage, and all I could think of was the expression on my mother's face when I was torn from her arms. She'd wanted me back. At that moment I could see her again, clearly, reaching for me.

Maybe I would find her when this was done. Maybe *she* would find *me*, and wrap her arms around me, and I would be home again. I did not think the universe could be that kind, but I wanted my mother, and I could hope.

My throat ached, my nose clogged, tears ran down my cheeks that I could not wipe away.

The rat-keepers took up their positions at the four corners of the cage, and from three points along the top of the arena, three seru began to drum. To the slow, steady booming, the oracles stepped across the sand floor of the Arena in single file. All talking within the Arena ceased; all eyes focused on the marching avatars of Vran Vrota; Hawkspar, Tigereye, Ruby, Windcrystal, Amethyst, Sunspar, Sapphire, Emerald, and finally Raxinan moved slowly and steadily toward the center of the stage, where cage, rats, and keepers awaited.

My bowels knotted, and I feared that I would lose control of them as the seru carried me to my fate; that I would shame myself and *then* die horribly.

When the procession reached the center, the drumming stopped.

Oracle Hawkspar lifted a hand. "The Holy Dyad has been questioned, Vran Vrota's choice impugned by some of my fellow oracles. My acolyte has been called false, and I have been called false with her."

I doubt that anyone in the Arena breathed. I know that I did not. I had never expected Hawkspar to take such a confrontational approach toward her colleagues.

"My acolyte has *volunteered* to undergo the trial of rats. If she dies, I will be proven false, and will step into the rat cage after her. After my death, the Eyes I wear will choose another to replace me."

We all gasped. This was a thing unprecedented, that an oracle should volunteer to follow her acolyte into the rat cage.

"Should my acolyte be shown to hold Vran Vrota's favor, and my honor be proved intact, it shall be my right to declare the consequences."

Here, I thought, she would call for the acolytes of those who had doubted her to face the trial of rats, which was not truly fair, since only two of the four *had* acolytes. Fairness, however, is a thing never seen or even considered within the walls of the Citadel.

However, Hawkspar broke with all custom and all history with her next words. "I therefore decree that, should my acolyte be found to be the true choice of Vran Vrota by surviving her trial unharmed, the following oracles will immediately be stripped and bound to face the trial of rats this very day and hour: Oracle Ruby, Oracle Windcrystal, Oracle Sunspar, and Oracle Emerald."

Pandemonium erupted in the stands at this decree. No one had ever—*ever*—suggested a situation in which four oracles would be thrown into cages with starving rats to test Vran Vrota's devotion to them. It wasn't likely to happen. Odds favored the Citadel getting a new Oracle Hawkspar. But Hawkspar was the highest ranked of the Nine Living Goddesses. She had the right to command others, even her equals, to do anything she was willing to face herself.

Which should serve as a reminder for the truly stupid, if nothing else: Enraging a living goddess of war leads to unhappy results.

The oracles were visibly stunned. The four Hawkspar had publicly accused stepped apart from those not named, and gathered in a furious knot to one side of the cage, whispering at each other. Their words did not carry, but the hissing did. Had one of them drawn a knife and cut Hawkspar's throat right there, I do not think anyone would have been surprised.

But I only had a moment to consider their discomfiture. The drums started up again, and the six Seru Onyx who had guarded me and bound me pushed me to the ground, face-up, and took their places beside me; two at my knees, two at my waist, and two at my shoulders. They linked hands beneath me, counted three, and stood. I was marched out to the beat of the drum, feetfirst, head dangling, into chilly air and hot sunlight and the stares of all the Citadel.

No one spoke. It is a solemn thing, the trial by rats, and faced in silence. The oracles permit no cheering, no jeering, no cries of sympathy. Those who attend are there for their own betterment; it is their duty to experience the discipline meted out to their colleagues so that they do not fall into the same error.

I had no idea what they were supposed to learn from my death. Not to be chosen by an oracle to be her successor? Not to volunteer?

That latter would probably make a good lesson, in truth.

We reached the cage, and two of the leather-clad rat-keepers undid the heavy locks that would keep closed the iron gate.

I wanted to scream, "Don't put me in there!" I wanted to beg for rescue with everything in me. I did not.

Hawkspar had said, *To the damned, courage is better than truth.* She had sent that message to me at who knew what risk. I had done my best to interpret it. I had made my choice. I had chosen the path of courage—or madness—and it was too late to turn from it. Why, then, shame myself and Hawkspar before I had to? Screaming would not save me, would not change a single second of my fate. It would only offer comfort to those who wanted my death. They'd have their comfort soon enough, when the rats dropped onto me and began to gnaw. I'd scream enough to satisfy them then. The women fed to rats always did.

All I could do as the Onyxes slid me in and my bare skin touched rough, cold metal was close my eyes and pray. To Jostfar, who did not know me, who was the god of a people who had once been mine. Through Ethebet, his warrior, she of the path of sword and sacrifice. I had been born Tonk, and I would die Tonk. And if I did not shame myself, perhaps my mother would know me as her daughter in whatever place I might exist after death was done with me.

When I lay with my knees jammed into my chest and my head barely inside the box, the door closed behind me, and I heard the sickening click of the padlocks.

The beating of the drums quickened their pace. All four rat-keepers marched to the cart, and each picked up four rat cages. They returned, set down three of their four cages at their feet, and placed the connectors over the openings that would lead into my cage. Each placed a hand on the lift-up door that would permit the rat inside to move from the back of his cage into the front portion that contained the connector.

The drums beat faster and faster, but never as quickly as my own heart. It hammered against my ribs as if trying to escape.

And then, at their peak, the drums abruptly fell silent.

Hawkspar's voice echoed throughout the Arena. "On my command . . ."

I clenched my jaws closed, squeezed my eyes as tight as I could—as if those feeble attempts would keep the rats from my eyes or my tongue—and silently begged my mother to find me.

". . . first rats *now!*" Hawkspar said, and I heard the scraping of four metal doors, and the squeaking grew to screeching as claws skittered down four metal tubes.

Four heavy bodies dropped onto me. Sharp points dug into my skin and scrabbled over me, and I felt cold, wet noses press against my flesh, and greasy fur sliding across my breasts and belly and face, and scaly, heavy tails draping along my skin.

I heard gnawing.

But I did not feel gnawing.

"Second rats . . . *now!*" Hawkspar shouted.

And more rats screeked and scratched and landed atop me.

Followed by more.

And more.

I made no sound, kept my eyes tight closed and my jaws locked, and the rats did whatever they were doing.

"They're eating the ropes," I heard one of the seru whisper.

"Will they go for her when they're done with them, do you think?" another one whispered back.

I, too, wanted the answer to that question.

Already, though, this was a trial of rats unlike any I had ever witnessed. Usually, the screaming started the instant the first rats landed on their victims, and stopped by the time the fourth round of rats hit.

Though I was terrified, I had promised myself I would wait until the pain became too much—worse than being whipped—before I screamed. But there was no great, terrible pain.

There were the little pains that came from lying on top of my tightly bound arms—the wires of the cage dug into my skin, and my weight pressed down on the muscles and bones of my arms, twisted so tightly behind me. Both arms were starting to feel like they'd caught fire. There were pains from the constriction of the ropes.

In the stands above, I heard whispering that neither the oracles nor the seru stopped.

I felt the ropes around my knees and ankles fall away, and it occurred to me that if I moved very carefully, I might be able to get the rats to eat away the ropes that bound my arms. I did not want to roll onto a rat and get bitten however— the smell of my blood might start the feeding frenzy I had so far avoided.

I rolled, a finger's-breadth at a time, and the rats moved around me and over me, digging with their claws, prodding with their noses, squeeing and squeaking. I felt their weight start dragging at the ropes on my arms and around my wrists moments later.

I sat up cautiously, and the rats kept eating the rope that coiled on the floor, paying me no attention. The whispers in the Arena grew louder.

Suddenly Oracle Windcrystal screamed, "You've only thrown four rounds of rats in there with her. More rats! Throw in more rats if this is to be a true trial. And not rats that have been fed—who are you trying to fool with this charade?"

Hawkspar said, "Are you sure that is what you would wish? All that you demand of my acolyte may be demanded of you in turn."

"Of course I'm sure," Windcrystal shrieked.

"On my command, then . . ." Hawkspar said, her voice even and unworried. The rat-keepers went after more cages, and brought more rats. I moved myself away from the corner of the cage because I did not want any rats to drop directly on my head. I sat hunched along one wall of the cage, my back to the rats, my arms around my breasts, my knees to my chest to protect my belly, my heels jammed tight against my buttocks.

"Let me see that rat!" Windcrystal snarled, standing at one corner and inspecting a cage. She pulled a hairpin from her hair and poked the rat with it. I could hear that rat squeaking and snapping. "That's better," she said, and poked the other three rats at that rat-keeper's feet. She stalked to the next sera and prodded her rats until they were frantic. In like fashion, she visited the other two seru.

"You'll be sure to let me borrow a hairpin for *your* rats," Hawkspar said. "Since I have no need for hairpins of my own."

Windcrystal just laughed.

"Fifth rats now!" Hawkspar commanded, and the rain of new rats began.

They were different than the first four rounds of rats, because they were angry. I hid my face as the snarling and screaming began, as bodies twisted against mine, fighting and scrabbling.

Then they were eating each other, and the air around me grew thick with the stink of blood and offal. They fought atop me as well as beside me, and I became smeared with bits of their fur and skin and flesh. But not a single creature bit me. Or scratched me.

At eight rounds, Hawkspar stopped. She walked over and stood by the cage, waiting in silence.

"Why are you stopping?" Windcrystal demanded. "The trial is not yet over."

"We have tried her with eight rounds of rats," Hawkspar said. "Eight."

"We have more rats."

"We do indeed. But the longest trial of rats in history has been twelve rounds."

"We'll go twice that if we must."

"No, we won't. Vran Vrota has spoken. The Blessed Dyad has chosen this girl as my acolyte, and as my successor."

"That is not for you to say."

"Oh, but it is. The girl *volunteered* for this trial, Windcrystal. Therefore, while I have thus far humored you, you exceed your authority. She has been proven by twice the usual number of rats. *I* now require her removal from the cage. And when she has been removed, four clean cages will be brought out, and you and the other three who called me a liar and unfaithful to the Order will prove your own faithfulness."

The leather-clad rat-keepers cleared the Arena of all save themselves. They opened the door to my cage once both gates at opposite ends were shut.

I stepped out carefully. The few surviving rats attempted to escape, but the rat-keepers caught and caged them.

Windcrystal barreled out of the gate and over to me the instant the rats were out of the way. Her hand clamped around my upper arm like a vise. And she shook me, screaming, "She isn't untouched! She's scratched and bloody. This is no choice of Vran Vrota, Hawkspar. This is a *fraud*! She has not passed the test. Throw her back in and I'll select the rats to try against her."

She slapped me, and I felt her fingernails slash across my face. I felt them dig into my arm as she shook me.

Hawkspar turned to one of the rat-keepers and said, "Fetch pails of water." She walked over to Windcrystal slowly and stiffly, but watching her, it did not seem to me so much that Hawkspar was old at that moment as that she was livid.

She said, "Take your hand off my acolyte."

Windcrystal did not; instead she tightened her grip, and her nails bit deeper. "Did you think you could fool me with your stunts?" she said.

"I think that your hand is still on my acolyte, and Vran Vrota wells up inside me. I think we shall see how Hawkspar, Living Goddess of the Eyes of War, will do loosed against Windcrystal, Living Goddess of the Eyes of Justice. Provided, of course, that Vran Vrota will still stand by you to lend you power after all your many betrayals."

"You're nothing but sticks and gristle, Hawkspar," Windcrystal said. Her grip didn't loosen in the slightest.

"My faith is greater than my flesh," Hawkspar said.

My head started to hurt. She looked at me, still gripped by Windcrystal, and on her lips a deadly smile curved.

Around me, the world grew suddenly dark. Pain stabbed behind my eyes, and from a distance, fading away, I heard screaming.

And then, with a snap, the darkness was gone, though the screaming remained. Windcrystal knelt on the ground at my feet, the stump of her right arm jammed against the black silk of her robes, while wet black stains spread across them. The screaming was hers.

The rat-keepers returned, lugging two buckets of water.

"Pour them on my acolyte," she said. "Make sure no spot of blood is left on her."

The sera doused me with the first bucket of water. It was icy, and with the crisp wind blowing in the Arena, I felt my teeth starting to chatter.

"Now the second bucket. Get the back of her this time."

The second bucket of water hit me and I yelped. Not that anyone would hear me, since Windcrystal continued screaming.

One of the Onyxes had raced across the Arena. Now she ran back and handed me a warm, thick towel. "Dry off," she said.

On the ground at my feet, Windcrystal writhed and howled and commanded Vran Vrota to give her back her hand.

The Holy Dyad did not.

I dried myself, stunned by what had happened, and by what was still happening. I could not believe I was still alive. Hawkspar had said she had marked me as chosen by the Eyes. I wondered, though, how the other Oracles had studied me and had not seen what she had done.

And I could not imagine how Vran Vrota had refused to protect Wind-crystal from Hawkspar's fury. What were these Living Goddesses, truly, to behave as they were—and what was Vran Vrota to let them? Why would the Dyad abandon one chosen vessel while publicly favoring another? And that one a goddess who worshipped another god entirely in secret?

When I was done toweling myself off, Hawkspar said, "Walk with me."

She and I started back to the Oracles' Gate, and as we stepped across the sand, the drums started up again with the slow, steady booming that had characterized the oracles' walk into the Arena that first time.

I listened to it, and felt it shiver through my bones. The other oracles stepped out of the gate as we approached, and lined up against the closed door. All of them were there.

"Observe her for yourselves," Hawkspar said. "She has not a single bite on her. And not a single scratch. Not even a mark from Windcrystal, who was doing her best to mark the girl with her nails. The rats devoured rope and each other, but did not touch the acolyte."

Above our heads, the drums thundered their slow pulse.

Tigereye said, "She is untouched."

Amethyst said, "She is untouched."

Sapphire and Raxinan both said, "She is untouched."

This left the three remaining challengers. Emerald said, "I agree. She is untouched. I was mistaken."

Ruby said, "I, too, was mistaken." But her mouth twisted in a bitter line when she said it.

Sunspar held her hand over me, though she did not touch me. I felt cold penetrate my skin, felt it seep into my muscles, felt it chill and slow my blood and my heartbeat and my breath until all the world around me seemed to stop. She looked into me and through me.

The rat-keepers moved past us, removing from the Arena the cage in which I had lain.

"She is . . . untouched," Sunspar said. "But I am unconvinced that it is the will of Vran Vrota, Hawkspar, that kept her untouched."

"Once you are done with your own trial of rats, then, Sunspar," the Oracle Hawkspar said, "you and I may pursue this further. In private. If you so de-sire. For your question then is not about my acolyte's acceptability or in-tegrity, but mine."

"Indeed," Sunspar said, "it is. It has been for quite some time now. So perhaps once this farce is finished, we shall meet privately to . . . *discuss* . . . our differences."

The chill of Oracle Sunspar's examination of me did not leave me when her attention turned to Hawkspar.

It clung to me, too, as the seru wheeled out the clean cages; as the oracles disrobed and permitted themselves to be bound—all save Windcrystal, who fought like a wounded animal as the leather-clad rat-keepers brought out more well-starved beasts.

I did not watch. I had been in one of those cages, and with the clang of the last door and the click of the last padlock, I could feel myself back in it again. Could feel the rats falling on me.

I heard screaming. So much screaming. The Blessed Dyad had wearied of at least one vessel and was allowing it to be devoured so that Vran Vrota could choose a more suitable one.

To my ears, it sounded like more than one.

9

Aaran

Taag av Sookyn was running a steady eight knots north-northwest without windmen's assist, threading the passageway through the Five Brothers Islands that lay in the Path of Stars. The ship was five days out from Midrid, and Aaran thought the crew was settling in nicely.

Aaran worried about his kor, or officers. He'd managed to fill his berths, but he had not done so with men he would have chosen in other circumstances. Aaran's kor daan, or first, was a good Dravitaak Tonk named Ves av Imaaryn, an Ethebettan with years of experience in the kor. He'd never been daan before, but he'd been raan, or second, on the *Dyn Glytaak,* and he came with excellent recommendations.

Aaran's raan, Ino Tortaaknavyn, had fought in the sea lanes around Beyltaak during the Feegash Purge, and before that, he'd been a naval officer in the Confederate Forces. He had some gray to his hair, but he was steady, and with a daughter killed and a granddaughter taken by a Sinali slaver, he was motivated to see the journey through.

But Aaran's kor wogan, or master of marines, was Ermyk av Beyrkyn; Ermyk had come to Aaran at the Buttered Bread and asked for the job when he'd heard the rumors of a trip into the Fallen Suns to rescue slaves. He brought a dozen men who'd fought under him with him. He wouldn't say what drove him to seek out the most dangerous possible journey when setting out from Midrid that season, his clan tattoo had been stripped from him and every man with him.

Aaran had only been able to get one apprentice windman in Midrid, a lad named Besik who had limited experience. The boy had managed a good enough blow in their way out of the Midrid harbor, but Aaran couldn't rest until, three days out, they put in at Five Brothers on the Path of Stars on the advice of one of his communicators, and took on Faryn Wo, a north Franican Tonk from one of the Pangaree Clan families up that way. Faryn said he hadn't seen enough of the world yet.

In all, Aaran had ten officers, and four of them were Tonk. He dared not count Ermyk, who had been exiled, nor any of the other exiles, as true Tonk.

He'd been less lucky with his sailors. Aaran's crew came from the scattered corners of the world—he had a Mixol and a Hva Hwa, a half-breed Najulite, a couple of Mindan Reformist Tonks who made a point of their pacifist bent, three Bhekians (two of them nephews of Makkor's), and a dubious assortment of Eastil, Greton, and Kadine wharf rats without pedigrees. Mixed with those were Ermyk's exiles, and a handful of fellow Tonk Ethebettans—but those were all Tand Tonks, mostly from the old clans. They had been stranded in Midrid without money. What they had done to get intentionally abandoned by their shipmates, they would not say. The possibilities gave Aaran nightmares. As did their taciturn eagerness to put Midrid at their backs.

The *Taag* had good seas that day, and good winds. The marines were scrubbing and cleaning and refinishing every interior surface of the ship, driven by Ermyk, who shared Aaran's vision of what the ship could be. They were joined by the off-duty sailors who weren't on their sleep shift.

The cooks were busy, food smells covered up some of the drowner stink, and Aaran was taking a break from supervising to simply catch his breath.

Ves came to lean on the rail beside him and Tuua as they cruised past one of the nameless thousands of tiny outlying islands that made up the Path of Stars.

"Fine day, isn't it?" Tuua said. "Sailing into adventure, a wind at our backs, sun in our eyes, a good ship beneath our heels. What could be better?"

Ves shrugged. "I for one would bypass any hint of adventure in favor of a guarantee of a quiet journey with success at the end," Ves said. "My dreams along the Path have been restless."

"I'm inclined to agree," Aaran said.

Tuua turned his gaze from the fair islands and balmy skies and lovely blue sea long enough to say, "What fun will it be if you make your first voyage as captain with no tales to tell after?"

"I'll still be breathing?" Aaran grinned at Tuua. "When I look in these blue waters, dead men's eyes look back at me, cousin. I've a ship now, and debts to pay, and promises to keep. The voice that was calling to me—she haunts me. She's so frightened, so desperate, in such terrible danger. Every day takes us closer to her, but every day takes her closer to oblivion. As much as we're hurrying, we need to go still faster."

Ves said, "If you weren't afraid, you'd be a fool. This is not a gentle puddle-jaunt we've set ourselves upon. I've heard tell of the Fallen Suns from men who sail them. If dead men look at you now, wait until they reach up from the sea and wrap their hands around your throat."

Aaran studied his daan with narrowed eyes. "Thanks for that," he said. "I'm sure to sleep better at night with those words echoing in my head."

And then, from somewhere in the belly of the ship, a man shouted, "Hey, you thieving bastard!" And over the creaking of the ship and the wind singing in the lines, Aaran heard running feet—two pairs of them, starting from what had to have been forward storage, galloping straight to the back, and then upward.

The aft hatch burst open, and a scrawny boy shot out of it as if propelled by a catapult. Behind him, one of Aaran's wharf rat Eastil sailors, red-faced and furious, shouted, "Grab the little stowaway!"

Tuua, Ves, and Aaran all jumped between the boy and any possible escape routes. When he tried to dart between Aaran and Ves, Aaran snagged him around the middle and held him aloft.

"Unlock a cell in the brig for me," he shouted, and the sailor who'd been chasing the boy said, "That's just the thing for him."

The kid, wild-eyed, fought and kicked and scratched and yowled, but Aaran dragged him down into the aft hold, where a two-celled brig lay.

The wharf rat, whose name was Drum, if Aaran was remembering correctly, held the cell door open. Aaran walked into it with the flailing, cursing boy and threw him on the narrow oak bench.

"Drum," he said, hoping he had the name right, "lock the door and go upstairs. I don't want you to see what happens next, you understand? Just make sure you're back down here next bell to let me out again."

Drum looked surprised. Genuinely surprised, as if he expected some punishment for the boy, but nothing so severe that he might be sent way. "Yes . . . ah, yes, Captain." He locked the cell door behind him, and Aaran could hear him head away.

Aaran studied the boy. Black hair, green eyes, pale skin not freckled by the sun. The boy's clothes were filthy, too big, mismatched. He wore good-quality shoes, though they didn't fit him.

He was a thin boy, probably about ten years old, with old scar tissue and pink, newer scar tissue around his wrists and neck. The look of the scars on such a small boy made Aaran queasy.

The boy glared at him with loathing in those green eyes.

"You're in a bit of trouble, boy," Aaran said in Trade speech.

The boy said nothing.

"You'll want to talk to *me*. I'm captain of this ship, so there's no higher authority from whom you can beg mercy, and I'm not in a mood to be patient with thieves. We're in warm waters, now. Sharks aplenty here, and other things that would find someone like you tasty."

The kid crossed his arms over his chest and turned his face away from Aaran.

"Well, see," Aaran said. "That's why I sent the sailor away. I don't want him to see what I'm going to do to you if you don't tell me who you are and why you're on my ship."

"You can't do anything to me worse that what's already been done," the kid said. He spoke Tonk, though, not Trade. But he wasn't Tonk.

Was he?

Aaran grabbed the kid's left hand and pried the suddenly clenched fingers open. No clan mark.

Spoke Tonk with a good clean Hyrian accent. And yet *wasn't* Tonk. Tonk was no common tongue for the non-Tonk to learn. People spoke their own language, they picked up Trade, and they'd learn one or two regional pidgins to get them through the tricky bits.

But this kid spoke Tonk like someone who'd been speaking it for years.

"There's where you're wrong, you see," Aaran said, switching to Tonk. "So far you're still breathing. But I have the right to make that not so. After all, we're at sea, and all you've shown me so far is that you're trouble I don't want to have."

The kid looked him straight in the eye and said, "If it makes you happy, kill me. You still can't hurt me like they did."

Aaran sat on the bench opposite him. "Who?"

"If I tell you that, you'll take me back, and I'm not going back."

Aaran laughed. "I'm not taking anyone anywhere. We're not on a pleasure cruise, boy. We're going to war, and I'm in a hurry to get there. I might dump you at the next civilized port if you act decent—from there you could go wherever you wanted. But there's no way I'll take you back where you came from. I haven't the time."

Arms crossed, body rigid. "Beat me. I won't talk."

"You think so, do you?"

"My father beats me. My uncle. Some of their friends."

"Why?"

The kid was quiet for a long time. Then he said, "Because they like to."

Aaran knew about drunks who liked to beat their children. They grew up to be wharf rats, and then ship's runners, and then sailors. He had a good double handful of such men onboard.

Aaran looked at the boy, sitting there on the bench in his too-big shirt. And he realized the kid had no reason to trust anyone. If a child couldn't trust his own father, who *could* he trust? The name of the kid's father didn't matter.

He said, "All right. I won't push you for details about what happened to you. But if you ever want to talk to me, you can tell me." He propped his elbows on his knees and rested his chin in his hands. "So. Here you are, and you're going to have to have food, and clothes to wear, and if you're going to be eating, you're going to be working. You want to get off at the next island we pass that has a town on it?"

"Not very much," the boy said. "I want to go a long way away."

Aaran said, "How old are you?"

"Ten."

"I swear . . . hearing starts to fail when you get to be twenty-five. I didn't hear you very well, I'm afraid. A boy can sign papers to work on a ship if he's *twelve* years old. How old did you say you were again?"

The kid looked downtrodden for a moment, and then hopeful. "Twelve?"

"You're pretty puny for a twelve-year-old, you know?"

"Yessir. I'm small." He nodded.

"But twelve? You're sure about that?"

"Oh, yessir. I'm twelve."

"You have a name?"

"Um . . . what is a good Tonk name?"

Aaran grinned at him. "You speak good Tonk, kid, but you don't *look* Tonk. You've got no clan mark, you wear your hair short and ugly, and I bet you haven't chosen your saint yet, either."

"Can you make me a Tonk?"

"Only Jostfar can *make* you Tonk," he said, and laughed. But the kid didn't laugh. He didn't have any idea who Jostfar was, of course. "We'll see about you becoming Tonk. It's not easy, but it's not impossible, if you want it enough. First, though, we have to make you not Marqallan. All right?"

The kid nodded, puppy-eager.

"You can be Eastil. *Anybody* can be Eastil, and sometimes that seems not such a bad thing. For now, we can call you Eban. That's as much an Eastil name as anything. Eban . . . Cooperson. The Eastils have as many Coopers and Cooperssons as they have everything else combined. And you could pass for Eastil, once we shave off that idiotic haircut and put you into a sailor's clothes. I'll let you sign papers to work on the ship as a . . ." He looked at the kid. Aaran had been almost ready to tell him he could be a rope rat—but the kid looked too frail. Within a month, rope rats knew the language of a ship, how to climb and how to fall, how to hang on, where to run when things got nasty. This kid's hands were as soft as a girl's. Or a keeper's. He'd spent a lot of time being hurt, not a lot of time running outdoors in the streets with friends. He'd toughen up in time, no doubt. But Aaran didn't want him to die in the process.

"You want to learn how to be Tonk, you think?"

"Yessir."

"Right. I'll sign you on as assistant keeper, then, and you can work with my cousin Tuua. You'll be on rope-rat half pay until Tuua says you're worth more to him."

"I'll get *paid?*" the kid asked.

Aaran could see a smile trying to show up on the boy's face. It was heartbreaking, really. The boy—well, Eban . . . might as well get used to thinking of him as Eban—seemed like a good kid. That didn't mean he was, but those rope burns and torture scars on Eban's arms told Aaran the father's side of the story wouldn't be worth hearing.

On deck, the next bell rang. "Drum's going to be down here any minute. How old are you?"

"Twelve," the kid said.

"What's your name?"

"Eban."

"Eban what?"

"Cooperson."

"And you want to sign articles and work your passage?"

"Yessir. More than anything, sir."

Aaran stood up as he heard a hand on the door to the cells. "Maybe you'll even do well, if you work at it. For now, listen more than you talk, watch as much as you listen, and stay out from underfoot. You'll learn a lot from Tuua. First, though, you're going to visit our kor feer. You know who that is?"

The kid shook his head.

"He's a master healer. He'll do things to fix the hurts your father and the other men did to you. He'll make you as strong as magic can. The rest, you'll have to do on your own. You have to trust him, though. He won't hurt you. No one on this ship will hurt you. You understand?"

The kid's eyes were huge, but he nodded.

"All right, then. While you're with the feer, I'll go talk with Keeper Tuanir, and tell him he's to have a helper."

Acolyte

I trained with Hawkspar in diplomacy, in the uses of power, in dealing with kings and emperors and great generals. Everything I had learned of language she said was barely enough. She would throw half a dozen languages at me in as many minutes, asking how I would approach a king in one language, how I would refuse a gift in a second, how I would put a general in his place in a third.

She pushed me on the tactics and strategies of war, drilled me on the great battles of a dozen armies and two dozen navies, and demanded that I work out problems that previous Hawkspars had solved, finding good answers for them out of my own knowledge of history. She said the Eyes would give me assistance, but they could only be of true value to someone already strong and intelligent.

And she told me the near future, of the Tonk warrior who sailed to rescue us, of a power-mad prince who would come to our doorstep begging my aid, and of the dangerous path I would have to walk to take half a hundred Obsidians, a goodly handful of the Citadel's other seru, and a hundred Tonk children away from this place.

I thought I was doing well. I could imagine that in a month or two, I might begin to feel as if I wasn't entirely lost. That in six months I might have learned enough to continue learning on my own.

But seven days after the rats ate Ruby, Windcrystal, and Emerald—sparing, unfortunately, Sunspar—a dozen Obsidians came to my cell, told me that it was urgent and that I must hurry, and led me, wearing nothing but my sleep tabi, through the darkness from the Brevon dorm to Hawkspar's quarters.

Hawkspar lay on her mat, pillows propping her up. I thought when I walked through the door that she was dead already, so pale and still was she. But as I stepped across the threshold, she turned her face toward me and said, "Obsidians, leave. Remain outside the door, guard us, and when you are called, hurry to me with all speed."

I knelt beside her. "Oracle, should we not call the Moonstones?"

"No," she said. "I die tonight because I choose to. Because this, at last, is the time when the river flows from me to you with the strongest, clearest current. I have things that I must tell you, and you must never tell them to another until the day comes when you must pass on the Hawkspar Eyes. Listen closely. This is your life, girl, and the life of every Tonk who lives or ever will."

I sat close to her.

"First know that Ossal was no woman monk, no faithful follower of the Cistavrian Order of Marosites. Every word you have heard about the origins of the Ossalenes is a lie, though only Hawkspar can reach the truth, for only the Hawkspar Eyes are powerful enough to permit the truth to be found.

"Ossal was the son of a king, a second son sent off to the Cistavrian Order to learn the disciplines of magic. He was a bright boy, but from his earliest years, twisted. He sought knowledge, but only so that he could use it to become powerful. When he had learned enough magic to give him the great power that he so desired, he returned home. Here. To the Citadel of the Ossalenes, which was, back then, his family home. Or one of them. He came here, and using the magic of the Marosite monks, he killed his parents, his brothers and sisters, his nieces and nephews, and any kin who might have dared lay claim to the throne he coveted. Then he set himself up as the new king. This wizard king set about conquering the people of neighboring lands. He took for himself the most beautiful women, and sought to enslave them so deeply that they would only ever be able to do exactly what he bid of them.

"To this end, he made the first Eyes. He took gemstones, bound them with his magic, and forced them upon unwilling captives. And when they wore the Eyes, they became . . . biddable."

"Biddable?"

"His primary interest was in using these women as sex toys."

History is full of men who have used women as sex toys. It was one of the things the Ossalene seru made sure we understood. "Ah," I said.

"But as he won more territory, and gathered more women, he decided it would be amusing to make these toys of his healers, gardeners, craftsmen, and warriors—all while still enjoying playing his perverse sex games with them. And eventually he decided to create some as his fortune-tellers, capable of revealing for him all aspects of his past and future, so that he might gain even more power, and more wealth, and more women.

"He created the first eight pairs of Oracle Eyes, and they gave the women power unlike anything their predecessors had. Through these women and their Eyes, he learned how to create new weapons and new arts, how to have his people grow more and better food, how to heal his warriors more efficiently. Each pair of Eyes was better than the last, each opened up new worlds to him. And with each pair that he created, his art grew. By the time he got to the final pair, the ninth, he had learned entirely new ways of shaping the power of the Eyes. He poured everything he had into the final pair: all of his art, all of his science, and all of his passion and his darkness."

I didn't like the sound of that. "Which pair would that be?"

Hawkspar's mouth twisted in a parody of a smile. "These Eyes, of course. The Hawkspar Eyes."

Of course.

"The Hawkspar Eyes gave the first Hawkspar the power to draw in and win over the other wearers of Eyes, to bind them together into a cohesive unit, and to lead them in slaughtering Ossal, though the first Hawkspar died leading them. Ossal's death was a fine thing, and after he was dead, the next Hawkspar caused all the Eyes of sexual enslavement to be destroyed. Ossal's toys took over the Citadel, and offered their skills as healers and teachers and eventually as fortune-tellers to the outside world. To some extent, they followed Ossal's Marositism, though they changed the religion enough that the Ossalenes would not be a recognized branch of the Cistavrian Order from which they sprang were they not faithful in sending tithes to the faraway Cistavrian Cathedral at Ons. Wealth and power have kept us . . . acceptable.

"And as word spread of the Ossalenes' power in seeing the future, they became rich. Powerful in their own way. But wearing Eyes carries a price, and wearing the Hawkspar Eyes, the largest price of all."

I nodded and waited.

She said, "So here are some warnings you must take to heart when you are the wearer of these Eyes. First, Ossal is dead, but he is not gone. The magic by which he created the Oracle Eyes bound him to them. Each of the nine pairs of Oracle Eyes can become a gateway for his spirit, and centuries in a hell of his own devising have made his spirit even fouler and more twisted than it was in life. The stronger the Eyes, the stronger the connection the wearer feels toward him at certain times. And the more connected you become to the Eyes, the more power his spirit has over you."

I shivered. Hawkspar's cell was cold, but the chill that came over me at that moment started from deep inside me and shuddered its way out.

"Why didn't you tell me about this before?"

"Because it is the price you pay to save your people. All power has a price," Hawkspar growled. "But with the Eyes, you can choose when and how you will pay. We haven't much time. Events gather on the horizon, and you must be ready to meet them. *So listen.* When you wear the Eyes, you will be able to see the flow of time. This holds a danger for the weak—time is beautiful, and the wearer can fall into the fascination of watching it and never come out again. An oracle can be seduced into her own past, back to a time when she was safe and happy, and she can choose never to leave. Her body will starve, her mind will waste away, and in short order she will die.

"But you are not weak, so for you, this is a lesser danger. Avoid visiting your own past."

"But remembering my name . . ."

"You cannot go back to find it. You cannot go back to see your family again. You *cannot.* If you remember your name on your own, take it back. But don't let yourself fall into the trap of searching for it."

"That danger has nothing to do with Ossal."

"It doesn't. It is a minor danger—the danger of *watching* time. If you avoid losing yourself in the watching, you can stretch out your life to vast, unnatural lengths. The reason I am so very old is that, save one exception, all I have ever done is watch time."

"That sounds a simple enough rule to follow. Just watch."

She snorted. "For *me* it was a simple rule to follow, for I was a spider sitting in the middle of a web. Events and the men who caused them came to me. You will not have that luxury. You are going out into the world. And in the world, you will be forced to act. The Eyes also permit the wearer to step between moments in time and alter outcomes. And this, if you are to succeed, you will have to do."

She turned her head away from me, and grew so still I thought she had died. I put a hand on her wrist to see if her blood still coursed, and she said, "I'm not gone yet."

"I feared . . ."

"Don't. I'll tell you when my time is done." She turned back to me. "You can, with the Eyes, rearrange the flow of Time's river. It is difficult, arduous, and painful—and when you do it, the Eyes call to Ossal's spirit and bring him to you. Stepping into time opens the gate that separates you from him.

Your youth and strength should permit you to accomplish much between moments. But understand that when you are exhausted, you will falter. And when you falter, Ossal will attempt to take your flesh and throw your spirit into oblivion. He will try to own you, and if he succeeds, you may not be able to get yourself back. When you must take the step of walking into time, be prepared to fight for your very existence."

"You did this?"

"Once. I had good reason. You and I are here now because of it. But the aftermath was . . . horrible. He is a terrible creature. A nightmare with hungers that have grown huge from long abstinence. Do not give him any opportunity that you can avoid."

I nodded.

She sighed out, long and slow, and I could feel her watching me.

"That's all?"

"I wish it were." She sat, the embodiment of stillness, and I waited, wondering, with slow dread seeping into my body. "The Eyes hold one other power. According to the Hawkspar knot-records, this power has been used only once, and only for the overthrow of Ossal himself. It was the power that killed his body. Hawkspar can, if the legend is true, call into her flesh the power of all the Eyes. She does this by in some fashion forging paths between the Hawkspar Eyes and all the other eyes, both oracle and seru."

Her eyes fixed on me, and my heart stuttered in my breast.

"I have seen the manner by which this might be done. Doing it will make the Hawkspar vessel a goddess in fact as well as in name, for the time that she can hold the paths together. But doing this will bind the Hawkspar vessel to madness and certain death. Understand that this is the path of sacrifice, and if ever you must use it, you will be finished. When the power drawn from the paths you have forged flows out of you, you will be lost. Doomed. The Eyes will own you, and there will be no step you can take that will give you back yourself. If you take this step too soon, the Tonk will lose you. Losing you, they will lose everything."

My fingers clenched on the fabric of my sleep tabi and twisted. "You see this as my fate, don't you?"

Hawkspar said nothing.

"You see this as my fate, don't you?" I repeated, feeling terror rising within me.

"You choose your fate," she said at last. "You choose the fate of the world, girl. Be sure you choose wisely."

And then she turned her face from me. "Tell the Obsidians to attend me. It is time."

"You're dying?"

"I'm done. And you must be made ready. Bring them."

I ran to the door and pulled it open. I had not even a chance to say a word. The Obsidians knew. They streamed past me. The tiny room filled with them, while a dozen more dragged me away, silently, back toward the acolyte dorm.

We were not even halfway across the yard when the ululation went up, the keening of grief that is the sound of an oracle dead. The bells began to toll, and the Obsidians hurried me faster. "Run, Mouse," one of them said, grabbing my arm, and I realized that I heard Redbird's voice. That she was beside me. "For the love of Jostfar, run. You cannot be seen like this. You are now the Hawkspar Elect."

Aaran

Aaran woke from a nightmare in which the faceless girl he pursued was screaming, in agony, terrified. In which he was racing to save her, but was too late.

Too late.

There had been flames. Rivers of blood. The clash of metal on metal, the scream of the dying.

The nightmare had carried with it both the stench of death and the ring of truth.

He sat up, and in the loft above him, a sleepy head popped out of a cubbyhole and said, "You need me, Cap'n?"

"Go back to sleep, Potyr. I had a dream. I'm going out to walk the deck for a while. You're off duty for the rest of the night."

"Thanks for that, Cap'n." The head withdrew, the little door pulled shut with a click. And the door to the second runner's cubby popped open, and a bit of moonlight poured out. "Will you be needing me, then, sir?"

"Nor you, either, Neeran. I'm restless. Nightmares. Nothing that needs to bother your sleep."

"I was reading," Neeran said, and waved a book down at him. "One Keeper Tuuanir recommended. *Ethebet the Morii: Tales of Adventure from the Saint's Early Years.*"

Aaran sighed. "Tuuanir *wrote* it," Aaran said. "And I thought for a few years the Ethebettans were going to disown him for it."

"It's a grand tale," the boy said. "What wouldn't you have given to know her? To fight alongside her. She must have been glorious."

"Enjoy your book," Aaran said. "Don't get into any fights with the ship scholars over it; Tuuanir hasn't sold many on his choice of sources for that thing yet."

He walked out onto the deck.

Ynyar av Beylan, kor adas, or master of the watch, was leaning on the captain's stair, the series of rises that led up to the captain's deck just behind the prow. He turned when Aaran stepped out, took one look at him, and said, "You felt it too, then?"

"Felt what?"

"The wrongness of the night."

"I woke from a nightmare with the thought that we needed to put some more wind behind us," Aaran said.

Ynyar leaned on the rail, staring out to starboard. "Your nightmares, my waking fancies. It all may be of a piece. Come take a look at this."

Shadows moved across the surface of the sea. In the moonlight, they moved like smoke, dancing and writhing, curling around the bow of the ship, slipping toward the back, then racing forward again. They were not of the water; neither were they in it. They never quite touched the light chop, they never fell beneath.

"What are they?"

"Makkor's log lists a place near the end of his journey where the spirits of dead men clung to his ship, telling of the mountains of treasure from sunken ships buried beneath."

Aaran watched the shapes move. They hadn't the look of men. But he'd never seen spirits in the physical world. "Is that what you think they are?"

"No, Cap'n," Ynyar said.

"I dreamed of fire," Aaran said. "Fire, and disaster, and us not reaching the slaves."

"Truly?" Ynyar worried at his bottom lip with his teeth.

Ves av Imaaryn, the kor daan, came to join them. "You noticed them, too? I think I know what they are."

"Oh?"

"I've not seen any dead fish on the surface yet, nor have I smelled any-thing foul. But the water is rough, it's dark and the wind is steady on. Those signs may be hidden. If we lower a bucket overboard and quickly bring it up, we'll know."

"What are you thinking?" Aaran asked.

"Fire under the sea," Ves said. "We have volcanoes in plenty along the Sea of Sorrows. There are volcanoes at the end of the Path of Stars, too. I think we might be sailing over something about to happen."

Aaran called a sailor to lower a bucket into the water. By the time he pulled it back up, a small crowd had gathered. Ves put a finger into the seawater and pulled it back out, swearing. "Hot," he said, and sucked on his finger.

"Get the windmen," Aaran told Ves. "Get both of them working, and push us forward as fast as we dare."

Along Aaran's skin, fear raced, but it wasn't his fear. It was her fear. If he closed his eyes, he was with her. In her. Her skin was his skin; her sounds, his sounds; her vision, his vision.

Something horrible was racing toward her. Pain and blood and the clash of metal.

Behind him, the wind picked up. The sails filled, the ship bit into the sea and raced faster.

It wasn't fast enough. That was all he could think. If fire and ash erupted from the sea, if towering swells ran under the ship to break as huge waves across the near islands, if the sky burned and darkness devoured midday, he could only think of those things as warnings. Something terrible lay before her, and no matter how hard he fought to reach her, he would not be quick enough to save her from the doom that stalked her.

10

Acolyte

The oracles convened in the center of the Arena on a dark, cold night three days after the death of Hawkspar, with Tigereye, the new Ruby—one of the younger penitents, and a complete surprise pick by the Eyes, the new Windcrystal, Amethyst, Sunspar, Sapphire, and Raxinan all present. The new Emerald's Eyes had not yet melded with her, so she remained in the infirmary under the care of the Seru Moonstone.

I walked into the center of the Arena under my own power this time, to face my own Gata Ossala Shen, though it took every bit of my will to do so. Obsidians walked beside me—Redbird on my left, another conspirator, Starweed, on my right.

In the center of the Arena stood a great pyre, and on the pyre lay the dead Oracle Hawkspar, her Eyes still in place. She would be burned to ash, Oracle Tigereye had explained to me, and once that was done, her Eyes would come to me.

I had asked if they would not be destroyed by the fire, and Tigereye had just laughed. "They have survived countless vessels and countless fires. They'll survive this one, too."

I had a duty that I was supposed to be pursuing, and my getting the Eyes was an essential part of that duty. But I cannot say that if the fires had shattered the Eyes into pebbles and dust, I would have wept.

I was selfish, I know. Selfish and unworthy. I could do the whole Litany of the Undeserving from the morning prayers by rote, and I had no doubt every word of it would be true.

But as I stood there watching them lighting torches, one passing the fire on to the next, the oracles chanted a prayer that consecrated Hawkspar's body and returned it to the earth, and that asked that her soul be found worthy since she had served in selflessness and faith. It echoed of continuity that had followed down the line from the first Hawkspar—the one who had won for the women of the Citadel a form of freedom, no matter how far they had strayed from its principles over the intervening centuries.

I was to be a part of that line, and I was the part that would break the chain. I could not believe that I would survive my future. I could not think it likely that I would return to the Citadel, though after my death, the Hawkspar Eyes might. This Hawkspar could be the last for whom the old prayers were prayed.

I was breaking something that could not be fixed.

So I prayed that I would be worthy of the power that I was about to receive, and that I would not fail in my task . . . and that my task was worthy, as well.

I did not let myself think that I had already seen the last sunrise I would ever see. The last sunset. The last red in a rose, the last green in a blade of grass, the last blue in the sea. I'd spent days thinking on that, while I prayed in Hawkspar's chapel and worked my way through the knot-books she had set aside for my personal use, reading everything I could get my fingers on. I knew what I was losing, and I would have given anything had someone else been the person who could have carried out the tasks that lay before me.

But Hawkspar's records let me see that she had marked me as her probable choice even before I had been bought from the slave traders. Her carefully tied journals let me follow her years of studying the paths I took, my character, my interests, my allies and enemies.

She had always watched for others who might be better suited to the task ahead, and she had found several candidates. But in the end, everything led her back to me.

This was my task. No one else could carry it for me. It was bigger than I had understood. My chances of success were poorer than I had imagined. What was at stake was more than just the Tonk.

I watched four oracles light the fire as if they were one person with many arms. They lit it, and stepped back, and the Obsidians nudged me forward. I took the few steps that brought me into the oracles' circle. They began another chant, asking that I be found worthy, that I serve with honor and courage and integrity, and that I give myself over to Vran Vrota and the Ossalene Order with goodwill and a cheerful heart.

I could have told them there was nothing cheerful in my heart at that moment, but they didn't ask. Instead, Tigereye called me to her, and bade me kneel. For the first time I could see around to the other side of the pyre, and there was a stone altar there. And knives. And several Seru Moonstone waiting.

My eyes. I could not bear to think about what would happen to my eyes.

I clenched my fists tight—so tight my knuckles hurt. I wanted to run. How had so many before me done this? How had they found the courage to stay still instead of fighting or fleeing? Their courage was more than I had, and unbidden, my eyes blurred with tears, and I could not stop myself from thinking, *Last time for that, too.*

I would have vomited had the seru let me have anything to eat or drink before the ceremony, but I had been made to fast for a full day and a night.

The chanting stopped, and the Oracle Tigereye said, "You have been chosen by the Hawkspar Eyes of War to become the new avatar of the Eternal Dyad, the new Goddess of War made flesh. From this day forward, you sacrifice all that you are to Vran Vrota and the good of the Order. Vran Vrota has chosen you, and we, vessels of the other aspects of the Sacred We, welcome you into our midst."

She stepped back, and Sunspar walked over to stand in front of me. Sunspar sneered down at me and said, "You proved yourself by trial. Your Eyes have chosen you." And under her breath, she added, "We'll see how much they like you once they have you."

In their turns, the other oracles came to stand before me, and acknowledged that I had earned the right to be one of them.

Then Tigereye came to stand before me again, and she commanded me to remove my acolyte robes. Behind me, I heard the dead Oracle Hawkspar crackling away. I smelled the smoke, and after I undressed, a shift of wind changed the direction of the fire, and sparks stung my bare flesh.

When I stood naked before all of them, Redbird brought me a gray sack dress—the same robe worn by slaves. I stood there with the heat of the fire behind me and the cold of my fear inside of me, shivering, and Tigereye held aloft a simple copper goblet and said, "This bitter draught we have all tasted, and its fruit we have known. It is the gate of passage between the old and the new, and the path by which you will traverse this final road, and the door that will open for you the new world that lies beyond this one." And she handed me the goblet.

"Drink," she said.

In the reflected light of the fire, the liquid in the copper goblet looked like the eyes of the Obsidians. Black, but transparent, catching the light and twisting it. Its smell was pungent, overwhelming. Breathing its fumes, I felt myself grow dizzy.

"Drink," she told me again. And, not unkindly, added, "It sends the pain away for a while."

So I drank—all of it—in one convulsive, gagging swallow, and felt my tongue go numb even as my mouth seemed to catch fire. And the world turned sideways on me, and I heard a voice shout, "Catch her, get her to the table!"

And then . . .

Dark dreams that I could almost touch. Voices whispering inside my head. Colors and lights and shapes, all of which swirled around me in taunting mimicry of . . . something. I was searching for my name.

In a place without shape, without rational form, without describable texture, I was walking past names. Names uncounted, uncountable, all of them discarded, unused, unneeded, unwanted. If I could only find my own, I could have it back. But it was not there, or perhaps it was but I did not recognize it. I wandered all alone, overwhelmed by the vastness of the place in which I found myself and the hopelessness of the task I had been given.

But by whom?

I had a name. I had no name. My name was everything, it was nothing. It was gone.

I ached, and then the ache became sharper, and yet sharper. The ache became agony, became nails in my skull and fire behind my eyes and fire *in* my eyes so great I could feel myself trying to claw them out. The Eyes were coals in my head, burning me to ash as the Oracle Hawkspar had burned.

Aaran

Pain. It was all pain, and wandering in darkness. He could feel her—the girl he was fighting so hard to save—and something was wrong with her. Something horrible had happened to her. He was too late. Too late by far. She was fading, drowning in poison, while a monster stalked around her, looking for a way to reach her. To hurt her. To violate her.

Aaran had a sword in his hand, though he could not remember how it had come to be there. He raced forward, across ground that looked solid but that reached up to grab at his ankles with every step he took.

Push harder, a voice whispered behind him. *Fight for her. She will not survive without you.*

He turned, and behind him saw, for just an instant, a Tonk woman dressed all in white, her face painted for war, but not with ash. With streaks of white instead. Her hair was white, her eyes the cold, pale blue of a winter sky.

For only an instant he looked at her, and then she was gone, and the monster was gone, and the girl was gone, and he was thrashing in his bed, trying to work his way out of a tangle of sheets.

And both runners were peering out of their cubbyholes, their expressions identically worried.

"Do you need something? Anything, Cap'n. We'll run for it," Neeran said.

"I'm fine." He untangled himself and stood. "A restless night, and too much hot sauce at dinner."

The boys both vanished back into their cubbyholes, the doors closed, and Aaran considered that sharing open quarters with forty other men at a shift was less bothersome than partially sharing quarters with two nosy boys.

He stalked out to the deck, made restless by the nightmares, unwilling to face sleep again. He judged from the track to her that the girl and all the slaves with her were about fifteen days off, if the wind and weather held. She and those with her had survived for so long.

Surely she could hang on for fifteen more days.

Hawkspar

Something horrible and thick and foul crawled down my throat, and oblivion came to me again.

It was a voice that woke me the next time. "You have been long asleep, Oracle, and you have not been restless, so the Oracle Tigereye bade me check to see if you could speak yet."

Everything was darkness. Everything was darkness, but worse, it was darkness full of pain, and beyond the pain and the blindness, it was without any special magic to compensate for my agony and my anguish and my loss. I was no goddess, no vessel of gods, no magnificent light-filled being, as I had imagined I would be. I was nothing but a woman—now a blind woman—whose head and eyes ached. Hawkspar had warned me this might be the case when first I awoke. She'd also warned both Redbird and me that under no circumstances could we permit anyone to know of it.

"Where am I?" I asked.

"In the infirmary," the same voice said. "I am Sera Moonstone Pale. You've been with us for two days now, but you seem to be healing well at last."

I was not heartened by that. My eyes were gone, but the new Eyes for which I had sacrificed them as yet did nothing.

"Does the Oracle Tigereye wish to speak with me?" I asked, but I got no answer. At least not immediately. I heard soft footsteps coming toward me—two pairs of them. And the voice of Sera Moonstone Pale said, "She is awake, Oracle." I had not even heard the sera leave.

"I have come to talk with you," Tigereye said. "A ship has sailed into the harbor, and you have been requested."

My first thought was that my rescuers had arrived and had foolishly come to the front gate, and that I would be helpless to meet them, or to get all those who would have followed me away from the Citadel.

But Hawkspar had prepared me for this.

"The prince, then, requests my presence already?" I asked her, though I did not want to hear what she would say.

A pause followed my question. "Prince Sheoua, of the Islands of Silver Hand, stands at the gate. He has sought out the advice of War on two previous occasions. She refused to grant him audience both times, declaring him unfit for her visions. He has been a long-wooing suitor with little to show for his great affection. Perhaps Vran Vrota will lead *you* to accept his offerings and send him on his way a happy man."

It had begun. This was the prince whose appearance would set into motion the last events the old Hawkspar had foretold. She had schooled me carefully in the steps I had to take in greeting him. In what I should say. In how I should act.

"Keep him waiting at the gate," I said. "Send word to him that I am considering his petition for audience, and that I will notify him of my decision."

"When should I tell him you will do this?" Tigereye asked me.

"You shouldn't," I said.

The pain gnawed at me, pounded behind my skull, drove like great metal spikes into the places where my eyes should have been. I could not bear to lift my hands to my face, to touch the damage that had been wrought there. I could barely breathe, the pain weighed so upon me.

Tigereye sighed heavily and said, "We could use Sheoua's gold. It will spend as well as any other prince's, and he is eager to give it to us."

"I already know what he wants," I said. "I have not yet decided if I will give it to him."

"You will do what is best for the Order," Tigereye said. "The manner of your choosing tells me this can only be the case. And that the Eyes have accepted you so quickly; that is a great blessing."

"It would appear so." I managed to sit up and swing my feet over the side of the bed, though when I did, a wave of nausea brought bile to the back of my mouth. "While you are sending a messenger to inform him of my intentions, I shall also need Moonstones and Obsidian Leap Bronze Flotan to assist me in preparing to meet with him."

"I'm here," Redbird said. "And the Seru Moonstones are all around you."

"Is the pain still with you, Oracle?" a sera asked.

"It overwhelms me," I told her.

Silence, a pause, and the sera spoke again. "This is milder than the elixir you drank at the Ceremony of Eyes. It will permit you to move, to walk about, and to think clearly, and still it will ease the worst of the agony."

She pressed a cup into my hand and I drank it.

It burned down my throat, spreading warmth as it went. I waited. It began to nibble away at my many hurts, to settle my stomach, to pull the stakes from my eye sockets.

"Better?" the Moonstone asked.

"Getting there," I told her.

Abruptly, I was so dizzy, I had to lie back down again.

Within me, around me, through me, sudden fire burned—but cold fire unlike anything I could have imagined. I felt weight, a rushing movement within and around and through me, and in the middle of it, Prince Sheoua stood. I felt the evil in him; I felt his corruption and brutality. I was in a river with him, the two of us standing in the same place, with the bitter-cold fire of time burning around the two of us. I could feel it flowing forward, and I discovered that I could let it carry me with it. Sheoua moved with me through the current, and I watched him sail in the stream of his choosing, burning and raping and slaughtering as he built for himself an empire within the islands around us.

I fought clear of that stream, with its visions of horror and death, and found myself back where I started. Facing him, the burning current pouring around us.

There were other streams. They flowed off in a dozen directions, and forked, and forked, and forked again. I could not follow them all.

I snapped out of the trance as abruptly as I had fallen into it, and found the Moonstones trying to wake me.

"I am not ill. I had a vision," I said. "Of Prince Sheoua."

In my head, I could still hear the voice of the previous Hawkspar, instructing me in my duties. "Much of what you do is for show," she had said. "And so long as you are the Ossalene Oracle Hawkspar, you have to put on a show for everyone—even the seru and the other oracles. Sometimes especially them. Once you are Hawkspar of the Tonks, perhaps you'll be able to do as you please."

I had a show to create. And I hadn't much time. I was too sick, too in pain, to go out and face the prince. But he did not need to see me immediately, in any case. Hawkspar said he needed to wait.

So I would keep him waiting.

I lay in the soft bed, so different from the mat on the floor I'd slept on for most of my remembered life, surrounded by sounds and smells and textures and darkness. The darkness, absolute and unyielding, was the centerpiece of this new world of mine.

The truth that lay before me terrified me. I who had yearned above all for my freedom, and who had foolishly thought that escaping the *place* that bound me would make me free, now found that no matter where I ran, I would carry the means of my own deeper enslavement with me. The Eyes were my masters—they would define what I could do, where I could go, how I could live. But slavery is such a funny thing, for the chain binds the man who holds it as much as the one who wears it. In my darkness, brushed by cold fire, I felt the first stirrings of the other half of the slavery, the part where I might grab the chain and yank back.

Aaran

The *Taag av Sookyn* sailed along Makkor's recommended path, avoiding the places where he had encountered cannibals, pushing hard. The volcano had erupted well after it was behind them—the *Taag* had suffered some cinders through her sheets, but the volcano hadn't been huge, and they were far enough from it that they suffered no real damage, and no loss of life.

It sat behind them like an omen. Before them lay an area on Makkor's charts where he had not found safe passage, where he and his men had fought their way through with injury and loss of life.

Aaran was going to have to try another route for that part of the voyage, and once he got out of Makkor's waters, he could not be certain he would ever find his way back.

When he reached out to the girl, sometimes he couldn't find her, and then he lived in terror that she was dead. If she were dead, that cold place in his gut insisted, his link to Aashka died with her. When he could find the girl, her pain drove into him so completely that he could not hold to his link for long before he had to back away and shield himself from her. Something terrible had happened to her. But it was not the thing she most feared, for still, when she cried out, she begged him to hurry. That they were almost out of time.

Every bit of magic he could muster suggested that she was right.

11

Hawkspar

A gentle hand shook my shoulder, and a voice whispered, "Oracle. Oracle? The other oracles are in a state—there's a . . . a . . . disturbance at the gates, and you are wanted."

I woke to an absence of pain. The Eyes—I did not feel them as things apart from me. They were not burning coals inside my skull any longer, not spikes driven into my skull, nor were they foreign lumps of stone. They felt right.

Normal.

I could not see, of course. But for the moment I was grateful for relief from an agony that had plagued me even in my dreams.

I sat up, wondering why I would be wanted for a disturbance at the gate. That was, after all, the sort of thing Obsidians dealt with.

But then I remembered Prince Sheoua, whom I had kept waiting.

The Eyes pulled at me, and I followed their pull into the dark streams and swift, cold currents of time.

I felt the presence of Sheoua again, and with him many soldiers who stood at the Citadel gate.

So he came with his army, did he? In spite of myself, I smiled. Hawkspar had spun that out as one possibility—for my purposes, the best one.

The time had come to start the previous Hawkspar's final show.

"I will have my bath now," I said in the commanding voice of a woman who would be treated as a goddess, "and black robes of silk, beaded and be-jeweled, and necklaces of sharks' teeth and the teeth of wolves, and the Silver Islands war headdress. For a brazen prince knocks at our gate who would dare make demands of a goddess. He believes his time has come. And I believe perhaps it has, though not in any fashion he will appreciate."

The words were mine. And yet they were not. They were freighted with the rhythms of generations of previous Hawkspars, with an arrogance that did not come naturally to me, but that no doubt would as I learned the secrets of the Eyes and how to exploit them. For the moment, the Eyes and the weight of history wore me much more than the other way around.

This was what Hawkspar had said I had to avoid if I hoped to lead my comrades to freedom and find the hidden enemy of the Tonk.

I had to learn to command the Eyes.

In the meantime, though, I had careful instructions laid out by my predecessor, which went as far as she could take them.

"Shall I send word to the other oracles?"

"No. Send word to the prince. Tell him when I am made ready, I shall meet with him at the gate. Tell him also that his hope lies in pleasing me. Carry my words, Sera Onyx, fast as your legs will take you."

In the wake of my demands, a great commotion started up. Feet scurried, water poured into a tub, women shouted everything from "Bring the robes!" to "Fetch the oracle's bath slave!" to "Towels! And rosewater! And mint leaves fresh from the garden!"

Everyone ran. I sat on the edge of the bed, my feet barely touching the floor.

A hand reached out to take mine, led me to the bath, and helped me to undress, and step into the water. Hands other than mine washed my hair, bathed me, perfumed me, and toweled me off with alacrity and gentleness.

Women and girls I could neither see nor sense lifted my legs while they put underthings and shoes on me, allar and hakan-allar, bo-allar and rak-tabi, rayan and cepa and finally oracle's cloak.

The tremendous weight of layers of exquisite, bejeweled fabric bore down on me. Rattling necklaces dropped around my neck, and massive headgear balanced upon my head. Swords clanked as women strapped them around both my hips, and higher notes rang out as my attendants placed daggers at my waist.

Blind I stood there, ready to take my next step, but uncertain how I was to move. I had followed instinct and Hawkspar's instructions to that point, but had just reached something she had passed over.

"Oracle?" Redbird whispered.

"Yes?"

"May I offer you help?"

"I can't *see* anything," I told her. "I can feel the rivers of time, I can follow their flow into the future, but I haven't the faintest idea how to find a door without stumbling to a wall and feeling my way toward it."

"Sight, such as we have it, is tricky," she told me under her breath. "Your mind will eventually catch the trick of it. In the meantime, though, rest your hand on my elbow, and two columns of Obsidians and a corps of drummers will take you to the front gate in style."

It was good advice.

"We'll do that," I told her.

She shouted, "Obsidians, form up, two columns, weapons hidden. Half before, half behind. We're escorting the Living Goddess to the gate."

In such fashion, with drummers beating a threatening cadence, we went down to meet an impatient prince.

He stood at the gates, and I knew that behind him stood enough men to storm the Citadel of the Ossalenes and overrun it. I could feel the weight of his men's stares, and catch the pressure of their whispers and their expectations in the time currents that swirled around me like a winter storm. I understood the danger these men were to my future plans and to the future of the Citadel, as well.

The prince thought he could command me. He had to learn, immediately and viscerally, that he and his men had no power in that place.

Obsidians opened the inner gate, which was wide enough to permit the passage of only one man at a time, and then only if he knelt when passing through it.

My finger beckoned, and my mouth said, "Come, O Prince, you who have traveled so far to seek my counsel. Come, and hear what I will tell you."

I heard the movement of many men. My heart began to race. I raised my voice. "Only you, O Prince. Your soldiers are not welcome here. The Citadel is neutral ground; no military force may tread our paths unbidden."

And then the voice of a man, big and strong and arrogant, speaking in the language of the oracles, but with strongly accented words. "You are not the Oracle of War, you girl. I know the Oracle of War, face and voice, and I would know what game she plays with me to send a snippet in her place."

I raised an arm and smiled. "Careful, foolish prince. The last to accuse the Hawkspar Eyes of War of falsehood were oracles far more powerful than you; they died eaten by rats. I would not see you fall to their fate. I still have use for *you*."

The prince seemed unworried by my threat. "Pick your targets, men," he said.

I told the two columns of Obsidians, "Take them before they can fire. Kill every second man, disarm the survivors. Go."

I watched what happened next through the currents of time; the Obsidians poured around me in two streams, out through the single gate before a single heart could beat a single time. The Obsidians on the walls above leapt to the ground in the same instant, dropping around the prince and his men. Their speed was inhuman, impossible. This was their magic, a clean and deadly power. They tore through Sheoua's men like scythes through millet. A hundred men lay dead before one could loose an arrow; the remainder were rendered weaponless as the Obsidians, with the speed and efficiency of long practice, formed a chain—as a few enemy eyes finished blinking, as a few enemy hands began to realize that they were empty—and tossed them over the cliff.

All but a dozen Obsidians poured back through the doorway to resume their stances. The remainder grabbed the prince, carried him bodily through the gate, and closed and barred it behind them. They threw Prince Sheoua facedown on the stones at my feet, and resumed their places, though this time with weapons drawn.

It seemed a long time before the screaming outside the gate began. It was only an instant.

"We do not tolerate threats," I told him, and put my foot on his head. Beneath me, he struggled to rise, and I heard blades move through the air, and a faint, frightened whimper. "You will send your surviving men back to their ships to await our signal. You will be stripped and bound, your head will be shaved, and for three days you will lie within the Oracle Tower, where you will think about the error of your manner, and the mistakes you have made. On the third day I will speak with you. What I have to say may or may not be what you wish to hear."

The Obsidians stripped him and bound him right there, then paraded him to the small front gate. From the gate, he told his men, "Wait in the ships. For three days, wait."

He seemed shaken and humbled by the number of dead men littering the path to the Citadel. From the cries of dismay, his men certainly were.

Aaran

The *Taag av Sookyn* passed out of sight of the last identifiable mark on Makkor's chart, a small island crowned by a squat black tower. From that point on, until they could reach the places Makkor had marked as safe they road uncharted waters.

Aaran gathered the crew around him on the deck, and said, "We're well into into the Fallen Suns. Civilization lies behind us, and both risk and reward ahead. From this point out, two men will ride the foremast higharm at all times, watching for danger. Eight marines will keep the watch, walking in pairs. Every man here will bear arms at all waking hours, and will have your weapon within arm's reach while you sleep. With Makkor's charts, we knew where danger lay. But in avoiding that danger, we don't know if now we'll sail through better waters, or worse."

Aaran took them north as far as he dared, keeping visible islands from the Fallen Suns off their port side. But after a day, Aaran realized that he was cutting into what little time he had to get to the girl who kept crying out to him. He could feel her desperation. She needed him to hurry, she didn't have much time. In his dreams, he saw her.

She haunted his sleep, and more and more the closer he got to her, she haunted his waking thoughts.

He had to go faster. Get to her faster. All his ambition and all his goals inexplicably depended on her salvation. She was a slave, but more, somehow. The closer the *Taag* sailed, the more he began to suspect that she was very much more.

He sent the *Taag* northeast, threading his way through small outlying islands. The watches kept their stations, but the weather favored them and nothing untoward attacked. They passed an island covered by buildings black as night that gleamed in the long rays of the rising sun. The stone, polished like mirrors, reflected the water and the sky so that at times it seemed to be a mirage, and not a true city at all. But the harbor before it was busy, and Aaran kept the *Taag* at a distance. He could see neither familiar banners atop the masts, nor any ships of familiar build. And since he could not hope to know how an outlander ship would be received, and since the *Taag* needed no supplies, he and his men were safer well away.

The islands clustered closer together, and became larger. And then, still running northeast, the *Taag av Sookyn* reached what appeared do be a wall of land running from horizon to horizon. The track he followed with the Hagedwar led straight through it, but he could not see any harbor, any cove, any sign that he could follow his track.

Baaksa, the Tonk who had the tillers, said, "Is this where we'll find her?"

"No," Aaran said. "Set us due east. We go *through* this land."

Baaksa said, "Cladmus says when you are the arrow that cannot hit your target, learn to make a target of the place where you fall."

Aaran glanced sidelong at him. "Which is one of the reasons I'm not Cladmussan."

"So you would have us sail through solid land."

"I would have us keep on our present heading and see what reveals itself when we're nearer it."

Baaksa shrugged.

As they came closer to the land, it seemed to come apart. Suddenly Aaran could see long, narrow inlets running southeast. He allowed himself to slip into the Hagedwar, and for a moment he felt the path before him. The water ran shallow through some inlets, deep through others.

He had Baaksa correct course for the deepest channel. They sailed north for one bell, then straight east for half a bell, and then into the inlet and southeast.

The land pushed in close on both sides, running almost straight up. Aaran looked for movement, for buildings, for clearings. For fire. The sun was setting, and he had an uneasy feeling about this place.

Ves came to stand beside him at the prow.

"Good deep channel," he said.

Aaran nodded.

"Makkor's log says he came through here on a bad one. Clogged up with sandbars toward the middle. They hadn't much draft, but even so, they hung up. And that was when they nearly didn't make it."

Aaran pushed away from the rail and turned to give the kor daan his full attention. "What do you mean, they almost didn't make it?"

"It was through this chain of islands that he reported cannibals. They were well south of here, but I've done the calculations, and this has to be the same chain. Same land features. Same northwest-to-southeast passages between islands."

He eyed the darkening cliffs off his port and starboard, and grimaced. No telling what lay beneath those unbroken canopies of trees.

Aaran sent one of the sailors to quietly gather all hands on deck, armed and prepared for danger.

"We have a clear channel through this passage, all the way from one end to the other," he told them, keeping his voice low. In the darkness, all he could see was the towering bulk all around him and the glitter of the stars above. He could feel both ends of the passage, but he could not see them. The ship seemed to be sailing on a choppy lake.

To either side, the sea rolled like distant thunder against the cliffs. Over that steady roll, sound still carried on the still night air—the flap of the sails as the windmen fought to keep them full, the singing of the wind they made through the lines, the creak of boards, the movement of bare and booted feet padding across the deck.

On both sides, he could feel eyes watching their passage.

He'd felt it before, and he'd been wary. But now . . . well.

Cannibals.

Surely there would be no cannibals.

"Everyone is up and on deck until we get through this passage," he said. "Every free hand bears weapons, we make no noise, all quarters watched at all time. Archers fire on any vessel that tries to approach."

"Has someone seen something?" the Eastil marine who took up port watch asked, sounding nervous.

"No. But Ves thinks this place may be near where Makkor and his men fought off cannibals," Aaran said.

"Cannibals." The word whispered and hissed across the deck, chilling the warm, heavy air.

The free hands, those who were not already standing watch or sailing the ship or making the wind, took up positions.

And then they rode in silence for a long time, with the natural wind dying away to nothing and the clear sky clouding over to hide the stars by which they'd steered.

Aaran sent his tracker back to the steersman's castle to keep them in instant communication. This was not a place where they wanted to run aground.

Behind them, a soft boom rolled like distant thunder. It died away, and in the breathless hush that followed, not a man aboard the *Taag* moved. At last, Aaran breathed out, sure that it was thunder.

And then, off to port, he heard a couple of patters, a soft thunk. Intentional sounds. The sounds of men.

Then silence.

Tuua had taken up a place at Aaran's left, with the boy Eban at *his* left. Hands grasped hilts, archers nocked arrows, and though Aaran heard Tuua whisper, "Steady, we'll be all right," to the boy, not another man so much as breathed.

The ship slid forward, and nothing else happened.

Time passed. Aaran exhaled slowly.

Others around him straightened, shook out shoulders, took the pressure off hits or put bows at rest.

The *Taag* kept steady on her course.

Nothing. It had been nothing, Aaran thought.

And then, from the starboard side, two heavy thrums. A low, rolling, thundering boom. Short, sharp thrums, higher pitched.

This time, the port side answered with more booming.

A pause, and then the starboard side.

The port side.

The starboard side.

They were talking to each other, Aaran realized. The messages were a code, or a language.

"Did Makkor mention drums in his log?" Aaran asked.

"No," Ves said. "Not a word about drums."

"Perhaps these aren't his cannibals, then," Aaran said. Whatever the men in the hills were, though, they didn't sound friendly.

The drums roared louder, and louder yet.

And then, in an unexpected silence, Aaran heard a sound like paddles in water.

"Ready Greton fire," he shouted over the drumming. "Fire one globe with a breaker."

"Ready Cap'n," a sailor to the rear of the ship shouted.

He felt the watching all around, and he and his were blind in the darkness.

"Fire," he shouted.

The globe of Greton fire vanished into the darkness. Aaran counted a slow five—and fire exploded well aft of the ship and high in the air. By the light of it, he saw something he wished he could have made his eyes take back. Long canoes filled with men covered the water like a blanket of ants on the march, pouring down from the hills, moving into the water. They covered the water behind the *Taag*. Beside it. Before it.

Aaran felt his mouth go dry. "All men aft," he shouted. "Launch Greton fire."

The fire from the first globe had hit a scattering of the long boats. Where it hit, it burned, whether on men, or on wood, or on water. When boats sailed through burning water, they caught fire. The air filled with screaming and the roar of war cries from those uninjured.

As the globes shot into the air and exploded, fire rained on more and more of the pursuers. Those who burned, quickly turned into torches. Those that had not caught fire quickly fell behind.

"Men port and starboard, arrows by volley! Men forward, catapult and chains!"

Ermyk, the kor wogan, called the volleys and kept his archers moving steadily; one line would fire and fall back, the next would step forward while the first rearmed and drew.

By the pale green blaze of Greton fire, he watched men writhe and burn and die, or leap into the water to avoid their burning boats, and catch fire in the burning water. No matter how many leapt, how many fell back, though; no matter how many died transfixed by arrows or ripped apart by the catapult shot, it wasn't enough. More came, and more after that. They reached the *Taag av Sookyn*, and began to climb in swarms.

The windmen kept the wind going, the ship surged forward fast as they could send it, but the archers had to give way to swordsmen, and had to take up swords to save their own lives.

The first invaders over the sides died. And the second wave as well. But by the third wave, the attackers were putting men onto the deck, and Aaran's marines were forced to fight one on one. Up in the rigging, the off-duty sailors still doubled as archers. The on-duty men kept sailing.

The clang of swords and knives and the screams of the injured and dying rang in his ears. He fought, sword in one hand and dagger in the other, and felt the kiss of a blade along his spine . . . but not one meant for him.

He fought, his men fought—all order gone, all sense of the shape of the battle vanished, with the deck slick with blood. In the darkness, by the still burning glow of Greton fire, men died beneath his feet and he stood on them to kill more.

And then, the rumble of thunder again.

In the hills to port and starboard, in the canopy of trees high above the narrow straight, the drums began to talk. Those attackers who could fled over the sides of the *Taag*, vanishing into the darkness.

Their boats bled away into the night.

In the east, Aaran saw a single, pale, thin line—bleak gray against black. Dawn came, and with it, open sea, the sweet, blessed openness of water without land.

They were through.

Hawkspar

For two days, I paced in my sleeping quarters, stepping along the wall with my fingertips dragging the stone. While the darkness was everywhere the same to me, I'd found my way around my quarters, which held nothing more than shelves of the previous Hawkspar's knot-journals and a sleeping pad. There was little in there upon which I could hurt myself. I'd been into my private chapel, but there I cracked my shins on the hard benches.

I had a penitent who ran for me. She brought me food, or walked with me to the upstairs dining hall where the oracles sometimes took their evening meals together.

Once each day I would gather Obsidians around me and make the trek to the green glass tower. Each time I did, the prince would begin to scream at me.

This time he saw me and howled, "I'll have your hide for this, you stone-eyed whore. I'll throw you to my men and let them have their fun with you, and then skin you myself."

"You are not yet contrite," I told him, sounding insufferably pompous. It was my intent to anger him. To frighten him, to shame him. I did not want him to change his ways. He would be no use to me if he became a better man, and I would feel badly about the future I planned for him if he renounced his horrible past actions.

I did not imagine the prince would like the experience any better than I had, nor did I think it would humble him. He did not seem to me the sort of man who would allow himself to grovel once my foot was no longer on his throat.

I made sure slaves kept him clean, but this was more for my convenience than for his comfort. My sense of smell had grown sensitive with the loss of my eyes, and the stench of his filth offended me.

I did not permit him food; neither would I allow him anything to drink, save water.

I intended to let him go when I was done with him. I would send him back out there with his warships and his soldiers and his newborn hatred of the Citadel, the Ossalenes, oracles, and everything we did and stood for.

I was making an enemy.

When I was done with the chained prince, my penitent led me across the common and into Oracle House, up the stairs to the room where oracles took their meals. I was dressed in fine clothing, and from the rustling of silks and the clattering of beads and jewels, I knew the other oracles had come wearing their finery.

I could not see them, though, or see myself. They kept asking if I had found my sight yet—evidently visual sight always came later than time sight. This made no sense to me, but all of them claimed to have experienced the same thing. All of them who would speak to me, of course. Sunspar loathed me, and kept her distance.

The others told me the sight would be different. Useful, but different.

The slaves filled our plates, and some of the other oracles began to chat with each other. I sat silent among them, fumbling with food I could not see.

Sunspar said, "If you're still blind, it would seem the Eyes haven't much use for you at all."

The others snarled at her and made excuses for me. Or said nothing. I simply struggled to get food from my plate to my mouth. It was such a simple thing, or seemed so until one no longer had the sight to do it easily. Then it became a monumental task.

Tigereye, seated to my left, cleared her throat.

All other conversations died.

"We are concerned," she said, "about your plans for the prince. His navy, waiting on our doorstep, grows restless, his soldiers march in front of the gate, and the Obsidians report forays by small teams, all moving around the base of the Citadel looking for other ways in. If you do not give the prince what he came for, his men will, at very least, destroy the town below. We hold the high ground, but that does not mean that they won't try to take that from us."

"This will get ugly," Sunspar said. She sounded accusing. "There will be bloodshed. Have you thought how you will deal with it?"

"Yes," I said. "I know exactly how I'll deal with it."

From the Tower, we heard screaming. The green glass monstrosity was playing with its latest toy again. I did not want to know what it did. I remembered its glass faces moving around to watch me, its glass hands reaching out to touch me; the memories were more than I could stand to contemplate.

I reminded myself that the previous Hawkspar had laid out this last plan before she died. I was following it as perfectly as I could.

On the third day, I went to the Tower and sat in the throne that formed there for me.

I had the Obsidians wash my captive prince and bring him before me—naked, shaved, in chains.

"We are displeased," I told him, pitching my voice as Hawkspar had taught me. "You have come to us before offering us gold and jewels, lands and slaves, and each time we have taken nothing of yours and turned you away from our gates because of your arrogance and your pride. This time, we gave you an opportunity to learn humility. To come before us with a meek spirit and a bowed head. Had you done so, we would have gladly offered you all that you desired."

Sudden power surged through me, unbidden, and I heard the prince gasp. I did not know what he saw; I could not guess what I had done. But when I spoke, my voice became deep and loud and dangerous. Like thunder, or the sound of a waterfall when the river has flooded.

"Now," I said in that terrible voice, "you will ask of me what you came to ask. And I will tell you what you must know. And then—and hear me well when I say this—you will leave this place, and you will not pause in doing so. You will not look back, you will not hesitate." My voice growled even deeper. "And under no circumstances will you ever return."

Abruptly I could see.

Not as people see who have eyes. But—I could see time, where before I had only felt it. I could see it flowing before me and behind me and all around me, dancing in rivers and pooling in eddies, tumbling down cliffs, flooding plains. If I had ever thought of time before, it was to see it as a line. Time is no line. It is a pageant, all of it happening at the same time. A wilderness of rivers, cliffs, marshes, eddies, and whirlpools, lit from within, radiant and wonderful and terrible. It is beautiful. Extraordinary. Compelling.

Time flowed into and through itself. It backtracked. It crashed and careened and scattered. It overflowed banks, got stalled. Lived.

Before, I had felt my way in darkness along its wild banks, and I had grasped only some small part of what time was. At that moment, I saw that at every point, it could be changed. It could flow from one strong stream into a hundred or a thousand rivulets, each going somewhere different, all going simultaneously.

And I could see not just the flow of time, but the little twigs and rocks, and the big boulders and cliffs, that made the steady streams diverge.

Before me again lay the future in which the pompous Prince Sheoua went to battle against the nation whose islands neighbored his, and won the battle and the war, and annihilated his enemies. Only this time I could see banners and battles, bodies stacked like cordwood, the march of dense armor. I saw him powerful, joined with villains who were themselves growing in power. Ruin for many lay in the path of Sheoua's success.

I saw clearly the shape of the diversion I had created by delaying for three days his navy's movement. His enemies had gained critical ports, moved powerful forces into strategic locations. I saw how those forces would, if he could be induced to attack in haste, ambush him and destroy most of his navy.

I saw what I had done with Hawkspar's guidance. I saw how, in the future, I could do it on my own.

For the first time, I understood what power oracles could have. The moment was not a fleeting thing, not unchangeable, not fated. The river of our existence had currents where it was most likely to go, with events pulling before it and pushing behind, but a single well-placed twig could divert a part of it.

The prince stood before me, and for the first time, I could see him, too, after a fashion. He'd been present for me before as smells, mostly—whether unwashed or washed. I caught heat as I walked up to him. Heard his raging, and the clank of chains.

But now I saw the shape of time as it flowed around him, and so saw the shape of him. His love of power drew in dark waters. The horrors he had committed in his past painted him in the blood of innocents; the horrors he intended for the future twisted him into a monster. His people he saw as an extension of himself, and his great desire was to spread them through the northern islands, to subjugate every people not his own. To murder the men, rape the women, enslave the children.

I knew his sort. He had never been a slave. He had, however, created whole armies of them. And I could break him, and free them from his hands.

I had reached into the stream of him and touched his hatred and distrust for me. For the Ossalenes. I had sharpened it, made it keen and fierce, twisted him back on himself so that all he could see was a reflection of what he was. He looked at me, but saw me as himself.

So I was going to tell him, at last, the truth he had waited so long to hear. I would set the truth to destroy him.

I said, "Ask your question, foolish prince."

I could feel his rage brushing against me. Wrapping around me. Threatening me. He was in chains because at that moment he would rather kill me than have his answer—but since he could not touch me, he would ask his question.

"I seek war with the Chevaks, whose islands lie next to mine. I have my ships prepared. I am stronger than the Chevak potentate, better equipped, richer. I have more men. I want you to look at my war and tell what I must do to win it."

His chance of winning the war he sought against the Chevaks had passed in the days I had held him and his ships in our harbor. He had lost them for the present. With his forces, he might yet have won a hundred other wars, and he might have come around from the other side of time with allies—in ten years or thirty—and overrun the Chevaks.

But those were not the questions he asked. Asking the right question, I saw, was more difficult than getting the right answer.

From my lips poured the truth. "You will win this war against the Chevaks by walking away from it. By turning tail and sailing home, O Prince, and putting your ships to sea as fishing boats, and setting your warriors to tilling the earth and caring for their wives and children. You will win this war by fleeing like little girls before a mighty storm, for if you seek this battle, your day as a mighty power will pass, and it will not come again."

What prince desires to hear that the prize he seeks cannot be his? What prince listens when told to set his eyes on different trinkets?

Not that one.

"That's your answer?" he screamed. "That I must go *farm*? That my men will *fail*? What treachery is this that you throw in my face, you who would not speak to me for ten years? *This* is the advice for which I have so long waited, you useless woman?" His voice dropped to threatening tones. "Hear me now, O Oracle of the Eyes of War, weak and pathetic liar, hater of men. I will go to war against the Chevaks, and crush them, and overrun them, and own them. And when I have done, I will come back and own you."

"At your pleasure, then, O Prince. You know our words on the matter; but we would not keep you from your fancies."

The Obsidians who had dragged him in now dragged him out. He would be tossed, naked and in chains, out our front gate, and we would give the signal for his men to come get him. I wished, knowing the sort of man that he was, that he could be given back to them as bones and tatters.

I could have fed him to the Tower, and he would have joined the silently screaming faces and reaching hands that lived within the glass. But much as that would have pleased me—and it would have pleased me a great deal—I had to set him free. I could not use him dead. Living, he would be a solution to a problem that had not yet presented itself, but that would shortly arrive.

It is fact, and fact known to all who know of us, that the Ossalene oracles speak truth. Only truth. We refuse many, for not all men deserve the truth. All who petition us and are admitted to the Tower, however, hear the truth, and most walk away. The Order of Ossalenes does not often send their suppliants out in pieces.

Done too often, that would be bad for business. Done for clear reasons, it evidently has the opposite effect, for our business has been steady for as long as people have yearned for the future and Ossalenes have had the Eyes to see it.

I sent the prince away, and stepped out of time's river.

I could still feel the new power within me, though. The change that had overcome me as I read the future for him, as I saw him standing within the cold blue fire, was not undone.

I sat in the throne within the Tower, and gradually my surroundings came into focus. Everything was darkness still—I had no beautiful rays of sunlight, no glorious colors, no patterns or textures. My world remained blackness, utter and bleak. But I could see the weight of things, and the density. Objects near to me came into very sharp focus; farther away, they seemed to blur. I could see what lay beyond my walls in all directions. I watched the other oracles going about their business, and the slaves, and the penitents, and the seru. I could see the prince, dragged down to the gate and pushed through, being dressed in fine robes by his slaves, and attended by his warriors.

I could see the shape of the island, and all the many passages that honey-combed it. I could see inside myself—could watch my heart beating and my lungs expanding and contracting.

I could not see the radiance of the sun. But I could see more.

13

Aaran

Silence lay in the *Taag av Sookyn*'s wake.

On the deck, silence, too, as the men sorted the dead from the dying, and enemies from friends. The bodies of enemies went over the side without ceremony. The injured among the enemy men were killed quickly, and tossed, too. The *Taag* had no room to carry prisoners if Aaran hoped to rescue slaves, and tossing living but injured men into the shark-swarming sea would be no kindness.

Alwyn, the kor feer, had desperate rounds, attempting to save men horribly wounded in the fight. Most lived; Alwyn did not have the power of the five Tonk master healers. He could not rebuild what was gone, but he could repair what was broken. Still, five sailors were dead, as was Majim Likely-Done, the kor jaagyn, or shipwright. Which meant that damage to the ship would become a greater risk to all who survived.

Three more men, including Drum, the Eastil who'd caught Eban stealing food, were missing.

Aaran stood on the officers' deck, built above the officer quarters, and worried about the fates of the three missing men. They might have fallen into the sea during the fighting. They might have been carried away by the hordes of men in longboats, to face whatever fate those men had planned for the crew of the *Taag*.

It tore at Aaran that he couldn't go back for them; that he had no other ships to help him, that he hadn't the manpower or the weaponry to take the battle to those bastards and destroy them. When they hit the narrowest part of the strait, his men should have launched Greton fire into the trees to either side of the *Taag*. The cannibals could have burned.

But by the time they were working their way through that narrow, fighting had already moved to the deck, and no one could chance letting Greton fire fall into enemy hands. It had been hurried off the deck by that point and hidden away in the guarded armory.

"You're quiet," Tuua said, joining him on the deck.

"I worry that the three missing men might face horrors, and I ache that we cannot save them from whatever they face." His mouth tightened. "We should have had the whole of the pack at our backs, Tuua. We shouldn't have been sailing these waters alone. In all the years I sailed with him, I never thought Haakvar a coward. But I think him one now. Four wolves could have sailed through there without losing a man. We could have cleared that passageway to make it safe for the next ships. We could have opened a way through the Fallen Suns for the Tonk, and claimed it."

Tuua put a hand on his shoulder. "You know what Ethebet says."

"No," Aaran growled. "I don't. But I suspect I'm about to find out."

Tuua said, "'There is no good that does not birth an evil, and no evil that does not birth a good.'"

"Easy for her to say. She's been dead a long damned time."

"We could have had a whole pack with us. But we did not, and perhaps, though it was not for the good last night, it will be for the good in the days yet to come. I sometimes wonder at the way events seem to work for ill, yet work in the end for good. Had we come through with four ships, perhaps we would have been marked as enemies and engaged by the navy of that tall black city we slipped so carefully past. Perhaps we would have fallen afoul of Sinali hunters before we even got out of the Path of Stars. We cannot know what evils we avoided by being only one ship. We can only know what evils we did not."

Aaran studied his cousin with a steady gaze. "I'd like to see some of the good in our hardship. I'd like to see where this has worked for us."

"Trust that it has. You'll find out how when you least expect it."

That was a worry, then, but not a worry he could do anything about. Jostfar had the working of serendipity as his burden. Aaran had cannibals and captive slave girls and markings on Makkor's chart that suggested Aaran had begun sailing the Dragon Sea, which he'd assumed to be a *mythical* place where dragons and sea serpents and ship-devouring octopuses lived, where giant birds dropped out of the sky to lift full-grown men to their nests to feed their young. But which, if Makkor's chart was correct, might not be a mythical place at all, and might include not-so-mythical monsters.

It just looked like sea to Aaran. Islands behind, water ahead.

They would have to do burials at sea for the crew. It would not be long until evening. The men would be sent off with the evening prayer. It was for that hour that both Aaran and Tuua waited.

"So . . . how is your young helper?" Aaran asked.

"He's got a good hand with a pen, and he can read Trade, though he has no idea what to do with Tonk yet. I'm teaching him now." Tuua frowned. "I'm surprised to find a scrawny little wharf rat like him so well spoken, too."

"Has he told you anything about himself?"

"Not a thing, beyond that he's twelve and he's never going back to Midrid as long as he lives."

"We'll, we won't make him. He works hard?"

"Does everything I throw his way, doesn't complain—I get the feeling if I asked more of him, he'd find a way to do it. I like him."

"He tell you he wants to be Tonk?"

"He mentioned to me that he told you that. Did you explain to him that becoming a Tonk isn't like becoming an Eastil?"

"I told him." Aaran grinned over at Tuua. "I also told him you'd teach him. I figure if he's in the chapel with you all the time, he'll have at least a chance to learn what it means to be Tonk. If he wants it enough to work for it, you and I can bring him into our clan."

It wasn't usually done that way. In the rare instances when a morii earned the honor of becoming Tonk, a taaklord or clan chieftain usually did the honors. But a captain of a ship or a keeper could do it, too.

Below, the men finished scrubbing the deck clear of blood, and officers started carrying the wrapped and weighted bodies of the dead crewmen up from the crew commons, where they had lain in state.

Aaran and Tuua went down to the deck to give them a send-off fitting of Ethebet.

Hawkspar

I dreamed of him—the beautiful man who came to rescue us. He sailed across the sea in a glorious ship that sparkled like the sun. He was tall and powerfully built, forceful and admired by his men. But when he turned, I could not see his face.

He came to me, and touched me with his hands and with his lips, and I embraced him. In my dream, he thought me beautiful. In my dream, he yearned for me in the ways that men yearn for women—all the ways the Ossalenes are quick to scorn, and to deny, and to forbid.

But when he came for me, I would no longer have to pretend to be an Ossalene. I could become a Tonk and claim the birthright that had been stripped from me, and I could discover the secrets of a man's body, the pleasures that I knew of only as the sins that Vran Vrota did not permit to Ossalenes.

When I woke, I knew that he was coming. I could not feel his touch as I could in the dream, but something existed between the two of us that had not been there before. I could see the line of magic that swirled out from me like a glowing thread. I could follow it through the sea. I could follow it beyond the point where I could actually see, to the point where everything became a uniform blur of even density. And then, if I held myself above the flow of time, I could follow it all the way to a ship that raced toward us across the sea.

He was there. Hawkspar had not lied to me. He came for us, following my plea for help. He came to me.

Awake, I was grateful to have a form of vision back, even if it was an uncomfortable form. To look at a person and see her as layers, as air pockets and watery tissue and solid bone, made people unpleasant to look at. I could not see only the outside, no matter how hard I tried.

I could not see just a surface of anything anymore.

That had advantages.

I called Redbird to my chapel.

When she arrived, I wrapped the chapel in the shield that blocked other oracles and seru from seeing me or what I did.

"He's getting closer," I told her. "With his ship."

"I understand."

"We're going to go into the passages under the Citadel. We have to start getting ready."

Redbird said, "You have your vision now?"

"Finally. It came to me while I dealt with the prince."

"Then you know we cannot hide what we're doing down there. There is no place within the Citadel that the seru cannot see," the Obsidian said.

"Save those things hidden within shields like this. But you cannot shield the corridors and the catacombs."

"I don't intend to. Secrets are not our problem. What we're doing, we'll do publicly. I am an oracle, and I will make it known that I do not wish to live as my predecessor lived. I want to be surrounded by riches. By treasures. By things that are fine and lovely."

Redbird laughed. "Why? You cannot see things that are fine and lovely. Everything is darkness, always. Texture and smell and scent are treasures to us, but gold and gemstones and great works of art are as valueless as common rocks and metals and wood polished but unpainted."

"We need not value treasure. Others do. This will be a final gift we give to the Ossalene Order on our way out the back passage, Redbird."

"Oh, Mouse," she said, and hugged me. "I had feared your power had changed you."

"No." I said. *Not yet,* I thought.

"You will gather all our people together, and all the little Tonk slaves who will be going with us. When rescue comes, we will have to gather them in a short time and get them to the ship under terrible, deadly conditions. So you and I will walk together now, deciding what route we will take. And I will tell you how we will help our friends and destroy our enemies in the process."

I shut down the shield around the room, and Redbird and I went out to walk together. We paced through the gardens—flowers lacked much appeal when they were only shapes and smells. The eye delights in their forms and colors and hides away small flaws and imperfections that become clear when they are viewed in layers all at once. Still, a walk through a garden with the sun on my face and the sound of falling water in my ears and the fragrances of so many warmed blooms in my nostrils soothed me.

That I could walk on my own comforted me even more. I found pleasure in the fact that I was no longer helpless. These were good things, and I accepted them.

The walk took us in the direction I wanted to explore. South of the Seru Garden, between the laundry fountain and the root cellar, there sat a tiny circular stone storage building with a locked door. Redbird had keys and unlocked the door for us, and we proceeded into its cool shelter.

In the floor, hidden from normal sight, lay a trapdoor. It was wide enough to permit the passage of two people at the same time—or perhaps three if they were small. And it required descent down a steep stair in order to take the traveler to the passageways beyond.

"Is there another way into this series of tunnels?" I asked Redbird.

"The cliff," she said. "The storage room in the kitchen."

"The cliff will not help me. That's an egress, to my way of thinking. Is the storage room entrance any bigger?"

"No. It's the same as this."

That would be a problem. It meant that I would have to have an excuse to have most of the people who would be leaving already in the passages when trouble started. Timing would be tricky, and explanations trickier. I would have to give it thought. Hawkspar had told me what I would have to do—but this far into the future, her guidance had been more vague. I would have to determine on my own the best way to accomplish my goals.

Beyond the bottleneck of the trapdoor, the cellars and passageways were spacious. We walked along the main corridor, heading south toward the cliff and the island's secret second harbor. The corridor was roomy and clean, carved out of bedrock. In shelves along its sides, the seru had stored dried herbs, root vegetables, cold-storage fruits, and such commodities as a community of nearly eight hundred needed to operate. Much of what the seru kept down there could rightly be called siege stores. We passed dried, smoked, and salted meats, jars and vats and bolts of cloth, weapons, utility items like ropes and string and nails, tools, spare cages and cage-making materials, and other common supplies. But we also passed several enormous storerooms filled from floor to ceiling and back to front with treasures: boxes and crates and trunks filled with gold and jewels and items that I guessed to be art objects collected by previous oracles.

The treasures were what I had come to see.

"We have great riches," Redbird agreed when I noted some of the contents of the cellars. "I do not know that we are wise to keep them in this fashion."

"We'll find them useful."

"Truly? I would think such things could only be a useless burden."

Hers was a good observation, and I smiled at it. She could no more see a smile on my face than I could see one on hers, of course. But she would discover how true her words were soon.

The corridors went on for a long distance, and I imagined the Obsidians leading whole flocks of children and young women at a run to safety while pursued by those who would be trying to stop us. There would be pursuit; I had no doubt of it. And some of our number would likely fall.

How best, then, could I hope to save the majority? Those who were risking their lives to trust in me—and I never forgot my own trial by rats, or the fates that would await those who tried to escape but failed—deserved the best chance at freedom.

At last we reached a small door carved into the end of the stone corridor. Beyond it, I could feel the narrow paths that wound down to the small, hidden dock where I would attempt to direct our rescuers.

Little girls were going to be running in a herd down the two paths, and if they did it in the dark, they were going to pitch over the cliffs and die shattered on the rocks below. If our rescuer could arrive in the daylight hours, we would not lose so many.

Some . . . we could not help losing some, I thought. There was no rail on either path. The paths could certainly be wet toward the bottom if the tide was low, and could be slippery all the way from the top should we have a storm.

I needed to find a reason to meet with all the young women who would be escaping with me—and at the same time, not one by one. I needed to meet with my predecessor's conspirators, too. I had to find an excuse to bring all of them—but *only* them—together at the same time.

I needed to think. To move over the currents of time, to search for a clear direction.

"We have to be getting back," I told Redbird. "I need to think about this. Make sure the doors lock and hinges stay well oiled and that a key is down here, hidden someplace where you and I both know to look for it."

"I will."

Sunspar and four Obsidians waited for us when we stepped out of the round stone entry room.

Sunspar strode up to me and shoved her face so close to mine I could tell she'd eaten leeks, and worse, that they hadn't agreed with her. Her perfumes, soaps, and skin oil added layers of sweetness that made standing so close to her even more unpleasant.

"I would know," she told me, "what you and a Sera Obsidian were about down in the storage cellars."

I took my coldest tone with her. "You would know about us that which we have no interest in sharing. A goddess of war owes nothing to a goddess of secrets. But we do not speak our business to such as you." And then I turned to Redbird and said, "We have indicated that which we would have for our chambers. Bring all of it immediately; get such help as you require from the slaves. Do not tarry, Sera Obsidian, for our temper is short and our wrath long."

And with that, Redbird and I pushed past the Oracle Sunspar, who stood silent and furious.

I had little interest in making a friend of Sunspar. My people and I had not much time in which to accomplish a great deal.

When we were well out of earshot, Redbird said, "The oracles have lost the warring spark they once had, and I think none save Sunspar will stand against you in what you plan; they will do as you direct. But not all here will let you act unhindered. Among the seru, Order and Discipline will present problems. Individual others may, as well."

"Some may."

"Yes. Order and Discipline wield much power over others, and as well, over . . . darker things. Not all value the idea of freedom, for themselves or for anyone else."

We walked in silence while I considered that some of the Ossalenes would constitute a deadly threat to me and mine. Not only did we have to protect the innocent who would stay behind from the storm that was about to descend on the Citadel, but we would have to protect the innocent who would flee against their own people, as well as the dangers of that same storm.

The sun had set—I could not feel it on my skin, nor could I find it in the sky. To my eyes it had seemed huge and powerful. To my Eyes, it was a tiny dot, confusing in its composition, spherical instead of disklike, with a powerful weight that seemed to pull me toward it. No chariots drove it through the sky, as I had been taught by the seru. How it had changed seemed to me a symbol of how *everything* had changed. It had moved outside of the realm of what I knew to be true, and forced me to see that I did not know much at all.

14

Hawkspar

I watched Redbird and the Tonk slaves toiling in the cellars. I had told Red-bird to make sure the largest and heaviest and most costly of the treasures were moved toward the front of the tunnel, and to have them placed where they could be clearly seen.

Small, easily portable treasures, as well as particularly fine costumes of state that had been worn by previous Hawkspars and other oracles, I had put all the way to the back, next to the secret door. These would be kept conveniently near the key, and covered with rags and ropes and other things of no importance so that, until we needed them, they would be inconspicuous.

My story to the oracles was that I intended to have the gaudy, grand treasures placed in my quarters. To give the story a bit of verisimilitude, I made sure that some of the Ossalene hoard actually did arrive there.

Over the next two days, I acquired hanging tapestries, a gilded jewel-encrusted bed with tall posts and heavy hangings all around, and thick soft carpets—those I actually liked. I took off my shoes and walked around on the floors in my bare feet, and my mind pretended that I was a child again walking on soft earth and thick grass.

All the while, I could feel my rescuer coming closer. Closer. Racing trouble.

Meanwhile, across the water, in islands not so far from mine, I could feel Sheoua engaging the Chevaks in battle, disengaging, running. Sheoua and his fleet took drubbing after drubbing, ran and hid, were found out again, lost more ships and more men, and fled yet again. Each time they fled, their path took them in our direction.

This was as it needed to be.

Every shower I took, I sent desperate words to the rescuer who followed the trail I had made: *Hurry, for there is not much time,* and *Come by the back stair,* and *Keep secret, keep hidden.*

A magic wind carried the man who answered my call—one his men created themselves—so that when the sea fell still as glass, his ship sailed on. He would reach us. But would he arrive when we needed him? He had to reach us neither before nor after Sheoua turned his surviving ships into our main harbor.

It was all very delicate, all too precise. I needed our rescuer to arrive in the daylight, at the same time as Sheoua; I needed good dry weather and not rain; I needed conditions that I was not likely to get; and everything that did not go my way would cost little girls and young women their lives.

I sent word to the villagers—*Trouble comes. Take that which you value and hide in the low caverns.*

Sheoua and his men would find the village deserted. They might burn roofs, and some furniture, but the village was carved of living stone. They would accomplish little before, in frustration, they brought their fight to the Citadel.

I could find no comfort where their fates were concerned. *We save who we can save,* I told myself when worry kept me from sleeping. I wanted a way that would make everything come out right. And no such way existed. So I repeated my mantra: *We do what we can, and acknowledge that no matter what we do, we cannot save them all.*

It was not enough, even if it was true.

What sort of a world is it where some must die so that others might live? What sort of world is it that demands the blood not just of the willing and the evil, but of innocents, that freedom might be gained?

In my chapel alone, having set my plans in motion, I could do nothing else. So I prayed. I did not pray to Vran Vrota, nor even to Jostfar. Instead, I prayed to Ethebet, the Tonk saint of war and childbirth, who was a stranger to me. I prayed that she would keep the little slave girls safe as I stole them away, and that she would protect the penitents who had trusted me, and that the seru who joined me would find their way to safety. And that I would survive this as well. I had paid for the freedom of others with my eyes, and with pain and nightmares and lurking dread—but at the very least, if the Eyes were to haunt me for the rest of my existence, I wanted them to do it away from this place with its rat tortures and beatings and all the rest of its pious horrors.

In my chapel, I formally renounced Vran Vrota and consecrated myself to

Jostfar through Ethebet, using what little I knew of the ritual, making up what I didn't. I had a bowl of incense and wood shavings, water, and scented oil. I had a swatch of hair I'd clipped from my head; I understood that pulling was the preferred method of sacrifice, but my hair was still too short to pull. I burned incense and hair, prayed my prayer, and stood afterward hoping that my prayer would be heard.

And to myself, I hoped Ethebet of the Tonk was not a saint who admired fear.

Aaran

Aaran paced the deck, feeling the *Taag* drawing near its destination.

They had crossed a windless Dragon Sea, and by the time islands came into sight again, both windmen were weary. Aaran wished he could have lured a third on the trip so that during bad times, each could have taken a shift for work, a shift for sleep, and a shift for relaxation. As it was, the two men had little more than time to throw food down their throats when they woke, and time to do the same before they fell exhausted into their hammocks at the end of their shifts.

They were unhappy, the men in general were unhappy—they had expected adventure in crossing the Dragon Sea, and that they had found. But they had wanted glorious riches, too, and wondrous prizes for all their efforts.

The crew—especially the moriiad—didn't like the sea's stillness, which made them think of curses. They muttered as they went about their work, and eyed Aaran with increasing distaste.

Aaran heard some cheering when the man on high watch spotted the first land. He consulted the Makkor's chart. Makkor and his brothers had used Bhekian measurements, which complicated the process of reading it, but if Aaran had figured out the bearing marks on the chart correctly, he ought to be bringing the ship into the first line of islands at the northeasternmost edge of the Dragon Sea.

Aaran wasn't taking them forward based only upon the charts, of course. He also had his thread to the girl who cried out for his help.

The nature of her call had changed. When he'd first felt it, she had been small and helpless. Now, though he could still feel fear and helplessness in her, he felt other things as well. A change in her nature, the presence of darker elements, an unnerving thread of power.

He was close enough, he thought, to venture reaching out to her through the Hagedwar. He was not sure that she would know what to do when he spoke to her. He was not the most gifted in the arts of the communicators, and he could not be certain that he could make her hear him. He had the same base knowledge that anyone who studied the Hagedwar obtained. He could connect to a mind that was not shielded against him, he could speak and sometimes make himself heard. Sometimes he could hear what was said in return.

If nothing else, he thought he could let the woman know he was on his way and, from the feel of things, almost to her. He could make her feel that her rescue was not far off.

He hoped he would be able to hear her, too. He wanted reassurance. He wanted to know that the undercurrent of power he felt was some aberration, and that he was not taking his ship and everyone on it into a trap.

So before they sailed into the islands, while the wind was still gone and the sea lay like glass and the crescent moon gave what little light it could offer, he bade the windmen rest awhile, and all the crew to stand guard against anything that might approach them while they were becalmed. With that done, he retired to his cabin, wrapped himself in the Hagedwar, and followed the line to the girl.

They were not terribly far away anymore. He had promised he would come for her, and here he was, almost to her.

Within the Hagedwar, he touched her lightly with his thoughts. He connected—far better than he thought he would. Something in the magic that she had sent out, bound by a third presence he could only describe as ghostly, let his clumsy, limited communicator skills establish firm contact with her. He was stunned by it. He could feel himself as her. He could feel his chest rise in rhythm with hers, could hear what she heard, could feel something soft and silky in her hands. He couldn't see anything. That was odd—to connect so well in other ways, yet see nothing.

She was walking somewhere, hurrying.

I'm almost to you, he said.

He felt her stop walking as her body went rigid.

Well, at least she could hear him.

Don't be afraid, he told her. *I'm coming to get you and the rest of the slaves.*

I know who you are, she said. *I've dreamed you. But you sound different in my head than I thought you would.*

So do you, he told her. *You sound very young.*

She ignored that. *When will you reach us?*

If I'm judging distances correctly, I should be with you by midday tomorrow.

We'll be dead by then, she said. *The men who are coming to kill us will be here when the moon touches the horizon. If you are not here by then, nothing you can do will save us.*

Men who were coming to kill them. So this wasn't going to be a simple rescue. Was there such a thing as a simple rescue?

I have men with me, he said.

Do not think to engage our enemies in a fight. The man who comes to destroy us has five ships full of hardened warriors with him.

And Aaran had one ship with a handful of Tonk warriors, a batch of Eastil wharf rats, and a scattering of other moriiad from across the many seas. All right, then, he wouldn't be able to march in as the conquering hero and kill off those who had come to kill her and those she wanted to save.

You must come by the back stair, she said.

He'd felt that in the pleas that she'd been sending through the water. The back stair.

The south-most harbor, and up paths cut into the face of a cliff? He had felt these things in the current of magic that bound him to her.

Yes, she said. *But remember, if you are not here when the moon is at midpoint, you will find nothing but our bodies strewn across the ground. Or worse for us—for they might wish to take us captive, and we would rather die than that—you might find nothing at all.*

Aaran broke off his communication with her after a final reassurance that she could depend on him, and a word to her to have her people ready.

And then, when she could no longer hear him, he settled in to worry.

He figured the distance, and the *Taag av Sookyn* would have to cover it at painful speeds. If they had a storm and the winds behind them, they might reach the hidden harbor on time. Or if the weary windmen could work together and give everything they had, he might still hope to bring the ship to her prize before it was too late.

But the skies were clear, not a breeze blew, and suppose he exhausted his windmen in the process of reaching the island. The *Taag av Sookyn* would race into the harbor and load up with rescued slaves and perhaps some treasure, and turn to get out. Only without wind or windmen, it would be dead in the water.

Only—enemies were sailing to attack her people.

They had wind, then.

Something cold shivered its way under Aaran's skin and lodged in his gut.

The moriiad had been insisting the whole time they'd been crossing the Dragon Sea that the windless calm was unnatural. Aaran had suggested they were a superstitious lot.

But if a nearby navy was able to proceed under sail to attack the island Aaran wanted to reach, then why did they have wind when the *Taag av Sookyn* didn't?

Were the moriiad right? Was the *Taag av Sookyn* under a curse? Was this the price he would pay for sailing a drowner ship? He had accepted the weight of guilt for taking the grave of his brethren to sea because he'd had no other choice. But in doing so, had he doomed this rescue mission, and once and for all killed any chance of finding and freeing Aashka and bringing her home?

He went on deck.

And found that circumstances had changed.

"There's something out there, Captain," one of the Eastils said, pointing east, where a curve of land showed over the horizon.

Aaran saw a wall of fog that rolled slowly across the glassy sea, and within it dark shapes, twisted and indistinct. He heard low rumblings, but they had nothing in common with thunder.

Ves stood with his hand on the hilt of a sword. He turned at Aaran's approach. "You have your rest?"

"I wasn't resting. I was communicating with the woman we're to rescue. We have trouble ahead."

"Trouble beside, too."

Aaran nodded at the fog. "You have any guess what that might be?"

"Not a bit of it, Captain, nor have I any stomach to find out. Those shapes and sounds make my belly knot up."

"Mine as well." Aaran shouted, "Marines on deck! Both windmen, stations now and give us everything you have!" He ran back to the Tonk who'd manned the tillers. "We've a need to fly to our goal and away from that which pursues; I don't want to find out what that marching fog is hiding."

Aaran ran to the steersman's castle and said, "Take arms. I'm going to track and steer at the same time." He gripped one tiller in either hand, and his feet dug into the high deck that formed the back half of the roof of officers' quarters. The sea didn't fight him.

Tracking, riding half in and half out of the Hagedwar, he got a better feel for what was coming.

The fog rolled toward them faster. Much faster. And the shapes within it grew more menacing. They were alive. Big. They coiled and roiled, formed and submerged and reformed, and he couldn't get a grasp on what they might be, but his balls tightened and his gut twisted and he knew that they weren't friendly natives rowing out to offer girls for sex and food for trade.

The sails filled, snapping to life.

Slow at first, because it had been becalmed, the *Taag av Sookyn* crawled forward. It took both distance and time to build up speed. But the windmen were giving everything in them, and if the *Taag av Sookyn* did not leap forward like a young horse, she put her shoulders into the harness like a plowhorse who knew its business.

To the east, the tendrils of fog clawed closer, and within, Aaran began to hear screaming.

The shapes were nothing human, but the screams sounded like men tortured and begging for mercy. Those human sounds were distant and faint at first; nevertheless every hair on Aaran's body stood up in recognition.

The sailors still on deck were up in the rigging, shifting the fansails and angling the pillar arms to catch every bit of breeze, dropping extra sheets, clinging to the lines.

Praying. He could hear a dozen languages not his own and not Trade, and most he didn't know. But he knew the sounds of men treating with their gods. He knew fear.

Eyes open and forward, hands on the tiller, Aaran sent his own thoughts winging to Saint Ethebet, asking for courage and strong arms and strong swords should his men need them, and then to Jostfar, the one god of the Tonk, for such blessings as he could spare to those who did his work, and such protection as he could offer to those, both rescuers and captives, who needed it.

And then he returned his focus to work, for Jostfar blessed, but men pulled the load.

Aaran watched the fog rolling closer, but sliding a little to the rear of the *Taag,* and heard the screaming growing louder. His heart beat faster, the prow dug deeper and harder, and the sails snapped and the lines sang and the boards creaked. He gripped the tillers.

We'll get there or we won't, he thought. *And all we can do is all we can do.*

One thing was sure, though. The *Taag av Sookyn* would be taking a different route home than the one by which she'd arrived. Aaran swore to that.

Hawkspar

Our would-be rescuer had spoken to me. He had touched me. He had slid beneath my skin—I'd felt him there. He came for me, and I found myself giddy from his touch and shivering from his voice.

Even after he had gone, I could feel him. I had been wicked. I had let myself follow his touch back to him, and I had permitted myself the pleasure of touching him back. He was strong. Big and strong and brave. Good-hearted. Young. Reckless. Randy. He had known women, and he had enjoyed them, many of them, and I let my body feel what his had felt, and pretended for the few moments I could that he was touching me that way, doing those things to me, and that I was responding as those women had. With wantonness. With pleasure and wild abandon.

We in the Order were forbidden the touch of men, and were forbidden to think of them. As a penitent, though, I had thought of them. I had watched the princes and the kings and the mighty warriors march across our paths, and I had lusted after their powerful bodies, their muscled legs, their strong arms. They were always so mysterious, and so tempting.

Sometimes I would catch them looking at me, or at the slaves or the other penitents, and I would see the hunger in their eyes.

When I was a penitent, I was forbidden to dream, but dream I did. I was forbidden to lust, but I did that, too.

Now that I was an oracle, I was supposed to be above the lusts of the flesh. The Eyes were supposed to keep me from wanting. But they didn't.

For those few moments that I slid beneath his skin, he was beautiful, this man Aaran who came to save me. I wriggled into his past and indulged myself; his touch was glorious, his caresses all-consuming, his smiles something to live for, his desires something to die for.

But I shut him away before I could become too enraptured. Death raced toward us, and I had much to do to keep it from catching us.

Sheoua with his battered ships and his limping crews lay on the other side of an uninhabited island only a dozen leagues from ours. I could not see him clearly. Too many layers stood between us. But I could make out his five remaining ships, and the fact that they stood at anchor while his medics treated those on board who suffered.

Prince Sheoua was moving all his injured men to one ship, and putting the healthy ones on the other four. They were going to let the one ship with its wounded stay behind in safety.

So four ships would attack us.

They would be on us quickly, choosing to attack in darkness. I wondered at their choice. Darkness favored us, because our Obsidians knew neither darkness nor light. They saw the same, always, and what they saw with their Eyes in the middle of moonless night far exceeded what archers and swords-men with could see with eyes of flesh.

I needed to watch what he and his men intended next. I called the river of time to me, and stepped in, and pushed the current to carry me forward along the direction it would follow if we did not conquer them when they attacked us.

Sheoua did not plan to destroy the women of the Ossalene Order, I dis-covered. He and his many men planned to find their way through two outer walls in the Citadel that we had thought unbreachable. A visible decoy force would draw our defenders away from those two points with a loud diversion, and while the Obsidians and the Onyxes were diverted to a messy battle, two side forces would run in and grab every young woman they could find. I watched Sheoua stealing slave girls and penitents, and then those of our Or-der who were not primarily fighters—the Moonstones and the Granites, the Amethysts and the Rosestones.

I followed this course of time forward still farther, and saw the slaves and penitents sold to slavers or raped and killed, the seru tortured, the oracles al-ready dead. All who remained within the walls of the Citadel, fighting, would perish.

Well, the walls they intended to breach would not be easily defended. But knowing how they planned their attack, the Obsidians who remained behind—nearly all the Obsidians from my predecessor's part in this conspir-acy, plus all those who had never known of a conspiracy—would have a sig-nificant advantage.

But I needed to give them more.

I followed path after path through the currents, following those that ended in triumph as well as those that ended in failure. Hawkspar had not been able to give me more than generalities about this last phase of my time as an Ossalene oracle.

I sought every advantage for the women I would leave behind, and when I'd catalogued them to my satisfaction, and put together what I believed would be the best possible plan, I stepped out of the waters of time. I had one final deception to carry out.

15

Hawkspar

I rang the bells in the warning sequence; I rang them loud and long, and watched through the occluding veil of stone as slaves and penitents, acolytes and seru, and eventually oracles, burst from doors and headed to the House of Holies, the only enclosed space in the Citadel that would hold every inhabitant at the same time.

When I finished, bell-deafened, I hurried to the Seru Garden. Redbird waited for me there. "All of ours are underground," she said.

I told her, "Then join me. We must make sure that those who remain behind can save themselves."

We ran to the House of Holies, burst through the great arched doors, and raced to the front of the grand edifice. And I took a place behind the great arching bench. My hands rested on the rails, and I said, "Listen well, for we have little time, and much to do if we would survive this night."

I did not need to shout, or even raise my voice. The stage had been cleverly designed to carry the quietest speech from the front of the building into the wings at the sides and to the distant benches in the back. My every word would reach every listening ear.

"Prince Sheoua and the remains of his vanquished navy approach; he is intent on revenge, for he blames the Ossalenes—and me in particular—for his defeat. I warned him that if he fought the Chevaks, he would lose; he chose to fight them anyway."

I heard murmurs of understanding from some of the other oracles. Evidently giving good advice to people who chose not to follow it was not something only I had experienced.

"He has more fighters than we have, and he thinks to surprise us with them. If you follow my directions, however, he cannot defeat us."

Sunspar said, "You brought this upon us."

"I'm always pleased to know that one of our own stands in the same camp as the enemy," I said, and now the murmurs of agreement, from both oracles and seru, reached my ears. Good. The fewer the number who actively supported Sunspar, the more would survive in what came.

"I have divided the Obsidians into four groups. All four groups have already armed and taken their places—at the point where the enemy will create a diversion to attempt to make us believe that is his point of attack, and at the three points where he will attempt secondary attacks.

"He is bringing five ships against us—four into the main harbor to our north, and one into our secret harbor in the south. He will split his forward forces into three groups, with one group attacking the main gate to the north, one group attacking the west wall, and one group attacking the east wall. The fourth group—the rear force—will attempt to swarm the long stairs and breach the back gate. *My Obsidians are going to let them.* We have planted explosives within the tunnels, and when the tunnels fill up with the enemy, we will light the wicks and explode them. Do not, therefore, pursue any of the enemy that enter the tunnels."

Sunspar said, "Then that was the purpose of all your people in those tunnels over the last two days. You discovered that you'd made a mistake, and now you're scrambling to fix it."

I leaned harder on the wood. "Not at all. Hawkspar my predecessor found Prince Sheoua a nightmare in the making. Had he been permitted to follow his chosen course of action, everyone within our group of islands would have fallen to his growing empire—and all of us would have been raped and tortured for his amusement. That fate still awaits us if we lose. However, Hawkspar my predecessor believed that we had an obligation to protect the innocent in the lands around us; therefore, we have dealt with Prince Sheoua in a manner that has nearly destroyed his military might. When the Ossalenes have finished with him today, Sheoua will be dead, his army destroyed, and the people he had already enslaved, free.

"To that end," I continued, "Onyxes and Bloodstones must fight alongside Obsidians at the front gate, and on the east and west walls. Put up resistance at the outer gate, but when it is breached, fall back through the Arena, close the inner gates, and loose the starving rats. When they fail, Ossalene archers will shoot fire arrows into the remaining troops. If the wall is breached, Obsidians, Onyxes, and Bloodstones will have to fight hand-to-hand."

"What about side defenses?" the new Windcrystal, who was being asked to commit her Onyxes, asked.

I said, "Defenders on the east and west walls are soaking the ground outside the Citadel with lamp oil. When the majority of Sheoua's forces have been committed to that ground, more flaming arrows will set the men on fire."

I took a deep breath. "Some may survive to get inside the Citadel. This is where every fighting sera will be critical. Non-fighting seru and oracles need to take the acolytes, penitents, and slaves into the Onyxes' underground chambers and seal the entrances. Should the fighters fail, you will be their last line of defense; you should consider that capture may not be preferable to death."

I heard the gasps. I took a deep breath. I didn't want to say what I'd just said, but the seru needed to understand how much was at stake. Having warned them, I offered what comfort I could. "I don't believe that you will have to make this choice, however; the future strongly favors the Ossalenes over Sheoua. If we are triumphant, the Obsidians will ring the 'Solar Triumphal' on the bells when Sheoua is defeated. It will then be safe for you to come out."

By then, of course, my chosen people would have sailed with me. Sunspar and her Bloodstones would not be able to turn her forces against us. All who remained could make a convincing claim of having been duped. There should be no bloodshed between Ossalenes. The Order would go on much as it had before; and the Obsidians would report that they had been instructed to protect everyone—from the slaves to the oracles—until "the Hawkspar Eyes of War" returned. I never intended to go back. But I would die, whether sooner or later. If they were so inclined, Redbird or the other Obsidians with us could then return the Eyes to the monastery.

Silence followed my pronouncements, broken at last by sniffling from one of the little slaves. "I don't want the bad men to take us again," she sobbed. "I want to go home to my mommy."

I understood her so well. I wanted more than anything in the world to go home to my mother, too. It was all I'd wanted since the day I was ripped from her arms, and my heart went out to the child. I stepped down from the vantage point behind the kneeling bench, and picked her up, and hugged her. This was an enormous breach of protocol, and oracles and seru gasped. But I didn't care. I patted her back and rocked her in my arms and said, "Hush. Everything will be all right."

Holding her, feeling her head rest against the curve of my neck while her thin arms draped over my shoulders, I wondered what sort of future she would find when all of this was done. Would she and the others who stayed behind in the relative safety of the Citadel be better off? Or would we, who sought freedom?

Aaran

The fog and the screaming horrors within it had fallen behind.

As they sailed into the hidden harbor, with the red sun falling into the western sea and bloodying it, he considered that his windmen were exhausted. The sea still lay like glass all around him, with no breath of natural wind to fill his sails.

He would be sailing from the harbor onward, toward monsters, cannibals, and Jostfar only knew what other nightmares, and he would be doing it on the power of drained windmen and nothing more.

Maybe Jostfar would grant him a sudden storm, favorable winds, a handful of new windmen.

But probably not. The ship would be full of panicked children, and heading into terrible danger, and it would be sailing crippled.

This was the voyage Haakvar didn't want to make.

Well. Four ships would have been better than one. And four experienced Tonk crews could have brought along enough spare windmen to keep the ships moving forward.

Aaran looked up at the last bloody flashes of sunlight on the bone-white cliffs towering over his head. A small dock lay before him and to the starboard side. A narrow ledge high above, directly over the place where the ship docked, marked the presence of an entryway. And two paths, neither of them wide enough to offer safe passage to any but goats, led up to it. Carved into the surface of one path were arrows pointing up. In the other one, he caught glimpses of arrows pointing down.

But the sun finished its crawl below the horizon, and long shadows enveloped the last bits of cliff. At a distance, he heard war drums. Their steady, slow pulsing echoed across the water. They were distant from him, and he did not feel them as an immediate threat. But he suspected that they signaled the arrival of the warriors who, with their four mighty ships, were preparing to attack the captives he intended to rescue.

"Make fast," he ordered, but he kept his voice down. He and his crew worked stealthily, tying up tight to the dock.

They were going to have to go up one of those paths. Going to have to come back down the other one. In the dark. His skin crawled. He was as much at home in the sea as a fish, but the very idea of his men climbing rocks in the dark on dry land gave him visions of destruction and death and mangled horror.

The drumming in the distance picked up speed, and he heard pipes beginning to play. They were girlish pipes to his way of thinking—high-voiced and melodic. They had little in common with Tonk pipes, which had warrior voices, other than that they were loud.

He wouldn't complain, though. The pipes and drums made stealth unnecessary.

"We have to get up to the doorway at the top of the cliff. We have captives to rescue. A lot of them. And treasure to claim, too, though I don't know how much we'll find here, or how much time we'll have to find it. The captives come first, though. I'm thinking we can arrange pulleys and ropes from that shelf up there, and lower the heavy things down. Maybe some of those slaves who won't be able to negotiate the paths."

"You didn't say anything about captives," one of the Eastils said.

"We're liberating slaves," Aaran said. "Tonk slaves, a lot of them. We'll get a good reward for it. But we're rescuing them from a sort of monastery, and I'm reckoning that monastery is as full of treasure as anyplace else that collects money for the gods, and then keeps it for the priests."

The Eastil grinned. The Tonks didn't have such places; the only things of value a raider would find in Tonk houses of worship were books. Eastil lands, however, were loaded with them.

"Right, then," he said. "Slaves and gold. What better booty could we hope for?"

"The *slaves* are Tonk, and under my *protection*," Aaran said, letting his voice carry to the men on deck. "Whatever harm one of you brings to one of them, you'll suffer a hundred times worse yourself." That wasn't the sort of thing a captain would ever have to say to a Tonk crew. Rape and pillage weren't the Tonk way. Some looting, maybe, if the target warranted. But Ethebet had no patience with rapists, or with those who slaughtered the innocent and the helpless.

A rabble crew of foreign motley needed different handling. And the grumbles told Aaran he had been wise to address the situation immediately.

A couple of the sailors took ropes and rebar and pulleys and mallets and began working their way up the face of the cliff, braving the gathering gloom without lights. While they climbed, Aaran put the rest of his men into teams—one that would gather the captives as they came out and direct them to either the makeshift lift or one of the two paths; a second that would get the captives off the deck and into the holds below; a third that would bear arms and work its way into the passages behind the escaping captives, both to make sure that they weren't attacked from behind, and to gather such loot as they might find while bringing up the rear of the retreat.

From the top of the cliff, he heard his men setting the rebar eye-ring into the stone. It took only moments, and then the first rope end came snaking down onto the deck. A second followed. Then both ends from the rope on the other side landed. The crew had found a cargo crate in the meantime, emptied it, and were setting solid metal hooks into the top of it that would allow the ropes to hold on to it firmly without fraying or wearing. Two sailors were rigging the block and tackle. Aaran figured they could fit ten children at a time into the lift. He had one sailor climb in, and directed the rest to get him to the top as quickly as they could.

Aaran timed the trip, and figured he could move fifty small children down by that route in the same time that the older children and adults came down by the single down path. He wanted to keep the up path clear as long as he could, in case he had to send more men up to fight. Neither path was wide enough to permit two people going in opposite directions any hope of passing each other. He didn't want to have his men be forced to choose between pitching children off the cliff and watching their friends and comrades die in enemy hands above. Using both paths for downward travel would halve the time it took to clear the captives. But he decided foresight suggested less hurry would offer a better chance of long-term survival. When all were up who were going up, he'd direct his men to start having everyone use both paths for evacuating the landing.

He heard a metallic creaking, and a shadow in flapping black robes stepped out onto the shelf. So the door was open.

He directed his armed team up first. "Hurry," he said. "Get behind them, stay behind them, keep them alive."

The men took off up the path. They did not make a swift trip of it, but no one fell to his death on the journey. The team that would sort and direct the captives followed next. The third team manned the ropes.

When the heavy door opened, orderly lines of children of all sizes, and of women in flowing robes, moved out onto the landing. They seemed calm. He could hear screaming coming from high above. He could smell smoke. But he saw no signs of panic.

Aaran's men and several women lifted children into the crate, and his throat tightened. He prayed quickly that the rebar was secure, that the ropes were true, that the pulleys were sound, and that the crate would hold together.

And then the first of the littlest ones started down toward him.

Meanwhile, a single shadowy captive was working down the inner path, inserting torches into sockets along the cliff face and lighting them. The flickering shadows gave him his first glimpse of the creature, and that first glimpse gave him pause. She had the form of a woman, even if that form was mostly hidden by billowing black cloth. But something was hellishly wrong with her face. With her eyes, which seemed completely black until she turned her head, at which times they seemed to light up and turn as bloody red as the setting sun had been. He did not think it a good omen. He wondered if he and his men had been lured to their doom by monsters.

But the children landed on the ship's deck, and they were just children.

Little shaven-headed children, none of whom he guessed would be any older than six. Their left palms bore Tonk clan marks. They chattered to each other in a language that was not Tonk.

The crate had held a dozen of them, and Aaran's deckhands hurried them into the passenger quarters, where Tuua and Eban would offer them comfort and reassurance and food. Food, Aaran guessed, being the one thing that would give them the most reassurance that they were going to be all right.

The black-eyed creature finished lighting her torches, walked over to Aaran as if she could tell without difficulty which of the men on the dark deck was in charge, and bowed.

In formal, archaic, oddly accented Tonk, she said, "I am one of the . . . guardians."

"I'm Aaran, the captain of this ship."

She bowed again. "Thank you. I must go."

"The children are that way." He pointed her to the forward companion-way, which would take her down to the passenger quarters and the little ones. But she shook her head, leapt into the air, and threw a kick that, if it connected, would take the top of a man's head off. She laughed. "You must guard children until Rosestones come. I fight *men*." And then she ran—*ran*—up the path, inhumanly graceful, to take death to the raiders attacking the monastery.

She scared Aaran. He'd bet she was going to scare a lot of the men on the ship.

Her presence ought to cut down on the possibility of men on a ship behaving badly in the presence of young women, however. He wondered what in the hell she was.

He watched as gray-robed youths with stubble for hair began filing along the down path. They were clearly unsure of themselves, and their progress was slow.

The crate, meanwhile, delivered its second load of children. These were a bit bigger, a bit older. All still shaven-headed, all still wearing what Aaran could only think of as gray grain sacks.

The crew got them off the decks, and as they did, the first of the captives making their way down the path reached the dock, and stepped warily to the deck.

From beyond the walls that lined the top of the cliff, Aaran could hear screaming. Booming drums and howling pipes, the crash of metal, the thuds of something big hitting stone.

The captives coming down the paths kept their eyes forward, stayed at a steady pace, little gaggles of older children in a line between a lead adult and a following adult who became the lead adult for the next little cluster.

A lot of people were coming down that narrow path, faster than he would have imagined, in a more orderly fashion than he could have believed.

The crate made its way up to the top of the cliff, and captives were hurrying across the deck now, each following the path of the one before as if they were ants on an ant trail, disappearing into their hill.

They all looked the same to him. Plain, their hair either completely gone or else the merest stubble at the top. None of them had the terrifying, weird eyes of the woman who had set the torches. Aside from her, though, none of them had a clear, identifiable gender, either. They might all have been young boys, or all young girls, or some of each. They were slender but not starved, clean, frightened, and simply dressed.

On some hands, he caught flashes of Tonk marks, but not on all.

The screaming grew louder, and closer, but those coming down the steps stayed steady, responding to the adults who walked among them and issued orders in a language Aaran couldn't even begin to guess at.

Above, Aaran saw the line of children trickle to nothing, to be replaced by women in robes of a multitude of colors, instead of the uniform black and gray and brown that preceded them.

They moved more quickly, at a trot that made his throat tighten.

Behind them came his men.

No more little children waited at the top of the ledge. Instead, treasure started making its way down, fast and reckless. Men at the bottom caught the crate and poured its contents into the drop chute that would dump everything into the upper common cargo hold. They'd sort later.

The stream of people pouring out of the monastery, he realized, was larger than he'd anticipated. Every woman and every child carried a bag or pack—nothing large. But they were going to need space, and while the *Taag av Sookyn* had a generous passenger hold, he was going to be exceeding its limitations severely.

Above, the shouts of men suddenly came clearer. He realized those shouts had started coming from the tunnels. Some of them were shouts in Tonk, some in Trade, and some in a language or languages that he did not know. He heard the ringing clashes of swords.

Ah, Ethebet, here it came.

His men on the deck lowered the next crate full of treasure so fast that the ropes slipped through their hands. Treasure poured onto the deck, some of it going down the chute, much of it spraying and clattering across the wood where it would serve as obstacles for the sailors and, if they were needed, the marines. Aaran swore.

If something had to fall partway down the cliffs, better the treasure than children, though.

Then the men he'd sent into the tunnels came back out, moving fast. They and the men who had run the operation at the top of the ledge came down both paths, moving with less assurance than the strange-eyed women.

And after them, more women, these exclusively wearing black. They ran down the paths as his men cleared them, and jumped gracefully to the docks, silent and inhumanly fast. And then they vanished down into the passenger hold as if they knew which way to go.

He watched a lavishly dressed woman turn at the top, take a torch, and toss it into the tunnel. She and a black-robed woman then closed the heavy door, wedging something into three different places along its edge. Finished, they turned and raced at a full run down the paths, jumped to the deck, and ran directly to him. The woman in the elaborate garb said, "Go. Quickly. It's going to explode any moment; we need to be well clear."

Aaran shouted urgent retreat and raced to the tillers, the deck crew cast off, and the windmen gave them a hard breeze.

And the *Taag* was off.

The well-dressed woman—who for all her assurance was startlingly young—and her companion in black strode back to him. He could not see many details of her face, but she, too, had frightening eyes. She said in flawless, if accented, Tonk, "I'm Hawkspar. I'm the one who called you. Thank you for risking so much to come for us. We will move out of your way for now, to permit you to work. But when we are to a point of some safety, I must talk with you."

"And I with you," he said. He steered the ship clear of the little harbor's mouth, and as he did, heard a rumble as if the earth were blowing itself apart. He looked behind them and caught a glimpse of fire erupting from the tunnel mouth, and of debris exploding toward the ship. He cut it hard to port, hearing the splash of objects going into the water behind him. He hung on, the windmen blew, and he steered the *Taag*'s tail out of the path of danger.

Almost quickly enough. Almost.

Something big slashed through the hull well above the waterline. He felt the ship shudder, and he swore. Men below shouted.

They couldn't stop to assess the damage. A fleet lay on the other side of the island. To keep everyone alive to face the next day, he and his men needed to put as much distance as they could between the *Taag* and the war going on behind it.

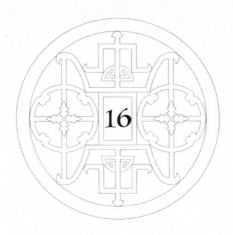

16

Hawkspar

I would have stayed to thank the captain again, but we were still in grave danger, and he and his men were working to get us out of it. We did not know our way around the ship; we could not offer assistance yet.

Still, we were out. Away from the monastery, away from Citadel and Ossalenes and bells and ritual.

We were out, and we had cleared the tunnels of the enemy on our way out. Though I could not be certain that the remaining Obsidians, most of whom stayed behind to fight, had managed to destroy Prince Sheoua and his army, they were winning when we left. Hugely. I held on to that, and prayed Ethebet would be with them. I did not want to abandon anyone to Sheoua.

But his attack would bind together those who remained. The rats would not feed on children anymore; the oracles would be less willing to offer their visions to anyone who had the wealth they desired. His death would make them stronger; it would remind them that they had once been a warrior rite, and could be again.

Too long a peace and too much wealth and adulation had made the oracles weak, save only my predecessor Hawkspar, who had kept the Obsidians strong and remembered where she came from, and where her acolyte would one day return.

We had not left them helpless.

I comforted myself with this thought as Redbird and I went down into the passenger quarters.

Below, the little girls clung to each other and wept, terrified. Their memories of shipboard time were very fresh in most cases, and they would have a hard time feeling safe aboard another ship, even when they were in rooms, and not bound by chains.

The older girls watched me. So, too, did the seru, in their own fashion.

I removed the oracle cloak with its elaborate hood. I took off my rak-tabi, and tossed my cepa to the floor, where I carefully stood on it.

"Do as I have done," I told them. "All of you. Take off badges of rank, take off such portions of your robes as you choose. You will no longer be required to dress as Ossalenes. You will no longer say the litanies or the prayers of your captors. You are free. *We* are free. Those of us who were born Tonk will find our way to being Tonk. Those of you who were not may reclaim the religion of your people, or any other that suits you. There will be no more rats in cages for us, no fires, no branding, no beatings. If you know your names, say them now. Take them back. If you don't know them, you will . . ." I faltered. "You will take new names." I clenched my hands tight in my sleeves. "Tonk names. You are free," I said, knowing that for those of us who wore the Eyes, this was not, and would never be, true. Those unmarred by Eyes were free—slaves, penitents, and acolytes. We confirmed Ossalenes could only envy life without the poison of shadows reaching out for us in our sleep and in our waking moments. But we could be happy that we had given freedom to the little ones. They would never wear Eyes.

We could hold that truth in our hearts as comfort.

I said, "As soon as we discover how we can be of service on this ship, we will take chores in partial recompense for our rescue. In the meantime, comfort each other. Talk about things you remember from home. Tell stories, tell secrets. You are not penitents or acolytes or slaves anymore. You are children, and we will do what we can to find families for all of you."

The seru had put aside one cabin in the passenger hold for my private use. I couldn't keep it just for myself, protocol be damned. The cabin had six bunks in it, each of which would hold three or four little girls at a time, or two or three big ones. It also had three overhead storage shelves, each of which was exactly the size of a bunk, each of which could be converted into bunks for our purposes. We had few belongings—those we had brought could serve as pillows for our heads. The Ossalenes and I did a quick count. We had one-hundred fifteen unconfirmed girls with us—slaves, penitents, and acolytes. Of the confirmed, we had fifty-seven Obsidian Eyes of Protection, two Granite Eyes of Maintenance, ten Moonstone Eyes of Healing, six Amber Eyes of History, five Beryl Eyes of Growing Things, and ten Rosestone Eyes of Learning. We had neither Bloodstones nor Onyxes. We

had me. We had a total, then, of two-hundred six women in a space designed to sleep forty-six. We could expand the sleeping quarters by the simple expedient of using each storage shelf as another bunk. It would be hard
wood, but Ossalenes started out sleeping on hard stone, with the thinnest of
mats between us and the floor.

It was to our benefit that we were well used to close quarters and discomfort.

I figured the spaces. We had twenty-three top shelves. Each of those
could sleep four girls. That would take care of the ninety-two smallest and
nimblest girls. We had forty-six regular berths. We could squeeze twenty-
three girls into six of those. The remaining forty berths we would divide
among the seru and me. Ninety-one women total.

We could either sleep two and three to a berth as the unconfirmed, or we
could sleep in shifts. I favored the idea of sleeping in shifts. We had done
that in the monastery to some degree. The Obsidian and Moonstone seru
always slept in shifts. The others did as need dictated.

However we decided to split up our sleeping, we would manage.

I had the seru divide the girls into groups by size, and I informed the
smallest that they could bunk with any three other girls they wanted. When
they were grouped in fours, we assigned each a berth, and told them to get
some sleep. We then formed groups of the older girls, most of whom were
penitents and the rest of whom were acolytes. We assigned each group to a
separate cabin. And then the seru and I divided ourselves into pairs and
triplets and crowded into the rest. All of us had been awake a very long time.
We agreed that whatever sleeping arrangements we might later make, for
that night we would crowd in together.

Redbird and I bunked together, back-to-back.

"I can't believe it finally happened," she said.

"I know."

"I wish it could have happened before we had to take Eyes, though," she
said.

I knew our freedom had come because we had taken Eyes—and so did
she. But I knew what she meant. I understood it completely. I wished that I
were still one of the acolytes, crowded four to a bunk directly across from us.
They whispered and giggled, and I envied them their freedom from knowing the future. I wished I had that same freedom.

We lay in silence, listening to the foreign sounds outside—water lapping
and surging, wind snapping the sails, shouts of men, the drumming of feet

on wood. We felt the ship rocking from side to side and front to back. We could hear the water, so close. Could smell it. Could feel it beneath our feet, falling away to vast depths as we moved farther from the Ossalenes.

We had power, and at some point, these men might find our power useful. They might come to appreciate us for what we could offer them.

We had our mission to pursue. We had hunters to hunt, destroyers to destroy. A lie to reveal, a truth to tell.

And all I could think of, in spite of that, was that I was on his ship, that my rescuer had come for me at last. That if I wanted to, I could get out of my bunk, I could walk up on the deck and find him. I could touch him.

Well, if I didn't mind climbing over Redbird to do it.

Aaran

They ran hard for three full bells, traveling east as straight as they could, weaving back and forth between uncountable islands. He wanted to get out of the islands soon, and drop down into the empty center of the Dragon Sea. Once the *Taag* pushed south of the equator, the ship would be able to risk the trade lanes. The Sinali would have no doubt claimed the whole of the Kervish Ocean as part of their empire if they could have, but south of the equator and west of the Fallen Suns, navies other than their own prowled the waters and prevented the bastards from overreaching.

They got well clear of any ships that might have been pursuing from their adventure at the monastery. Then Aaran pointed them south and handed over control to Ves and the rudders to Baaksa.

He slept, a dreamless sleep, desperately needed, and woke to music.

One of his runners was gone, he noted. And Neeran stood with his ear pressed to the door, a wistful expression on his face.

Aaran sat up. "You look miserable."

"They're dancing," Neeran said. "Celebrating the rescue."

"Ves found us a safe harbor, then."

The boy nodded. "Safe anchor, in any case. We've found a good deep channel between islands, well enough away that we can see anything coming. And we've a clear day. And the cooks have been cooking since before daybreak, and down in the attable, we've some of the finest food ever, Potyr says."

"And you haven't had any."

"No, Cap'n."

"Go on. And you can stay when you're done. I could do with some song and dance myself."

When he went out on deck, two of the Eastils had set up with narrow sailor's fiddles, three-stringed instruments designed to take up little space under a hammock but still make a fair amount of noise. The two playing—he recognized one as Ratter, but still didn't remember the name of the other—were fair hands with strings and bow. Two young girls, their hair cropped so short Aaran could see their scalps, danced, though watching them, Aaran could see the moves of warriors in the steps they took. They spun and stomped and kicked high and low; one would vault over the other, then the second would vault over the first. They were silent as they danced, and the expressions on their faces were of intense concentration.

Aaran, fascinated, leaned against a rail and watched them.

"When they get older, they learn to do that with sharpened swords," a voice said beside him. Aaran turned, and found himself face-to-face with one of the young women they'd rescued the day before. She was dressed in silks and richly embroidered cottons—extravagant fabrics. Her clothes were golds and browns and ambers, and he realized that they matched her eyes. Her stone eyes. Her hair was short and black, slightly wavy, very glossy. He tried to concentrate on that, and on the slender line of her neck, and the sweet curves of her jaw, and the softness of her lips.

He wanted to keep his mind on all those things, but his gaze kept straying back to those eyes.

She said, "Out of the Order's robes, I no doubt look very different. I'm Hawkspar."

"I'm . . . ah . . . Captain Aaran av Savissha."

"I know. One of your men pointed me to you. I came to thank you for coming for us."

"Well," he said, made awkward by not knowing how to look at her. "Well, you don't owe us thanks. This is what we do. We're Tonk. We find our own."

"Still, you risked great danger to come to us. And will risk more danger getting us away from . . ." She paused. ". . . From all of this," she said at last, waving an arm in a gesture that seemed to encompass the whole world. "Thank you for listening when I called," she added, and her voice went soft.

He stared at her. "You're the girl who called to me?"

"Yes."

He was quiet for a long, uncomfortable moment. He didn't know what to say.

"I'm not what you expected?" she said. Her lips curved in a smile of wry amusement.

"Not . . . precisely."

"I'm not what I expected, either, if it makes you feel any better. Nor am I the same as I was when you first answered my plea for rescue. I had my own eyes then. Not . . . these."

"What happened? I got to you as quickly as I could. I knew you were afraid, but I had no idea they were going to . . . torture you. Or blind you."

She turned her face to the fiddlers, and to the dancing girls, whom he realized were not a great deal younger than she was. A few years, perhaps. She said, "I wanted nothing more than to find my way to freedom, and to take with me all who dared to escape, before we were forced to choose the Order, and with it, the Eyes. But you were not too late. It was because you answered my call, because rescue was finally on the way, that the Eyes came to me. And that I accepted them."

His stomach growled loudly. He winced. "Have you eaten?" he asked her.

"Not this morning," she said. "I woke to the sound of music, and came straightway to speak to you. Thanks should not take second place to comfort."

"Then would you be my guest for morning meal? While we eat, you can tell me what happened. I'm desperately curious, but desperately hungry as well."

She laughed. "As am I."

He found himself wanting to ask her all manner of rude questions about those stone eyes, and how she seemed not to be blinded by wearing them. But he held his silence and led her down into the belly of the ship, to the attable, the large open room that took up half of the maagen deck, where at long, narrow, built-in tables and fixed benches, the men ate while the cooks toiled in the galley to the fore.

Aaran headed for the galley window, where the cooks sent out the trays and bowls. He told Hawkspar, "Let the cook give you his choice. We have masters of pot and kettle with us—you won't be disappointed."

One of those masters, the head cook, heard him speaking and came to the window. "I would have sent yours up through the dropwaiter," Barwyd said, looking reproachful. "We take care of our captain here."

Aaran said, "I am so well taken care of, you'll make me fat before long." He watched as the cook filled his tray personally. "Barwyd, man, you're not to try to make me fat in this one meal."

And the cook grinned. "We're celebrating today, Cap'n. Eat wide and deep. We have good treasure, captives rescued, dangers evaded, and home our next port. You've earned the day, and a full belly with it."

Aaran laughed. "Well, thanks. Those are things worth celebrating, though home remains a long way off."

The cook shrugged, handed him his tray, and began to fill one for Hawkspar. "Then celebrate the day, for we never know which will be our last."

Hawkspar took her tray from the cook, and said, "My thanks, master chef." She bowed slightly.

Barwyd grinned. "I'm honored."

They took seats, squeezing in between sailors and marines and little girls and women with stone eyes, and Aaran dug into some of the best food Barwyd had ever put together. He'd done magic with dried fish and dried pork and dried vegetables and Ethebet alone might guess which spices and other sundries.

For a short while, Aaran satisfied himself with his food, for Hawkspar seemed intent on her own. At last, though, she sat back and put her knife down, and he said, "You were going to tell me about . . . what happened to you."

"Only a bit of it," she said. "Most will wait for a time when we can speak in private. Here, I'll say that I was not the first slave taken into the Ossalene Citadel who plotted escape, nor was I the first to plan to take others with me. The Oracle Hawkspar who preceded me was another such—though she did her scheming after she inherited the Hawkspar Eyes."

Aaran wanted to ask her about those, but he held his tongue, hoping she'd go into detail.

"When it became clear to her that the war she planned to end lay far in her future, she began watching for other Tonk girls who showed promise. I was one of her choices—I was defiant, yet cautious; I won the allegiance of others of my station; I had a plan and I put it into action without getting caught." Hawkspar sighed. "Though part of my not getting caught was, I think, because Hawkspar intervened with magic, and hid my worst actions from those who had reason and duty to stop me."

"Friends in high places are a good thing," Aaran agreed. "Though only if they stay friends." He couldn't help but think of Haakvar, his mentor, his friend, his champion—who had become his enemy over this very girl.

"There is that," Hawkspar said. "In any case, Hawkspar presented to me a story that I could not ignore, and offered me her protection to get me and those Tonk who would come with me out of the Citadel. But to accept her protection, I had also to accept the pain and the responsibility of the Hawkspar Eyes."

And that seemed to Aaran a good enough opening. "You both shared the same name as the stone eyes you wear?"

"In my predecessor's case, that would be 'wore.' There's only one pair of Hawkspar Eyes—when she died, they came to me."

He was quiet for a long time. Then he said, "Oh." He wished he had not asked. She wore the eyes of a dead woman. That was at least as awful as being captain of a drowner ship.

"The Eyes let me see possible futures and how to reach them," she said. "At some point, I'll tell you the futures I see for the Tonk. It is because of these futures that I accepted the Eyes; I did not want them, or the burden that goes with them. But I am Tonk, and there are things I must do."

Aaran was intrigued. People talked about seeing into the future, but as far as he knew, no one had actually done it—at least not with any accuracy. Hawkspar talked about futures, though, instead of a single future, so perhaps she had no real power, either.

It didn't matter, he decided at last. He'd listen to her tale, and take her back to the Tonk lands, and then he would say good-bye, because that was what he always did. Unless, of course, his sister was already on the *Taag,* and safe and well, still disguised as one of the Ossalene women aboard. After the celebration, he would ask Hawkspar if she knew anyone who bore his sister's name.

Later, though. There was time, and he wanted his guests to enjoy the celebration of their freedom.

He watched Potyr teaching one of the shaven-headed girls a Tonk dance out in the crew commons. He went through the steps slowly once, and she danced the steps back at him, flawlessly. A little flustered, he nodded to the piper who played for them to pick up the pace, and he danced at speed. And the girl danced right along with him.

And then she mimicked his gesture to the piper to pick up the pace yet again, and she danced alone at a speed that left Aaran stunned.

Behind her, other girls her age stood, and as the piper brought the tune around again, they followed the steps at that blazing speed as if they'd been doing that dance their whole lives.

"How have they done that?" he asked.

Hawkspar had been watching with him. "Learn simple dance steps?" she asked. "They're trained from their earliest days in the monastery how to memorize dances. It's part of the training that determines who will become an Ossalene, and who will remain a slave. They learn quickly because those who learn slowly have already been weeded out—have been sent back down to the slave market, or sold outright to buyers who have approached the monastery for girls acceptable for work. The sorts of work they might be acceptable for, the monastery never questioned too closely." She sighed. "We all heard stories. We feared that they might be true. I've learned since becoming an oracle that we didn't even hear the worst of the truth. There's very little in life that is more dangerous than being unneeded."

"So." Aaran felt the darkness of her world seeping into his. He didn't want it. Not right then. He had no doubt that before he dropped her off in Beyltaak, or whichever harbor the clans were sending captives to by the time he got them home, he would have heard all about the grim lives of the Ossalenes. But this was a day of celebration. He said, "I take it, then, that you dance?"

She turned her face toward him. He felt certain she could see him, though he could not guess what she might see. She grinned, though, and said, "I can dance *you* through the floor."

"Can you?"

"Faster than you can breathe."

"Would you care to wager something on that?"

"What could I have to wager," she asked, still smiling, "that you might fancy?"

"For my part, that you take dinner with me in my quarters, and tell me the whole of your story when the two of us have the privacy that will let you do it justice."

"And if I win?"

"I'm not sure what I have that you might fancy."

Her grin spread wider, in the sort of way that made a man wonder at the security of his coin purse, his back, and his testicles. "I do. Though if I win, I'll tell you privately."

He felt something itching down his neck. A little twitch there that suggested he might be making a mistake.

But those who had been eavesdropping on the two of them stopped making any pretense of it when the word *wager* was mentioned. And in the few instants in which they set the terms of their bargain, the whole of the crew common was listening, with every man, woman and child fallen silent.

"I will not wager my ship," he said.

"Nor would I ask you to. No, my prize will be small and personal, as yours was."

Mouth dry, palms sweaty, he raised his left hand to swear out the wage.

She raised her left hand as well, and he saw the mark on it—the impossible mark of a clan long lost, but never forgotten—and for a moment he could not think of a single word to say.

And then, behind him, Ves shouted, "Up on deck, to judge the captain's wager." He clapped Aaran on the shoulder, laughed, and led a small stampede that took more folks than Aaran would have dreamed up on the deck to watch his silly wager with the woman he didn't know, but thought he might want to know.

He shed down to boots and breeches. She handed off a whole string of outer garments to that black-clad obsidian-eyed woman who followed her everywhere, ending up at last in a white tunic that fell to her hips, and that was of a material so thin he could see her breastbinder beneath it, and ankle-tied baggy pants. She stood, her feet bare, her uncovered arms hanging loosely at her sides. Watching her taking her things off had been an education in weaponry. She'd had blades hidden under the sleeves of her robe, fastened to each forearm; a long dagger fastened in a neat sheath between her shoulder blades; the two swords; two boot daggers; and a sort of whip-cord-and-ball arrangement that had fallen out of a hidden pocket somewhere in all those folds of shed cloth, which her assistant, or retainer, or whatever title the black-eyed one bore, scooped up and slipped quickly into one of her own pockets.

He thought it probably wouldn't be the best of ideas to attack an Ossalene.

And then the fiddlers finished rosining up their bows, and Ves, laughing, declared in ringing tones, "Cap'n and the lady before you have set terms of a dance contest. First to dance the other through the floor—and we'll be the judge of when *that* happens, won't we?" This statement was met with such laughter and applause by the sailors and marines that Ves had to stop, and wait, and hold up a hand at last to silence them. "As I said, first to dance the other through the floor will win. Cap'n chose as his prize a dinner in his cabin with the lady."

Applause, hoots and cheers, ribald remarks.

"The *lady*, on Ethebet's hand, has chosen to declare her prize after she has won. In private."

Whistles, more cheers, and no end of interested looks.

Aaran felt his cheeks heat up, and knew his face had to have gone red as heartberries. He tried to grin around at the audience, and then looked at Hawkspar standing before him. She was young, elegantly made, finely curved, smooth-skinned and high-breasted. She had her head tipped to one side, and on her face, he could see the faintest ghost of a smile.

"You want to be winning then, Cap'n," one of the marines said. "They'll have their prize in some mighty frightening ways, women will."

"Shall you lead first, or shall I?" he asked her.

"You go first," she said. "I would not have their fun over for them too fast."

"You're so confident, then," he said.

And she lifted her chin, and that smile of hers spread wider.

"'Marrying Maadryn,'" he called to the fiddlers. And they began to play. The men clapped in time with the music.

The tune he'd chosen started fast, and got faster. He'd thought to be easy on Hawkspar, until he saw that grin on her face. And then he thought, well, perhaps he'd show her a thing or two right away.

He spun and stamped, jumped into the air and clapped, jumped into the air and kicked his legs out to each side, dropped to the ground in a crouch, then kicked high into the air. He watched her, and she was following along behind him, only one measure behind every move he made, as fast and graceful as if this were a dance she'd done all her life. Well, maybe it was. Not the way he and his clansmen did it, though. He got to the fastest part of it, and then added in the bit that he was sure would throw her. He flipped backward, spun with his heels tucked tight, over his head, and kept spinning, unfolding neatly to land on his feet. Exactly one measure later, she executed the same move flawlessly. And he, who had been in one of the simple, circling moves of the dance, realized that he'd just shot the biggest arrow in his quiver, and she'd caught it in one hand and snapped it in half.

He wasn't sure what she was going to throw at him, but he had an uncomfortable suspicion that he wasn't going to make as good a showing as she had.

When the fiddlers stopped, the people on deck applauded and cheered, but Hawkspar just stood there, her face turned toward him, her forehead furrowed in thought. The applause, the laughter, and the banter died down to silence as his men grew curious about what she was doing.

She turned abruptly, and pointed to one of Aaran's marines. "You," she said, "come stand in front of him." She then pointed to the black-clad shadow who followed her everywhere. "Redbird," she said, and Aaran thought, how did that creature ever get a name as cheerful as Redbird? "Take your place in front of me." And she turned to him. "You cannot watch my steps a moment ahead in time," she said. "So to give you an opportunity to win, I will do one step of the dance, and you will watch me. You will then do the step. I and mine will watch you. You do not have to exceed what I do to win. If you get through the routine once without striking your man so hard that he goes down, I will consider that you have won. For the first time I did this dance, my partner toppled on the second move, and I was disqualified."

"Is it actually a dance?" Aaran asked.

"It is. I will do it for you at full speed, and with music, so that you can see how it goes."

He nodded.

She stood, her slender body backlit by the morning sun, and took one slow, deep breath. Then she said something in that language most of her people spoke, and the stone-eyed women on the deck, and the tall girls, and the shaven-headed children, began to clap, quickly, and in a complicated rhythm. The older ones began to sing.

And Hawkspar began to dance. She lifted up on one bare foot so that she balanced on her toes—he could not imagine the pain of that, but realized he was going to get the chance to discover it firsthand. She kicked with the other foot, high over the head of the much taller Redbird, and spun as she kicked, and leapt as she spun, so that for a moment she was airborne, twisting through nothing, her arms wrapped tightly around her, one to her chest and one at her back, the other leg then soaring over Redbird's head, and then she landed lightly, and from that move, which he already knew he would fail at, she came down on both feet with her back to Redbird. Her back arched, she flipped over backward onto her hands toward the unflinching Obsidian, and then from her hands, twisted so she would be facing Redbird, and flipped to her feet, which came so close to the other woman's face before they landed on the deck that Aaran found his heart in his throat. She immediately leapt straight up, her hands landing on Redbird's shoulders. She vaulted over the other woman, rolled to standing on the other side, spun-kicked the back of Redbird's head, missing striking her by what could have only been the breadth of a single hair. The clapping got faster, the singing sharper and more urgent. Hawkspar vaulted front to back over Redbird again, this time landing on her feet and spinning, her right leg out, the heel of her right food going so close to the tip of Redbird's nose that Aaran could not see light between. Around she went, spinning faster and faster, her heel never striking, never showing air either. And then her hands were on the ground, her feet kicking up into the air, striking at the rock-still woman before her, pulling back. She did some dancelike moves with her hands, which Aaran thought pretty until he realized that they were meant to be done with swords in hand. He swallowed hard, realizing with a sword of any length at all, those blades would have been whipping as close to flesh as her feet had been instants before.

And then, abruptly, she stopped. She called a quick command to the singers and clappers, and the abrupt silence held the audience in thrall for a long, stunned moment, before his men broke the hush with wild cheers and thundering applause.

She smiled only a little at the recognition. When the noise died down, she told him, "It's a better dance when two dance it, and when both are armed with their two swords. And it can be danced much better than I do it. Any of the Obsidians can dance me to ground."

Aaran exchanged worried looks with the marine Hawkspar had planted in front of him. "I can't," he said, turning to her. "So that I don't kill one of my men uselessly proving that fact, I concede defeat. I would have either broken myself or him on the first move." He smiled a little, both awed by her athleticism and entranced by the erotic pictures the physical prowess she'd demonstrated painted in his imagination. He bowed to her. "There is no shame in acknowledging the art of one's betters."

She laughed. "I like to win," she said. "I could have picked an easier dance."

"Why should you have? I picked the most difficult one I knew. I like to win, too."

"A favor I will ask of you in the future, and that favor you must grant me. I promise you it will be neither bigger nor more risky than my having dinner with you in your quarters would be."

"As dangerous as that?" he asked her, and smiled. "I don't know that I should honor the bet, then."

Some of his men laughed.

Hawkspar smiled. "To seal our bargain, I agree to have dinner with you in your cabin anyway. That way, when I ask my small favor of you, you will recall that I was a generous winner."

"Very well, then," he said. "I'll accept your terms."

There was more laughter, some ribald remarks aimed at him, and his own men telling her to be sure to take her swords with her when she went to dinner with him, that she would surely need them.

She laughed, and he casually steered the two of them up to the captain's lookout at the bow of the ship, where they could be alone.

Hawkspar

We stood at the front of his ship, on the high deck just behind and beneath the enormous carved wooden horse head. Below us, the celebration continued, with sailors asking Obsidians to teach them to dance, and a great deal of hilarity at the disastrous efforts and failures that resulted.

"I must ask you something," the captain—Aaran—said. "I know that not all of the women we rescued were born Tonk, but I believe most were."

"Yes," I said. "Most of those who have come on this mission are Tonk."

"Mission?" he said, and then cleared his throat. "Never mind that. For now, I must tell you that I'm looking for someone. I've been looking for her for a very long time. My sister—she was taken by slavers when she was young, and I've been trying to find her ever since. I have hope that she might be among the women I rescued. Her name is Aashka. She would have been about your age," he told me. "Perhaps younger."

I called Redbird to me. She had been waiting nearby; the Obsidians would not leave me unguarded, and Redbird, my friend for so long, was one of my personal guard by both my choice and her insistence. On duty, she was always near.

"Oracle?" she said, approaching.

"He has a sister named Aashka, who was enslaved. He hoped we might have heard of her, or that she might be among our number. She would be about our age. Have the Obsidians check each of ours who is of the right age. See if she is among us, or if her name is known."

Redbird hurried off to gather the Obsidians, and I turned to him. "I dare not offer much hope. She might *be* among ours," I told him. "She might be among the women who stayed behind. *I* might be her. We would not know her by her name, though. We have never been permitted to use any names but those the Ossalenes gave us. Many of us no longer remember the names we bore as children."

"You don't."

"No. I have no idea what my mother and father called me, or what my brothers and sisters called me. I cannot remember much at all of that time, or that life." I turned my face away from him and said, "But in any case, I would hope for her sake that she was never found by the Ossalenes. We were not, as a rule, well treated. I would hope her fate was better."

Aaran said, "Thank you for asking."

Below us, Redbird and two other Obsidians took up their posts again. I saw other Obsidians hurrying up to them, then walking away.

And finally Redbird broke away from the other two and approached me. "None knows her name, or remembers if the name Aashka might be her name. At the captain's convenience, those who are of about the right age who do not remember their names will gather, that the captain might see if he recognizes them."

"You would do this now?" I asked the captain.

He was quiet for a very long time. "Today is for celebrating," he said at last. "My men have had nothing but hardship this voyage. Your people, too, deserve a day to rejoice. And I . . . I could use happiness, too. While I can hope that she is among us, I can still view this day with wonder and joy. If I know for certain that she is not, then for a while hope falters again."

"Hardships and pain are easy to find," I agreed. "I would not despise a day of happiness."

My motives were not pure when I said this. I wanted to touch Aaran. It was a foolish thing, but for me he was layers and gaps and lines of bone and shadows of muscle, and in places he blended with the ship, and with the water beneath, and with the enormous sea creatures that coiled and glided beneath even the surface of that. I wanted to feel *him,* to feel the solidness that the Eyes would not let me see. I wanted to draw some picture in my mind of him, something that did not include the roots of his teeth locked into his jaws and the shapes of the sockets that held eyes that were, to me, almost not there at all. He had a face, but I could not see it. So I wanted to feel it.

He had come for me. I had called to someone, anyone, and at last, after so long, this one, this fine strong man, had heard my plea and had come.

I reached out a hand and let it rest on his arm. He was warm, and beneath my fingers his skin was covered with a soft furring of hair. His skin was smooth, the muscles hard beneath the smoothness. Intriguing.

I longed to touch the rest of him. I wanted to explore him, to discover how a man might be different than a woman. I wanted to slake my endless, boundless curiosity on him. He was a mystery, and I yearned to uncover him. If my mind did not know what to do, my body seemed to have already come to an understanding of the possibilities between us. I moved closer too him, close enough to feel the heat that radiated from his skin.

"I've thought of you often," he said, his voice gruff in my ear. "You haunted my dreams. My waking moments."

"I waited for you for so long. I had begun to think you would never find me. Never find us."

"The instant I heard your call, I knew that I would be the one to answer it, no matter what price it would take for that to happen."

His fingers interlaced themselves with mine. Our palms touched, and I felt as if I might stop breathing right there. As he touched me, the whole of the world changed its complexion. I knew darkness lay in my future. I had seen as much. Darkness lay in everyone's future; that ceased to matter when he held my hand.

He raised his other hand, and ran a finger down my cheek, along the line of my jaw, over my lips.

"You are not as I had thought you might be. And yet, I find that you are beautiful nonetheless," he said.

I told him, "You don't have to lie. I know the Eyes are ugly. It was to avoid ever wearing them that I called out so long for rescue. But in the end, I made myself a volunteer. It was part of my mission."

He brought his face closer to mine, and stepped nearer me. "Don't talk of missions just now," he said. "I am weary of missions."

I could feel the heat of his skin through his clothing, touching me.

In that moment, filled with heat and hunger, I desperately wanted . . . something. Though I could not put a name to it, I ached for it.

The men on the ship fell suddenly quiet, and I heard footsteps running toward us before I caught the form of the man who raced in our direction.

"We have . . . something . . . coming at us, Cap'n. We need you."

Aaran swore. "I'm so sorry," he whispered, and stepped away from me.

I followed without being invited.

"Out there," the sailor said. I could make out the bones of the man's arm, lifting, the bones in his hands curling. One finger outstretched.

And the captain turned in the direction that the finger pointed. I did, too.

Aaran

Aaran peered across the sea. The islands were disappearing. Quickly. Everything was fading into a gray blur.

"A storm?" he asked. "It doesn't look like a storm. The sky is still clear."

And next to him, Hawkspar said, "A line of dead men comes toward us. And a ship that floats upon the sea of their bones."

He turned to stare at her. "You can see what's out there?"

"Some things. Things that are watery blend with the water to me—I cannot see them. But things dense as bone, I see quite well. I can see what comes. And as well, what is already here."

"Here?"

"I saw the first two when we stood upon your tall deck beneath the horse's head. Great sea beasts that circled beneath this ship. But I did not give them any importance. They did not seem interested in us. Now, though, others are gathering with them beneath this ship, curling tentacles up toward us. They are, I think, bound to the one who pursues us across his sea of death."

One of his men screamed, "Behind us! Beside us!"

Aaran looked, and saw that in every direction, the grayness encroached, swallowing islands, swallowing the horizon.

Aaran turned in all directions, realizing that he had been careless and overconfident, and that because of it, he had allowed his ship and everyone on it to become trapped.

He'd eaten. He'd danced. He'd stood in sunlight on his own ship, captivated by the line of a woman's throat, by the delicate curve of her ear, by the soft fullness of her breasts. He'd been fascinated by the sweet curves of her lips, and curious about the golden brown glints in her eyes, which did not bother him so much when he let himself just accept them.

He'd been resentful of the sailor who'd called him away from her.

But the resentment and his desire ebbed together. He stared out at the sea, and down into the black glass of the water that gave him back nothing but the reflection of his own ship, and his skin started to crawl. Monsters. Tentacled monsters? The great squid had been known to rip ships apart.

And he could not even say that the danger he faced was that known one. They still navigated the waters surrounding the Dragon Sea. The depths could hold some new and more horrible nightmares.

The *Taag* had picked up a light breeze and Aaran was giving the windmen a well-deserved rest. He turned to Ves and said, "Get the windmen going. Quickly."

And then he turned back to her. "What, exactly, do you see?"

"At this very moment, fish with toothy maws big enough to swallow a man in one bite pace this ship, running deep. I count half a dozen of them, and with them, three curling balls of tentacles that, when they uncoil, are longer than this ship." She closed her eyes and bowed her head, still for a long moment. He waited. Abruptly, she started speaking, but her voice had taken on a distant quality. "They could attack now, but they await the coming of the master whose pets they are. The master wishes to claim the bounty this ship carries before you and it are destroyed. He is coming." She stood very still, her head still bowed.

Aaran had gone so far to save Hawkspar, and all those with her. And in her he had found something he wanted to explore.

And now there were monsters.

He told Potyr, who with a runner's instinct had attached himself to Aaran's side the instant trouble started, "Get Ermyk. Tell him I need him and his men. We're about to be under attack."

Hawkspar spoke again. "The warlock—this vile oathbreaker who deals in the dead—comes by fog. He knows your name. He knows your ship. He travels surrounded by the screams of his victims, and he sought to meet you once before."

The fog curled closer on all sides. The day had become silent as oblivion, all wind dead, all life aboard and away from the ship hushed with fear, hoping to escape detection. Hawkspar's description twisted the final knot in Aaran's gut.

"Oh," he said. *"Him."*

She smiled a little, the corners of her lips curling like the tips of a drawn bow. "He let you get away then, because he discovered that you carried no treasure that he might wish to take. Now . . . now your ship carries his favorite treats."

"Gold? Jewels?"

"Women. Girls. And especially . . . objects of power. Once—perhaps a hundred years ago—this wizard sought to meet with the Ossalenes, hoping to enter the Citadel in the guise of a friend, so that he might kill the oracles and steal the Order's Eyes. The Hawkspar of that day saw his intended duplicity, and the Citadel gates did not open for him. He was sent away with arrows, catapults, and fire. Now he senses that we are with you, and he hungers for what you have obtained that he, with all his magic, could not."

"Great. A jealous wizard. I wish we had Senders and Shielders with us."

Hawkspar straightened and turned her face toward him. "I have warriors I can offer to you. Our Obsidians fought with your men yesterday, and killed as many of the enemy as your people did."

He hadn't been up there with the fighting. He'd been down where he had to be, in his ship, ready to give the orders that would set the *Taag* on her way should the rescue attempt turn into a disaster.

But Aaran had seen Hawkspar dance. And she claimed herself less than the least of the Obsidians.

And the men had talked—of black shadows that had dropped on the Citadel's attackers, of silent death that had ripped enemy heads from their shoulders and moved on before rescuers who had been about to die could even identify what it was that had saved them.

The Obsidians.

Three of the stone-eyed women stepped forward. They had been standing in the shadows, Aaran realized, but for some reason he hadn't noticed them until they were ready to be noticed.

They made his skin crawl. Unlike Hawkspar, they had no feel of softness about them, no gentleness hinted in movement or gesture. They were like arrows drawn, swords unsheathed, catapults winched. Hawkspar said, "Redbird, stay with me." To the other two she said something in a language Aaran couldn't catch, and both women flowed away inhumanly fast; their movements were almost impossible to watch. They reappeared moments later, followed by a stream of black-clad women. Aaran judged their numbers the way he would have an enemy force, and guessed about fifty of them stood before him.

They wore twin swords at their hips and the braids that hung down their backs had been capped with metal balls. Their black eyes gleamed, bottomless in the reflected light.

"These women are at your disposal," Hawkspar said.

Aaran wasn't about to be picky. "I'll put them below as final forces if my men fall."

Hawkspar said, "Use them in the first lines, as you use your own men. They are especially trained to fight against magic. They can accomplish feats your men cannot duplicate, or even imagine. The warlock dares attack you only because he does not yet suspect what they can do. Their Eyes give them power he will regret."

Aaran had sixty-three marines, and he'd planned to fight them in a first and a second wave. With the addition of Hawkspar's Obsidians, he could decrease the number of marines in each wave and increase the number of waves, and keep fresh fighting forces at the front. He figured quickly, and came to the conclusion that he could have three waves of almost forty fighters each. Forty of his own fighters on the deck would take all the space there was. He had qualms about fighting with women, but the black-eyed creatures had comported themselves well in the fight in the Citadel tunnels.

His runner skidded to a stop in front of him. "The windmen are at their places, and I await your orders."

"Wait in the cabin, Potyr. Tell Neevan he has orders to stay in there as well."

"Yes, Cap'n." Aaran did not miss the disappointment in the boy's face as he turned away and slunk across the deck like a chastened dog.

He turned to Hawkspar. "Send some of your fighters below as a defense for the children—"

She interrupted him. "Fifteen Obsidians guard that small space, and the passage leading to it. My people are well guarded. Those who stand before you now are entirely at your disposal."

"Then have your people split into three groups. Each of the groups will join a group of my men, and they will fight together. We will have one wave on deck and two in reserve at all times," he told her.

She bowed slightly, and he caught the hint of a smile at the corners of her mouth. "As you command," she said, and turned to her fighters. She gave them quick, sharp orders in that other language, and they flowed away like liquid, into three groups.

He asked her, "Can you still see through this fog?"

"To me, it is the same as it was."

"In which direction, then, will we face the least resistance?"

"Aside from straight up?" she asked. But she pointed. "That way."

He did not know if she pointed east or west, north or south. He knew only that she pointed toward their possible escape.

The sea lay black beneath him, made blacker by the fog-blanketed world through which no sun could penetrate. He could track a channel, and steer the ship through it, so he ran to the steersman's castle and displaced Baaksa, who once again had the tillers.

The sails snapped full as the windmen began to call up as much of a gale as they could manage. In the riggings above, men unfurled tragadyl sails and snap sails to catch the extra wind. Aaran drove the ship through deep water keeping it from the reefs and sandbars that laced the treacherous nest of islands in which they'd taken their rest.

The *Taag* plunged forward.

Not quickly enough. As the wind whistled through the rigging, something in the air changed. Aaran could smell cold and sour rot. Fog, suddenly glowing, curled around him.

He did not fear natural fog. But a fog of light was another matter.

Screaming. Close and sudden, and in all directions. Sound battered the *Taag*, forward and back and sides all at once.

The fog grew brighter, and in the midst of it, Aaran saw the twisting shapes of reaching men, flesh falling from their bones, eyes clouded or eaten away, some mere collections of rag-draped bones. They all screamed, though, and he was grateful that he did know the words they cried out in their anguish.

Massive tentacles whipped up, over the sides of the ship, grasping and feeling. Aaran shouted, "First wave forward!"

A tentacle slipped out of nowhere and wrapped itself around his waist; its strength crushed the breath from him. Aaran slashed once with his sword, raised it to slash again, and then Hawkspar leapt into his path, blades flashing in the evil glow of the fog. She moved faster than his eyes could follow, and when she stepped away, the tentacle was cut from the monster's body. It went limp around him and fell to the ground, and he sucked in air, his ribs aching.

"Worse comes! Get away from the edge!" she shouted.

He stepped back, his sword ready, and saw, coming up behind him, a man in a boat spun of light. The man stood in the center of his little coracle, with the hands of dead men dragging his ship forward at terrifying speed. This had to be the mighty wizard, but he looked nothing like Aaran would have expected. He wore simple clothes—plain pants, a rough shirt such as any Tonk farmer would wear while chasing his herds, coarse boots. The wizard held nothing in his hands. They were spread wide, palms up, fingers splayed; he would have looked welcoming had he not traveled in such dire company.

He grinned at Aaran.

Aaran heard the battle continuing behind him. Heard his own men shouting, heard the clang of swords, heard the Obsidians speaking in their incomprehensible tongue, and he knew that he should turn. Help them fight.

But he could not look away.

The man and his illuminated coracle rose free of the water, and sailed a sea of dead men's arms, passed hand-over-hand toward Aaran.

"Bada da hedu," the man said. *"Sheki da hedu gosha shpa emi. Shemik emiab glespakat, gees hedu od geesak ema sphevimamo ema pikpu emi didogado hofu."*

And in Aaran's ear, the voice of Hawkspar said, "'You have come. You have brought to me that which I have most desired. Give over to me the treasure you carry, and your ship alone of all the ships that have trespassed my territory I will permit escape.' This he says. And I and mine are what he most desires. If you pass me to him now, and all the Ossalenes aboard your ship, he will do as he says he will do, and you will be permitted to take the children, and the hold full of other treasures, and flee to safety."

Aaran had not come so far and worked so hard to give the women he'd fought to save—Tonk women, most of them—to some monster. He had not followed Hawkspar's desperate plea to hand her to the horror he faced.

Aaran might not have got what he wanted, exactly, but he wanted what he'd got.

"Why don't you step off your little boat and come talk with me. Man to man," he suggested, and heard the woman beside him translating his words for the wizard.

"'If I did as you asked, you still would pose no threat to me,'" the wizard said, translated by Hawkspar. "'But as I hold the upper hand, I think I'll keep it.'"

"Well enough," Aaran said. "If you won't come parley like a man, you don't deserve to be treated like a man. You can't have what is mine. You can't even have what isn't mine. The women stay, the treasure stays. And you go."

The tracker who'd trained him, Fergan av Radavan, had spent time making sure Aaran had a good foundation in the uses of the Hagedwar, not just tracking and basic communication, but also attack and defense. He said that in desperate times, the tracker ended up being all things to all men, and if Aaran wanted to be a good tracker, he'd keep that truth in mind.

So Aaran shielded himself against attacks by magic—not a simple task— and caught the coracle that floated just above his head, and swung himself up into it.

The wizard stared at him, then spewed angry-sounding words. The translation came quick enough—"'Those who touch my boat die.'"

"By Ethebet, I didn't know that," Aaran said. "Had I, I'm sure I would have fallen over dead."

He swung his sword, whipping it side-to-side once, then thrusting. He tore through his enemy's clothes but did not seem to cut flesh. If he had, the man was bloodless.

"Orsheka hedu te dega badi fendogo goro!" the wizard howled. But this time no translation followed.

Aaran couldn't look around to see what had happened to Hawkspar. The best he could manage was a quick prayer to Ethebet.

He had a fight on his hands; the wizard glared at him and unsheathed a sword of his own that had been tucked on his back between his shoulder blades. When the wizard lifted both arms to grab it, Aaran lunged at him with a neat forward and down stroke that should have skewered him through the gut. That it didn't—that in fact his sword point hit his enemy's gut and skidded off as if it were water beading and bouncing on a griddle— scared Aaran.

The wizard grinned at him, and Aaran had only the time to realize that his enemy had filed his teeth to sharp points before he had to fight off a powerful downward blow meant to cleave him in half. "Bastard," he snarled.

The wizard's blade snaked off his and Aaran slashed quickly across the monster's throat.

Again, he might as well have spit on his enemy for all the damage the blow did.

That two-handed blade was flashing back at him—a sidestroke this time, and he barely arched back out of its way in time. He could have been two Aarans had it connected. Both shorter.

His sword wasn't working as it should have. Aaran didn't trust gimmicks and tricks, but he was at the mercy of a man who was a better swordsman than him, and who had a better magical shield—one that protected him from physical blows. Without a trick or two, Aaran was going to die in the next handful of blows.

He knew a trick or two.

He bent the light around him. It was a coward's move, and served little against a man with magic at hand—unless the man had never seen the trick before. But from the look of the wizard's face when the light streamed around Aaran and he appeared to vanish, this wizard never had.

Well and good. Time to see what might be accomplished by a man the enemy couldn't see.

18

Hawkspar

Aaran had stepped into the wizard's coracle, and the dead hands of the wizard's many victims held them up. They were not taking Aaran away from me. But they would. I could see that the wizard planned to toss his body into the sea, to join the rest of the dead.

Time swirled around me. I stood half in its river, half out. I could hear the screaming, I could see the dying, and the dead, and the dozen different paths in which everyone was still dying, dying, dead. What I could not see, trapped against the aftermast with giant creatures of the deep feeling across the deck for me, was the path in which we did not all end up dead. In which the escaping members of the Order were *not* dragged into lifetimes of torture and horror by the disgusting, twisted man who'd brought his pets to steal us. In which the brave men who'd come to find us did not end up as corpses carrying the bastard's little boat above the waves until they rotted into pieces.

Time. I knew that I could change things, if I was only willing to pay the price.

The Hawkspar before me had told me that I could hold time, that I could, if I chose, step within the spaces between an instant.

All rivers led to Aaran's death, to the destruction of the *Taag* and everyone on it, to the annihilation of hope for not just those aboard this ship, but farther out, for the Tonk, as well.

It was for this moment, and ones like it that would come, that I had been chosen. So that I could make the necessary sacrifices. So that I could step between the seconds.

I had swords in both hands. I let my body flow with the movement of the ship, and made the rushing water stand still. And I held that moment. Fought for it. The pain defied belief—but in that moment, nothing around me moved, yet I moved.

I was cold, colder than I had ever been in my life. I fought my way through air that suddenly resisted my forward progress as if it were hands grasping at me, and I pushed to the back of the steersman's castle, over the rail to the gombaar deck, where dead men and the coracle, Aaran, and the wizard stood frozen, fighting. I fought for breath against the blinding pain, fought to breathe the thick-as-blankets air, crawled beside the wizard through a thicket of bones and rotted flesh, and pushed myself into the little boat. I fought the weight of my arms and the weight of the swords, and I swung.

Seivein dance, two swords leaping, dance done always before with the long, wrapped reed blades. Done now blind, with the black-on-black-on-black shapes of man versus man lifted by dead men before me as weights against my skin.

The blades danced, hard; the shock as they struck screamed through my arms and down my spine and added to the agony in my head. Screaming, howling, fire lanced through my skull. I danced in a world of absolute silence—there is no word for the stillness when time stops, unless it is *death*. My blades struck again. Head, neck, chest, belly, arms of the vile bastard who had come to kill Aaran, and I felt the blades hit, slice through him, but they did nothing. Nothing. He stood there, frozen as still as Aaran, and my blades passed through him, and still he stood.

I danced seivein then against the dead men beneath my feet, slashing through arms and hands, cutting bone and tendon and such meat as remained.

And nothing. Nothing. The dead resisted me, too, and the pain grew worse and worse in my eyes and my skull until I could not find the strength to hold time's flow anymore. It slipped away from me as if through my fingers, and pain enveloped me, and I fell backward, out of the coracle, onto the gombaar deck, into the midst of the rotted living dead.

Before me, things happened all at once. The wizard fell into pieces, dead, and the dead men who had lifted him fell back into the sea, still screaming, and submerged beneath the waves, silenced at last, and his boat crumbled to dust, and Aaran fell to the deck beside me, and the monsters that the wizards had forced to his will fled back into the deeps from which they had come.

Leaving the living and the dying and the dead behind. And Aaran above me, his face turned down toward mine.

"You have blood on your blades," he said.

The pain, like spikes through my skull, did not lessen when I released the time I'd held. It clung to me, a starving jackal gnawing my bones. I fought through it for words, so that I would not lie at his feet like some stupid creature.

"Blood," I managed. "Yes. I fought the wizard who came for us."

"He fell apart," Aaran said. "How did you do that?"

"Time," I whispered. "I . . . caught the piece of time where we were and held it. Not long."

"Held time." He sounded intrigued, but not afraid. I didn't think much would frighten him. Beyond what we had just been through, of course. He was watching me, or at least, the shadow of his face turned toward me. "Are you hurt?"

"The Eyes hurt me when I use them." I tried to stand, to show him that I was stronger than the Eyes, but I collapsed again. The pain sucked the strength out of my arms and legs, turned my spine to water, left me too weak to do anything.

He picked me up in his arms. Oh, his touch was all I'd yearned for, and I wanted to cling to that moment—but not at the price of trying to capture time in my hands again. He was warm, and powerfully built. My swords went clanging back to the deck because I was too weak even to hold on to them, and he stepped over them, and carried me down from the gombaar deck, down onto the main deck, down the passenger companionway into the passenger common. The little girls were hidden there, tucked behind the six doors in the long bunk rooms. I could make them out, huddled together clinging to each other and weeping.

"Tell them the monsters have gone," I told him. "They don't know."

Aaran pounded on the doors. "You're safe now. Safe. Your oracle is back again."

He took me into the passenger common, stretched a hammock in front of the friendly little fire that burned in the stove there, and carefully placed me in it. He brushed my hair back from my forehead with a gentle touch, and whispered, "Rest. I'll have one of the cooks bring you broth. And we have a medic who can help you with the pain, perhaps. I can't be sure—we've never had any experience with something like those Eyes."

"Well, neither have I. The Seru Moonstone are healers, and they have much experience with the pain the Eyes cause."

"Moonstone?"

"The women with the white eyes, who dress in white."

"Oh, Ethebet. I'm sorry, I'm so sorry, but just looking at them makes my skin crawl. There's something more horrible about their eyes than . . . the ones with the black eyes, or the red eyes . . . or—" He faltered.

"Or my Eyes. I know." I could feel his horror. I knew it well enough from life with the Ossalenes before the Eyes came to me. They are unnatural things, terrible things.

"I'm sorry. I don't mean to be such a braying, thick-headed jackass. I didn't want to hurt you."

"You didn't. I didn't want the Eyes. Not ever. I took them because there's something I have to do with them. Something the previous Hawkspar saw through them, that concerns the survival of all the Tonk."

His hand held mine. "Relax. It isn't important now. Take deep breaths, and I'll go get one of your Moonstone seru. Everything will be all right."

And he let go of my hand and left.

I was left feeling foolish. In pain, and foolish. He had seen me collapse; he thought me weak.

I rested in the hammock, in front of the little stove. Warm, at ease. The hammock swung back and forth, and the ship creaked gently, and I heard voices coming and going, and feet thudding on the decks above and below. The sounds were comforting. Gentle, distant, muffled by the wood. I was not alone, but I was not crowded either.

The Moonstones would not be able to hurry to my side; I already knew this. They would be dealing with worse hurts than mine, working side-by-side with Aaran's healer. The dead they could do nothing for, but the dying—well, the Moonstone Eyes gave them a great deal of power where the dying were concerned.

And I was not dying. I was merely in pain, and the pain would probably pass on its own. If it felt like the whole of the universe had shoved its way inside my head to explode, I could still give myself some comfort by knowing that I was exaggerating.

I wondered if I could distance myself from the Eyes. If I could turn them off for a while, and not have them affect me.

If I could do that, I would be completely blind, of course. But the rivers of time flowed through my skull unchecked, and bits and pieces of events and scraps of people flashed on the blank wall that was my personal vision.

A man stood within my mind, deep in the water. I could not see any detail of him. I could not get a feel for him, except that he was strong. Old. He lay in my past.

I turned, and found another like him. Dark, strong, old. In my future.

And a third, like the first two, lay in my present—but he was dead. Destroyed. I could make him out when I looked closely. He was the wizard I had killed. He was not gone. Dead, but not gone. His spirit lingered, bound by something he could not escape. He had become one of his own dead men, a spirit that could not rest.

The one that lay in my past was bound to me, and was with me. He had come into my mind through the gate I had opened when I held time at bay.

She had warned me, Hawkspar had. She had told me there would be a price for using the full power of the Eyes.

I had known. Though I could not get close to the shadow within me, I knew he had come. And I could sense that he would not leave. I'd opened the door behind which he had waited, and I had let him in.

I knew him. He was the wizard of the Eyes. He had, in a sense, made me.

The shadow in my future was bound to someone else . . . someone I did not know. But I would have to stand against him.

He was a wizard, too. He did not know I watched him. But the first did. The second did.

The third would come to feel my presence soon enough.

I shuddered, wishing the room could be warmer, or my pain less. Wishing that I could be someone else, perhaps—the girl I had been before the Eyes came to me.

"Oracle?"

I could not place the voice. One of the little girls, but I did not know which one. And I was trying not to look with the Eyes, because looking hurt so much. "Yes."

"Are you going to die, Oracle?"

I sighed. "No. Why would you ask such a thing?"

"The sounds you were making were so . . . frightening."

Sounds. I was lying there making sounds, and did not even hear myself, at least not until I thought about it. Once I listened to myself, I heard the whimpering, and the moaning. How lovely. I was scaring the children and I, with not a cut on me, sounded no less in agony than the dying.

Feet thundered down the companionway, and then Aaran's voice touched me again. "My healer is working, as are yours. Many of the injuries were terrible; they'll be longer before they can attend to you, and yours made it clear to me that nothing I might do would help you. Still, I thought perhaps I would bring you something that I've used to ease pain—maybe it will help somewhat while you wait." I caught his movement next to me, and the shape and weight of his hand pouring something from a bottle into a mug.

For an instant, a rancid smell curled around me, but then it vanished, replaced by sharpness and the biting aroma of the infirmary, and the stinging astringency of the solutions used to clean wounds.

"Have a sip," he told me, and put the mug to my lips.

"That's something that should treat wounds on the outside," I said, "not pain on the inside."

He laughed. "It's my favorite gyriik—caribou milk fermented with herbs, strained and bottled and aged for twelve years. There's none finer."

"You drink it?"

"When I have the privilege. It's hard to come by."

"And you're not dead yet." I sighed. "Yes, let me have a taste."

"Sip it," he said. "It burns."

It did. It burned all the way from my mouth down my throat and into my gut. I choked, and sputtered.

"It's strong," he said. "But once it gets in the blood, it can ease a world of hurt."

I could think he was right. It flowed through me, spreading warmth. The taste had been terrible, but the sensation that came after the taste was remarkable.

"Another sip?" I asked.

The shadows of two dead men watched me, receding as the warmth filled me.

He put the cup to my lips. I would like to say that the second sip wasn't as bad, but that would be lying. If I crawled on the ground and licked the dirt, I would find no worse tastes.

But I lay there and felt Aaran's vile-tasting gyriik start blanketing the worst daggers of my pain. Dulling the points, putting softness between me and them. The river of time receded, as if I were stepping back from its banks. The voices and the images, the ghosts and all the many horrors of what might happen and what might have happened slipped back, and hushed a bit.

"Oh," I murmured. "That's better. More, perhaps?"

"Finish what I've poured," he said. "And then tell me about your Eyes, and how you and these other women came to have them. Where they came from, what they do."

"You have nothing else more important to do?"

"The healers are working, the ship is—for now, anyway—not moving, and anyone who needs me knows where to find me. And I'm curious."

I took two more sips that burned their way through me. I thought if the tiny mug he'd held up for me had helped so much, surely more gyriik would be even better. But I didn't want to appear greedy. I'd tell him as much of the story as I knew, and perhaps partway through ask for more.

He refilled the mug and sipped from it himself.

"The story isn't all that long. The Citadel of the Ossalenes was once the estate of one of the island kings. A son of that king, whose name was Ossal, converted to Marositism, and then joined the Cistavrian Order, which against the teachings of the rest of the Marosites, practices magic. By the Ossalene accounts, Ossal became powerful in the creation of magical weapons and magical tools. He also fancied young women, and kept a large harem of them for his amusement."

"Harems," Aaran said. "Right. I think it's understood that most men would love to have a harem of young women. Just the way we're made."

"Would you?" I asked him.

"I find parts of the picture appealing," he said. "Then I consider my vast talent at annoying women, and consider the consequences of having a whole herd of angry, if lovely, creatures coming after me with murder in mind—and I decide that I would be best off enjoying the company of the world's beauties one at a time." He sighed. "Maybe two at a time on a really good day."

Two. "Oh." A woman wants to hear a man say, *All I've ever wanted in the world was one woman—the right woman.* Not, *Everything with legs and breasts, just not all at once.*

He started laughing. "You asked me what I would want. I was honest with you. And now you look horrified. I'm trying to find my sister, and until I find her, I don't have the opportunity to stay in one place and be with one woman. Maybe someday I'll be able to do that—and maybe someday I'll want to."

His sister. Yes. If she was not among us, then he would return to devoting his life to the search for her.

I sat up in the hammock and discovered that the pain in my head had become a little thing. Replacing it, however, was a spinning sensation that made me feel as if the ship were rocking forward and backward and side-to-side and upside-down all at the same time. I lay back down.

I said, "You quickly grasped the problem with harems. Ossal, who had used his magic to destroy his father and all his father's offspring so that none could challenge his right to the throne, was not so quick in realizing the danger, however. He created the Eyes that we now wear—the story is that at one time there were more than two thousand pairs, and that many of those pairs were designed to make the girls biddable."

"Ah," Aaran said. "Not enough that he should be a king. He wanted to be a god as well."

He seemed to have a clear picture of the man who had created the Eyes. Clearer, perhaps, than I had.

"He had women to care for his every need, for his health and his protection and his amusement, the growing of his food, the tending of his flocks, the maintaining of his surroundings. And then he decided that these slaves, bound to him by the magic of their eyes, unable to be unfaithful to him or to escape him or to argue with his slightest whim, were not enough. He wanted to know the past and the future. He wanted to see all of what was, all of what is, and all of what might be and to find ways to control the whole of time. He dreamed of being king not just of his islands, but of the whole of the world. So he made the Eyes of the Oracles."

"And got some *very* special slaves."

"More special than he wanted. The oracles could see not only what he was, but what he had been, and what he could become." I laughed a little. "Worse than that, they could see clearly how the future might be changed to crush him. They led him, with advice carefully given, into a trap in which he was slaughtered, and all his soldiers with him. At his death, the bond that bound his slaves to him cracked, but did not break. The oracles and the seru, though they did not yet think of themselves in that way, closed up the Citadel. They locked themselves away from the world for a time. Tried to find out who they were, and what they might do. And how they might be fully freed of the spirit of dead Ossal."

"It seems that the king should have been able to figure out that women who could see into the future might be interested in finding a way of shortening his." Aaran sipped slowly at his drink.

"We seem, rather, to have stretched it for him. It is a weak bond between those with lesser Eyes. All of the slave Eyes, that served no purpose but to turn women into sex toys, were destroyed as the women who wore them died. The seru Eyes connect to him, but from all the Hawkspar before me had time to tell me, the connection is not strong. With the Oracle Eyes . . . well. If we allow ourselves to delve into the full power the Eyes offer, we strengthen the connection between us and him." I let my body bask in the warmth inside me and outside me, and smiled. All of that was so very far away. "Power has its price," I told him—but at the moment that saying seemed to have little to do with me.

"When you started calling for help . . . ?"

I lay in the hammock, gently rocked by the sea, warmed by the fire, surrounded by people who were not trying to kill me, and by those whose lives I had saved. As much as anyone could be safe floating on a speck of wood in the middle of a vast unknown world, I was safe. "I was powerless. Just a little girl with a knack for Tonk magic."

"And then you received your stone eyes, and they let you stop time."

"And I'm not like the other girls anymore. Right." I turned my face to him. The pain had subsided enough that I could try to see him; I wanted to catch as much of who he was as I could. I wanted to see what others saw—I wanted to see the outside of him, the colors of him, but all I could make out were the solids and the liquids and the air spaces, layers and densities. I had no idea what he looked like. "My mentor died. And I received her Eyes. It was not a pleasant thing, and she gave me right of refusal when she chose me. But she saw something—something that involved the destruction of the Tonk. And she offered me the task of preventing time from taking the path she saw. Or at least preventing it in this stream."

"Why you?"

"Because I was born Tonk. And will be Tonk again, as she was Tonk. We were both captured by slavers in our youths—I when I was very young. She chose me because I was a troublemaker not tempted by power. Because I'd figured out a way out of the Citadel, and had people ready to risk their lives to fight for our freedom with me."

He reached out and took my hand. My left hand. I had thought he meant to offer me comfort, but instead I felt his fingers trace the mark on that palm, the one I had shared with my Hawkspar predecessor.

"Eskuu," he whispered.

"My clan, though I don't remember it. My mentor bore the same mark."

"Eskuu was lost to the Known Clans some thousand years ago. The whole clan sought new lands and a new future, took horses and seeds and sailed into the west. And were never heard from again. We thought—always believed—that the Eskuu were devoured by the storms and none survived. But here you are." He sounded excited. "Where were you? I cannot tell you the excitement there would be if the Eskuu returned in force, and brought back the fedderhorses and the books of their passage."

"I don't know where my people lived. As I said, I was taken young. We have girls who were taken as slaves when they were older. I don't know if any bear the same mark I do—I was never that curious—but if they do, they might remember."

"A clansman of the Drifted, returned. It's amazing. I would have thought it impossible."

He sat there for a while holding my hand, his finger tracing over and over the mark on my left palm.

He sat that way for a long time. Then he said, "But you mentioned a threat."

"That someone seeks to destroy the Tonk, and is succeeding."

"There are a lot of Tonk," he said. "In a lot of places. The nomads still roam the plains of Tandinapalis. And our sailing ships and horses have taken us across the world. The Old, the Transitional, and the New Clans covered much of the world. My clan, which is Viiku, has several taaks in the Confederacy of Hyre, which has now allied itself with the Eastil Republic . . . but the Confederacy is Tonk to the core, and has maintained the old ways." His hand squeezed mine one last time, gently, and let it go. "So . . . what threat do you see?"

And I had to confess my own failure. "I don't. Yet. My mentor saw it with these Eyes, but she was much more skilled in their use. She saw that the Tonk are fighting a war they don't know they're fighting. All I see is a coming darkness—and three wizards bound to my fate. Two are dead but not gone. One of them we killed today, one is Ossal, who made these Eyes. The third waits in the future, and I don't know who he is or how I shall meet him—only that he does not bode well for my future. More than that, I don't know. I still have only the strength and skill to navigate the waters that flow around me a little way in any direction."

I heard Aaran stand, and heard the chair he'd sat in scrape back and click as he slipped the ladder back of it over a hook on the wall.

"I'm going up to see how everyone is doing. I'll check in on you later. I have not yet counted our losses—this I must do."

I wanted him to stay, but around me I could catch the shapes of healing and tragedy. He was right; he needed to be other places. "Thank you for sitting with me, and for sharing your drink with me. It was dreadful. But it helped."

"You only have to start worrying when you like the way it tastes," he said, and laughed. I loved the sound of his laugh—deep and warm and strong.

And then his boots clattered up the companionway at a near run, and I was left with myself for company, and the little girls still hiding in the berths, too afraid to come out.

I sat up again, and the room still felt like it was spinning in every direction at once. Like the captain, however, I had duties. I had brought those little girls to this place, and I had the responsibility to make sure they did not shiver in needless fear. If I had to crawl from cabin to cabin, I would do that.

19

Aaran

Eskuu. Hawkspar was Eskuu.

Aaran couldn't shake the disbelief. It was like knowing in his bones, knowing from everything he had ever seen and ever heard, that there were no more fedderhorses in the world. And then stumbling across one, alive and kicking, gold and black stripes gleaming in the sun.

He wondered if the fact that there were still Eskuu meant that there *were* still fedderhorses.

He could have the men do some work on one of the holds—put in a few stalls. Great Jostfar, if they showed up in Beyltaak, say, at the horse market, with even one breedable, papered fedderhorse, his fortune would be secure. His reputation would be . . . godlike.

Aaran played for a moment with the idea of going in search of the land of Eskuu and fedderhorses, but he couldn't think he would find any Tonk slaves there.

He hadn't eliminated the possibility that one of the women aboard the ship was his sister, but it didn't seem likely. He considered that she might have been one of the Ossalenes who stayed behind, but that wasn't likely, either. He needed to check the clan marks on the hands of the girls and women aboard; perhaps all the Drifted had come home. Perhaps, hidden in the islands where men did not dare to sail, some Tonk had found a way to survive. If that was the case, then there would be other expeditions.

Meanwhile, he and his men had saved more than two hundred women and girls, mostly Tonk, who had been captive, had managed to sneak them out under the very noses of a raiding king and his pillaging scum, and away, too, from the monastery that would never have let them go. The Tonk would have to send people to deal with the Ossalene Order—the Tonk did not tolerate the enslavement of their people. But dealing with the Ossalenes would not be Aaran's mission, either.

He had to get the captives he had to safety.

And he had to find Aashka. If she wasn't on the *Taag*, she was somewhere else.

Tuua saw him step out of the passenger companionway, and crossed the deck.

"What's the news?" he asked.

"Bad," Tuua said. "Ves is dead. Neeran is dead. Otaam is still alive, and the Moonstones are working on him, but I cannot believe he has any hope of surviving."

Otaam was the ship's tracker. He was of only middling talent, but having him alive meant someone to watch the passageways while Aaran slept—someone to keep them off rocks, if not someone to find them the best route through an entire region. Aaran, still stunned that he'd lost his kor daan and one of his runners, prayed that he would not lose his tracker, too.

"Who else?" he asked.

"Baaksa."

Their one true steersman. They had other men who might do the job, but none who'd had training in it. He nodded. "Who else?"

"Four marines. Seven sailors. Some of the warrior women. One little girl who hid on deck instead of going below."

And if any of the dead women were Aashka, he had lost her before he found her.

Aaran rang the death bell—a slow, steady tolling of the ship's bell that summoned all who could attend to the final rites. He rang it until everyone who could walk and was not tending the injured stood on the deck. Then he steeled himself against what he would face, and walked aft, where the men and some of the women had washed the dead and laid them out in state on the deck.

And there was Neeran, always so quick and willing and eager; a boy on his first voyage, a young wharf rat who had signed papers because he saw his future in the sea. The boy had no one back home to notify—he'd said he was an orphan, and if he wasn't, he'd had his reasons for the lie.

"Who first?" Tuua asked.

"The boy. He'll be the hardest to get through. And then the little girl. Do the women want the Tonk words said, or have they another prayer to offer?"

"We are all Tonk here," the Obsidian Redbird said, and Aaran jumped. He did not know that she'd been standing behind him. "Born that way or not, we are your people now."

Aaran nodded, and Tuua said, "As you wish it, then."

Tuua knelt on the deck beside Neeran, and put one hand on the boy's narrow chest. Aaran stood at the child's head, wishing Neeran didn't look so young, so small, so helpless. Wishing they had someplace for his body other than the cold depths of the sea.

Wishing that someone somewhere would weep that he was gone, and understand what a good boy he had been.

The boy wasn't Tonk, but he was *theirs*. So Tuua said the prayer for a Tonk warrior for him.

> "Jostfar silent but near,
> Ethebet, hand of the sword,
> Guardians of the souls of your people,
> Take Neeran Old-Walk home,
> To horses and meadows and family
> And the long halls of the honored.
> Give him place, and name,
> And rest for a time.
> Remember him,
> And that he served in life,
> Honored living.
> That he is in death,
> Honored dead."

"Gitaada," Aaran said, in unison with Tuua and the other Tonk officers gathered around the bodies, and with the sailors and marines who had fought and lived. And with the women and girls, who whispered "Gitaada," with the rest.

Aaran said, "The spirit is gone to the Summerland. The body remains, but is not the boy. We honor the life of Neeran Old-Walk, and grieve his passing. We are made less by his absence."

Aaran folded the shroud around the boy's body. So small, so young. He hadn't listened to Potyr, who had passed on Aaran's order that he seek safety. He had died fighting, a dagger in his hand. He'd been a brave child. He'd deserved a long life, and great adventure.

Aaran forced himself to concentrate on the task at hand; on folding the corners, on wrapping the cords, on tying the knots. Each step had to be done with respect, in the old way. Each step took concentration—and it was as he squared the corners and carefully tied the falcon-head knot at each point down the midline that he understood why. It was a way of stepping back. Of building a wall between the living and the dead, of making the death about form and custom, so that it could be borne a piece at a time.

Aaran finished the wrapping, which was always the captain's duty, and nodded to his officers. Six men would not be needed to carry the boy's body to the rail of the gombaar deck—but six men would carry it, because that was the way a warrior went. Two officers, one marine, and one sailor stepped forward, and along with Tuua and Aaran, carried what remained of the boy to the rail.

Aaran bore responsibility for the next part of the ritual. When the after-deck filled with everyone aboard ship save the healers and the injured, Aaran said the old words:

> "His spirit is with Jostfar.
> His flesh is as nothing.
> He was born of salt and tears,
> In a gush of brine and blood.
> His flesh is one with the sea,
> And the sea will keep him."

Aaran tried not to look as the wrapped body hit the water, as the lead sewn into the shroud bore it down, beyond vision, beyond retrieval.

He would remember Neeran. Even if the boy had no other family, he'd had a family on the *Taag*. And Aaran stood in as his father. No father would forget his own son.

And so it went. The little girl. Ves, in whom Aaran had just been beginning to discover a friend, and a man he admired. Reynor Deepwater, who had become the new head steersman, and who had been steady at the tillers, level-headed.

And on, and on.

One by one, Tuua blessed the spirit with the prayer of souls, Aaran released the flesh with the Final Grace of the Sea, the men lifted the bodies and sent them to the deep. The little splashes always chilled him.

Death showed little mercy, offered little grace. It only took, and in place of what it took, left ghosts of sound and fragments of scent, little shapes that caught the eye and brought back memory and pain. One of the sailors who had fiddled on the deck, amidst the dancing and laughing, went still and silent into the deep, his music dead with him. "Marrying Maadryn" was going to echo in Aaran's head for a long time. The tune, the way everyone had gathered around, clapping, the way Hawkspar had leapt and stomped and flashed through the dance, following his lead, never missing a beat.

And then that little splash, and everything that had been the fiddler was gone, and only the empty spaces filled with ghosts of what had once been remained.

Death made no distinctions.

They turned back, and Aaran looked at the line of dead still waiting. And took a deep breath. He was their captain. He was the last family for every one of them. He would honor them. Keep them in his heart. Remember the sacrifice each had made, and grieve the loss of each.

Men went to the sea because they had no place else to go. Because they had no one. Because of a thousand different reasons—but all of the reasons meant that they were mostly alone. But on a Tonk ship, everyone had family—everyone was family.

He worked his way through his officers, his sailors, his marines.

And then he reached the first of the women. She looked like she might be the right age to be Aaran's sister. Her hair was the right color. He knelt beside her and turned over her left hand, and felt his throat tighten and his breath grow short. She had been Clan Viikuu, the same as he was. He rolled her over on her stomach and carefully lifted the neck of her shirt to check the marks between her shoulder blades. Her name marks *mua* and *haa*. She had no saint mark—she had been taken captive before she was old enough to claim a saint.

"Not her," he whispered, and the fear drained out of him, leaving him dizzy and sick with relief.

None of the other women could have been her. They were the wrong age, or the wrong clan, or the wrong appearance.

Hawkspar made it up on deck for the burials of the women who bore Eyes. She did so supported by two of her Obsidians, and he could tell from the pallor of her skin that she was far from well. But she knelt next to each of the women after Tuua had said his words, and added, "Your Eyes will go with you. You will be the last of your line. May your soul find comfort in that."

At last it was over. The decks cleared of all save those who were working.

Aaran gathered his officers in the attable and called in a handful of men who were to be promoted. Right there, he gave such new assignments as he had to. Ino Tortaaknavyn stepped into duty as the new daan to take the place of Ves av Imaaryn. Aaryn left his kor wogan, Ermyk ave Beyrkyn, in charge of the marines, but also made him kor daan.

He would make do with one runner. Neeran would not be replaced this voyage. Aaran found a sailor with good carpentry skills, a solid older Eastil fellow named Bobik Two-Bricks-Down, and made him shipwright. A few Tonk sailors—Reformed Mindans all—were deeply offended that a non-Tonk was elevated to an officer's rank when Tonk men were available. Aaran told them curtly that wood and metal didn't know race, religion, or creed, and when he was making a man shipwright, neither could he.

Death had come, it had gone. Life moved on.

Hawkspar

I stood in a pool of darkness, as if at the bottom of a deep well. Above me, I could see light, but nothing I could do would let me reach the light, escape the deep pit, or move in any direction. I was bound after a fashion that I could not discover, and helpless, and I knew that I was not alone.

"You belong to me," a voice said very close to me. "You wear my Eyes, you are my slave. You have opened the door to me, and welcomed me in, and now I claim you, flesh and bone and sinew, mind and magic. I own you, and you cannot deny me what is rightfully mine."

He laughed, and I shivered. I heard madness in his laugh, and evil.

And then he was upon me, a spirit, but thick as liquid mud, pushing into my nose, my mouth, my ears, between my legs, forcing the air from my lungs, strangling me, choking me.

I flailed. I fought him, not with the art of an Ossalene warrior, but with the panicked, useless strugglings of a child overpowered by a monster.

He was in me, around me, filling me, and I was dying. Dying.

Light poured around us, and in the light, he began to thin. To melt off.

I dared to look around, to see what weakened him.

I was in the meadow, with the flowers, the horses, the woman dressed in white who stood far away, watching.

Ossal, for I knew he was Ossal, began to sizzle like water poured on a hot griddle. He began to scream. "Mine," he shrieked. "She is mine."

"She is Ethebet's," the woman in white said.

They were both gone. I lay in the bunk in the passenger quarters of the *Taag av Sookyn,* crowded next to Redbird, in a room filled with others who all slept with varying degrees of noise. My throat hurt on the outside. My nostrils and ears ached. The place between my legs was a throbbing agony.

I tried to tell myself that it had been a dream, that in opening the gate that had separated me from Ossal, I had not released something that had the power to physically destroy me.

But I ran my fingers lightly over the skin of my throat, and I could feel places so tender they seemed likely to bruise. It had been no dream.

Ossal had found his way to me, and had sought to take me by surprise.

I wondered how I would deal with his next attack, or what I would do to prevent that attack. No one had awakened. No one—not even Redbird— had sensed that anything was wrong. The woman in white had stepped in and saved me. But I should have been ready. I should have been prepared to protect myself.

Aaran

A day passed, with the ship moving slowly southward, safe enough in a deep channel, keeping well away from islands and anything that moved. The windmen worked their shifts, but they were not encouraged to any great feats. The injured aboard the ship were mending; the Moonstones had astonishing skill with magic.

The *Taag* got a bit of wind, and the raised sails bellied out and the ship began tugging forward. The windmen stood down, resting in reserve against future need.

Aaran set an easy course, running due south across the wind. That would keep the *Taag av Sookyn* in the center of open water for a while. At their current slow pace, for several days.

He didn't look forward to running through any of the islands again; he'd tracked out a dozen deep channels back into open sea, but the way home would be long compared to the way in, and he couldn't know which parts of it would take him past more cannibals, or past horrors none aboard the ship even knew to fear.

He found Hawkspar in the passenger commons, and invited her be at his cabin door at fifth bell, for the dinner she had promised to share with him.

He told his officers to fend for themselves for the evening meal. And then he spent the rest of the time between when he entered his cabin and when the fifth bell rang showering in the gombaar, and dressing himself in his best clothes, and then—realizing that Hawkspar was unlikely to recognize his best clothes—dousing himself with a musk oil that the natives of Firewalk Island got from a species of deer that lived there, and that they declared made a man irresistible to a woman.

He sent Potyr down to the temple to study with Tuua and his protégé for a while.

The bell rang, and she knocked before it had finished the fifth clang. He opened the door, and took a half step back.

She glowed like the sun, dressed in something that resembled the Ossalene garb in cut and form, but was threaded with gold and studded with gemstones—gleaming emeralds and rubies and blue-black stones that matched her hair.

She'd done something with her hair. It was up, which emphasized the slender, graceful length of her neck, the smooth line of her jaw, the sweet curve of her face.

She smiled, and he realized she also had fine white teeth, even and well cared for. Something about the finery and the hair and her stance emphasized to him that she was very young for a woman who commanded such power. Certainly a few years younger than he was. "I dressed," she said. "You did not say if it was formal, but in the Oracle House, we dressed for the meal. I hope this is appropriate."

"You look beautiful," he said, startled by his sincerity. Even with those stone eyes, he discovered, she was beautiful. He tried to imagine what she had looked like before. And then he forced himself to put that thought away. She was who she was. And he needed to get to know her, and understand her—and for many more reasons than that he felt drawn to her.

He led her to the private companionway in his quarters that took them down into the captain's grand hall. The room was his alone to do with as he pleased. Unlike much of the rest of the ship, he could dine there in silence, alone, or seat himself and all his officers. Food came up through the dropwaiter in the center of the table, and the room itself had its only entrance through the companionway down from the captain's quarters. Which meant that those in the grand hall were guaranteed privacy.

He led her around the table where he did his navigating, and down the step stairs. She had no trouble getting from place to place.

"How does your head feel?"

"Better," she said. "That drink you gave me worked wonders. Though it did make the world feel as if it were spinning so quickly I could not even lift my head. The feeling wore off—but I confess I did not find it entirely pleasant."

Something wicked in him whispered, *Let her try Kerfuu wine. That will make her head spin.*

He took a deep breath, chasing the wickedness away. "I only gave you a few swallows. Gyriik is a strong drink."

"It smells a great deal like medicines we use to clean wounds."

"Well, it would. Alcohol all smells much the same, no matter what you use it for." He paused. "You've never drunk alcohol? Wine? Beer? Mead? Liqueurs? Brandy?"

"Water," she said, sounding quite certain about that. "Slaves were only permitted water. Penitents, also. The same for acolytes. And the oracles at table had different drinks, but I did not care for the smell, or for the way those women behaved when they had been drinking their drinks. So I stayed with water."

The wicked voice came back. *Never drank anything but water. Think about that, would you? She'd be warm. And supple. It wouldn't really be taking advantage, would it?*

He silenced the voice again. Rang the dropwaiter bell, and in a moment heard the rope creaking. Her face was turned to the center of the table. "How very clever. Ropes and pulleys, and a big box with trays in it, and one boy down there to pull it all up. And thus your food comes to you hot from the kitchen, instead of being run up through the ship, and outside across the deck, and back inside and down. I had wondered how you got your food in here."

He studied her as the trays came level with the table. He tapped the bell, and the boy down in the kitchen stopped pulling. He could also have trays delivered directly to his quarters if he wanted to eat at his desk; the ropes ran straight through the grand hall to his quarters.

"How did you know how it worked, or how many people it took to get it up here?"

"It's all part of that seeing but not seeing. I have lost color. I've lost surfaces. But I can feel densities and movement and shapes at a distance, even through other objects. People are nearly as clear as water to me. I can see through the sea as if it were a faint haze. Through wood is not so hard.

Through stone, harder, but not impossible. Through metal, very difficult."
She shrugged. "I would *love* to know how the ship looks. But I can see how
it works."

Aaran put her plate in front of her, and rang the bell. The dropwaiter descended, and the round cutout that filled in the hole in the table dropped
into place.

She could see through things.

Could see if someone was hiding weapons, certainly.

Could see monsters under the sea—he'd already known that.

Could see through the walls of ships, so that men might have no privacy
around her.

Could see . . . through clothes?

Could tell if a man was . . . interested in her?

Oh, Ethebet, preserve him from women who saw too well.

She was eating—dainty bites with knife and fork, pauses in between each
bite. "This is remarkable," she said. "What is it?"

"Smoked hawfish. They only run in the spring where I come from. And
when they run, they come up the rivers from the sea to spawn. They're a sta-
ple in Hyre, especially in the southernmost regions, where the weather is
coldest. They're deepwater fish the rest of the time—once they're back in
the oceans, no net can reach them."

"The meat has a bite to it. I like that."

I have a bite to me, he thought, and felt like he'd been drinking too much
of his own gyriik. "So tell me about life in the Citadel."

"Some of it wasn't bad. For those of us who showed aptitude, there were
classes. Learning languages and history, fighting, etiquette in a hundred different cultures, the strategies and tactics of warfare, a smattering of magic,
how to rule. There was a great deal of scrubbing things," she said. "There
were parts I would rather never think on again. Too much of it is not suitable to discuss while digesting. You tell me about you. About life on this
ship. About what it looks like, about what you look like. Colors. Give me lots
of colors. I miss them most of anything, I think. Sunrises and sunsets and
flowers and leaves. They aren't the same now."

"They wouldn't be, I suppose." He sighed. "The ship is a beauty. Old, and
made in the old fashion, with a big horse head carved on the neck at the
fore. Real horsehair for the mane, too, which I thought a nice touch when I
first saw it. The ship itself is polished wood, a rich gleaming dark brown that
has been varnished and revarnished for more than a century now. But the

prow is gilt, and the horse head atop it has a gold nose and gold ear tips, and eyes of faceted garnet."

"Garnet. A red stone," she said. "Odd color for the eyes."

"And after the horse, there are the sails," he said, immediately changing the subject. Where Ossalenes and odd eye colors were concerned, every single thing he could think to say sounded wrong. "They're crimson, every one of them, and when the light shines through them, they glow like fire. So gold and crimson and gleaming brown, we cut through the blue water like a jewel. She's a lovely ship, the *Taag av Sookyn*. Inside, most of the walls are painted white, because it would be dark in here otherwise. The portholes are small, and there are none on the working deck."

"That's the deck below ours, right?"

"The one with the attable."

"Right," Hawkspar said. "And the kitchen, and all the marines."

"A handful of light tubes bring in some light from the top deck to the working deck, and lanterns burn there whenever anyone is there, but it's still dark."

"I miss the light," she said softly.

He sighed. "The best place on the ship, though, is up on the ratlines, or sitting astride the foremast snaparm and clinging to the mast, looking out over the sea, with the deck so far below it looks like a toy. You might as well be flying. Sometimes, you can feel yourself wanting to let go. To leap out over the water and become some great soaring bird."

The expression on her face was rapt. "It sounds wondrous."

"As long as you don't let go, it is."

"What would it be like to let go, though?" she asked, more to herself, he thought, than to him. "To feel the wind against your skin, to soar, to be a bird?"

"Until you crashed into the water or the deck, I'm sure it would be lovely," he said. "But water feels like rock if you land on it from high enough up."

"You know this?"

"I missed a handhold once," he said. "When I was much younger. And I went over the side. They managed to scoop me back in—good thing they were quick with the catchman and the gaffe, though, because I couldn't move my arms or legs, couldn't breathe, and every muscle in my body felt like it had been ripped from the bone. I couldn't have tread water to save my life. My hide was one big bruise for weeks after."

"How terrible. And yet you did not leave the sea. I think if something like that had happened to me, I would never have had the courage to step back on a ship."

"My sister is not yet home. It wasn't a matter of courage for me. Staying on the sea was a matter of necessity."

"When you first heard my plea, you thought perhaps that I was her?"

He shook his head. "I knew you weren't. You shared no common memories with me. And she's younger than you, by perhaps a year or two."

"I don't know how old I am."

"I'd guess you were twenty. Maybe twenty-one."

"Which would make her nineteen or twenty now. You've been looking so long?"

"She was eight when she was taken. I hope she might be one of your number."

"Oh, you don't hope that. You don't want her to have spent twelve years with the Ossalenes. Not so much as a single day. Horrible things happened to those who displeased the seru and the oracles, and equally horrible things to those who pleased them too much. The best hope of a good life in the Citadel was to be plain-looking, and quiet, and unremarkable. Not too smart, not too talented, not too pretty."

"And yet you are pretty, and intelligent, and I imagine talented as well."

For one long moment she said nothing at all. Then she laced her fingertips together on the table before her, and in a careful tone, said, "And I've been beaten so often the scars on my back feel like a washing board. I've been fed to starving rats, and it was only some secret magic my mentor summoned that saved me from horrible death. As a reward for being good at languages and studies, and for having the initiative to figure out how to escape from that place, I had the privilege of being offered the opportunity to have my eyes ripped out and these shoved in their place. Now for the rest of my life, I'll see things I don't want to see, and know things I don't want to know. And experience pain worse than any beating I ever got for the honor of being Hawkspar."

"And you did this because . . . people you didn't know were in danger."

"Family I didn't know," she said softly.

"A hidden war, you said. A vast conspiracy. By whom?"

"I don't know."

"Tuua—that is, my cousin Tuuanir, who is the ship's keeper, and who has most of Ethebet's teachings memorized and who has a fancy for politics, might be able to steer you toward likely candidates. If you care to seek him out."

"I will. It would make this easier, if I knew which part of the river to search for the future and its cure."

She had done what she had done with no guarantee that she might succeed. Suffered great loss with full knowledge that she might have suffered in vain. He stared at her. He understood her far too well.

He stood and stepped around the table, and pulled her up, not thinking about what he was doing, or why. He held her close, and after an instant, felt her body melt against his. He stroked her hair, and felt her shiver.

She was warm. Soft in all the right places. Well rounded, giving, firm and curved and enticing.

He ran a finger lightly down the back of her neck, and she sighed. "That makes my knees feel like they're going to fall out from under me. Do it again."

He did in again.

"Are you still hungry?" he asked her.

"I don't think I could eat another bite."

"Would you . . . come up to my quarters with me, then?"

She paused for a moment, and he found that he was holding his breath.

"Yes," she said then, and she sounded certain. Better yet, he knew she was sober.

He put a hand on her back, and followed her up the stairs and into his quarters. He had a wide berth—the only one on the ship that would comfortably fit two adults. He had two comfortable chairs. And his table. And a bench with windows that looked out over the sea. And a loft above, empty for the moment. He locked the door.

And then he turned to her. "Come here," he said, and she came to him, smiling.

Hawkspar

He wanted me. It was all I knew, all I needed to know. Somehow, he had managed to leave his shock at the hideous Hawkspar Eyes behind. Somehow, he had found something in me that spoke to him the way everything about him spoke to me. He was standing before me with his arms spread wide, saying, "Come here," and it was all I could do not to throw myself at him. I forced myself to walk as though I were a sane person, and not a creature driven mad by the magic of his touch. The back of my neck still tingled from his fingers.

He curved both arms around me and pulled me tight against him, and lowered his head to press his lips against mine. I had never felt such a thing, nor imagined it. I licked his lips, tasting him, and he made a little growling noise in the back of his throat, and bit me lightly.

I could feel his teeth. His tongue. I wanted to feel more, and at the same time, I felt foolish. What was I supposed to do?

I ran a hand over his chest. It was so different from my own. Mine was the only body I'd ever felt, and I'd thought all of them would be much like it. We saw men in the Citadel, but seeing is not touching.

So I reveled in touching him. Where I was soft, he was hard. He was so much bigger than me, and his arms around me were thick and roped with muscle. And far stronger than I could have imagined. He picked me up again, and I was no longer so consumed by pain that I could not enjoy the experience. He carried me to his berth, and laid me on the firm mattress, and bent over me, and once more pressed his lips to mine.

I bit him. Lightly. I did not, after all, want to hurt him. But I'd liked the feel of it when he did it to me.

I did not expect the response I got.

He laughed and clambered on top of me, and pushed his tongue through my teeth to lick it against my tongue.

My body seemed to have gone mad. Every part of my skin was covered in chill bumps, hair was standing on end, my breasts tingled, and low in my belly, I felt things tightening and relaxing.

Anything below our waists the Ossalenes had taught us to ignore. Never touch, except for the bleed times, and while washing, and little gods help the girl who spent too much time in the shower washing. The seru would drag her out of the water naked and beat her right there.

But I was shivering with desire, wanting and longing and not even sure what it was that I so desired. My mind didn't know. But it felt like my body did.

He found the knotted bo-allar at my waist. That flat knot had taken me an age to learn, but he had no problems undoing it.

Well, no—why would he? He was a sailor. They lived in a world of ties and knots and bindings.

After he tossed the bo across the room, he slid the heavy jeweled rak-tabi over my head, and let it drop to the floor. And then his hands were sliding the overblouse off, over my head, and I raised my arms to help its progress, then felt along his chest to the lacings of his shirt. I undid them, and tugged them free from his belt and breeches, and he lifted up from me long enough that he could shed both shirt and jacket.

My hands slid across his chest then, and my fingers were shocked by what they found. Soft hair, curly and short, covered his chest. His shoulders were smooth, as was his back.

His upper arms likewise were as smooth as mine, but his forearms were furry.

He felt wonderful.

"How many clothes do you have on?" he asked me. I heard laughter in his voice.

"Bo-allar, cepa, rak-tabi, tabi, rayan, allar, hakan-allar, pantlets, breast-binder, barutis, and soltis."

He made a clicking sound with his tongue. "We could be here all night."

"If we were, would that be a bad thing?"

"Not for me," he said, and brushed a thumb across my cheek. His hands were big, and rough. Calloused, hard. They felt strong like the rest of him. And that strength excited me. "I hope not for you."

"Not for me, either."

"Good." His voice, already deep, sounded deeper. My heart skittered. We felt like we were racing somewhere, and I didn't know where it was, but I wanted to be there.

His hands then worked at the hakan-allar—my warrior pants—and he said, "By every Eastil god begat by man, how do you get this off? Is there a magic spell upon the thing?"

I put my hand over his hand and slid it to the side. "Buttons on the outside. Hooks and eyes on the inside. It is the way things are done." And I sighed a little, for truly, it did not need to be the way things were done for me. Not anymore. I was shed of the Order, shed of the Ossalenes, shed of the Citadel. Shed of all save the Eyes, and them and all their darkness I was stuck with.

This was not the time I wanted to think about any of that, however. I helped Aaran get me out of my pants, and then slipped off my allar—my underblouse. And he made a noise in the back of his throat like a petted cat, and said, "By all that is good, you're a lovely thing. Jostfar help me, the curves on you."

He tugged my breastbinder off, and buried his face between my breasts, and I held his head while my heart hammered, and while he licked and nibbled his way from nipple to nipple, and then back.

I moaned, and he made that wonderful purring noise again. "You like that?"

"Oh, yes. Truly."

"What else do you like?" he asked.

I didn't know. I'd never been in this position before. "Anything. Everything."

He sat up, still straddling me, his face turned toward me. He was very still.

"Something about that seems not quite . . . do you know what . . . anything . . . ? *Anything?*" He was faltering, stumbling for words. "Perhaps you don't . . ." And he sighed heavily. "This is awkward. But when you have been with other men, what . . . sorts of things . . ."

That certainly aroused my curiosity. I'd not thought there would be terribly many options. I wasn't sure what we were heading for, but my body had liked the idea of going wherever it might have been. And I'd been eager to follow along. Aaran made me feel good. I wanted more of that.

So . . . what other things were there?

"There haven't been any other men," I said.

A pause. A silence. "Well, no, with you locked away in that place with only other women around, I don't suppose there would have been." And I could not miss the intrigued note as he asked me, "Well, what sorts of things did the women you have been with do?"

I tucked my hands behind my head. "We were forbidden to touch each other. Or ourselves, save when showering."

He laughed softly. "But the difference between what is forbidden and what is done—"

"In the Citadel, there was no difference. It was the job of the Seru Obsidian to enforce the rules. They could see everything we did, all the time, no matter where they were. They knew, and they would come for transgressors, drag them out into the dormitory squares, and beat them with whips. Those who attempted to transgress too often were sold as whores, or simply fed to the rats as an example for everyone else. There were . . . very few examples. We weren't stupid."

"Sweet Ethebet. How did anyone survive such a life?"

"Our thoughts were our own. We spent a lot of time thinking."

He ran a hand over my shoulder, and his touch sent shivers all through me. "No one has ever touched you?"

"Not with intent. Not since my mother."

"And you would . . . let me touch you?"

"My heart tells me it will tear itself apart if you do not," I said. In truth, not even in fighting could I remember it hammering so vehemently against my breastbone. I could barely catch my breath. The blood in my veins felt like it was jumping.

He rested one hand flat upon my belly, and I shivered at his touch. "You will not catch a child from me," he said, "nor any of the poxes or ills that can come of lying with another. I wear beneath my skin an Amulet of Tagor, sewn there so that I cannot forget it. It will protect you."

"You want no children?"

"I want," he said softly. "But I cannot have. Ethebet requires of her warriors that, if they sire children or bear them, they take responsibility for the lives they have brought forth. I seek my sister, and until I have found her, my oath and my responsibility are to her and my dead parents, to Jostfar and Ethebet. I will not abandon my own children, so I cannot have them."

"It sounds a lonely life," I told him.

And he whispered, "Sometimes I lose hope. Sometimes, more in these last years, I think that she is gone, that I will never find her, that all my searching is for nothing, and all my sacrifice the same."

I closed my eyes, and with my hand placed on his hand, I let his desperation carry me above the river of his time. I could not see clearly where it took me; I did not delve too deeply. I wanted only a simple answer, and that I could find, without detail, without pain or danger to myself. "You'll find her," I told him. "I see it."

"I would give anything to know that was true."

"I am an oracle," I told him. "You don't understand what that means. But if I say I have seen a thing and it will happen, it will happen."

His hand slid over my breasts, down to my belly, lower. He stopped, just as I was certain that he was going to uncover for me the mysteries of the sudden, yearning ache between my legs. "Thank you," he said. And lay beside me, his hand still.

I wanted the hand to move. To keep moving. To do . . . well, whatever it had been about to do before he stopped. I sat up and put my face on his chest, tickling my nose and chin with hair. I found his nipples, so tiny compared to my own, and licked one of them. He laughed and squirmed away from me. "Don't," he said. "That tickles."

I licked again, and he squirmed harder. "No. Really. I hate that."

So I bit him. On the side of the neck, once, a little harder than he'd bitten me. And he growled, and rolled over on top of me.

A shaft, long and hard, unlike anything I had on my body, prodded one of my thighs, and when he pushed my legs wide with his knees, I felt it move against me, pointing to my ache, my hunger, as if it knew. This was the mystery, I thought. This was men and women, and the secrets between them.

He nibbled one of my earlobes, then whispered, "You could be a minx, I suspect."

I did not know what a minx was, but I wanted to be one, if it meant that he would keep touching me.

He rolled us over upon his bed, so that he was on the bottom and I on the top. And he lifted my hips so that long shaft rested between my legs, slipping and prodding. I shut my mind and let my body lead. I embraced him, and through a steady but bearable pain that accompanied the pleasure, pushed myself onto him and filled myself with him. I moved slowly, and so did he, and the pain became less, the pleasure more.

We began to move together, and all the world receded from that room; all knowing, all caring, all past, and all future. We were the whole universe, the two of us, and for a while all the darkness fled. With my eyes closed, I saw colors; they pulsed with our movements, so that we seemed to dance this new dance within a garden where we were the flowers, endlessly changing. His fingers dug into my hips as he moved faster within me. My back arched and my toes curled and I locked my thighs around him so tightly he had to fight to move—and the fighting was as thrilling as the power of locking him tight.

I lost all control. I thrashed against him, mindless and hungry, and he buried himself in me like a swordsman with the final stroke.

All, everything, nothing; I had flesh and no flesh, I was the air and the ocean, I was immortal, and I was a dayfly living and dying and born again.

He pulled me down onto his chest, and held me, and stroked my hair. I shivered, holding him still inside of me for as long as I could, as if I could keep him there forever, until at last he pulled away and my body shuddered a final time. He rolled on his side, with my back held to his chest. It was the perfect moment. I would have stopped all of time to stay right there, right then, in his arms for all eternity.

Had I suspected what would come next, I would have tried.

But the warmth swallowed me, and my eyelids would not stay open, and my mind drifted down into stillness.

Three shadow shapes surrounded me, moving forward and back, first reaching out to prod at me, then pulling away. Three poisoned monsters, two dead, one worse than dead, attenuated and spare, twisted and ugly. None of the three seemed to be aware of the other two; all of the three moved in a vile parody of the dance of flesh that Aaran and I had known.

They were pulling at me. Tearing at me. Trying to force their ways into me.

I sought the meadows in which the woman in white had chased them away. I sought her, hoping that she would save me. But I was alone.

Aaran was gone. The ship was gone. I made my way to my feet, and moved away from them.

If I was to escape them, it would be because of what I did.

As young students, we had been taught by the Ossalenes to shield ourselves against magic. To shield our minds, our thoughts, our souls, and our flesh from evil. I knew the trick so well—it was how I had sent my pleas to Aaran. It was a simple thing. Pull in the strength of earth—but there was no earth.

Then water. Pull in the power of the sea, the restless churning energy. Draw its essence into my flesh, and from the sky pull down the radiance of the sun. Fill myself with both until the power was ready to pour out of me. Send it spinning outward, into a radiant sphere—

The light, the blazing blue-white light, sent all three of them scuttling back.

I woke. Aaran still slept, his arms around me.

I needed to understand what was happening, why the wizards, all three, came after me, how we were bonded, how I could free myself.

I touched Aaran's arm, and turned, and ran a hand over his face—strong nose, full lips, high forehead. My hand called him lovely, even if the Eyes gave me nothing but guesses. I thought I could be happy forever in his embrace. I wanted to wrap myself around him, and wake him, and take him again.

But awake, the movements of time slid through me and around me, the harsh currents of a bleak, cold river. I could see my own end—not the how of it, not the details. But the underlying cause.

The gate that I had nudged open, I would have to fling wide and tear from the hinges, so that all its horrors could rush in at once.

I would have to use all the power of the Eyes to save the Tonk. And with every step I took into that power, a little more of everything that was me would peel away. I would become a husk of myself, a creature human on the outside, something else entirely within.

And before long, every last bit of me would burn away to ash. To nothingness.

There would be no river that flowed with Aaran's embraces, with his touches, with his warmth. Not for me. There would be no happy future filled with moments like the one I was clinging to with increasing longing. The best moment I would ever know was the one that had just passed. All the rest would be poisoned by the truth that what little joy I might glean from a moment would be taken back, so that not even memory remained.

I moved carefully away from his embrace, sliding slowly down the bed so as not to wake him. I gathered up my clothing, and put on each piece, but not carefully.

Perhaps we would have another time together. Perhaps a few more. But in the end, I would be nothing but flesh that moved the Eyes, flesh that faltered and fell away into madness. Eventually, I would not even be that.

In that moment, I discovered true darkness. The loss of the light had been nothing, I realized, dressing silently. It had been only a little taste of my future, a forerunner of the realization that the people I loved, and those I was coming to love, would only survive if I embraced my own destruction.

I let myself out of his room carefully, closed his door without a sound, and hurried to the passenger quarters, and to my own narrow bunk. For a while, I hid myself in it, mourning the existence of a future I did not want, and dared not deny.

The little girls were playing tag, running from the passenger commons into the crew commons, and their thundering feet and endless laughing were near to driving me mad. They'd discovered that, no matter what the Seru Obsidian and Onyx might dictate about running, the sailors were willing to excuse anything, and to stand between the children and discipline. Several of the men had taken to spending their off-watch hours making dollies of braided rope and patch-cloth for the smallest of the girls, and were patiently trying to teach all of them a language they called Trade, used, according to Aaran, in western lands, as well as in the harbors of places farther away that traded with westerners. It was also the language the sailors and officers spoke to each other in sailing the ship, though it had nothing in common with Tonk, the language the captain and many of the ship's officers spoke among themselves.

The previous night lay behind me like a weight—half miracle, half heartbreak. The happy half of me kept reliving my moments with Aaran; the more realistic part of me focused on my duty and my future. Dark thoughts, those.

The mood of the rest of those aboard the ship was bright. A hard wind had come up and we were sailing due south, and apparently quite quickly. The sailors had holds full of treasure, and they were already trying to figure their shares. Most of the seru, other than the Seru Moonstone, had discovered the pleasures of not having anything in particular that they had to do, and had taken to sunning themselves on the officers' afterdeck—the deck atop the officers' quarters.

And the children were happiest of all. Men aboard the ship scrubbed and cooked and cleaned and fetched. So the girls, slaves and penitents and acolytes alike, spent their time singing and learning to tie sailors' knots and climbing in the rigging and struggling to speak Trade.

They had retaken their names, those who remembered them. Slave and Penitent and Acolyte and Sera became Margit and Toshee and Bodeshooka, Iaena and Aanryn and Saatget and Avyn.

I kept Hawkspar because I had nothing else, and could think of nothing sadder than to give myself some pretend name and act like it was mine. And Hawkspar had a power to it that I would, one day, need. While I was Oracle

Hawkspar, I was as mighty as any emperor, my word as much honored as the words of many gods.

But I'd had a name once. I dreamed of somehow getting that one back. Unless I did, I would live and die Hawkspar.

I had much to do that day. Sighing and reliving the previous night, either its good parts or its bad ones, would not get my work done. I left the passenger commons and walked into the crew commons. Theirs was a larger space than ours by far, filled with raised-edge tables and benches, a warm stove, men off their watch sitting and talking, children running.

I found the door to the temple, and found Tuua, the keeper, moving about replacing books on shelves.

"Hello," he said. "You would be . . . one of the seru?"

"The Oracle," I told him. "Hawkspar."

"You're the one, then, who called us out on this voyage—the one who has so fascinated Aaran." I heard faint laughter in his voice. "I'm Keeper Tuuanir av Savissha dryn Nakri. But everyone calls me Tuua."

My name would have once been something like that. Long.

"Tuua," I repeated. "Your cousin suggested I come to speak with you."

"Did he?" Tuua turned toward me, and with a gesture, indicated a bench on one side of a table. He took the bench on the other side, and we both sat.

"I have a . . . a desperate mission," I told him. "I am searching for a hidden war, and to find it, I need the last fifty years of Tonk history. I need to be able to narrow down the specific threads of time that will show me the danger—my predecessor found it, but there was no way for her to pass her information on to me. The flow of time into the future does not offer landmarks or tolerate markers."

"Fifty years? Aiee—which Tonk would you know about?"

"All of them," I said.

"*All* of them! Woman, there are twenty-three clans of Tonk alone, though three of them have drifted beyond our ken."

Aaran had thought the same thing—had said that my clan was one of the Drifted.

I held up the palm of my left hand, and heard Tuua's breath whistle out. "Eskuu. By Ethebet, Eskuu—breeders and keepers of the lost fedderhorses."

"Horses again," I said. "What is it about those horses?" I held up a hand to stop him before he told me, though. The Tonk seemed mad about horses; I remembered them, but I had not been around horses for most of my life, so I did not understand the obsession.

And I had my mission.

"I don't want to know about the horses, actually. Not now. Just the history."

"That's just it. I can't give you a history. There is no one history. There are thousands—the twenty-three clans, some lost, the tribes that belong to those clans, the taak-dwellers and the herd-riders and the sailors all have their own histories. We share a god, a language, a faith, and a law. But we do not share a history."

"Do you share an enemy?"

Tuua laughed. "We share the grand ability to *make* enemies." He drummed his fingers on the table. "The Tonk of Hyre were plagued for three hundred years by the Eastils. They allied with the Eastils when the Feegash overran them both. When they'd ridded Hyre of Feegash, the Sinalis began raiding the shorelines with their slavers. The Tand Tonks battle the Northmen, and on their east coast, the Valgards. Tonks in Greton were exiled some few years ago by the Gretons; Tonks in Velobrina are constantly fighting the inroads of the Allied Velobrines into their southern territories, and the Waanduun barbarians to the north. And in Franica, pick the Tonk enemies from the Freeboardmen, the Balchose, and the Sanours. I do not think there is a place in the world where the Tonk reside in peace. But that is the way of the world. It is the same for all peoples in all places."

I sighed. What he had told me would help me not at all.

"You'd be better to ask who are the friends of the Tonk," he said.

"Who *are* the friends of the Tonk?" I asked him.

"Reliably? Only the Tonk."

I considered that. "In all the history that you know, have the Tonk been without allies?" I asked him.

"No. The last . . . hundred years or so . . . those have been hard years everywhere the Tonk live. I cannot point to a reason; there is no one reason. Different problems arise in different places, and . . ." I saw his shoulders rise and fall. "In earlier years, the Tonk had many allies, but for one reason or many, they fell away. Things change. In the future, no doubt, we'll have allies in plenty again."

I thanked him, and rose, and went on my way, wondering at the coincidence that all the Tonks he knew of were warring with neighbors or suffering some outsider incursions at that point.

He thought all peoples suffered the same problems, but as I tested that statement, I found it false. The Sinali, for example, had been allies with the

Bhekians for time out of history. They had good relationships with various nations in Franica, too, and with some of the kingdoms in the Fallen Suns. Some of the kingdoms within the Fallen Suns, for that matter, had lived in undisturbed peace for remarkably long times.

That all the Tonks in all their scattered homes found themselves beset by different enemies at the same time smelled, to me, of deception and conspiracy. Somewhere.

21

Aaran

Aaran went about his work in a fog of doubt and misery.

He'd gone up to Hawkspar twice to talk to her. To ask her why she'd left his bed, to offer apology for his behavior if, like so many women, she was having morning-after thoughts.

She'd held him, and he'd kissed her. And then she'd backed away. She excused herself from her presence the first time claiming a need to check on the little girls in her care. The second time, she'd said the flow of time was much in her mind. She'd been distracted. Worried.

He should not have been bothered. He already knew that she would be a temporary part of his life—that he would take her to Hyre and leave here there with the rest of the rescued captives, and likely never see her again.

He should have been fine with that.

He'd sworn his life to the rescue of Aashka over the dead bodies of his mother and father, over the burned campground where they had been summering with the flocks and his only sibling. He'd sworn in his own blood, to Tuua, that he would not rest until he found Aashka or he died in the attempt.

So he had never permitted himself to consider permanence. A woman he might keep.

Love.

It was not for him. He'd made his peace with that. He took his comfort expediently. He accepted the limitations of his life, because those limitations came tight-bound to the goal that gave him purpose.

And yet every time he heard Hawkspar's voice something inside of him shivered.

When he'd touched her, he could see himself wanting to touch only her.

"Captain? We're seeing gulls ahead."

He had not yet questioned Hawkspar about what lay in the southmost islands of the Fallen Suns.

She had been aware of the layout of the islands, of which kingdoms or tribes were most likely to be found in the areas they passed through. He'd discovered this, and had meant to put her knowledge of the area to good use—and then other things had distracted him.

He turned to Potyr, who had been whittling at his side, and said, "Please ask Oracle Hawkspar to come to the foredeck lookout, will you?"

Potyr nodded, and turned and raced down the companionways and vanished into the depths of the ship.

Aaran didn't turn around moments later, when he heard her footsteps behind him. He pretended he didn't know she was there.

"You sent for me?"

He turned, schooling his expression to calm, so that he would not betray his irrational delight in seeing her, and then keeping it there even when he remembered that she could not, by her own admission, make out facial expressions. "I had meant to ask your assistance earlier. We're soon to pass into the south islands of the Fallen Suns. We have a sailing chart of questionable usefulness, no old logs or records to consult, and only rumors of the vaguest sort on what we may find there. I'd hoped you would know about the people in this area."

She stood there for a moment, resting a hand on the back rail of the deck, bracing as the ship rocked and plunged through a moderate but worsening chop. "I know the history of this area, up until fairly recently. We were instructed in the customs and religions and politics. I cannot promise you that what I know is current, however."

"Anything you can offer me will be more than I already have," he said, and saw the corners of her mouth quirk into a tiny smile, swiftly gone.

"Of course. Bring your chart, and something I can write with, and I will do what I can to assist us all through this place." She paused, and lifted her face toward the sea, and breathed in deeply. "I don't smell land. Nor do I see it."

"We're not that close. The lookout noted sea birds. We have another day's sailing, I think, until we pass into the islands."

And still she was standing there, face lifted to the sea, and something about the intensity of her expression and the way she stood unnerved him. "Not another day, though, before you reach the Iage."

"The Iage?"

A thoughtful frown. "Master boatmen. We dealt with them from time to time. They sought out the Eyes of War—they are much taken with expanding their domain. And, too, they brought gifts for the Eyes of Discovery, Tigereye, always wanting her to find them new ways to kill their enemies. They are clever, dedicated warriors, and unlikely to be gentle with any who try to sail their waters without paying tribute." She turned her face to him at last, and said, "You're going to need a negotiator."

"I'm a fine negotiator," he told her. "And that is a duty the captain bears."

Her body tensed. "No, Aaran. Captain. No."

"You dismiss me so? Why would I not be negotiating?"

"You don't speak Iage, do you? Have you skills the Iage might choose to employ in exchange for free passage?"

"I don't speak Iage, but I have skills. I'm a Hagedwar masterclass tracker, one of only a handful in the world. I found you, after all. It's no simple thing. How long before I found you had you been calling for someone to come save you?"

She said nothing for so long he thought she hadn't heard him. And then she whispered, "At least twelve years. Maybe thirteen."

He'd been all ready to flaunt his prowess for finding something no one had found for a month, or six months, or perhaps a year. But he tried to make sense of no one crossing the powerful spell she'd cast for twelve or thirteen years, in an area he knew lay close to the Southern Trade Current. "Are you sure?"

"Every day from the first day my first instructor taught us how to bind and cast a spell, every single day, without fail, from that first day until the day you came, save only those days when I was too hurt or too sick to shower, I sent out my prayer for help. I bound it with my sweat and my blood and my tears. It became my one link to my people." She hung her head. "Would that I had bound my name with the prayer, that I might have remembered it."

"Your name."

She nodded. "Had I said it every day, even just in my mind, I would have it yet."

He felt a burning at the back of his throat, and a suspicious tightness in his breathing. His eyes itched and he rubbed at them surreptitiously with the backs of his hands, grateful that she could not actually see him. What manner of man heard a woman tell of a simple daily prayer and found himself at the edge of tears?

Not a warrior, for certain—a veteran tracker of slavers and hunter of the enemies of the Tonk. Not a man who had heard every pathetic story ever told, and had one of his own just as bitter.

"Well," he said, and his voice cracked. He took a deep breath, and started again. "Well, it's well for you, then, that I came."

But . . . twelve or thirteen years? How many trackers had traced that plea in that time? Had found where it went and had not followed, out of fear or out of lack of interest? How many times over could she and these with her have been rescued? How many times over could the women who knew of the plot to destroy the Tonk have been discovered, brought out into public, and their knowledge made known? How many Tonk lives—everywhere— might have been saved?

He had asked among the women of the right age if any of them were named Aashka. He had looked for the tattoo on the left palm that was like his own, for the Aayn and the Eyn tattooed between shoulder blades.

Aashka was not among the women he had rescued from the Citadel. And no one knew if she had even been among them, because they had never dared whisper their true names one to the other. If Aashka had passed through the Citadel of the Ossalenes, none had marked her passage. None would remember her, none could point him to the place where her body lay, or to the slaver who had bought her. For that matter, she could be there still. And he would never know.

But Hawkspar said he would find Aashka. He wished he could have faith.

"You're sad," Hawkspar said, and he jumped.

"I don't get sad," he said. "I have too many things yet undone to allow myself that luxury."

She held her silence for a long time. When thinking they were done speaking, he turned to leave, she said, "I will negotiate with the Iage for you. I will offer both my own services as oracle and yours as master-tracker to them in exchange for the lives of those aboard this ship, and unmolested passage." She stood there with her head down, with her hands tucked into her complex robes, prim and distant and cool as some Mindan goodwife, and he thought of her nearly undressed on his bed, wanton and eager.

"I would be most grateful for your assistance, Oracle Hawkspar," he said, and heard his voice tremble with longing.

She turned without another word and walked toward her quarters.

He watched her leave, wishing he had touched her while she stood there. No. He didn't love her.

Hawkspar

The Iage came to us in moonless dark, silent as ghosts in the wind, sliding in their longboats up to the ship, grappling their way over the sides, landing on our darkened deck in bare feet.

They had thought to come unnoticed, to slay us as we slept, to take the ship and all on it as their spoils.

We met them with the formal ceremony of the Iage negotiators—with a table and benches on the deck, with the ship's officers and me gathered around it, with tea and ale and food spread on the table, because to negotiate with the Iage, first the would-be negotiators had to provide a banquet. The cook and his assistants had labored in the galley for the better part of two bells, getting everything right. I told them which foods could be included in the treat, and which could not. Thus, pork and fowl were present, and smoked and dried and pickled fish, but beef and cheese forbidden. Ale made without grapes they could serve, but any fruit of the grape was hidden well away. We offered breads both leavened and unleavened, and beans spiced to ferocious hotness—a specialty of the cook's and a favorite of Aaran's, he assured me.

The beans were a hidden bit of tactical superiority. I had thought I'd die eating them—I'd mistaken them for food when in fact they were clearly the invention of some vile demon. Yet the captain and his men ingested them without a whimper.

This they could use against the Iage. Beans were a much favored Iage food, and the Iage were of the belief that men proved their manhood by tests of courage and strength and the endurance of pain. I thought the beans would bring them to their knees faster than bouts of knife-wrestling on the afterdeck.

The captain rose as the ruffians climbed over the rails, and one of the captain's runners lit the lamps at table, revealing the fine feast that we had set for them.

The captain bowed, and I bowed. I said, "I, the Oracle Hawkspar, Eyes of War, late of the Citadel of the Ossalenes, greet you. My companion, Ship

Captain and Hagedwar Master-Tracker Aaran Donin av Savissha dryn Tragyn, offers you welcome aboard his ship."

They stood there, stripped to the waists and with their knives clamped in their teeth, surrounded by armed men with swords held at attention and by Seru Obsidian dressed all in black, and presented with a very attractive banquet spread, and they assessed the situation quickly. They put their knives point-first into the captain's beautifully scrubbed deck—I could feel him stiffen at my side as the blades thunked point down into the wood—and they bowed.

Their leader stepped forward. "We had not known such as yourself traveled these waters, Oracle," he said. He bowed deeply. "We have thought often of the Eyes of War; we would never have presented ourselves thus had we known you graced this ship."

I translated for the captain, then said, "I did not choose to make my passing through these waters a public matter. A war awaits me that I long to reach, and I have little time to tarry, no matter how fine the gifts offered."

I made a point of mentioning fine gifts. The Iage were used to paying quite well for their military information. Passage through their waters would be a small, almost disrespectful gift, compared to the hundred slaves they once gave the Citadel, or the trunks of gold and jewels. We'd take it, of course. But I did want to place them on a less-than-firm footing before negotiations started.

We sat at table. Rather, I sat first, then the leader of the Iage sat, then Aaran sat, then the Iage second sat. Everyone else stood around with weapons in hand, pretending that this was a social event instead of interrupted slaughter. It was the sort of meal that would give most people indigestion. And I knew the captain's pepper-devil beans were waiting.

The captain's kor wogan, Ermyk av Beyrkyn, was dressed as a cook, though beneath those clothes he'd hidden enough weapons to take on the Iage single-handed. He served us. We first received small bowls of pig's-foot jelly sweetened with fruit. Following that, eel soup and leeks, which I quite enjoyed. The cook had added bitters to the broth, and chervil, and I found it quite heartening. Following that, a baked sailfish stuffed with crab meat and seasoned with more of the cook's spices. Something about them stirred memories deep inside me. I could not say for certain that I remembered the food, but it *seemed* familiar.

Then a bread with oil and garlic and salt, baked to crispness. And then the beans.

I had been given different beans, a kindness by the cook. He'd taken sympathy on the blisters on the roof of my mouth and assured me that he knew how to make beans that were not a weapon. And I had a bowl of those. I bit into them, and I swear, they were near as deadly as the beans I'd had three days before that had made me weep.

But no man of the Iage would feel himself winning face if a woman—even an Oracle of the Eyes—were too weak to eat such mighty food.

I sipped my tea and wished for more of the bread, which would have eased the pain somewhat, and vowed at my earliest opportunity to have a word with the cook about what was and what was not a lethal amount of hot pepper.

Meanwhile, however, the captain had started digging into his enormous bowl of beans like he had never seen food before. And the Iage chief and his second attacked theirs with equal enthusiasm. For about three bites.

Then the pain caught up with them, and first the chief and then his second put down their dippers. They sat with their faces turned toward the captain, watching him eating. One mopped at his eyes with his napkin. The other drank all his tea in a gulp, and handed his mug to Aaran's second for a refill.

"You are not eating your beans," the Iage chief said to me, his voice accusing.

"I am but a woman," I said, "and this dish is man food. I am not strong enough to eat it." It seems to me that if the enemy who has come to kill you suddenly hands you his knife, you should stick it into his ribs at the earliest opportunity, and then twist it a bit. So I did.

"Man food?"

I said, "Oh, for certain, good Chief. This is a courage food of the Tonk—a warrior's meal."

Aaran asked me what they were saying, and I translated. He nodded, and said, "Tell them I'm ready for a second helping. And that we have made enough that he and all his men, and I and all my men, will have some of this fine warrior fare together." He clapped his hands, and the cook and his assistants stepped onto the deck with a huge cooking vat of the beans, ladles, and the square wooden bowls used aboard ship because they didn't slide on the square, raised-edge trays, and in truly bad seas, they almost never broke.

I translated quickly. The Iage chief and second turned their faces toward each other, and murmured an exchange that managed to sound panicked, but that was too quick and too low for me to catch.

Around me the rivers of time swirled and flowed, and I found myself at a splitting point in the river. "Careful now," I told the captain. "Neither you nor your men can mock them if they fail at this, or they will pull other weapons out of their clothes and we will all be dead before we can draw our next breath. They will eat, because they must. But—and I swear this—no man may dare laugh, nor any woman. Pride is a dangerous thing among the Iage."

The Iage chief stood and told his men, "Eat—each of you. Match them bite for bite, and don't shame me."

Iage warriors and the *Taag's* marines walked side by side, two by two, to the bean vat, and each received a bowl filled near to overflowing with the beans. They returned to their places around the deck, this time paired man to man.

And began eating the peppered beans.

I heard whimpers masked by coughing, little choking noises, wheezing, strangled muttering. And over all, the steady clicking of dippers against the wooden bowls. And then the clatter as each man put his wooden bowl on the deck and resumed his position.

"Tell him his men are most brave and rugged warriors," I said to Aaran. "And be quick about it."

Aaran raised a glass and said, "I salute the brave and valiant warriors of the Iage, with bread and ale."

While I translated, the cook and his assistant brought up the bread and ale, and began passing that around. And if the Iage ate the next course with unseemly quickness, or drank the ale in embarrassing quantities, none of our people made any sign of noticing.

The feast continued after that, with a roast swan taken by one of the sailors by bow and arrow as it flew overhead. And with steamed flounder. And an enormous smoked ham. And yams salted and sugared. Smoked conies by the brace. A thick dessert soup of chilled jellied cranberries and fresh peaches liberated from the Citadel stores.

By the end of it, the Iage were sitting around the deck, too full to move. Which had been the plan all along.

Our marines sat, too, but they had received much smaller portions than the Iage, so while they'd been instructed to act as the Iage acted, they were nowhere near as close to being incapacitated.

It was, all in all, a fine and effective feast. And since we had not been included on the groaning board, I had to consider the first part of our encounter a success.

The second part would be up to the captain and me.

The Iage chief leaned his elbows on the table and sighed hugely. "I and my men thank you for your hospitality, which was both grand and unanticipated."

I passed this on to the captain.

"You are our welcome and honored guests," the captain said, "with whom we would trade favor for favor."

I translated that, too. The captain and crew were being careful to say only what the Iage could hear—it's always risky dealing with those who trade widely, because they have a nasty habit of picking up languages you wouldn't expect them to know. And of demonstrating their knowledge of a language only after something unforgivably insulting has been said in it.

The Iage were not as circumspect, however. One of the chief's men sitting outside the circle said to another of them, "As well they fed us. This lot looks too tough and stringy and old to make good eating."

I did pass that on to the captain. His face snapped toward me, and in Tonk, not Trade, he said, "They were going to *eat* us?"

"I thought I'd mentioned that," I said.

"They're cannibals? I thought the *west* islanders were cannibals."

"Some of them are. And some of the south islanders are as well."

The chief said, "He has questions about his guests?" Which told me that the chief had at least a rudimentary knowledge of Tonk.

"One of your men noted how unappetizing our ship's crew would have been."

"If your captain is offended by this, I will—myself—kill the man who spoke, and your ship's very fine cook can prepare him."

"I think, rather," I said, "that the captain is pleased his men are too tough to make good meals. It is the way of Tonk warriors, and that is, to them, a compliment and not an insult."

"Ah." The chief smiled broadly, and I passed this exchange on to the captain, who laughed.

Yes, we were all fine friends around that table.

In most cases, the next order of business would be the challenges, to ensure that the Iage dealt with real men and not weaklings unworthy of their time. I waited, knowing the chief could require a challenge if he so chose. If he did choose, I'd told Aaran that he wanted to suggest an eating contest— the *hot* peppered beans. He had assured me, in fact, that the beans could be made even hotter than those that would be served at the banquet. I wondered what manner of men would seek out such food.

But apparently the chief had considered the beans served at table to be enough of a warning about the men he dealt with.

"So—what favor would you trade for, that you have treated us so kindly?"

he asked, skipping the challenge phase entirely. I had been able to see that as one possible outcome, and I was pleased.

"Safe passage south," the captain told him. "Escorted by your men." We had discussed this beforehand, he and I, and I'd convinced him that this was the best solution, though he didn't like it. Aaran wanted to travel through alone, because the *Taag* would sail so much faster unaccompanied by rowed longboats. However, the Iage already had their treaties and through-ways worked out with the competing powers in the area, and no matter how talented a tracker Aaran might have been, he could not track through lines of political infighting.

"Safe passage. And an escort. For that," the Iage chief said in a thoughtful voice, "we shall need a powerful future from the Oracle Hawkspar, Eyes of War."

I waited, pretending to consider the offer. First, the talents of the oracles were never priced lightly. A true view of the future is no small thing. Nor could I be seen as eager to accept this offer as if it favored our side. An escort through the southern islands was not the equivalent of a hundred slaves, and the Iage knew it, and so did I. Not being eaten by the Iage was worth considerably more than a hundred slaves, but I could not suggest that I considered that a factor, and the chief, having just been well fed by our crew, could not suggest it either.

It still *was* a factor, of course. Though treated well, the Iage were entirely capable of finding an unintentional infraction against their complicated religion or mores as a reason to attack and devour those on board the ship if it suited their goals; they'd made an art of finding excuses for breaking their treaties with their neighbors in the past. If they knew we had a shipload of young girls and women in the hold belowdecks, they would consider that a wondrous excuse. Iage men kept harems, and were not picky about how they got them. For this reason as much as for their dinner habits, their neighbors bore them no affection.

All penitents were taught the story of the Iage. And the Kee, and the D'gadigi, and the Mfar, and every other culture the Order had dealt with since men first found their way to the women with the Eyes, in search of a clear path to their future.

I knew only too well with whom I dealt.

I knew, too, that the Iage chieftain had to believe he got the better of the deal. If for a moment he thought that we had come out ahead, we would discover that we had committed some taboo, and would be overrun by thousands of Iage.

So I made the most of my reluctance to part with such a powerful thing as the reading of the time rivers.

"Have you slaves to add into this bargain?" I asked him. "Gold or jewels? Silks or laces? I would not think to ask for a hundred slaves or their equal, of course, for your escort though these dangerous waters is no small thing. Yet and all, charting your path through the troubled river of time is no small thing, either."

He bowed to me. This was familiar territory for him, if not for me, and he was much more familiar than I with the many ins and outs of negotiation. "I had thought," he told me, "an escort of five hundred men for the days it will take you to traverse these waters to the Great Deep would be an equal to the exchange of goods for your path."

Which it would. I did not like the sound of this, though. Five hundred men in escort was far too many. It was a war party. If we traveled with a war party, one of two things would happen. One, we would find ourselves in the midst of a war with some local tribe the Iage wanted to overrun—in which we would be forced to engage ourselves on the side of the Iage—and we did not wish to do that. Or two, the Iage would, citing some breach of taboo, use their massive superiority in numbers to overrun us in the middle of the night watch, and that would not end well.

I sat there for a moment, formulating my words carefully as I prepared to pass this pending disaster on to the captain. "They have offered us an escort of five hundred men," I said at last. "A great honor."

Aaran considered that for only the briefest of instants. "Tell them I am honored beyond all honor by their proposal, but we could not hope to repay such a debt. I grieve at our poverty, and ask for a simple guide of a dozen men, asking that the chief forgive our lack of success on this voyage, and understand, too, that I cannot allow a woman to pay my debt for me."

He was clever, was Aaran. I would never have considered the merewoman angle.

I passed this on to the chief, and he sat there for a moment in nonplussed silence.

"The Oracle is not your master?" he asked at last.

"I am a passenger only, traveling via this ship to a war of immense size, where I will offer my guidance. I . . . paid a fare to travel thus."

"In truth? It must be some magnificent war you seek. I have never known the Eyes to leave their Citadel."

"It is a war that could consume the world," I said. And that was truth, if I'd understood my predecessor.

Again I passed on our conversation to Aaran, and he said, "Such deals as you make with him will be only for your safe passage. We will pay as we can for his small escort."

The chief was surprisingly understanding. "Very well, then. For your safe passage, O Oracle, a short look into the waters you alone can see, and the answer to this question. How do we conquer the Ekadites in three days? And for the captain . . . I do not understand what he has to offer of value equal to our guides."

"Tell him you'll lay out the future for him, and I'll draw him a map of the paths he must take to arrive there safely."

And the chief found this idea intriguing, and after a quick demonstration of Aaran's power, conceded that this was a deal worth a dozen men and one boat for a handful of days. And my safe passage, of course.

I slipped into the twisting churning waters of time. We were in a bad place—in the waters of a physical river, I would have called it a rapids. I should have been watching all along, for not only could I see a dozen different ways in which the chief would attempt to betray us, but I also saw that someone onboard the ship—one of our own people—had betrayed us already.

I tried to see how. I fought for it, looking for the link between a treachery that sought us at that moment and the betrayer who had sold us, and I struggled to lay out the chief's planned betrayals in such a way that he would be shamed . . . but not too shamed . . . and would honor both the word and the spirit of our agreement.

The hideous thing about being in a rapids is that if you lose your footing, you find yourself swept into the water and banged against rocks along the way. It works the same when fighting the waters of time.

The pain grew hideous; I was reading too many things at once, digging deeper than I had a capacity for, seeing too much, feeling too much. Blood and death and lies and corruption, old plots and new plots and a thin pale thread of faith and honor that hung above me like a rope, if I could just grab it before I drowned.

I reached. Clung. Became aware that I was whimpering and clutching my head and my eyes.

I pointed at the chief. Pointing is a grave insult to the Iage, unless of course you're an oracle. "You plan to have your five hundred men follow us. Use us to make your war against the Ekadites. You plan to claim that we have eaten of the cow and the caribou in your presence, so that you can claim bounty on this ship. You plan to plunder whatever treasure we might have aboard, and sell the ship to your allies. And you were alerted to the possibility of our coming by your allies, some of whom are hidden away on this ship, under the guise of sailors. You never intended to honor your agreement."

The Iage chief stood and shouted, "Now!" and over the sides of the ship swarmed men who had crept up on us while the Iage sat in their feast-bloated stupor, and we sat thinking we had gotten the better of them.

Our marines were quick, and my Obsidians even quicker. *They* had not eaten at all, and, hungry, were sharp and hard. It all became a blur. I grabbed a knife. My head throbbed, and I wanted to do the trick again where I stopped my place in the waters of time, then moved through it. But I could not. I could barely stand.

The chief leapt across the table and grabbed me, but Aaran moved faster than I could trust my senses to believe, and I felt the gout of the Iage's hot blood on my skin.

The bell on the ship rang like doom itself, and the deck flooded with every able-bodied sailor, and with the Onyxes and the fight-trained acolytes as well. Blades clanged, men screamed, and I stood in the center of it all, in the way, unable to do anything of value, furious at myself for being so weak that I had not been able to follow the river of time to this moment *before* we found ourselves in it.

I was useless. Worthless. I had done nothing but set us up for the betrayal the Iage had planned all along. The captain would have done better without all my knowledge and advice. And I thought I was going to prove of some use to the Tonk? That I had any place among them?

I was a fool.

And the next thing I knew, I was a fool grabbed by a couple of the captain's marines and dragged toward Aaran's cabin through the thick of the fighting. "Captain's orders," one told me. The second jumped into the captain's cabin with his blade swinging, and got two of the Iage hiding there in one arcing slash. They checked the many hiding places, determined that the quarters were safe, and bade me lock myself in, while they would stand guard outside.

I could hear the fighting, muffled but still horrible. I could feel time pushing at the backs of my Eyes. Unbidden, images spilled over me of my people taken back into slavery, of the men who had risked their lives to save us dead—horribly murdered—of myself a captive and concubine of the Iage.

I fought the pain. It was pushing me to my knees, but away from the fighting I could slow down everything that was pouring into me and washing over me. I began to understand why oracles would only meet with one man, and would do it away from everyone else in a stone-walled room. Distance mattered. Silence mattered. Being able to feel water from one river, instead of something that felt like an onrushing sea tipped out of its bed, mattered most of all.

The pain did not recede. But I did find an eddy in the waters of time where I could stand still. And where I thought I might be able to stop the waters. I did not know how long I would be able to hold them, but I knew that if I did not do something, the main channel of the future I read would hold, and we would lose everything that mattered to us.

My sacrifice. My choice.

I made time slow. Slower, slower, and then the waters stopped, and the cold descended around me again, and the air grew so thick it seemed un-breathable, and I waded through it to the door, unlocked it, moved with certainty to the few Iage I could identify as key warriors. Men without whom the Iage would be leaderless. I remembered my lessons of my first fight in time held still, and did not waste all my energy on one man. I slashed through the neck of the first with his own sword which I had ripped from his hand, and ripped open the belly of the second, and rammed the blade into the belly of the third. Two remained, but I could not reach them. I fell to my knees, and the weight of the waters washed over me and the pain of the rocks upon which I was battered smashed the world into silence.

Aaran

Aaran found Hawkspar lying with the dead and near dead, nowhere near his quarters, and with a bloody sword in her hand. The marines he'd set to guard her swore that they'd seen her safely locked into his quarters and that she had not come out.

But she had a way of ending up where she was not supposed to be, a fact he found both frustrating and unnerving.

She was hurt. She'd been stepped on more than once, and he could see that one of her arms was broken, and could hear a grinding in her ribs when he picked her up. She was covered in blood, too, and some of it was her own. He carried her into his quarters and called two of her terrifying white-eyed healers in, demanding that they attend to her before they saw to anyone else.

He assured himself that this was simply so that he could be sure that the Tonk would have their seer.

But it wasn't that, nor was he fool enough to try to deceive himself for long.

He wanted more from her than the visions of her stone eyes.

He wouldn't take it. He couldn't have it. But he at last was willing to admit that *she* was what he wanted, what he hungered for. He did not know why. He could not begin to guess what it was about her that so deeply touched his soul. He did not look forward to discovering how he would sail away from Hyre without her, in search of his missing sister, and spend the rest of his life with an unrequited love that he had to that point managed to avoid.

He was a fool.

"She's badly injured," one of the Moonstones, who mostly struggled to speak Tonk, told him. "There are tears in her . . . I don't know what you call. Inside. She bleed inside."

He spoke slowly. "Save her. Do whatever you have to do. I'll give you whatever you need. But you can't let her die."

"The gods and goddesses decide that," another of the Moonstones said. "We no make promises about what we can't keep."

The Obsidian Redbird stood at the head of her bed, unmoving. She did not acknowledge his presence. She simply stood there, hands on the pommels of her blades, and he had the feeling that she watched everything, both inside and outside his cabin.

He left Hawkspar with the Moonstones and Redbird, and set marines at the door again. Two of them, with strict instructions that none save those in the room with her at that moment be permitted to enter.

Cleanup was a little slice of hell. He and his sailors and marines and officers tossed the Iage corpses over the side without a second thought. But his own people—and Hawkspar's—those bodies could not be dealt with in such a cavalier fashion.

And there were a lot of them.

He'd started the voyage with nearly a full complement. He'd lost a third of his officers—including Ino Tortaaknavyn, his second daan—near half his sailors, a third of his marines, and both cooks and all four assistants. The Iage had gotten into the galley and slaughtered them all.

Besik, his apprentice windman, was missing and had to be presumed dead—his loss would hurt the *Taag* more than Aaran dared consider. Faryn Wo, the remaining windman, was hurt, but Aaran thought he would recover under the Moonstones' care.

But nine Obsidians lay dead upon his deck, and three Moonstones. Four Rosestones, who with the dead Obsidians, had given their lives to protect the rescued girls. They had nearly succeeded.

The Iage had managed to get into one of the passenger cabins, and had slaughtered a dozen of the younger girls before the Obsidians and Rosestones broke down the door. Still, just over a hundred survived.

That was something.

But the bodies of twenty-five dead women and children lay on his deck, and with them, the bodies of forty-one crewmen and officers.

Some of the survivors were badly injured. Hawkspar bore so many wounds the Moonstones couldn't even tell him everything that was wrong with her. She wouldn't wake up. He feared she would die.

And he and his shorthanded crew now had to get though the islands without the assistance of the Iage. They weren't crippled. But they were badly hurt.

Tuua, wounded but still functioning, limped from body to body and gave the dead grace. The sailors who could scrubbed the blood from the decks, and the marines worked alongside them.

Several of the older girls had taken over kitchen duties, noting as they did that they, too, knew their way around kitchen and pantry. They'd been inventorying stores when he checked in on them, and putting together a simple first meal for those who labored above.

Aaran went from group to group, checking. Alwyn, his healer, still lived, thank Jostfar, and the surviving Seru Moonstone were unhurt. They had their hands full with the wounded. The *Taag* was not, Aaran knew, at the end of its dead. Some of those still living barely clung to life, and before the sun set again, they would be joining their comrades in the sea.

The survivors struggled on in varying states of the same shock and grief that he felt. They were worried for friends, devastated by the deaths of friends. No one had been spared loss.

Tuua had finished the words for the dead; Aaran found him in the temple, sitting with Eban, who was weeping.

Aaran raised a brow, and Tuua patted Eban on the shoulder and said, "I'll be right back."

"What's wrong?" Aaran asked.

"One of the Seru Rosestones had taken him in and mothered him; evidently along with having a dreadful father, the boy had no mother. And that sera was killed in the fighting."

"We lost a lot of them," Aaran said, and he was thinking of Hawkspar, in his cabin with two Moonstones working frantically to save her, and with Redbird hovering like a mother bear over her hurt cub.

Tuua said, "You bear a deep grief. What are you not telling me?"

"I've lost officers who were friends. I've lost crew who were fine men. There are dead women and children on my deck."

"And a hurt woman occupying the bed in your cabin."

Aaran paused. "Well . . . yes. I fear for the Oracle Hawkspar's life, as well."

Tuua said, "The dead are gone beyond our reach. We can mourn them, but we cannot help them. The injured we are doing with what we can. I am hurt, true, but the Moonstones are extraordinary healers, and Alwyn is solid as well, and between them, you need not worry for me. After this, I'll be able to walk around on the deck with a few fine scars, so that I may go shirtless without shame, like the sailors and marines."

His mouth curved in the ghost of a smile. "But young Hawkspar . . . I thought the rumors about you and her might have had some truth in them."

Aaran turned his back on his cousin. "No truth. We've rescued her, she's a passenger, she thinks she can help us win a war we didn't even know we were fighting. I . . . admire her courage. And her tenacity."

"Right. Of course you do."

"I do."

"I've known you all your life, Aaran. I've seen you in your best times and your worst," Tuua said. "I know when you're telling me the truth—we're blood, after all. So, every time you look at her, your *admiration* shines in your face so that your expression becomes one of besotted idiocy. We all look like that when we're consumed with . . . *admiration.*"

"Don't mock me."

"I'm not blind. Nor a fool. If you want her, why not pursue her? Why not be honest about it?"

"You know why we sail."

Tuua said, "I've not forgotten. Your sister, our vow. The hope that we might yet find her alive."

"And I have never let myself fall in love. Nor have you."

"I've fallen in love a thousand times," Tuua said. "And broken my heart a thousand times less one."

Aaran turned to study him. "You're in love now?"

"Deeply. With a girl who was one of the penitents. Her name is Jarynan."

"And when we reach Hyre, you'll see her off on a dock somewhere, and never see her again while she goes on to find a husband and make a life for herself and have a house full of fat babies without you," Aaran said. "You can look at that future and live with it?"

"I don't know that I can," Tuua said. "And I'm not sure it's the future to which I'm willing to resign myself."

"You're going to stop looking for Aashka, then?"

"No."

"You're going to marry your Jarynan, and leave her alone to fend for herself for months or years at a time while you search the seas for Aashka?"

"Not that either, I don't think," Tuua said. And now he sounded uncertain. "She's Tonk. I'd thought to make her my assistant after this voyage, and sail with her."

"And we'd have a mutiny the same day. Or shall all the sailors and all the marines bring their wives, too?"

"I don't know," Tuua said. "I don't. But I think this time I don't want to have my heart broken."

Aaran turned to look at him. "She won me before she even met me, Tuua. Before I'd even seen her, I knew her voice, I knew her need, and I knew her courage. I didn't know her name, but she doesn't know it either— but without her name, I still knew enough to cross through hells and death for her."

He looked down at his hands, at the big, scarred knuckles, the calluses, the cuts and healing wounds. "I didn't do it to find Aashka, Tuua. I told myself I did, because that is why I've done everything I've done since the day we both became men. But what I told myself was a lie—even if it wasn't an intentional one. I did it to find *her*. And now that she's here, I want her even more. I want her, and I don't want to have my heart broken, either. What if she dies? What if she vanishes into the heart of Hyre, and doesn't wait for me while I complete my vow? This isn't what I wanted. Not ever. I didn't let myself fall in love, because I had my duty. And now I am in love, and I don't know how to live with that."

Hawkspar

I hovered in a hell I had made worse—I'd shoved the gate to Ossal's cage open wider with my failed use of the Eyes, and I had welcomed him closer to me. We struggled across his endless dark plain, with him touching me in ways I did not want to be touched, with me striking out at him in ways that had no effect. The woman in white did not save me.

I could not break his darkness, I could not escape his territory, until sharp pain at last reconnected me to my body. With the memory came my thoughts of the sea, the ship, Aaran . . . oh, Aaran . . .

. . . And shielding.

With the fury of a sea storm, with the brilliance of the sun, I brought my own blazing light into Ossal's darkness, and at last he fled.

Two Moonstones were leaning over me when I opened my eyes, and I heard one of them sigh with relief. "How are you?" she asked me.

I hurt. And not just my head, not just the Eyes. I hurt everywhere. I tried to move, but my legs wouldn't respond, and my arms wouldn't respond, and when I tried to breathe in to say something, the pain in my chest set me to coughing, and the coughing hurt so much I thought I might just die.

I managed, between coughs, to squeak out a faint, "What happened to me?"

"You fought."

I thought I recognized the voice of the Moonstone who spoke. "Seya?"

"Yes," she said. "You fell. And apparently many men stepped on you while they fought over the top of you. They broke more than a few of your bones."

"Why . . . can't I move?"

"Your arms and legs are weighted and restrained while we mend the bones. Your head we've pinned on a hard board between pillows, for your spine has breaks in it, too. And your ribs . . . well, we couldn't do much to help you with the pain there, for you have to breathe."

"Not well, apparently," I said.

"Better than you were," Seya said. She was one of the few Moonstones who had taken back her name. Many, like me, had forgotten theirs. "You don't have little pink bubbles coming from your mouth every time you exhale. We thought you were too badly hurt to live," she added.

"I'm grateful for the pain," I told her, and let her form the wrong conclusion. "I'm quite happy still to be alive." And then I asked, "Has the captain been in?"

"He brought you here, and he's been by to check on you twice a bell. He's been in a foul mood."

I could imagine. I could imagine, in fact, that he was in a foul mood with me, since my failure to spot the treachery in those around us had led me to give him some very bad advice. We would have been far better off to have attacked the Iage while they were still in their little oar-powered longboats. Aaran had mentioned Greton fire as a fine weapon and one they had plenty of, and I had told him that the islands in these parts were full of Iage, and we were better off negotiating with the send-out party.

I had a lot to answer for.

And would clearly have the opportunity to do it, for Aaran slammed through the door right then, demanding, "Any improvement? Any?"

"I'm awake," I said. But that started another coughing spasm, and the sera had to give me water laced with something bitter, sipped through a reed, to soothe it.

"Out, all of you," he snarled, and the Seya and the other Moonstone, and even Redbird, whose hand I had felt on my shoulder the instant I woke, hurried out.

"I would have words with you," Aaran said.

"I'm so sorry," I told him. "This was all my fault. If you want to toss me into the sea, I'll completely understand. I've earned no better."

"I . . . what? You think I want to throw you overboard? I want no such thing."

I said, "Oh. But it was my bad advice, and my difficulty in navigating the time rivers, that led you to let them on board."

"I didn't come to talk to you about what happened. I came to talk to you about the future. About the two of us."

"Now?"

"If now is all we have, I will have said this, at least. I love you, Hawkspar. I don't know what to do about it, because I am bound by oath to find my sister, and life on the sea is no place for a woman. But I love you in spite of duty. And if you told me that to have your love, I would have to forsake duty . . ." His voice broke, and I could hear the anguish in his voice. ". . . Then I would break my vow, and be Tonk no more. If you demanded it."

He loved me. And I loved him. And because I loved him, I could not let him suffer as he was. "We both have our duties, Aaran. Yours is to find your sister, and make pay those who stole her away, and murdered your parents. Mine is to die stopping a war."

In his quarters, silence lay between us like an ocean. "Die?" he whispered at last.

"Yes. If I succeed in stopping those who seek to destroy the Tonk, I will die from the sacrifices I must make to do so. If I fail . . . well, it will be because I died before I could succeed." I felt his hand moving on my forehead. "I can see my own future. It has only two paths. One is short, the other shorter. There is no third way."

"I do not accept an immutable future." He was silent a long time. "So many dead. We lost so many, and you seem so weak. Seeing you like this . . ." He tensed. "How did the Iage find us, Hawkspar? They came in force when we were still far from land, and they came not as a scouting party, but as a war party. That as many of us lived as did, I can only consider a miracle. So how came they to discover us?"

I did not know that question. I had not thought to ask it. "Bring the Moonstones back. I will search the past for your answer, but I want them here when I do, in case they have to revive me."

He went to the door—he did not have to go beyond it. They and Redbird stood just outside, talking with the marines who guarded it.

I didn't want to look—pushing the Eyes was going to add even more pain to the pain I already had. But delaying looking would mean that I would have to dig deeper into the past. The waters of time flowed away, and those who had caused so much death and destruction moved farther from our reach with every moment.

When the Moonstones were in place, I let the river of time flow around me, let myself slide into it. All the voices and pictures flashed around me, all the possibilities of the moment. But I did not want possibilities. I wanted facts. The past, and what had transpired there.

I waded upstream, where the river narrowed to a hard, fast current, a single powerful thread that pushed against me with all the weight of time itself. The past does not welcome intruding eyes. And I was pushing where I was not wanted.

But I pushed anyway, and with my efforts came the pain. I ignored it, looking for the moment when those aboard the *Taag* were betrayed, and the method by which that betrayal had been effected. I pushed, and pushed—and three days back, found what I sought, though it was not where I would have sought it, nor was it what I would have expected.

Three men huddled together in a deep hold in the *Taag,* hiding where they had no business being, doing what they had no business doing. They were in contact with someone far away, and I could not push that far. It was not the Iage . . . and yet somehow it was, for from what they did in the hold, the Iage came. Three men—if I reached hard and clung to them against the current that battered me, I could catch a few sharp images. "Hagedwar," I said, as foreign words formed in my mind. "Reform Mindan. Three traitors. Sailors all."

And then I lost my grip, and smashed downstream into the present, and enveloping fire.

Cool fingers held my head, and pressed against my closed eyelids. Voices murmured, and someone put a reed to my lips, and I sipped. Fire on the inside, in my mouth, down by throat, into my gut, and the hottest edges of the pain in my skull cooled. Just a little.

The voices took on shape. "Is it like that for them every time?" That was the captain.

"No. She's a very new oracle, and she hadn't any training from the previous Hawkspar before she inherited the Eyes. She's pushing herself too hard—pushing into time too deeply. With experience her pain will lessen. Will become, in most cases, bearable. Now, though . . ."

And the captain's voice again. "Can she do herself any permanent damage?"

"She can. She runs close to doing it, I think. Sometimes oracles fall into their time river and cannot find their way back. They live in the pain, and drown in it. They either go mad, screaming of spirits haunting them, or sometimes they simply die."

"Oh, Jostfar. I didn't know."

"*She* knows." Seya said. "If she looked for whatever it was you sought, it was because she thought it was important."

"It . . . was. Is. Though I can't believe what she said."

"The future is a tricky thing."

"I asked her about the past."

"That you can believe without question. The oracles are ever complaining about the many seductive wanderings of the present and the future. But the past, they say, is a hard, deep, single channel. If she found what you sought there, it is exactly as she says it is."

No one said anything.

My pain ebbed further, and I realized that the captain had given me more of that fire-drink of his. The Moonstones had done their best for me, too.

"I'm . . . better," I told them.

My voice was a pitiful croaking thing, but they all seemed glad enough to hear it.

"Is she safe?" Aaran said, not to me, but to them. "Is she well enough that you could leave us for a while?"

"We can dare a short absence," a Moonstone said. And I heard the door closing, and knew we were alone.

"You . . . do you remember what you told me?"

"Of course," I said. It was a whisper.

"You . . . said . . . *traitors.* Reform Mindans. Three of them."

"Yes. And the blue sphere with the . . . blocks in it. Triangles and squares."

"That's the Hagedwar. It's a . . . a sort of magical tool. But . . . *Mindan?*"

"Reform Mindan."

"But that's *Tonk,*" he said. He sounded hurt. Bewildered. As if what I was telling him was so near to impossible that he could not bring himself to even consider it. "You're suggesting we were betrayed to our enemies by . . . *Tonk.*"

"I'm not suggesting. The past is what it is."

I lay there, with the pain ebbing and flowing like the tides of an angry sea, and waiting for him to explain why the idea of Tonk traitors was so impossible. Everyone had traitors, didn't they?

"Tonk," he said, as if I hadn't heard him the first time.

And I realized that in not understanding his bewilderment, I had discovered the truth about myself I didn't want to admit. I knew a lot about the Tonk. But I had no idea what it meant to *be* Tonk.

"You say this as though it ought to mean something to me. As if I should understand. But I don't. Why should the traitors on your ship not be Tonk?"

"Because we are a people," he said. "We have stood together since the dawn of recorded history. Before that, even, when all we had were the rotes and the long sagas. We have been everything to each other. We would cross any ocean, fight any battle, to save our own from outsiders. Tonk, no matter where they might be, no matter what clan or what saint, are always Tonk."

It was, in a way, what my predecessor had been trying to tell me. She'd said I had family, and that was what Aaran was talking about, wasn't it? A family, spread over the world, with people who would take you in no matter whether they knew you or not, because you were theirs. I was, in his eyes, theirs. I bore a little mark on my hand and had in my memory a brief childhood with parents and siblings who had been Tonk, and in his eyes, that was enough. It made me Tonk. Family. Worth sailing through terrible dangers and risking his own life to save.

That he hoped to find his sister was not, at the moment, the issue. Many a man did not go looking across the world for a lost sister, but instead handed her up to fate. Cried, "She's gone, alas, alas," and then went back to his fields or his fishing or his herds.

Aaran was not such a man.

He was Tonk. In his eyes, all Tonk were like him.

I would do better not to let myself think on what sort of man he was. I wanted something that my duty to this family of mine—and his—would not let me have.

But he had come to rescue me. Because I was Tonk.

And the traitors were Tonk.

I told him, "I cannot say why they have done this thing, but three Reform Mindan sailors used the magic of . . . Hagedwar . . . to communicate with your enemies. To plan this betrayal."

"So they contacted the Iage? How could they have known I would come this way?"

"They didn't contact the Iage," I told him. "Someone else. I got no images. No faces, nothing clear. Only a word, and it from the men on this ship."

"The word?"

"Feegash," I said.

"No!" he shouted. "No Tonk, ever, would knowingly aid the Feegash."

He stood, pushing away from the berth with angry motions, and he began to pace a short line through his quarters. "Reform Mindan," he said after a while. "Three of them." He paced some more. *"Feegash."*

Hawkspar

I could have tried to follow all he did next, but I did not. I was exhausted. The things the seru were doing to my bones to get them to mend quickly were not only terribly painful, but they were also exhausting. So I slept. I had no idea how long, but the sound of the door to the captain's cabin banging open woke me.

"If I stood the men from the ship before you, could you tell me which three were traitors?" Aaran asked.

"I can. I'll know them when I see them again."

He brought six men before me, all shackled and guarded by marines. I would not have marked them as any different from the other sailors aboard the ship. They were big men, relatively young, healthy. I had passed them all in the time we had been aboard, going through the crew commons and sitting in the attable eating our daily meals. None of them had marked themselves as special in my memory before. But I had no difficulty seeing which of them had marked themselves with treachery, with Feegash, with Iage.

I could not point. It would have made things easier. Neither could I nod with my head. "First on the left, second on the left, and last at the far right," I said, and heard the marines gasp, and heard one whisper, "She *knew*."

"We'll try them," Aaran said. "The one who helps us most will live, the other two we'll hang. Chain them apart from each other, one on the top deck, one in the holding cell, and one on the working deck. Keep every other human being away from them. They're to have water. Nothing else."

He had the three innocent men released, and the marines took the three guilty men away. Aaran stayed behind.

"You had six of these Reform Mindans on board?" I asked him.

"No. Only three."

"Then why did you bring in six men?"

He sighed. "Because the men I brought were Tonk, and the men I ordered to bring them were Tonk. When we hang them, we'll be hanging Tonk men. Our own people, accused on the word of one who is Tonk . . . but who has not been raised Tonk." He walked over to the side of the bed, and pulled up a chair. Sat, rested his hand on my shoulder. He began to stroke my skin. He didn't seem aware that he was doing it.

I said, "You needed to prove to them that I had not falsely accused them."

"I had to prove to them that you could identify the three men you had told me about. Either the traitors will accuse each other, or they will go free."

I laughed a little. "You're still not certain of the value of what I saw."

"I am. But if I hang three Tonk men without evidence that anyone else can see, I'll have a mutiny on my hands. From what remains of my officers and the Tonk sailors and marines, in any case."

"Three? I thought you were going to hang two, and let the third live."

He didn't say anything for what seemed to me a very long time. Then he said, "This is how it will go. Each of these three backstabbing cowards will offer up some evidence in order to be the one who survives. Each will be told that one of the others gave us more. We will in this manner get everything that we can out of each of them. And each of them will demonstrate his unworthiness to live in what he says about the others; he will prove that he had a hand in the deaths of his comrades and his friends, his brothers and the innocents we had on board. All the men aboard the ship will know what each of the three has said and done."

"Yes. Of course."

"Each of the three will pay with his life."

I lay there considering that. "But that doesn't seem right to me. They were told one of them will live."

His voice was heavy as he said, "What is right? That I send these men to their deaths before I know everything they know? You say there is some secret plan to destroy the Tonk, and if ever there were a people who would hold such a plan, it would be the Feegash—evil, lying, cowardly bastards that they are. These three traitors are, if my suspicions are correct, enemy soldiers for the Feegash. If that is the case, they are the first such we've found, and every Tonk needs to know about them, and know everything they know. I could torture them—I might, if they are not willing to talk to save their own skins. But torture is hard on the men who must carry it out, and I'd rather not put my people through that."

I could not say that I had seen any evidence of fairness in the universe to this point. I'd watched children whipped to death, and fed to rats, and sold to slavers who would rent them as whores until they died.

But I had not thought the captain a man who would not keep his word, and it seemed to me that this put him, at least a little, into the company of those I had just escaped. Those I had refused to become.

"You're disappointed in me," he said, and I realized that he'd withdrawn his hand from my shoulder.

"It isn't my place to be disappointed," I told him. I was trying to find words that would let me say what I was thinking, and not make myself a fool in the process. "If you kill all three of them after saying you would kill only two, do you not . . . make yourself the same as they are?"

And he laughed out loud. "That's what you think? Three men betray their own people and cause the deaths of a third of my officers and near half of my crew. I see to it that the three men guilty of this horrific crime prove themselves guilty before I see them executed. Then I see them executed. And I am like them?"

Put that way, I seemed to have made myself a fool anyway.

"This is war," he told me. "War is never pretty, it is never kind. It is not won by the gentle or the thoughtful, or by those who would keep themselves above their enemy in spirit. It is won by those men and women who are willing to do what has to be done." He said, "You are the Eyes of War, you say."

"I am."

"Then what war have you seen where the kindest prevailed by being kind?"

I had seen the flashes of the wars that were and that would be tossed at me by the Eyes. And I'd read the histories in the knot-books, and had learned the oral histories.

"There are no such wars," I said at last. "There are only wars in which those who were stronger, or had better weapons, or who were better deceivers, overcame their enemies. Any kindnesses came after, when the conquerors had the choice to destroy their enemies and all that their enemies held dear, or to let them live. Mostly what came after was as horrible as the war itself."

He sat with his face turned toward me, restless. "You have charted the courses of other men's wars?"

"No," I said. "I'm too new for that. I had an opportunity, but the man who sought my advice was an evil man, and his enemy was more worthy. So I kept him in place awaiting my word until his chance to conquer his enemy had passed. Then I gave him very good advice. I told him to leave off his warring or he would lose."

Aaran leaned forward. "What happened?"

"He warred with his neighbor anyway, and he lost most of his army. The rest came after the Citadel, and this petty prince was busy attacking us when you arrived and rescued us."

"That was him?"

"That was him."

"So your experience in guiding the outcome of a war has been to prod a king to lose one."

"My experience has been to save a decent people from genocide at the hands of a vile monster."

His voice dropped so low that I could almost not hear it. "And if I execute all three of the men who caused the deaths of your people and mine, will you think me a vile monster, and seek to help my enemies?"

"No," I said. "Since my childhood, I have been able to feel the Tonk with me each sunrise and each sunset. I felt a bond with them that gave me hope, that kept me from despairing or giving up or accepting my fate. I called out for my people, even if I did not know who you were. And my people came. *You* came. I know you are no monster. I do not know the Feegash. You speak of them as if they are evil incarnate. But even if the Feegash were not wicked, but for some other reason sought the destruction of the Tonk, still . . . you are my people. My family. Should I help those who would destroy you?"

He leaned over and placed a kiss on my forehead. "You'll find your way through this. As will we. I cannot ask you to simply trust me when I tell you that those of our people who would assist the Feegash against us have earned death many times over. But when we have time, I'll tell you what the Feegash did to the Tonk, not so long ago. It may help you understand."

He left, and I lay in my pain and thought about war, and the Eyes of War, and what I was to be about.

24

Aaran

Aaran conscripted the stronger and more agile of Hawkspar's girls as help, to fill in for the missing crew. They were tough girls, used to hard, thankless labor and long hours, and they caught on quickly to the business of lines and sails and winds.

He felt strange seeing them scrambling up the rigging and onto the masts like boys. They'd gleefully disposed of the robes of their order for sailors' clothes, and had taken to the heights with a joy that he could well understand.

Freedom waited up there in the riggings, looking out at a world curved round the edges and spread before your feet like you were a god. The far horizons beckoned, and the scraps of land promised adventure. And these were girls who had been caged up the whole of their lives, and adventure sang its song to them as it did to men.

Counter to everything he had ever known about women, the girls complained less than his men. They weren't as strong, but they were twice as willing to take risks. He wondered about that. About their fearlessness that bordered on the edge of recklessness.

Hawkspar was up within days, and hobbling. The Seru Moonstone insisted that she would be completely sound a few days hence; their work was easily as good as anything his healer could have done.

The *Taag av Sookyn* was making its way north-northeast with the plan to turn due east as soon as they were well away from Iage territory. They'd had to backtrack a bit, but Hawkspar's information on the areas suggested that a relatively safe corridor lay not far out of reach. They might slip through it without running afoul of any locals. And outside of Fallen Suns, they could pick up the Trade Current and run south toward Greton. Then west again.

And home.

Hawkspar joined him in his cabin.

"You sent for me?"

"How are you feeling?"

She gave him that half smile he had come to recognize as wariness. "Better. I'm no longer tied to a bed, which has done wonders for my mood."

"I have a favor to ask of you," he told her. He'd debated asking her this, but he needed to have her on his side without doubts on her part or his. From what he'd been learning from the traitors, the Tonk were in more trouble than he'd ever guessed. She could be a weapon that could even the balance for them. She couldn't move the Tonk ahead—they'd long ago fallen behind in this war they hadn't even suspected. But to win more than her half-hearted acquiescence, she had to see what it was she was fighting for, and why she mattered.

"I'm going to do a questioning of each of the three traitors today. I want you to come with me and listen to what they say. You're to act as if you can tell when they're telling the truth."

To the wary half smile, she added raised eyebrows. "To some extent, I can."

"Truly?"

"If I submerge myself in the time river, I can see if what they're telling me lies within the channel of the past, or outside of it. I'm not sure if I'll be able to give you my judgment on all three men in one day—the pain from the Eyes might be too great for that."

"They all say much the same thing, varying in only small details. If you can verify the words of one, you will have come close to verifying the words of all."

She added, "It would be good, perhaps, if I heard their stories. I would like to . . . understand."

He took her to the holding cell, where the most talkative of the men was being held.

"We're going in to talk with Kerwyn," Aaran told the marine guarding the door.

The marine said, "I'll chain him, then. Wait here, please." When he came back out, he stepped aside, and Aaran led Hawkspar into the dank, foul-smelling cell. The man inside sat on one of the two benches, manacled—wrists and ankles—to the wall behind him.

"Have you decided?" Kerwyn asked Aaran as soon as he was through the door.

"I've brought the Eyes of War with me. Her Eyes can tell whether you're lying or not. You're to tell me everything you know, and she will judge the truth of it. She will then listen to the stories of the other two. And then I will decide who lives and who dies."

"But I've given you the best information, haven't I?"

"You have if it's all true," Aaran said. "So tell her what you told me, and watch your words. Today is not the day to lie."

The traitor swallowed hard and looked nervously from Aaran to Hawkspar. Aaran wondered how many lies he'd told in his previous confessions.

"I was brought into the plot against my will," Kerwyn started, and Hawkspar interrupted him right there.

"He's lying," she said.

Kerwyn's head whipped back and forth, and sweat beaded on his forehead.

"She can see your lies, you fool," Aaran snarled.

Kerwyn shuddered, and started again. "None of us were brought into the plot against our will." He paused, and when Hawkspar didn't say anything, his shoulders slumped and he continued, "The Reform Mindans broke off from the Mindans following the Feegash War. Minda was good to us when the Feegash were in charge of Hyre. Trade was good, ships came into our ports from around the world, and gold flowed in like water. Shops flourished, the taaks could afford to rebuild, and the Mindans gained immense power within the Hends."

"What he says now is true," Hawkspar said.

"He has managed to leave out a great deal. While the Feegash ruled Hyre, slavery came to Tonk lands for the first time. Daughters and sons were sold into concubinage, perversions made their homes with those who held power, the Feegash attempted to erase all Tonk culture, and eventually many of our people were consumed by a twisted magic that held their minds prisoner within their own bodies."

Her face was turned toward him. "And everything you say is also true." She looked both stunned and horrified.

"The greddscharf—the mind-slavery—was the work of one man, and he was eventually killed. The Feegash who remained could have stayed and made us rich," Kerwyn said. "Instead, they were chased to the last man from our lands, and the trade ships and the gold followed them to other shores. The Confederacy of Hyre was once again a pariah among those who traded on the sea. And if we had a new alliance with the Eastils, what of that? Endless warring had impoverished them as much as it had impoverished us."

"You see the truth of this," Aaran asked Hawkspar, and she nodded. "Keep going, then," he told Kerwyn.

The man said, "Some of the Mindans were satisfied to see the Feegash go. Others, however, wanted them to return, so that we could be rich and powerful again. It was over that issue that the Mindans split. Minda is clear in her teachings: that war is evil, that those who pursue it for any reason are evil, that peace and prosperity are the true signs of her favor."

Aaran remembered hearing something about a schism in the Mindan ranks, but Mindans never went to sea in privateers. They were aboard merchant ships often enough. And he'd lived at sea since he was sixteen. So if he'd thought about it at all, he'd simply thought it an odd bit of news about Tonks who, following Minda as they did, were just barely Tonks in his mind.

He'd never imagined that the Mindan schism might be Tonks fighting over the right to support Feegash interests over those of their own people.

Kerwyn said, "We joined the Reform Tonks because what they said made sense to us. That peace was always a better path than war. How could anyone disagree with that? That war was always evil and always wrong. That everyone deserved prosperity, and that whatever we did to bring prosperity would bring Minda honor."

"He believes what he tells you," Hawkspar said, her voice soft and puzzled. "To get to what he believes, he's been lied to, and he has lied to himself. But so far as it goes, he thinks he's telling the truth."

Aaran looked over at her. Her hands were on her lap and her head was bowed. She looked delicate and frail; she'd lost weight while she was healing from her injuries. But she seemed to be suffering some sort of quiet distress, as well. Being in the presence of the Mindan was sitting poorly with her.

Kerwyn said, "Of course I'm telling the truth." He turned to Aaran. "I don't think she knows what she's talking about."

"She found you and your two fellow traitors," Aaran said. "Just keep talking. Get to what you actually did."

The bastard had the balls to glare at him. Aaran didn't let himself be bothered by it, though. Kerwyn would get the end he'd so justly earned.

"We were in Port Midrid when your ship arrived. There with the *Calligaffa*, a merchanter heading back toward Hyre from a mediocre trade run. We were the *Calligaffa*'s communicators, and our captain, a Reform Mindan like us, heard that you were looking for sailors. And that you were heading into the Fallen Suns. You sounded like you were on more of a treasure run than a slave-rescue run, but the captain said our allies wanted communicators on that ship. That if you were heading into the Fallen Suns, you were trespassing on Feegash trading territory, and the Feegash didn't want you or anyone from your ship coming back with stories of the great wealth to be had there. Or anything else, for that matter."

"So you came aboard with the sole purpose of seeing that no one aboard the *Taag* survived the trip?"

"That's right. But we would have saved some of those little girls, I think," he said.

"No one is going to applaud you for saving little girls just to give them to the Feegash, or sell them on the market. It's only been fifteen years, you fool. We haven't forgotten what the Feegash did."

"They're slaves," Kerwyn said. "They've never known anything but being slaves."

"Jostfar recognizes no slavery—in his eyes all souls are born for freedom."

"In this, Reform Mindans disagree. Not all creatures have the capacity for freedom, and those who do not should be cared for as slaves."

Aaran bit the inside of his cheek to keep himself from saying what he thought of that; instead he said, "Tell the Eyes of War the rest of your story, that she may judge the truth of it, and keep your heresies to yourself."

"The three of us waited for our time. We helped with the taking of the cargo and the rescue of the slaves, because we had been instructed to do so. When it became clear that you had all the treasure you would claim, we notified the Feegash of this, and they told us to notify them again when we could mark a point of passage. We did so; it was by our chance or good fortune that you moved into the terrain of the Iage, with whom they have traded and treated for many years." The bastard kept looking from him to Hawkspar, back and forth. He fidgeted and every time he did, his chains rattled, and his story came to a halt.

"That's not all." Aaran ground his teeth. He had not yet hit any of these spineless traitors, but his fists were aching for one good shot at them. At the moment, he was holding out the hope to each of the three that he would be the one to best betray his fellow traitors, and live; that pretense would end soon, though.

Part of Aaran wanted to torture the three men himself for the lives they had cost. Part of him, though, remained aware of Ethebet's edict, that unless no other alternative would bring the truth, proven enemies should be traded quickly, or killed quickly; they were not toys for a cat's play.

Kerwyn shivered. "We did as we were told to do. Marked the important men on the ship, so that the Feegash could let the Iage know who to kill first. We told them about the cargo, so the Iage would be sure to get all of it off."

"And by cargo, you mean . . ."

"The treasure. The slaves. The stone-eyed freaks. Anything that would bring a profit."

"And you three? What did you do then?"

"Hid in the deep common cargo hold, as we were instructed to do. We were to be rescued when the Iage had finished with everyone else."

"They would not have been," Hawkspar said suddenly. "They would have served as meals for the Iage dogs. The Iage have no use for traitors, not even to cook for their own meals. They fear the cowardice might come through in the eating. They don't worry so much about their dogs, I understand." She turned to Aaran. "Has he offered anything else?"

And Aaran said, "This one had a few things about the girls they intended to keep for themselves—but since they wouldn't have lived once off the ship, that is of no real importance."

Hawkspar nodded. Her hands unfolded from her lap, her shoulders came back, her head came up, and her voice changed. It grew deeper, and firmer, and louder. "I judge his words true, and his intent behind them the betrayal of every living soul aboard this ship. He had a willing hand in the deaths of those who fought to protect those still living; he knew full well their deaths were planned, and helped to mark them as the first to be sacrificed."

"He hasn't given us as much as his friend Hebaas," Aaran said. "We know what he's given us is true. But it isn't all he knows. Or if it is, then he was less important in this than Hebaas."

"You said I had given you the most," Kerwyn shrieked.

"This one knows the Feegash who tells him what to do," Hawkspar said. "Kerwyn has contacted that Feegash more than once from this cell, even as he has been confined in here. He still fights to betray us all, and believes that his Feegash masters will get here in time to save him."

Aaran turned to stare at her, the full horror of what she'd just said slashing into him like blows from a sword.

He told Kerwyn, "You'd best let me know now who's coming for you. And what the name of your Feegash friend is. Because I'm guessing all three of you have the same information, but the one who gives it to me first has the best chance of surviving to see tomorrow."

Kerwyn was sweating in the damp, cold room. His voice shook. He said, "My Feegash . . . supervisor . . . his name is Janjigral. He's an ambassador to Merigona, one of the leading diplomats there."

"Merigona, which won't trade with Hyre."

"That's the point. That's why we're doing this thing. We're fighting for Hyre's right to be the same as other countries. They all think the Tonk are madmen," Kerwyn said. "They think we're still nothing but nomads chasing herds. I tell you, as long as we permit the damnable nomads to cling to their old religion and their old ways, no country will so much as consider our worth as a trading partner."

This was all new to Aaran. "So," he said, keeping his voice calm. "The Feegash are working to . . . eliminate the nomads?"

Kerwyn nodded. "Filthy animals, the lot of them. Our people have marked as many of the nomads as we can get close to—the Feegash use our markers to send the Sinali slavers in to burn out the camps, kill the adults, and steal the children. They'll have us rid of them soon enough."

"Really?" Aaran was ready to kill the man right there, but this—*this* was the reason all three of them were still alive. So that he and his crew could discover the extent of the betrayal that had been going on around them, unknown, for years. "How long have Reform Mindans been marking nomads for the slavers?"

Kerwyn wasn't even looking at Aaran. He was looking at Hawkspar. Staring at her, his eyes squinted tight, every bit of his body tense.

"Two years," he said.

"A lie," Hawkspar said.

"Lies count against you. You have two now."

Kerwyn looked back to Aaran, and his terror was clear. His skin had turned pale, his eyes showed white around the edges, and his hands twisted against each other. "I had nothing to do with the marking. I swear it."

"That isn't what I asked."

He was silent so long that Aaran rose. "If he won't tell us, one of the other two will."

"It was the first thing the Feegash had them do, the first Reform Mindans. Perhaps—six or seven months after Talyn destroyed their leader."

Which meant that when his sister was taken, it was because the clan had been marked. She hadn't been lost to a random raid, but betrayed by her own people to the plan of enemies who had marked *his* people for destruction.

Aaran took Hawkspar's hand and stood. He had no time for more revelations, not with the ship marked and Feegash or their allies on the way to destroy it and everyone on it.

When he walked out of the cell, he told the guard. "All three of them are to be hanged immediately. They're still in contact with the Feegash and have been planning another ambush against us. No frills, no words. We shall hang them from the higharm, make sure they're dead, and then toss them overboard as fast as possible. The sharks can feed on them." He kept a tight hold on Hawkspar's hand, dragging her forward at a fast pace.

"You don't want to know what else they know?"

"I do, but I can't afford to. As long as they're alive, the Feegash know exactly where we are and what we're doing."

"Yes," she said. "There is that." And then she turned those odd eyes in his direction and said, "This was more to you than just finding out the depths of their treachery, though. This was . . . very personal to you. Why?"

"I can't talk about it," he told her. "Not now. We have other things to worry us, and I cannot allow myself to . . . to consider the full meaning of what I've just found out." He'd never considered before that his sister might have ended up as a Feegash concubine, but now he could think of nothing else. Yet he had to. The lives of everyone aboard depended upon what he did next.

The voyage was cursed. The ship—cursed. He should never have accepted a ship that had betrayed its crew to their deaths and buried them all. Never. But he had, and this was the result; disaster upon disaster, death and pending death.

"Go back to your quarters," he told Hawkspar. "Form everyone who can fight into a perimeter around those who can't, and keep everyone in quarters. Doors barred, not to be opened except to my voice, or—"

"I can tell friend from foe," she said. "Through the doors. I'll need no special password from you."

"Right. Of course." He cleared his throat. "I don't know when we're to be attacked, but all three men knew that the hangings were to be tomorrow at dawn. I would guess our greatest danger will come after dark."

"Yes," she said. "If the men are dead, will not the Feegash lose sight of your ship?"

"They might."

"More than ever, you need as many of my Obsidians on deck as I can put there. And you need to have me with you," she said. "You need to have my Eyes, Aaran."

Hawkspar

I did not think he would see reason. I was certain he would look at what I was offering him and tell me that he did not need my help. That whatever he had to do, he would do alone, while I protected my people—as if we would have any hope at all if we huddled belowdecks while the ship was overrun.

But he said, "Yes. Yes, I suppose you're right. You should come with me. How's the pain?"

I felt a silly pleasure that he'd thought to ask. "Not as bad as it's been. Worse than I'd prefer."

"Before I can witness the execution, we're going to my quarters," he said. "And there I'm going to look through the Hagedwar at this ship and its people, and see if I can find the marks the traitors have left on us for the enemy to follow. If I can erase them, we'll shift our course, and perhaps if we're very lucky, evade the enemies coming toward us."

"I can look a short ways into the future. See what is most likely to happen, try to find good branches that will let us avoid the worst of it."

We shot up the companionway almost at a run, his hand still clutching mine, me moving faster than I was ready to, but managing to keep my feet nonetheless.

In his quarters, he sat on one side of his wide berth and placed me on the other, with my back to the built-in wardrobe. "Don't push yourself too hard," he said. "See what you can without causing yourself pain. If you think we should, I can have one of your Moonstones standing by."

"I'll be fine," I told him. "So long as I look but don't touch, I should have very little pain at all." It was selfish of me, but I wanted to have him to my-self for the few minutes that I dared.

"Good luck to you, then. And wish some luck my way."

I reached across the bed and squeezed his hand. "You have every good wish I can think of."

He closed his eyes, and in the midst of all my darkness, I suddenly saw a light—the first light I had seen since the day I got the Eyes. It was not like sunlight. It was a cool, glowing blue that flowed out of his head like a bubble, then expanded until it surrounded him. I ignored the waters of time for a moment; I would slide into them eventually, but this was the magic he'd spoken of, and I could actually *see* it. It was a beautiful thing. Within the blue sphere, a warm red cube emerged, and expanded until it, too, surrounded him. And then, within the cube, a yellow tetrahedron, and then a golden one, both lying on their sides, intersecting with each other, but fully encompassed by the cube.

When Aaran was done, he sat within the center of the intersected tetra-hedrons, and though he was still a man, he was something more. He was spirit, glowing and radiant and beautiful, and if I had not already loved him before, I would have fallen for him then.

I ran my hand over the outer surface of the blue sphere, and felt its power. I shivered at the touch of it, at the purity and the intensity of the en-ergy that filled it. I felt music through the tips of my fingers that sang to me of home and forever, of life and creation and eternity and infinity. I pushed my hands through the sphere at a corner, and brushed the red cube. It was control and focus, the identity of humanity, the weight of birth and death and knowing that the existence of the flesh is finite—it was a filter for the wild, compelling power of the blue. And within the red, yellow, and the dreams of humankind for greater things. To do better, but more than that, to *be* better. And gold, and in the gold, the mind of the infinite, reaching out to the spirit of mankind.

I wanted to step within this beautiful construct, this magic. I wanted to fall into the blue that was the View and soar forever, and reshape myself within the red, and dream beyond my reach in palest yellow, and touch the soul of Jostfar in gold. I wanted this song to flow in me and through me. I wanted to become a part of this music that I heard for the first time, and that yet was the most familiar song I'd ever heard, that was my breathing in and out, and the weight of sunlight on my skin, and the sound of growing trees, and the power of water.

This place in which he sat was my home, was all of our homes, if only we could reach it.

He said, "You can see me."

His voice shook me from my reverie, but it did not touch the beauty that vibrated through my reaching hands.

"I see you. And this magic you have made. It's the most beautiful thing I've ever felt."

"It's the Hagedwar." He paused. "You feel it?"

"As if it were the part of my life that has been missing since I was born. The blue calls to me."

"It does that. In Tonk magic, that's the View, and if you go in alone, you won't come back. It's too compelling, and too beautiful."

"The red, the yellow, and the gold shield you from the naked power of its song."

"You can see that?"

I said, "I can see more than I even imagined existed. But . . ." I pulled my hands back, and the blue called to me not to leave, even as I moved away. "I'm not looking into the future, and you aren't looking at the ship."

"No." I realized that he wasn't speaking to me with words. His voice spoke only inside my head. "When we are past this trouble, if you'd like, I will teach you the Hagedwar. I don't know what use you would find it or what effect it would have on your visions of time."

He could give me the wonders I felt? The music of the universe? He could just *give* it to me? "If we have time, I want you to teach me," I said. "I'll do anything to know how to create this magic."

I forced myself not to touch it again, though it was as hard a thing as I had ever done. The blue whispered its music in my fingertips, and sent it shivering over my skin so that when I listened, I could see the world transformed into shapes of light and sound and taste and smell that ebbed and flowed; I could not understand how sound or taste could be a shape, or a weight or a desire, and yet they were, and they called to me to join them.

And then darkness slid against me, touching me, licking at me. Ossal had found me in this place, and he wanted into me—into my flesh, into my desire, so that he could touch the beauty of Aaran's magic. He wanted it for himself, as hungrily and as desperately as I wanted it.

I was awake and strong, and I could deal with him. I cast a shield and banished him to darkness.

But the encounter crushed my hopes as quickly as they had been born. I could not have the Hagedwar, for if I had it, then Ossal would have it. And Ossal, who desired most to walk upon the earth in flesh form again, would use it for evil.

I brushed my hands against each other, willing the seductive beauty away from me. Like Aaran, it was not for me, no matter how much I desired it.

I put my mind to my own task, and at last the river of time flowed around me again, and I acknowledged its presence and waded into its cold, harsh depths.

Little joy lies in the flow of time. There is all about us too much pain, too much failure, too much struggle and doubt and tragedy and grief. Light and joy flow through those waters, too, but their pictures are harder to notice in the midst of terrible devastation.

And devastation lay at the fore of our main channel. The waters of choice and betrayal bore us toward a rendezvous with three ships—Sinali war frigates by their sails and build, upon which waited hundreds of fierce marines, hardened veterans. The ships were sailing in a favorable wind, and set to intercept us just after the last light of day faded. They knew where we were, they knew how many of us they would find and what weapons we could bring to bear against them, and they knew, as clearly as I could see, that we had no chance. They had us. They knew where we were, and even if we changed course, the magic with which the traitors had branded us would let them track us as if we were their Lady with the Lamp, their fixed and shining star.

When they caught us, they had but one instruction. Every living thing aboard our ship had to die. They would kill the men with a quick, brutal efficiency.

The women and girls would die a slower, uglier death.

If it came to that, I would kill every one of my people myself, rather than let those monsters at them.

But perhaps we could keep it from coming to that.

I fought my way out of the strong channel into the side branches, looking for a branch where we escaped.

It took a great deal of looking. We had little hope. Our deaths mattered to them—to the Sinalis and the Feegash—because we had uncovered a secret that had been hidden for fifteen years. They would do *anything* to keep it hidden as long as possible. They had been doing *anything* for quite a few years, I suspected.

But there was one thin, shallow channel. It grew so thin in places I doubted we could follow it. But we had no choice but to try.

"We are likely to die at first true dark," I told him. "But if you would live, I've found one route we might follow with at least some hope of success."

Aaran stopped what he was doing.

"Your communicators have to let your people in Hyre know what you've discovered about the Reform Mindans. *Right now*—this is more important even than finding the markers they have hidden on this ship. You must send news of the testimonies you have taken and the executions you are carrying out, of the betrayals, and the names of the betrayers, both Tonk and Feegash. The names of the Feegash allies, the names of the Sinali ships that are almost upon us. I have them, I'll give them to your communicators."

"Now?"

"Now. The Feegash have traitors everywhere, and they'll hear what you're telling. You must get this message out to every communicator you have, and instruct them to pass it on to everyone. Everyone. Including Mindans and even those you suspect may be Reform Mindans. There can be no secrecy in this discovery, no chance that it might be hidden away. You cannot let any secret go unspoken, though, because they will use any wedge, no matter how small, to hide themselves again. They will lie, they will deny. But that is for another time. For now, bring forth the truth and spread it to all the winds."

"Then what?"

"Find the rest of the marks the traitors hid on this ship, and break them as quickly as you can. And I will seek the route across the sea that will let us evade the three Sinali frigates that come to kill us all."

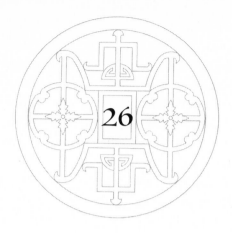

26

Aaran

The drums rolled long and slow, the "March of Death." All sailors knew it, none ever wanted to hear it. They crowded on the deck with the Ossalenes, with the little girls solemn and frightened, and the adults still and watchful.

The sails were reefed, the ship sat briefly on the currents, adrift in the sea without direction.

And up from the holds, the traitors stepped forth. Each wore his complement of chains and manacles, each moved between his escort of cold-faced marines. Aaran stood at the mast, sword in hand, waiting while the drums rolled in a steady rumble, and the men fought, even to the last, to escape.

Aaran wondered briefly where they thought they might escape to. If they jumped into the sea with their metal chains around them, they'd drown in an instant. Or perhaps they knew enough of the Feegash magic of transport that they could transport the chains off them, if only they could break free of their guards.

But they didn't break free. They stood in the center of a wall of men and women and children, and not a face staring back at them bore pity. They were betrayers who had brought unnecessary death to their own people.

"We are gathered to witness the executions of the following sailors: Sedaar Degooryn and Den av Diiri, both Reform Mindans born to the Tonk people, both claiming Saint Minda, have by their confessions admitted treason against the Tonk people, and the attempted murders of all aboard this ship." Aaran took a slow breath. "Kerwyn av Maaitaak, Reform Mindan born to the Tonk people, claiming Saint Minda, has confessed to treason against the Tonk people and to the attempted murders of all aboard this ship. He has also implicated the Feegash, enemies of all Tonks, as the allies of the Reform Mindans, and has named his associates within the Feegash."

Aaran heard gasps from the other Tonk aboard the ship. He understood their shock and disbelief. The Tonks had not welcomed the intervention of the Feegash when first they came to Hyre, offering to negotiate a peace between the warring Tonks and the Eastils on the other side of the border. But after their attempted enslavement of all the people on both sides of the border, after stripping the wealth of two nations to line their own pockets, after they were uncovered as the debased, vile scum that they were, no true Tonk could look at a man born Tonk who sided with Feegash dirt and say he was Tonk anymore.

Aaran continued, "These three are made clanless, nameless, peopleless. We do not know them, we do not acknowledge them, and we do not give them prayers or words now in the hour of their deaths. They are cast aside. If Minda wants them, she'll have to find them herself."

The sailors up on the higharm dropped the nooses and grapples, and all three men, still in chains, were hoisted by grapple up to the deeparm. There sailors wrapped nooses around their necks, and the drums began to roll for them. No one cried out for mercy. Not a soul breathed any word at all. They stood watching, a solemn crowd finding no pleasure in this necessary killing— in this removal of beasts from their number. They watched because it was their duty to their fellows aboard the ship. They desired justice, and justice, like freedom, required acknowledgment of its consequences.

Aaran stood next to the ship communicators, crewmen who used the Hagedwar to send out the progress of the executions of the traitors, just as they had previously sent out every bit of information Aaran and Hawkspar had been able to glean from the traitors about the betrayal of the Tonk.

Aaran studied his crew, satisfied by their demeanor. He would have had the man who made sport at that moment, or the one who jeered, beaten. This was no moment for celebration or for mocking. This was a dark task, made necessary by treason. But what had to be done did not have to be done with pleasure.

He raised his sword and the drums leapt to life again, this time a loud and terrible thunder. Up on the deeparm, all six sailors who held the convicts in place signaled their readiness. He dropped his arm, they pushed, and all three men toppled from the deeparm to hang just a bit above the deck, their necks snapped, their bodies twitching only for a few moments.

Aaran ran each through the heart with his sword—the final assurance that all three were truly dead.

He made the air cut that stopped the drummers, then called up to the sailors on the higharm, "Cut them down."

And to the sailors who stepped forward, unbidden, to deal with the bodies, he said, "Cut their heads off. Throw them overboard. Take the chains off first, weight them with ballast. Say no words for them."

He watched the men work quickly, wrapping the bodies in with the ballast, tying the shrouds shut, tossing them over without ceremony.

So it was. So it went.

He started to walk back to the steersman's castle to give the crewman his new heading, when out of the still-gathered crowd, a sailor lunged at him, knife drawn. No sound, no warning; he caught the movement from the corner of one eye, and then, as he started to turn, a fast, low shape lunged in front of Aaran's attacker and did something too quick to be seen. Aaran's attacker flipped through the air, and Aaran realized that the one who had flipped him was Eban.

"You can die now!" the boy screamed, and drew his own knife, and cut the attacker's throat.

Aaran had a fleeting sense of how near death had stepped to him. The man—who had gone by the name of Tagrish Boxmaker—lay on the deck, bleeding out, his eyes glazing and fixing even as he still feebly waved the knife.

"Don't touch his weapon," the boy said as Aaran knelt by the dying man. "The blade will be poisoned. They always are."

Aaran studied Tuua's young apprentice with a wary expression. "Which blades are those? And how would you know this?"

"He's a Feegash assassin. I didn't recognize him until he pulled out the knife and ran at you. He changed his appearance—grew a beard and longer hair. But I've seen him before."

"And where would a boy with no past he'll admit to have met a Feegash assassin?"

Eban said, "In my father's house."

Which set Aaran back on his heels. "Your *father's* house."

Eban nodded and hung his head. "I'm Feegash. I am the youngest son of a concubine my father killed. I had no value to him—I wasn't a son of any importance, so he lent me out to visiting friends, along with my sisters and a lot of half sisters, and some of my other half brothers." His voice dropped. "I lived. A lot of them didn't."

Aaran's heart went out to the boy. "We know about the Feegash and their . . . entertainment," he said, feeling both angry and disgusted. He looked at the kid. No wonder the boy hadn't been willing to say anything about himself before. Aaran had thought him simply a wharf rat with a drunkard father he feared. That Eban was a Feegash kid taking refuge among Tonks—who'd have believed it?

"The men don't pay any attention to children; they don't care what we see or hear. We're just toys to them, and they have so many toys we become part of the house. I saw things and heard things, both with him and with his friends."

Aaran rose and pulled the boy to his feet. "Walk with me," he said. "I want to talk with you." And to two of the marines, he said, "Just throw the body in the sea. Don't bother with wrapping or weights. Let the sharks have an easy meal."

The boy trotted along beside him as he went to his cabin. He sat the boy at his charting table, and took a seat at right angles from him. "So when did you learn how to kill a man?"

"The Ossalenes have been teaching me," Eban said. "They're good fighters. I need to know how to fight, too."

Aaran nodded. Tuua said the boy was a quick student, and eager to learn anything anyone would teach him. "I'm getting a feel for what the Feegash are doing. But perhaps you can help me. What I can't understand—yet—is why. Why do they want all of us dead?"

The kid again stared at him, as if that ought to be the most obvious thing of all. "Because you're never going to see things their way," he said. "My father and my uncle talk about that all the time. About how the Tonk haven't changed in centuries upon centuries, and how they aren't going to change now. How as long as there are Tonks, you're going to be this . . ." He looked frustrated. "*Amijanbja bnar.* I don't know how to say it in Tonk. It's a big thing in the middle of a river that stops boats from going on the river. The water runs, but no one can use it. You're that thing. And my father and his brother and their friends think that the whole world ought to be their river."

"And if they can't get us to be like them, and they can't make us slaves, they want us all dead."

The kid nodded. "If you dare say what they're doing is bad, they want you dead." He put his elbows on the table and said, "They think they're the best people in the world. They're horrible."

"I've seen some of what they've done."

The kid pulled off his shirt and turned his back to Aaran. "Have you seen this?"

The kid's skin was a roadmap of scars: the puckered furrows of whip lashes;

the narrower lines where someone had carved obscene pictures of the things men might do to little boys; round burn holes and brands. It was, Aaran thought, a wonder the kid was even alive. He had never seen anything like it.

No wonder the boy never took his shirt off in front of anyone.

He turned, and to his horror Aaran saw that both the boy's nipples were gone, too, and that the front of him was as brutally scarred as the back.

"Jostfar's heart . . ." Aaran wiped a hand over his face and said, "Sit." He tried his best to sound reassuring. "Tell me who these men are, your father and his friends, and when we return to Midrid, I will guarantee not one of them ever touches another child."

"If I tell you their names, they'll know you have me. They'll find out. They're *diplomats*," he said, as if this was the most terrifying thing in the world.

Aaran's people had experience with the Feegash. Perhaps diplomats *were* the most terrifying thing in the world. "This is what Feegash men do to their own children," Aaran said softly. "I don't want to think about what they do to the slaves they buy."

His mouth went dry. *Jostfar,* he prayed, *don't let her have fallen into Feegash hands. Please.*

The horror of his sister's possible fate had never been more clear to him.

Eban said, "You look sick."

"My sister was stolen by Sinali slavers when I was a boy. I've been sailing in search of her ever since."

The kid gave him a pitying look. "I'm sorry. Knowing is bad. Not knowing is worse, I think. I had a sister I liked. She was three years older than me, and she was always kind to me. And one morning I woke up, and she was gone. I never saw her again. I probably know what happened to her . . ." He hung his head and stared at his hands. ". . . But I don't know that I know."

"I'm sorry," Aaran said.

"I want to be Tonk," the kid said after a moment under his breath. "I want to make them stop it. The horrible things they do. They say none of it matters—that there isn't any good or bad, that it's just what people do. But it matters to us. It matters to the people they do it to."

Aaran said, "It does. We're all born to be free. Being some sick bastard's plaything is no part of being free." He stood and patted the boy on the head. "Come on. You're supposed to be helping Tuua. He and I will talk—he'll tell me when you know what you need to know. So learn, all right? Being Tonk is something that starts in your heart and flows into every part of your life. It isn't a name you take. It's a whole life."

"I know," the boy said. "I want that life."

As Aaran went back out to check on the windman and the progress of the *Taag,* Aaran thought that the kid would possibly make a better Tonk than a lot of those who'd been born to it.

It should never be easy to be Tonk, he thought.

And he considered the Reform Mindans, who wanted ease. Slaves and a steady flow of wealth, no standards, no criticism. No shame.

It was that, he thought, that had marked the Feegash as worthless, and that now would mark the Reformists, too. They wanted to live in a world without shame. Where anyone could do anything wicked, and everyone would simply smile, or look the other way, and say it was fine.

Shame had value. It kept men decent in their dealings in public and in private. It protected the weak from the strong. It civilized.

The Feegash were in dire need of civilizing, Aaran thought.

Hawkspar

I stood by the captain as he frantically passed information to his communicators. Those communicators had the same light inside them that had surrounded Aaran, the same beautiful magic that was, to me, a door that led straight into the whole of existence. It was, in each of the two of them, small. But perfect. Same colors, same shapes, same power. I could not reach out and touch it, though I wanted to.

They'd already passed on the names of the Sinali ships that pursued us, their location in the sea, the names of their captains and the Feegash diplomats aboard them. Everything we knew about the Iage, too, though that was little enough.

Now we were passing on the names of the Feegash diplomats—two brothers—that Eban had given us. We were not announcing the boy's presence on the ship—only that a reliable source had implicated these two Feegash as being important in the plot against the Tonk. And we were letting everyone know that our ship had been marked by the traitors, that we had managed to remove the marks, but that we might not survive—that we were still being pursued and that the deaths of all on board was the goal of our pursuers.

The word went out, with the communicators expressing the shock and disbelief and dismay of most of those receiving the messages. Standing in the communicators' bay that sat just below the steersman's castle, I allowed myself to slide back into the river of time. I followed events back to the narrow, shallow channel I'd located. Time was shifting around me, banks eroding and channels reforming. My chosen channel—the one in which we lived and escaped—was growing faster and deeper as chances that time would flow that way improved.

It wasn't the main course yet, nor even close to it. But hope grew in me.

When we were done, we returned to Aaran's quarters, with Redbird settling outside the door with the marines to stand her guard.

I was scattered. I had pushed the Eyes too hard that day, and I was not strong. Not yet.

"You're hurting," Aaran said.

"Merely tired."

"I don't believe you," he said.

"Believe. I have been tracking our future, looking at possible paths, trying to pick those most likely to lead us to safety. I finally discovered such a path. It will be a miserable journey."

Aaran said, "Miserable would be an improvement on final."

I didn't argue.

I just said, "We have to sail due east, straight into the wind."

He stood there, quiet for a moment, then I heard him start to chuckle. Then to laugh out loud. "That'll slow them enough that we'll have a chance to get out of reach."

The Sinali ships had no windmen. If we, with our one, sailed straight into the wind, they would have to tack to pursue us, while, even shorthanded, we would be able to sail forward in a straight line. Even if we did not make great speed, we would still make better progress than the Sinalis, whose sharply zigzagging path would slow them to a crawl.

If we could get far enough ahead of them, we could, perhaps, lose them, and then swing around and creep safely out of the Dragon Sea.

"So the question is," Aaran said, "will Faryn hold out long enough for us to get beyond their reach?"

"He moved the ship when there was no wind," I said.

"He did. But he had help, and had the Trade Current working with him, and no wind to fight against. This time, he'll be alone, and he'll have to create an envelope around the ship and funnel the existing wind into it. The Trade Current will drag us a bit southward whether we want to go south or not. To go due west, which is head into the wind, we will be fighting everything."

"You know we could die here," I said.

"I've lived with that truth since I first sailed away from shore. The sea is no friend of man or ship. We sail in spite of the dangers, always knowing the next minute could be our last."

I did not want to push him. I did not. I knew in my heart that what I wanted was something I could not have; yet I knew in my bones and blood and flesh that what I wanted meant the world to me. While the ship sailed west, everyone would be waiting. Waiting and tense, armed, watching. They would need Aaran, perhaps, to check from time to time that everything went as planned. The ship was shorthanded, and I had seen him take the tillers more than once.

But surely there would be time. A way. Surely he and I could be together once more.

Our lives rode on a thread, and I looked to see if getting what I wanted would cut that thread. And it wouldn't.

I wanted him.

Standing before him, I unbound my shoes, and pulled off my clothes. Aboard the ship, at these lower latitudes, we of the Order had found all the many layers of our robes too much to bear, and had taken to wearing only a tabi and penitent's hakan-ara—these being made of light cotton instead of heavy silk or wool. So in an instant I stood before him in just my breast-binder and pantlets.

"Ah," he said. "You—what are you doing?"

"I have seen many futures in which I am used roughly and viciously by many men before they at last kill me. As many more in which the seru and I kill all the girls before we kill ourselves so that we do not suffer the fate they plan for us. I have seen one still unlikely future—the one we pursue now—in which we escape. There are so many ways that we can fail at this, and only one in which we can succeed. We may not have much time. If we survive this night, I know we cannot have each other. But for tonight, we could . . . pretend that we will love each other for the rest of our lives. If we only live until tomorrow, it will be true."

"Even if we lived forever, I wouldn't have to pretend," he muttered, and then his hands grabbed my shoulders, pulling me toward him, and his lips pressed against mine, hard and hungry, and he pulled me toward the bed, and pushed me down on it, and leaned over me. "Wait here," he said, "I have to set Faryn and the steersman our new course, and I will be back. Don't move."

His footsteps rang across the floor, and the door opened, and the humid, hot, salt-tanged air of the southern Dragon Sea wafted in. I could hear him on the other side of the door, telling the marines there, "No one in, no one out. No exceptions."

I followed his progress—dark on dark on dark, shapes and weights as he ran the length of the ship, vaulted up the officers' companionway three steps at a time, charged up the steersman's castle, stood almost no time, went vaulting down the steersman's ladder into the empty windmen's room, and next I heard the ship's bell ringing. It was a sharp sound, penetrating. It carried without difficulty down to the attable on the working deck, and into the passengers' sleeping quarters.

Sailors came running from all directions, managing to reach him at nearly the same time.

Another moment, and then Aaran was running across the deck again, and back to me.

To me.

I shivered, with want and anticipation and feelings for which I had no words.

He hurried through the door again, and this time dropped the bar into the brackets.

"You're still here. You have not changed your mind?"

"I have not."

He stripped off his own clothes as he came to me, leaving them in piles on the floor. For a moment I felt like a penitent again, threatened by terrible consequences for even the slightest infraction against the Order's endless rules on neatness. And then I felt deliciously wicked for straying so far from them.

He sat beside me on the bed, and his hand reached out and touched me on the shoulder. Rubbing, stroking. It was a wonderful, glorious thing, the touch of his hand on my skin, and better when he unbound the ties of my breastbinder and tugged it off me.

"Oh," he whispered. "Beautiful." And pressed his lips to mine, and ran his hands over my breasts at the same time.

His mouth had moved to my breast, and I stroked his hair. Pulled back, braided in a complicated braid. Thick, coarser than mine. His teeth nipped lightly at my nipples, and in spite of trying to be quiet, I cried out.

He moved over me, touching me until I thrashed and bucked beneath his hands and his lips, his teeth and tongue. I bit the bedclothes to keep from screaming, and wrapped myself around him, and cried out, wild with pleasure. A storm built inside of me, more fierce than the first time, more compelling, more consuming.

He rolled us over again, and lifted me, and my legs wrapped around him, pulling him against me. He laughed, and slid into me, and began to move in and out, slowly, carefully, and all that came before faded away. I clutched at the bedclothes, clawed the bed and his back, shoved myself against him. Inside me the storm rose higher, waves crashing, winds howling, thunder roaring, lightning cracking. I screamed, and he moved faster, and I begged for more. More. Heat and hardness and slick wetness, pounding and arching and pounding together and pulling apart.

He drove into me, then, and I moved with him until everything collided at once, the storm crescendoed, my body locked tight and the universe inside my head blew apart. He kept moving, driving, hammering, faster and harder, and I locked tighter. Nothing had ever felt so good. Nothing had ever been so loud in my mind, so much, so strong. I was outside of myself as he stilled, as his back arched, as he cried out and we clung together, suspended as the universe fell around us in pieces.

Then came silence, and he moved slowly to lie upon me, his weight a blanket, while the storm in me subsided.

"I keep not expecting that," he whispered after a while.

"What?"

"You," he said, and turned his face toward mine, and kissed my cheek. Gently.

I kissed him back. Lips, no tongues, just the merest brushing of skin to skin, like butterfly wings in a lightly cupped hand.

We lay together a little longer, and then he kissed me again. "Dress," he said. "And sleep here if you would like. I have to go back to the ship, and make sure all is running as it should be."

"I won't sleep," I told him. In truth, I was so full of energy that I felt as if I'd never need to sleep again. And I, too, had duties I needed to be about. "I'll look a little forward in time and see what I can tell you."

"You're wonderful. Wonderful." He pulled away, and started for the door. "If we're both still alive tonight, I'd like to share dinner with you. Here. Alone."

I thought about him in me, and us together.

"Yes," I said.

27

Aaran

Jostfar help him, he was so in love with her.

Aaran went about his duties on the ship, but she was the only thought in his head. People kept talking to him, and he kept not hearing them—not the first time or the second time they spoke, and sometimes not even the third time.

His men made pretense in mistaking the cause of his distraction.

The boy up on the higharm had all three ships in sight up until darkness fell. At last sight, they'd been falling badly behind. All three had their lanterns hanging unused and cold, to hide their positions in the dark, and to make seeing the *Taag* easier, should someone carelessly let light show for a moment.

Aaran caught a change in the scent of the air, and a twinge of pain in his forehead. He frowned.

He sought out the steersman. "Still heading due west?"

"We are." Young Nemick, not much past wharf rat, had the rudder. The ship was shorthanded, and the boy was holding. Aaran bit his lip, but said nothing. Nemick said, "Making as good headway as could be expected, though I could wish for better. It helps a bit knowing that the Sinalis are beating to follow us."

"It does."

"Faryn says he's having a hard time of the headwind, though."

Aaran looked down the latter-hatch and said, "You going to hold?"

"Headwind's bad and getting worse," the windman shouted up at him. "It's a bitter fight I'm having here. I think we may be pushing into a building storm."

That was what he'd smelled and felt in his sinuses. He smiled a little. A
storm might not be the worst thing that could happen to them, if they could
get well into it. Ships could hide in storms. Enemies could end up scattered
or reefed or sunk entirely—especially those that didn't have trackers and
windmen. He could hope for a storm, perhaps, in which he could double
back and sail the *Taag* right by the pursuing Sinali ships and out the easiest
point of the Fallen Suns, where it looked like he would only have to run
through a single chain of small islands, and those decently far apart.

He watched the western sky, and saw it flickering in the darkness. Lightning, a ways off. But coming.

He breathed in and smelled the change.

It was big, he thought. Pushing wind a long way out.

Aaran slid for a moment inside the Hagedwar—long enough to see that
the Sinali trio was tacking southward at the moment. He said, "All right,
then. Set us east northeast under sail, and let Faryn have a break. We'll put a
bit more distance between us and them, then turn hard and double back
with the wind due west when the storm hits. We'll give it everything we
have, and hope we get around them and lose them for good before they
catch on to our trick."

The ship's bell rang the hour; one shift of sailors changed places with
fresh ones, the officers on watch gave their reports and handed off to the
next watch.

Aaran called to Ermyk, who was getting off watch, "Have the off-duty
officers meet in my quarters for dinner."

And he went down to the galley to instruct the cooks to send up meals for
five right away, and to make two special meals to send up on the next bell.

He had to talk with his officers. But he had to be with Hawkspar again,
too.

The surviving officers gathered in his grand hall, a grim and silent group.
Aaran suspected it would be some time before they could look at the empty
places around the table and not think of how some of their own had betrayed the missing to their deaths.

When everyone was seated, Aaran opened a half-nob keg of fine black
ale, and poured the mugs to full. When each man held his drink in hand,
Aaran lifted his glass and said, "To the honored dead."

"To the honored dead," the voices around the table echoed.

"And to making the guilty pay," Aaran said.

"To making the guilty pay." They sounded stronger and surer that time.

He drank, and they drank, and then he sat.

"We'll not dance around this issue. We had four traitors on this ship. Three of our own, and a Feegash assassin who chose this day, for Jostfar only knows what reason, to try to kill me. He could have had a part in other deaths on the ship. We've lost a lot of good people this voyage, and we're still a long way from home."

Alwyn said, "We could lose more. We could lose everything tonight."

"No," Aaran said. "We might all die, but we won't lose everything. Whether we live or die, all the communicators in Tonk lands around the world have by this time received our messages about the treachery of the Reform Mindans and the involvement of the Feegash. Our own communicators are under marine watch in case we have yet another traitor somewhere in our midst, and they're already receiving reports that confirm what we discovered. The conspiracy was big. But now most of it is in the open. At least we think it is."

"Then the Feegash truly have been working with Tonks?"

"Yes."

"How is that possible?" the master of arms asked. "How could any Tonk side against his own people with those villains?"

"There's no knowing," Aaran said. "Maybe these are men who were twisted during the time the Feegash held their minds in thrall. Maybe they are simply men without spines, or convictions. Minda has never been a saint who inspired great things from her followers."

"No. Perhaps we should cut all Mindans from our number."

He couldn't deny having thought the same thing. The Mindans had always been the Tonks who wanted to push all other Tonks into the Mindan fold, to make everyone into a nation of merchants and shopkeeps who valued gold and peace above freedom.

But Minda was a part of the Five, and had been for the history of the Tonk. Jostfar *needed* shopkeeps and merchants. He just didn't need to have them running things, in Aaran's opinion.

Traitors, though? No, Jostfar had no place for traitors.

"So what do we do to find any other traitors among us?" Ynyar, the master of the day watch, asked.

They ate in silence, and Aaran considered the question. "We ask some of the women of the Order to look for us. To use the Eyes. They share our fate; perhaps they need to be taken on as full crew in this journey, and share our rewards along with the risks."

Each man around the table considered the effect this would have on the size of their shares at the end of the voyage. "The men might raise objections. Part of their shares are going to come from risking their lives saving the women you're considering as crew."

"Women aboard a ship are unlucky," Ermyk said.

Aaran stared at his kor daan. "They're *already* aboard the ship," Aaran said. "They're already working. They aren't going to become any unluckier if we pay them."

Ermyk grinned. "Less money for each of us is a bit of bad luck."

Aaran swore. "Are you Mindan, too, kor daan, that your heart is in your pocket with your gold? We've discovered a conspiracy against *our people*, and we have what might be a new weapon to help us fight this conspiracy, and you're going to mention the lessening of your share?"

Ermyk made a face, then laughed. "Jostfar forgive me, I'd blame my Mindan mother but I know better. Even she pulled a sword and fought the Feegash when we ran them out of Roovintaak at last."

"There's your answer then, or should be," Aaran said.

They ate a while longer, and then Ynyar said, "But maybe not full shares, eh? Since they weren't aboard for the first half of the voyage."

Aaran sighed. "Half shares, man. Did you take me for born yesterday? Is mine a fool's face?"

"Thought you might have been looking to pull your woman in for a full cut."

"She's not my woman. She's her woman."

"Well, anyway. It was what I thought."

"No. I'm not trying to give shares you've earned to someone else as a gift."

They discussed the day, then—executions and the attempted murder, their run from the pursuing Sinalis, which might yet end in their destruction. They were weary, all of them and afraid more than they cared to admit. Hopeful, too, especially with a storm building that would both make them harder to pursue and let them run out of sight of even the sharpest-eyed sailors.

The Sinali had no trackers. At least these Sinali had none. Considering that they were allied with Tonks—Reform Mindans though they were, there might still be men trained in the use of the Hagedwar and capable of taking their training aboard enemy ships for the benefit of the enemy.

That was a worrisome thought.

28

Hawkspar

I wish I could say that I withstood the storm like a seasoned sailor. But I didn't, and neither did most of those with me. We'd had our feet firmly underneath us for most of our lives, and finding ourselves climbing waves big as houses sent almost all of us to our beds, puking and retching in between long stretches of being terrified that we were going to die any minute, or wishing we were already dead.

I'd never experienced such a thing in my life. I tried to imagine living on a ship, and facing storms like these as a matter of course. It made my belly knot. What kind of life did these men live? How could they bear it?

Aaran had been living like this since he was just a boy, to fulfill a promise he'd made. To find his sister.

I'd known he was a brave man. An honorable one. But I'd never imagined how much courage keeping his promise must have taken.

The wind sounded like demons loosed from the hells. The thunder roared so loud it seemed the ship should blow apart just from the sound of it. With every crash, the children would scream, and by Jostfar and the Five Saints, I wanted to scream with them. We lay in the dark, clinging with both hands to our berths, terrified to let go lest we be tossed to the floor like beans shaken from a jar. It was all I could do to keep breathing steadily.

I was quite sure I never wanted food again. And that was when I realized I'd missed the captain's dinner.

Well, I hoped he would understand, that he would forgive me.

And then the next wave of nausea hit me, and I just hoped I'd fall out of my bunk and knock myself unconscious so that I didn't have to know how horrible I felt.

The three demons surrounded me—Ossal and the wizard I had slaughtered and the one who still needed to die. I knew to shield myself from them, but when I tried, I found myself cut off from water, earth, air, and sun. They had changed the pit in which we struggled, and I did not know how they had done so.

But they were not hurting me. Not even trying to hurt me. They simply circled me, while in my head a voice whispered, Look at them. Look at them, Ethebet's daughter, with your Eyes and with your mind.

I turned, and caught just a glimpse of the woman in white. She smiled at me, and then she was gone, leaving me in the dark with the monsters.

I stared at them, poisonous shadows all, power-hungry monsters whose obsession stretched their lives to unnatural lengths and bound their souls to this dark place both alive and after their deaths. I did not want to see them. I did not want to take a chance of calling their attention to me, or further opening the barriers that protected me from them most of the time. But the woman in white had told me what I needed to do.

I relaxed myself and allowed my connection to the Eyes to open, and began to feel time flowing around me. In the cold waters, I sought echoes of the man who I had killed to save Aaran's life. I had touched him—we shared a connection in time. I located him without much difficulty, and found the moment he had last lived, and the instant that he had died. And then, out of perverse curiosity, I followed the instants after his death, and saw his flesh ripped from his soul, and his soul dragged into darkness, bound between life and afterlife by a thousand frail threads.

I had seen such threads before, connected from Ossal to the Eyes he made. I followed one of the little threads binding the sea wizard, and found that it connected him to a skeleton that wandered aimlessly beneath the sea. I tracked another, and another—and at the end of each thread discovered another skeleton, moving along the sea bottom, or over a stretch of land, circling or crawling or walking, never with apparent purpose.

I shuddered, recognizing what they were. They were the screaming legions of the dead that had borne him across the sea—no longer directed by his will, but still bound by his magic, even as he was bound to them.

I broke away from that wizard, and, because I had seen Ossal more closely than I cared to, I tried to look at the still-living wizard. He had spun webs around himself so that I dared not get too close. But like the other two wizards, threads bound him—even though he still lived—to the oblivion that lay between life and

afterlife. His fate when he died was sealed, I thought. I could not touch him to dis-
cover what magic he had cast that would consign him to the dark, cold hell; I could
only be satisfied that something had.

But I wanted to know why he showed up in my future. I did not know him. I
had no ties that bound me to him. And since, for the moment, he was paying me no
mind, I let myself float backward on the waters of time, from the vague point
ahead where he and I met, back to a place where he connected with anything or
anyone else I knew.

And I found him bound to Aaran.

In that moment the dream, if it had been a dream, ended.

I woke to blessed stillness. No thunder, no howling wind, no roaring sea, no pounding rain. No screaming children.

The gentle creaking and sighing of the *Taag*, the regular treading of feet over deck boards, the smells of the soap the sailors used to clean things aboard the ship, voices speaking normally some way off. I sat up.

The room smelled clean, and I was alone in it.

I sat up, sniffed my clothing, and found it malodorous, reeking of sick and fear sweat.

So I rose, and pulled out my bed drawer, and from the left side found my underwear and a clean tabi, and from the right side clean hakan-ara.

The practices of slaves and penitents translated well to the life of oracles. We who could not truly see benefited greatly from having been trained for a lifetime to put our clothing in the same places and the same order every time.

I took my clothes and trudged up the companionway, still feeling weak and sick, and walked along the ship to the afterdeck and the gombaar, which held the board full of holes hanging out over the open sea—the ship's privy—and beside that, the washing room, where I could shower myself with salt water, and then rinse off with a few wipes from fresh water.

I cleaned up and rinsed out my dirty clothes at the same time, grateful for how good it felt to be clean.

And then I went in search of Aaran, to see if I might discover how he connected to the third and final wizard of death I would have to fight before I, too, died.

29

Aaran

"You look surprisingly well for one who was so recently so sick," Aaran said.

Hawkspar stood on the deck with the sun glinting blue off her black hair and picking out the gold bands in her eyes. The eyes still made him uneasy, but she did not.

"A shower and clean clothes cure a world of ills." She turned her face toward the sea. "We have escaped?"

"We seem to have. My hope is the three ships pursuing us kept plowing deeper into it and were lost at sea. My hope is unlikely to have much of a tie to reality, of course." He chuckled a little, still gleeful about the success of his gambit.

She didn't laugh with him. Instead, she said, "I've found something odd. A connection you have with a . . . a monster. A wizard bound to pain and death. His life and yours are somehow connected, and have been for a very long time. I would have tried to follow the connection back to where it first began, but I was afraid to do more than float above the time threads connected to him. I'll . . . face him. Eventually. And one of the two of us will die in the encounter."

Aaran started to protest, but she took his hand and said, "I do not need him to find the connection. I have you. And if I hold your hand, and travel back along the flow of time, I will be able to connect deeply enough to discover the truth without risking my life. Or my sanity."

"I can leave Ermyk in charge for a time," Aaran said.

She seemed to him taut as a strung bow, quivering with barely bridled excitement.

"What do you think you've found?" he asked.

"At the moment, my suspicions are groundless. Let me look through time and find out the truth before I say anything."

"Very well, then," he said, and left the command to Ermyk, and followed her into his quarters, banishing both Potyr, who had been following him, and Redbird, who had been following her, to the outside with the marine who stood guard.

They sat at his charting table, facing each other across a corner. She pulled his right hand onto the table and interlaced her fingers with his, and then she gave his hand a squeeze. "I don't know what I'll find. As I think about it, I have some ideas, but they may be wrong. If at any time what I discover becomes more than you want to know, tell me, 'No more,' and I will cease." She stilled. "I'll begin now," she told him. "You know what to do if something goes wrong with me."

"I do."

Though she was sitting right in front of him, solid and warm and real, she seemed to fade as he watched her. Her breathing became so shallow he almost couldn't see it, her face went pale, her eyes stared unblinking. She said nothing for a long time, and fine beads of perspiration formed on her forehead, giving her a sheen like wax.

Aside from the faint, regular flaring of her nostrils, he would have sworn her a statue, well formed and well painted, but not alive.

And then her lips parted. "I have followed you back a very long ways, to the place where you and your family last parted. I am in the encampment where you hugged your parents and your sister when no one watched, and then mounted your horse and rode off to join Tuua. The moment of connection with the wizard comes when you hugged your father. So I am following him forward now, slowly, to see if this is the right path. If it is not, I will trail him back in time."

Aaran swallowed hard. He said nothing, because she said speech made it harder for her to find what she sought. But as she said the words, he was right back there with his family the last time he saw them all alive. His little sister with her bright eyes and deep dimples, taunting him about him becoming her big sister instead of a man. His father, clapping him on the back, telling him he would do well. His mother, chin up, managing to smile at that moment, though her lips trembled as she did so. Bidding him be careful.

The sounds of the camp just before sunrise, on that day when several boys would ride out to seek their manhood. The vibrant colors of sunrise, the hush just before the sun crept over the horizon, the whole clan turning to face east, saying together the blessing of the day.

He could hear the hushed voices, *"Haabudaf aveerzak"* floating on the breeze.

He could smell camp smoke and horses. Spring smells of damp earth and growing things. Running water nearby.

He blinked back the tears.

"A month forward from your parting, the slavers have come. From your father, after he fell, they took a medallion he wore. They placed it upon your sister. The medallion is the connection to the wizard I seek. They took all the children and young women, and killed the rest."

Yes, he thought. Remembering coming back, triumphant, a man at the end of his three months' trial. Finding the herds scattered, bodies that still lay where they'd fallen, pecked apart by crows, destroyed by sun and rain. And his sister missing, along with others. Searching with the other young men for family, for survivors, and taking their story to the nearest taak, only to discover that slavers had been raiding the southern coast for months.

"Forward," Hawkspar said. "A rough voyage, but your sister has not been chained in the slave holds with the others. She has been kept in a cage on one of the upper decks. She is given food and fresh water regularly. No one touches her."

"Why?"

"The medallion she wears is important to the men who guard her."

And in his gut, Aaran felt a sick clenching. The medallion. He suddenly remembered it. His father had taken that from the body of one of the Fee-gash he killed during the war. He had worn it as a trophy all the rest of his life. He didn't talk about it, but he'd said it was his reminder of who the enemy was.

And Aaran's father had never suspected how true that was.

"The rest of the captives on the ship have been sold in a market, but your sister has been taken from one ship and placed on another."

And then more silence.

He tried to think that the medallion would not matter. He tried to believe, but in his heart he knew. There would be a price for the taking of that medallion, and Aashka would be the one to pay it. He stared at Hawkspar, willing the next words out of her mouth to be, against all odds, good ones. Words that would give him hope for his sister's fate, words that would make him think that he might yet find her whole and well. Happy. Safe.

"From this ship, in a fair harbor, she travels in a long caravan. She is still in her cage, though they take her out and walk her twice a day. It's big enough that she can stand. She is not touched, she is well fed."

But that did not give him hope. It filled him with terror. They were keeping her well for a reason. He did not want to know the reason. He did not want to. He had to.

He closed his eyes and waited through the eternity of Hawkspar's next silence, his mouth dry, his palms damp.

"She has been taken to a grand house. The women there dress in brilliant colors, the servants in dull brown, the men in black."

And all he could think was *Feegash*.

In the wake of the Feegash betrayal of all of Hyre, every Tonk learned about the Feegash. Children learned how to identify them, and old histories became new again. The ways of the Feegash, what they believed, and how they lived were made a part of every parent's education of his children.

There would, the Tonk promised themselves, be no second Feegash betrayal because of trust.

And yet, here they were, with the Feegash using their position as congenial peacemakers for many of the world's nations to translate those nations' trust in the Feegash into vile misdeeds against the Tonk.

Hawkspar's hand tightened in Aaran's, and he heard her quick intake of breath. He opened his eyes and saw her horror.

He did not want to know. He did not. But he had to. He held his silence; she said she'd tell him what she saw. He'd said he wanted to know. In a moment she would tell him what she saw.

She sat there, her grip growing tighter, not a word coming out of her mouth, and he fought to ask her. And fought to tell her not to tell him anything.

Her shoulders tensed as if she were warding off blows. She winced. She began to whimper—soft little noises in the back of his throat.

Still she breathed; she was not suffering the symptoms that marked the backlash from using the Eyes.

Maybe this was not about his sister; maybe Hawkspar had drifted into something else. Somewhere else.

And then she gasped, "Oh, Jostfar," and slumped against him, weeping.

"What happened?" he asked her, his words barely making it out past his blocked throat.

"No," she told him. "No. I can't tell you. I can't even say the words, Aaran.

It's more than I can bear. She still lives. She is in the keeping of the wizard I must destroy. She is . . . she belongs to another man, whom the wizard serves. If we can reach her and kill those monsters, we can save her." Her hand clung to his so tightly his fingers throbbed. "We have to go get her," Hawkspar said. "Now."

In all of it, Aaran made himself focus on the words *She still lives.* His mind skittered past the fact that what was happening to Aashka was so terrible that a woman who'd been dragged from her murdered family, enslaved, beaten, fed to starving rats, and had her eyes ripped out could not even tell him what it was. He could not let himself think about that.

She still lives.

He would reach Aashka. He would kill the Feegash. All of them, or some of them. The ones who were hurting her, at least. They would pay.

And he would bring his sister home, and somehow, everything would be all right. Somehow. He would make it all right.

He wrapped his arms around the still sobbing Hawkspar, and tried not to remember the stories of what the Feegash had done to their captives in Hyre. He thought about the boy on his own ship that had been a toy for his Feegash father and his father's friends. Horror tightened his throat and knotted his bowels. But that sort of dread wouldn't help him. It wouldn't help her.

"Are you in pain?" he finally asked Hawkspar.

"Some. I'll . . . manage. Leave me in here, for a while, if you would, while you go . . . do whatever you must do. Send me one of the Moonstones, and let me have a sip of your drink. I'll . . . I will calm myself, and . . ." Her voice broke and she covered her face with her hands again.

"We were going to take all of your Order to Tonk territories."

"There's no time," Hawkspar said.

"It's been fifteen years."

She rested a hand on his arm. "If you waited fifteen more years, she would still be there. Or thirty. Or maybe a hundred. However long they can keep her alive. But . . . no. Have your communicators contact a Tonk ship that can take the children and one of the Obsidians, and the Rosestones, and one of the Ambers to a safe harbor. The rest of us will stay and fight with you. You'll need us," she added. "The one who owns your sister is the Feegash leader, as much as their power resides in a single pair of hands. He is the one who directs the allies of the Feegash against the Tonk. You will need us, and many, many more than us."

Aaran scooped her into his arms and deposited her in his bed. He covered her, gave her some of his gyriik to drink, and told her to be still. "Then I'll have a double benefit for killing him, if he's the Feegash leader as well as the one who stole my sister away," he told her.

He left to get her healers and his communicators and to start after Aashka, trying all the while to concentrate on the fact that she was, against all odds, still alive. And not on the questions Hawkspar refused to answer about her condition.

He was halfway between having sent the Moonstones to help Hawkspar and locating a communicator to send the message she'd requested—the lot of them were probably down in the attable eating—when something struck him.

Eban had mentioned that his father and uncle were diplomats.

What were the odds that they knew the senior diplomat of the Feegash, the man who held his sister?

He reversed course halfway down the companionway to the attable, and ran back to the temple. Tuua wasn't there, but Eban was, painstakingly reading aloud from a history of the Viikuu Tonk that Aaran knew Tuua had written. Tonk wasn't the easiest language to read, even for native speakers, but the kid was making his way through it.

"Eban," Aaran said.

The boy put the book down and looked up. "Yes, Cap'n? Tuua said he had to check on patients, but that he would be back shortly."

Aaran took a seat on the bench across the table from the boy and said, "I was actually looking for you. You mentioned your father being a diplomat. And your uncle, too. I need to know if you ever heard them talking about a diplomat named Kafrij Son of Fanbjan."

"I've heard of my uncle," the boy said sadly. "But if you have, that means that he's found me, and has offered you a deal to get me back."

Aaran felt the air in the room go thin. "Your uncle? He's your uncle?"

The boy looked puzzled. "You truly did not know that?"

"He's the bastard who holds my sister."

The boy put a hand over his mouth, and beneath the tanned skin, grayness crept in. "Oh, no," he whispered. "My uncle is . . . he is a very bad man."

At first, Aaran couldn't even think, beyond the shock of realizing that he had someone on his ship who might be able to lead him straight to his sister.

And they were, after all these long years, going after Aashka.

But then Aaran considered the bigger picture, and he started to get scared.

Eban wasn't some random Ba'afeegash kid. He was the kid of the brother of the first diplomat of Ba'afeegash. He might not have been a kid that anyone liked very much, but just having him aboard—if his presence were discovered by the Ba'afeegash—would be perfect justification for a major Feegash incident.

If the diplomat bastards hadn't used some of their magic to get him aboard.

He closed his eyes and rubbed at his temples.

The kid was scarred all to hell. Imagine for a moment that the Ba'afeegash decided to claim that those scars had been inflicted by the Tonk. Or decided to kill the kid, and present his scarred body to the world as proof of Tonk atrocities.

There were Tonk deep healers who could remove all the kid's scars, grow him up a little and put some muscle on him, maybe change the color of his eyes or his hair. None of them—and there were only five that Aaran knew of in the whole of Hyre—were on his ship. The deep healers were all military, all of them with highest trust status—and all of them personally trained by the woman who had brought Hagedwar magic to the Tonks.

Talyn Wyran av Tiirsha dryn Straad. One of the two heroes of the last battle against the Feegash, which had been both a small battle and, conversely, the winning of the war.

Every Tonk knew her story. A lot of Tonks knew it from inside her eyes, and wished they didn't. She'd come through unthinkable pain and suffering to bring her people out of slavery, and had given them a remarkable gift at the same time: the enemy's magic, done better than even the enemy could do it.

It was because she had unraveled the secrets of the Hagedwar that ships could have trackers. Individual communicators. Windmen. It was because of her that every ship could have its own healer, and not just a medic whose only real option in emergencies was to amputate. Her gift of magic had meant Tonks born to magic no longer risked their lives in the View, twenty at a time; no longer fell into the seductive places between life and afterlife, to leave their bodies behind forever.

She'd made it possible for people who were not born to magic to still do magic, and had increased the size of the Tonk magical defense in the process.

She had changed the face of peace and the face of war for her people.

There were more than a few who whispered that she could have changed it more, had she wanted to. That when she taught the Hagedwar, she didn't teach all of it.

The presence of five Tonk master healers who could perform absolute miracles—and their high military clearance—lent some credence to those rumors.

He wondered how to make the Hagedwar do more. He wondered if he could figure it out. He'd been a quick student, and he was better than average in using the thing. He only knew a part of what it could do, of course. He'd watched the windmen work and sat with them from time to time. In an absolute emergency, if there were no qualified windmen aboard, he *might* be able to manage something without killing everyone aboard. He sat in on communicator sessions and had practiced with the communicators on emergency signals and a few other basics. Healing—well, he knew nothing at all about that. It was too far outside his area. He wouldn't even know which interstices in the Hagedwar to use.

But cross-pollinating seemed to have worked well with Tonk magic and the Hagedwar. Aaran was a better tracker than most because he had the Tonk magic in him, too.

He found himself wondering if the Seru Moonstone, who already had their own brand of healing, could be taught the Hagedwar, and could figure out a way to use it to do the same sorts of magic the master healers could do.

He went to talk to the communicators, to have them send in secret for a ship to take the children to safety, and to beg help from any Tonk wolfship—to announce that he had found the enemies of the Tonk, and that only an armada would hope to prevail against them.

He would talk to Hawkspar about teaching her Moonstones the Hagedwar later. And perhaps her, as well.

He would not let himself think about loving her and losing her. He would not think about her claim that her destiny was to die. He refused to accept that the future would not offer the two of them a chance together. For the first time in sixteen years, he knew, at least generally, where Aashka was. He was going to rescue her.

And he would not believe that the woman who had found Aashka when he could not had no chance at a brighter future than war and an early death.

He would not let that happen.

Hawkspar

I lay in Aaran's bed, and as soon as he was gone from the room, I clutched my head and cried. I could not chase the pictures of his sister and her fate from my head. I could not stop hearing and feeling what the Feegash diplomats did to her. I could not stop hurting for her.

The river of time ran through me, cold and bitter, and I could not escape the images it still poured at me.

Aaran and Aashka's father had killed the brother of the man who came eventually to lead the Feegash. But even before he assumed the top position, Diplomat Kafrij Son of Fanbjan and his brother Hirsem had both held tremendous power. When she fell into his possession, Kafrij had made very sure that Aashka understood why he and his associates were doing what they were doing to her. He'd been careful to justify his every action, to declare himself as doing nothing more than carrying out justice for the Feegash who had been so badly treated by the inhabitants of Hyre, and especially by the Tonks.

She had just been a little girl. She could not understand.

I'd flowed past as many years as I could without letting the horrors brush against me. But I had to understand the *why* of the nightmare that flowed around me.

My life had been marked by these people—these Feegash—too. They'd been paying the Sinalis for years to hunt down Tonk children and enslave them. I had not understood this before, but the Feegash had always considered the nomadic, independent, world-spanning Tonk a threat to their plans to create the world of their vision. The Feegash needed a world filled with sheep, and the Tonk were wolves. So, long before their invasion of Hyre under pretense, they were paying the Sinalis and other peoples who permitted slavery to specialize in acquiring Tonk slaves. They paid a little premium on each one. They only accepted authentic clan marks for their bonuses—which was why the slavers slaughtered all children younger than two. They were too much trouble to keep, and they didn't bear the necessary clan marks.

I'd been gathered under their systematic eradication program. The Feegash truly didn't care whether the children lived or died, so long as they were no longer Tonk. Scattered and shorn of their beliefs and their heritage, the Feegash believed Tonk children posed no threat. The Feegash allies killed all adults. Some saved left hands to collect bounties.

I'd not understood before the nature of my enemy. I'd not seen what the Feegash were.

Now I knew.

All peoples have among their number the good and the bad. It is the nature of humanity, and cannot be changed. But some cultures are by their nature evil; this I had not understood. I had seen evil men. I had never before been forced to confront a culture that trained its men to be evil, and rewarded them for their evil as if it were good.

I did not fully understand the Tonk culture or my own people. I was still struggling to make sense of where I'd come from and what that meant. But I understood that I had become a player in a war that mattered; in a fight between a way of life that was at its heart profoundly evil, and one that I believed to be mostly good.

I understood at last why my mentor had fought so hard to win me to her cause when she discovered what the Feegash were doing. She had been too old and too physically weak to do what the Eyes of War would have to do. By being the Eyes of War, I had already helped the Tonk cause by bringing Feegash involvement and Feegash treachery to light. But in the days to come, more would be demanded of me. I could already see how the river ran, and in its branches where the Tonk survived, I stood centered in the stream with Aaran at my side.

I could see my own death in every future, even in those where the Tonk eventually won out. I could see pain and heartbreak for myself along the way. I could see points of sacrifice, though I could not see the events that caused them.

I lay there, wrapped in blankets, knowing what would be asked of me and knowing the price I would have to pay to give it, and I was terrified. I wanted to give the Eyes to someone else. I yearned to be a slave again, with no responsibility for lives other than my own—and not even a real responsibility for that.

But every time my mind shied away from my own future, it landed squarely on Aashka's present. And on the Sinali ships out in the oceans and seas of countries I'd never heard of, looking for unsuspecting Tonk clans that had been marked for slaughter.

I could not hide from my future, no matter how much I wanted to. I could not leave other children to Aashka's fate, or even to mine. I'd taken on this duty, and no matter how much I hadn't wanted to then, and how much less I wanted to after finding out what vile creatures I had to face if the future would be better, no one else could do what I had to do.

Acceptance of my duty, I was coming to understand, was part of what it meant to be Tonk—to belong to this far-flung family I was only beginning to know.

Aaran

Aaran quickly heard back from his plea for help. The Rovintaak wolf-pack had been hunting not far from where Aaran and the *Taag av Sookyn* escaped the last of the islands of the Fallen Suns. They were breaking off their hunt to join up with the *Taag*.

Through the communicator codes and secret channels, other wolf-packs scattered through the Kervish Ocean, the Copper Seas, and the Formiterranean Sea, confirmed that they were on their way, and designated meet-up points. In addition, another lone wolf like Aaran's had agreed to step in and ferry the captives back to safety.

Aaran sat in his quarters with his communicators, marking points and times, charting their course, feeling more confident as he put together a fleet that, if every ship arrived, would number more than sixty ships. Enough to wage a war even on Ba'afeegash, he thought.

One of his marine guards banged on his door. "Cap'n," he yelled. "Tracker calls an emergency."

Aaran, with half a crew and with the holes filled for the moment by girls and young women, had no illusions about his readiness for another emergency. He leapt to his feet and ran to the steersman's castle, Potyr at his heels. There, the tracker knelt before a charting page, his eyes closed, his hands drawing the lines and angles of troughs and peaks beneath the sea that would act as navigation markers.

"What have you found?" Aaran asked Otaam, who was finally healed enough to have resumed his duties.

"The Sinali warships," Otaam said. "We didn't lose them in the storm, and they've been using the favorable winds and currents since to catch up with us. They were running a parallel course when I spotted them, but just moments ago they split off from each other. It looks like they're going to try to trap us."

Aaran swore steadily. And then, looking at the placement of the three ships, he started to grin.

He cast his own track, and drew in the positions of the six ships in the Rovintaak wolf-pack. "The Sinalis don't know they're out there," he said to Otaam.

Otaam looked at the positions the three Sinali ships were taking, and the placement of the pack. And he said, "Cap'n, we're placed to bury the lot of them."

"We are, indeed," Aaran said. "If we can get a bit of space between us, anyway." He turned to Potyr. "Get all the communicators in here, fast as they can move," he said.

The boy took off like a mad hare.

When the communicators arrived, Aaran had them transmit an offer for shared hunting and spoils—which the Rovintaakers readily accepted. He then dragged Faryn out and set him to the sails, channeling as much wind as he could in a direction that made clear to the slavers that they'd been spotted, and that the *Taag* was attempting to evade.

They were heading almost due west, where a scattering of little islands formed the easternmost edge of the Fallen Suns. The Sinalis should think that the *Taag* was hoping to take cover in the islands in order to lose its pursuers.

With luck, they'd speed up their pursuit, abandon all pretense of stealth, and fall into a nice, tight line. Aaran would then attempt to lead them into the trap the Rovintaakers would set.

He sent word to Hawkspar, and she joined him in the steersman's castle.

She looked thin and pale. In the two days since she'd located Aaran's sister, Aaran had seen the color go out of her face, and had noticed the Obsidian, Redbird, start hovering around her like a shadow, becoming increasingly worried and protective.

When he managed to talk privately to Redbird, she told him that Hawkspar had hardly eaten anything since she had located his sister.

"You need me?" Hawkspar asked.

And Aaran thought, *Always*. He said, "We did not lose the Sinali warships that were sent to destroy us. They're close behind us now, and though we are drawing away from them at the moment, we will not be maintaining that speed. We're going to turn and fight." He took a deep breath. He'd thought to ask her to look into time and tell him how he might make sure the battle went well, but when she was right there in front of him, he could not. He feared for her; she should not ever look so fragile.

She didn't wait for him to ask her, though. She said, "Give me a moment," and took a seat next to Otaam on his bench. Her eyes closed, her hands lay flat across the chart Otaam had been working on. "Avoid the black-sailed ship," she said. "Do not engage it under any circumstances."

She opened her eyes again. "We may do well in this," she told him. She got to her feet, and started to leave. Her knees sagged, and she looked like she might topple forward, but quick as Aaran was to get to his feet, he was not as quick as Redbird, who caught Hawkspar, and put an arm around her waist, and draped one of Hawkspar's arms around her own shoulder. "You have to eat something, Mouse," Redbird said, and half-walked, half-carried Hawkspar away from him.

He could not even afford to pursue her. He had a battle to plan.

It came not long after dawn the next morning. The *Taag*, having slowed over the course of the night to make sure the Sinalis kept up, ducked around the point of the third island it passed. The wolf-pack waited, hidden just behind the mass of that tiny island and two others.

When the *Taag* passed the hidden ships, Aaran turned her to one side, and with the careful use of anchors, mimicked foundering on a sandbar.

The Sinalis, sensing the opportunity for a kill, came racing in.

And the wolves descended on them.

Aaran turned the *Taag* around, and—having passed Hawkspar's warning to the wolves to avoid direct engagement with the one black-sailed ship—brought his crew, with marines augmented by the Obsidians, to bear against the next-largest of the warships.

These were no slavers, and the fights were fierce. Both sides had Greton fire, both had catapults and archers, and in the end, the battle was decided not by skill, for all represented themselves well, but by who had the sailors quickest at getting sand on burning wood or cutting away burning sheets—and who had the most weapons in their holds. Simple numbers won the day.

The Tonk wolf-pack watched the Sinali ships until they burned to the waterline. Then they spent two days engaged in repairs of their own ships.

They had no treasure to show for their battle, and they'd lost men. But three Sinali warships and every warrior aboard them were destroyed. That was worth some celebration.

Hawkspar

We reached the first of the meeting points Aaran and the captains of the various wolf-packs had plotted out. We maintained a steady course while the Tonk fleet pulled alongside us. One ship, the *Seevyn Aragga* (or *Beautiful Dancer*), cut itself out from the line of wolf-ships that would be accompanying us, and tied on to us. We transported all the children and young girls who had been penitents and acolytes, and a few Ossalenes as guardians for them.

We had debated sending off our moriiad crewmen and trying to replace all of them with Tonk crew, but in the end, Aaran trusted the results of my search forward in time; I insisted that none of the moriiad who had fought with us and survived to that point would betray us. So we would be the lone ship in the growing pack that would carry moriiad.

Aaran and the marines gave shares to each of the seru, and to each departing girl who had worked as crew. None of the shares was large, but they were something. And none of the girls had ever owned anything before. The remaining crew then slogged our current salvage and treasure into one hold, to keep it separate from anything new we might get.

After that was done, we took on desperately needed replacements from both the *Seevyn* and the other ships in the pack. We got another windman, a dozen marines, as many sailors, and a new qualified steersman. We didn't get any new officers, though we needed them. And we didn't get a new runner, though not because none was offered. Both Aaran and Potyr agreed that they would not replace Neeran.

All the new crew were Tonk—and none were Mindan, Reform or otherwise—and all signed agreements that would make them party only to shares of loot collected after they joined. They brought their own shares with them, and we had to catalog and separately store these new shares where they would not get mixed in with the *Taag's* treasure.

To me, it felt like delay and more delay. But Aaran had assured me that the best way to keep a crew loyal through hard times was to make sure to take care of that crew's future. Which meant guarding the sanctity of the shares.

Our course would take us to three more meet points in quick succession.

We would, at these points, add in new ships to the secret armada. Those ships that reached us in time would sail with us—those who did not make the meet points could attempt to catch up later, or simply return to their hunting. We were going to run down to Greton as planned. Resupply there at a handful of different ports so that no one would notice our numbers. Then regroup and sail north up the coast of Tandinapalis, to the mountainous Askag Bay, which Aaran said would be our closest connection to the mountain-walled city-state of Ba'afeegash. We would resupply in Danaskataak, the northernmost taak in Tandinapalis. Our ships would harbor there, and the Obsidians, our marines, and as many of our sailors as could be spared would go overland to Ba'afeegash, which in all its centuries of existence had never fallen to outside attack.

How we were going to deal with our enemy when we arrived, none of us could say. I could see nothing useful in the way of battle plans in my forays into the future. That time still lay too far ahead for even vague details to emerge. I could only see that in some futures we went and we conquered, and in most we went and were destroyed to the last man.

Tuua came to sit beside me after the children were gone. I'd promised them I would find them again if I could. I knew as I said the words it was a promise I was unlikely to survive long enough to keep.

"You seem worried," Tuua said.

"The future is not a place I enjoy spending much time in right now," I told him. "It's an ugly place."

"We made it past the slavers and out of the Dragon Sea; we'll get through this as well."

"I could tell you all the different ways that we don't, if you'd like. And the ends to which we will most likely come, individually or as a group."

He laughed. "I think I'd rather you didn't do that. I'd rather hear all the many ways we'll win, and how we sail home with the Diplomat Kafrij's head dangling from the teeth of our figurehead."

"The carved horse head at the front of the ship?"

"Yes. That's why they're carved with their mouths open, and why they have hooks in their bottom jaws. For a long time, sailing home with the heads of enemy chieftains hanging from the figureheads was a proud Tonk tradition. I think in this case it's one we should renew."

I liked the thought of that.

"If I can see that in our futures, I'll be sure to tell Aaran how we can follow that stream instead of all the others."

He rested a hand on my shoulder. "You don't see much good for us, though, do you?"

I considered my words carefully, but in the end my choices were to either lie or tell the truth. I was not, and had never been, a liar. "We don't have much chance of winning," I told him. "The strongest branches of the stream lead to our death and to the destruction of the Tonk, though the manner in which that comes has changed drastically."

He said, "Has it?"

"It has. Before your . . . our . . . people knew about the involvement of the Feegash, the Tonks were weakened by raids from Sinali ships, but destroyed at last by betrayal from within. The Reform Mindans carefully worked their way into positions of power, then permitted an influx of foreigners—"

"Moriiad," Tuua told me.

I corrected myself. "They permitted an influx of moriiad to assume positions of importance within Tonk institutions. And the moriiad eventually assumed power and made being Tonk illegal, in little bits and pieces. It would have taken about a hundred years until the last Tonk died."

"And now?"

"The biggest streams now lead to war, with all the Tonk from all their many homes banding together against the weight of nations. In these futures, the last Tonk dies in about fifty years."

"That's not an improvement."

I considered. "You wouldn't think so, would you? But in a funny way, it is. The waters of time had carved a deep, fast channel leading to the demise of the Tonk. There were almost no streams that led to any other future. Now that we have shifted the river from its bed by letting the Tonk know what they face, about half our futures lead to our destruction. The other half lead to hope. To a world where Tonk are still Tonk at the end of this."

He sat for a long time considering that. "Certain gradual, silent extinction over a hundred years, or a fifty percent chance of keeping our freedom, and a fifty percent chance of dying while fighting for it. You're right. This is better. It gives us something to do even if we lose."

I laughed. That was such a purely Tonk perspective—something I was gradually learning, but had not yet managed to fully embrace.

And then we were ready to see the transport ship off toward Hyre. And to get underway ourselves, with the first battle we would face moving closer with every racing instant.

I listened to the girls aboard the other ship shouting their good-byes and wishing us luck. Then, as they drew away, the sounds of the ocean, wind, and lapping water erased their voices.

I let the rhythms of the ship soothe me; men's voices shouting, the snap of sails as they filled with wind, the singing of the lines, the creak of wood, the rush of water. This time we were part of a fleet. Not so vulnerable. Not carrying traitors anymore. Everyone aboard the ship wanted to see us win— even those of our crew who were not Tonk, but who had heard of the magnificent wealth of the Feegash, and their endless strongholds lined with gold, and who wanted at least a chance to see if all they'd heard was truth.

Aaran joined me at the prow on the private captain's watch-deck after we were underway.

"Having second thoughts?"

"And third. And fourth," I admitted.

"You could have gone with most of your people. We know who the enemy is now. We'll find a way to root the bastards out."

"You'll have a better chance with me along," I told him. I did not let him know that he would have had no chance without me. That somehow, though I could not yet see how, I would prove critical in any possible success. I did not let him know the many ways that I could see either of the two of us die, either, or my own futures in which my only wish was death. He knew we did not face good odds. All the men knew. I found them admirable. They knew as well as I did that we would be outnumbered, and most likely that we would not win—and yet they had all come.

I felt pride, then. These were my people. I'd never truly felt that kinship before. I'd had no connection with the Tonk, save prayers morning and night— and those do nothing to tell the measure of a man, or a culture. It's how he acts when he thinks his god isn't listening that will tell you a person's worth.

These were strong, brave people.

I was grateful to be one of them; I was slowly discovering how much that meant.

31

Aaran

They sailed for a week and a day, making each point, picking up those ships that waited there. Never as many as they had hoped, but always more than they'd had before. And when they stood off a dot of an island—a mere pinnacle of rock in the center of the deep sea that the Tonk called Jostfar's Icepick—they acquired the last ships that would be sailing with them.

Communicators passed messages from ship to ship, trying to set up the organization of the fleet, but at last it was agreed that all the captains needed to meet in person, and that Hawkspar, who had discovered the information that had brought them all together, needed to meet with them.

With a certain amount of confusion, then, those called to the meeting began to make their way to the chosen meeting place—the private officers' attable of the enormous, new-built *Ker Nagile*, named after the famous Tand warhorse and sire of warhorses from the ancient War of Stones and Snow. Hawkspar was nervous about presenting what she knew, so they left early. She insisted, saying the Eyes told her it was what they needed to do to win the captains to the tasks ahead.

The *Ker* was a gorgeously appointed ship, and one that Makkor and his sons had finished not long before Aaran had come ashore in Port Midrid. It had a sleek horsehead prow, four masts, a deep arrowhead hull, and more speed than any of the other ships in the makeshift fleet could hope to match. It boasted catapults and boarding arms and massive winching crossbows and huge stores of Greton fire, and berthed a crew of a hundred-forty sailors, twenty-four officers, and a hundred-sixty marines. It sailed smoother and steadier than any ship Aaran had set foot on, and he almost lusted for it. Almost.

It was not his, and—for all that he still more than half-believed it was cursed—he had come to love both the graces and the quirks of the *Taag*. But the *Ker* was what all wolf-ships would someday be. Lean and quick and stable. And big.

He followed one of the *Ker*'s runners to the officers' attable, where he stopped and stared. The attable was enormous, high-ceilinged, and well appointed. In all his life, Aaran had never seen such a vast amount of space set aside just for the officers. It had three dropwaiters. It had beer on tap. The benches were padded. It was magnificent. And, as nearly the first to arrive, he got to stare around it to his heart's content.

"Lovely, ain't it?" one of the two men seated at table asked, watching Aaran's face with evident amusement.

"As fair a ship as ever I've seen."

"The *Ker*'s captain had a fine ship. The story is that he saw this one as it was gliding out of dry dock, and all but ran over the builder to be first in line to buy it. And with his deep pockets, he was last in line as well."

"Lucky man," Aaran said. "Wouldn't hurt to be rich, I suppose."

"It wouldn't," the man agreed. "You captain one of the ships from the Rovintaak wolf-pack, don't you? I thought I saw you come over on one of the Rovintaak longboats just behind me."

Aaran shook his head. "I'm Aaran av Savissha," he raised his left palm, presenting his clan mark. "We've been sailing with the Rovintaakers, but the *Taag av Sookyn* is my ship."

Both captains fixed their attention on Aaran. "The . . . *Taag*? *Av Sookyn*? You're the *Madman*?" one asked.

That nickname hadn't gone away in the past weeks, then. "So I've been called," he said.

"And you're still alive? You're all the talk around the Path of Stars. Story was that you sailed into the Dragon Sea and wizards ripped you apart. We all thought sure you were dead days after you left Port Midrid."

That was one of the interesting effects of maintaining secrecy while using the communicators, Aaran thought. He'd passed the codes that proved he was Tonk, and proved his ship was a wolf-ship in good standing and with papers in order, but to keep anyone from betraying him, his identity and the name of his ship had remained secret from all save the registrar—the man who controlled the codes for the wolf-ships. So no one knew precisely where Aaran had found his information, or who he was, or who his ship was. They had been able to verify his first batch of information—regarding the treachery of the Mindan Reformists—themselves, which was why they had come when ship Wolf-808-Solo said if they did not act quickly, the Tonks would fall under the Feegash plot to destroy them.

The captain raised his left palm and said, "I'm Dyur av Derstaag, captain of the *Vinik Han.* Delighted to meet you. Good of you to join in this fight— probably a happier place to be than chasing ghosties in the Fallen Suns, eh?"

Aaran squelched a grin. "Actually, I'm the captain who called everyone here."

The other captain was staring from his companion to Aaran and back. His head bobbed like a marionette's. "You're the man who found out about the shit-swilling Feegash and their treachery?"

"No. But I'm the man who rescued the woman, Hawkspar, who did." Aaran glanced toward the door. "She'll be along shortly. She found a lad who wanted to show her around the ship, and since she was enchanted by it, she took the boy up on his offer."

And Dyur laughed. "You rescued her, eh? Well, the little beauties do get their tails into some interesting fixes, don't they? Hawkspar . . . that almost sounds like an Eastil name. I still don't trust that lot, but their women have as good ears as any women do, I suppose." Apparently he was assuming Hawkspar had gotten her information via pillow talk.

"She's Tonk. The name is a title." Aaran smiled. He didn't feel any need to warn the men that the woman who was coming was not some delicate little flower, some wench who made her way from bed to bed and gossip to gossip. It would be, he thought, a great deal more fun to watch as the truth dawned on them.

On the companionway stairs outside the door, a thunder started, the heels of many boots descending at once. Aaran and both the other captains turned toward the open door, and through it streamed a veritable tide of ships' captains, all of them silent, and most of them looking shocked.

"There are women aboard this ship," one of the men said. He sounded scandalized. "Stone-eyed, monstrous women."

And then a chatter of voices all at once.

"They're acting as if they own this place. They were . . . rude when we suggested this was no place for women."

And, "They parade about the decks as if they were thinking of taking lease."

And, "What fool brought them, and why them?"

Aaran wondered if Hawkspar had refused to come down into the officers' attable with him because she had known in advance that this would be their reaction. He shouted, "Attend! Attend me!" but captains were better at giving orders than taking them, and he had to step onto a bench and shout at the top of his lungs before the other men silenced themselves and turned to face him.

He introduced himself once again, but did not give time for the greeting exchange that would have been polite under most circumstances.

"I am the man who called you here," he said. "The one who voyaged into the Fallen Suns and rescued more than a hundred slaves, many of them Tonk, from the Ossalene Citadel. The women on this ship right now will be joining us shortly, and the Oracle Hawkspar will address you."

"Women, man!" someone shouted. "What were you thinking?"

"Hawkspar is the reason we know the truth about the Feegash. She is the Oracle of the Hawkspar Eyes of War, and for her ability to see clearly into the past, the present, and the future, kings have offered gold and lands and slaves and even marriage. She does not offer her visions to everyone. She pays a terrible price each time she seeks the future. But she helps us without charge and without obligation."

"Why?" Captain av Derstaag asked. "Why are we the beneficiaries of this help of dubious worth?"

"Because she's Tonk," Aaran said stiffly. "As is the Seru Obsidian who guards her. Both of them, and most of the Ossalenes who remain on my ship, were stolen away by slavers as small children, and sold to the Order." His mouth twisted with anger. "All of you know the story; most of you know it personally. We share this pain. And so does she. She took on the Eyes she wears because the previous Eyes of War, also Tonk, discovered that we were at war with an enemy that chose not to declare itself. That oracle was too old to travel with warriors to do what had to be done; she died in a manner that makes me think it was by choice, and Hawkspar accepted the mutilation she has suffered so that she could offer herself for the survival of our people. Give her the respect that she has earned for her sacrifice."

They stood around him, faces disbelieving, chastened, or marked with pain.

And then a voice Aaran had not expected to hear again rang through the hall.

From the top of a table on the opposite side of the attable, Captain Haakvar said, "So. The Madman erupts from the Fallen Suns with a wild tale of rescuing women who can see the future, and calls us across the seas to fight a battle these so-called oracles claim will save us. Had I known it was you who had brought us here, neither I nor my fleet would have come." He glared at Aaran. "You're barely a captain, tracker, and only because you took a ship on credit and named yourself one." Haakvar pointed at the other assembled captains and said, "I cannot speak for many of you, but I can speak for those of you who sail my ships. We will not stay for this . . . joke."

Into that silence, Hawkspar and Redbird swept, led by a handful of awed-looking junior officers.

Hawkspar's sheer presence cleared a spontaneous path, and she joined Aaran on the table. She went a step farther, standing on the tabletop itself. It wasn't a thing either of them could have done in his ship—but in this magnificent new warship, some decks enjoyed ceilings as high as homes, or nearly so.

Hawkspar turned to face the majority of the men in the room and raised her left hand. The gasp that followed marked their introduction to the fact that she was Eskuu—the first Eskuu anyone in the known Tonk territories had seen in time out of mind.

She said, "Captain Haakvar, you will sail with us, as will your other ships, because if you do not, then the Tonk cause is lost. And as you are neither a traitor nor a coward, the survival of your people means more to you than your own life."

She turned her face from one side of the room to the other, and Aaran could see that the men who were watching her shuddered. "I know my presence on this ship and with this fleet disturbs you," she said bluntly. "I know this is not the way of things, and under better circumstances and in better times, we would have not the need of it. But we have the need of it now. I am the Oracle Hawkspar Eyes of War, raised from the time of my capture and enslavement to be an Ossalene. I had a name once, but I do not know it anymore—you may, therefore, call me Hawkspar. You will have noticed my Eyes."

This she said in a haughty, deadpan tone that made Aaran wish he dared turn to stare at her. He wanted to see if the corners of her mouth were twitching, the way they did when she found something funny.

"They are stone," she continued, "enchanted artifacts made by a fool of a wizard back at the dawn of history. They are ugly, and they hurt, but they permit me to step into the waters of time and follow them where they flow, both forward and back. I can see what was, but I can also see all the many ways that things might be, and catch them as they change."

"I doubt that," Haakvar said.

And Hawkspar said, "I know you do. So let me tell you something that will convince you. When you were a young man, you stood before a woman you hoped to marry, and promised that you would take Minda as your saint, and be the shopkeeper she and her parents hoped you would be. You went so far as to walk with your beloved to the temple to put Ethebet aside in favor of Minda, but when you were there, you stood before the shrine of Ethebet, and in the Meditations of Saint Ethebet written on the wall, found something that convinced you to turn to the woman beside you and tell her that you would not—could not—marry her."

She paused. "Her family, who doubted your commitment to Minda, were quite relieved. They used her heartbreak as an excuse to hurry her into a marriage to a man they considered more suitable. She has had a good life, and has been content with the man her parents chose for her. And all your life you have wondered if you made the right choice."

Haakvar stood on the table across the room from her, his expression stunned. "No one knows of that."

"I do," Hawkspar said. "Further, I know you made the right decision. The future is not done with you, Rya Haakvar. You greatest encounter with destiny still lies before you."

Voices clamored around the room, men who wanted, in light of this revelation, some word of their own secret pasts, and their own unknown futures.

But Hawkspar held up a hand to silence them. "My visions of the past and future are not a game, good men. I pay a price in pain, and other prices more dear, every time I push hard into the waters for one clear view. I told Haakvar what I saw because Captain Haakvar's participation is critical to the success of the voyage we embark upon. But you are not here for your amusement. You are here to learn of the voyage before us, and why we must go forth."

Aaran watched her, awestruck. She was magnificent as she spelled out the dangers she had told to him, as she presented to the assembled captains the risks they faced and the doom that might yet devour them all.

He wanted to think that she was his. His heart believed it wholly, and refused to be dissuaded. But as she talked flatly of the dangers before them, and of her own certain death, either as the battle raged on, or when it was won, he at last believed her. Something about the matter-of-fact manner in which she presented her case finally made him understand that the little time they would have aboard the *Taag*, and perhaps the time while they fought the Feegash, was all the time they would ever have.

And sad and futile as Aaran knew it was, he loved her even more.

Hawkspar

I'd seen before we even left the *Taag* that I would have to make a dramatic entry. I'd known I would have to spend myself freely in reading Haakvar's past. I knew that if I did not do these things, he would abandon Aaran for the grudge he still held against him, and we would be lost before we'd even begun. Ten ships sailed with him, ten he owned besides the *Ker Nagile*, and without them we would have sailed with sixteen ships. Not enough. The fleet we had with us, not even half as large as the fleet Aaran had hoped to assemble, might be enough. If we were quick, fierce, and steadfast. And very lucky.

We needed them all.

So I presented my visions with every wile my predecessor had taught me. I used my voice, I used my passion, I engaged each of the captains individually by addressing some point of the future that I could see mattered to him. I brought them all into it, but the pain behind the Eyes grew as I did. It became bad, and then fierce, and then an agony so great I thought I might stop breathing right there.

But I could not quit. I could see that they needed something more from me, and though I could not discover what it was, they did not yet have it. I bore the pain and kept going.

They asked me questions about the Feegash, and about our voyage, and I sought, and they asked more, and I sought more. Behind the Eyes, the pain billowed—there were too many people, too many streams, too many places where the currents of one life conflicted with the currents of other lives. I was fighting to keep myself upright; they asked important questions and I knew we needed the answers to them. How would we find our way around the outer perimeter of Ba'afeegash? How would we hide the fleet? How would we find the man responsible for this treachery in a strange city? How would we keep harm to innocents to a minimum? What happened if we failed?

Every question mattered.

But I had not the strength to answer them all, and behind the building pain, something inside of me snapped. I toppled backward, and collapsed.

I fell into darkness. I crashed beyond knowing, into Ossal's prison.

"I'll have you," he said, and I could feel him grinning. "I'll become you."

It was, I came to understand, the whole of his desire. Not to have me, not to use me. But to be me. To be flesh again, to be free of the darkness and the infinite nothing. If he won, he would escape, and I would remain.

Aaran

Aaran noticed that she was looking pale. He caught the first sheen of sweat on her forehead and on her upper lip. He saw her breathing faster and shallower. But he didn't realize she was in real trouble until, right in the middle of a word, she collapsed.

Her whole body went limp and neither he nor Redbird were quick enough to catch her, though Redbird's dramatic leap from floor to table—vaulting across two unsuspecting captains to get there—certainly caught the awed attention of those present.

"Get me cold water," he shouted. One of the junior officers, who had stayed to observe, fled, and quickly returned carrying two buckets of cold water.

Aaran dipped his finger into it and licked it—it was fresh, not salt. He cupped his hand in, and sprinkled it over her face.

She didn't move. She barely breathed. The men gathered around him, and a low murmur filled the room.

"What's wrong with her?" Haakvar demanded.

"Did you not hear her tell you that she pays a price for using the Eyes? Or did you, perhaps, think she exaggerated her suffering to win you over? I've seen the hells these things put her through," he said. "Because she needed to reassure you, because she knows how much this matters, she tore herself apart for the lot of you."

"She won't die now, will she?" some fool at the back asked.

Aaran looked up at him. "Do you mistake me for Jostfar, who knows such things?"

She breathed, but only faintly. Her skin, usually warm and golden brown, was cold and the color of raw wax. Sweat soaked her. She did not twitch. She did not cry out. But her muscles were locked tight, he realized, and with every fiber of her being she gave the impression of fighting desperately for her life.

He turned to Redbird. "We need to get her back to the Moonstones. Quickly."

He scooped Hawkspar into his arms. Holding her, he could feel the tension in her body. It frightened him. This was not exhaustion. It was not pain. It was something worse, something sinister that he could not begin to guess how to reach.

Redbird stared at Hawkspar, fear clear on her face. And something else, too. Yearning? Love?

Aaran would have thought more about that, but Hawkspar suddenly gasped, and her eyes opened.

"No," she whispered.

"Hawkspar?"

She shuddered. Inhaled slowly. "No," she said again. "Don't take me. I can't leave here yet. They were asking me our safest path. Let me find it for them. Then we can return to the *Taag*."

Aaran watched Haakvar, who had moved to the front of the crowd. He was staring at Hawkspar, and he looked both wary, and concerned. "Young lady," he said at last, "you need not tear yourself to bits over this. We can wait until you feel better to give us your answer. We have time."

And then he saw a faint smile curl at the corners of her mouth. "No," she said. "We don't have time at all."

Hawkspar

"Get someone to write down what I say," I said. "I caught glimpses of what lies ahead before I . . . fell. It's . . . very complex."

One of the junior officers bolted again, returning with a sheaf of paper, ink, and several pens.

I relaxed my body and sank into the flow of time. I let its current pull me a little way forward. I looked for snags and sandbars and eddies, and I found, after a time, the truest, safest channel for our needs. "Five great, busy harbors lie about the coast of Greton. You know them." I fought to discover their names. "Gerstaggen," I said. "Himbrellan, Forth, Yammelrud, Meggren. Five ships from the fleet must go to each, arriving one each day for five days, berthing as far as possible from each other, resupplying, and leaving within two days. No crew may be permitted to walk on the docks, no matter the temptation. Two ships in each group should fly under false sail—those making harbor on the second day and on the fourth. No communication must pass between any of the ships during the seven days that the resupply takes place. Even if these rules are followed, there will be some danger."

I followed the stream deeper. "No captain of a true-sailed ship may say other than that he's hunting slavers. The false-flagged ships may say either that they're pursuing treasure along the Tonk coasts, or that they're mercenaries from one of those pacified Franican nations answering a call down in the southern Tand and hoping for good pay and a good fight."

I heard the scribe scratching quickly. I did not move out of my stream, but I let the current flow around me for a moment while he caught up.

Haakvar said, "At the moment, there are twenty-seven ships in this fleet. There may be more."

"There will be no more," I said, "and two of those who have joined us, *Dark Fire* and *Wolf Bite*, have resupplied recently, and must not go into harbor under any circumstances." I could hear startled remarks from the captains of the *Dark Fire* and *Wolf Bite*, confirming that I was correct in what I saw. "They will stand well offshore at a place called the . . ." I had to stop and fight for the name I needed. The safe point was a sailor's idea more than an actual location, and in the currents of time men called it by many things. I gave it my best guess. ". . . the South Current Convergence Point?"

A babble of voices, then, confirming that they knew the location.

"All the ships, on safely leaving harbor, will sail there. And then we must sail north through the Gold Channel to the Brindle Sea, traveling by night and hiding along the shores by day. This is done, is it not?"

"The Gold Channel has been a pirates' and smugglers' haven since men first sailed the seas," said a voice I had not heard before. "We know it well."

"I apologize that I have no personal knowledge of these places," I said. "It would be easier for me to be sure I was correct in all details if I did." I did not let myself sink too deep into the current. I did not let myself *feel*. I stayed apart from what I saw, so that it could not reach back to me and suck me down into the dark places with Ossal again, or pitch me into the hands of the other mad wizards suspended, forever alone together, in that horrible place.

"Things become complex when we reach Askag Bay. Somewhere along the inner shore there is a Tonk trading place, a far northern hold for those who prefer the southern plains. Danaskataak?"

"I know of it."

"It has come under attack by slavers recently, but the Tonk there were more prepared than most places. Many of them died, but they killed all the slavers, rescued the captives, and burned the slave ships to the water."

"Good."

"From them, you will borrow horses to ride north through the high hills to the mountains that surround Beyltaak. You will free the horses, they will return to their people, and then we will go up the mountains."

I stopped. The currents at this point branched and branched and branched again, too many variables breaking off in too many directions for me to choose the safe, deep channel.

The scribe finished his writing and said, "I'm ready, Oracle."

I opened my eyes. "For now, that has to be all. Beyond, events become too spread out, too small, for me to offer guidance with any accuracy."

They thanked me. Profusely, sincerely—all of them. It was, I realized, my suffering that they had needed to see. They did not understand it, but they had to know it, and they had to believe it was real. They had no previous knowledge of oracles. But they knew magic, and that no magic came without a price. They had to see my price—and if they only saw the tiniest outward signs of the fate I faced, still, that had been enough. They would not know that I would be denied the man I loved, that my death would not be some gentle moment in which I simply ceased to be, but a horrifying descent into madness, pursued by demons who had once been men; that time itself would swallow me up and drown me in its endless surging possibilities until the currents stripped away every bit of me, and left a babbling husk oblivious to everything but the world's pain.

They did not know.

But I did.

Hawkspar

The *Taag* was one of the ships that had to resupply. We needed fresh water most of all, but also our share of Greton fire and other war materiel. And some fresh fruit.

I sat belowdecks, not even in the passenger common, where I could be approached, but on the single, armless chair in the room I had claimed as my own, private save only for Redbird, who guarded me. With all the little girls and penitents and acolytes gone, the seru who had stayed had their own bunks, which gave them twice the storage space they'd had before, and almost none of the noise. I'd claimed the smallest room as my own—a place where I could put up a shield and keep the waters of time at bay. I felt the shadow of my future sliding close to me. I heard the lure of time itself calling to me to drown myself in its endless possibilities and find my release from struggle and pain.

Time is too beautiful, and the *now* is so very hard to bear.

We sailed into Meggren under our own flag. The other women and I took turns peering out the companionway hatch, trying as best we could to get the feel of the place into which we sailed.

My first impression was of smells, and of the bitter cold.

Meggren lies far south along the continent, and Aaran, who was with us, said that in early winter Meggren Harbor froze. We were there in late spring, though, so we were seeing the place on the right end of winter, hard as I found that to imagine. I felt snow on my skin, not soft and gentle flakes, but stinging, biting pellets that came down with a steady earnestness I found frightening. The men aboard, however, seemed quite happy. According to

Tuua, this was like the weather back home for most of them. And that was, apparently, something they had missed. I could not fathom why.

"Meggren's a gorgeous place," Aaran told me. "They build mostly with wood here, but fancifully. Tall peaked roofs, and fair spires with bulbous bases. The wood is mostly pale—aged now to silver. But they've painted portions of their buildings in red, orange, and purple, which are the sacred colors of the people who live here. Meggren is home to the Hamdan Gretons—one of a few separate peoples who manage to occupy Greton peaceably."

"My view is of unthinkable numbers of ships and masts and clusters of buildings, and beyond that, low, rolling land."

"This part of Greton is nearly flat. North, it gets rougher."

"I don't like flat land very much."

Aaran laughed. "You'll develop a keen appreciation for it when we have to go trekking up into the worst mountains in the world to finish off the Feegash."

"Perhaps."

I did not tell him that, with the limits of my vision, flat land felt much like the sea. Directionless and bleak. He looked at the stars and knew where he was. I had no guides, and so drifted in the little wooden shell of the ship, feeling the hugeness of the vast ocean around us, before us, behind us, beneath us. Feeling the monsters of the deep gliding down there, tracking us and watching us, out of our reach but perhaps contemplating us as a light dinner between their midday and their late-night meals.

I understood now why the Oracles and the seru did not venture away from the Citadel. Walls made their world manageable. Kept it in neat borders, with a small, defined sky, a neat slice of land, a bit of harbor, some cliffs. It must have felt very cozy to someone not looking for a way to leave it. They must have felt quite safe.

I could not imagine the sea ever—not sailing the deeps, where sometimes it was water so far down that I lost the bottom, and it might have been nothing but water stretching down forever, a wet version of the sky above.

"You'd like the place if you were to go to it. The folk are decent enough, the food in the taverns and hostels is amazing, street vendors cart about hot drinks and hot meats that they will sell you for near nothing. They speak a reasonable version of Trade—it falls happily enough on the ear."

"You go all these many places, and you do not worry that you are far from your own people."

And Aaran laughed. "I'm Tonk. Even alone, we're never far from our people, or far from Jostfar. That is one of the great joys of being Tonk."

"I wonder if I shall ever feel that way."

When we were assigned our dock in the deep bay, we passengers had to go belowdecks and stay there. Everyone knew that Tonks did not sail with women, and the presence of women would raise questions. Make us memorable. We did not wish to be memorable.

Belowdecks, sitting in the passenger commons, some of the seru and I fell to talking. And because the rules of the monastery no longer bound us, we fell to talking of men.

"Some of the sailors have been most kind," Rabi, one of the Seru Moonstone, said.

Obsidian Keenyn, a tall, broad-hipped woman, said, "There is a marine named Gabaan who sits and talks with me. And we have . . . touched. He is most patient, and yet, I find myself wanting him to be less patient. I am so curious. And sometimes . . . hungry, though that does not seem the right word."

"Gabaan seems a good man," Rabi said. "I have seen the two of you sparring together. He has a grace about him, and he never tries to hurt you the way Sera Obsidian Dance Copper Soritotara back in the Citadel did."

Keenyn sighed. "He sits with me at table some nights and tells me of the fights he's been in. He's been rescuing slaves for a long time—slavers burned most of his village. I mean his taak."

And Rabi sighed. "They have such sad stories, most of them. Like ours, but on the other end. We were the ones taken, they the ones left behind. Doesn't it make you feel better to know that all this time, the ones left have been looking for us?"

It did for me.

But Gnadable, who was not Tonk, but an islander, a Sera Amber who had insisted in staying with us because she wanted to record this history of our trip in her knot-books, said, "You're Tonk. Your men *were* looking for you. I'm Nito Absi, and I've heard no word of any Absi men searching for their lost and stolen. Nor seen any Absi ships armed with marines out sailing the seas to fight the slavers."

"The oceans are big, and we haven't been over most of them," I said, a bit amused. "It's easy enough to believe that they could be looking in a thousand places for you, and still have not found you."

"I don't think that's it," Gnadable said. "I remember being Absi. I wasn't taken by slavers, but by Absi men who took us away to pay off debts our fathers or brothers had incurred. We'd always been told that if they came for us, we were not to fight. They never needed to kill anyone to take us from our families. The day they took me and two of my sisters—they *said* for my father's debt—they pulled the three of us off the streets in broad daylight, waved their swords around, and everyone shrank back. Not a single man stepped forward to fight them, not a single one. I never saw my family again after that day, and I don't think even they cared."

I sat trying to imagine that. My parents fought for my siblings and me. Died for us. Everyone in the encampment had. It was the clearest picture I'd had of them. How would it have been for me if all I could remember was them backing away and leaving me to my fate?

I would have hated my family, and my people. I would have hated them a thousand times over.

"The men nearly sold me with my sisters as whores. But then one of the seru showed up, and paid extra for me. Just me." She sat there, silent, for a long time, and we three Tonks said nothing. "That's why I'm studying with Tuua to become Tonk. I don't want to think that some day I could stand back and let those vile beasts take my children off to horror simply to save my own life."

"Being Tonk is better than being of the Order," I said. "I remember almost nothing of my life before. But Tonk *means* something. The Order never stood for anything. Profit, I suppose, for services rendered. Some fine songs passed down to us from ages before. Hours kept, and liturgies said. But can any of you tell me the meaning of the Liturgy Axa Nidella? We said it every day, and I have yet to understand why."

No one had an answer.

I glanced up through the deck, seeing movement where none should have been, and I discovered that strangers had stepped onto the *Taag*. Five big men wearing armor of metal rings hidden beneath animal-pelt coats, and knives tucked away against their bodies, out of sight. Our people looked soft and watery compared to the dense metals of these men. I did not like the way they walked. Nor the way they looked. And I watched one of ours slip away from the deck and hurry down the passenger companionway.

It was Tuua.

"Trouble," he whispered. "Meggren has been overrun by Feegash mercenaries in the harbors, claiming the right to inspect all Tonk ships. The Feegash say the Tonks have been inciting the Sinali and pirating through waters protected by Feegash treaties. They're looking for trouble."

"They're hiding knives and armor under their coats," I said.

Tuua said, "I'm not surprised. They claim this is simply a routine inspection, but I think they mean to take us."

I hurried into the time river. This was the danger I had seen, not clearly limned before. Feegash mercenaries. Those we sailed to destroy, here at the wrong place and the wrong time, not looking for us particularly, but for all Tonk.

And they did mean to take us. The currents were strongly split; in half, they did take us. In half, we got out of this mess and sailed way.

One variable would determine whether they merely made nuisances of themselves, or whether the lot of us would be dragged away to Feegash prisons to face trial for . . . what? What?

I fought to clear the murk in time's waters, to understand what I was seeing. And then Eban, dressed in Feegash clothing, was prodded into court as a witness. Against us.

"Jostfar bless us, Tuua! Get Eban into the deepest hiding place on the ship and keep him there and quiet, or we're all going to be executed for kidnapping the son of a Feegash first diplomat. Hurry, man! You have almost no time left, and the rivers are shifting against us."

We needed a diversion. I ran to my room and over my simple garb tossed on the outer wrapping of grand Oracle robes. "Stay," I told my companions. "Except for you, Redbird. Follow me. We're going to be Ossalene Order all the way."

We hurried up to the deck via the crew companionway, since that was the way the Feegash were heading. To inspect the ship, they were saying; they would find us, instead.

I reached the top of the companionway just as they were getting ready to descend, and heard all five of them gasp.

"Who are you? Explain yourself immediately," I said to them. But not in Tonk. In Sinali.

Fierce stone-eyed women wearing elaborate robes and speaking in the tongue of the Great Empire do give men pause. And thank Jostfar for that.

"Pardon me," the man in the lead said. I heard him swallow hard. "Who, exactly, are you? You . . . aren't Tonk, that's for certain." His Sinali was passable, but nowhere near as good as mine.

I kept my hands tucked into my deep sleeves, and reminded myself that under no circumstances could I let any of them see the palm of my left hand. "I am the Oracle Hawkspar Eyes of War, Goddess Incarnate of the

Ossalene Rite of the Cistavrian Order of Marosites, from the Citadel of the Ossalenes."

"The . . . who?"

Behind him I heard one of the men whisper, "Gods' balls, Sergeant, *I've* heard of the Ossalenes, and if you knew more of the world than where to find booze and whores in Sinali, so would you have. They're absolute terrors, they are. The Sinali empress goes herself to visit the Oracles; they don't go to her. That's how big they are. If we create an incident, the first diplomat himself will . . . well . . . *you* know."

I was not meant to have heard that, and so I pretended that I hadn't. Instead, I said, "You ask many questions, little man, and yet I have refrained from demanding to know who you are."

The silence that followed was either awkward or frightened; both suited my purposes. "We're Feegash mercs, posted to harbor duty," the sergeant said.

"As for who I am, emperors and kings and regents seek me out when they need to see a true future." I made certain to put the weight of the Order and my deep scorn equally into those words. "I am known by name to the High Red Empress of the Sinali Empire, and King Rostgavir of Bheki has come personally to my chambers thrice in his lifetime, bearing slaves and gold and treasure of immeasurable worth. So, little men, why do you block my way? I demand to speak to that pissing irritant of a captain, and you impede my progress?"

"You're a seer," the not-terribly-clever sergeant said.

"If you tell me what I am, I shall tell you what *you* are, little man, and what you are is doomed."

"Are you threatening me?"

"None such. I merely report the past, the present, and the future as I see them. I have urgent business with this ship's captain, who has been well paid to get me promptly and without incident to my destination, and now he pleads low supplies, and to my way of thinking, you people look like an incident. I am *most* displeased."

"Beg your pardon for asking, Oracle," the sergeant said, "but what would your mission be?"

I was scrabbling through the waters of time, digging for the right answer. The one that would get him and his men off our ship. An ally of the Feegash, one of their puppets.

"The city of Rajarmalad, in Cartajarma. You know it?"

"Rajarmalad has been a Feegash friend for centuries," he said. "Why did your captain not tell us you were bound there, or that he carried envoys of another Feegash friend?"

"Perhaps for the same reason he failed to tell us he had only stocked half our requested supplies of fine Regallan soap. Or that his ship would not have sufficient fresh water for us to bathe in comfort daily. Perhaps because the man is a blundering jackass."

"He's here to resupply with water and . . . *soap*?"

"He finds that embarrassing. Would you find that embarrassing?"

I heard his men suppressing snickers. "No, Oracle," he said, but there was a hint of a chuckle in his voice, as well.

"We travel to Rajarmalad," I added, "to set up an outpost for the Order there."

"The Order of the Eyes inhabiting a Fee— I mean, ah, that's tremendous news. Seers on their way to . . . to tell the future in convenient locations."

"With a ship full of nice soap," the funny man in the back said, and again I heard the sounds of barely suppressed laughter squeaking out of them.

I put a hand on the sergeant's chest and let his time flow around me. There truly was not much of it left. "You mock me? And yet, if I choose, I can tell you how to live past tonight. If you follow your present course, the woman with whom you are . . . ah . . . keeping company, will betray you. You dare not touch her again, out of either passion or vengeance, for she is not who you think she is. She pretends to be a commoner, but she is, in fact, a daughter of the vice chair of trade, with whom your diplomat treats. Having found out most of what she wanted to know about your mission from you, she has invited you to a dinner and bedding tonight."

He gasped. "You knew of . . . of her? And my plans?"

"Emperors do not pay a kingdom's riches to those who cannot deliver what they promise. I deliver," I said. My tone was haughty. Aristocratic.

Oh, sometimes being an Oracle is a fine thing. I think the bastard Feegash damn near pissed his pants right there.

"Then I should not go?" he asked.

"The instant you step through her doors, you are a dead man walking, for whom there will be no retreat. Would you live?"

"I . . . would," he said. "I have no wish to die at a woman's word."

"Take your friends quickly away from this place, for she has marked all of them for death as well. Put as much distance as you can between you and Meggren, and as quickly as you can, because when you fail to appear at her dinner, she will send assassins after you. If you leave immediately, you and your friends have two out of three chances of living to fight in great wars. For every moment you tarry, your chances narrow horribly. If you're still in Meggren by the next bell, you'll die before the morrow, no matter where you might hide."

The man before me and his four fellow guards turned to each other, and in a flurry of debate I heard only snatches of their muttered conversation.

". . . pass this one through?"

". . . soap . . . you want to die for soap?"

". . . should stop with the captain, or we'll be in trouble . . ."

". . . I'm not going to die for that bitch . . ."

And the sergeant whose future I'd read, and to whom I had lied so handily, turned to me and dropped to one knee and kissed my hand. "I would give you gold or jewels if I had them, Oracle. I'm told by my men that is the way of it, but I'm a poor soldier."

"Your people and my Order share powerful friends," I said quietly, tucking my hand back into my sleeve and hiding it away before he decided he wanted to kiss my palm as well. "Live a long and courageous life, and consider that my repayment."

He rose and whispered, "Thank you," again, and then fled with his cronies, slowing only enough to snap at Aaran, "The next time you're hauling allies or restocking soap, you fool, say so and spare us all a lot of bother, won't you?"

"I . . . will?" Aaran said, though he didn't sound certain about it at all.

While the one mercenary berated him, one of the others took a board from his hand, appeared to mark it, and said, "You're cleared, and your cargo. Get your soap and go."

And then the mercs hurried off the decks as if pursued by wolves and wizards and the walking dead.

I stood, unmoving. Waiting. Tracking them through increasing crowds, plotting their course. They were heading for another wharf, and the wharf would take them to a ship which would take them away from both their duties and their captain.

And they would die this night anyway. In a fight against their fellow mercenaries.

I fought the pain of the lie. The necessary lie that saved our lives. I despise liars, yet found myself a liar whose lie carried weight because it has always been known that the Oracles of the Eyes speak the truth.

I had become a new sort of Oracle. A liar.

Was this also what it meant to be Tonk? To deceive enemies, standing on the power and prestige of my position, in order to save my own people? My family?

I wanted to slink back into the passenger quarters and hide myself on my bunk and soak myself in my shame. I'd felt no other way to save us but I'd betrayed the sole core of being an Ossalene oracle to do it.

But Aaran was hurrying across the deck at a fast clip, and I waited to hear what he had to say.

"What happened?" he asked me. "I heard your nasty remarks about me, but I'd thought we were going to keep you and your people well hidden, and glide through here without making waves."

"We won't make waves," I told him. "All of those men will be dead before sunset. I . . . sent them to their deaths with a lie."

"You're damned dangerous," he said.

"Be grateful they did not see what we hid belowdecks. We would have all been hauled into their stockade and held there until they could send the lot of us off to Ba'afeegash to be executed."

"Executed? We have nothing they consider contraband. Not yet, anyway, though when our holds are loaded with Greton fire, we'll be in trouble if ever we're boarded."

I took his hand in mine. "That's not precisely true. We hold the nephew of the Feegash first diplomat aboard. He has by now been reported kidnapped, and if anyone among the Feegash finds him in the company of Tonks, you can be sure they'll have all our heads."

34

Aaran

The Great Pack stood off the South Current Convergence Point, and all save one of the ships that had joined the pack had arrived safely.

The only ship not to report in, however, was the *Ker Nagile*, and she was a day past the latest date she should have arrived.

Aaran and the other captains met aboard the *Taag*, down in the common at-table. They had two choices: assume that The *Ker* was fine and simply running behind, or assume that it had been taken and that Haakvar and all his people were captive and would be tortured for whatever information they could give.

They could, of course, give a lot.

Aaran sat at the head of the council of war, with Hawkspar at his side.

"If we go on, we could find ourselves running into a trap," av Messyn of the *Muus Zir Ip* said. He stood, leaning over the table before him with his hands planted on it as if he could no longer bear his own weight, glaring down the table's length at the rest of them. "Without Haakvar, I don't see how we can keep going."

Belkraag of the *Dark Fire*, an independent ship like Aaran's, said, "We keep going because if we don't the Tonk will be wiped from the face of the world like a stain."

"I second going on," Dyur av Derstaag said. "The *Vinik Han* is Haakvar's, just like the *Muus*, but if Haakvar's dead, are we to give up the fight because of it? Better we should fight in his memory, I say."

They'd been at each other for some time, and no one had faced what Aaran saw as the real issue. "I don't think we should go on, and I don't think we should go home," he said at last.

"You want to sit here until every hostile ship in the region figures out this is where we're sitting and comes to destroy us?"

"No," Aaran said. "I think we need to go to Greton. Not all of us. Just one ship, secretly, though with as many marines as we can squeeze aboard. I say we go back to Gerstaggen, get the *Ker Nagile* and her crew at dead of night, and kill anyone who is holding them."

"A raid? You want to raid Gerstaggen?" Dyur, who had been staunchly supporting what he saw as the true Tonk way, turned to stare at Aaran as if he'd lost his mind. "*Gerstaggen Harbor.* The largest and most heavily guarded of the harbors of Greton, wherein, I'll note, port authority is already well armed with catapults loaded with Greton fire and massive winching crossbows bolted with Greton fire, and soldiers with swords and spears and archers with an unlimited supply of . . . *Greton fire.* You *don't raid Greton.* It's nearly as much a law of nature as that things tossed up do come back down."

"Laws of nature are made to be broken."

"Tell me that *after* you've flown around the room, lad."

Aaran looked over at Hawkspar, who sat quietly. He still felt the urge to drag her back into his bed and have his way with her every time they were in the same room together, as well as a lot of times when they weren't.

It was, however, an impulse tempered by visions of a future in which he was forever without her. That vision, paired with endless longing and painful desire, made for uncomfortable moments whenever they were so close.

He said, "I'll go in, and take the Oracle and her fighters with me. They can . . . move without being seen. Or at least Hawkspar can. If we can sail into harbor, she can get our people, kill their captors, and I'll have marines and the Obsidians in place as backup if things go bad. We'll send a clear message if we run into trouble we can't handle, and anything you do after that will be up to you."

"Move without being seen, eh? I don't believe that for an instant," av Messyn said.

"Since it's *my* life and my *crew's* lives I'll be risking on this plan, why don't you just not worry about how reasonable what I'd be doing sounds?"

He wanted to hit a whole herd of captains, most of them Haakvar's. He wanted to trample the smug bastards whose dubious expressions couldn't have been more clear. They didn't know Hawkspar. They hadn't watched a sea-walking wizard crumble to pieces before their eyes the way he had. They didn't know.

He couldn't tell them. They wouldn't believe him; what he had seen was simply too strange.

But *he* knew. If their people were in the hands of enemies, Hawkspar and the Obsidians were the ones who could get in, get them, and get them out again.

"The trip up the coast against the currents is three days if you don't run against bad winds. Back, it's a day. Plus a day in harbor."

"One night," Aaran said. "With the ship away from the harbor, and us going to land in longboats, and everyone else waiting behind to send in reinforcements if we need them . . ."

"We're to sit here another six days? Figure seven or eight if we assume at least one day of ill winds." Loostan av Hys of the *Red Wake* stood up, his face going redder and redder, and slammed a fist on the table. "We're to just *sit* here, in a place known to every sailor on the sea, braiding ropes and carving wood and stitching our clothes like a whole shadda full of women. A whole fleet of us. Sit here and wait for someone to come along and sink us."

Aaran said, "Yes. Sit here and be sunk. As if you *were* a whole shadda full of women—and evidently Mindan women at that, since Ethebettan women would no more sit helplessly by then Ethebettan men. If there's a man here who would sit idly by while these ships were under attack, I haven't met him. If one of you is that man, and can't imagine fighting, I think it would be best if you'd turn around and go back to your women's shadda."

He stood on the bench. It was against etiquette in a room full of equals to be the man higher, but etiquette didn't seem to be slowing down that old blowhard av Hys.

"You might wish to remember that we're all going off to die, men. Some of us might survive, but I have it on good authority that, saving we get a miracle, most of us won't. Hawkspar says she expects she'll die in battle. She can see paths where she doesn't, but she cannot guarantee that we'll end on one of those paths. We can pursue them, but the enemy can change, which will force a change in us." He took a deep, steadying breath, and forced his voice lower. Calmer.

"We go to win a war, and probably to die winning it."

"You hurt my ass, av Savissha. You stab me like a festering boil every time you open your mouth," Soder av Fonjin of the *Wolf Bite* said. It was the first thing he'd said the entire meeting. "You are, I am certain, the madman who will be the death of all of us. And yet I'll follow your lead. Your pursuit of this business unveiled more treachery than we'd ever suspected, and you've managed to keep your skin on your bones until now." He stood, too. "I'll stand with you."

"I'll stand with you," av Soortaak of the Rovintaaker's *Homsryn* said.

"As will I," the captain of the *Nels* stood, as well.

Around the long table, captains began to stand, usually without comment, but sometimes with.

Av Hys sat down, of course. Aaran wouldn't have expected anything else. Nor could he be said to have universal support otherwise. But when the movement stopped, he had more than two thirds of the room standing with him. And the other third looking unhappy, but not looking like they were going to bolt from the room, take their ships, and sail home.

"Eight days, then," said av Hys from his sitting position. He of all of them looked most resentful.

And av Fonjin, who thought Aaran was a boil, said, "Quiet, man. You're not captain of captains, and you do not speak for any but yourself. I'm in favor of giving the lad the time he needs, and seeing how this plays out. Fifteen years the Feegash have been working against us undiscovered, and maybe longer—"

"Much longer," Hawkspar interrupted, making av Fonjin jump.

He glanced at her nervously, then continued. "And you're going to give the one who discovered their secret an ultimatum and a deadline? Really? And had he not found out their treacheries, you would have died thinking our problems with Sinali slavers were no different than any others' who suffer their predations. You would have thought the blockades against our trading were a separate issue, and our people slaughtered when traveling into other lands yet a third issue. Neither you nor anyone else would have put all of them together, when there is no visible connection between them, and seen the hand of the Feegash over all."

Aaran wasn't sure he cared to be considered a boil, festering or otherwise. But he was grateful to have someone with av Fonjin's experience speaking in his favor, so that he did not have to do it all alone.

They went on at some length after that, setting out their codes and contact methods, arguing about approaches and manners of determining where the captives, if there were captives and not a ship full of dead men hanging on the docks, might be held. Debate, most of it insubstantial and speculative, only some of it useful.

But all debates must end, usually when the hour is late and dinner has been long overdue, and Aaran finally got the captains off the *Taag*, knowing that he still had to speak privately with Hawkspar, whose support mattered to him most of all.

Hawkspar

I would never have refused him, and the Eyes told me his path, which he was blazing himself, was the best possible one for us to choose. So I found myself sitting in a longboat with all the Obsidians and all the Onyxes, being rowed to shore with the captain by a crew of well-armed marines. We'd been given our choice of weapons—the best the *Taag* had to offer.

We had a less than perfect night for such an adventure, according to Aaran. He said we had bright stars and clear skies, and about a third of a moon treading its path across the sky.

To me, bright daylight would have been no more hindrance than blackest night. When I found my stopping point within the time river, the whole world stopped, nor did it matter if I stood and danced in front of everyone I saw. When I set the waters flowing again, it would be as if I'd never been. Or considering the pain this business caused me, I would topple like one dead on the floor in front of some enemy, and time's river would roll its mighty current over me, and I would end up a casualty.

Either way, though, my success was subject only to my own abilities, and would stand or fall by them. I was immune to unfortunate circumstance.

The Obsidians and the Onyxes, whose job it would be to physically contact any captives and survivors I located, and, when I had done my part, to get them away, had a harder time before them. For them, light cast by the moon and lanterns and torches in the great city of Gerstaggen would be of some import.

Nevertheless, with their Eyes, they could speed their movements within the flow of time, and make out what lay inside buildings, behind walls, and around corners. They were silent as owls on the wing, and if they could not truly see, still, their Eyes made up for the handicap.

Outside the walls of the city, we stopped and hunkered down. The marines set up their perimeter, and I stepped into the time river, connected with the harbor, and followed it back to the day the *Ker Nagile* sailed into harbor. Then I let the current carry me forward, and I watched.

The *Ker Nagile* crew hadn't followed instructions.

A handful of sailors had managed to sneak off the ship, and they went out whoring and drinking. The whoring would have been fine had they not gotten drunk; the drinking might even have ended well had they not then ended up in the arms of whores. One of whom was an informant for the port authority, and that one heard the sailors' words that "those Feegash pissers are going to vanish off the surface of the world" with more than casual interest.

She'd taken his indiscretion to the harbormaster the instant the sailor was asleep in her bed (and took the initiative of tying him to that same bed with remarkable skill and practiced speed against the possibility that he might be wanted for questioning).

And, because she was a clever girl, and he'd been a less than clever man, she took note of the fact that he was Tonk, and remembered which ship he had come off.

Between what he said and the fact that the port authority noted a run on sales of Greton fire, and a heavy purchase by this ship, a Feegash diplomat had been sent for. He hadn't arrived yet, but was on his way. The Gretons didn't have a trade ban with Tonks, but Tonks weren't favored customers, either. They paid higher prices, and in times of scarcity, had their orders filled last, not first.

But I was heartened that the Feegash diplomat had not arrived.

By carefully tracking back and forth through the current just past, I could see that he had been given only notice of an emergency, without detail. This is a normal thing, since diplomatic incidents can be created if something is broadcast by communicators about someone—or about a whole people—that then turns out to be untrue. The Gretons did not want any diplomatic incidents. They sold what they made to anyone, and it was their discretion in their dealings that made everyone willing to buy from them. The finest weapons in the world are of less value sometimes if the enemy knows you have them.

So.

Everyone on the ship was now housed in a comfortable clean ward in the prison. The prisoners were well treated. They had not been questioned. Their keepers were following the protocol of a carefully neutral nation, which will permit all sorts of dirty work within its borders, but will not publicly sully its own hands, or allow itself to be caught furthering one cause over another.

Their good treatment would, of course, end with the arrival of the Feegash diplomat.

And he was making haste. His party was coming overland from south Greton via horse. He would arrive on the morrow.

We had to have our people away before first light. Not just away from the prison, but away from Gerstaggen. We'd have to liberate the *Ker Nagile* as well, for we could not hope to get all the captives out to the *Taag av Sookyn* on our longboats.

I'd been tracking the futures as we approached the *Taag*'s hiding place. Following the progress of the Feegash diplomat, following the waters along the ever-thinning streams that led to our successful rescue of our people.

I could not track the streams to the cause of the thinning. We were doing what we needed to do, and yet at every turn, our odds of success worsened.

And if we failed here, our war was over. We could not destroy our enemies or save ourselves if we did not get our people to safety.

"You're worried," Aaran said.

"Terrified. Something is wrong. Something I can't see. We have almost no chance of winning this, Aaran, and when we left the South Current Convergence Point, we stood at nearly one chance out of two."

"What could you possibly not see?"

I turned my face to him, wishing again for normal sight. I could not hear sarcasm in his voice, but could not believe that he might be asking that question seriously.

"The waters of time are not a clear stream. They can be murky. Messy. Littered with so much busyness and confusion that it's entirely possible for the one critical piece of knowledge to slip by unseen." I closed my eyes tightly and rubbed my forehead. "That almost has to be what's happening now."

"Your head hurts?"

"Yes. But not from the Eyes. Just from simple frustration. What am I missing? How do I not see it? I'm going to look again."

We were closing on the shore. I could be interrupted by our landing, but I had to look again. The happy side of this, if I cared to see it that way, was that the stream that led to our success had become so shallow and thin that useful knowledge would have a difficult time finding a place to hide. I was desperate enough to look at it that way.

I dropped into silence, and lost the rocking of the boat, the sounds of the oars, the crash of the breakers, the hiss of surf growing nearer. Suspended in silence, with time flowing around me, I looked once more from our people, to the caravan carrying the approaching diplomat, to the impounded *Ker*

Nagile. Nothing. Nothing changed, nothing different. Nothing wrong. But the stream thinning, weakening, growing shallow. We were almost out of time; the danger lay where I was not looking. I did not see. Could not see.

And then I tripped over the thread I had missed. The thread that had garnered no attention.

One of our people was apart from the others, but on purpose. He was not being tortured, was not in pain, had not had anything horrible happen to him that would have caught my attention. To all outward appearances, he was another member of the crew, waiting rescue or doom, whichever came first.

He wore Ethebet's nine-part braid, and knew her principles to mouth them, and he had conducted himself bravely in previous fights.

But beneath his outward appearances, he was one of the enemy. Reform Mindan. He had been put in place with the Ethebettans long ago, had claimed a conversion from Mindaism. And he had waited for the moment when he might do the enemy's cause the most good. That moment had come. He had somehow managed to get himself put into a cell apart from the others, and he had at last gotten word to some Greton official that he was working with the Feegash and wanted to be taken out so he could give his statement. And the Greton official was on the way, in person, to hear what he had to say, and to consider the merits of putting him aside for a separate meeting with the Feegash diplomat.

A traitor in the midst would make everything so much less messy all around, from the Greton perspective.

I shook myself free of time's grip and clutched Aaran's arm. We were already on shore, and I was standing. I hated the disconcerting feel of coming back to different surroundings than I'd left. "We have to fly," I said. "One of the crew is a Reform Mindan traitor, and if the Greton who is there to meet with him hears what he has to say, we're done. Dead. The war is lost."

"He's . . . in the city now."

"It's worse than that. He's almost to the prison doors."

Aaran was not a man to throw up his hand at bad news. I had to give him that. "Archers, take out the men on the wall as soon as the marines are in place beneath it. Marines, as soon as the bodies fall, up the wall and over, kill anyone in your way, and get those gates open. You," he said, and grabbed my arm, "ready yourself to go through, and get back to us as quickly as you can."

He did not understand how quickly that would be. But he would.

Then we were racing toward the wall, the fighters of my Order and I far more comfortable running through the darkness than the *Taag*'s warriors with their normal vision.

I would that our comfort translated to speed. We were wearing sailors' clothing—the robes of our Order would have been an impediment. But we, even the Obsidians, were not as quick of foot as the men. They were at the wall and up and over it, with bodies already on the sand before us, when we reached the gate. Just in time for it to open.

Aaran, who had paced himself to my speed, said, "Be careful. And hurry."

And again, I had to school myself not to laugh.

I shook off the world around me and stepped into the river of time. Into the silence. Found and caught the now, the instant in which I and the flow of time intersected, and hung on to it, while around me the world froze and chilled, the air thickened, silence became absolute.

From my repeated trackings through time, I knew the lay of the streets, and I ran down them, for though I had within that instant sufficient time to do everything I needed to do, the weight of holding to that instant against the pressure of the rest of time crushed down on me. I could not hold my place against the currents forever.

Rough cobbles lay beneath my boots, but my soles made no sound in striking them. The weights of people frozen in the street, night birds and bats suspended over my head, fires cold as ice stiff in mid-flicker, fell behind me as I pushed through the thick air to the prison.

The doors were not locked. One stood open, with men inside it and outside it on the steps. None showed any clear direction, so I slit the throat of each in turn and dragged the bodies—or what would be the bodies once time resumed and they died—into the prison. Their weight was a nightmare, a vast unthinkable burden. Each of them felt like pushing a house up a mountain, but at last I got them moved. In the street, no one was nearby who might have noticed the instantaneous vanishment of six men. For that I was grateful. The rest of our unsuspecting enemy could be left to fall where they died.

I closed the doors behind me and went from guard to guard, slitting throats.

I would say that I experienced great remorse at what I did; that in those moments I regretted the families they no doubt had waiting for them at home, regretted extinguishing their hopes and dreams, regretted taking their lives. I would say this, because it would make me look the better person. But it would not be true. I thought only of how I could make certain all were dead before I raced back to Aaran to let him know the prison was cleared for the rest of our people to move in.

It was them or my people, and I chose my people. Not the Tonks I had never met. They were an ideal to me. Something fine that I could admire at a distance.

No. I fought for those I knew. The men on the ship who had fought through hells to get to me and save me. With whom I had fought aboard the decks of the *Taag* against enemies before. With whom I would fight again.

I could claim to have killed those men for some fine ideal, for the millions of strangers who would live free because of my actions. But that would be no more true than it would be to say that I regretted killing the Gretons when I did.

I think once my view of humanity was much wider. Back in the Citadel, with the vast, high walls around me and all my dangers known, I had the luxury of seeing all people as more or less the same. If I did not care deeply about any of them, I still maintained the thought that I cared the same for all of them, and thought myself wise and good for doing so.

Now, I cared deeply about a few. I had committed, body and soul, to those I could truly love. And with commitment and caring, my broad view died.

He who loves all in theory loves none in truth. The words ran through my mind, and even as I knew they were not mine, I realized I believed them. I was living them.

I killed the Gretons because they would have killed the men I fought with. Cared about. Loved. Loved as friends, as comrades, as mine. The men of the *Taag* were my men. All the family as I had. *Those* were my people, and they were the whole of our war to me.

I searched everywhere. I did not want to leave anyone who could race out into the streets screaming for help.

And it was as I was making sure I had missed no one that I found we were already too late.

I came to the cell where the traitor had been hidden. I'd planned to kill him as well, so that he could never tell anyone anything. And he was already gone. I thought of the open door. The men about the stairs. I had not looked at them; there had not been time. But I did not think any of them had been Tonk. They had, I was almost certain, worn the short-cropped hair favored by Gretons, and not the nine-strand braid of Ethebet. The braid he had betrayed.

If he was gone, then the man who had come to meet with him was also gone. Out the open door, in some direction I could not guess. Out of sight, perhaps already out of reach. My Eyes could not make out a Greton and an Ethebettan walking together at any distance in any direction.

We had been quick. We had been tremendously quick. And still we had been too late.

If I could have let go of my single moment in time, I could have pushed my way back up time's stream to find out where the two of them had met and drifted with them to find out where they had gone. But I could not do that. The weight of the moment I held crushed me closer to my breaking point with every breath I struggled to take. I would not be able to do that and still get back to Aaran and the waiting rescuers.

I could not tarry.

We had to save the rest of our people. Even if all else was lost, we could not leave the crew of the *Ker Nagile* in the hands of a Feegash diplomat. We could not abandon them.

I had not missed any of the Gretons in the building. I could do nothing more right then. So I turned and fled, the breath sobbing in my lungs, and fought my way back to the gate.

I grabbed Aaran's arm, let go of the moment that I'd held, and felt the warmth and thickness of sound roll over me, felt the air fill my lungs easily.

"The Obsidians can track to where I was," I said. "You and your men follow them. Run. Something has gone wrong, and if I am not at the dock when you get everyone aboard the *Ker Nagile*, presume I am dead, and the traitor is dead with me. And sail without me."

"Without you? We can't. We have to have you."

"No, you don't. I'm only one person. Don't argue. Just go. The Greton got away with the traitor. I have to track them down. I'm the only one who can."

"Then we've lost already and there is no need to hurry."

"Yet hurry anyway, as if we still had hope. Fight as if we still might win. And pray with all your heart I find a miracle."

35

Aaran

They split into three groups, each taking a different route and hurrying with a different Sera Obsidian. Aaran ran behind Redbird. The streets were almost empty, the groups were small, and no one paid them any attention. In Aaran's group, they acted as four simple traders within the walls; no one pursued them, and they pursued no one. They exhibited neither fear nor guilt.

He could only be grateful no one could see his thoughts.

Hawkspar was back there somewhere, knowing already that they'd lost everything. As Aaran knew it. The rest of his crew and Hawkspar's people still thought they fought a battle they might win, though; nor would he tell them otherwise.

He didn't know that he had it in him to pray for a miracle. She'd been his miracle. He'd pulled her out of her cage, and she'd given his people a truth they needed and a way to conquer it.

Now that was gone. He had the cold night air, and the warm steam of his breath puffing out into the cold night air. His hands, his body, his mind— they all still belonged to him.

His future, though, *that* some inconceivable Tonk traitor has sold into the hands of the enemy, knowing he was selling the destruction of all the Tonks as he did it. Knowing, and thinking that he knew better, that his handful of traitors would still go on with their lives enriched by the gratitude of those who'd bought them.

Traitors never did seem to see the price they would end up paying before it actually overran them.

Aaran couldn't understand that.

They reached the door of the prison to find it open just a crack, and one of the Onyxes guarding it on the other side. "Your men are finding keys and unlocking cell doors," she said. "The Obsidians are looking for the best way to move so many people at once through town without drawing attention."

"The other prisoners?"

"Seeing every guard in the place fall dead at the same instant with his throat cut, and no sign of what cut it, has made them a well-behaved lot. Your men have convinced them they'll be best served to sit in silence well away from the door in their locked cells and wait for rescue by the day guards. They wouldn't want to be thought to have had anything to do with us." And she smiled a smile that would have looked at home on a wolf.

Everything was working well. Incredibly well. And yet, they had already lost. If all of them died here, they would no more affect the outcome of the war, for good or ill, than if they tried to take their fight to the walls of Ba'afeegash.

It was over, and the captives grinning as they hurried to freedom were as doomed as the families back home who did not suspect the horrors that would roll over them when the Feegash spun out some tale of Tonk barbarity to convince their allies to overrun Hyre.

But she'd said, *Hurry anyway, as if we still had hope. Fight as if we still might win. And pray with all your heart I find a miracle.*

He'd pray for her. He thought he'd used up his miracles.

One of the Obsidians had pinpointed the location of the impounded *Ker Nagile,* and was sketching out for the archers the locations of the handful of men who guarded it. Aaran could not look at her as she did it. She had her head up and her black eyes stared off at nothing while her hands moved one of the warden's pens across the back of a sheet ripped from the prison ledger.

"Are we ready?" Aaran asked.

"We've found a problem," one of his men said.

"What?"

"The traitor is gone."

This was the moment when he could not fail them. He put a confidence into his voice that he did not feel, and said, "That's not a problem. Hawkspar is killing him now. And the Greton, too. That's why she didn't come with us."

They accepted that. He said it, he was the captain, he had evinced no shock at the news.

He was a fine liar, wasn't he?

But if everyone around him had to die, he'd as soon they did not do it at the hands of a Feegash pervert and torturer who'd styled himself a diplomat. He could focus on that and, if all his people reached the safety of the *Ker Nagile,* snatch some small victory from the fangs of defeat.

The victory of the moment.

He sent another prayer to Ethebet in Hawkspar's name. *Give her blade a perfect edge and her feet wings.*

Hawkspar

Time was my enemy. Implacable, hateful. And yet I had to win it as my ally.

I crouched inside one of the two gatehouses, out of sight, my head beginning to throb and my body aching already. I slipped into time, pushed against its currents back to the moment where I'd found the Greton official, did not think about the pain. It was a hard push; I was weaker than I should have been.

I did not have to push for long, though. Once I found him and marked him, I followed the Greton back downstream, flowing without any pressure on me at all. I watched. He hurried up the stairs of the prison at a run, snapped an order to a guard as the man opened the door for him, and they ran—*ran*—down the corridor. The fat, puffing little official then had the Tonk prisoner bound hand and foot, and shackled. And taken through a service passage out of the prison proper, and into the building next to it, and from there, down stairs into a room with two chairs, one table, and the sort of paraphernalia that would make a man think he'd chosen to side with the wrong people after all.

One part of me hoped the Gretons would amuse themselves no end hurting him. The other part of me knew I dared not let them.

But the Tonk had already talked. I could feel the shape of what he told the Greton. I could feel its ripples in the shifts of the currents around me, the inevitability of the Feegash victory over the Tonk that grew with every word he'd spoken. I could feel the river that sprawled before me widen and deepen until, where the Feegash and the Tonk were concerned, its course became the only course. Little trickles might slide a tiny way away from the main stream, but they led nowhere.

Still I marked the Greton and the traitor, and as the Greton rose and opened the door to allow entry of a third man—still not the Feegash diplomat—I marked him, too.

We had lost. All we had done so far had come to nothing. Meant nothing.

War would come to the Tonk, flooding over them as Feegash allies slaughtered them wholesale to eradicate the dangerous vermin. They would die because they clung to families, religion, and loyalty to their own people, as things with worth. Because they insisted their own ways were better than those of the Feegash, who had already managed to convince much of the rest of the world that common men could not be trusted to have a voice in their own governance, or a say in their own futures.

The idea that common men might not only wish to decide their own lives, but might also have a god-given right to do it, was an idea the Feegash intended to kill. And now they were going to succeed. Quickly.

I should run to the *Ker Nagile* and let them know that we had nothing left to do but gather those we could save and flee. Find some hiding place, and hide the books and the culture and the religion and the lives of a whole people who had created a civilization that had endured ten thousand years.

Hide it all away, and hope that someday the world would have a place for men and women who stood in Aaran's beloved Hends and spoke their thoughts as equals.

And I knew that the world would never make room for such people, because the powerful of the world always had need of more slaves. And free men did not take well to the yoke.

I should have gone back to the ship. I could see the spread of time before me, and it held no hope. I'd found no miracle for Aaran.

Still, I could not give up.

I rose, shook off time, and kept my Eyes focused on the three men in that room. Three men who were still the only ones who knew the truth.

I trotted through town, keeping my eyelids down and my face averted whenever I drew too near anyone. I went to the back door of the building where the three men still talked. Checked to see if it was locked. It wasn't.

And then, already hurting, with my head aching, I pulled myself into the river and seized my moment and held it. Anchored it as tightly as I could.

The bone-dead-deep cold stopped everything, and the air fought my lungs. I did not have it in me to run through the weight of time anymore. I walked, already weary, through the building. I did not kill any of the men around me. Not this time. I had no need. They did not threaten me, and they did not threaten my people. The threats lay below, and I moved down steps that seemed to stretch into infinity, pursuing them.

Because . . . because . . .

I had no because. I had seen time, and in time, no hope remained. No thinnest trickle of that mighty river flowed in a direction that might let me think I acted for the greater good—for the Tonk good.

All the people I loved—Aaran and Redbird, Tuua and Eban, my flock of little girls sailing toward what should be safety, the Obsidians who stood by me and fought because I told them we had to fight, and they believed in me—all of them were walking dead. In every rivulet of time I saw them dying, dying, dying, and me helpless to stop their deaths.

The Feegash had already won the war and the whole of the world would bow to their evil, fall into slavery, and serve as Feegash toys to be broken and discarded at will.

It is no gift to see the future when the future has been lost. That which I was about to do was nothing but useless action. I knew it, and yet I took it.

I stepped into the room and found the three of them there. The two Gretons and the Tonk traitor, frozen in a tableau meaningless to me because I could not see their faces. I could not see if the Gretons hated this treasonous Tonk, or if they liked him.

It did not matter. I was no longer there to win a war; I was there to mete out justice to the man who had sold his own people into oblivion. Because of him, the river had shifted wholly against us, and we would not gain from his death. But he would not profit from his betrayal.

I killed them all. I would have hoped for quickness and efficiency, but I could not manage that. The cold was freezing me, slowing me, making breathing too much to manage. I dragged myself from one to the next, lifted my arms that weighed more than trees, dragged with the knife that felt frozen to my hands across throats harder than iron.

I succeeded, and knew they would die.

But I knew I was going to collapse, as well. I could feel the world narrowing in on me, and the pain crashing down on top of me. I had only a little more time.

I shoved the knife with which I had killed them all into the outstretched hand of one of the two Gretons. That would give them all something to puzzle over.

And then I opened a box that held torture implements, and crawled into it, and pulled the lid down on top of myself.

For a moment I lay with time's swirling waters around me, and looked to see if, against all hope, I had changed the future. If I had managed to create the miracle I'd told Aaran to pray for—the miracle the Tonk needed to survive.

I had not. The Tonk traitor and both Gretons who knew what he had discovered lay dead just outside the box, and still the Feegash owned the future.

36

Aaran

Hawkspar wasn't back. Aaran and his people and the crew of the *Ker Nagile* had successfully infiltrated the ship, killed the three men who guarded it, quietly lowered the corpses overboard into the harbor in weighted shrouds, and then made ready to cast off. Everyone was present and accounted for, save the traitor and Hawkspar.

He knelt on the deck and drew out the Hagedwar, and sought her through it. Gerstaggen was the biggest city in Greton, and one of the largest Aaran knew. But he knew Hawkspar—he was certain he would be able to seek her out, to identify her even among the hundreds of thousands of others who filled the walls of the city.

But he couldn't. He could find no sign of her. If she were dead, he wouldn't be able to find her. Nor would he find her if she were somewhere that he didn't know to look. But she could have gone anywhere; he didn't know where the Gretons would have taken the treasonous Tonk. Having no starting point, he had to look everywhere, and in the end he feared that there was simply too much area filled with too many people for him to succeed.

If she were dead, he wouldn't be able to find her. That thought hit him again, but for the second time he pushed it away. He didn't need or want it.

She had told him if the hour when they were to meet came and went and she had not arrived, that he was to presume she and the traitor were dead. To go on without her. She had told Aaran to hurry as if they still had hope. And to fight as if they still might win.

He'd always been good at finding people. He was a tracker. He could find anyone, anywhere.

Except in death.

If she were dead, he could not find her.

He couldn't make excuses anymore.

He blinked back tears, and around the knot in his throat walked back to the *Ker Nagile*'s captain. "All are aboard who are coming aboard, Maar. We dare not wait any longer."

Maar was a good man. "She's the whole reason we know we have traitors in our midst. She's the entire reason we know the name of our enemy, for the first time in uncounted years. We should go back for her. At least for her body."

"She said to leave her. She's the one who can see the future, Maar. She told me if she wasn't here, to presume both she and the traitor were dead, and to go. To fight the war as if we intended to win it."

Maar gave a long look at the docks. Then he signaled his men, who silently cast off, and the *Ker Nagile* sailed away.

Aaran found himself relegated to the position of passenger. He took his lack of purpose while on the *Ker Nagile* without complaint; at the moment, he needed quiet and answers, if such answers might be had.

He went first to the temple. Unbraided his hair, separated out a single sacrifice lock on his front temple, braided that, rebraided the rest of his hair into Ethebet's braid.

The keeper said, "Do you need anything?"

Aaran nodded. "I have a sacrifice to make."

The keeper went to his cupboards and pulled out a sacrifice bowl, a handful of cedar shavings, and a small cake of incense, and carried them over along with a small lamp, already lit.

"Thank you," Aaran said.

The keeper was studying Aaran's face. Not too hard to miss the tears that kept welling at the corners of his eyes, no matter how hard he fought to blink them back. "Prayer for the dead?" he asked softly.

"I hope not," Aaran said. The words were sticking in his throat. "Prayer for the . . . missing. I won't believe dead until I must."

"Jostfar hear your prayer," the keeper said, "and Ethebet speed the words." With the grace of a man used to dealing with the grief of others, he sensed he was intruding, and moved out of the way to leave Aaran to deal with his dread and grief as best he could.

Aaran set the sacrifice bowl into the depression in the altar before Ethebet's shrine. For a long moment he stared at her ikriis. Her eyes were painted a rich, deep sea green. Unlike the ikriis of her in his ship, which had been painted originally for a temple on land, this Ethebet was horseless. She stood in traditional warrior's garb, feet wide to balance her on the back of a great black whale, proportionally tiny to demonstrate Ethebet's power.

Around her neck she wore starfish and bloodred shells, and in the hand that traditionally held a weapon, she carried a harpoon.

And she was smiling at him.

Ethebet in her ikriis never wore a smile. And yet here, she smiled, and her smile seemed to him to say, *Have faith. I'm here. I hear you.*

He put the incense atop the cedar shavings, and lay the bigger sticks over that. When everything was ready, he lit the shavings, and when the sticks were burning well and the smell of the incense filled the small temple, he grasped his sacrifice braid with both hands and yanked it out. The pain hurt all the way into his eyes and nose. He could feel a trickle of warm blood start down the side of his face.

He lay the braid over the flames. And at first, all he could think to say was what he had already said. Aloud he prayed, "Give her blade a perfect edge, and her feet wings."

But the eyes of Ethebet looked down on him. Kindly. He did not often think of her as kind. But that faint smile encouraged him to add, "Keep her safe because she is ours. Because she will be yours, if you have not claimed her already. Because she works for the good of the Tonk and we need her."

And then he heard himself add one other thing.

"Because I love her."

He'd not intended to say that, not to Ethebet, and certainly not to himself. He'd not intended to ever allow himself to think it again, because she was not the woman he could have. And yet, no matter how much he denied it, he now stood facing the loss of her. The truth that he would likely never see her again, though, forced him to face the other truth, the one he'd wanted to deny.

He did love Hawkspar. He'd promised himself that he would never give his heart to a woman until he had fulfilled his promise to his sister and his parents—to bring her home.

The fire died out, leaving the temple reeking with the stink of burned hair overriding the faint memories of cedar and incense. In the sacrifice bowl, black ash still glowed red in places.

This keeper did his altars differently. He had the oil in a vial on the left side and the water in a larger vial on the right. He found that out when he picked up the oil vial first.

He put it back, poured a little water on the embers, and waited for the sizzling and the smoke to die away. Then he took one of the sticks, dipped it in the oil, and stirred the damp ash. On his forehead he drew the figure for Ethebet, on one cheek Hawkspar's clan mark.

His face marked, he turned away from Ethebet.

At the temple door, he looked back to thank the keeper, and Ethebet's ikriis caught his gaze.

Perhaps it was the change in angle, or a shift of the light. But she no longer seemed to be smiling. She looked the same as every other Ethebet ikriis he'd seen.

Hawkspar

I am
  We are
  You are not
  This is mine
  I've waited too long. You will stand aside. I am you now, and you are nothing.
  Nothing.
  Nothing.

I was not me. Ossal was me, and pushing me into the utter, shapeless, formless darkness that felt to me like death, only without the hope of *after*. To the place where he had for so long lain. Some religions have a hell. The Tonks do not. But there are evidently ways to make your own hell, for the creator of the Eyes had done a fine job of fashioning his. He no longer wanted it. He wanted to give it to me instead.

And this time he had the advantage over me because I was weak, and to do what I had done, I had to blow the door between us wide open, and I would never be able to shut it again. I had drained myself, paid too much of who I was and all that animated me to push the Eyes, to use them, to make them give me what I needed. He'd had centuries to gather strength. He tried it at the various doors of his Eyes from time to time, but all his might would not supplant a soul bound tightly to flesh, or an unbroken will.

I'd given him too much to use against me, though. He'd been able to watch me and ready himself for the moment when I could not shield myself, when I could not fight.

The coming defeat of the Tonks at the hands of a world led by Feegash had bent me. Yearning for Aaran and a love I could never have had twisted those bends. The sheer physical strain of holding time, reading time, fighting to change time—those had snapped my weary metal in a dozen places. I was nothing but shards, and shards consigned to hell, while the creature who had created the abominations that were the Eyes slid into my exhausted flesh.

I could see the lines that connected him to the Eyes, and the Eyes to me.

But I could clearly see the lines that connected him to the other Eyes, as well.

To very many others. To all the scattered Ossalenes. And those Eyes did not connect to him through me. Even as I lay separated from my flesh, in the dark, able to move neither back to my body nor forward to the peace of the Summerland I could feel before me, I could see those other Eyes pulling at him like hundreds of anchors. Dragging him back into his hell and out of my body.

While I was weak, he might have a faint hope of holding the ground he'd gained.

But in the hell of utter nothingness, in the silence that transcended death, nothing hurt me. Nothing tore at me. And I began to regain my strength.

He would not hold me for much longer. Would not try to keep me back, to shove at me, to steal my body and my life because he had been too much the fool to appreciate his own when he'd had it, or to appreciate the value others might attach to *their* skins.

He would not hold. His theft would not hold.

With a snap that made my skull ring and the Eyes throb, I wore my skin again.

And woke up.

I don't recommend sleeping in a box filled with tools of torture. It makes defining the sources of one's pain far too difficult. The closed lid of the box makes breathing a chancy feeling thing.

And the voices outside of it, raised in fury and dismay, let me know I was not getting out of it right then.

I lay there, and let myself sink into the moment. Not to toy with it, or try to reshape it. Just to get a clear view of who was talking, and what the situation was out there.

"How could they be dead? I have come all this way, across country, at great personal discomfort. You tell me you have a Tonk who claims to be Reform Mindan. Who claims the Tonk plan to go to war against the Feegash, and who claims to be able to prove it. You told me you had an entire crew of prisoners upon whom I could test the truth of his words. You told me you had captured a ship filled with Greton fire and other items we *suggested* you not sell to those barbarians."

So this Greton, too, knew something of what the traitor would have said. And he'd told the Feegash the subject of the emergency he'd declared—so much for Greton neutrality—and in context with the presence of recent Tonk purchases of Greton fire and other war materiel and the sightings of Tonk warships in this region, where no Tonk warships were being reported in clear Communicator channels, the Feegash would certainly figure out the rest.

Jostfar alone knew who else these two had talked to.

"We had everything we said we had," a Greton said, anxious voiced and pitiful.

The Feegash's voice grew louder. "And yet, when I arrive, what do I find? The prison broken into, all your men killed, some ludicrous story given by the prisoners about how they all fell over with their throats cut, and all at the same moment, no less, with not a hand to touch them. And how not a single one of the prisoners saw another cursed thing. The ship is gone. Your informant is dead. And from the looks of it, the one who murdered him is none other than the man you claim called me via emergency communication to get here as quickly as possible. It appears he killed the informant, and then he killed your chief warden, and finally killed himself."

"We suspect that the Tonk are in collusion with demons, Your Excellence. That these demons somehow controlled the minds of the prisoners, and perhaps of my men as well."

"Demons? You're dealing with a stupid rabble of religious fanatics who haven't had an original idea in ten thousand years, and the best you can offer me by way of explanation is *demons*?"

I found I didn't care so much for my own discomfort when the entertainment outside was so good. I lay there, listening to him, hoping I could get something useful from this situation while I gathered my strength.

The Greton said, "We have no other explanation. The Tonk were reliable trading partners with the Gretons for many years. We never knew them to be fools."

"You would trade with them instead of us and our alliance?"

"We would trade with any who sought our business. We have maintained our neutrality in order to do that—something that I would think a Feegash diplomat above all others would understand."

"The Tonk are not people. They're animals who figured out how to walk on two legs."

Were we really? I considered how I might best teach him otherwise.

The Greton said, "As you would, then. Animals or men, we never knew them to be able to control minds, or make men see things that they could not have seen, either. I'm an educated man," the Greton added, his voice stiff. "I have studied the four elements, the four humors, the writings of the philosophers of Greton, the pillars of mathematica. And if I am neither a geometer nor a physick, still, neither am I a superstitious peasant. But I cannot explain what they have done, unless a demon was present. Can you?"

"Oh, certainly. I think," the Feegash said, and his voice suddenly held a silky, insinuating note, "that the name of the demon we need to pursue here is *money*. Who could have seen to it that the Tonk were freed, that their traitor died without telling us anything he knew, that no one lived who could—or would—give an honest account of their escape? And how much money would it take for a city official to arm his enemies and let them slaughter his own men?"

"What are you suggesting?"

"How much did they pay you? And where have you hidden it?" I heard him laugh softly. "I'll have the truth of you, man. Your only say in the issue is how much I enjoy myself getting it."

And I heard his footsteps walking across the floor toward the box I was in. *Ah, hell.*

I was in no shape to fight the flow of time, to grab a moment and hang on to it, but if I didn't, the Feegash diplomat would have his truth without having to lift a finger.

So I slipped and scrabbled and grasped after the *now,* the here, and clung when I caught it, and fought to hang on to it as the lid lifted and the Feegash stood over me, staring down at me, slowing, slowing.

And frozen.

I would have killed him while he could see me, could see the clan mark on my left hand, while he could know that he'd died at the hands of one whose family his people had destroyed. That he was paying.

I would have hurt him. I would have hurt him the way some other Feegash diplomat had hurt Eban. I would have reveled in his hurt; I would have made him the recipient of vengeance for an entire people, for dead named and nameless.

But I could never hurt him enough, could never kill him enough, to satisfy my heart. So I slashed his throat with the knife I'd used on the Tonk traitor and the two Greton officials, the knife the two of them had argued over. I put it into the hand of the Greton official. But him I did not kill. How much better for my people if the Gretons should fall out with the Feegash over the murder of one of their mighty diplomats at the hands of a Greton city official already suspected of killing a Tonk informant and freeing a shipload of Tonk captives?

Where I could stir dissension, I would. The war might be over for the Tonk, but that didn't mean I had to quit fighting.

I pushed up the stairs, my lungs burning from the cold and the difficulty of pulling in air. I took a knife from the sheath of a guard standing by the back door, hid it inside my sleeves, and got myself a block away from the trouble before I had to let go of the moment and allow the relative warmth and fluidity of Greton in the midst of an early spring snow snap back around me. I leaned against a building just to catch my breath and steady my legs; then, I walked with my hood pulled forward to hide the Eyes, and ambled my way toward the docks, trying to hide the fact that I was hurrying.

I didn't know how long I'd been . . . wherever it was that I went. Moments, maybe. Surely not more than that. I felt the sun on my skin, though, so I knew I'd been in the box for a while.

I tried to tell myself that they would still be there. I'd told them to go without me if I didn't make our meet point in time—but I'd thought I'd be dead.

Only I wasn't dead, and was, in fact, in rather good shape considering the night I'd had. And I wanted to go home. To the *Taag*. To the family I'd found.

But I was still well away from the docks when I could tell no Tonk ship waited there.

This time when I leaned against the wall, it was because I felt like someone had punched me in the gut.

I was alone in Gerstaggen. On Greton. And no one would ever look at me and think I was normal. I could not pass as a Greton, or anyone who might belong in the city. Darkness was the only friend I had left in this place, and even darkness had abandoned me for a while.

The city was a jumble, though. Big and tangled and full of hidden places. I had an advantage over those who belonged here—I could see which of those hidden places were empty before I went down into them.

Head down, hood over my face, I began to walk, careful not to bump into anyone, and at last found a basement warren in a vermin-infested house that had no occupants, and, from the absence of any food or fresh water, seemed likely to have been without them for some time. I went in through a window that had a broken shutter, and found myself a comfortable corner.

And for a while, stupid though it was, I wept.

Hawkspar

Perhaps tears are not the waste of time they seem. They lulled me into a sleep I needed.

I was back in the field of wildflowers and tall grasses. It was beautiful, with a brilliant blue sky full of high, wispy clouds, with the colors of the flowers and the grasses so rich and deep it seemed more real to me than the gardens in the Citadel ever had. In the distance, I could see people moving. Children playing. Horses galloping in herds, free and wild.

As I stood, slowly turning, taking in everything and filled again with indescribable joy to find myself there, I realized she was coming toward me. The woman dressed all in white, with white feathers in her warrior's braid and white paint on her brow. She was a warrior of the Tonk, by her braid one of Ethebet's. But when she held up her left hand in greeting, it bore no clan mark. So who was she?

She smiled at me, and from nowhere there appeared a white rug on the grass before us, large and thick and woven through in complex designs—white on white, but when I looked at it, I could almost think I was looking through milky glass at a whole living world that lay beneath.

"Will you break bread with me?" she asked. Never had she asked this before.

I nodded, unable to find any words. She was both fierce and beautiful, filled with a radiant light that made her so much more than human that I scarce dared meet her eyes. They were blue; I'd noticed that before I looked down. The deep blue of the middle of the ocean—bottomless, knowing eyes.

I managed to whisper, "Are you Ethebet?"

She settled herself across from me on the blanket, and a meal appeared—jerky and a bean-and-fat stew, bitter greens, flat bread, and bowls of water.

I knew the food. Knew it in my soul. My mother had cooked such stews and greens inside our shadda, and made flat bread like this in the clay oven outside; and my father had dried and smoked the same sort of jerky. I could smell this food, and it made me weep again. For all that I had lost once. For all that the Tonks—my Tonks—had lost again because I had failed them.

The woman laughed. "I am a messenger only. You are Ethebet's daughter, to whom Jostfar and all the saints owe a great debt. Ethebet has sent me to thank you, and to warn you."

I shook my head, my gaze still cast down. "She owes me nothing. I failed."

"Have you?" She handed me a bowl of the stew, a plate of the jerky and greens, and one of the bowls of water. I heard merriment in her voice, and looked up at her. She smacked the hard bread on the plate that held it, and it broke into a dozen pieces. "Take, eat," she said.

She seemed almost ready to laugh aloud. She ate the bread, and so did I, and at the first slightly smoky taste, I was a child again, sitting at my mother's feet while she stood, chopping vegetables, handing me down little nibbles of the bread to keep me still while she finished our meal. I could almost reach out and touch her, she was so near to me.

And I wanted to, so much.

I managed to choke down the bread with a sip from my water bowl, and the messenger smiled at me. "Eat. Eat. You have a long journey yet before you are done. This meal will give you strength to do all that you must do."

I wished it would. Dream food is never filling on waking. But I ate, and was home and safe again while I did. And as I ate, she talked.

"You think you have failed, because when you looked before you, all you could see was failure."

I nodded. I couldn't say anything. My mouth was full of jerky.

"Think of this, then. What you see is the river of chances—of what may be. Those things that will likely happen flow through deep, strong channels. Those that are unlikely to happen run in rivulets, don't they?"

I nodded again.

"But if something could only happen in one way, at one moment, if carried out by one person, what would that stream look like?"

I finally swallowed the bite of jerky. Took a sip of water. "I don't know."

"There would be no stream at all. Some futures are so unlikely you have to dig the streambed as you go, by living it. But once you have dug, child, the whole of the river can follow you through."

I sat staring at her, trying to catch the import of what she was telling me. "There was no hope," I told her. "I killed the traitor *and* the men he confessed to, and I looked into time, and nothing had changed."

"So you did. And so it hadn't. And yet, before you left him to find those three men, you said to your good captain, 'Hurry anyway, as if we still had hope. Fight as if we still might win. And pray with all your heart I find a miracle.'"

"I did not want him to despair, and despairing, do something foolish."

Her smile grew merry again. "There is always hope, if you have the courage to look for it. After you killed the Feegash and left the knife with the last Greton, you didn't look again." She sighed, and added, "You'll need a great deal of courage in the coming days. And a willingness to see what others won't, and fight for what you see. Sometimes you will have to fight for things not even you can see. But so long as you walk with Ethebet, you are never alone." She took my left hand in both of hers, and traced the clan mark on my palm. Fire burned into the mark, and for a moment it seemed to me to glow with its own inner light.

"That was my warning?" I asked.

"No. Your warning is this: If you are to find your way through to the end of the task Ethebet has set you, and the task you took on your shoulders when it was offered you, you have one more sacrifice to make, and it is greater than the last. If you do not make it, everything you and all the Tonk have suffered, everything you have done to that moment, will be for nothing. And yet it is a sacrifice that any warrior might refuse, and not be despised." She rose, and I realized that I had finished eating.

I stood, too, and the blanket was gone, and she began to fade in front of me, and the field of wildflowers seemed to fall away, faster, and faster.

"Yet you did not lie to Aaran av Savissha. There is always hope."

I woke, back into the utter darkness of my blindness, with no idea of how long I'd slept, nor of why I'd had such an odd dream. And I was hungry, of course; so much for the hope that my dream food might have some substance, since the dream had been so real.

But the woman in white . . . I found myself wondering if her words, at least, had some reality to them. I found myself yearning for hope.

So I let myself drift into the waters of time. I did not push nor struggle. I simply immersed myself and let all the possible futures swirl around me, thinking as I did of the Tonk, and the Feegash. The river had changed. It once again split, with a wide channel in which the Feegash won and the Tonk were no more. But the narrower channel in which the Tonk won and conquered the Feegash was back, and it was strong.

I slipped upstream, watching, and saw that the Feegash, hoping for advancement and a transfer to a place more hospitable and refined than Greton, had told no one of the great coup he was about to pull off. And the Greton prison warden, fearing reprisal for having broken with Greton's policy of neutrality in order to convince the Feegash to drop what he was doing out in the hinterlands to race to Gerstaggen, had told no one about the secret he held in his prison, save the interrogator and his assistant. He would tell no one, either, because when he'd discovered the Feegash diplomat dead and the knife in his hands, he'd realized that he would be handed over to the Feegash for questioning. Knowing what he knew of the Feegash, he promptly killed himself.

It was done. Over. The traitor's poison had been stopped before it could destroy us all.

The voice of the woman in white was inside my head. *Some futures are so unlikely you have to dig the streambed as you go, by living it. But once you have dug, child, the whole of the river can follow you through.*

I pushed myself to the point in the river where the waters split.

And there I found the three events that dug the channel and let the water run through. First, I had gone back to the prison knowing it was hopeless, and had killed the Tonk traitor and the men who knew what he'd told them. Second, knowing that even doing this had changed nothing, I'd killed the Feegash diplomat who had come to find out what he knew, and my actions had resulted in the Greton prison warden killing himself. And, third, Aaran had sent the *Ker Nagile* back to the fleet without me.

That stopped my self-pity at being left behind right in its tracks. If Aaran had not pushed the captain of the *Ker Nagile* out of harbor when he did, all would still be lost.

I had saved hope for the Tonk. And so had Aaran.

No more tears on that account, then. If the only way the Tonk could survive was if I ended up abandoned in Gerstaggen, well . . . I could hardly complain about the unfairness of that.

I had to get out of Gerstaggen, though. My trick with the knife would certainly make things miserable for a bit with the Greton official who had ended up holding it, and the importance of the dead Feegash diplomat might even cause a complete breakdown in Ba'afeegash's diplomatic relations with Greton.

But maybe not. Maybe they'd come looking for anyone who didn't belong, and with the Eyes, anyone could see I was one of *those* people.

Traveling time flows, I could see the ways by which I survived that mess. However, there were also so many paths where I didn't that they all started to blur. It would have been so much easier if I could have just drifted into the future a bit to see one perfect line of actions I could take that no one else could interfere with, that would get me out of Greton with my head still attached to my body.

I let myself drift into the future, farther along the stream in which I survived. It hazed quickly into a completely indecipherable mess. Too many choices, too many directions, too many places where I could put one foot wrong and get myself killed.

So I sought out Aaran's stream. I had followed him so often, watching his life run, worrying about all the dreads and horrors that seemed to be awaiting him. I knew the feel of him, the shape he took in time's river.

And I found him. Unlike my tangled mess of a future, his currents ran straight and clear.

He was going to sail to the South Current Convergence Point, meet up with the rest of the fleet, retake the helm of the *Taag*, and then convince the rest of the fleet to follow him up the Gold Channel, just as they'd planned. I could see him and the *Taag* on the other side of Greton, tucked away into a tiny bay, sails lowered, as he and some of the rest of the fleet waited for nightfall.

In a bay.

Close to shore.

Where, if I could just get across Greton, I might catch up with him. He had to sail around the whole of it, and going up the Gold Channel, he would be running against the current.

If I could get across Greton.

Traders would travel from Gerstaggen overland, wouldn't they? Traders and travelers, marketers, entertainers, priests . . . I ought to be able to find my way to someone who would help me. Or direct me. Or introduce me to someone who could.

I had no money, of course. No form of trade that I dared make public. I would be an outsider of the worst sort to anyone who saw me.

I knew of cultures where men hid their faces, and those where women did, but in every case, their eyes were visible behind their veils or scarves. I could certainly cover my whole face including my eyes. But if I did, who would trust me enough to provide me passage?

I did not even know the names of places where I might ask to be taken. The name of the tiny bay where Aaran would hide? I not only did not know it, but could not ask about it for fear of raising curiosity about the place.

At least, however, I had a direction and a goal. I would find some way to run east. I would do everything in my power to be in that bay when Aaran reached it.

I would not let myself consider what would happen to me if I failed.

38

Aaran

Down in the passenger quarters, the Obsidians wept and prayed and fasted. They'd braided their hair in Ethebet's braids, and made sacrifices in the chapel, and marked their faces with ash in Tonk fashion, abandoning the gods of their Order and pinning all their hopes on Jostfar. The head of Hawkspar's personal guard, Redbird, spoke to him in tones of loathing when he addressed her; she blamed him for not holding the ship in Gerstaggen, for not going back to find Hawkspar, for leaving their indispensable oracle.

For not letting the Obsidians know, so that at least they could also be left behind to search for their missing leader.

Aaran blamed himself, too. He leaned on the rail, staring out to sea. He'd given up trying to make sense of anything, given up hoping, given up feeling. He thought drinking himself into a stupor might be a solution, except he wasn't on his own ship, and didn't care to make a fool of himself on another man's.

So he lost himself in the wind and the waves and the endless, directionless blue-gray where sea met sky without even leaving a line to mark the transition.

"How are you going to tell the rest of the fleet that she's gone?" Haakvar asked.

Aaran didn't turn around. He wasn't going to answer—any answer required effort, he was weary from the weight of breathing. But simple politeness demanded some response. "I don't believe she is."

"Gone? You don't think she would have met us at the dock had she still be alive? You were sure when we left—that she wouldn't be coming, that she had fallen. We would never have left her if I'd known you had doubts. If she's fallen to enemy hands . . ."

"You think enemy hands could hold her? How?"

The captain had seen every guard in the prison fall dead without a sound. There had been no sight of the woman who had done it, but Aaran had been quick to tell him and his men that the oracle who had brought them this far had also effected the most difficult part of their rescue. "You make a point. Still, if you thought she yet might live, we should have gone back for her."

Aaran shook his head. "She said that if she did not meet us as the dock, we should go on. We waited—we waited as long as we dared and perhaps longer than we should have. I tracked for her. I sought her out." He hung his head and closed his eyes. "Had she lived, I would have found her. I found her the first time from half a world away."

Rya Haakvar leaned against the rail next to Aaran and looked him directly in the eye. "So she is dead. And yet you said you don't believe she's gone."

"I don't. That's the pure madness of it, isn't it? I searched for her, and she was gone. Gone. Utterly erased, no part of her spirit within my reach. I *know* she's dead. And yet I don't *believe* she's dead. My heart keeps trying to insist that if I looked for her again, I'd find her."

"So have you?"

"Looked for her again? That way lies madness," Aaran said softly. Nor did he exaggerate in positing that end. He did not forget the trackers who had pushed past the safe places at the Edge, trying to follow a loved one through death to whatever came after. Some died in the process, following too well. Some stepped back from the twilight borders in time, and lived to tell their tales.

Some trackers, however, fell into spaces or mazes or mirrored halls where they could no longer see the way back. They struggled inside private hells, seeking ceaselessly something that had moved forever beyond their reach; their bodies roamed, their hands picked at their skin, their hair, their clothes, they did not know enough to eat, though if fed, they could swallow. They saw well enough to avoid falling into holes, but they never recognized what they saw. It all melted into the shapes of the world that had trapped them.

He would not follow any of those routes—would not out of desperation chase in death someone he had failed to adequately embrace in life. He was without her; that was the price of war. But he had been without her for most of whatever time they could have had. And that was the price of his own cowardice, that he had only been able to fear what life would be like without her, and had not been able to rejoice in what it had been with her.

Aaran stood there a while longer, then turned to tell Haakvar he'd been wrong about the way he'd treated her. He discovered that he was alone again.

Ahead somewhere, the *Taag* would be making way for the South Current Convergence Point. Now the *Ker Nagile* was making good time.

When they arrived, Aaran was going to have to tell everyone that they had lost their oracle—that they no longer had any sight into the future. No edge, no direction, no real chance. Because that was the truth, wasn't it? She'd told him to keep fighting, but without her, they were fighting blind.

He didn't miss the irony of that.

Hawkspar

I want to be safe. It's such a simple thing in concept. You find a place with four walls, a solid roof, high windows, a strong door. And you hide yourself inside it, and nothing will bother you, and you will not die.

Such a simple thing in concept.

But I was running through Gerstaggen after dark, keeping myself well away from the busy streets and the marching guards, heading east, east, ever east, and even though I knew where trouble was before it marched around corners, still I felt like I was the sole mouse in a city full of cats. I was small and fast and careful, but they were hungry and everywhere.

Twice guards turned suddenly out of streets where I'd thought they would be marching in straight lines, and suddenly I found myself with trouble behind me and trouble before me.

Both times I managed to flatten myself against inset doorways; I was not found only because of luck and darkness. I could not hope for more luck. What I needed was less city.

I stumbled across a caravaner who shouted at men loading wagons. I listened, hiding first against a wall and then under the axles of a loaded wagon.

"We're an hour more than late, you worthless daughters of poppy-drunk sluts. You balless sack-headed snivelers. If you loaded any slower, my cargo would be moving *off* my carts, you pigs. Clear it is that you're not the lads with a profit dribbling away as the ships to Tandina sit empty in harbor, while villages along the way pay another man for fineries they won't need when I arrive."

The laborers, big men all, took the little caravaner's endless cursing at them in good humor. They ribbed each other, and said, "Left your balls at home, did you?" and "I thought you had naught but sacking between your ears." And they trudged, their loads huge, their backs bent.

I could not understand their good humor. Had the man shouted at me as he shouted at them, I would have left him to do his own hauling.

I was grateful they were not faster, though, for from the long stream of his invective, I pulled out a few useful facts. He was heading east. He'd already bribed a guard to count his load at half its value, to save him from heavy taxes. He needed to be out the gate before sunrise.

That was enough for me. I found one of the wagons that had already been loaded full of bags of grain. I climbed aboard and crawled into the center of the cargo, and built myself a hiding place well covered on all four sides. And then I curled up and slept.

I awoke to rocking, and thudding, and the warmth of the sun on my face where it should not have been. The buildings that had leaned in toward the road or crazily away from it on all sides, their stone walls shifted over time into dense, tilting masses, were gone. So too were the cobbled roads, the narrow walkways, the wells and lines that hung overhead layered with laundry. Gerstaggen, then, lay behind us. We rolled through wide-open country—rolling low ground, bare of trees. I guessed that it would be covered with grass, but grasses did not show up well to my eyes. They were too much water, not enough dense matter.

I heard someone coughing, almost on top of me, and froze, holding my breath.

"I can see you, you know," the voice said. Male, amused, thick, and deep. And threatening. "Pretty sleeping girl in man's clothes. I figure, you sneak onto this caravan, it's because you want to provide services for the lonely men making their weary way across the—"

I sat up and turned to face him, and opened my eyes.

And he shrieked like a girl. I was most gratified.

"I think," I said, "that you do not wish to upset me. I was seeking a way out of town that would get me safely past the guards. But it was only because I didn't want to hurt anyone when I left. Not, you understand, because I was afraid of them."

That wasn't as true as I would have liked it to be, but it was true enough.

"What's wrong with your . . . eyes?" he said, his voice hoarse.

"Not a thing. Don't you like them? You thought I was pretty."

He was moving away from me, slowly, as if I might strike suddenly if he turned and ran.

"You're a devil, aren't you?"

I grinned at him. "Don't you want to come find out?"

"No," he said, and jumped off the back of the wagon, and went running to one of the outriders, shouting.

So I was no longer a secret. I should have amused myself less at the expense of the man in the wagon, but it seemed to me a thin line lay between frightening him too much and not frightening him enough. I did not want to end up dead in the ditch at the side of the road. That had seemed possible.

It still seemed possible.

The man had pointed, but he wasn't coming back this way. The outrider was, though.

"You," he said. "You don't belong here."

"I know."

"You have gold to pay your fare like the others who ride with our protection?"

"No," I said. "I have nothing."

"Of course not. And what are you willing to offer for your fare? Nothing? For I assure you, our protection costs money, or something of equal value. We can take your fare out in trade, or you can stay behind and take your chances with the hillmen who roam these parts. I like your chances better with us."

"So do I," I said. "But we might need to define trade."

"Women have only one coin good as gold. You're no beauty," the outrider said, trotting along the cart where I road, "but I venture in a dark enough room there would be few who would protest that."

"I think I should speak to the man in charge," I said.

"You think you'll get a better deal from him? Little, noisy Beckgert? You think he'll bed you himself?" The man laughed. "Beckgert likes no woman so well as gold. And he has no more heart than the sacks of grain you sit among. If he finds you've slipped yourself into his caravan without paying, he'll leave you by the side of the road, and you'll deal with the hillmen. You'd rather have us, trust me."

"I'll trust myself," I said. Though I did not. I did not, in truth, know if I was strong enough to hold time in place, or to fend off Ossal should he come after me again. But I had no choice. I embraced the power of the Eyes, and caught the moment within the time stream, and held on, until for me it slowed to bitter coldness and vast weight of limb and breath and blood, and then I pushed myself forward along the caravan to the front. There I found the little man who had given everyone else such a miserable time while they loaded cargo; he rested in opulent comfort in a huge carriage at the front of the caravan. I opened the door, slipped inside and made myself comfortable on a fine, soft leather seat covered with lamb's wool, and arranged my clothes to be as presentable as I could. Draped my cloak around me, pulled my hood forward so it hid most of my face, and made sure that I was looking down.

And then released the moment that I held, and warmth and breath flowed into me again.

To the sweet sound of the outrider down the way shrieking. And the man before me sucking in air, then snarling, "How did you get here?"

"It's how I can help you that should be of interest to you," I said, and looked up at him, pulling back my hood.

The Eyes. They're worth instant attention in even the most difficult situations.

"Eh . . . eh . . . eh . . . ," he said.

"I can see the future. Yours, if you'll trade me safe passage in your carriage for as far as I need to go."

He could have scoffed, of course, but the outrider came galloping up right then to shout into the carriage window, "There's some sort of witch-woman in the caravan, sir."

My involuntary host muttered, "Right on the mark, is that Kivir. Sharp as three round rocks. A pissing genius, that lad—and if you want any pissing done, he's your man." And he leaned to the window and said, "Yes, then. I seem to have found her." He waved Kivir away, then leaned back in his seat, his face turned toward me, and in a conversational tone said, "Evidently not worth much beyond the pissing, though. So. You'll trade me my future for your passage, is that it?"

"That's it."

"And I'm taking it Kivir told you that you'd find no mercy from me; that I'd throw you to the road to take your chances with the scoundrels who live in these parts, is that it?"

Again I said, "That's it."

"Kivir was right about me."

I sighed. I didn't want to have to convince him.

"You'd have been better to let them have their fun with you," he said. "This is a bad place to be stranded."

I was going to have to convince him anyway.

Even with the sleep I'd had among the grain sacks, I was too achingly tired to do what I needed to do next. I hurt inside and outside. My short trip from the back of the caravan to the front of it had cost me dearly. But the quickest way to convince a man that he doesn't want to hurt you is to prove to him that it is in his best interest not to.

I would be quick, I told myself. Mightily quick.

So into the cold of frozen time I leapt again, to find and catch and hold and anchor the moment. His mouth was open—I'd caught him mid-word. I fought the cold, which seemed each time I struggled though it to get sharper, more impossibly freezing. I made the two steps across his carriage to him, and grabbed the whip tucked beneath his seat. I positioned him so that I could bind his wrists and his ankles together. Then tipped him on his side, stuffed the corner of his heavy wool, silk-lined cloak in his mouth, and held the knife that I'd stolen from the guard back in Gerstaggen to his throat.

Let go of the moment, and wished I could look into his eyes and see the expression there. I didn't like to guess.

"I won't be getting out of here and walking to my destination," I told him. "I know you're frightened. You should be. I could have killed you easily while I was tying you. Could kill you easily now. But," I let my voice drop, "I'm tired of killing. Tired of men falling dead all around me. So I think you're going to be very quiet, and we're going to work out a deal whereby you get something valuable for your transit—and so do I." I put my hand to the heavy material in his mouth and said, "You don't want to make any loud noises, now."

I pulled the cloth free, and heard him start weeping.

"I'm not going to kill you. I wasn't going to tie you until you decided to be a jackass."

"You're . . . most generous."

"I know," I told him. "If I untie you, you do understand that I can do exactly what I did before, only the next time rather than tie you up, I'll simply cut your throat for being too much trouble to deal with."

The silence following that was long enough that I feared he might have fainted.

"That's it, is it?" he said at last. The words he'd no doubt meant to sound brave, but the timid squeak in his voice betrayed him.

"That *is* it."

"Well, then. I'm a reasonable man. Can see the inside of my own pockets, can't I? Can see where my profit lies. Tell me my fortune, then, and you'll have a comfortable trip to wherever it was you wanted to go."

He still thought that I was a charlatan. Well, so long as he behaved himself, we'd have a happy ending yet, he and I, no matter what he believed.

I said, "This takes a moment," and sat with my face toward him. I touched his hand and let his time flow around me and embrace me. His stream was strong, full of determination and hope. He was not the man he let people think him. He had a wife and several daughters in his home, and he was heading there after this trip. I could feel his love for them, and his fear that one daughter who had been sick when he left would be sicker when he returned. Or that, perhaps, she would have died; he ached with dread at the news his wife might have waiting for him.

All the things he did, he did for them. He took every precaution to get his caravans through, he counted every piece of silver that crossed his palm, he bargained and struggled and saved and scrimped because he had half a dozen dowries to finance if he hoped to see each of his girls happily married to decent men.

I had not wanted to like him. I'd wanted to find that he was the sharp-tongued, miserable creature I'd thought him. He had clouds in his future that suggested his love for his family would make problems for me, but I could not see what those problems were, or how I could avoid them. I could, for the moment, work to both our benefits. I could, perhaps, find ways to be well away from him before those clouds began to rain on me.

"Your youngest," I said. "She can either get better or she can die, depending on what you do. She will still be sick when you arrive, and her chances will seem poor. But if you will do what I say, you can save her."

"I'll do anything I must," he said.

"Take a horse and go home immediately. Your home is actually not far from here, though out of your path. Send away the healer you've hired for her. The man is a pretender with no knowledge of healing, and no intent to see her healthy again. Everything he does is to keep her as near death's gate as he can get her, because while she is ill, his wants are all met—he has your money, your food, your roof over his head, and his eye on your second daughter as well."

"I'll kill him," the man snarled.

I shrugged. "You'd save more lives than your daughter's if you did. Take away from her all the medicines he's been giving her. For three days, give her clear water and fresh green foods only—no meat, no milk, no cheese, no grain, no wine. She'll grow stronger, but the cause of her sickness is in her lungs. To clear them, you'll have to force her to get up and walk, and you'll have to make her cough until she looses all the poisons and coughs them out." I paused. "To test my truth and know it for what it is, when you get home, ask first for the little dog your daughters love."

"Ippe?"

"It died yesterday. It was killed chasing a cart from your courtyard. If you ask first of this and find it to be true, you will know all else I told you is true as well." Oracles rarely gave such proof, but this time, the life of an innocent was the only thing at stake. No kingdoms, no greedy kings, no matters of questionable ethics. This was a simple problem, with a surprisingly simple solution.

"I understand," he said. "You'll come with me."

"You won't need me."

"No. But I know who you are, and what you did—and I'm willing to help you greatly if my daughter lives."

"I have little time to tarry. I have a place I must be, and the hours run through my fingers."

"You have a place you need to get?"

"Yes."

"Then if what you tell me is true, I can get you there faster that any other means. You can spend three days in my home, and still arrive with time to spare. If you know how to ride a horse."

"It's been a while, but I was born to the saddle." I sighed. "I'll come with you."

39

Hawkspar

We rode hard, on two tough little horses, with two replacement mounts trailing us. He had us stop regularly, cool his beasts, change tack to the more rested animal, then ride hard again. Even so, I did not think the horses would survive such brutal treatment.

He had a groom, though, who ran out to greet us and took the horses away, and Beckgert's wife came running out the door as we crossed the walled yard. She threw her arms around him and clung to him, weeping, and he embraced her, then led both of us into his home.

As I had instructed him, he asked first about the dog. It had died in the manner I'd stated. Beckgert grew grim.

He bade his wife stay where she was, and led me through his home. I could feel the spaciousness of it, and smell flowers everywhere.

Beneath the sweet perfumes, though, lay the stale, rancid odor of sickness. Of heavy drugs, and oiliness.

"Back this way," he told me, and his hand moved over the pommel of his dagger. "Cover your head with your cloak, keep your head down. I want to see this, I want you to be there, and I want him to think you are a weary abbethe of the Lady traveling in disguise."

"What do I need to say, then?"

"Say nothing. They don't talk, except to speak offices for the dead and to sit by the roadsides or in chapels giving the messages of the Lady."

"Well enough. I know how to be silent."

I hid my head beneath my hood and walked behind him, head down.

At the door of the sickroom, a man slight of bone, tall of stature, with little muscle to give him presence, met us. "Master Beckgert, good sir, she has been restless and in pain, crying out in confusion. I have managed only moments ago to get her to sleep. I fear that for all my care, she worsens."

"We share the same fear," Beckgert said, his voice curt. "You have been giving her medicines to get her to sleep, have you?"

"Certainly, good sir. The best medicines. I have withheld water from her, for she cries when she swallows it. I have made sure to bleed her once a day."

"Bleed her."

"It is the newest thinking, Master Beckgert. That ills of the blood, which she clearly has, are best dealt with by letting the blood out."

"How much have you . . . let out?"

"One bowl per day. The recommended amount."

There was little left of the girl in the bed. I touched her hot skin, felt it dry as paper beneath my fingers. She had wasted to nothing. I could hear her labored, rasping breathing, and the wetness in her lungs, and every time she exhaled I could not believe she would find the strength to breathe in again.

"You have no need for an abbethe here yet, Master Beckgert."

"Brother Danrgard, I believe I have. For this abbethe, in any case."

Beckgert called down the hall to his wife, shouting, "Lebettis, go and get Vardie for me, please. And run. I must know something."

He turned to the healer, walked over, and rested a hand on his shoulder. "You have done so much for us, Brother Danrgard. But I think it is time to let the girl find her way to whatever end she may have."

"No," the healer said, and I could hear the edge of despair in his voice, and in his next words, the taint of something sly. "No, Master Beckgert, you must not be willing to give up. For does not the Lady of the Plains demand that we abjure despair. That we embrace life and reject death until death comes for us."

"Death came for my little Peppika long ago," Beckgert said. "We'll deal with him today."

And into the room ran another girl, this one full of life, strong and solid. "You sent for me, Appa?"

Beckgert said, "I did. Brother Danrgard leaves us today. An abbethe of the Lady has come to speak words over Peppika. And I wondered if you had any idea how we might reward him for all he has done for her. He fancies you, you know."

The pause that followed this statement stretched on.

Danrgard cleared his throat and said, "I had . . . not thought my . . . affections . . . common knowledge. That I had . . . ah . . . hoped . . . nay, dreamed to . . . ah . . . *marry* Vardie."

"Marriage. Is that how he sought to sell this to you?" Vardie said with loathing in her voice. "Marriage. There has been no talk of marriage. He sneaks up behind me and pinches me," Vardie said. "Tells me how he would like to have me between his sheets, or maybe flopped over the bales in the barn. How we could do it right on the floor in here, because Peppika would never know."

"Meant respectfully," Danrgard said, voice rising in pitch. "It doesn't sound as well said as *she* says it—a man fancies his wife not always primly dressed in her bedgown . . . and . . ."

"Quiet, please, Danrgard. If there have been any misunderstandings, I'm sure we'll sort them out." And to Vardie, he said, "So he touched you, then—"

"Respectfully," Danrgard insisted.

"—without your invitation or consent?"

"Yes, Appa."

"It wasn't like that," Danrgard said. "Would you take the word of a mere woman over that of a healer? A professional man?"

"Yes," Beckgert said, and there was no humor or patient deception left in his voice. Now he was angry.

"Then if I am no longer wanted, I'll have my fee, and be on my way."

"I think not. I think you'll be staying with me for the sum of three days. The woman I brought with me will take care of Peppika, using her methods. And while we watch Peppika's progress, you will watch, too. You'll be under my roof for the duration, in the tower rooms for now. You can keep company with the watch while they're up there."

"You're . . . imprisoning me?"

"I've been given cause to believe you have been hurting Peppika with your treatments, rather than helping her."

"Who would have told such a foul lie about me?"

I turned away from the girl on the bed.

"I would have you meet the Oracle Hawkspar," Beckgert said.

I threw back my hood and turned my face to Danrgard. And heard his gasp. "Your eyes . . . ," he said. "You're not an abbethe of the Lady."

"Not even a little," I agreed. "I see things," I told him. "The future. The past. It's an ugly magic, obtained at an ugly cost and with much pain, both in the getting and in the keeping. Still . . ." I reached behind me and from a shelf full of vials pulled the one he had depended on most. The one that my Eyes had told me was, more than all the others combined, making Peppika sick.

I handed it to Beckgert. "Have him drink the whole vial."

"No!" Danrgard shouted. "That's medicine for the sick. It's no thing for a well man."

"Have him drink it," I repeated.

Beckgert said, "I'll hold it for three days. And if Peppika does better in three days under your care than she did for nine months under his, he and I and a few of my men will go out back and spend a little time with this bottle. And, perhaps, other things."

"You can't make me do anything I don't want to do," Danrgard said, and the words hadn't even completely crossed his lips when the sickroom filled with big, muscle-dense, bone-heavy bodies. Beckgert's wife had evidently called more than Vardie to the room.

"Upstairs with him," Beckgert said. "Lock and bar the door."

Feet thudded on the heavy board floors, and up solid wood stairs, and with them went the wail of Danrgard, who was still shouting protests.

I turned back to the girl. Peppika.

"Water first—cold water for drinking, and hot water for bathing. I'm going to need a lot of it."

I would have given anything to have one of the Moonstones with me right then.

40

Aaran

In Aaran's dream, Hawkspar sat beside him, her hand resting on his chest. "Your heart beats more slowly than mine," she told him. And then she leaned over him and kissed his lips. "I love you, you know."

"I know," he whispered, and in whispering, woke himself up. He was alone. On the wrong ship, away from his own men, away from work that could distract him. And all he could think about was her. In two more days the *Ker Nagile* would make the South Current Convergence Point and meet up with the other ships. Aaran would tell the other captains the news, that the one they had most depended on had fallen by the wayside. He would tell them that before she died, she told him they should keep fighting. He would never tell them all hope was lost, that the entire Tonk people were on their way to their deaths. He would not pass that on, because it would not change what they did. They would still go into battle.

They would simply do so with heavy hearts.

It is better not to know the day of your own death, he thought.

Aaran rolled out of the bunk and landed lightly. He stretched and yawned. No light came in through the porthole—night still held sway over this part of the world.

He would not be able to sleep. That kiss had felt so real. Her hand on his chest and her soft voice had made his heart race.

He'd tracked her once, and she was gone. Beyond his reach.

But she'd gone in search of a miracle, and in the dark of night, alone, with only defeat and despair before him, he suddenly had to hope that she had found it. It made no sense. He could not justify what he was going to do; not to anyone. He planned to risk death to search out an answer to a question that he already knew.

"I'm praying for that miracle," he said to himself, to the Hawkspar who had been in his dream, to his missing sister, to the men with whom he'd worked and trained and fought all the many years who would never accept the suicidal madness of trying to track the dead.

He settled on the floor. Promised himself that he would pull back in his search before he crawled all the way out of his body and left the corpse on the floor for someone else to find. And then he closed his eyes and drew into himself the power of the sea beneath him and the sky above him, the living, breathing energy of the world. He spun out of it the glowing blue sphere, and within the sphere, a fiery red cube. And within that, two intersecting tetrahedrons, one of gold and one of yellow. The powers of the universe flowed through the shapes of his Hagedwar, refracting and separating the energies of all existence the way prisms broke light into rainbow colors.

He expanded the Hagedwar until it was huge, and he sat in the very center of it, enfolded in yellow and gold and red and blue. From where he sat, the light surrounding him was brilliant white, pure and clean. And the songs the universe sang flowed through his skin, caressing, soothing.

He wanted that comfort to keep him anchored. To keep his spirit in his flesh. He wanted something to make the pain he was going to feel not so bad. He needed a miracle. That didn't mean he was fool enough to think he'd find one.

With the Hagedwar in place, he then let his spirit drift. He was looking for the shape of her; he knew it so well. He had marked her to find her before, and in doing so had marked himself with her. She would always be the only key that could fit into that one lock he had forged.

His search would require time. He started in Greton, in Gerstaggen, in the places where she had been last. Her traces still lingered there; they would for some time yet, at least for him. He could feel several explosions of violence linked to her presence, moments when everyone around her died simultaneously. And then—

He had lost her before, but now he found clear marks of her presence, in the last room with a brutal, instant death. The Feegash diplomat. She'd killed that one, and he had been alive when Aaran sought Hawkspar before. He had been alive and Hawkspar had been dead, and now . . . the diplomat was dead, and the trail to Hawkspar moved on.

How could that be?

He couldn't imagine. But he followed.

She was moving east. East.

As if she hoped to cross Greton and meet up with the ships on the other side?

He tried to figure distances—she was more than a month at best speeds from the nearest point on the opposite coast; he wondered if she hoped the ships would sit at anchor, hidden in the many little coves and bays of the Gold Channel, while she caught up with them. He wondered how that would affect their war against the Ba'afeegash, if they did wait.

As it was, they would be arriving after spring had cleared the mountains and passes around the country of deadly avalanches. A month to two months later would put them into summer—which would give the Tonk a safer and more pleasant trip in, certainly, but which would require the war be decided quickly, before the first snows of autumn. The weather at high altitudes could destroy them if they tarried too long.

Still . . . she'd survived. If she lived, could the Tonk still have hope? The diplomat was dead, the traitor was dead, everyone who had been anywhere near the traitor was dead. Had Hawkspar found—no, had she *made*—their miracle?

He tried to reach her, as he had reached her before, when she had still been in the Citadel and he had been racing to save her. He wanted to hear her voice, to reassure her that he knew she was there.

He had no great skills as a Communicator—that portion of the Haged-war was a struggle for him to comprehend and connect with. He tried, but the magic that had connected them through the water and bound them together—the magic that had been born of her desperate prayers and strengthened by the previous Hawkspar's intervention, was gone. Hawkspar had ceased to pour prayers for rescue into the water. He could find nothing else about her to connect to. He could not move into her, feel what she felt, hear what she heard. He could only find the place where she was, and feel that she was still alive.

He decided he would, as soon as he could, take one of the ship Communicators off the Tonk listening duty and set him to trying to talk to Hawkspar. The fleet needed to know what she would have them do, if she would require them to wait for her to reach them, or if she had some other plan. If she had found their miracle.

He shook off the Hagedwar, and breathed in air that didn't clog in his lungs for the first time since the *Ker Nagile* left Gerstaggen Harbor.

And ran up the stairs to wake Haakvar and tell him hope had been reborn.

Hawkspar

Peppika started coughing on the morning of the second day. I'd spent the day before pounding on her back with cups held upside down, as I'd seen the Seru Moonstone do with stubborn cases of lungfill; they did it to break up the congestion. She'd started waking up the night before, desperate for water. I let her drink a little at a time. The first two times she'd vomited anyway, but the third time, she managed to keep it down.

And when she started coughing . . .

I was grateful I could not see what she brought up. The sounds were bad enough. Still, her sisters and her mother took turns cleaning her up, and letting her drink water. Her temperature still ran high, and she sounded like she might tear herself apart with the coughing. But on the evening of the second day, we had her up and walking, leaning on me on one side and her mother on the other. And her father stood in the hall and wept. Peppika had not been on her feet in months, and every movement hurt her. She was, however, moving again. Awake again. A little walking skeleton, who on the third day started eating greens. And talking.

"I owe you her life," Beckgert said. "That's of more value to me than any number of crossings of Greton."

"She'll be a long time getting better. And it will be painful for her. Don't let her linger in bed, though. Make her use her arms and legs, make her lift things and carry. Her body will give her back only what she's willing to take."

He patted me on the shoulder. "We'll do all of it. Would you stay to see Danrgard die for his crimes?"

"No," I said. "I long for friends and familiar food and talk of familiar things."

"Then you shall have it," he said. "Where do you wish to go?"

"The east coast of Greton."

"It's a long coast."

"I know. But the place I want to go is not much of anything, I've been told." I dared not tell him the place I truly wanted to go, which was called the Pirates' Dance. It was a dangerous stretch of coast on which a line of sharp cliffs full of caves fronted, not on rough and crashing seas, but on cypress-clogged marshes full of poisonous snakes, huge insects, grotesque flying monstrosities, and other hideous beasts. It was the first place I could see the Tonk fleet pulling aside and resting.

So I told him I wanted to go to the town nearest it. "Specifically," I said, "I want to reach Bragguiydshevhurd. If word I received is correct, three of my Order's sisters are there, but will not be there much longer."

"Bragguiydshevhurd?" He chuckled. "We call it Brurd. I know the place. I even have friends there. It's a decent enough town to do business in, though it's still a bit small."

"What I don't know is how you'll get me there in time."

"It would be poor repayment for my daughter's life if I did not get you there in time."

I'd thought the same thing, but hadn't said it. He'd not given me much choice, and the time rivers suggested that I would make it to the coast in time if I stayed the three days and helped him.

But I could not see *how* I would make it.

"You'll be going by courier," he told me. "You'll ride along one of the courier routes that cross Greton in several directions. You'll use my passage account, and be accompanied by my son-in-law, Weggnrad, whom I would trust with your life as with the lives of my children and grandchildren. By day you'll ride the courier routes, on courier horses. You'll be tagged as cargo, with guaranteed delivery. You'll be in Brurd in six days. You could not have gotten there in less than twenty by any other means."

Six days.

If he could get me to where I needed to be in the time he claimed, I might even find myself with time to wait.

Six days, and I would discover whether or not Aaran had looked for me. Had tracked me. I prayed he had, because if he had not, he would not know I was waiting for him.

I had to tell him that we had won past despair. That we had hope.

Beckgert told me I would be tagged as cargo. I was to impersonate Beckgert's oldest unmarried daughter, Seperka, who had received word that her husband-to-be had to sail to his plantation in northern Tandinapalis, and who would have to leave her for more than two years if she was not able to meet and marry him in the short time he still had in Greton. I was told that, because of threats to the family, various security measures had been put into place, and that part of that security in getting her to her wedding on time would be me pretending to be her, and going by a public and different route.

It was, I understood, a mildly risky proposition. Beckgert told me he was confident I would be safe, considering the way I'd demonstrated my talents to him. I was inclined to agree. In exchange for this final favor I was doing him, I would receive free passage on what Beckgert claimed was the most expensive, but fastest, transport route in the entire world. And a disguise that would keep me safe from people who would have much more cause to hate me than Beckgert's daughter.

Beckgert's wife, Lebettis, gave me special bride-to-be garb called a culappe to wear that was traditional in her culture. It completely hid the outlines of my body, and every bit of exposed skin, including my hands and face. The hood came with a gauze mesh face cover that I was not to lift except when I was completely alone. Lebettis said the fabric was dark green, and that it hid my features, especially the strangeness of the Eyes. This was important to me.

She showed me how to wear the culappe, and told me that under no circumstances should I let my face or any other part of me be seen.

I quickly checked my future. Whitewater all around, countless things that could happen, none that seemed any more likely than any other. I could see it all ending in success, in failure, in death. But I could see nothing clearly, no event I must be wary of, no person I must not trust. I saw danger, danger everywhere, but nowhere reliably, so that I might know what to avoid.

Beckgert introduced me to his son-in-law, Bont Weggnrad, whom I had not met before, and we exchanged bows. He was a wiry man, not much taller than I was, but tight-muscled. He'd broken a few bones, I could tell, though a long time ago. They'd healed with big knots in them.

Finally, it was time to go. I had to face the fact that, save for my short ride with Beckgert, I had not been on a horse in a very long time. I was strong and healthy and flexible and fit, but even that short trip had left me aching in unusual places. I was uncertain how my body would tolerate a long, hard ride.

We mounted up on Beckgert's horses, which one of his grooms would keep at the first station to maintain until Weggnrad delivered me and rode back.

We rode that first evening at a leisurely pace.

I hadn't forgotten riding. I knew the moves, the way of reins and knees and heels and throat. The horse responded easily to me, and I quickly found my way through his gaits, from walk, to trot, to canter, to gallop.

"The fact that you can't see makes me wonder how you ride. But you do seem to know how to do it."

"Hard to explain," I told him. "I can see, after a fashion. Everything is black to me, but it's different weights of black. I can tell where the holes are in a field, and where you broke your right arm a little above your elbow. I can tell rock from paper painted to look like rock. I can tell which men are mostly muscle, and which are all fluff."

He cleared his throat. "You can . . . see through clothes?"

I shrugged. "Clothes and skin. I see people as bone and muscle, and not much else."

"That can't be very pretty."

"It's all black on black, and it's better than seeing nothing at all. When they first put the Eyes in me, I thought I would be true-blind for the rest of my life."

We rode for a while in silence, going at a steady trot because there was no real hurry. We would not be logged in and traveling the Courier Road until morning.

"Did it hurt?" he asked.

I didn't have to ask what he meant. "Yes. A lot. It still does. They drugged me when they took my eyes and put the stone ones in, but when the drugs wore off, it was nothing but pain for a long time. Now . . . it can still be so bad sometimes that I think I'll go mad from it."

"Why did you have it done?" he asked.

I wasn't sure if I should answer. When at last I did, I said, "I did it because it was the only way I could protect my family."

Weggnrad was quiet for a long time. "I understand that. I would do anything to protect mine."

We rode at an easy trot for a while, and then Weggnrad, my companion for the next six days, said, "You're wearing sheepskin thigh pads, aren't you?"

"Yes."

"I thought Beckgert would remember to outfit you with them. Did he see that you had powder?"

"No."

"I'll get you some at the station," he said. "If you haven't been in the saddle in some time, this is going to be a painful experience for you. We'll be covering about twenty-five long leagues a day, running daily through four to five stations, and changing horses at each station. You'll hurt."

I turned my face to him and said, "I'm used to pain. But thank you. I appreciate those things that make it less."

He didn't say anything else for a long while.

The station turned out to be a small building with large stables. I walked around it, getting the feel for the layout and trying to understand the pattern underneath what felt, at first, like chaos. Weggnrad said he was putting me down on the Courier Road log as "cargo, bride, Beckgert's daughter" and explaining that I had to be delivered at fastest speeds to one of Master Beckgert's favorite clients, who had requested me as a wife, and who wanted me to accompany him on an expedition into the small nations of northern Tandinapalis to locate and discover interesting trade goods. Since this mission did fit with the fact that Beckgert's second daughter would be marrying the aforementioned client and going on the described trip, anyone checking the story would find it matched the truth in every checkable detail. The fact that she was traveling in secret, heavily guarded by a sea route, Beckgert wanted to keep hidden.

This trip would be beneficial all the way around.

So I kept to a stretch of wall behind a fence, pacing and watching. Men and horses galloped in, grooms raced to take the horses and then spent tremendous time and care in cooling them down, rubbing and cleaning them, tending their feet. The men got less attention. They went inside to seek out the source of the delicious smells that rolled out from the station's open doors. More men arrived, and more horses, more grooms scurried. No one left, though, and at last I realized that these men would be bound to the station until first light; they did not have eyes like mine, that could identify the emptiness of a leg-breaker hole in tall grass in darkness. I had only darkness, ever, but I was no longer ever truly blind.

Having paced along the wall until I got my legs working again, I went to find Weggnrad.

The men around me deferred to my special status, either tapping their foreheads in polite greeting or bowing while wishing me "Gold and healthy children in equal abundance."

I said nothing—I'd been instructed that women who wore the culappe never spoke to any but their intended, or to the one responsible for guarding them in public.

I bowed instead, and finally located Weggnrad with two other men, getting information on the state of the road ahead of us. When they saw me, the men told my guardian they would speak with him later. I started toward the room where food was being served, but Weggnrad caught my elbow and surreptitiously swung me toward a set of stairs that lay in the opposite direction. "Up," he whispered. "I have to move my hand quickly."

Because, of course, no one could touch me.

I climbed the stairs, reached a landing, and waited for him. The corridor before me ran the length of the building, with dozens of doors on either side.

"Tenth on the left," he said, and I walked along the corridor, thinking how very much like ship's quarters it was. The spaces were tiny, and when I opened the door, I found the room that I would have to myself, with my unfortunate guardian sleeping on a cot outside the door, to be far more cramped quarters than those aboard the *Taag*.

"The beds are not bad," he told me. "And the food is good. You'll have to eat up here, though. You can't be seen with your veil lifted—and that's the only way you'll be able to eat at all."

So I waited, and Weggnrad brought me food—a lot of it.

I took off my gloves and threw back my veil, and took the tray he proffered, and thanked him effusively. It smelled wonderful, nor did he skimp on portions. Then he sat in the hallway on his cot and with his back to me and ate his own meal, while I sat at a table no bigger than an apple crate. He'd kept the door open, though, so that we could talk over our food.

"What is it like where you're from?" he asked me.

"It was a small, warm island with high stone walls, temperate in the summer, cold enough in the winter. The place was lovely, but the life was restricted, and I detested confinement and wished to avoid the future the oracles had planned for me."

"Did you?"

"No," I said. "I wear the Eyes."

"And before you were an . . . oracle . . . what were you?"

"A slave. Then a student."

"And before that?"

"Too young to remember," I told him.

We ate in silence for a while, and then he asked me, "So were you in Gerstaggen in time to hear about the uproar they had there?"

"I might have been, but if I was, I missed the excitement. What sort of uproar?"

"I wish I knew," he said. He sounded disappointed. "I heard some Tonk were captured who then escaped. And some traitor Greton who they paid to free them died."

"Ah," I said. "I wish I'd heard something of that. It sounds interesting. Who are the Tonk?"

"You don't know the Tonk?" he asked. "They're a funny sort. Just about everywhere, it seems. You have to be one of them to know them. It isn't that they keep to themselves—they show up around the shipping yards where I pick up goods for Beckgert from time to time, and if you speak to them, they'll give you good day. But they aren't . . . I don't even know how to put this."

While he thought about it, he took a bite of food, then, when his mouth was full, decided that would be the time to explain. "You see them and they're always in their funny-looking clothes, with these horses that you'd give your off n— um . . . your off *hand* to get one of, and they're polite enough, but you always know that you aren't them. And that they don't have any particular interest in seeing you become one of them."

"Why were they captured?" I asked.

"I don't know. They seem an inoffensive enough sort if you don't cross them. But I hear the Feegash have taken a dislike to them."

"Ah. The Feegash. Not the best people to anger."

"That's naught but God's truth," he said with startling fervor.

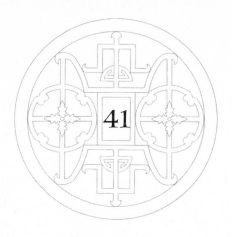

41

Hawkspar

The next day started early. Weggnrad was banging on my door with a fist when I shook off sleep. All around us, I heard men's feet hitting the floor as they jumped out of their bunks, and I heard them running along the corridor and clattering down the stairs. I yawned and stretched and Weggnrad opened the door just a bit, and said, "Put this on your legs."

He'd thrown in the powder he'd suggested I use. I was grateful, and said so. I hated to admit it, but Weggnrad had been right. I *hurt.* I was sore in places that I didn't even know I had. I could just imagine how I would fare after five hard days of riding, and not riding just for the space from sundown to dark, but from first light to last.

I powdered my legs, put on the fleeces, and dressed.

We ate lightly and from the first rode hard. The horses were well gaited, and I sat them well enough, but each time we rode up to a new station and one set of grooms raced out to take our tired, sweating horses, and another set came running up leading a set of fresh, dry horses, I struggled more to dismount, and twice as hard to remount.

We were nearing the third station at midday, and even through the veil, my mouth was full of grit and I was tired of the stink of my sweat mixed with road dirt and horse sweat. I ached everywhere. Weggnrad seemed to be having none of the problems I had. He was happy to talk, happy to pace himself to my horse, which seemed the slower beast, or else was merely the less well-ridden, and he was full of stories. If he suffered from dust from the hard-packed, dry clay trail, he didn't show evidence of it.

"... and then we had to fight off a whole crew of scoundrels from the south," he said, and laughed.

And an arrow lodged itself in his chest, and he went off the horse in one slithering, sickening drop, and dragged along the trail with his head banging on the ground. I fought to find my way into the Hagedwar, to catch my moment. And on a galloping horse, in pain and trying with all my might just to keep my balance, I could not. I could not find the peace and quiet I needed, for around me the trees rained men, and branches slapped and stung me.

And I was afraid.

I had not seen the men, so well had the dense branches of the copse into which we'd ridden hidden their less-dense forms. The brigands blocked our passage and when the horses skidded to a stop to avoid the barrier they'd formed, one man grabbed Weggnrad's horse, and one mine.

I could hear no sound from Weggnrad; I had to guess him dead. Which meant I was alone, with at least ten men. When one of the brigands grabbed me and yanked me from the saddle, I slumped against him and pretended to faint.

Other men were digging through the saddlebags, shouting angrily about us having nothing of value with us.

"A bit of gold in the man's bags. Nothing but clothing in the woman's and it's man's clothing at that."

On the ground, though, and supported by my enemy, I could find stillness.

"So the only thing of value is her?"

"Appears to be."

Could retreat into time's waters, could spin the Hagedwar, could slide into it, away from my captor passing me off to some other man.

"Get her pants off her then. Is she dead?"

"I can't find any blood on the bitch, but she isn't moving."

I reached out and caught my moment as the men around me started to tear my clothes off. I struggled to hold it as the breeches came down, as the shirt slid up, as I heard one bandit say, "Yeah, yeah, oh God, yeah, she'll do."

And held it as the cold came, as the stillness descended, as my would-be rapists and probable murderers froze into stillness.

I managed to struggle free from them. They had not been holding me tightly because I had not struggled. Nonetheless, frozen, their hands turned to iron, and it was all I could do to break free.

I fought my way to my feet, pulled up my clothes. They were not innocents in this, nor would Weggnrad be the first man they'd murdered, nor I the first woman they'd attempted to rape. I could have bound them and left them in the middle of the Courier Road for the next man along to find. But I was not in a mood to be generous. A good man lay dead on the ground.

I cut their throats, wondering a little that I had become so easy with death. I thought for a moment that I was wrong to use the advantage that I held over them; that moving among them with the twin knives strapped to my wrists, slashing and stabbing, I took unfair advantage. But that was only a momentary stupidity on my part.

There were ten of them. One of me. Any weapon I had, I had to use.

I didn't let go of my moment until I was sure I'd killed them all—I knew I was too tired to fight my way back into the still places and struggle through the leaden cold again. I feared weakening myself enough that the mad wizard would find his way back through the Eyes to push me into his hell again.

I got myself to the horses, and looped their reins around tree branches; I couldn't afford to go chasing after them. That took the last of the strength I could muster. I had to let control slide through my fingertips. The warmth of the spring day and the sunlight seeped into the cold that had consumed me, sound rolled over me, a breeze that had caught the first green scents of new growth blew around me. I breathed easier. And I made my way to Weggnrad, who lay on the ground, his foot still caught in his stirrup. I put my cheek to his nose and mouth, but he did not breathe, put my ear over his heart, but it did not beat.

I crouched over his body, angry. My benefactor's daughter was a widow for Beckgert's generosity, and the man who had done his best to be kind to me was dead. I worked his foot lose from the stirrup. He was a big man, I a small woman. I would have put him back across the saddle if I could have. I tried. I tried until I wept, but his body kept sliding down against me. I hadn't the strength to lift him so high. I envied men their strength.

I leaned against the horse, and that was when I heard hoofbeats on the Courier Road, coming fast.

I stood there surrounded by dead bandits, mostly dressed still—I hoped—in the green culappe, with my guardian dead at my feet, a brigand arrow through his chest.

One rider approached from the east.

And I did not know if I should hide or show myself.

His keen eyesight decided the situation for me. "Woman!" he shouted. "Need you assistance?"

"You arrive too late," I shouted back. I knew I was not supposed to speak, but I also was without the guardian who was supposed to speak for me. I hadn't the faintest clue what the etiquette in this situation would call for. These were not my people. This was not my place.

He galloped up and stopped, his face aimed toward the bodies scattered across the ground. He whistled softly, then said, "What in the name of God happened here?"

Which was an obvious and relevant question. And not one I'd prepared myself to answer.

"Ah . . . I . . . I . . ." I hadn't the faintest idea what to say.

That, in fact, seemed to be the right approach, for he dismounted, dropped his reins to the ground, and walked over to me. "Your husband to be?" he asked me.

"No. He . . . was taking me to my husband."

The man turned away from me, facing again toward the bodies that littered the ground like autumn leaves. "He was a hell of a fighter. How did he *do* this? Each of them with one slash across the throat deep as the devil's road, all of them fallen with no other mark on them, and him with an arrow to the heart. And no blood on his hands." He paused, his face turned toward me, and I knew he was staring at me. I had blood on *my* hands. I could feel the stickiness of it as it dried. It was Weggnrad's blood, but all blood is red. "How *did* he do this?" I could not miss the suspicion in his voice.

"I don't know," I said. "I fainted when a man dropped out of the trees onto my horse and grabbed me."

The courier's face stayed turned toward mine for what felt like a long time. Then, at last, he sighed. "Yes, of course. You're a woman; you would faint. The only explanation I can find, then, is that some man or men arrived to save you and your guardian from certain death, but left before he—or they—could be rewarded."

"That must have been what happened," I agreed.

He walked over to Weggnrad and me, and said, "I know him. This is the son-in-law of Master Beckgert. He'll be crushed at this news; he loved this man as a son."

I hung my head. The weight of death is sometimes too much to bear. I did not know how I might have saved him—this event did not show as a possibility in the waters of time that had flowed around me that morning. His death might have been, like the Tonk chances of survival before I ran back to kill the traitor, an event caused by the actions of a single man's choice at the moment. Something that could not show in the rivers of events, but that could change everything.

Had I seen, I could have acted. There had been nothing to see.

The actions of one man, or one woman, could alter everything. That thought terrified me even as it had uplifted me before. I could see more clearly than most those events that had the weight of numbers behind them, of men moving in unison with shared goals and shared dreams. I could track how those events would unfold, how they could be moved, how they might be bettered or made failures by other masses of men. But the individual with vision and heart was proof against my gaze. Was capable of surprise, and devastating effectiveness. I had been that lone individual, and now I had been made to suffer by that lone individual.

I held a future painted in broad strokes. But the miracles and the nightmares would happen or be prevented between those strokes, in threads too small to see.

I seemed have at my disposal the most valuable knowledge in the universe—the answer to the question "What next?" And yet, I knew nothing.

"Help me get him on his horse, will you? We'll get him and you to the next station, and I'll see if the couriers can give you another guardian to get you to your destination." He turned to me. "And of course, officially, you and I never spoke. *Officially.*"

"Of course." I paused, and moved to help him with the body. "My thanks for that."

42

Aaran

"Make sure the points of the yellow and gold don't extend beyond the red cube into the blue sphere," Aaran said. "I trained with a man who trained with none other than Talyn herself."

"Talyn?"

"She was the first Tonk to realize the Feegash were trouble, and to discover what kind of trouble, and she was the first to defeat them. And she discovered how to use the Feegash Hagedwar."

Redbird struggled to hold her Hagedwar in place. She said from time to time shadows intruded, and she was distracted. She would not tell him what sort of shadows, and he could not see them.

But overall she did well.

"How long will it be until I can use this thing to talk to the Oracle Hawkspar?" she asked him.

"I don't know. I can't reach her. The Communicators can't reach her. Something about the Eyes, they say, blocks them."

"So I have to learn to use this thing *with* the Eyes, which none of you can teach me."

He sighed. "I'm sorry."

"I'm not," she told him. "It's a chance. She's still alive, and this is a chance. It does not break my heart," she said grimly, "that you need me, Captain. It would not have broken my heart had you left me behind to find her. I *would* have found her. And now she would not be alone."

Redbird was not going to forgive him, he knew. But he had to concede she had every right not to. The *Ker Nagile* had already been well out to sea when the Obsidians discovered Hawkspar was not aboard. He hadn't been thinking about them when he gave the order to cast off. He hadn't been thinking at all; he'd just been doing what Hawkspar had told him to do.

"When, then," Redbird persisted, "will I be ready to go to the Communicators and learn from them?"

"When you're able to track her on your own," he said. "Because you won't be trying to reach someone at a set point who will then be able to receive your coordinates and your direction and establish a back connection to you. You'll have to find her, with her a moving target, and you one as well. Only once you've found her and put your own marker on her will you be able to reliably reach her."

Redbird's obsidian-eyed face was remarkably expressive, Aaran noted. She would be damned glad to be done with him.

He sighed and took her back through the exercises. Form the Hagedwar, move through it, settle in the proper quadrant, locate the practice marker, track the marker. Over and over and over. She might not like him, she might suffer from odd distractions, but she had the patience of stone itself, and she was tireless, and focused with a ferocity that he found almost frightening. He was grateful she and the rest of the Obsidians were on the side of the Tonk. He would hate to be against them.

When at last he ended their training session, Aaran spent a time tracking Hawkspar across his chart, marking her location after two days of travel. She was making tremendous time. Impossible time. He could not understand how she was crossing Greton at such a pace. In spite of stopping during the hours of darkness, she would actually reach the first of the hiding places he and the other captains had chosen at about the same time the fleet, hampered by unfavorable winds and their run against the hard, fast currents of the Gold Channel, would reach them.

All the ships of the fleet had celebrated her. She had won the *Ker Nagile* its freedom, she had somehow survived, and she was racing to rejoin them. They saw her as their good luck charm, their magical figurehead. He did not know how they would react to her if they fought the Ba'afeegash and lost. To him, they seemed to be ascribing too much power to her.

He heard a knock at his door, and when he shouted, "Enter," the marine guarding his door stepped into the door frame and said, "Keeper Tuua and his apprentice, and Communicator Waandar to see you."

"Let them in," Aaran said. He checked his log and made a series of little marks on the chart, showing the progression of the *Taag* into the channel at each bell.

They would make better headway after they were past the narrows, he told himself. The currents were worst there. Where the Gold Channel widened out into the Brindle Sea, currents would cease to be a real issue. Then the only question would be the winds.

"Good morning, Tuua, Waandar, Eban," he said, standing to greet them. "Have seats. We can have a meal brought in; I'm hungry enough to eat the full moose, you know?"

"Eban has news," Tuua said. He looked grim. He took one seat at the table, and motioned Eban into another one. "About his father."

Aaran raised an eyebrow. "*Eban* does?" He turned to the boy. "What is your news, then?"

"I've gotten good with the Hagedwar," he said. "Waandar has been teaching me to communicate—listening only, for now."

"Eban is a quick student," Waandar said.

"Considering who the boy's father and uncle are, that may not have been the best of plans."

"He taught me how to use the Hagedwar so I could spy on my father."

"That's risky," Aaran said. He gave Tuua a questioning look, trying to not let the boy see.

"It would be if we didn't have Eban back-shielded with Tonk magic," Tuua said. "We thought about that before we even began training him. Waandar knew how to teach the boy to focus on the ties he shared with his father; events that they'd experienced together. And Eban has been very brave about going into the pain his father cost him to hunt the bastard down."

What Tuua was describing was essentially the process of Eban trailing a torturer using the blood the bastard had spilled from Eban's body. Aaran couldn't imagine doing such a thing himself; he was amazed at the guts the kid had to have displayed to put himself back in the middle of the torture.

The method would work, of course.

"What did you find?" he asked.

"My father let me loose certain that I would do what I did. Run to a Tonk ship and find passage. Only now he can't find me. So they're telling the Feegash friend nations that Tonk pirates sent a ransom notice. That I'm some important boy, and that you said you'd kill me if the Feegash didn't make the Tonk . . ." He glanced over at Tuua. "What was the word again?"

"A favored nation."

Aaran said, "So you heard this, too?"

Tuua nodded. "He passed what he was hearing on to me but I could only catch the parts that were said in Sinali to the whole assembly. Still, from what I got, the Feegash are claiming the boy is dead already, and a martyr. 'Sacrificed to the barbarity of the bestial Tonk' was the phrase they used. They're rallying their allies to go to war against Tonk everywhere waving him as their banner. No negotiation with kidnappers."

"Conveniently not mentioning that the boy was not kidnapped but ran away, and that they're responsible for stealing our children to be their slaves and murdering our adults."

Tuua smiled. "How would mentioning those things benefit them? How has telling the truth ever benefited them?"

Aaran muttered, "I think that's what diplomacy is. Lying long enough to get the knife between the other man's shoulder blades first. I hate diplomats." He stared down at his chart, which showed the distance between him and Hawkspar—the distance, as he thought of it, between failure and success, or between destruction and survival.

If he couldn't reach her or she couldn't reach him, he could not believe the Tonk could win the war. The Feegash had stacked too many odds against them. Had made things too big, too all-encompassing. The Feegash would offer deals and bribes and treats, trade daughters or sons or gold, lie and lie and lie and lie, and in the end most of the known world would call the proud Tonk—the oldest civilization in the world—animals.

The Tonk people would be enslaved, their vast libraries burned and in the end their grand and ancient idea—that all citizens deserved a voice in their lives, the right to choose their own destinies, the right to be responsible for their futures, their successes, and their failures—would die.

Aaran knew what he and the small fleet went to battle for. He knew its worth, he believed the cause worth the sacrifice of his own life and the lives of those who fought with him, just for the chance to prevail.

But he desperately wanted to know that at least some chance of success existed.

His fingers traced the complex shoreline of Greton, sliding back and forth along the line of glossy black ink. She was out there, and she was traveling with ungodly haste to meet up with him. Was her speed because she knew the Tonk might prevail? Or was it because she knew all hope was dead, and that their best chance lay in turning tail, fleeing back to Hyre as quickly as the winds would take them, and gathering up their loved ones and whatever possessions they might save, and crawling into exile, to wait for better times?

"You're a long way away," Tuua observed.

"I am. My heart is with Hawkspar right now. I pray hourly that whatever force it is that moves her across the land at such speeds does not fail her."

"I hope she can help us take our battle to the snakes' nest. But in the meantime, have you any thought what actions we might take against all the rest of the world, who will be moving against us in this decent season, rather than debating and waiting while they lose the advantage of good weather?"

And Aaran thought, what was there to do? The betrayal of the world's kingdoms and principalities would come as no surprise to the Tonk. They kept their spies in the world's many courts, as did everyone else.

They would find out what they faced.

The fleet could offer nothing to help them more than what they were already doing. If Aaran and the Tonk Great Pack could crush Ba'afeegash—something that had never been done before—they could, perhaps, win over the rest of the world eventually.

But so long as the Feegash occupied their poisonous mountain nest, and so long as they yearned to remake all the world in their image, they would conspire against the Tonk, for they despised everything the Tonk held dear, and held dear everything the Tonk despised.

"We can stay our course," Aaran said at last. "We can hold true to our mission. If there is any hope for our people at all—whether we can get Hawkspar back or not—that hope lies in our actions, and our faithfulness to this mission."

"Then what we must do, we will do." Tuua rose, and the boy and Waandar stood a beat after him. "As Ethebet says, 'Men are not measured lying down, but standing.'"

Hawkspar

We had to take a slower pace. The horse that bore Weggnrad's body was skittish, and tied though the beast was to my rescuer's saddle, he would not gallop at speed, but kept shying away and rolling his eyes.

The slower pace allowed the courier to talk easily, however, and I quickly got the feeling that he was not a man who often found himself with a captive listener—and better yet, one who could not talk back.

". . . so then—ha, ha, I wish I had only been there to see it—my mother's sisters brought out their sacrifice. They'd found a young man, some fool who is the sort to listen only to what he wants to hear and never to what is said—you know the sort. My own half brother was like that, as a matter of fact. Ha! I could tell you stories about him. He was forever getting his father, my mother's second husband, riled about something that he had done that he thought was what his father wanted, but never was anything like. He gave the goat some green hay once . . ."

Here he burst into such laughter that he choked and gasped and had to drink water before he could resume his odious tale.

Weggnrad had been a pleasant enough companion. He hadn't talked much, but he'd managed to start one story and finish the same story. I'd not appreciated what a gift that was until I met Heebart. It was Heebart with some long name after, and a handful of titles or badges or honors; I hadn't been able to tell which. And all this had started because Heebart, discomfited by the presence of the dead man in the saddle behind his, and awkward about traveling with a woman made guardianless by bandits mysteriously dead, had thought he would entertain me for a while with the amusing story of how his family had come by its unusual name.

Which I still didn't know. I couldn't remember, at that point, if he had gotten around to telling me his last name, much less why he'd thought it was so unusual. His voice, not rich or deep or pleasant but high and nasal, had become an inescapable unpleasantness, like my aching thighs and lower back, both terribly unused to riding horses quickly over long distances. Or like the dust that got inside my clothes. He became an insect whine right up against my skull, and if I could have, I would have swatted him.

Which makes me sound ungrateful for his help, and I wasn't. I was merely ungrateful that he was the one who had come along to help me.

And on he droned. And on. And on.

I did wish I could remember his name. Someday I would want to tell people about him, and I wanted to identify him fully, as Heebart Pigsnout, or Heebart Dullard of the Tedious People, or however his people styled their names. I wanted to say his name, and have a listener from half a world away cringe and say, *God as my witness, I was waylaid by that man once and I thought I'd have to cut my own head off and toss it from my body to get out of range of his voice.* Just once. Just once I wanted to know that others had suffered what I suffered.

Finally we came over a rise, and a station lay before us. I would have lifted my head and sung praises to Jostfar and Ethebet, had I not been attempting to disguise my origins.

"You'll be wanting to stop here," he told me. "They'll find someone to ride with you soon enough, though they will surely wish to contact your father first to let him know of your dilemma, and the death of his son-in-law."

Which reminded me that I was complaining about a dull man, while a good man was dead just behind us. Instantly guilt descended upon me that I could so quickly turn to my own petty concerns when the tragedy of others rode behind.

Heebart was no doubt correct. The Association of Couriers would no doubt want to have me wait while my "father" was notified of Weggnrad's death. I, unfortunately, did not have time to wait for all the niceties to fall into place. No matter how badly I felt about Weggnrad, and no matter how much I hurt for both Beckgert and his daughter who would soon find out she'd been widowed, I could not stay to see that all went smoothly. I had to be on my way. I could not be certain when Aaran would reach the cove I aimed for—not even by standing in the center of time itself could I tell how the winds would blow or the ocean currents run in the upcoming days. I'd lost the time to make one station of my three remaining stations for the day, but could still hope to make two more if I could avoid delay.

I wondered if I would be able to follow the Courier Road on my own. It had, so far, been a clear track most of the time. But I would not have been able to pick my way through the copse to where the track became clearer on the other side. Part of the route I suspected the couriers had memorized. Part might change depending on conditions. And to have access to the horses I had to have permission to ride the Courier Road. And to reach Aaran and the rest of the fleet before they had passed me by, I had to have access. I had to be approved. I could not play games with time, because I could move only myself against the weight of a caught moment. I could not move myself plus a horse.

But how could I, a lone outlander woman disguised as a would-be bride, forbidden to speak, win the couriers to my cause? They did not love the Tonk. They did not love the Ossalenes. They were neutral in theory, but sliding toward becoming Feegash satellites in fact, and I could not hope to find among them those who hated the Feegash as much as I had come to.

When the groom ran up and grabbed my reins, I dismounted like an old woman creeping down stairs. I made pathetic little whimpering noises, and hobbled silently into the station, leaving Heebart to deal with Weggnrad's body and the horses and those things which we'd carried in our saddlebags. I had Weggnrad's paperwork, his courier seal, his road pass, and his lodging chits—all things designed to make exactly the sort of thing that had happened to him that day less likely.

I hobbled up to the stationmaster's desk and stood there, facing the stationmaster, wondering how I should do what I needed to do.

I expected Heebart to come in at any time, to pass on the information about Weggnrad to the man before me and make some sort of introductions. But instead one of the grooms banged through the door.

"Heebart dropped off that woman there and Bont Weggnrad. They were ambushed in the Biltod Wood. Heebart says he managed to kill the ten men who were attacking them and rescue *her*, but he didn't get there in time to save Weggnrad. He said he'd pick up his reward for killing the bandits on his way back."

"Heebart Frogass?" the stationmaster said. "That long-winded bastard did something besides talk? I don't believe it."

There. I was happy. That tedious man had inflicted his horrible pointless maunderings on someone besides me. And that someone hadn't liked him, either.

Well, I was a bit happy, anyway. Heebart Frogass had apparently abandoned me to whatever fate I could work out for myself here in the middle of nowhere. And he'd claimed to have killed ten bandits, for which he'd also claimed a reward he hadn't earned, and all because he figured I wouldn't be able to tell anyone what had really happened.

"We're going to have to send for another guardian for her," the stationmaster continued. "Her husband-to-be will just have to wait until we can get her an appropriate escort." And then he turned in my general direction and said, "I cannot speak to her, of course, but I know she will understand that she will have a place to stay in one of our rooms until her guardian arrives, and will have food brought up to her, and will be given the run of the baths and such during the midday hours. And I would hope she would find those arrangements suitable for the next several days."

I didn't. Those arrangements wouldn't be suitable at all.

I put my head down and thought.

And sidled over to the stationmaster. "Ask the groom to leave, please."

His head whipped around to face me, and he gasped.

"This is not a breach of etiquette, I promise."

His head was toward me, but he said to the groom, "Go outside, Broogin. I've something to deal with in here."

I waited until Broogin stomped across the floor and out the door, slamming it behind him.

And then I lifted the veil.

"I'm only the decoy for Beckgert's real daughter," I told him. "She is going by another route, because Beckgert feared she would be the target of . . . kidnappers. And assassins. So I was sent by this route, publicly, pretending to be her. And she went privately, hidden away and with no notice given. But in order for me to do my job, I must be permitted to stay publicly visible, on the road, showing up where I'm expected to be. Anything untoward could permit the attention of those who have reason to hate Beckgert to fall on her."

"I . . . I . . . yes." He faltered. "I understand. But . . . your eyes. What's the matter with your eyes?"

"They give me certain abilities. *I* am the one who killed the ten bandits. Weggnrad was shot from ambush before we even reached them; I had no chance to save him. But I killed all the men who had gathered to steal Beckgert's daughter away."

"What kind of abilities?" His hands played with something hard and thin. A pen, a scribe—I couldn't tell. But he ran it back and forth in his hands, and twisted it, and rolled it between his fingers. He'd not seemed a nervous man until he saw my eyes.

I shook my head. "If I showed you, then I'd have to kill you."

Silence.

"Can you . . . see . . . with those eyes?"

I studied him. "In your back left pocket of your breeches, you have three coins and two pieces of paper. You have two more coins stuffed inside the heels of your shoes. You have metalwork done on three of your teeth, and a missing left small toe. And once, a long time ago, you broke the bones in your right hand. It looks like you might have punched a man in the face." I turned my face toward his. "I see quite well. Just not the same."

"I'll have a horse readied for you."

"Do you have anyone capable of riding with me? I don't know the route." I handed him Weggnrad's papers and courier seal.

He read them silently. Scribbled something in his book. Then said, "I'll have Broogin accompany you to the end of your journey. He's not finished earning his seal, but he can ride under Weggnrad's for this journey." The stationmaster added, "We'll have had verification of the ten bandits by now—there will have been other riders coming in from your route. Assuming all is as you've said, do you want your reward here, or when you get to the final station? I'll write it up for you as a cash-on-demand note."

I was willing to risk carrying cash. I was becoming confident of my ability to defend it. "I'll take it now."

"Then I'll go check our verification. Go up to the first room on the right and I'll have a boy bring you a meal. I'll tell Broogin he's riding out today, and we'll get you back on the road. Or have you eaten?"

"No. I need a meal."

He hurried off, and I went upstairs, pleased that I had managed to get myself back in business again.

We made the Buke Ravine station not long after darkfall. Broogin was a pleasant enough companion, much more so because he knew he could talk to me. I wasn't a real bride-to-be. Like the stationmaster, he wanted to know all about the Eyes. I lied. I let him think they were simple weapons. That with them, I could see ways to kill men that no one else could see. It was, in its way, a true enough statement, but it didn't make me one of the oracles, and it didn't mark me as a member of the Ossalenes, and it didn't put me in a position where he wanted anything from me. I was strange and frightening and clearly dangerous, and that was enough to keep him both polite and at a distance.

With his curiosity about the Eyes appeased, he told me about himself. He had a little brother and a little sister, had never done much before he joined the Courier Service, had thought it would be a life of grand adventure, but had so far been disappointed because the well-paid couriers hung on to their jobs and the only way to advance was when one of them retired or died. The Courier Service was a new thing. Greton had only been running it for about three years, and the Feegash thought they should take it apart because it was an expensive proposition, and instead hire Feegash Communicators.

But, Broogin pointed out, it would be a little difficult to send a bride-to-be at such speed to her husband with Feegash Communicators. Or to quickly get the medicines and other physical objects people across the country had found so useful. The Feegash could send nothing more than words, and the Gretons were less than enthusiastic about turning over any portion of their communications and transport network to foreigners.

I thought them wise, and said so.

I kept my use of the Eyes to short, light bursts of the future, as I had throughout the trip, focusing only on Aaran and his progress. The physical act of riding through changeable weather drained me of energy—the same energy that I would need in abundance to fight Ossal and hold him at bay if I used the Eyes any more than I already was. In my sleep, time swirled constantly around me, and voices babbled in my head. Ossal had backed into his cage following our last encounter, but I remained aware of him, and of the spirit of the corpsewalker, and the still-living monster I had yet to confront. They were close; I did not want to bring them closer. Even awake, the waters of time sometimes brushed me at unexpected moments because of my near exhaustion, and I would suddenly find myself submerged in the life of someone not with me, or near me, or relevant to me. I could see where previous wearers of the Eyes had succumbed to madness, and I could feel how easy it would be to fall myself.

So I used them as little as I could, knowing they would consume me eventually, but that I had to survive to carry out my mission before they did.

We took lodgings come evening, fell into our roles as silent bride-to-be and guardian, and got a good night's sleep.

The sixth day, our final day, I told Broogin I'd appreciated him riding with me, and asked him how much he would receive for making the trip. He shrugged. "The same thing I'd have made working at the stables. I'm just pretending I'm a courier, I'm not the real thing."

"You've been the real thing for me." I reined in, and rode off the Courier Road. I dismounted, reached into my left saddlebag, and took hold of the reward I'd received for killing the ten bandits. "Here," I told him when he rode up to me. "I have no use for this, and I suspect it would benefit you a great deal."

He sat astride his mount, not moving. Saying nothing.

"Take it. I don't need it," I insisted.

"That's . . . the reward money you received for killing those bandits, isn't it?"

"It is."

"Is it true that you saved Beckgert's daughter's life?"

"It is. But how did you hear about it?"

"If I tell you, I'll die." And then I heard him swear under his breath. "Get farther off the road. Well off. Trouble will be along shortly, and we don't want it to see us."

I'd never got the feeling that something was wrong with Broogin, but I did at that moment.

Still, I had faith in my ability to defend myself. So he led, and I followed.

When we and the horses were completely out of sight of the road, he said, "You remember Weggnrad? You know who he was?"

"Beckgert's son-in-law."

"No. I mean, do you know who he really was?"

"No," I said. "No idea."

"He was one of the main Greton agents working for the Feegash. His wife saw some sort of mark on your hand that made her think you might have had something to do with those Tonk barbarians who made such trouble in Gerstaggen. Weggnrad volunteered to escort you so that he might find out what you knew about what had happened, or at least find out why you were in such a hurry to get where you were going."

I suddenly felt like I might be sick. "And you know this how?"

"I read the note he carried with his seal. The couriers carry mission papers, so that if something happens to one of them, the courier who picks up the mission will know what he'd been doing. In Weggnrad's mission paper . . ." He stopped, and I began to think he would have nothing more to say. Then he sighed and shook his head. "Well, I cannot *not* tell you now. You've been most kind, and this sort of betrayal . . . no matter who you are, it isn't right. The note you carry says that you are a Tonk traitor, and that Weggnrad thinks, because of special weapons you carry, that you are the killer sought by the Feegash for the deaths of many good men in Gerstaggen, and that you were supposed to be permitted to reach your destination, and then you were to be immediately killed once you had made contact with your contact. And the mixed army of Gretons and Feegash that is following you one station behind—but that is now only a long league or two behind us, since you are so close to Brurd—was to fall upon and utterly destroy whomever it is you've ridden so hard to meet."

"Oh, Ethebet, preserve us all."

"You can see after a fashion, but you can't read, can you? Of if you can, you can't read words written on a page."

"I can read knots tied into silk string," I said. "I can read with my fingers, but not with the Eyes."

I leaned against my horse. I might have betrayed the whole of our secret war. Weggnrad was dead, but the army he'd summoned was almost upon me. "Am I still carrying the same note?"

"Yes."

"Oh . . . my sweet gods," I said, falling back on the oaths of the Order.

"I'm sorry. I was told by my stationmaster that if I got you safely to the last station to turn in the horses, I could return home and be given the commission to ride the Courier Road that I've been waiting for so long. That Weggnrad's seal would be mine, and I would become rich in my turn."

"But you didn't."

"No. I read the mission paper. I don't think you're a Tonk barbarian—you haven't once acted like you might want to skin me and eat me." He hung his head. "I think you're a good woman, and you have been kind to me. But now I don't see much future beyond that they'll kill me when I go in to face my stationmaster. I didn't just fail to get you to the last station in one piece. I told you what they planned to do once you got there."

"What will happen if you don't show up?"

"It depends on how I don't show up. If I'm already dead, what could they do? If it looks like I turned traitor, the important Gretons are likely to hunt down my family. Torture them. See if anyone else might be thinking about not following our Feegash allies into ever deeper treachery."

I stood considering that. "So you couldn't come with me, or your family would suffer?"

"You'd take me with you?"

"I would."

"But you're right. The Feegash would convince the Gretons to let them torture and kill my brothers and sisters, my parents, my grandparents, my aunts and uncles and cousins."

"So for you, being dead would be the best thing?"

"I'm having a hard time seeing it that way. For my family, though, me being dead would be better." He stood there, face turned away from mine. "I guess if you could do it so it wouldn't . . . hurt. . . ."

"Killing you would be a terrible way to repay your kindness," I told him. "I was thinking more along the lines of tying you up and hitting you on the head and leaving you and your horse by the road."

"Really?" He considered that for a moment, and brightened. "You would do that for me?"

"I would. And I'll bury the gold by the road, where you can come back later and dig it up. You deserve repayment for helping me."

"Are you a Tonk barbarian?" he asked.

"I'm a living goddess," I told him, pushing him to the ground and using rope he'd tied to his saddle to bind his wrists and ankles. "I can see the past and the future, and I'm trying to save the whole world."

He giggled. It was a nervous-sounding giggle.

I sighed. "No," I said. "I'm not a Tonk barbarian. I've never skinned and eaten anyone. I'm just a woman in a hurry to meet a man. I know a few good fighting tricks, and I caught wind of the army coming up behind us, and blamed you for it. So I hit you over the head and tied you up. They can't blame you for that."

"They could fault me for living, I suppose," he said.

They could. But the only way I could help him out of that dilemma was to kill him. "Tell them you reminded me of *my* brother."

"Do I?" He sounded surprised.

"You do. But most young men remind me of my brother. He was tall and handsome and kind, and he was murdered when I was a small child."

With him tied, I dug a quick hole at one corner of a large, oddly-shaped rock, and dropped the reward money I'd been given into it. To make sure Broogin would be able to find his reward, I then made three fresh chips into the face of the rock, evenly spaced, with the treasure hidden on the right side of the third one.

"You'll be able to find this again?" I asked him.

"Yes. Thank you. Thank you so much."

I returned to his side and knelt by him. "Good should be rewarded by good. Remember where your treasure is, young Broogin. And remember that not everything you hear by those in power is true."

I brushed his hair back from his face, wondering if Broogin was handsome. If he did look anything like the big brother I so vaguely remembered.

And then, before he knew what I was about, I hit him on the back of the head with the pommel of his dagger, the sort of injury someone taking a boy by surprise would inflict.

His body went limp. I checked to make sure I hadn't killed him. I hadn't.

I left his horse standing beside him, ground-tied, and rode away on mine, back to the road, back to heading toward Brurd.

Around the next corner, I got off the road again, backtracked, and rode north. A slow lope this time, because my horse had been ridden hard, and there weren't going to be any handy stable boys to replace him with a fresh one. I had a ways to go, and this horse needed to last.

When I was well away from Broogin and with a clear shot to the Pirates' Dance, I would take enough time to find a hiding place and slide back into time's waters to see if I might catch the way the future flowed. I had little hope of finding anything useful, though. The last time I'd checked, I was still in whitewater. I was back to digging my own channel, not knowing where it might take me when I arrived.

I hoped it would take me, eventually, home.

43

Aaran

"Pindas and Cartajarma have allied with the Feegash, Captain," Holyn said. Aaran, Tuua, and the second Communicator sat in the station just beneath the steersman's castle. He looked grim. "Word is they've built up forces to cross over the Brittlebreak Strait into Hyre; they were going to try to cross on the Republic side, but that Hva Hwa king of theirs put out his army and deployed his magics, and they realized the Republic is no longer sympathetic to enemies of the Tonk. So now they're trying to find a weak spot to cross over on the Confederate side."

"So now we have enemies across the strait. That's not good. Better than on the other side of the Kraata Mountains, but not good," Tuua said.

"Before, all we had against us were the Eastils. Now . . . we have the Eastils on our side but the rest of the world against us." Aaran rubbed his temples. "It's not going to go away if we wipe out the Feegash. Not now."

Holyn leaned his back to the wall and looked at Aaran, eyebrow raised. "You think not?"

"No. Because the Feegash have convinced the rest of the world we're barbarians. If we wipe the pogging Feegash out, we'll look exactly like what they say we are."

Tuua shook his head. "But if we don't wipe them out, they'll destroy us—with their policies, with their allies, and with their lies."

"I know that. I have no good answer. I don't even have a bad answer."

Holyn shrugged. "They're killing us now. Our only option as I see it is to kill them, then clean up the mess that ensues as best we can."

"If we can get Hawkspar back, maybe she'll have a third alternative that she can see." Aaran stared at the rough table where the Communicators worked, but he wasn't seeing it. He was seeing her; dark-haired and slender and deadly. He ached for her.

"Don't count on it." Holyn took a sip of ale and said, "I'm going back into the Hagedwar. There's more happening, and I want to be sure I don't miss the main points."

"Who are you reading?"

"There's a message station set up full time in Beyltaak now. They have Communicators in there reporting events as they happen, and then repeating briefs from elsewhere, relaying everything important so that anyone who had to shut down would still be able to find out what was happening later. The Hagedwar Magics units are up and running, but they're also bringing back all the Sender and Shielder units. They and the Republic are actually working together on this—the Republic has all its units activated, too, and they're working in council with the Confederacy on joint defense."

"So all of Hyre is on full war footing."

"All of Hyre. All of southern Tandinapalis. Franican Tonk territories, the Velo Tonks . . . everyone is armed and ready." Holyn nodded. "And we're still traveling dark. Almost none of the defensive units and none of the public knows about us, so there are calls from all over the country to attack Ba'afeegash, attack Cartajarma and Pindas, attack Sinali. Everything looks scattered, and it's well known by the Feegash that we have not sent any of our navy beyond our own seas—that Tonks, or in the case of Hyre, Tonk and Eastil navies, patrol the Tonk lands exclusively, defending against all comers."

"How does it sound like it's going?"

"The Tand clans are already seeing action. The Tonks in Tandinapalis are in a worse position than we are. They have the whole of the Great Plains where enemies can attack by land, and immense shorelines to patrol. Publicly, they're following the same policy that Hyre is. Maintain a strong defense."

Aaran said, "Defense is a game of attrition. They're going to have to go on the offensive to survive this."

Holyn took long swallow of his ale. He closed his eyes for a moment, his brow furrowing. Then he sighed and looked from Aaran to Tuua. "Privately, I'm sure they are. I *pray* they are. The Feegash have allied with the Hjorma and the Lagakodi, who are now getting paid to do what they would have done for free."

"The Feegash have publicly allied themselves with the Hjorma?" Aaran could hardly believe that.

The Hjorma, the most horrific of the Northmen peoples, worshipped a pantheon of the most bloodthirsty gods Aaran had ever heard of. Their gods demanded human sacrifices in brutal fashion for every aspect of their existence, and their priests kept Hjorma constantly at war, raiding other tribes in the Great Plains and the jungles up by the equator to get the sacrifices they claimed the gods demanded. The Hjorma ripped the beating hearts out of infants; raped men, women, and children to death; skinned people alive; forced prisoners to eat their own body parts. They would turn on the Feegash in an instant if ever they got the opportunity; they knew no more of loyalty than they knew of compassion. But they were willing to fight against the Tonk, so the Feegash would call them civilized.

In truth, most of what the Hjorma did in worship of their gods was no worse than what the Feegash did for sport.

"There are reports of border fights," Holyn said. "But these are not official. Most of what's going on in the Tand is encoded, I suspect. And we don't have their current codes."

"The Tonk in Franica and Velobrina?"

"We know of instances where clans have been attacked from all sides and wiped out. One where a Mindan settlement attempted to negotiate a truce, and Franican negotiators agreed to settlement, then slaughtered the lot of them when they stepped out, unarmed."

"Glad you're not a Mindan?" Tuua asked.

"By Ethebet's blade, yes."

"Me, too." Aaran stood up straight and gave Holyn a quick bow. "I'll let you get back to your work. Make sure as much of it goes into the logs as you can."

Holyn picked up his pen again, and said, "Good luck to you, Captain."

Aaran, who had been turning to leave, stopped and looked back. "Luck to me?"

"In finding that third solution."

Up the ladder and out on the aft deck, Tuua said to Aaran, "I want to make a pact with you, cousin."

Aaran stopped and turned. Those were the exact words he had said to Tuua, over the bodies of their mothers and fathers and Tuua's siblings. They had made their pact, and they had lived the rest of their lives by it, but neither had ever uttered those words again.

"What would you have of me, cousin?" he asked.

"I would swear to Jostfar by Ethebet's sword and braid that we do not rest until we have destroyed the Feegash and their allies."

Aaran stood there, biting his lip. "I'm torn," he said. "My head tells me to swear with you. My gut, my heart, the raising of the hair on the back of my neck, tell me wait. This is not the third way. There is a third way, Tuua. There has to be."

Tuua looked at him for a long time, saying nothing. And then, silently, he turned and walked away.

Redbird was teaching the rest of the Ossalenes, from Moonstones to Ambers to Obsidians, the Hagedwar. She could not reach Hawkspar, either, but she said she was certain it was some failure on her own part to understand the full intricacies of linking the Eyes into the Hagedwar magic. She believed one of the other disciplines, or perhaps simply another Obsidian might make the connection she could not make.

She'd gotten happier, he noted, since she started being able to track Hawkspar. He was relieved. She and the rest of the Obsidians were eating again, and most of the ash had worn off their faces. The whole lot of them were still going to the chapel every day, Tuua said, starting right after the morning's *hadudaak aveerzak* and going until the *gitaada*. One Ossalene was in front of Ethebet's shrine at all times, praying.

He had to admire their dedication, and their devotion to Hawkspar. He wondered at how hard Redbird drove them. And wondered, too, that not a one of them complained.

Ever.

He hoped he might inspire that utter, unquestioning devotion from his own men. He feared that the time was coming when he would need it.

Hawkspar

I'd ridden through the sun-warmed chill of daylight and into the miserable damp-soaked cold of darkness, and I'd managed to reach the cove where my latest little peek into time promised Aaran and the *Taag* would hide.

I'd never been afraid of land before. But I was afraid of the place I'd come to, and so was the horse.

The Pirates' Dance stank. It smelled of rotting vegetation and sour water, sickly sweet flowers and carrion—those last two frequently together, so I avoided brushing against large plants, for fear that one of the carnivorous monstrosities might be large enough to devour me. The chill air didn't seem any deterrent at all to the buzzing, singing, chirping, hissing things that lived there. I was stung and bitten and scraped by all manner of tiny insects who found their way into my nose and mouth and ears. Probably the Eyes, too, though I couldn't feel anything there except along my eyelids.

Once he was cooled down, I took all the tack off the poor horse and chased him away. He seemed happy enough to go.

I then balanced on the edge of the cliff and tossed saddle and bridle and crupper into the water far below, where it all sank to the bottom. I kept the saddle blanket and the supply kit; those I thought might be useful while I waited. I wanted to find a good hiding place and rest there until the *Taag* arrived.

So I studied the cliff, and found several caves of varying sizes in its face. Some were just holes that went back a ways. They all seemed to be full of live things, and I was suffering enough from the biting and stinging insects already. I didn't want to dislodge a cloud of bats, or something even less savory.

One cave, though, was large, and had been hollowed out by men, who had built dock structures inside. It was empty, and it looked like it would be an excellent hiding place. I worked myself down the face of the cliff carefully, testing each handhold and foothold, and with not too many bad scares managed to get myself into shelter.

I found a good ledge inside the cave, put the horse blanket down, and settled in to wait. My best read of the future suggested the *Taag* would find harbor in my little cove before the sun rose. That I was almost through with running, almost through with waiting, almost back to my home and my people. I suffered greatly to sit still, so anxious was I to hear their voices and be among them again.

I spent my stillness in fretting about Aaran.

I wondered how things stood between him and me.

Would we be nothing but colleagues and comrades at arms after this separation?

Would his heart have changed toward me?

I was surprised out of exhausted reverie by the sound of oars dipping into the water at the cave mouth. It was on me before I could even think about the meaning of it. It glided beneath me, and the men in it kept silent, working their oars. I wanted so much for it to be sailors from the *Taag*. But I dared not assume.

A small ship lay at anchor outside the cave. I could barely make it out—the rock all around me played havoc with such vision as I had. It did not seem large enough to be the *Taag*, but some of the other Tonk ships had been about that size, and size in a place like the Pirates' Dance, with trees that seemed too huge and tall to be real poking out of the water, with insects as big as my hand, and with nothing normal or known to measure against, is tricky. Things that seem near can be far, and things that seem far can be near, depending on what size the mind thinks they might be.

I wanted one of the men to say something. I wanted them to speak in Tonk, and when they did I would shout my joy.

But they proceeded at steady pace right by me, and I made no sound. Perhaps they were my people, quiet because they were moving through unknown territory with possible enemies before them. But perhaps not.

I had no wish to kill those I could simply avoid.

Neither had I any wish to be killed, and with my exhaustion, hunger, and physical pain, I did not know how long I would be able to freeze a moment should the need arise. I could very well find myself dead. I was using the Eyes as little as possible, but I dared an instant for checking on the progress of the *Taag*, which with the rest of the Grand Pack was almost to me, and an instant to check the progress of the army that pursued me—they were scattered by trying to cover as many of the coves as their numbers would allow, but five had found some sort of barge hidden along the shore, and had worked their way down the cliff face to it. They were at that moment setting out to reach the hidden ship.

I came out, chilled to the bone, feeling strange and light-headed. The ship hidden in the cove was not the *Taag*, but it could be a threat to the *Taag*, as could the five men, Gretons or Feegash or perhaps both, who slid quietly across the water.

Behind me, I hear the sound of the longboat bumping against the dock.

And then voices. In a language I did not know.

I could not risk the Eyes again. My weakness, my hunger, my pain, my exhaustion, the wearing effects of the cold, the light-headedness that suddenly plagued me—all could permit Ossal to take over. Or perhaps not even Ossal. Perhaps the madness that would one day devour me might devour me right then. I could not guess whether the sailors in their little sloop would be more of a danger to Aaran than the loss of whatever help I might give to the Tonk fleet, should I be lost in the madman's hell. Or should I die.

I stopped being cold. I started sweating.

I decided that I could crawl out of the cave the way I had crawled in, and hide along the cliff face, and see what I could find out about that ship. Perhaps it was harmless.

Perhaps I could even get onto it long enough to get some water. My canteen was empty, but the smell of the water in the swamp made me retch.

So I focused on the handholds and footholds in the wall. These had been carved by men, not the sea, so they all angled down into the rock, and they'd been roughened to provide some traction against the slimes and mosses that grew in profusion on the rock face. I kept my ears open. The men behind me at the hidden dock sounded like they were moving crates. I hoped they had a lot to move, and that they would stay busy a long time.

I crept across the rock wall, grateful that the handholds were above the tide line. After encountering some sort of crab in one of them on my way in, I'd ripped the veil off my outfit and tore it into two pieces. These strips I'd wrapped around my hands before going farther. And my hands were still well wrapped on my way back out. I didn't want to encounter any of the sea's stinging, biting, poisonous little creatures.

Outside, I crept down to where the ancient cliffs gave way to the snake-tangles of the sea cypress roots. They were ugly trees, and that they and this bay and estuary backed up against a cliff face that had been battered and cut by an ocean spoke to me of rough changes in this land. Violence between ground and sea, and shifts in currents. The silting of the channel.

I wish I could have truly seen the place—light and color and radiance—and not just read it by its density and the way the bogs and knobs and roots reached like clutching hands toward me. It might have been beautiful, had I still had eyes.

I could make out the ship hidden between the trunks, though. It was long and lean, and without the solid stone of the cave between me and it, I could see that it was armed heavily. I did not recognize its style, but it clearly was not Tonk. It had no fanciful prow, no graceful curves, no multiple masts and complex spiderweb riggings.

Sitting at anchor, it reminded me of a thief hunkered and hiding in shadows, low against the ground. I didn't like it. It was trouble, clearly. And trouble that would be here waiting when the *Taag* and other ships of the Tonk fleet came sliding in.

I watched the five men on the raft work their way closer to it: I was interested in their progress. The men might be Greton or Feegash, but either way, they were enemies of me and mine. I wished them ill in their encounter with the ship they approached.

And then I caught movement and shifting weights and densities at the edge of the Eyes' visual range. The mouth of the bay was, I knew, some distance from this estuary. The *Taag* and at least some of the other ships of the Grand Pack were seeking shelter. And me.

I wished then for something I could do to reach the hidden ship and reveal it to my people. I wished that I might somehow disarm it. I wished I might disable the five Feegash cronies who sought me.

If only I had a bow and arrows, a bag of quicklights to fashion a flaming arrow to launch into the enemy's furled sails.

And a stable platform from which to fire.

I could not be everything, or do everything. I knew that. But I was stuck like a dizzy bug on the face of the cliff, with tangles of roots my only possible path across the water to the enemy ship, and that path not one I could follow to a clear end. I tried to untangle the maze, but every route I tried to plot out led inevitably to a blockage, or a huge open sheet of water, and either way, beyond those obstacles I could not pass.

I began to shiver and heard my teeth start to chatter. I hoped that the sound wasn't as loud as it sounded to me.

Meanwhile, the *Taag* sailed closer, and behind it a goodly string of other ships. I could not yet feel any hint of the sun on my face, so I suspected nothing would warn my people about the hidden enemy.

Behind me, from inside the cave, I heard the echoing of voices. That unknown language again, and the splashing of oars. I might do something with them, perhaps. Maybe I could force them to reveal themselves.

I was close enough I should have been able to throw something and hit one of them. If I could cause shouting—especially if I could do it without revealing my own position—I might prove of some use.

I felt around on the cliff face and worked loose a small stone. Then I shifted my position to get steady holds for my left hand and left foot, and slowly swung the right side of my body out from the cliff.

I didn't have the chance to throw my rock to alert my people.

One of the men on the raft coughed, and on the darkened sloop, lights suddenly shined over the side, illuminating the raft and its occupants.

The sloop opened fire. I heard the twang of bowstrings, the thump of a catapult, various splashes, and screaming. The raft began to burn, and the men on it. I saw them jump into the water—and saw monstrous creatures I had mistaken for fallen logs erupt out of the water, spread massive jaws wide, and drag them beneath the surface almost too fast to see.

I shuddered. Under no circumstances did I dare go into the water. My grasp on the cliff face suddenly felt weak, and untenable. My lightheadedness got worse.

I was hot again.

And then catapults on the deck of the *Taag* launched lit tarballs into the mast of the hidden ship, and Greton fire onto its deck, while arrows from my Obsidians up in the masts rained into the longboat that had raced out at the first sound of trouble to get back to its ship. The men in the longboat screamed and rowed faster, but one by one the oars stopped. Then the longboat stopped.

Meanwhile, the men aboard the low ship tried to mount a resistance, but all the ships in the bay fired in on them.

I tried not to hear the screaming from the decks of the burning sloop. It didn't last long. None of it lasted long.

While the sloop yet burned, I saw a longboat from the *Taag* lowered into the water, and saw a dozen men get in. They rowed straight toward me.

And at long last, I heard Aaran call out, "We'll get right under you, Hawkspar. Don't move near the water until we're there."

Even with them beneath me, I almost didn't make it in. My arms and legs were shaking, and as I tried to let go, the dizziness overtook me, and I lost my grip and began to topple forward.

Many strong hands caught me, and voices I knew said my name.

Redbird.

Aaran.

I sagged against one of the gunwales and closed my eyes.

"Hawkspar? Are you all right?"

I needed water. Food. To warn Aaran about the possibility that other enemies on land might find this position before morning or during the day, in spite of my care in hiding my trail. I needed to sleep knowing that my back was guarded, and that I could truly trust the people I was with. But words would not form in my mouth. In that moment, when I needed to say so much, all I could do was touch the wood of the Tonk-made longboat and know that whatever happened to me, I'd found my way home.

Aaran placed a hand against my forehead and said, "She's feverish. We need to get her back to the ship and the healers."

The sailors rowed, and Redbird held my hand, and I just lay there, grateful. I didn't feel sick. In truth, I didn't feel much of anything at all. A sort of blissful numbness and lethargy stole over me. I didn't have to fight anymore, didn't have to think, didn't have to act. I could simply be still and breathe, and no one would try to kill me. Or if they did, someone other than me was on hand to stop them. I cannot begin to explain how pleasant that sensation was.

Home. Home, *sweet* home.

I spent the entire week that we sailed up the coast toward Danaskataak, however, hideously sick. I'd gotten some form of swamp fever common to the area, and apparently I was lucky it didn't kill me, or maim me, or turn my mind to pudding. I'd never heard of such a thing; Aaran's healer told me locally it was known as the pirate madness.

Which made me wonder, if they knew they risked such a disease, why anyone would be a pirate. Of course, at the time I was wondering that, I was also seeing huge insects crawling around inside my head and cringing from tentacles that writhed toward me from the ceiling. Everything I thought that week made perfect sense at the time.

When clarity returned, none of it did.

Redbird had been with me all along. The other Obsidians said they thought she never slept. She told me how she had tried to reach me using the Hagedwar—Aaran's magic. How the other Obsidians had, and the rest of the Ossalenes. Something about that bothered me, but I could not figure out what. Freed from fever, I was not yet well, and thinking was hard.

Finally upright, I learned from Tuua that the ship hiding in the bay was a Pergassak spy ship, from Pergas, one of the dozens of little countries on the east coast of Velobrina. Pergas has long been a friend of the Feegash, and unlike most of the countries under Feegash influence, Pergas had a well-disciplined communications system. If they'd been permitted to spot us, they could have destroyed our mission.

Because Aaran and the captains of the other Grand Pack ships were constantly in conference with each other, Tuua took upon himself the task of getting me back on my feet and walking again.

"The captain has been distraught the whole time you were gone," he told me.

It was good to hear. Knowing you're needed is always pleasant. I wanted to think that I'd been missed for myself, though I had to assume that the loss of my skills to our mission had been his real concern.

I told Tuua as much.

He laughed. "I think *you* were his concern. You don't know about the charts he kept, tracking your progress across Greton, estimating our time to you, trying to find ways to make sure we could get to you." He tucked his arm under mine as I lost my balance—I was not yet back to being comfortable with the movement of the ship beneath my feet. "He hasn't eaten well; he hasn't slept much. And you do not know how happy he was when he became certain that you were alive."

"Since I have been back, he avoids me."

"He went to your room to check on you constantly while you were sick. He got so little done he has been running to catch up ever since."

"I don't remember him in my room."

"That's because you were *sick*. You don't have a clear memory of how sick you were. You danced a bit too near death's edge." He turned to face me and rested a hand on my shoulder. "I speak for my cousin, but I have no doubt as soon as he has his preparations made for this war, he'll speak for himself." Tuua turned again, and as I leaned on him, we strolled along the clear spaces on the deck. Both the ship's healer and the Moonstones insisted I get fresh air. "He loves you. He told me he said as much to you, and that he wants more than anything to spend the rest of his life with you."

"That cannot happen, you know. I have . . . I have only a little time left."

"I know. He knows, too. He has already told me that, while we are in Dananskataak, the kor daan will run the ship, and he and you will be occupied elsewhere."

My heart filled with hope. It shouldn't have, but I could only imagine the two of us together, away from everyone else. Would so much happiness make the pain of what would follow even worse? I hoped not.

"Tell me about him," I said. "Things he would not think to tell me."

We walked in silence for a while. I thought perhaps Tuua had decided to tell me nothing, that perhaps he viewed my request as asking him to betray Aaran. But suddenly he said, "He and I were yearmates in our clan. When we rode off to our coming of age, both of us had already fallen in love, he with a girl the same age as him named Rokaanis, and me with Denee, a year older than me, already a woman of the clan. I had sworn to Denee that I wanted to court her if I passed my tests of manhood. Aaran had already been secretly courting Rokaanis, and was determined that he loved her above all women, and always would."

"And these girls were taken slaves," I said, a painful comprehension settling over me.

But Tuua said, "No. They were among the dead and violated when we returned. We did not vow that we would never love again. Pain, I think, made us believe no such vow would be necessary. It seared our hearts with the images of how we had failed them. How we had not been there to save them. They'd fought for their lives, and they'd lost. And he and I and the other boys of our clan who came back men built our dead a fair pyre, and put their bodies atop it with the rest. And then we stood there, a dozen sixteen-year-olds trying to be brave, and lit the fire, and watched everything we had ever known and everything we had ever loved go up in smoke."

I closed my eyes, feeling tears sting. So many of us had so much loss behind us. A generation of adults murdered, a generation of children vanished.

And Aaran had lost more than I. He'd been old enough that he realized more of his loss. He'd had family, but he knew them as people, not just as a vague forest of legs, the frequent hug or kiss, a memory of laughter. Aaran had a girl he'd loved. Friends he'd lost. I'd been so young the whole thing was a handful of sharp images for me, and a sense of confused emptiness.

"I'm so sorry. For both of you, for your losses. I don't know how people would be so willing to do what the Feegash have done—to try to destroy an entire people."

He gave me a quick hug. "We don't need to understand evil. We need to recognize it for what it is, and destroy it."

I walked with him for a while. "Is there good among the Feegash? Is there something there we should save?"

He turned to me. "Save? The Feegash? Are you mad?"

I walked with my head down, wishing that I could not see the layers of the ship beneath my feet, the creatures swimming under the ship, the sand and rock beneath the creatures.

I remembered the world when it seemed solid. When time was a simple, steady thing, when walls were trustworthy and floors had a comfortable heft, when I did not feel like bone and gossamer moving through a world of spirit and liquid. I remembered when the world seemed real.

It didn't seem real to me anymore. It was ghost and shadow, slippery fluid, changeable time, sand through my fingers, water spilled from a glass.

And in it, Aaran and I danced around each other, trying to step out of shells of remembered pain, and seeing in the future more pain.

"He should not face more loss," I said.

"Life is loss . . . and getting through it. You will eventually hurt him by dying, or perhaps he'll hurt you in the same way. But either way, you see him too clearly. You see what he was, and is, and will be. He loves you. But he fears you, too. How can he not?"

"I see everything too clearly," I whispered. "And I see nothing at all. I would be as I once was. I would put the Eyes away from me and give up the power they bring, and I would see sunrises and sunsets and never the truth that lies within the actions of men."

"But you can't do that, either."

I stopped. "No. I can't. I took this burden on not understanding what it was. I only knew that it mattered. Now that I see what it is we face, I am every day more deeply bound to this task that has been set before me. I have been given a gift, Tuua. I have been given the power to save my people. And the opportunity to use that power."

We walked in silence. My sides ached, and though the salt air was good for me, I was already wearied from one simple trip from the fore of the ship to the afterdeck.

"How do you feel about Aaran?"

"I love him," I said. "This is the worst of times for love. The worst of situations. I am the least suitable of women." I lifted my chin and said, "And I can barely even call myself Tonk. I know so little, remember so little. I feel like I'm home, but at the same time, I feel that I haven't earned it."

Tuua helped me back down the stairs. "Consider that now may be all you have. Unless those Eyes of yours give you better news than what we've all been anticipating."

"They don't."

"Then I'll give you a musing from a lesser philosopher, and let you make of it what you will. 'All of time is now. There is no other, no better, no finer moment. There is no other moment at all.'"

And then we were down the stairs, and he turned me over to Aigret of the Moonstones, who took one look at me and said, "You're to have a hot drink now, and sit. And then you're doing another breathing treatment."

The hot drink would be something that tasted horrible, and the breathing treatment would hurt, for I would be exhaling air into a bladder I could barely get to stretch, and she would not give me a moment's peace until I had stretched it to her satisfaction. And then the drink would make me so sleepy I would fall into my bed and lie there like one dead, until someone came to wake me again.

I would have neither the time nor the inclination to consider Tuua's words for a long while.

44

Aaran

They'd reached Askag Bay, and the town of Danaskataak. Tonk merchants greeted them on Tonk docks, speaking Tonk. Aaran took Hawkspar around—she hadn't been to a taak, ever. He took her first to Ethebet's temple, and watched her walking along the rows and stacks of books, fingers trailing the covers, her face wistful.

"I wish I could read them all," she said. "I wish I could read any of them."

And in a burst of gallantry that he hadn't intended, he said, "I'll read them to you."

They went to a shop where he helped her pick out traditional Tonk clothing. To eateries where she got to taste the local Tonk dishes. To a dance in the Faaverhend, where for the first time since she was a child, she heard songs sung to pipes and drums that her family had known and sung. He watched her weep.

She walked through the proscribed stables where horses that could be sold to none but other Tonk were kept, and ran her hands over horses, and told him what she remembered of the horses she'd ridden as a child. Of their golden color, their dark stripes, their shaggy manes. Eskuu horses, fedderhorses, that had still existed when she was a child. She ran her hands over the flanks of the Danaskataak horses, and smiled.

All of it sang to her. In the few days they were able to pretend they had a future together, he got to see her not as the Eyes of War, not as a creature half of magic, but as the woman she could have been. Was, before she took on the burden of the Tonk's survival.

If he had loved her before, he loved her twice as much after. He could see himself living out his life with this happy, laughing young woman. She was so far away from the mystical, from magic. Everything was almost new to her, and he got to bring it to her and let her rediscover who she was, and who she had always been meant to be.

"I want to stay here," she said one afternoon. The sun beat down on them, and he'd just been thinking that it never got so hot in Hyre, that the trees were all wrong, that the sky was the wrong color and the sun in the wrong place.

But it was Tonk. The first truly Tonk place she'd been since she was stolen from her home and her family and the future she should have had. She kept saying, "This is how it felt when I was a child. This was how things were."

She loved getting up before sunrise and stepping out into the street, and with the rest of the people who were out and getting ready to go about their day, saying her greeting to the sun. She loved raising her hand, and hearing the exclamations of shock when people saw her clan mark, and came up to her asking her if she was truly Eskuu.

"Hyre has the same walls," he'd told her. "The same temples, the same ways. But in Hyre, we have true winter, with snow and ice, and summers when the sun never sets. I would show you the fields where I hunted as a boy, and the temples of Kopataak. The temples have all been rebuilt after the Feegash treachery of fifteen years ago, but they're magnificent. Most of the old books have been replaced, and new ones added. And there are taverns for Senders and Shielders that have taken in the new magics now, too. You'd love them. The food is better than anything you'll find anywhere else, and . . ."

"And it's your home."

"After a fashion. Like yours, my true home is gone, but I'm a citizen of Kopataak. And as someone whose clan was destroyed, you could be taken in as a citizen, too. We could . . ." He stopped. He'd been about to suggest that they could have children together there. He'd envisioned a fine little horse house on a hill, looking down over the river. He'd imagined the two of them teaching their children to ride, and to go to temple, and to read.

But that was too far in the future to see.

Too far to even dare contemplate.

He slid an arm around her. He had avoided kissing her, or holding her; he had been afraid of all that he had to lose.

She turned her face up to him, and said, "I want so many things, Aaran. I want to have the future to enjoy them."

"We may not."

"We probably won't. Time wraps itself around me and whispers death to me. I have seen all of us die a thousand times in a thousand horrible ways. I can see possible survival, too. Not so many chances, and no matter how we win, if we win we still lose many of those we love."

"You and I may never have a chance to be together," he told her.

"We have that chance now. We have another day before all our supplies are ready to go."

"I . . . don't want us to be distracted."

She laughed, but the laugh had the notes of a sob in it. It was the saddest sound he'd even heard. "I'm going to be distracted no matter what. I know what it feels like to have you touch me. Desire me. Take me. I want that again, and if we wait past today, I may never again know what it is to be loved by you."

He took her arm and led her away from the dock and the ships, away from their friends and colleagues. "I don't know what's right. I don't know if we should wait. I have told myself I would never do this again; that you and I could never be. And yet, here we are and you are all I can think about." He stroked her hair and pressed his cheek against the side of her head. "I would love you forever, if I had the chance."

They went to an inn, him with his arm around her, her with her arm around him. He wanted her then. He got a room for them, and had a good supper brought up. Venison and bitter greens, diced potatoes with red peppers and eggs, and black bread, which was a specialty of the Tand clans. And clear, cold water to drink.

And when they were done eating, they stood in the room together, palms of their hands pressed together, bodies not touching but so close he could feel the heat coming off her.

And he looked into her eyes, and all that looked back was stone.

Stone that glimmered and sheened in the flickering light from the oil lamps in the room. Pretty stone, gold and amber and brown.

But stone. Her eyes were not windows to her soul. They were walls around it. He could not see into her, but she could see into him. She could see everything he had ever done.

"Aaran, what's wrong?"

He kissed her. "Nothing."

"Something," she said. "I felt you start to pull away from me."

"I didn't." He pulled her closer and kissed her again. He closed his eyes and banished hers. She was not her eyes. The Eyes. She was the woman he loved, and when he felt her relax and kiss him back, he could forget about them. He blew out the oil lamps, and darkness descended.

For a while, the world and all its worries fell away, and their universe was each other.

Hawkspar

Aaran, Eban, and I hiked with our packs on our backs, leading a heavily laden packhorse. We pretended to be a family; we dressed like peasants and traders from the area, and we kept our heads down, trudging along the wide, paved highway, following other laden horses and carts and wagons going in the same direction we were; and passed by others, minus their loads, heading in the opposite direction. The road was the Sijguik High Pass, famed throughout the world for its steady traffic and its smoothness. It led up into the heart of the mountains like a fat serpent, so broad twenty horses could walk abreast, straight to the Sijguik Gate, one of two public entries into Ba'afeegash.

I'd been told that Ba'afeegash was a nation scarcely two long leagues from one end to the other, yet it held a population of more than one hundred thousand people. I could not imagine so many people in such a tiny place. Citadel Island had held, with its village below and the hermitage above, less than three thousand people, and it had been much larger.

Peaks rose over our heads, and on those peaks I could make out guard towers. Guards paced along the tops of the towers, and from time to time I could catch them waving their arms in regular patterns while holding sticks.

"It's a code," Aaran said when I asked him. "They're keeping each other up to date on anything questionable that's coming up the road."

"We hope that wouldn't be us," I said.

"Indeed we do," Aaran agreed.

Eban would show us the place where we would step off the road. According to him, there was a single pass that connected the road to the Ba'afeegash Valley, where Feegash shepherds grazed their flocks. And near the place where this pass crossed into the valley, a gate called the Shepherds' Gate provided quick entrance to the flocks and herds in case of emergency. So long as no alarm had been raised about us, we should be able to go in through the gate without raising any notice, if we did it in twos and threes, and not too frequently. Once the gate had been barred, Eban said, it was impenetrable, as was the rest of the enormous city-state. But if some of us were inside, we should be able to find ways to get the rest of us inside.

Eban was in the lead with us because he was familiar with the terrain. He would take us off the road, and we would leave a tiny marker at the turning point for the rest of the marines, Obsidians, and sailors to follow. Each group, strung out down the side of the mountain like beads on a necklace, would then veer off casually, as if taking a moment to eat a meal, and would, once out of sight, continue along the hidden path to Shepherds' Gate.

I dreaded being so near our target. I feared the moment when I would have to sit down and slide into the waters of time again, and see if I could uncover the third way that Aaran kept talking about and that I kept sensing—the way in which we could take Ba'afeegash while sparing the innocent who we knew would be in there somewhere. Children like Eban; people like Aaran's sister trapped in slavery. The ones that the top Feegash used and abused.

We did not want to destroy them, which meant that we did not want to hit the crowded city with Greton fire. We had the Greton fire with us, of course. Each of us lugged a few of the carefully packed glass balls up the side of the mountain, and all of us were gentle in setting our packs on the ground, too.

Aaran had his tracking fixed firmly on his sister. He could not connect to her—the wizard who kept her in confinement had her shielded against magic. I had gone through him to her, but Aaran could not do that.

He did, however, have the mark I'd placed as near her as I could get. And since she did not ever move from the place where she was confined, he knew where to go to get her. His handpicked team of marines and Obsidians and one Moonstone would go in to free her; they walked in several groups just behind us. Behind them, we had more marines and sailors, and more Obsidians and Onyxes and Moonstones—only a handful of marines and captains drawn by lot, plus the Ambers, stayed behind to guard the fleet. They made up few of our total number.

We came over a rise, and suddenly Ba'afeegash lay before us. I had not known what to expect. I could not make out the whole of it, for part of it lay behind dense mountains; what I could see, however, left me stunned.

I had not been able to imagine how so many people could live in such a small space. But looking at the stone and wood buildings, I no longer had any doubt. In the section near us, buildings rose as high as six stories, and were shoved together so closely in places it would be impossible for a person to walk all the way around one without squeezing between its sisters on either side. These close-packed buildings gave way at intervals to park-like open spaces, but the greenswards, filled with trees and water, were walled off and gated, and each held a large house of two or three stories at its center.

I could not guess how all these buildings were used, but to the northwest I could see a place with open fields and crop rows. For the size of the place, the surrounding fields seemed terribly small.

But the Ba'afeegash would be dependent on imports for their survival, wouldn't they? If they had so many people living on such a small patch of land, they could not be a self-supporting nation.

"No wonder they have to be allies with everyone," I told Aaran. "They would starve in days if they didn't have these wagons constantly bringing them more food."

Aaran chuckled, but his laughter quickly died away. "They would," he agreed. "But a blockade of their roads would not do what we would want it to do. The poor and unimportant would starve, certainly, and be sent to fight against us for their own survival. They would be used as fodder by the Ba'afeegash mercenaries. The rich and powerful would have the supplies and the means to wait out any siege we might manage. And we have no supply lines. We're counting on raiding the Feegash in order to return."

We drew near the place where Eban would take us off the road. "Here," he said. Eban took my hand and tugged my arm, and I followed him over a deep ditch, up a grassy slope, and onto a small flat meadow ringed with rocks. Aaran lingered for a moment, painting an inconspicuous mark on one of the spires of stone that rose out of the bedrock at the point where we slipped away.

Then we followed Eban, with Aaran marking rocks as we passed them. Some of the marines were excellent sight trackers, but not all. We didn't want to lose any of our people when we were already at a disadvantage.

At last we came to a high green overlooking the Ba'afeegash Valley.

"This is as close as we'll get today," Eban said. "Come nightfall, the flocks will return to the city, and we can go down and graze the horses. But not now, or we'll raise the alarm."

I sat on grass with a slab of rock at my back, with the sun warming my face, soothing me and filling me with comfort, and I wished I could see more of the valley than the stark, toothy shapes of rocks or the lighter layers of loam and grass. I admired the delicate, meandering tracery the stream cut through its center. But I could imagine it vibrant green, and full of wildflowers in red and yellow and pink and blue. I could see our horses galloping over the ground, and sitting there, suddenly I saw the woman dressed all in white approaching me.

I knew where I was. I was sitting above the shepherds' valley, just out of sight of the watchtowers of Ba'afeegash. But the meadow before me rose up, growing wider and vaster until it rolled away in all directions in gentle undulations, with nary a stone spire or mountain peak to be seen.

The woman came to me and crouched beside me where I sat, not moving. "She loves her people," she said.

"Who?"

"Ethebet. She loves all of you who found your way to this place. Some of you will join her beyond life after this battle, but she asks you—her daughter now marked Hawkspar—to look without the Eyes." She reached out to me and touched the stone Eyes, a curious expression on her face. "They lie, you know. They show you only the streams the herd follows. But her people are not the herd, and this time the herd would trample heedless toward its own destruction. Look beyond the Eyes, daughter, and give your people a new way."

"Can't you tell me?" I asked her.

She shook her head, a sad smile on her face. "I am only permitted to tell you to look. I cannot tell you what to see."

She leaned forward, still crouched, and kissed my forehead once. And then she was gone, and the clear day with the bright sunlight was gone, and the breathtaking colors of the meadow and the flowers and the horses were gone.

And I sat in blackness once more, the heat of the day on my face and a warm rock at my back, a woman whose Eyes lied.

I was to seek out the third way for my people—the path that would not lead to their destruction, either with or without the concurrent destruction of the Feegash. I was to look for the path that would let us save the innocent. I was to look for a path that Ethebet's messenger insisted existed, but I could not look with the Eyes that had brought me this far, because the Eyes lied. They only showed the paths of the herd, which would lead to destruction.

Eban sat beside me. "You look worried."

"Do I?"

"You have for a long time. And I think only part of your worry is about the captain. I think the other part is about the battle."

I laughed a little. "I'd be a fool if it weren't."

"But you can see the future. You know how it will go."

"I know how it *can* go. Some of the many ways, and not all of them."

He said, "I wouldn't like that. I wouldn't like being able to see things that might happen, but not be able to fix them."

"Sometimes you can."

"Not always though, right?"

"Not always," I agreed.

We sat in silence for a little while. Behind us I could hear our people settling in for a wait. The horses clustered together, tethered and with their packs off for the moment; the men in little groups, talking softly. My Obsidians and Onyxes kept to our perimeter, on watch against things seen and unseen.

A cool breeze blew across my face and beside me, Eban shivered. "I wish we could reach the slaves."

"Why?" I asked him.

"Because they were kind to me. I'd let them know to get out of Ba'afeegash."

"They would talk to you? Even though you're the son of an important man?"

He laughed—such a bitter laugh in a little boy. "I'm not a favored son. I'm one of the throwaways to be used for whatever amuses my father or his friends. The slaves pity me. They would talk to me. They always did before."

I sat there for a while, contemplating the slaves of Ba'afeegash. Men and women and children who had suffered under the torments of their owners. Certainly some of them would not be willing to turn on their owners, but others might.

They would know things. Where keys were kept; which doors led to places we needed to reach; how we might best hit the ones we had come to kill without destroying those who had done nothing wrong.

How many innocents might there be in a city-state of a hundred thousand people? How many among those had served the whims of libertines and sadists? How many might stand and fight beside us, or at least help us in our battle, if only to open doors before running away?

If we came to slaughter them, we would make ourselves the enemy of all.

If we came to liberate them, however, we would be the enemy only of those who were our enemies.

I, too, wished that Eban could talk with the slaves inside Ba'afeegash's massive walls. But I could not begin to imagine how such a feat might be arranged.

Aaran

The Tonk huddled close to Hawkspar, as if around a fire. Cold mountain wind bit into them, and they shivered and shuddered, and at the periphery, Aaran heard muttered complaints, but they dared no real fire. The flames would betray their position to the Feegash. It didn't matter—these were not the best of conditions, but neither were they the worst he had ever endured.

Hawkspar had finished explaining her idea—that they find a way to talk with the slaves within Ba'afeegash's wall, and win them over to helping the invaders gain access to the Feegash elites.

Having explained it, she then opened the discussion to suggestions with a simple question. "How do we reach the people who might help us without betraying them to those who would gladly kill them?"

It was such a simple question. If they could answer it to their satisfaction, they would have cause to rejoice.

Aaran sat thinking about his sister, now only one city wall and a limited number of streets away from him. He wanted to charge the place with sword and fire and kill everything that moved to get to her.

Yet she was as truly out of his reach as she had been when he was on the other side of the ocean. He had no idea under what circumstances she was being held, nor had he any knowledge of what might be done to her if he were to charge in to rescue her.

He hated operations that relied on stealth and guile. He much preferred direct action, skill, and strength. He clearly would be out of his element in the upcoming campaign to overthrow the Ba'afeegash elites. Yet he would do anything to get Aashka out of there, to see her healed and well and safe

away from the monsters who had stolen her and kept her and hurt her for so
many years.

He did not allow himself to think about what she would be like. About
what might be left of the loving, laughing, bright-eyed child she had been
the last time he saw her. He hadn't let himself consider that in all the time
she had been missing he had moved forward with single-minded faith that
if she lived he would find her, and when he found her he would bring her
home. And everything would be all right.

Around him the men were throwing suggestions to Hawkspar, considering different ways that the Tonk might make contact with those held against
their will by the Feegash, to let them know that rescue was at hand and to
ask them to help as they could. They came up with everything from throwing
notes over the walls with an improvised catapult to dressing as shepherds
and infiltrating the city.

Aaran let them talk. He, his kor daan, and the other captains and *their*
firsts would filter everything, and he would pay more attention when it got
to the point of the serious hows and whys. In the meantime, though, he had
to find his sister.

So he slipped over to Hawkspar and whispered in her ear, "Show me how
to connect with Aashka. I need to track her to make sure I'll be able to find
her and get my men to her to protect her once we're in there."

Hawkspar turned her face to his, and those blank stone eyes stared at
him. "Yes," she said after a moment. "I'll show you. And I'll stay with you
while you find her."

She pointed Redbird to her position, then took his hand and rose, and
stepped with him away from the men and their tight war circle.

He led her a few paces away from the talking, and when he dropped
cross-legged to a sitting posture, she did the same. He wrapped his Hagedwar around both of them.

She said, "I'm pushing back into the past—just to the last time that I
found her. From there I'll let myself follow her forward to where she is now.
And when I've found her, I'll make sure the mark is at the same location I
gave you. You'll be able to read my send, right?"

"I'm sure of it," he said.

She shook her head, and he watched her taking slow, steady breaths. He
realized that she was afraid.

"You're strong," he told her. "You've recovered from your ride across Greton, from your fever. You don't have to go back very far in time." He made his voice sound confident and encouraging.

And she whispered, "That isn't why I'm afraid."

"No?"

"Aaran . . ." She reached out and took both of his hands in hers. "I know you've been going after her for most of your life. I know that you want to take her home and make her well. But I don't know that you can. I don't know that there is any mercy to be had in rescuing her now." She bit her lower lip, and his heart skipped a beat, and then another.

"I'm going to get her."

"I know," Hawkspar said. "You will. It's almost certain. I simply don't know if you will be sorrier if you fail, or if you succeed. You have to know, not just where she is, but how she is."

He watched her lips tremble and tears roll down her cheeks.

"You have to know," she said at last. "You have to understand. I'm going through him, to her. When I reach out for you, hold my hands tightly; so long as you touch me, you can feel what I feel, can't you?"

"I believe I can," he said.

She closed her eyelids over those gleaming stones and all expression drained from her face. She seemed to pause in mid-breath, to drift away from him even as her body stayed firmly anchored to the ground before him. He watched her face, and knew the instant that she found Aashka. Suddenly, her face became a mask of agony, and her whole body went rigid. Her hands locked into tight fists, her lips peeled back, and she began to make a mewling noise in her throat that effectively stopped all conversation in the war circle and turned every head toward her.

Aaran found himself fighting for breath. Hawkspar was feeling the pain that Aashka had felt. But not pain she was experiencing right at that moment, he told himself. She wasn't always hurting. She couldn't possibly always be hurting.

Hawkspar moved forward in time, and her face changed rapidly. Pain to repose to pain to fear to rage to pain. And on pain she stopped, and fought with her body to reach over to him, and take his hand. And what Aashka felt poured into him.

The pain nearly overwhelmed him. He was being boiled. He fought to control the scream that almost escaped from his throat. Ice, then, and more heat.

He could not hear any sound from her in his mind. But he could feel her presence. Her awareness. She knew what was happening to her. She was awake. She couldn't fight, and somehow she couldn't flee. Not even into her own mind. Whoever had captured her had found a way to lock her into the horror of the torture, to keep her with her torturers.

She did not respond to words that he sent her through the Hagedwar. He could not go into her thoughts, but he could touch the experiences that she wore like dust on her skin. He could read much of her from that—and nothing that he read was still human. She had become living pain and rage and awareness, fear and abyssal despair. He could find no sign that she understood what was being done to her. He could brush no tatter of hope. Could locate no memory of anything other than this moment and the last, and the pain that lay there.

He tried to reach out to her, to offer her some comfort, some shield from whatever pain her captors were inflicting on her. She didn't notice him. She didn't respond at all.

For the first time, he realized that he might be able to go in and save her body, but that even though she still lived, he might never have his sister back.

He shook off the Hagedwar and knelt in the darkness, hunched like an old man, shivering and heartbroken. And he wept, silently at first, and then in ragged sobs.

Hawkspar crouched beside him and wrapped her arms around him. She pulled him close and murmured in his ear, "There is always hope, Aaran. Even though we cannot see it, even though all avenues seem closed, there is always hope."

"She's gone," he whispered. "There's nothing left of her."

"We'll do what we can. She and Jostfar will do the rest."

He thought of the Tonk master healers back in Hyre. Perhaps Talyn or one of the other four could save her.

Hawkspar was right. Hope remained.

He sat up and took a deep breath. He'd known all along that he might not be able to save her. He'd *found* her. That was something. And his determination to reclaim her was unchanged. He would slaughter every bastard within those walls if he had to in order to get to her. He would get her out of there, or he would die trying.

But he could not let himself think of her as the whole mission. For the moment, he had to see her as the symbol of the evil the Feegash wrought with their actions. She was the personification of the price his people paid simply to exist. They were hunted, reviled, slaughtered, and enslaved because they would not accept the Feegash yoke, nor the Feegash philosophy that all gods were the same and that good and evil were the same, or were matters of local interest and custom that varied as men defined.

The Feegash denied the existence of innocence.

In the end, the vast differences in their two philosophies could be illuminated by that single point. The Tonk believed in protecting the innocent from harm. The Feegash—declaring none innocent and thereby deserving of protection—raped their own sons and daughters and the children of others for amusement, tortured their wives and concubines, enslaved their neighbors, betrayed their allies, declared their power the only arbiter of justice, and their will the only law. The Feegash said, "He who hates my enemy I shall embrace as friend," and maintained alliances based only on mutual hatreds, then discarded those alliances as soon as their allies became inconvenient . . . or had something the Feegash wanted enough to encourage them to leap into alliance with their one-time allies' enemies.

The Feegash knew no loyalty. They knew only the convenience of disposable partners and partnerships. Sooner or later, they bit every hand that fed them.

Aaran sat up and got himself under control.

Aashka stood as the symbol of what the Feegash did to the innocent. She was Aaran's beacon, his shining light leading him forward to destroy people who would choose to see no difference between a warrior and a child, who would claim depravity nothing to be ashamed of, and who would then dare to hold themselves up as the model all others should follow.

Below him lay the place from which this poison emanated. It was not a contained poison—it had spread beyond the walls of Ba'afeegash, and others had adopted the morality of convenience as their own, because excusing evil was always easier than stopping it.

The Tonk might fail in their assault, Aaran thought, but at last the Feegash treachery had been laid bare, and the Tonk knew their enemy by name and they would not permit more of their people to be slaughtered or more of their children to be stolen away without facing the cowards who used puppets to persecute them.

Aaran stood and Hawkspar stood with him.

"Whatever else happens," he said, "the Feegash are going to stop hunting us through their proxies. We're going to deal with them face-to-face."

Hawkspar

I sat in on the war council, which went until nearly dawn. Our warriors covered both slopes of the one valley that lay out of sight of the road, the city, and the shepherds' valley, while the captains and the kor wogans—the marine masters—prodded their trackers to map out the locations of Feegash communications centers, guard posts, military strongholds, and most important for our purposes, locations of the prominent men of the Feegash. The diplomats in their mansions, the wizards in their colleges, the rich merchants and the officers in their comfortable retreats.

Men with scribing talent copied off these maps for units to use. I did not know what they managed for light, but someone among them apparently had a trick with the Hagedwar that gave them a way of seeing what they were doing without alerting every Feegash guard and soldier around us of our presence.

"I say we go in over the wall from three points," a kor wogan from one of the other ships said. "Drop into the city, make our way first to the communications points, take all of those out simultaneously. From there, spread into groups. I'd like to go after the military and the diplomats at the same time, because if we hit the military first—which would be tactically sound—the diplomats will scurry like rats and we'll have to track them down one at a time."

It sounded reasonable to me, and in the time river this plan clearly allowed us to wipe out the Feegash. But it led to most of the rest of the known world banding together to attack and annihilate the Tonk.

I said as much, and felt the stares of the men around me as clearly as if I could see them.

"You have a suggestion, then?"

"Win the people to our side. The same thing I suggested before."

"And you see that working?"

I wanted to say yes, that this was the solution that would allow us to conquer the Feegash and at the same time win over enough of the world that we as a people would not be annihilated. The problem was that I could not see this future at all. Which meant that either it was the true third path the woman in white had suggested to me, or else that it was a foolish idea I had that would lead us nowhere.

Eban said, "I could slip in tomorrow when the shepherds come out. I know the city. I spent most of my life here before my father took a foreign assignment. I could tell people you're coming. The right people, people who will want you here. I know other children who can get places that I can't. Adults don't see us. Not unless they want to hurt us. To the important people, we're almost invisible."

Tuua and Aaran sat on either side of the boy. I could hear the urgency in Eban's voice. I thought his was the path that could lead us to safety, but I had no evidence upon which to base this hunch. I could not see how it played forward in time. I could not see any sign of this path at all—and that, of course, was because it was utterly dependent upon the success of one person, and then upon individual actions from those who would meet with the boy.

Tuua said, "I don't want him going in alone."

One of the captains snorted. "I should think not. Send one of the treacherous little brats back into his lair and trust him to work for our good?"

"I'd stake my life on his integrity," Tuua said. "I don't want him going in because I don't want them to catch him and hurt him anymore. He's not one of them. He's Tonk in all but name."

"So he'd have you think." The captain laughed. "Why don't you go in with him? Keep him safe while he introduces you to all the poisonous little spiders scuttling around in there just waiting to become big spiders."

"I'll go in with him," Tuua said. "I like that idea far better than abandoning him to those monsters himself."

Aaran turned his face to me. "How do you see this, Oracle Hawkspar?"

And so it rested on me. I could lie. I could say that I saw the outcome of the two of them going in before us was our best hope. They would not know; they could not tell what I could see from what I couldn't.

I even wanted to lie.

But in the end, all I could say was, "I think this is how we should proceed." *I think.*

They weren't accustomed to the speech of oracles. *I think* to them was no different than *I see.* If I said it, they would assume I had some better view of the outcome than they had, when in fact this time all I had were views of two outcomes of variable degrees of disaster, and a strong feeling in my gut that the proposed third path would give us something other than more disaster. I couldn't very well tell them about the visitations of Ethebet's white-clad messenger, or about that brief time when I could once again see as others saw. Those had been dreams. I believed they were true dreams, but I could not make a convincing argument for my instinct. My intuition.

I had the Eyes so that I wouldn't need intuition.

Aaran said, "The oracle has spoken. We have seen her visions become truth time after time. Therefore I say we send in the boy Eban and with him Tuua, Ethebet's Keeper of Words, and a handful of Obsidians as guardians."

I wanted to cringe, hearing that intuition presented as if it were Oracle's Truth, instead of an oracle's wild guessing about what lay within the Eyes' blind spaces.

But Eban hugged Tuua, and the two of them shed their packs, hid their weapons, and huddled briefly out of my earshot with Aaran and the marine kor wogans. No doubt to choose their targets. Redbird, meanwhile, hugged me quickly and promised she would stay safe and keep them safe. Then she picked five Obsidians to go with her.

And then they were up and hurrying down the steep hillside into the shepherds' valley, on their way to the gate. After which, we all would wait for morning, doing nothing more than hiding ourselves and praying for their success.

We spent a day lying flat in the tall grass, the sun beating down on us, remarkably hot even though the air had a chill to it. We could have had worse weather—it could have been raining or snowing—but by the end of the day I felt as if my face would split. My skin was hot to the touch and it stung.

I was as grateful as the rest when night came, and I was the first to mark the figures that slipped out of the gate as the shepherds moved their flocks in, that pressed themselves flat to the wall out of sight until the gates closed, then broke into a run and charged toward us.

They moved quickly to our hiding place and kept voices low, but I could hear their excitement.

Tuua said, "They have a well-developed underground, though until now it has been used for nothing but smuggling children to freedom. But with word that we plan to free them from the elites, the news has spread like wildfire; the slaves, the children, the wives, the concubines, the underclass— they will all do what they can to aid us. But we must go now. We'll go over the walls at the three points we'd planned, and attack communications, and then the military and diplomats simultaneously. We'll use the password *kejihar* at doors and the city will open for us."

I moved close to Tuua and read him, let myself slip into the time stream, flowed with him through the path he'd carved to his future. It led us to triumph, though I could make out nothing about what happened after that. Still, he had done well.

We traveled in predetermined squads. I had insisted upon going as a warrior as much as the oracle; I could not know how my strained and much-tried health would hold out but I wanted to be there if some skill of mine might turn the tide of battle in the Tonks' favor.

Tuua, Aaran, Redbird, and half of the marines and sailors from the *Taag* were in our squad, plus the Moonstone Daaryi to heal for us. Each squad had either one Moonstone or one Tonk healer, and a small contingent of Obsidians. We were well weaponed, well provisioned, and ready.

We charged forward, pouring down the hill at a steady trot, breaking into the directions that would take us to the three areas the trackers had identified as the least guarded along the wall.

My mouth was dry. I had been in fights before, but this was the moment when everything would begin to change. This was the moment for which I had given up my own eyes and taken on those of the oracle. For which I was becoming something other than human, and for which I had given up any hope of love. If we won here, it would be the vindication of my sacrifice. I would find a way to accept all that I had put aside.

If we lost . . . well . . . I would suffer a quick death. Any who tried to kill me slowly would not survive the adventure.

I ran steadily, in rhythm with the men all around me. I breathed evenly, grateful for the training in breath control I'd spent years on—for the air was thin and cold—and for the recent rest aboard the ship that had returned much of my strength to me.

I kept my focus on the knives in my sleeves, on the way my feet hit the uneven ground, on the moment, and never on the future. We were finally at the place where the Eyes had led us, at the first moment that would be a watershed for the Tonk, and I could neither dare nor bear to let myself slide into time's river to try for a glimpse of how we might do.

Like everyone around me, in each of the many squads running in one of the three directions, I was in the moment because I could be nowhere else.

We reached our target quickly, and the marines tossed the padded grappling hooks up on the wall in an instant. Sailors and marines swarmed up the ropes, and those of us who were less agile waited for the rope webbing to roll down. When it hit the ground, we clambered up and stood atop the parapet.

The marines had already killed the guards whose route passed over our section of the wall, and the sailors and Obsidians had swung like spiders down ropes on the other side to clear any men who were on duty within the towers.

We quickly found ourselves running along roads finished to incredible smoothness. They were neither cobblestone nor brick, but rather a fine aggregate of crushed stone and binder. I had never run on anything so even. We followed Redbird, who used her Eyes and her senses to keep us to clear paths, and she ran beside the marine with the map. We hurried along broad, straight avenues, keeping single file and close to buildings, making no noise.

And reached, at last, our first target.

A servant sat upon the front stoop of a building where the Feegash housed some of their communicators. Our lead marine separated himself from our group, for we kept out of sight, and said to the servant, "Kejihar."

The change in the man was remarkable. He went from still and slumped to quick and animated, indicating that we should follow him around to the back of the building. Our Obsidian gave us the "all's well" signal, and we rushed to follow. With the servant leading us, we charged into the building through the back door, followed guides to the communications offices, and quickly killed those we had come to kill.

We left with the servants behind us clinging to each other and praying for our success.

I could only hope that we would be so fortunate in our next encounters.

The night smells in this place were alien to me. The cold had its own scent, sharp and green, but faint. Wood smoke I recognized, and nearby open water. But the air seemed almost empty. Barren. I caught no perfume of flowers, no earthy tang of horses and goats and other beasts, no rich aromas of cooking foods, no sewage, no scent of sweat or incense. The barrenness *was* the smell. A city crowded with people that offered nothing to the nose, and nothing to the ears. Our boots on the smooth roads and walkways made a soft, muffled thudding, barely audible. Yet the fact that we heard it at all attested to the silence of this place. No music played, no people walked the streets arm-in-arm, or laughed their way from yard to bed. No groups gathered in the courtyards to dance or sing late into the night. No young lovers leaned against doorways murmuring endearments; no old married couples shouted so loudly the sounds echoed out their windows. I would have been reminded of my years in the Citadel, but even there, once darkness fell we had the singing at the hours, and the voices of seru as they went about their tasks, and the occasional talk of the slaves and penitents as they carried out assigned night duties.

I did not like Ba'afeegash.

I felt no fear or dread as we ran again, this time toward the mansion where Aaran's sister was kept. I felt nothing, in truth, but the urge to keep my breathing steady so that I could avoid any sharp pains in my side. I knew we were heading into the worst possible target.

The master of the city held Aashka captive, and he lived in a grand, well-guarded fortress of a mansion. Tuua assured us that he and Eban had ascertained that the servants' underground ran into this master Feegash's quarters, but I wondered what it would take for those so eager to help us to be frightened away from doing so. Or what price would buy their betrayal. Gold? Freedom? The oracles had a saying: *There is a coin for every man.* By this they meant that if the bribe was right, anyone could be bought.

I wondered now if the oracles had been cynical in their assessment, or merely correct.

But it did not matter to us. We were on our mission. We were the squad that would rescue Aashka and slaughter those who had stolen her away and enslaved her and hurt her so long and so horribly. Aaran had insisted that he and his handpicked marines go on this mission. He did not want to entrust either her safety or the deaths of her captors to anyone else.

I could not hear any alarms being raised. I could not, in fact, hear anything out of the ordinary at all.

One slip by any of our squads and that would change.

Redbird took us along the wall, stopping us twice as guards moved above us. We froze, barely even breathing, and they made their pass along our section of wall. We would not be going over this time. And I thought it likely that we would have to fight our way out—but we hoped to just walk in.

A servant loitered at the back of the wall near a narrow, massively reinforced door, drinking something from a bottle. He hummed to himself, and I thought he must be drunk—I had seen sailors with too much ale in them behave in the same fashion.

Again, though, our lead marine whispered the password, and the man transformed into a paragon of silence and energy. He indicated we should follow him and led us through the door in the wall and into the grounds beyond.

Sterile grounds. I made out the mazy shapes of hedges, and the dense lines of paved paths through what had clearly been designed as a formal garden. But the garden had no more life to it than the city. It held no riotous banks of flowers, no rustling leaves from weeping trees, nothing but spare,

clipped, shaped hedges, and hard paths, and in the center, a single tiny fountain that we in the Citadel would have mocked for its stinginess.

The man who owned this place was very fond of hard, straight lines.

The servant led us along one side of the maze, then he and Eban exchanged a few quick words.

"He'll let us in the side servants' entrance," Eban said. "And from there,
we'll follow other servants to the master's suite."

We had our lives in the hands of men who had little enough reason to
trust anyone, who might benefit greatly from turning us in to their masters.
All across this city, we were scattered into these groups, twenty fighting men
and a few ancillary people to each, and in each, we were going into unknown
territory with the foreknowledge of strangers.

If I'd been wrong in encouraging this approach, in saying I believed it was
the right one, I would be the death of the Tonk. Aaran and I would die,
Tuua would die, Eban would die. The men with whom I'd fought, the men
with whom I'd sailed, and far away, their lovers and friends and families, all
would be crushed by the world's armies and its rage.

I wanted the reassurance of the white-clad Tonk woman. I wanted a
promise that we would triumph.

I got only the same darkness. The same silence. The masses of moving
men before me, and behind me.

Men, women, and children sleeping in rooms to our right.

Weapon stores in rooms to our left.

Ahead, corridors that went from low and plain to high and vaulted, with
soaring stone arches intricately carved, and glass windows with complicated
leading, and passageways leading off to the left and the right.

We were walking now, weapons drawn. We made no noise, and even so, I
felt eyes watching us. The silence of the place bore down on me. I could not
escape the sensation that we were fooling no one. Walking into a trap.

I could see nothing that would indicate a trap. No soldiers armored and
armed and hidden along side passages.

Nothing I could point to and say, *That should not be.*

And yet the hair on the back of my neck stood up, and my heart raced,
and my mouth went dry.

I had not been afraid before.

But suddenly I was terrified.

The servants had been passing us off, one man or woman to the next. We
came at last to a huge chamber. In it, I made out the scattered shapes of simple

furniture clustered between wide spaces, a central hearth of an odd, open design, and beyond, three doorways.

The servant said, "Beyond, none but the master's body-servants and guards may pass. And they are not with us in this." He patted the kor wogan on the arm. "Our prayers and hopes go with you."

Eban translated, the kor wogan thanked him, and then we moved on, finally relying simply on ourselves.

I studied the three doors. Down the first lay another hallway, with rooms and cross hallways to either side. Behind the second I could make out the hazy shapes of two chambers, one directly behind the other and both connected by a single metal door. The walls in the second were so dense I could only make out the presence of space. I could not begin to guess the details of what waited within.

Aaran dropped back to my side as I was studying the third doorway.

"You have any suggestions here?" he asked.

I was terrified, my mouth so dry I had to try twice just to get out the words. "Something is wrong in this place."

"They know we're here?"

"I don't know. I would not think so, for the time to have taken us would have been as we were traversing the small, narrow passages behind. Here we have room to fight."

"Then what is it?"

I tried to let the future roll around me, but we were in a dry place again. Where we stood, we were digging our own channel, and the waters that flowed to either side of us had nothing to do with us.

We were digging our own channel. We stood in Ethebet's moments, when we made the future—we and those who stood against us. When the actions of the few determined the futures of the many, and when nothing at all had been decided.

We danced, I thought, on the point of a sword, and at any instant we could fall off.

Was that my fear?

No.

"It isn't where we are," I told him. "Not some wrongness in our direction. It is this *place*. One I know—one who stands in my destiny, waits for me here. Danger has already marked us."

Aaran turned his face toward me, still for a moment. "That's not good," he finally said.

"No."

"You think there are hidden traps? Pits, crushing walls, things of that nature? I've seen devices of that sort before."

"No. Nothing of that sort."

"We can't just stand here," he said.

"The central door is the most interesting," I told him. "It is also where I can see the least. It's an outer chamber with a well-reinforced inner chamber behind it. The left and right doors open into hallways."

The Obsidian and the kor wogan joined us. "I get security forces patrolling in the right corridor," Redbird said.

I hadn't looked that deeply yet. I kept being drawn to the central rooms. The source of my fear—my third dark shadow—almost certainly waited within. I could not turn back. I could not go forward alone.

And I could not begin to guess the nature of the trial that I—that we all—would face.

46

Aaran

Aaran tracked Aashka. He couldn't place her location—something blocked him. He knew she was in the house, but not where. He thought she might be in the room that Hawkspar couldn't see into. If something had been done to the room that blocked the magic of the Hagedwar, it would explain why he had never been able to find her until Hawkspar used the Eyes to track her through time.

Once he knew where she was, he could sense her.

If he saved her at all, he would owe her life to Hawkspar.

Hawkspar brushed against him as they worked their way around the perimeter of the room, staying soundless, to set up barricades against the left and right doors. They would deal with those later, but didn't want to be surprised by attackers coming in behind them.

The weight of her and the curve of her flank against his thigh distracted his as he changed position—he could still feel her lips on his, her soft body wrapped around him, him moving in her.

They could die here. The last time could be . . . the *last* time. For either of them. For both of them.

The three doors into the corridors were designed to open inward—possibly to prevent exactly the tactic the Tonk were at that moment using. The marines bound and wedged them closed using the tiny gaps between the doors and door frames underneath to slide in iron spring angles. The spring angles had been the clever invention of one Tonk sergeant tired of being surprised by doors that spilled out unexpected enemies. They slid under all but the closest-fitted doors, and the hinged angle popped up as soon as it was free. On the other side, a vise allowed the marine to use whatever wide, solid, handy object might be handy to form a cross-brace. The marines with Aaran were using those plain, massive couches. And with the doors being iron-bound and, Hawkspar assured him, of the solidest make, no one was likely to be bursting out of either to disturb the Tonk invaders anytime soon.

He ought to feel confident about entering the central rooms. But he didn't.

Like Hawkspar, something had him spooked.

The marine at the central door told the kor wogan, "The lock is a good one. For the sake of time, we're going to have to make some noise."

The kor wogan glanced around the room. The back corridor stood open, and none of the men would forget the presence of the servants behind them. For the time, they'd shown themselves to be friendly, but everyone knew that could change.

The marines were therefore in a split formation. Fourteen ready behind the entry man to burst through as soon as he cleared the door and fell back. Four behind, facing backward with swords in off hands and light crossbows with bolts drawn and cocked to clear anything that might attack from the rear.

Hawkspar, Tuua, Eban, Redbird, and Aaran were between the foreguard and the rearguard. And the entry man and the kor wogan would step in before them. The rearguard would stay at the door while the foreguard cleared the room, and then whatever lay behind it.

They were, Aaran thought, as ready as they could hope to be.

And he dreaded the next step his feet took.

"Do it," the kor wogan said.

The marine jammed lock picks back in his kit, took out a tempered steel wedge and a mallet, and with two clanging slams against the handle, had it off.

The door slammed open as the marines kicked it in and burst through into a room lit by dim gold light, filled with faint, sweet hints of incenses and perfumes, extravagant in its decor. The gold light highlighted the sheen of silks, the richness of velvets, the lush depth of tapestries, and the polished beauty of wood furniture. Which the marines kicked out of their way as they ran for the shape in the huge, elaborate bedstead.

But a naked man rolled from a wide, curved settee shoved along one side of the wall, and landed on his feet, and smiled at the marines who charged him. They froze in mid-stride.

Aaran could not see what the man had done to them. But it would have been done by Hagedwar magic.

The figure in the bedstead did not move.

"That was an expensive door you ruined," the man said. And he yawned and stretched as elaborately as a cat. "You'll want to pay for it, or the first diplomat will be most displeased." He looked around at them, and smiled.

Aaran realize that he couldn't move, either. Funny how he hadn't noticed that before.

Hawkspar

This was what I had feared. The men around me were frozen. Something bound them—I could feel it tugging at me, too. I realized that I could move away from whatever the man before us had done; I could shake it off and step out of it. I wondered if Redbird could do the same thing, or if I could only because of the Hawkspar Eyes.

She didn't move. But neither did I. I wanted to see what the man was going to do. While he thought he had all of us in his power, he might offer some bit of information that we would otherwise be unable to get from him. Or he might open the door to the back room, or wake the diplomat from his sleep.

So I steadied my breath, and relaxed my muscles as I had learned to do in training, and I waited.

The man before us was an odd creature. He bore scars on his skin, but these were not like the whip marks on my back or the marks of torture Aaran had described seeing on Eban. These were intentional. Someone had made cuts into his skin, and filled them with powdered metal. Gold. His entire body was decorated with curling spirals and dots of those embedded gold-dust lines.

I knew those spirals, and as memory clicked, my heart constricted. This man was the third wizard, the living monster who stalked with the two dead ones through my past, my present, and my future.

And as I could see the Hagedwar, so I could see the effect of these lines on his body. He was using them to draw and direct power into himself from whoever it was who occupied the huge bed behind him, and then to transform that power and push it toward us. He radiated like a small, pale blue sun, those lines glowing.

He'd been speaking Feegash, but looking at our group, he switched to Tonk. "You lads brought women with you," he said, and laughed. "How thoughtful of you."

His head angled down and he stared at Eban, who was taller and tanned, his hair bleached by the sun, his shoulders straight, his demeanor confident.

The bastard didn't recognize him as the first diplomat's nephew, or the Marqal diplomat's son.

"And a *child*," he said. "We simply *love* little Tonk children here. I have one over in the bed there."

And he was holding our warriors frozen by killing her. I could see him sucking the life out of her to do it. I didn't know if he had anything else useful to say, but I slid into time's river and grabbed my moment and pushed my way through the abrupt weight of air and the cold of the sudden stillness. The light of the power he drew from the child into his body, frozen in its arc, twisted like threads and spirals of wool being spun into yarn before my blind eyes. It was all I could see in the room except for the spirals in his body that it filled.

I lunged at him, both blades out, and slashed for his throat. My blade stopped in the air before it touched him, and the light that surrounded him slowly crawled up over my blade and my hand to touch me. And though I held tight to my moment, when his light touched my skin, his head slowly began to turn toward me, and I saw his jawbone hinge open, and as he began to move faster, heard his voice in my ear.

". . . aaascinating trick you have there, my lovely. And whatever have you done to your eyes?"

I could still move. But he could move, too.

Inside the Hagedwar, studying him with every sense I had, I could see how the magic he was pulling from the dying child built its wall around him. How he used it as a shield against me.

A sword materialized in his hand. How had he done that? His Hagedwar had a different shape than Aaran's. Two points of the tetrahedrons pushed out beyond the surface of the red cube, into the blue beyond. Did the difference in shape let him do things with it that Aaran could not?

I moved out of his way, blocking his first sword blow, stepping back as I did.

He moved toward me, and I saw something.

The arc of light, that blue glow of power that connected him to the child and my people to him, that hung in the air around him, broke away from him. He moved in time, but it did not.

And as he moved away from it, the shield around him broke. He felt it instantly, and I saw him stop, saw his head jerk around toward the power that had sustained him.

And he froze again, held in that moment in time.

I did not take chances. I cut his throat, then slashed through the spirals in his skin, and finally pulled his sword from his hand and drove it through his heart.

And then I released my moment and sagged to the floor, and the light that had run from the child to him flickered and was gone, leaving me in darkness again. Blessed darkness.

In the darkness, men surrounded me, and voices raised, and I heard a child scream.

The pain was whipping in on me, tangling around me.

Redbird was at my side, her arms around me, holding me up. "Live," she whispered. "Live. For me." The Moonstone Daaryi reached me next, and put her hands over my Eyes, taking some of my pain into herself; I heard her whimper once, and then she steadied and I steadied, and she and Redbird pulled me to my feet.

Aaran was at my side. "What happened?"

"I stepped into a moment, he pulled himself in with me somehow, we fought. And then he lost the source of his power, and I killed him."

"I mean, what happened to *you*?" he asked.

"It doesn't matter," I said. "I'm fine now. Keep moving. We're not done with all that's dangerous in here."

He pulled back from me, hurt.

I was going to hurt him much more, I knew. I felt myself getting stranger and stranger on the inside. I felt the currents of time always around me, I reached into them and pulled deaths and lives and despair and hope in endless quantities from the never-ending flood. My own life was falling away from me in pieces and shards, my own grasp of self being washed from me as if I were nothing but another bank in the river to be cut and eroded and worn to nothing.

I would not always be me. Aaran would, however, always be him. And whatever part of me remained would ache for him.

The rearguard marines and the Moonstone kept the child, a battered little girl, with them, behind their guard. The rest of us moved forward, following the same procedure, breaching the massive metal-bound door in the same manner that we had the previous one.

In this room, nothing smelled of incense.

Instead, I smelled death. Decay.

My skin raised in chill bumps and I had to fight to get my feet to move forward.

Here, though, no powerful wizard stepped out to greet us.

Instead, a man dressed in robes elegantly cut and embroidered over with thread of gold turned to us, and in a voice almost heartbroken, said, "She is dead. I kept her for so long, but suddenly—in an instant—I lost her. She was alive. My best specimen. I've kept her for fifteen years and she was perfect. Perfect. And now . . . now look at her."

He did not seem to register that we were the enemy. His back was to us, I realized, and he was staring at a body that hung suspended from his ceiling by thin wires. She wore a medallion around her neck.

He was staring at Aashka. Or at what was left of her.

She had been alive. Had died in an instant.

Had died in the instant that I had killed the wizard to save the little girl. I had killed her.

Aaran whispered, "Aashka," and drew his blade, and pushed through the marines that held the diplomat at swordpoint, though the diplomat did not seem to be aware of them.

"Aashka!" Aaran shouted, and the last of the marines stepped aside, and he swung the sword two-handed in an overhand stroke, straight down onto the diplomat's head. Through it. The diplomat stood for a moment, his head split in twain, a sword wedged into the base of his neck, and then his knees buckled and he dropped. Soundlessly.

Barely able to get words out of his throat, Aaran said, "Cut her down."

Her body was falling apart before us. The smell of decay was getting stronger.

My fault, my fault. And still I could not find anything I could have done differently. I stood behind Aaran, wanting to touch him and offer comfort, and I could not bring myself to do it. She would have known he'd come for her if not for me. He would have seen her alive once more if not for me. I hung my head and tears ran down my cheeks, and I wrapped my arms around myself.

I heard him say, "Get me something to wrap her in," and one of the men ran back to the outer chamber and dragged the bedcover back in.

The marines handled her gently. They wrapped her carefully, and Aaran crouched down and picked her up. My back turned to him, I could still watch him. He cradled what was left of her in his arms, his head down. Then he said, "Greton fire in this room, against the back. Greton fire in the next chamber. Leave the doors blocked—the bastard's loyal soldiers and servants are back there. If they find other ways out, we'll deal with them. If they don't, the fire will." He turned and walked toward the door to the outer chamber.

"You can't burn the left corridor," Eban said.

His head snapped in Eban's direction. "Why not?"

"His concubines and wives and children are there. Some of my . . . brothers and sisters . . . may be back there."

Aaran snarled, "Hold the fire," and carried his sister out through the outer chamber and into that vast arched central room. He laid her body on one of the remaining couches, and said, "How do you know this, Eban? How do you know where the concubines and children and wives are?"

Eban, trembling, answered in a whisper, "I was here . . . on loan. Once." And then his voice got even softer. "I'm glad you killed him. I'm glad you killed them both."

We had managed to forget, somehow, that all of this had been Eban's life before his father transported his household to Marqal and the child escaped to join us. We had not realized how very close to Eban's nightmares we had come until just then.

Aaran picked the boy up and gave him a hug. "Let's go find your people if we can," he said. "We'll save *someone* from this hellhole."

We went through the door as before, protecting all sides and with guards posted in the rear. Every man in the column covered an area the men before him were not. We cleared rooms one at a time—a horrible task, for some of them were torture chambers with victims in place, waiting the return of their torturers, and some were rooms where someone was dissecting the dead. Some were crowded, filthy quarters where women and children were kept. We passed bathing chambers and dressing rooms, too, and discovered a few rooms that were elegantly appointed, but empty. Eban said those were the rooms where diplomatic guests came to be entertained by their choices of wives or concubines or children.

Though for the most part the captives in these rooms were controlled by locked doors, there were a few guards. Some of these fought. Others threw down their weapons and begged mercy. The Tonk granted those who asked it mercy, until one man picked his sword up and tried to stab a marine in the back with it.

After that, there was no more mercy.

When the whole corridor was cleared, we worked our way back, setting the captives free—men and women, boys and girls, and infants in arms. Two marines, with Eban as their translator, detailed the servants to tend to the torture victims once they were removed from their restraints.

And then we stood, undecided.

"Is there anyone in the other corridor who should be saved?"

Eban shook his head slowly.

Aaran went back to the couch where his sister's body lay. "Burn this place down then. Burn every bit of it that will burn." He scooped her into his arms again, and we marched back through the servants' area, while he told everyone to get out.

Behind, the marines were tossing Greton fire down the corridor and into the chambers, closing the doors behind themselves as they retreated. When the servants were clear, they set fire to the huge central chamber, and then cleared out of the building down the servants' section. We got to the back of the grounds. And then I realized that I could hear fighting in the streets. Aaran laid his sister's body on the path, and told two marines, "Guard her, and keep order in here." Eban and Tuua stayed behind, and the Moonstone, who was doing what she could for the torture victims.

The rest of us formed up, drew weapons, and moved into the street.

Our marines, plus civilians armed with clubs made from broken chairs, boards with nails sticking out, farm implements, and even hammers and mallets, fought hand-to-hand with the elite Ba'afeegash mercs, the best-known mercenary fighters in all of Korre.

Ba'afeegash had more professional soldiers than any other nation in the world. Most of them, however, were serving overseas, pushing the Feegash agenda. The Feegash controlled their own people by making sure they had nothing to fight with. They kept the weapons in the hands of their enforcers, and so held their population captive to their every whim.

After being so long without challenges against them, the Feegash evidently believed that no one would dare carry the battle to them in their own land. Armed men and women stood side-by-side with Feegash slaves, who had risen up and were giving their support, fighting with whatever they could. And the outnumbered mercs were dying in the streets.

The effect on the mercs was astonishing. Some had stripped off uniforms and fled, others had turned against those who were killing their own people and were fighting with our men.

The result was chaos. Pandemonium. The grand mansions of the Diplomate were burning, the official buildings were burning, the bodies of diplomats and wizards were being strung from poles and trees and roof posts. As the mercs fell back and fled and drained away, the commotion in the streets turned to cheering.

I did not know how long I fought—how long any of us fought. Some of our people died, and many more fighting civilians lay where they had fallen. But through the tears, through the grief, still the dancing and the cheering and the celebrating went on.

People wandered through the streets, looking from face to face for loved ones who had been taken from them, and each time a mother found a child or a brother found a sister or a friend found a friend, I watched embraces and laughter and weeping all at once. And I envied them.

I would have given anything to be one of those people, to have had the chance to find my own brothers and sisters, my own mother or father. Yet, for all my envy, I rejoiced with them, too. They had paid so much, and for so long, for these moments of happiness.

I wondered what would happen to them when we were gone.

The diplomats in Ba'afeegash were dead or dying. The mercs within the walls of the great city-state were disbanded, scattered, or dead. Those who had held positions of power mostly hung in the streets, and the citizens of Ba'afeegash were looting swords and armor from fallen mercs and going after those who had managed to bar their doors and hide within their homes.

Over the coming days, we would clear out those who remained.

But we had not come to stay. We would be leaving, and unlike most city-states, Ba'afeegash had a presence that was felt everywhere. Most of its mercenaries were in the field; most of its diplomats in foreign posts, whispering in the ears of kings and potentates and warrior chiefs.

We had cut off the head of our enemy, but if we did not deal with it, the body that remained could grow a new head. We had to that keep from happening.

The downfall of Ba'afeegash, long claimed to be impossible, we had accomplished. But the destruction of the Feegash elite had only just begun.

47

Aaran

Aaran stood in the central Ba'afeegash square, in front of what had once been the Ba'afeegash law council building, but which had become a pile of stones and broken glass.

His men had scavenged the city for wood and built funeral pyres for the fallen marines, sailors, and Ossalenes.

What little remained of his sister lay atop the pyre beside him, and his men gathered around him to send her to Ethebet and Jostfar.

A few of them had spoken words of sympathy and hope, words of regret that they had not had the chance to meet her.

Tuua had finished his words of remembrance, for the child she once had been.

And then, to Aaran's surprise, Hawkspar stepped out and turned to face the men.

"I slept, and just before I woke today, I dreamed. I was in a broad meadow, in low, rolling hills, and the sky above me was blue and fair, and the meadow around me was full of flowers—red and yellow, blue and gold, pink and purple. Horses ran free, their hooves thundering in this distance like a coming storm.

"And a woman dressed in white, in the manner of the Tonk, with a sword at her hip and a staff in her hand, came to me. She has come to me before, but this time she came with a child—a little laughing girl. And she told me, 'This child has been with Ethebet for a long time. Her body remained in the world of the flesh, but her spirit has been in Ethebet's care. Set her flesh free, and mourn her passing only for a little while. Know that you who ride for Ethebet will see her again in Jostfar's land.'"

Aaran stared at Hawkspar. He had heard tales of the woman in white. He had once heard the famed Tonk heroine Talyn, who had been sitting in the Star's Rest in Beyltaak, telling a story to those around her of having been offered a choice between a banquet and the world, and water and a sword, by a woman in white. Talyn's description of the woman and the place sounded just like Hawkspar's.

The hair on Aaran's arms stood up.

Aashka had been safe? He had felt her body suffering. But he had not felt her. He had never felt anything about her that had remembered him. He had felt only pure pain. And he thought about the fact that as soon as her body died, it decayed. Her body was, lying atop the pyre at that moment, little more than dust.

The wizard, then, had kept her flesh alive. But her spirit had gone on long before.

He breathed easier all of a sudden. A burden lifted from his shoulders. He signaled for the torch, and suddenly Hawkspar turned to him and said, "You have to take the medallion with you."

"I have to . . . what?"

"The medallion your sister wore. The woman in white said that you have to take it with you. That you have to wear it."

Aaran didn't want it. He wanted nothing to do with that accursed piece of metal, for which his sister had been singled out and dragged to this horrible place to be taken by the first diplomat and premier of Ba'afeegash to be his personal toy.

But he climbed onto the pyre, and unwrapped her, and gently lifted the medallion over her head and dropped it over his own.

He climbed back down from the pyre, took the torch handed to him, and said, "I release you, Aashka, little sister, into the arms of our mother and father, into the care of Ethebet, into the fields of Jostfar. Run free, be joyous, and know that I love you. And I will miss you until the day I see you again."

He fought back tears, and put the torch to the base of the pyre, and watched as the tinder caught, and then the oil and the flames licked up the wood. He stood, with the smoke boiling into the sky, and thought of all the years he had spent on ships in search of her, hoping for word, hoping for a sign. Of the oath he had taken, that he would not rest until he found her. Until he saved her.

He'd kept his oath as best he could. It hadn't been enough, because from early on, she'd been beyond rescue. But he had sworn, too, to bring the men who had taken her to justice.

And he had made a start on that.

"Be well," he whispered, and his hand wrapped around the medallion that she had worn. "Be well, and be happy."

Hawkspar

I'd regained the time river. The waters that flowed around me when I stepped into it once again showed the currents of our possible futures.

I had hoped to see us triumphant. I had hoped to see the Feegash discredited once and for all. But none knew of the fall of Ba'afeegash save those within its walls. It was being kept secret.

The slaves, the flunkies, and those otherwise freed from oppression had taken over the gates and the treasuries, and were carrying on trading as they had before, pretending that their masters still ruled them. Supplies poured into Ba'afeegash as they always had, as did tribute from allies. Emissaries were turned away, with a story about temporary difficulties in the diplomatic headquarters; they were given official documents from the secretaries who had years of practice lying for their masters, and who now were telling one last grand lie to protect themselves.

The people of Ba'afeegash were carefully dividing up the gold and the goods of the city, and leaving in family groups. There was nothing in this foul, sterile place that they wanted—not the played-out land, not the poor grazing of the small fields, not the precarious location that without regular supplies from debtor nations would leave the population to starve quickly. And since we'd made it clear that we intended to topple the Feegash masters and destroy their regime, everyone understood that if we were successful, the supplies and tributes would stop coming.

And if we failed, the Feegash diplomats and mercenaries would return.

So, via two broad roads, in groups of ten and twenty and even thirty, families and friends who had found each other at last slipped out of the walled city, carrying their shares of hidden gold, good food, and such small trinkets as they wished to carry. They mingled with the traders leaving the city, bound for anywhere that ships might be paid to take them.

Some remained with us. *We* had another mission, one I had seen in the waters of time. If we succeeded, we would win the day, and our place in the world. If we failed, the Feegash elites would regroup and the Tonk would yet be overrun and our history would come to an end, and with it our people.

We kept with us some of the secretaries and the file clerks and the scribes. Those mercenaries who had turned against their ranks to save their own civilian families and had fought with us. The wives and concubines of the first diplomat and their children.

We were going to burn Ba'afeegash to the ground on our way out the door, lock the gates behind us, and hammer notices that Ba'afeegash was closed for business to celebrate a great triumph to the walls. And then we were going to hie ourselves with all possible speed to Sinali, which housed the Grand Hall of Nations, and in which the Feegash still held sway through their proxies. And there we were going to out-diplomat the diplomats.

The Feegash had left behind the complete details of their Five-Hundred-Year Plan for the total domination of the world. They were on year 324. They had been kind enough to write their plan down, make multiple copies, and have their servants file those copies.

We had the copies. We had the servants. We had the medallion of the first diplomat, and the undersecretary who had signed documents for him for years, and who had once had a wife and children he loved.

And we were on our way to our next battle.

Our communicators were sending like wild men, keeping everything in code but letting our people back home know what we had discovered.

The Tonk, meanwhile, were having a terrible time everywhere. In Hyre, the Cartajarmans and the Pindans had attacked from the north, the Sinali were bringing in fleets from the south, the Reform Mindans were sabotaging Tonk efforts from the inside—although they were not doing as good a job as they might have hoped, for most of them had already been banished from Tonk lands. Only those few that had managed to stay well hidden remained.

On the seas, in Tandinapalis, in Velobrina, in Franica, our people were beset by enemies. War raged everywhere.

And our people could not say anything about the fall of Ba'afeegash, because if they did, the Feegash throughout the rest of Korre would reorganize. As it was, they'd stopped receiving any communications from their own people when we killed off their communicators. Their code books were in place and several of our communicators were Feegash-fluent, so we brought the Feegash communication stations back to life and we spun out a nice little tale of the defeat of a major Tonk territory down in the nearby lowlands, and of the celebratory month-long orgy that would be ensuing. National Feegash holiday, we'd declared, and said Ba'afeegash communications would be via courier for anything but emergencies for all that time.

We ordered the farflung Feegash embassies to close their doors and celebrate with us. We'd left our communicators to deal with the emergencies in such fashion as amused them; they feigned being irritated at being disturbed from their drunken revelries, they passed on commands from the first diplomat and premier himself that had to be driving the field diplomats and the mercenary commanders to distraction. We had, for several weeks, shut down almost all Feegash activity. We couldn't touch their allies, though, so our people were still dying.

I wished I could have seen the smoke of the burning city as we set the last of it to the torch.

At last all the people save ours were gone—all of them comfortably well off from their masters' gold, all of them heading for new lives and new futures. I hoped they would find them.

I wished them well.

With a small contingent of amused ex-slaves dressed in the armor of the Feegash mercs parading along the tops of the walls to give the illusion that the city was still guarded, we shut and locked the Ba'afeegash's grand gates behind us on our way out the doors. The fake mercs had suggested that they wait one month, then file out the Shepherds' Gate in the dead of night. By then, we would either have won or we would have lost, and it wouldn't matter if the true fate of the fallen city were known.

Making our way down the mountainside, we told the oncoming traders and others who were bearing tribute up the mountain, "Big party. They don't want to be bothered for a while, and they're sending everyone away. Wait if you want, though. They have to open the gates again eventually."

So great was the fear of the wrath of the Feegash that not a single trader or tribute-bearer turned and started back down the mountain.

We raced down the road, taking half of it for ourselves and pushing those who went down ahead of us out of the way.

We had little time. The Feegash and the Tonk were the only two people who had Hagedwar Communicators, but the news of the fall of Ba'afeegash would not stay hidden for long. We had to get to our ships and sail to Sinali with our proofs of the Feegash betrayal of all their allies before the Feegash in the Grand Hall of Nations could stir the full wrath of those same allies against the Tonk and crush us with the might of the world's armies.

With good winds we might make decent time, though we would be sailing against the southern Trade Current.

We swept into Danaskataak and onto our restocked ships and launched ourselves out of Askag Bay with our windmen on steady shifts boosting already favorable winds. The seas parted for us as if Jostfar himself had smoothed them for our passage.

Tuua and Eban worked on some of the Feegash records in the ship's temple.

The rest of the records were scattered across all the other ships and their keepers. Our people were finding the best examples of Feegash treachery against those we hoped to win to our side, marking books with plots that had been used against the Feegash allies, and the results of the actions taken.

The marines and Obsidians trained on the deck for close-order fighting. The sailors practiced their fighting when they weren't sailing us toward our destination.

I even drilled, doing the exercises I had mostly neglected during our months aboard the ship.

I kept myself from Aaran's side, except when I could not refuse to meet with him. The time was coming when I would make the last sacrifice of myself. We were on the way, time and my predecessor had both been clear that this was my future, and I could not bear to be with him when I knew how quickly the magic of the Eyes would devour me.

He didn't seem to notice. He worked constantly. He and the other captains were working with the people they had rescued from the Ba'afeegash, honing the testimony they would present to the court of the Grand Hall of Nations.

I spent a little time watching the oracles and the Ossalenes who had remained behind in the Citadel. They were almost as profitable as ever, even without the Eyes of War. They'd put a girl in my place who wore false Eyes of hawkspar stone, but without the magic. She sat in audience and offered advice whispered to her from advisers who read the old Hawkspar knotbooks from their hiding places behind her throne.

They still dealt with potentates, they still entertained warlords, they still made great sums of money.

I could see that in the near future, Ossal would present himself to the monastery again, though I could see neither the how nor the why of that.

But the future beyond his arrival was all whitewater, and I grew weary of trying to penetrate it, so I ceased to try.

I turned to watching my own future. I couldn't see the places where I might suddenly veer, or dig my own channel, of course. But I could see my trend. I was consumed by the magic of the Eyes. Soon. Very soon. I fell into the madness and the brooding that spelled the eventual end of most oracles, and died badly. Always, no matter which way I turned, no matter what I did, shortly after the trial we were approaching, my channel went black.

But there was never a current that led me toward happiness. After all the tragedy Aaran had already been through, how could I let him love me and be subjected to watching me go mad and die? Was that any way to return his love?

I kept to myself, I prepared my own testimony for the court with everything I could gather about the futures of the people who were currently allied with the Feegash if they did not turn away from them.

I put together a knot-book like those I had read after the death of Hawkspar, treating on the Feegash and their iniquities.

And I waited.

The trip was as fast as the windmen could make it, as uneventful as any sea trip could be. We had one storm that scattered some of the fleet, but we regrouped quickly enough. We crossed paths with one Sinali slaver, and took as much time as we had rescuing our people and sinking the ship. But we took prisoners. Once we had done what we intended to do—if we succeeded—we would set them free. If we failed, we would offer them in a hostage exchange.

In such lonely fashion, with Aaran in his quarters and me in mine, we reached the southern tip of Sinali, the Magon Peninsula, and the province of Hai Ei, where, in the ancient city of Ei Angon Yeh, the Grand Hall of Nations sat atop a high hill like the crown on the head of a king.

48

Aaran

The city of Ei Angon Yeh, the Place of Courageous Men, rose from the rocky cliffs like a gilt mirage. Aaran was up the foremast on the snaparm, watching the shoreline off to starboard. When the *Taag* came upon it, first he caught a flash of gold. And then a shimmer of white, backed by green.

And then over the horizon arose the most astonishing city he had ever seen. It was almost like watching an enormous sun come up, it gleamed so in the sunlight. The white stone towers and buildings were topped with gold domes, gold pinnacle roofs, gold arches. Flags and banners snapped in the breeze from every high point, on top the azure spear of the Sinali empire, and below that flags from every Sinali province, and below those, flags of individual Sinali houses.

As they drew closer, Aaran could see the famed Trees of Life, rumored to be older than even Tonk civilization. They rose in the backdrop behind the walls of the city. Each of them was sacred, each had a name. The trees were called the guiding spirits of the empire, and some tales said they were haunted, and others, that they actually spoke with voices like those of men.

Aaran tried to equate the people who had built that glorious city with the men who had killed his parents and sold his sister to the Feegash. With the sailors who went from clan to clan, raping and murdering and looting and burning. He would have to remember that the men he would face within the court of the Grand Hall of Nations had set those other men against him and his. That the urbane gentlemen in the fine robes were pirates no less than the filthy ones in breechclouts.

He would be dealing with the wicked, the criminal, the vile, and the corrupt. And he had to win with honesty. It was the only card he could play—the only one he was willing to bet had never been played in that white-and-gold city before the gathered nations.

He would be the lead speaker for the group that would demand a hearing. He was not the oldest, but he was the one who had dared the Islands of the Fallen Sun to get Hawkspar and her people out, and to discover the truth that he intended to share with the members of those nations who were fighting and dying in a hundred little wars for the profit of the Feegash. He had taken the risks. He had earned the right.

As the *Taag* sailed closer, he could see men on Sinali warships in the harbors scrambling to put out to sea to meet the Tonk fleet.

"Truce and treat flags up masts now," Aaran bellowed. And on the foremast, the aftermast, and the castlepole, white flags with the single black circle in the center—the international sign of truce and treaty—snapped upward to billow in the wind. They rose an instant later on every ship behind the *Taag*.

"Marines on deck and arms rest!" Aaran shouted, and heard the order relayed via the bells. In a moment, the marines, in dress uniforms but fully armed, thundered onto the deck and formed up.

"Sailors on deck and arms rest!" Aaran called down, and as the bells rang a second time, those sailors not on duty charged onto the deck, well dressed but armed, and took their places. Tuua and Eban, the cooks and medic, the communicators, and other ship personnel came on deck with them.

"Passengers on deck and arms rest!" Aaran shouted one final time, and the bells ran the third signals.

The oracle and the Ossalenes did not run onto the deck. They walked in stately fashion, dressed in the full robes and hoods of their order. It was the first time he had seen them so dressed since not long after the *Taag* carried them away from the Citadel. All of them gathered together in a square on the raised afterdeck, each carrying a staff, all of them standing chins up and faces forward. The wind blew them, but they seemed unmoved, still as statues.

The Ba'afeegash on the *Taag* and the other ships of the fleet made their own small formations, too. While the Ba'afeegash women kept out of sight, the male Ba'afeegash put on Feegash black, the finely cut silk and velvet and linen and spun-wool clothes of the Feegash elite diplomat class. None of them *were* Feegash diplomats, of course. Those were dead if they had been posted in the Ba'afeegash city-state. Or, if they were lucky enough to be sent abroad, they were still on post at their various assignments around the world, or sitting in session in the Grand Hall of Nations. But that Tonk ships appeared to carry Feegash diplomats in great numbers, would, the captains of the fleet hoped, get them a hearing in the Hall without having to resort to violence.

He slid down the rigging and landed lightly on the deck, quickly straightened his own dress clothes, and took up his position on the officers' deck, between the longboats and just in front of the steersman's castle.

His people were ready.

Two Sinali warships came racing out, and out of the corner of his eye, Aaran could see others raising their flags to follow. The Feegash undersecretary who would be the lead delegate for the Feegash cause took the ship's calling cone in hand, and in Feegash, told the Sinali captains that the fleet had come with Feegash negotiators to bargain a Tonk settlement in the Court of the Grand Hall of Nations, and that the Sinali should put down arms and raise truce and treat flags.

The effect on the Sinali was immediate. Both ships heeled around, their truce flags waving as they did, and came alongside either side of the Tonk fleet.

On the docks in the Ei Angon Yeh harbor, men had stopped preparing the warships. They watched from decks and masts and watchtowers as the whole Tonk fleet sailed in, claimed dock space, and weighed anchor.

The Sinali troops that guarded the city were waiting as the Feegash marched off first—many of them walking for the first time in years, thanks to the care of Moonstones and Tonk healers. Behind the Feegash went the marines, excepting those few who would stand watch over the ship. Behind the marines went the Ossalene seru and the oracle, behind the seru, the keepers and their assistants, and behind the them, the captain.

All the sailors stayed aboard with the remaining marines. It would not do to march too great a force into the city. The thousand-strong marines made an impressive escort, but adding more than twice that many sailors would have been seen as a threat.

Aaran and his contingent were first off the docks, but as they moved forward, more and more Tonk poured onto the docks and marched forward. The centerline of Tonk marines carried boxes of documents. The Ossalenes carried staffs, and perhaps some of their hidden weapons. They did not wear the swords at their hips, though. Everyone else was armed, but with arms away and weapon hands raised across chests as they marched.

The Tonk were not, for the most part, marching men. They were by preference and long practice riders, guerrilla fighters, runners. But they could march at need, and they had drilled onboard to get precision marching down, because the armies of their enemies marched and stood in close formation, and regarded such armies as civilized.

So the Tonk were arriving in the guise of civilized men, presented and accompanied by Feegash negotiators, an Oracle Hawkspar Eyes of War, and an entire contingent of Ossalenes—most of those Obsidians.

This fight had to be won with words instead of swords, and Aaran and the other captains had played out this battle endlessly, both with each other and in their own minds.

This, finally, was the one that would count.

Hawkspar

I could hear the murmuring of the men around me as we marched off the dock and headed for the Grand Hall of Nations.

I could tell it must have been beautiful. It was amazing even from what I could discern. It towered over us as we made our way up steep switchback roads of stairs, between lines of archers atop walls and behind them. We lived for that moment at the mercy of the Sinali, under a flag of truce that they had never seen fit to honor before. I'd heard all the stories from the men, of Sinali warships coming in with their truce flags raised only to cut them loose and raise weapons when they were within range, of them cutting down unarmed men carrying flags of truce. I knew that the presence of Feegash dressed as diplomats, and to a lesser extent the members of my Order, which the Sinalis respected, were the reason the archers did not shoot the Tonks down to the last man.

I did not forget, either, that we were marching into the city safely enough, but if we failed to convince the members of the court of the merits of our case, we would be unlikely to survive our march back out.

I wished, briefly, that I had let myself indulge in time spent with Aaran during our trip. I knew we had less than even odds of surviving this visit into the halls of our enemies. But unlike the battle of Ba'afeegash—where we could have lost everything, but could not have won everything no matter what we did—this time the other half of those odds indicated that we could remove the cloud from the Tonk people if we performed well here.

The waters of time ran in every imaginable direction.

As we drew closer to the Grand Hall, I could make out the deep designs carved into the stones from which it was built. They were in relief, and they made sense to my eyes—but not a pleasant sort of sense. I saw friezes of men in chains being marched at spear point, men being beheaded, men being run through in battle. In their stone murals, the Sinali were always the heroes, of course. They paraded with the heads of their enemies on pikes, and ripped the entrails from men chained to stretching racks.

These were not a gentle people led astray by the whispering of the Feegash. These were people who had been brutal and violent on their own, without help from anyone else.

They had fit in with the Feegash plans.

We started up the main steps of the Grand Hall. It dwarfed us; it was on a scale so inconceivably massive that I realized our entire contingent would be able to gather comfortably under the pillars at the front. We were not much more than gnats in this place.

I didn't find that feeling pleasant.

When we reached the landing, a man hurried to me, and bowed deeply, and in Sinali said, "I am Do-es Ei-enyan, empress orator first to Ei Angon Yeh for the empire of the Sinali. Please forgive that I do not recognize you by your robe ranks, but unless I am mistaken, you are an Oracle of the Eyes, are you not?"

I turned to him. "I am. I am the Living Goddess Oracle Hawkspar Eyes of War."

"The *Eyes of War*? Never have we of the empire known an oracle to travel beyond the walls of your Citadel. We are most honored by your presence, Living Goddess Oracle Hawkspar Eyes of War. *Most* honored. You will be our guest while you are here. You will have the best of everything. The empress was notified of the presence of an oracle when you were still walking on the Path of Truth and Justice, and she commands me invite you to partake of her bounty, and treat you in her chambers as a beloved sister."

"I thank the empress," I said. "And when I have concluded my business here, I would be delighted to visit with her. I have gifts, unworthy though they may be, for her august glory."

He bowed.

I bowed. Dealing with the emissaries of empresses is a touchy business, especially when one is not in one's Citadel surrounded by a good wall, long leagues of ocean, and hundreds of Obsidian-Eyed warriors who would make rat hash out of anyone who became dangerous.

He said, "Your business here . . . You are speaking on the surrender of the Tonks?"

"I am speaking on a number of issues, and bringing what I know of the

future of our world before the peoples represented in the court of the Grand
Hall of Nations as a gift."

"A . . . " he faltered. "A *gift*? From the Ossalenes?"

We oracles were well known for being right. And for being touchy, and
difficult, and sometimes dangerous. We were not, however, known for our
generosity of spirit where the powers of our Eyes were concerned; rather, we
had a well-earned reputation for skinning our visitors for all they might be
worth, and more, if we could manage it.

"A gift," I said firmly, "though it will not be a happy one."

"Ah," he said. Oracles giving away bad news wasn't any more common
than oracles giving away good news, but at least the former fit in with the
Sinali philosophy that nothing good came free.

Cynical people, the Sinali. From the empire-building perspective, though,
I could understand where they could make a case for the success of their
philosophy.

"When you have presented your . . . news . . . the empress will make you
welcome." He bowed.

I bowed.

He said, "I have a simple question from the empress. Not a future. Simply . . . a question."

I caught the stresses in his voice, and realized that someone in this city
knew a Hawkspar claimant still inhabited the Citadel of the Ossalenes. She
would have preferred credibility, because she was where *Eyes of War* belonged, and I was not.

So I was being asked to prove that I was not a fraud. The question would
be laden with tricks and traps.

I said, "Ask her question."

"The empress was treated just yesterday for a health condition that had
left her most ill for some days. Was she treated correctly?"

I was surrounded by a throng of people, all of whose life currents collided
with mine. The empress was nowhere near. The emissary radiated a nervous
energy that gave me a headache.

I bowed. "You will hold out your hand, and I will touch it to read this bit
of the empress's current."

He bowed lower, and held his hand out. As my hand touched his silk
glove, I read backward as quickly as I could, and uncovered a veritable viper's
nest of lies and treachery and betrayal in the high court.

The empress had recently conceived a child by the man before me. Her own husband, the empress consort, had been away in battle, in which the empress had made arrangements for him to die. But the man with whom she had made arrangements had been killed instead, and she did not know if that death had been accidental or intentional, or if someone knew of her attempt to rid herself of the empress consort.

Her husband, meanwhile, had come home the admired hero of a battle that he had not been expected to carry, and favor in the high Sinali court had shifted from the empress to him. Talk of seeing him made emperor had reached her ears. If he were made emperor, the empress knew, her own power would vanish. He could put her away from himself, have her killed, marry a dozen other wives. Her own children with him would be hunted down and slaughtered, and the power of her family, and the dynasty that had ruled for hundreds of years, would end.

So the empress had called in her trusted medic, and had him create a powder that could be added to her husband's food. The powder would take three days to sicken him and kill him. The small dose his taster would ingest would have almost no affect, and even the effect it did have would be days in coming.

But had anyone seen or heard what she was doing? That, of course, she could not know. But I knew.

I said, "These things you must repeat to the empress, exactly as I tell them to you. Her smallest sickness, though it saddened her, is done with, and she will recover fully. For the larger problem, it is badly contagious, and yet it has not spread so far as it might seem. Her trusted medic is a worthy man, and his cures are good. If he can but give a second dose like the first, he will rid her of this disease and set her free. Her beloved and trusted minister of the spirits, who has grown close to her adored husband, should be . . . consulted . . . on this matter."

The empress orator first had grown still as I told him the necessary cure for the empress's "health"; his face was turned toward mine with fixed intensity, and he seemed not to breathe. When he heard the last of my words, though, he said, "Ah. Your Eyes see clearly, blessed Oracle, to see all of that."

He then bowed so low his head touched his knees.

"Give the empress my blessings, and tell her she is and will always be a dear friend of the Ossalenes." And I bowed. Just a little.

He turned and hurried away, a lean man dressed in layer upon layer of expensive silk.

Others in our party had been approached, of course. The Feegash, naturally, had found themselves facing diplomats of their own people. We'd known this would happen. All they would say was that they had been sent away from the celebration of the Feegash at the orgy in Ba'afeegash with documents of surrender and treaty, and that they had been instructed by the first diplomat and premier to present these documents directly and without delay to all the representatives seated within the Grand Hall of Nations.

All of this was, of course, true. Not true in the manner that the seated Feegash diplomats or any of the representatives of Nations would expect it to be. But the surprise was, to my mind, the best part of this expedition.

At last all our people had gathered atop the landing that led into the Grand Hall, and I wish I could say we made an impressive spectacle. I could only see us as a mass of individuals, and one that took up less than half the space on the landing. We waited while Feegash diplomats and others consulted on the landing with our Feegash, who were to a one posing as diplomats who had served previously in secondary diplomatic posts or as newly raised underlings. While the seated diplomats were uncomfortable with the arrival of so many underlings and seconds, and no familiar old faces, they could not deny that the last news they'd had from the home post had been of the fall of one contingent of Tonk, followed by a tremendous worldwide holiday for all Feegash.

And here were appropriately dressed Feegash who knew the diplomatic procedures and codes, who came with a whole fleet of tame Tonk running under flags of peace and, from their point of view, submission. And with them, the Oracle Hawkspar Eyes of War, who had never before in the very long history of the oracles stepped off her island.

It certainly looked like big news and a cause for more celebration by the Feegash. Like their long-held and long-hidden plans might be moving a few steps closer to fruition in one big leap.

We waited, men argued, I drifted a bit into the waters of time and felt all the countless dangers to us in the flow.

And saw the moment had come. I was called the Living Goddess, but I had never embraced the powers of a goddess.

They lay within me, and I could reach out and pull them to me—lines of light that had stretched long in the time since I left the Citadel. They went from our island to the Ossalenes around me, across a vast ocean to the Ossalenes departed from us. They were the strings that bound us all to Ossal's spirit, those lines, and I had done my best not to even think about them.

But I could not walk into the next arena of my life anything less than a goddess. This was my last, and greatest sacrifice, the one the woman in white had told me would come. I could pretend that I did not recognize the moment, and it would pass. Or I could burn myself to nothing taking those powers. My part, like the parts my comrades would play, was essential to the success of our mission, and if I did hide from my responsibility, we would fail.

I shook myself out of reverie and focused on where I was and what I faced. No one died well, after all. Dead was dead. At least I could do something valuable before I was consumed. I could save my people from onrushing destruction.

At last we were ushered through massive doors of solid brass, into a vaulted space so huge it dwarfed the lot of us. Voices echoed within like shouts in a cavern. I felt like an ant crawling across the vast plain of the Citadel's Great Chapel floor. From the balconies ringed above us into that celestial dome, I could imagine that I looked like that ant, too—if I was even that significant.

"Follow, please," a Sinali man said, bowing, and we followed, across the long, open space, to a wall of doors that seemed at first so tiny that we would have to crawl through them single file, and that when we at last reached them, were so immense we could have doubled the width of our columns from six men to twelve and still marched through with space to spare on either side.

I tried to imagine the men who had built this colossal building. I wondered at their imagination, at their vision, at their goals. They wanted to intimidate, clearly. And to awe. They wanted to shape the people who walked through this monument that they had built with hands and minds and muscles; to make them less than they had been. To humble them. I had no doubt that they had succeeded.

I was humbled.

It was just stone and concrete. Stones piled on top of stones, one after the other, concrete poured a certain way, shaped a certain way, arranged to a plan. It was a roof and walls. And yet I walked through the high vaulted corridor behind the Sinali guide, knowing that dozens of other corridors just like this one had led off from identical doorways, feeling small to the point of insignificance. Feeling unworthy of walking in these corridors.

I would have benefited from a few years experience in being the Eyes of War in the Citadel, I realized. No oracle who had spent several years being treated like a goddess would have permitted walking through a mere artful pile of stones to reduce her to inconsequence. She would have been a goddess still, and the stones would have been stones.

I breathed in deeply, knowing the time had come. I straightened my spine, and drew to myself the lines of light that connected me to the other oracles and to every Ossalene everywhere. In part, I drew in the tradition of hauteur and unapologetic power that had come down to me from countless generations of women who dealt with kings. I could not be small here. I could not be human. What was needed here was not the human me, but the creature who had become part of the Eyes.

I could be that creature.

I bound myself around with the raw magic that had formed the Eyes. It filled me. It embraced me.

It became me.

49

Aaran

Aaran marched into a half-bowl chamber bigger than any Faaverhend he had ever seen. Tiers of seats and long, curving tables rose like cliffs around him, and all of those seats were filled with men who stared down at the group filing into the chamber like executioners awaiting the word of the judge.

He was not ready for this. He doubted if anyone in the room was.

But they had their audience. He could identify some of the representatives by the cut of their clothes, but that wasn't necessary. The flag or banner or shield of each nation represented in the chamber hung from the dome above the men representing it. He knew that he and the people with him had what they wanted—an audience comprised of the eyes and ears of the power brokers of the world.

The Sinali waited until the last of the group filed into the chamber, and until the guards outside the massive double doors had closed them with an ominous, quiet click.

Then he stood before the assembly and bowed. "In this emergency session of the full gathering of men of goodwill representing the true nations of the world, I present the Feegash representatives of the first diplomat and premier of Ba'afeegash, and their captives, the pacified Tonk, here to present their case for surrender."

Aaran suppressed the smile he felt. The ripple of applause around the chamber, and the cold triumph in the glittering eyes of the buzzard-black–garbed Feegash diplomats, would change soon enough if he and his people did their work well.

The Sinali presenter stepped aside and Sakjin, in his role as voice of the first Diplomat and premier, stepped forward and unrolled the scroll that the Feegash and the Tonk had spent countless hours putting together with its supporting documents.

Sakjin bowed, and presented the scroll with its unbroken Seal of the first diplomat to the head diplomat of the Feegash, who had moved down to the front row center for a better view of the proceedings. The man nodded and turned to the assembly. "The seal is valid," he said in Feegashi. "What follows are the true words of the first diplomat and premier of Ba'afeegash."

He handed the scroll back to Sakjin and took his seat.

Sakjin stepped back and broke the seal—which Aaran had sealed with the medallion only the day before, once everyone agreed it was as close to perfect as they could make it. He lifted the scroll and read:

"Heretofore the Feegash people present to the nations of the world the treaty of the Tonk clan with the nations of the world, as negotiated with Kafrij Son of Fanbjan of the first family, first diplomat and premier of the nation of Ba'afeegash, and so spoken for all the Feegash people.

"This treaty replaces all previous treaties with all nations represented in these chambers, and claims provenance by signature over all Tonk Old Clans, all Tonk Transitional Clans, all Tonk New Clans, the Drifted Clan of Eskuu, and by proxy the still-missing Drifted Clans of Kyruu and Jiree."

That brought gasps from the audience. Nothing like the ones that would be coming, but the idea of a signature treaty that claimed jurisdiction over all Tonks everywhere was enough to set the audience back on its heels.

Aaran kept the grin off his face, as did his men. They stood straight and looked grim, which was their job for the time being.

Sakjin read through the list of clans and the signatures beside each, as well as the list of witnesses, each with their seal. Those seals had been great fun to collect.

It made an impressive, if tedious list. And a nicely forged one, too, Aaran thought. The hands of dead men wrote poorly, but their seals spoke just as well for the dead as for the living.

Sakjin then got to the good part. "As is customary in proceedings of this nature, where the complete capitulation of one people to the peoples of the world and the dissolution of that people as a sovereign entity is assigned by treaty, we will now read into the record the cases on file by which this agreement was reached. And as is mandatory in such cases, we require that all representatives who would have this held as binding for their nations remain present for the reading-in of the records as well as for the treaty."

It didn't look like getting people to stay was going to be a problem. At the words "complete capitulation" and "dissolution," emissaries had sent their runners fleeing from the chamber at full gallop, and already additional men were beginning to file in and take seats at their nations' tables. Aaran guessed that if the trend continued, the place was going to be standing-room only by the time Sakjin reached the part with the capitulation and dissolution.

All to the good.

"We now read into the record the agreement of alliance between the Mesahaqa nation and the Feegash nation, dated first of Ereagn, hour seven, in the year Toqin 73 of the Feegash calendar."

Up in the high seats, there was some stirring, and a ripple of distress. The Mesahaqa were not a known Feegash ally, and had been on the payroll of Ba'afeegash in exchange for making war on the Romefendags across their northern border. Aaran watched, privately amused, because the unhappy looks across tables were going to get worse. Down in front, the Feegash head diplomat shifted uncomfortably. That, too, was going to keep getting better—from Aaran's perspective, anyway. Sakjin read in the agreement where in exchange for a supply of Bessel-made catapults and crossbows the Mesahaqa agreed to raid the Romefendags and turn over all but political captives to the Feegash.

Mild uproar from the high seats, stunned disbelief in the eyes of the first diplomat.

Sakjin said: "We now read into the record the agreement of alliance between the Romefendag nation and the Feegash nation, dated third of Ereagn, hour fourteen, in the year Toqin 73 of the Feegash calendar."

Up in the high seats, only the fact that the Romefendags and the Mesahaqa were separated by the width of the room was keeping them from attacking each other. The head diplomat was sinking into his seat, knowing what was coming, though he clearly couldn't begin to figure out how under-the-table Feegash alliances were going to lead to the disbanding of the Tonk clans.

And when Sakjin revealed that the Feegash were also giving the Romefendags weapons in order to get free slaves from the Mesahaqa, attention started shifting. The Feegash had been publicly working toward a peace between the warring nations; there was suddenly a certain amount of interest in those buzzard figures scattered throughout the chamber from representatives of other nations. And with good cause.

A lot of folks in that chamber knew dirty secrets. And all but the Feegash present knew only a tiny number of them.

Sakjin began calling forward his assistants, armed with the records handed over by the marines who'd lugged them in, and he read. And read. And read.

While there had been murmurs of amusement from other nations at the embarrassing situation between the Romefendags and the Mesahaqa, by the time he had read out conflicting treaties between Sinali provinces, between Franican states, between the whole of Bheki and its smaller sister island of Dhakrit, each engineered by the Feegash for the clear end benefit of the Feegash, no one was laughing anymore.

The head Feegash diplomat stood and said, "As head of the overseas Feegash diplomatic community, I question the direction of this document, and the relevance of the material you're adding to the record in regards to the issue of Tonk surrender. I move, therefore, that we adjourn these proceedings until the Feegash field diplomats have the opportunity to confer with the Feegash voice, and go over the materials sent by the first diplomat and premier, to . . . better present this . . . testimony."

Sakjin, with the scroll in front of him and the wall of marines with boxes of records behind him, said, "As voice of the first diplomat and premier, I do not recognize you to speak, Afirt, nor do I recognize your right to question the materials assembled by the first diplomat and premier to present this case. You will remain in chamber, and you will be seated."

Afirt looked around. He was hemmed in by an increasingly hostile crowd. So, too, were the other Feegash diplomats.

In a dozen languages, Aaran heard other representatives telling him to sit down.

Sakjin said, "We have more supporting documents, and we will return to reading them into the record. However, at this time, we welcome the Living Goddess Oracle Hawkspar Eyes of War, of the Order of the Ossalenes, who will present the record of the first 324 years of the Feegash diplomatic plan as kept by the Order, and the future of the war and peace of the world, as a gift to the peoples of the world."

Several of the Feegash diplomats leapt to their feet and attempted to fight their way through the crowds to the exit. The head diplomat, for some reason liking his chances across the main floor better than up through the stands, jumped over the barrier that separated him from the Feegash and Tonk presenters, fell the distance to the stone floor, and missed his footing.

The sickening crack of breaking bone reached all the way to the top seats.

While the crowd of representatives forcibly returned the Feegash diplomats above them to their seats, three Seru Moonstone marched forward to the screaming head diplomat and crouched over him. Aaran, watching their heads dip forward and seeing their translucent white eyes begin to glow, was forcibly and uncomfortably reminded of the feeding of a pack of wolves on a downed deer.

The head diplomat quickly stopped screaming, and a chill ran down Aaran's spine. He could imagine them stepping away with nothing but dust in a man-shaped pile at their feet.

But of course that didn't happen. When they stood, they pulled the unwilling but healed head diplomat to his feet, and handed him, on two unbroken legs, over to the Sinali guards who had materialized out of side doors.

The guards marched him out of the chamber, then brought Afirt back in through the representatives' doors, marched him down the central aisle, where the standing audience crammed even closer together to permit him to pass, and reseated him down front. The two guards then stood behind him, and signaled that the proceedings could resume.

Aaran held his breath. He had known how every part of their presentation would go to that point, but when Hawkspar strode forward, and the marines and her own people bowed all the way to the ground as she passed, he had the sudden impression that a force of nature had stepped front and center. She was not the woman he knew. She was, instead, the creature he feared. The one she said she would become.

The woman he loved had left him—perhaps, like his sister, she no longer existed.

He bent, too, as she went past him. He had not intended to, but the force of her presence moved him. The waves of representatives above him, their foreheads going flat to the tables before them, and the audience dropping to its knees told him her power reached far beyond him.

Ageless and ancient, a goddess borrowing human skin for a visit, the Eyes of War stepped atop the small dais and from within one sleeve pulled out an arrangement of wood that she bent down and made into a tripod. She adjusted her staff within the center of the tripod so that it stood up. She rose and from the staff's top, pulled down two small wooden arms.

All eyes focused on her, fascinated. Aaran thought she could have been calling down lightning on the lot of them and such was the magnetism of her presence that not one of them would have moved.

From somewhere within that mass of skirts, she next removed a thick roll of knotted silk wound onto two carved rods about as wide as his forearm was long.

These she attached to the crossbar by means of a cord, and let the object unroll into a hanging. Black strands of silk hung knotted in irregular patterns and rows. He could make out no overall pattern in the arrangement.

But some in the audience evidently knew what the object she had hung before them was, for he heard scattered gasps and a sudden rush of whispering.

Hawkspar rested her fingertips on the silk strands and waited for silence, staring up at the audience.

Silence came quickly.

Hawkspar

I was infinite. Eternal. Legion. I drew my strength from the same source that would feed the madness; I knew this. But I also knew that my presence and my testimony would allow everything that followed to matter to those who held the fate of the Tonk in their hands. If I did not bind my audience into my tale as I had bound the knots in my weaving, the material we presented next to the gathered representatives of nations and empires would fail to move them, and all that had gone before would be for nothing. The Feegash might be temporarily discredited, but they would regain their stature. The Tonk would be wiped out and destroyed.

So I wrapped the power of the Eyes of War around me like a cloak, and let it echo in my voice as I spoke to the gathered crowd.

"I bring before you the oracles' record of the Feegash Five-Hundred-Year Plan, along with the paths it has woven through your own people and the prices you have so far paid to it."

"There is no Five-Hundred-Year Plan," one Feegash from up toward the top shouted.

I turned my gaze to him, and he froze. "In the same manner that there were no secret treaties between the Feegash and the assembled people here, there is no Five-Hundred-Year Plan," I said. "The first diplomat and premier of Ba'afeegash has kindly offered to us a copy of the Five-Hundred-Year Plan, signed with his word and his seal, to be entered into the record of this court and studied by those interested in the careful deceptions found therein. It is not my purpose, however, to read the whole of the plan to you, but simply to acquaint you with the overall purpose of the plan, and those parts of it that have been successfully carried out."

I wished I could see faces. With the full power of the Eyes brought to bear, I could feel the emotions of the room around me. I stood in the waters of time, submerged in the moment, and I could catch the rage and shock and betrayal in the assembled representatives, and the fear in the Feegash diplomats, and from behind me, glee and joy in vengeance long-awaited and now coming to fruition for the Tonk warriors and the Feegash who had been downtrodden and misused for so long. But being able to feel is not the same as being able to watch the eyes of those who had been responsible, as a people, for the deaths of my family.

I wanted to watch them shake, the Feegash bastards. I wanted to watch them quake and shudder as the truth poured out.

We rarely get what we want.

Sometimes, however, we still get enough.

I began running my fingers through the knots, reading the past that I had so carefully gleaned from time's currents. "In the fifth year of the Feegash plan, because of the first treaty of Hamin, negotiated by the Feegash between the Rance-Hawe of Old North Tandinapalis and the Pelosi, also of Old North Tandinapalis, the Rance-Hawe disarmed, as did the Pelosi. The Tand Northmen, who had paid a great deal of gold to the Feegash, then were able to invade and wipe out both Rance-Hawe and Pelosi."

The Tand Northmen later settled into cities, and became the Roshnan, who were still allies of the Feegash. There were no Pelosi or Rance-Hawe left to protest this treachery. But the Roshnan remembered how they had become who they were. And I wanted to establish the manner in which the Feegash worked. Many in that chamber would recognize the treachery, from one side or the other, but would never have made the connection before what happened to them and who was responsible for it.

So after story of the Rance-Hawe, I told of the warring Tand mountain clans who permitted the Feegash to assist them, and who found themselves subsumed by the highest bidders. And then, as the Feegash influence spread, of nation after nation pitted against one another, or disarmed in order to favor greedy third nations. Each section of knots told me of the next betrayal, and then the one after that. Every ally of the Feegash had at one point or another been on the wrong end of a deal that favored the Feegash—they were entirely happy to take secret money from all parties and then deliver only the results that favored their ends.

And the Feegash ends were quite simple. They wanted to eventually receive tribute and slaves from the whole of the world. They wanted their way to be the only way, and they made certain that anyone or anything that stood in the way of that long-term goal eventually failed.

The steadily mounting list of their treacheries drew gasps, and then angry murmurs, and finally—as all those people representing nations that had so far survived the Feegash plan heard of the dealings that would eventually destroy them—a dangerous undercurrent of whispers.

My fingers read knots in silk, and my words put forth images to my listeners that their minds could not refute, and could not shut out. They had been willing to profit by the betrayed trust of others, but had never thought that they would be made fools by the same tricks that they had so rejoiced to see used on others.

And yet, there they all sat, and among them sat the architects of their foolishness.

I began to hear murmurs that the Feegash diplomats should be taken out and executed on the stairs.

I raised a hand—my right hand. I did not wish, after all, to mark myself Tonk. Not yet.

Some of my story still remained.

"You cannot kill the Feegash yet. That time might come, but there are some who have been treated by the Feegash as you have, but who do not have representatives in this grand chamber to speak for them. You must hear their story as well."

And I told them the story of the Tonk, and the three hundred years of Tonk war with the Eastils in the other half of Hyre. Everyone knew this story, or at least they thought they did. However, they had heard it through the Feegash diplomats, whose people had for over three hundred years coveted Hyre. As I told the representatives of those nations allied against the Tonk about how the Feegash had negotiated a truce between the Eastil Republic and the Confederacy of Hyre, and how the Feegash diplomats had disarmed both nations with the Feegash mercenaries acting as peacekeeping troops throughout the process, and how Ba'afeegash had then turned its mercenaries on the unarmed population and enslaved both Eastils and Tonk, murmurs of recognition passed through the room. The Tonk ceased to be a swarm of madmen to those assembled, and became men standing against a common enemy.

I told of how the Tonk had been the reason the Feegash Hundred-Year Plan became the Three-Hundred-Year Plan, and finally the Five-Hundred-Year Plan. How the Tonk refusal to be pacified had kept not just the Tonk free for over three hundred years, but much of the rest of the world as well. The Feegash, not having the resources to fight the Tonk on their own, built up other nations to do their fighting for them.

"All you who stand in this assembly with nations that have strength of arms and strength of armies, all of you who call yourselves free men *and* allies of the Feegash, do so because the Feegash needed you for this moment. The moment when they could call your armies down upon the one people they could not conquer, could not bribe, and could not sell. You have been made the Feegash tool to hand Ba'afeegash the southern plains of Tandinapalis, the island nation of Hyre, the western islands of Velobrina, sections of Franica, and northern Tandinapalis. Their plans to betray you, disarm you, and enslave you once you have given them that which they most desire, and which they cannot obtain for themselves, are written into their Five-Hundred-Year Plan, which has been submitted for the record. The Tonk have saved you so far."

Then I told how the Tonk in Hyre had foiled the Feegash plot to disarm them, because by the requirements of their Saint Ethebet, the Tonk maintained weapons stores the Feegash did not know about. I told how they fought back. How they had been enslaved by magic, and how in the end, one Eastil man and one Tonk woman had found a way to break the Feegash hold on their people. How, had they failed to do this, the magic the Feegash had used to coerce, and in many cases destroy, the people of the two conquered nations would have spread and consumed the rest of the peoples of the world.

I then told about how the Feegash, failing at their Three-Hundred-Year Plan, rewrote it to strengthen ties to its allies, to engender in them deep obligations, and then to call for the payment of those obligations by commanding a war against the Tonk wherever they might be found.

"You have heard the past as it was, you have heard the future as it would have been. Now hear the present as it is from the same Tonk whose strength has kept you strong, and whose courage has done you one final kindness in spite of how you have treated them."

I stepped back. It was Aaran's turn to take the dais.

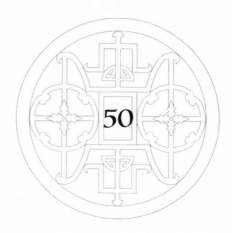

50

Aaran

Aaran had been watching the murderous mood building while Hawkspar spoke. He'd felt the power in what she said. He'd felt the truth of it all the way to his bones, and had seen that recognition of truth reflected in the eyes of the men who watched her, so still while they listened to her that save for their expressions they might have been carved.

When she raised her staff with the knotted silk record she'd been reading waving like a banner, and stepped down from the dais, he stared at her, dumbfounded. No one in the audience moved either, or looked anywhere but at her.

She stepped into the center of the ranks of Ossalenes, and lowered her staff, and the spell she'd woven over them all seemed to break.

He realized that it was his turn to take the stage.

Aaran took the scroll from Sakjin, walked to the dais, and stepped atop it.

"I am Aaran Donin av Savissha dryn Tragyn, Clan Viikuu of the Tonk people, and captain of the *Taag av Sookyn*. I also speak as leader of the Battle of Ba'afeegash, and conqueror of the Feegash people." From his throat, he pulled out the medallion that Aashka had worn—the sigil of the first diplomat and premier of Ba'afeegash—and pulled it over his head. He held it up high, for everyone to see.

In the front row, Afirt the fallen head diplomat of the Feegash delegation, recognized the medallion for what it was, and screamed.

Aaran dropped it to the dais, and, with a bit of flourish, stood on it.

Speaking in careful High Diplomatic Sinali, he read, "Having read or entered into the record kept by this assembled body of representatives the history and cases pertinent to this treaty, as is both customary and mandatory, I now state the terms of the treaty, wherein shall be declared the complete capitulation of the nation of Ba'afeegash to its Tonk conquerors, and the dissolution of the Feegash people as a sovereign entity."

A rumble of applause started somewhere near the back of the chamber, and spread, rippling and growing louder, until it was like a storm surf crashing over Aaran's ears.

He raised a hand for silence, but it wasn't quickly granted.

When finally the room stilled, he began reading again.

"Under the terms of the treaty, the city-state of Ba'afeegash has been razed to the ground within the walls, its wells poisoned, and its soil sowed with salt so that no one will inhabit those grounds again in the lifetime of anyone living, or the lifetimes of their children or grandchildren. The Feegash power brokers within the city itself—the diplomats, the military leaders, and the chief merchants have been executed. The Ba'afeegash women and children, as well as all slaves and citizen-servants, have been given generous portions of the wealth of the nation and set free to return to the homes and families from which they were taken, or to find new lives for themselves in better lands."

The applause started again as representatives realized that some of their own people, stolen by their neighboring nations but given to the Feegash, might be coming home.

Aaran waved the applause to silence again.

"The Tonk people, as conquerors of the Feegash people, recognize their right under the laws of this court to benefit from the treaties held by the people it has conquered, to collect the debts owed to the Feegash as its own, and to claim all the advantages rightfully given a successful conqueror under the law of the conqueror, which has been held as valid within these chambers for more than one thousand years."

The audience found its silence at that declaration quickly enough. The translators murmured to the delegates where necessary, but High Diplomatic Sinali was the official language within the walls of the Grand Hall, and few translators were doing more at that moment than leaning forward holding their breath, just as the delegates were doing.

Aaran cleared his throat. "I hereby give the terms under which the Tonk people exercises its right of conquest."

"All Tonk captives, servants, slaves, or prisoners within each nation or territory represented here are to be returned to their own people safely and with such monies and possessions as will permit them to begin new lives.

"All trading in Tonk captives and Tonk slaves by all peoples represented here will cease immediately.

"All raids, attacks, or wars on Tonk peoples or Tonk territories or possessions, whether at land or at sea, will cease immediately.

"Tonk lands will be held as sovereign, with borders respected by all peoples represented here.

"Finally, the Tonk people will acquire permanent seats equal to one full voting seat and one debating seat in this chamber for each of the twenty-one known clans, with one voting seat and one debating seat held in reserve for the two remaining Drifted Clans, the Kyruu and the Jiree, should surviving members of those clans ever be located.

"For each nation or people represented here who abides fully and freely with the conditions we, the Tonk people, have set forth, we will declare all treaties, debts, obligations, or alliances, whether secretly or publicly recognized, to be dissolved without cost or penalty."

This time, there was no stopping the applause. Or the cheering. Or the standing and dancing on seats and desks. The yoke in which the Feegash had held the assembled peoples had been heavy, the debts it collected had been steep, and the costs of those debts had just been presented to everyone in horrifying detail.

When Aaran and the other captains and the Feegash secretaries first went over all the rights the Tonk had as conquerors of the Feegash, it had been hard not to look at those treaties and debts as something to be used for every drop of gold and blood they might be worth.

But the first flush of vengeful glee had passed, and the words of Saint Ethebet had come back to all of them: *He who holds the chain is as much bound by it as he who is held.*

By her edicts, the Tonk did not keep slaves or permit slavery by any peoples living within their borders or under their law. And by her edicts they were guided once more. Those Feegash treaties were as much chains as any slavery. The debts would require debt collectors, and would collect hatred along with gold.

So the Tonk captains, and through communications with the clans across Korre, the taaklords and clanlords, had agreed to offer freedom to all who would have it.

From the still surging roars of applause, the assembly had found the plan to its liking.

Except the Feegash, of course, who were being manacled and marched quietly out of the chambers by armed Sinali guards and accompanied by Sinali shamans to make sure they didn't try any of their Hagedwar magic.

Aaran read the rest of the treaty—the details of when conditions would have to be met for the respective peoples assembled to be considered in compliance, as well as information about the Feegash who had presented the first part of the treaty, and who were released from any ties to the Feegash in power—to relative silence.

But when he read the last line, and rolled it up, and presented it to the Sinali master of chambers to be entered into the record along with the copies of everything else that the Tonk had brought with them, another wave of applause started, and thundered down like a summer storm.

Hawkspar

We were back in the ship, and the Tonk fleet no longer carried the truce and treaty flags. The captains had chosen temporary delegates to take the newly created seats in the Grand Hall of Nations, along with those communicators who would stay behind. Marine volunteers had gathered up their shares from their various adventures, and were offloading their belongings. They would form the first Tonk diplomatic escort, and would be responsible for the safety of our delegates.

We were not so naïve that we believed all the nations' representatives would be friendly to us, no matter how generous our gesture in offering to forgive debts. There would be those who were benefiting from the wars against our people who would want to continue reaping their profits. They would no doubt try to harm our delegates, or turn them; the diplomatic escort would do everything in their power to make sure our people survived in good health and safety.

Our communicators spent a busy few days presenting the news of our triumph in Sinali to all the clans scattered across the world. The wars continued for a while, because emissaries had to be sent to the fronts to inform the officers of the various armies to sound retreat.

For a time, the Tonk fought hard defensive actions, took and kept prisoners, and held the line, waiting. Waiting. Some of our people died fighting, knowing the peace had already been won, but holding the line to protect those who could not fight.

The news passed, though. The orders came down to officers, and cease-fires were called, and the tides that had assailed the Tonk began to retreat.

When we received word through our communicators that the last attacks on the Tand Asvikuu had stopped, we said good-bye to the people we would leave behind, and set sail as a fleet.

We parted company, though, with individual ships splitting off as tide and wind took them toward their own homes.

The *Taag* was heading for Hyre, with a cargo of freed Tonks slaves who had come from there before ending up in Ba'afeegash, and with holds full of riches. And with a freedom and a power that our people had never before enjoyed. The Tonk had, if only for the moment, no declared enemies. We were not at war with anyone.

We had won, and I had done my part to help us win.

I could not share the happiness of those around me, though.

There had been that one moment when, stepping on the ship after the Feegash were formally dissolved, Aaran and I had fallen into each other's arms and danced around the deck like fools and cheered.

But the Eyes had me, and realization dawned on both of us, and we pulled away.

I was already not the woman he loved. I was the creature who was devouring her.

I could no longer shield myself from the raw magic of the Hawkspar Eyes, heightened by the power fed them by every other set of Eyes in the world. To be the goddess in truth as well as in name; to lend my force to the Tonk cause, I had connected paths that became greater than me—that brought to full expression a magic that had been so powerful it had destroyed even its own creator.

I no longer needed that power, but power exists for its own sake, and the Eyes, fully opened, would not close. I did not have the strength to save myself. The Hawkspar Eyes dragged in images and voices from all of time and all the world—the past, the present, and the future—and those phantoms shouted or whispered or screamed in languages lost, and known, and not even yet in existence. And I could not look away. I ate alone, I slept alone, and as much as I could, I stayed alone—and I was never alone.

The presence of anyone real near me made things worse; even Aaran and Redbird, who were my family, stirred up the eddies of time around me.

Simply by being near me, the currents of their lives flowed into mine, and made the river I fought swell as if in a flood.

I kept them away because having them near hurt me. But more than that, I kept them away because I could not bear to have them see me the way I had become. I mistook the unreal for the real, the past and the future for the present. I cried out at terrifying specters I realized a moment later were not there; I babbled at people who rose from the waves and spoke to me or through me to someone else who had once been or who might someday be—or who, a thousand long leagues away, *was.*

The madness had not yet devoured me wholly. Sometimes I knew where I was. Less often, when I was. I still knew who I was and what I wanted. But that, too, I could feel slipping away.

I didn't give up. I fought. I pushed my way out of the voices, out of the seduction of all the times that might be, that were right then, that had been before, and I dragged myself far enough into the *now* that I could feel sunlight on my skin and breathe the air of the moment. I fought because some part of me remained human, and humans keep fighting. Drowning, we struggle toward the surface for one last breath, even if no one will ever come along to pull us out, because so long as we hope and fight—so long as we hang on— we do not die.

I fought. But death sat close to me, and every day closer.

Aaran sent his healer to me each morning, hoping that Alwyn would find a way to break the Eyes' hold without killing me. The Moonstones hovered over me as long as I could tolerate their presence, trying to undo what Ossal's magic had wrought.

But here is the truth of power; the lesser magic cannot undo the greater magic. In all the world, I doubted there lived a wizard great enough to undo the magic Ossal had wrought with the final pair of Eyes he made—the Hawkspar Eyes.

My death would break the lines that coursed through me. The Eyes would become weak again.

But I did not want to die.

Aaran

"How is she?"

Aaran turned toward Tuua. "Demon beset. Half starved. Lost in visions that make me think the Eastil hells might all be real. I sit outside her door, and listen to her talk to no one, and scream, and sob, and laugh. And then will come a silence, and I wonder if she has come back to herself. Or if she has fallen asleep. Or if she is dead."

"Alwyn cannot do anything?"

"No." Aaran turned his face back to the sea, and watched the approaching ship. It was small and fast, and after a moment he realized it had, in miniature, the same elegant lines as the *Ker Nagile*. "No one can do anything. She's going to die. She gave everything she had to save the Tonk, and instead of triumph and joy, she gets madness and death. And I, who love her, watch her crumble before my eyes, almost as if she were Aashka all over again." He clenched his hands on the rail, and said, "If you speak to Jostfar, ask him if I am poison, that my mere presence destroys the people I love." He turned, the bitterness consuming him, and said, "But you have found happiness. Jarynan, is it?"

"We're going to the temple in Port Midrid and make our vows," Tuua said.

"Yes. And on the ship, a dozen other men have found their futures with women they dared to love and get to keep. They will take their shares and go on to happiness."

The shares had already been divided. Aaran had first set aside what he would have to pay to those who had invested in his voyage, and then paid out shares. His men had done well; they could thank the Ossalenes for that.

Tuua said, "Good Jostfar. That's Makkor."

And Aaran's heart sank. "Oh, Ethebet hammer me once between the eyes."

Tuua said, "I rather like the old man."

"As do I. But I owe him a wife, or the full price of the ship."

Tuua said, "I'd forgotten all about that."

"As had I. It wasn't written in the log with our contracts. It was simply an agreement between the two of us."

"How much is the full price of the ship?"

"Enough that no one will get shares for the voyage," Aaran said. It seemed obvious to him that this would be the next thing to come crashing around his ears. He'd been on his maiden voyage as captain of a ship; he'd rescued a shipload of Tonk slaves; he'd found his missing sister and discovered a plot against his people—and aside from what he and everyone else had managed for the Tonk, it had gone to ashes. All of it. His sister was dead; the woman he loved, dying; and now he would not even be able to pay his crew, and so would guarantee that he could not hire another, and that his name would be a mockery, a synonym for failure as a captain, ever after.

The fine small ship came alongside, and Tuua muttered, "I don't suppose we could accidentally sink him."

"I think not." Aaran watched his men grabbing the tossed ropes and helping the ship come alongside.

Makkor Gurak-Golak-Dok-Hkukguh came up the side of the ship and dropped to the deck like a man a third his age. He spotted Aaran, grinned broadly, and came bounding over, embracing him with an enormous hug and a laugh. "Are you not the hero, lad, saved all the Tonk and most of the rest of us into the bargain?" And then he pulled back and studied Aaran. "And don't you look the hell and hard times? You should be dancing, lad. Treasure from the Fallen Suns, from what I've heard, and from the Feegash storerooms as well."

"It's not been a good voyage for me," Aaran said.

Makkor studied him through narrowed eyes. "I'm believing you," he said at last. "Did you have hardships on the way back?"

"His sister died when he reached her to rescue her," Tuua said, his voice low . . . but not quite low enough. "The woman he loves is dying."

Makkor's exuberance fell away. "I offer my condolences," he said. "That does not seem the way things should work." He sighed. "I'll not keep you, then—I'd hoped for a dance and a banquet when you reached the bay, and to fete my bride-to-be at the same time. But you'll not be wanting such festivities. You found a girl for me?"

Aaran started to say no. He was going to just give up and admit to failure. He didn't care. He would never go to sea again; he had nothing to go back for. He could give the old man back his ship, work passage to Hyre, and find a place there where he could be alone with his grief.

But then he thought of the old man, who wanted a companion. Who was lonely. Who had given Aaran the ship he sailed on a handshake, for the promise that Aaran would look for a wife for Makkor, or pay for the ship if he couldn't find one.

It had been an offering of faith and goodwill, and it had reaped massive rewards for Tonk everywhere.

"I have a great many women on the ship," he said slowly. "None who would agree to marry a man sight unseen. But I'll ask them to come on deck to meet with you, and you can talk with them."

Makkor nodded. "That will suit me."

He didn't ask if Aaran had the money to pay him if none of the women wanted an old man for a husband. Aaran appreciated that bit of forbearance on Makkor's part.

He went halfway down the passenger companionway, and found the Ossalenes in the passenger common sitting in utter silence. His gut knotted.

"Has something happened to her?" he asked. No one needed to ask what he meant.

Redbird, huddled disconsolate in front of Hawkspar's door, said, "There is no change. There is only the continuation of the sameness. But we near land, and the sera must know the orders of their Oracle. They only wait until a moment when she is calm to ask her what they are to do."

His life was not the only one in disarray. He said, "I have a man above who seeks a wife. He hopes for an islander, he says. He is the man who gave me this ship to come to your rescue when no one else would deal with me, and he did that in exchange for the hope that I might bring back for him a companion for these lonely late years in his life. I would ask of those of you who might care to have a rich husband that, as a favor to me, you go talk to him. You don't owe me, any of you. But . . . he's a good man. And he did a service to all of us."

A few of the women stood. One said, "None here dares say we owe you nothing. But we owe this man, too, for without him, you might not have found the means to reach us."

Another said, "If she says anything, call us back."

Five went. Three Obsidians, one Rosestone, and one Amber.

Aaran gave a final glance to Hawkspar's door. He could hear her inside, sobbing and screaming. He knotted his fists and followed the Ossalenes up the companionway.

Makkor studied the five of them, clearly taken aback by their appearances. They were all young and graceful, all strong and healthy. But they all bore the Eyes of the Ossalene Order.

He studied them. And then he said, slowly, *"Kurga gal glaksa yadnega gnee, rega ksoggingor hkgack pongi?"*

One—only one—of the women burst out laughing. She was one of the Ambers; Aaran had talked to her a few times. Her name was Gnadable. She spewed out a string of syllables that sounded like a cat trying to cough up a hairball in a hurry.

Makkor responded in kind, a big grin on his face.

And the girl answered him, smiling, too.

Hope. Aaran dared not breathe; he feared if he did, the same fate that crushed him at every turn would see what was happening and destroy it.

But that didn't happen. The Amber turned to the other Ossalenes and said, "I'm going to sail with him to Port Midrid. We'll meet you when you arrive, and I'll receive word of the oracle then."

Makkor came over to Aaran's side and said, "Consider your debt to me paid, whether she'll marry me or not. I like the look of her, but even if she decides she won't have me, I owe you as much debt as any free man today. Releasing you from your debt for the *Taag av Sookyn* will be my small repayment."

Aaran managed a smile, though from where they both stood, they could hear the screams below. "My heartfelt thanks," he said.

Makkor said, "You have enough to occupy your mind, it seems. I'll not add to it."

Makkor returned to his own ship, accompanied by Gnadable.

And Aaran exhaled. At least his men would get paid.

He handed off the ship to his kor daan as they neared Port Midrid's harbor. He could see the ribbons festooning every stationary object in the port, the bright streamers, the docks crowded with people waiting to see the *Taag av Sookyn*—the only ship in the Grand Pack to go there direct from the fight—so that they could cheer the warriors who had won them their freedom.

Aaran wanted no part of celebration. Ermyk av Beyrkyn could handle the crowds. He'd enjoy the adulation, no doubt find himself an armload of nubile young women who would treat him to a hero's welcome.

He went down the passenger companionway, and found the Ossalenes hugging Redbird, or each other, and weeping.

He could not hear a sound from Hawkspar's quarters.

One by one, the Ossalenes picked up their packs and filed silently past him, up the companionway.

"She's dead?" he asked Redbird when the last of them was past him.

"No. She is, for the moment, herself. She cut them from the Order and sent them away. Me, too, but I won't leave her." Redbird, pale and gaunt, with her black stone eyes red-rimmed from weeping and lack of sleep, said, "She asked to speak with you. She might still be herself when you go in."

He said, "Well. Then." Redbird opened the door, and he passed by her, and went in.

"You've come," Hawkspar said.

"I've been here all along."

"Yes. Part of me knows that. We're nearly come to land. This voyage will be over, and whatever waits for you in the future will be out there. Not in here."

"I love you," he said. "I don't care about the future. I only care about you."

In the darkened quarters, he could see only the faintest curve of her lips. "What little of me remains loves you, too. But I'm done, Aaran. I can't hold on any longer. It hurts to try. So I want you to . . . leave me. I don't want you to watch me die."

"I don't want you to die alone."

"I would give anything to die alone. It's dying in the midst of this chaos that weighs on me."

"I won't leave you."

She was silent for a long time. "Do you remember," she said at last, "the day we danced?"

"On the deck? Of course I remember."

"I won the bet," she said. "And I told you then I would ask nothing of you harder or greater than having a dinner together. I intend to collect my winnings now."

"No," he whispered.

"I ask that you leave me. That you not watch me die. That you not see what the madness does to me when it takes me completely. It is not such a hard thing, turning and walking away. When my body is done with this life, you may come back. Burn it, and when I am ashes, scatter them in a garden, where the sun is warm and the flowers are beautiful. And find some way to smash the Hawkspar Eyes into powder, or if you cannot, take them and toss them into the deepest heart of the sea. These things I ask of you as the man I love. But the leaving? That I claim as the winnings of our bet. If you are a man of honor—and I know you are—you will honor that."

She was gaunt. Skeletal. Starved, bruised, dying. He could look at her and see how near death she was, and still, in that moment when she knew him and herself, he could not believe that she could not—somehow—be saved.

"I love you," he said, and his voice broke. He could not think of her dead and still upon a pyre. He could not think of her lost and torn in her mind. And he could do nothing—nothing—to help her.

"Be well," she said. "Find happiness. In the future, you will find someone to love. I have already seen you with her, and in most of your futures you grow old together and are happy. You will not mourn me for long."

She lay back down, turned her back to him, and pulled her knees to her chest.

"I'll never love anyone but you," he whispered.

"It's such a funny thing," Hawkspar told him. "I have never been able to see your face in the rivers of time. Never the face of anyone else, either. But I can see her. She has blue eyes."

He would not believe it. He started to argue with her, but she said, "Go. Please. The river swells, and soon it will take me again. Have mercy on me, and do not see me as I am about to become. I cannot bear thinking that you might."

He would not leave her. He would join Redbird outside the door if he had to, and spend every last moment of her life as close to her as he could get. But he would give her a little peace of mind. He would leave the room as she asked him to.

As he closed the door behind him, he heard her say, "I'll never love any-one but you."

Hawkspar

I lay there listening to the voices in time washing over me, feeling the current pulling under, deeper and deeper into cool darkness. The ship had come to land, and the Ossalenes were leaving. Aaran and Redbird both sat on the other side of my door, though, and I knew neither of them would release me and live their lives again until I was dead.

I would never be better than I was at that moment; I would only get worse. The kindest thing I could do for both of them, then, was to die quickly.

I had knives, swords, the skill to kill myself. But I did not, and I could not be sure if it was because I didn't want to take that final step, or if the Eyes refused to let me. I had a way to end the misery quickly, though, and at last I took it.

I embraced the madness of the Eyes. I did not want to fight any longer. I was lost, I would die, and everything I loved would vanish for me as if it had never been. The inevitable came, and at last I opened the door.

My mentor had warned be about pursuing my own past; that if I went back to a place where I was happy, I would never find my way out again.

It was the choice I could not unmake.

It was the choice I made.

I pushed my way back into my own past.

I found the places where I was with Aaran, where we held each other, touched each other, and those moments were so sweet they broke my heart. I wanted to stay in them—but the still-living Aaran sat on the deck outside my door, and his presence stirred the tides that flowed through me. If I could find my way out to him, he would hold me again, and there would be more wondrous moments. He was too real, too living, for me to be satisfied with memory.

I pushed deeper into the current. And Redbird was with me, as we struggled through fight training, language training, as we learned the rudiments of the Ossalene rites, as we scrubbed floors and ran errands, as we lay side-by-side in the dark, stinking hold of the slave ship keeping each other going. Those were strong memories, but not happy ones.

I dove deeper yet.

Past my parents' deaths and my capture.

Back. To them alive.

They held me once again. They embraced me, and I was small and safe in a world that no one would ever touch. Ever. I could stay with them forever in the bright shadda, with the horses outside, with my sisters and brothers all around me. The smells of my mother's cooking filled the air, the sound of her singing, and my father singing with her, or laughing. The feel of horseback as he taught me to ride, my small hands on the loom as I sat in my mother's lap and she started teaching me to weave.

"Yeri," my mother called me.

And I remembered my name. Not just Yeri, but all of it. I had a name, a home, safety, people who loved me enough to die for me, but this time they would never die. I would never have to make my way alone again. This time my mother would still be holding me when I died.

Aaran

"She set you free with all the rest. Why didn't you leave?"

Redbird turned to Aaran and frowned. "I'm not with her because I'm bound to her. I'm with her because I love her. She saved my life—I owe her every breath I take." Redbird hung her head. "If I could, I'd die in her place."

Aaran leaned his back against the wall next to the door. Hawkspar was quiet for the moment. He could hope that she was sleeping, regaining her strength. He could tell himself, when she wasn't screaming, that she could yet get better. She wouldn't, and in his heart he knew she wouldn't, but for the moment he could still tell himself fairly convincing lies.

"Tell me," he said. "About how she saved your life."

Redbird sat on the opposite side of the door, her knees pulled close, her arms propped out straight atop them. She sighed. "She chose you, but we both lose her the same, don't we? I suppose I can tell you." And she shrugged.

"I was captured before her, along with a brother a little older than me. He died quickly, trying to fight his way to me. I lay in the dark for a long time. I was already weak when the slavers chained her next to me. By then, I didn't want to live anymore. There was no light in the hold, and I'd never been in such darkness, in such a stink. The slavers did not wash us. We lay in our own filth. They didn't care if we lived or died, and eventually neither did we. At least not most of us."

A tiny smile crossed her face. "But she cared. From the first day, when they tossed the food at us, she grabbed enough for herself, plus for the girl on the other side of her, and for me as well. If we wouldn't eat, she fed us. She talked to us—told us stories of sunlight and horses and mothers and fathers and brothers and sisters. She made up ways in which we could get out of our chains and run away. She was very young, but life was so strong in her that she passed some of it on to me. The girl on the other side of her died, but I didn't . . . because Mouse wouldn't let me. She kept talking about the day when good people would come and take us out of the darkness, and we would run in fields again, and ride horses, and find our parents."

He saw a tear run down Redbird's cheek.

"It was all she ever wanted. To find her way back to her own people, to have a family again. She gave me my name—I don't suppose you knew that. I've long since forgotten my real one, but it never mattered to me, because I had the one she gave me." Pursed lips, another shrug. "She was all I ever wanted."

Aaran could understand that. "You ever tell her?"

"No. I'm Ossalene. I was brought up from a very early age to understand that self-denial was a virtue, and that punishment came swiftly to those who failed to deny themselves. I was forbidden to own anything of my own, forbidden to claim a friendship, forbidden to hope for love. I understood from the beginning that I might love her, but it would never lead to anything."

Aaran thought about that for a while. In a way, it was not so different a story from his own.

Above, he could hear sailors singing, and people shouting and cheering. He heard Tonk pipes blowing, wild and discordant and passionate. His people loved and fought and touched and held on to what they cared about with everything in them—but to do that, sometimes they practiced self-denial, too. He had. He'd never thought he would love, and in the end, the love he'd dared lay dying.

"She's quiet," Aaran said. "I hope she's sleeping. I hope she isn't hurting."

Redbird turned her face to him, and he felt himself under cold scrutiny. "I hope she finds the sunlight and horses and family she yearned for. She won me my freedom at last, though I don't think I want it. She got me out of the Citadel. No one ever got away from the Citadel before, and she didn't go alone. She saved me, and a lot of others. So I hope the stories she told me come true for her, wherever she is. I hope she finds joy."

Aaran heard the clatter of boot heels on the companionway, and rose to his feet. "No one down here," he said.

A tall, lean woman with gray-streaked brown hair pulled back in Ethebet's braid leaned down to look at him. "My name is Talyn," she said. "Talyn Wyran av Tiirsha dryn Straad. A dream brought me here. The woman in white sent me."

Aaran's mouth went dry. Both Hawkspar and Talyn had talked of the woman in white who appeared to them in dreams.

"She . . . sent you?"

"I have little time to talk. Where is she?"

A chill ran down Aaran's spine. "What are you going to do?"

"The woman in white told me," Talyn said, "that I must greet the ship. That another was bound in the twists of magic spun too deeply, as I had once been bound. That another faced the hell of darkness caught between life and death. I've come to save her. If I can. If it isn't too late."

Hawkspar

My mother and father talked, and I sat on the rug-covered floor of our shadda, playing with a wooden horse an older brother had carved for me. I was warm. I was happy. Nothing changed, but then, it didn't need to change. I needed nothing but what I had.

And then a woman pushed her way into the picture—bent my world around me and said, "No. You will not die this way."

I could not ignore her, though I tried. I tried to hang on to the safe places, the comfort, my family, but the woman surrounded me with brilliant light in gold and red and blue, and the power and the brilliance of it dragged me back into time. Into cold, screaming currents that carried me, fighting, back to places of pain and fear and madness.

I fought, but the woman held me down, and shielded both of us—I could feel her magic, and I could see the Hagedwar she held around us both. It was different than Aaran's—the points of both tetrahedrons pushed all the way through the surface of the ruby cube and into the brilliant sapphire of the sphere. Because of the difference in its shape, it had a different feel, as well. It felt dangerous. Powerful and wild.

She touched me on the shoulder, and I tried to shrug her hand off me.

But she crouched beside me and said, "You'll not go this way."

And, with her Hagedwar shield spun huge and both of us wrapped within one gold point of it, she and I ceased to be two people, and became one, fully and completely. We breathed as one, we moved as one, we thought as one. All her memories poured into me, all my memories poured into her, and pain old and new overran both of us for a moment. But I felt joy in her, too, for things I could not imagine. She knew love and motherhood, family that spread in ever-growing circles, the comfort of belonging, the richness of having roots and a place that was and always had been her home.

I knew what she knew; I could see how Ossal had bound the magic of the Eyes to his own soul, and how he had thus trapped himself within the nothing that lay between life and afterlife. I could see how those bonds had been formed, and I could see how I could break them.

Her magic became my magic.

Her hands, or perhaps they were my hands, cupped Ossal's stone Eyes—the Hawkspar Eyes, the pinnacle of his creation—and one of us, or maybe both of us, broke the lines of power that had filled them with magic for uncounted time. Pain filled me, consumed me like fire, burned through me so fiercely it ripped breath from me, while a roar like the sea in a storm and the screaming of the wind and drowning sailors assaulted my ears and crushed my thoughts. The stench of death filled my nostrils, the taste of rot clogged my mouth.

And then—nothing.

Was I dead?

The voices fell silent. The rush of time's currents vanished. The weight of the ship, the movement of things beneath it, within it, beside it, above it, all went dark.

The world lay black and shapeless around me.

Everything was gone. My power, my strength, my magic. Gone. I was mortal again, human again, and fully blind.

I was alone inside my head except for the other woman. Talyn. The other daughter of Ethebet, the other sister of the woman in white.

"She would not leave you to fall into darkness," Talyn said aloud, and I knew she was speaking of Ethebet. "Not when I could step between and set you free."

"There are more," I said.

"I know," she told me. "I saw them leaving as I was coming aboard—and there are others that I felt while you were still bound to the Eyes. I can't do anything about them—not here. Not now. If we can gather them together with the other master healers, we can release those you brought with you. Those who stayed behind . . . I don't know about them."

I lay there, basking in the blessed stillness, in the absence of tide and current, in the release from the endless agony of other people's pain.

And then she said, "I'm going to touch your face. I'm going to remove the Eyes."

"Why? They're no danger now."

"They're not your eyes."

I didn't understand, but I allowed her to lay her hands over my face. She was still in my head, inside my skin, as much me as I was her, but I realized that I could not hear her thoughts. I could see her life, I could know what she had done, but I could not know what she was thinking.

Her hands then covered the stone spheres, and within her head—my head—we drew in the golden Hagedwar light around us, and power unlike anything I had felt before—clean, beautiful, sweet power, untainted by Ossal or his perversions or his madness—poured through us. As the light filled us, I knew what we were doing, and I understood how we were doing it.

It was beautiful. We reaching into me, into the smallest parts of me, where Jostfar had hidden the keys to how my body was made, and we spun out of the air and water around us, and out of bits of the music the held the universe together, new eyes. I could feel the hard stone dissolve, I could feel living eyes in place again.

She closed her Hagedwar, and we were two people again.

I slid my hands over my eyes, unable to believe that they were there.

But they were. I opened them, blinking in the darkness, and at first there was only darkness.

Then I began to make out shapes. Legs moving away from me, a door opening. A whisper in the hall; I could not hear what was said. But I could see the legs walking back in again.

I could see.

Colors began to filter into the room. Brown first—the rubbed wood of the bunk frame, gleaming and rich and worn and beautiful.

Then the rich black and the deep green of uniformed legs.

And then a face peering down at me—tanned, with green eyes. With a smile that flashed white teeth. With a braid of black hanging over his shoulder.

"Hawkspar," he said. "You're well? It's . . . you?"

I knew him by his voice. He was beautiful, and I would never have seen him so beautiful in my mind. I slid out from the bunk and touched his face, staring for the first time into his eyes, looking for the man I loved in those unfamiliar depths.

"No," I said. "Not Hawkspar anymore. Hawkspar is gone—the Eyes and the magic are no more. I'm Yeri. Yeri Karja av Ro dryn Hoda, of Clan Eskuu. And I have been waiting most of my life to see you."

He wrapped his arms around me and held me tight. And then slowly, slowly, he turned me so that I faced the window. He stared into my eyes, an expression of wonder on his face. And he said, "Your eyes. They're the bluest eyes I've ever seen. All along, you've seen this moment, Hawks— Yeri. All along, you've seen us growing old together. You simply didn't know that it was you."

Redbird waited by the door as we exited the room. She said, "You did it. You brought us to freedom." And she hugged me, and said, "I got my one wish. You'll live to see your stories come true."

We stood, with some awkwardness between us, and I said, "I am sorry you did not find your dream at the end of this."

She smiled, and I remembered her as the girl with brown eyes—not Obsidian black. Soon she would have brown eyes again. She told me, "I never dared to dream, Mouse. Not once. I lived on your dreams, and you kept me alive and brought me far enough that now I think I can find a dream of my own. Dreams don't need guarantees, I imagine. I think that sometimes just having one, and a chance to pursue it, might be enough."